Free Public Library
Dalton, Massachusetts

First opened, May 1861   **Accepted by Town, March 1885**

MARJORIE MORNINGSTAR

BY HERMAN WOUK

Fiction

Inside, Outside
War and Remembrance
The Winds of War
Don't Stop the Carnival
Youngblood Hawke
Marjorie Morningstar
The Caine Mutiny
City Boy
Aurora Dawn

Nonfiction

This Is My God

Plays

Nature's Way
The Caine Mutiny Court-Martial
The Traitor

A Novel by HERMAN WOUK

Marjorie
Morningstar

Doubleday

NEW YORK   LONDON   TORONTO   SYDNEY   AUCKLAND

MAR 9 1993

Published by Doubleday, a division of Bantam Doubleday Dell Publishing Group, Inc., 666 Fifth Avenue, New York, New York 10103

Doubleday and the portrayal of an anchor with a dolphin are trademarks of Doubleday, a division of Bantam Doubleday Dell Publishing Group, Inc.

2   4   6   8   9   7   5   3

0-385-04285-x

NOTE

Fictional liberties have been taken with place names, weather, eclipses, steamship schedules, dates, and so forth. All the characters of the novel, with their names and traits, are complete fictional inventions. Unintentional duplication of actual names of people or business organizations may have occurred. But any resemblance to actual people or events, in names, traits, or physical descriptions, is coincidental. Real names of hotels, apartment houses, restaurants, ships, and business organizations have occasionally been used where invented names would have sounded forced, but beyond that, the characters and events in those places are fictitious.

TO THE MEMORY OF
MY FATHER
ABRAHAM ISAAC WOUK
1889–1942

CONTENTS

PART ONE

Marjorie

Chapter 1. MARJORIE

Customs of courtship vary greatly in different times and places, but the way the thing happens to be done here and now always seems the only natural way to do it.

Marjorie's mother looked in on her sleeping daughter at half past ten of a Sunday morning with feelings of puzzlement and dread. She disapproved of everything she saw. She disapproved of the expensive black silk evening dress crumpled on a chair, the pink frothy underwear thrown on top of the dress, the stockings like dead snakes on the floor, the brown wilting gardenias on the desk. Above all she disapproved of the beautiful seventeen-year-old girl lying happily asleep on a costly oversize bed in a square of golden sunlight, her hair a disordered brown mass of curls, her red mouth streaked with cracking purplish paint, her breathing peaceful and regular through her fine little nose. Marjorie was recovering from a college dance. She looked sweetly innocent asleep; but her mother feared that this picture was deceptive, remembering drunken male laughter in the foyer at 3 A.M., and subdued girlish giggles, and tiptoeing noises past her bedroom. Marjorie's mother did not get much sleep when her daughter went to a college dance. But she had no thought of trying to stop her; it was the way boys met girls nowadays. College dances had formed no part of the courtship manners of her own girlhood, but she tried to move with the times. She sighed, took the dying flowers to try to preserve them in the refrigerator, and went out, softly closing the door.

The slight noise woke Marjorie. She opened large blue-gray eyes, rolled her head to glance at the window, then sat up eagerly. The day was brilliantly clear and fine. She jumped from the bed in her white nightgown, and ran to the window and looked out.

It was one of the many charms of the El Dorado that it faced Central Park. Here on the seventeenth floor there was no one to peer in on her nakedness but the birds of the air. This fact, even more than the spacious view of the green park and the skyscrapers, gave Marjorie a sense of luxury each day when she awoke. She had enjoyed this freedom from prying eyes for less than a year. Marjorie loved everything about the El Dorado, even the name. "El Dorado" was perfectly suited to an apartment building on Central Park West. It had a fine foreign sound to it. There were two categories of foreignness in Marjorie's outlook: high foreign, like French restaurants, British riding clothes, and the name El Dorado; and low foreign, like her parents. By moving to the El Dorado on Central Park West her parents had done much, Marjorie believed, to make up for their immigrant origin. She was grateful to them for this, and proud of them.

What a wonderful day it was for horseback riding! The warm breeze smelled of new grass, here seventeen floors above the murmuring auto traffic. The sky was bright blue, with little white tufts of cloud, and the green park was tufted with white too where cherry trees were blossoming. She felt unbelievably good as recollections of last night came back to her. She hugged herself with pleasure, crossing her arms and clutching her bare pretty shoulders with her hands.

Her dreams of the gawky days of thirteen and fourteen had come true, and more than true. Four years ago she had scampered and squealed with other skinny dirty little girls in the playgrounds of Bronx public schools. Last night she had walked on the moonlit grounds of Columbia College. She had faintly heard the young men who lived in the dormitories shouting and laughing, a wonderful rich male noise. She had danced in a wood-panelled hall decorated with colored lanterns and great blue flags, and sometimes she had been only inches away from the smiling band leader, a famous man. She had danced with dozens of boys. Even when the band was resting a victrola had played, and there had been more boys to dance with her to the thin scratchy music. One of them, the son of the owner of a great department store, was going to ride with her today in Central Park.

She picked the black dress off the chair and smoothed it gratefully. It had done its work well. Other girls had floundered through the dance in wretched tulles and flounces and taffetas, like the dresses her mother had tried for two weeks to buy for the great occasion. But she had fought for this tube of curving black crepe silk, high-necked enough to seem demure, and had won; and she had captivated the son of a millionaire. That was how much her mother knew about clothes.

There was a rap at the door. "Marjorie, are you up?"

"Just getting into the shower, Mom." She darted into the bathroom and turned on a drumming rush of hot water. Sometimes her mother came in and shouted questions at her through the shower curtain, but she didn't today. Marjorie returned to the bedroom and waited for a moment, watching the doorknob. Then she walked to the full-length mirror on the closet door, and draped the black dress against her bosom, pleased by the contrast it made with her naked shoulders and tumbling hair.

At this moment—it was quite an important moment in her life—she grew hot, and prickled all over. An intuition about her future came flooding into her mind, like sunlight at the drawing of a curtain. She was going to be an actress! This pretty girl in the mirror was destined to be an actress, nothing else.

Since entering Hunter College in February of the previous year, Marjorie had been taking a course of study leading to a license as a biology teacher; but she had long suspected that she was going through empty motions, that chalk and blackboard weren't for her. Nor had she been able to picture herself settling into dull marriage at twenty-one. From her thirteenth year onward a peculiar destiny had been in her blood, waiting for the proper time to crop out, and disturbing her with premonitory sensations. But what she experienced on this May morning was no mere premonition; it was the truth bursting through. She was going to be an actress! The daydreams of her childhood had not been mere dreams, after all.

In the light of this truth—for it was not a resolve, not a decision, but rather a sudden insight into an existing truth—all her life seemed to take shape. Puzzling things were explained. Contradictions melted away.

This was why she had triumphed at Columbia last night, and this was why she had been such a fish out of water all her life in the Bronx. This was why without effort she had been the star of all the playlets at school and in summer camps. Even as a child she had had a quick mind, a gift of mimicry, an excellent memory, and self-possessed charm. Some instinct had taught her early to imitate the speech of her English teachers. Long before her family moved to Manhattan she had been half mocked and half admired in the highly critical society of the Bronx gutters, where her nickname had been Lady Pieface. Now, in an amazingly short time, she had transformed herself into a Central Park West charmer, the belle of a Columbia dance. She had sometimes wondered at her own remarkable advance—her quick mastery of collegiate slang, her grace on the dance floor, her polished charm of gesture, above all her unfailing run of bright talk, which always sounded clever even when there was nothing in it. She knew that in truth she was still very much Lady Pieface of the Bronx playing a hastily learned part. But her performance

5

had been getting better week by week; and last night she had scored an unmistakable smash hit. The wonder of all this vanished, on the supposition that she was an actress discovering her powers.

She dropped into the chair at her desk, letting the dress fall over her piled-up unfinished homework. White steamy clouds from the shower, shot through with yellow bars of sunlight, were filling the room. Marjorie kept staring at herself in the mirror through the vapors, unmindful of the roaring waste of hot water. Had there ever been successful Jewish actresses? Of course: Sarah Bernhardt, Rachel—and now that she thought of it, rumor described half the great stars of Hollywood as Jewish.

But her name wasn't good. It wasn't good at all. There was wondrous resonance in *Sarah Bernhardt*, stark elegance in *Rachel*—whereas her own . . . Marjorie Morgenstern . . .

Then came the confirming flash, the white streak of revelation. Such a simple change! Not even a change, a mere translation of the German compound, and her drab name turned into an incantation, a name that could blaze and thunder on Broadway. She pushed aside the dress, seized a pencil, threw open her biology notebook to a blank page, and hastily printed

MARJORIE MORNINGSTAR

She stared at the name, sprawled in dark blue ink over the light blue lines of the page. She took a pen and carefully wrote, in the small, vertical hand which she was trying to master,

Marjorie Morningstar

For a long time she sat looking at the page. Then she wrote under the name

May 7, 1933

She ripped the page out of the book, folded it, and locked it in the rosewood box where she kept George's love letters. Then, singing, she disappeared into the foggy bathroom.

Mrs. Morgenstern had eaten breakfast several hours earlier with her husband, who was unable to sleep once the day dawned, Sunday or not. Calculating the time it would take her daughter to shower and dress, she placed herself at the breakfast table again a few seconds before Marjorie came out of her room. In her hand was a cup of steaming coffee. She was not lying in wait to grill Marjorie. Surely she was entitled to an extra cup of coffee on Sunday morning.

"Hello, Mother dear." Marjorie draped her jacket on the arm of a chair.

Mrs. Morgenstern put down her coffee. "My God."

"My God what?" Marjorie dully dropped into the chair.

"That sweater, Marjorie."

"What about it? Don't you like the color?" She knew what her mother didn't like. She had spent the last few minutes at the mirror worrying about the sweater. It perfectly matched her British boots and breeches and tweed jacket, and the russet band on her perky hat—all new, all being worn for the first time. It had looked charming in the shop, this cat-smooth russet cashmere, and the size was correct. But the fit was snug; mighty snug. Marjorie knew that a pretty girl in a tight sweater created a commotion. It was very vexing, she thought, and so silly; in the South Seas nobody would think twice about it. She had decided to brave it out. Her mother might not like the sweater, but Sandy Goldstone probably would.

"Marjorie, people will think—I don't know what they'll think."

"I'm a big girl, Mama."

"That's just what's bothering me, dear."

"Mom, for your information girls don't ride horses in pink quilted housecoats that make them look like tubs. They wear sweaters."

Mrs. Morgenstern, short and stout, was wearing a pink quilted housecoat. But this kind of argumentation was standard between them; she took no offense. "Well, Papa will never let you out of the house. Is that all you're having for breakfast? Black coffee? You'll be a nervous wreck by the time you're twenty-one. Have a bun, at least.—Who was at the dance?"

"The junior class of Columbia College, Mama, about two hundred and fifty boys, with girls."

"Anybody we know?"

"No."

"How can you say that? Wasn't Rosalind Green there?"

"Of course she was."

"Well, we know her." Marjorie said nothing. "How is it you're going riding? I thought your lessons were on Tuesday."

"I just decided to go today."

"Who with?"

"Billy Ehrmann."

"How come you're wearing your new riding habit?"

"Why not? Spring is here."

"You don't have to impress Billy Ehrmann."

"Well, I've got to start wearing it sometime."

"Yes, once you've learned to ride. But what's the point, just for a lesson in the armory?"

Here Mrs. Morgenstern was driving to a material point. Marjorie had been taking the armory lessons in a borrowed old habit of an El Dorado neighbor, Rosalind Green. Her mother had bought her the new outfit on the understanding that she wasn't to wear it until she graduated to the bridle paths of the park. Marjorie could lie to her mother cheerfully, and with a good conscience, but she had several minor lies going, and it seemed a weariness to take on another. "Mom, I'm not going to the armory. We're going riding in the park."

"What? You've only had three lessons. You're not ready. You'll fall off the horse and break your neck."

"That'll be something to look forward to." The girl put her cup down with a clink and poured more coffee.

"Marjorie, I am not going to let you go riding in the park with that fat clumsy Billy Ehrmann. He probably can't ride any better than you."

"Mother, please. We're riding with two other couples and a groom. We'll be safer than in the armory."

"Who are the others?"

"Well, there's Rosalind and Phil."

"Who else?"

"Oh, some fraternity brother of theirs." Marjorie was determined to let her mother know nothing whatever about Sandy Goldstone.

"Who?"

"Oh, some fellow. I don't know his name. I know he's a very good rider."

"How do you know that, if you don't even know his name?"

"For heaven's sake, Mom! Billy and Phil said so."

"Was he at the dance? Did you meet him there?"

"I think maybe I did. I don't know. I met a hundred boys."

"Is he a good dancer?"

"I don't know."

"Where does he live?"

"Mom, I'm late. I said I don't know the boy——"

The telephone rang, and with immense relief Marjorie sprang into the foyer. "Hello?"

"Hello, pooch."

The proprietary nickname and the odd twangy voice brought the usual pleasurable warmth to Marjorie, mingled this time with a dim feeling of guilt. "Oh—hello, George, how are you?"

"What's the matter? Did I wake you up?"

"No, George. Matter of fact, I was just going out, so excuse me if——"

"Out?"

"Just out in the park. Riding."

"Well, well. Riding in Central Park. You'll be joining the Junior League next."

"Don't be funny."

"Well, how was the Columbia dance?"

"It was miserable, thanks." Her mother, she saw, had come to the doorway of the dining room and was openly listening to the conversation. Marjorie made her tone more affectionate. "I never realized how young a crowd of college juniors could look and act."

"Well, sure, how old can they be?" said George with a relieved lift in his voice. "Nineteen, average. Less, some of them. I warned you you'd be bored stiff." George Drobes was twenty-two, and a graduate of City College. "Well, pooch, when am I going to see you?"

"I don't know."

"Today?"

"I've got a ton of homework, dear."

"But you say you're going riding."

"Just for an hour. Then I'll be at the desk all day, really, George."

"Take off another hour."

"Dear, I'd love to—it's just such a long trip from the Bronx down here, just for an hour——"

"I'm not doing anything. It's Sunday. It's been almost two weeks—— Look, I'd just about decided to go to the art museum anyway. I've got the car. I'll drop by. If you feel like it, we'll go for a drive in the country. If you don't, why I'll just go on to the museum."

"Well——"

"See you about one or so, okay, pooch?"

"All right, George, sure. Love to see you." She hung up.

"What's the matter between you and George all of a sudden?" said Mrs. Morgenstern with pleasure.

"Absolutely nothing. Mother, I wonder whether you know that people don't usually listen to other people's phone conversations?"

"I'm not people. I'm your mother. You don't have anything to hide from me, do you?"

"There's a thing called privacy, that's all."

"I hope the great love isn't beginning to cool off."

"It certainly is not!"

"I haven't seen him in such a long time. Does he still have that red nose?"

"He does not have a red nose."

"Bronx Park East is a long way from Central Park West," said Mrs. Morgenstern with a majestic sigh. Marjorie made for the door. "Listen, Marjorie, don't be foolish. The first time in the park anything can happen. Don't wear the new outfit."

Marjorie's hand was on the doorknob. "Clothes don't do anybody any good hanging in the closet." She opened the door. "Goodbye, Mom. I won't be home for lunch."

"Where will you eat?"

"Tavern on the Green."

"Listen," said Mrs. Morgenstern, "Billy's friend, this fellow who's such a good rider, will like you just as well in the other outfit."

Marjorie's heart sank. "I can't imagine what you're talking about, Mom. Goodbye."

Her exit, which she made with a fine airy wave of the hand, was spoiled as soon as she closed the door. She had no money. The stable was at Sixty-sixth Street, and she was late. She had to go back in and ask her mother for taxi fare. "Well, I'm glad I'm still good for something in your life," said Mrs. Morgenstern, "even if it's only money. What's happened to your allowance this week?"

"Mom, you know my allowance only runs from Saturday to Saturday."

The mother was fumbling in a large black patent-leather purse. "It's a good thing your father's business doesn't run from Saturday to Saturday."

"Might as well give me the rest of my allowance, Mom. Then I won't have to trouble you again."

"No trouble, I assure you." Mrs. Morgenstern drew another dollar and a half from the purse. She always managed, thought Marjorie, to make the payment of the allowance a triumph. Marjorie often felt that she would go hungry and barefoot rather than ask for her allowance again. A hundred times she had planned to gain independence by writing short stories, or tutoring, or getting a weekend job as a salesgirl. These plans usually sprouted just before she had to ask for her allowance, and tended to wither right after she got it.

"Thank you, Mother," she said, remotely cool and formal as she accepted the money.

At this moment her father came into the hallway, carrying the Sunday *Times* in a disordered sheaf under his arm. He wore a red silk smoking jacket in which he looked uncomfortable. Marjorie kissed him. "Morning, Dad. Sorry I've got to run."

The father said, "Horseback . . . Can't you find something less dangerous than horseback, Margie? People get killed riding horseback."

"Don't worry. Marjorie will come back in one piece. 'Bye."

Marjorie's father had come to the United States at the age of fifteen, an orphan, a fleck of foam on the great wave of immigration from Eastern Europe. In his first bewildered week in a wretched cellar on the lower East Side of New York, he had become friendly with a boy who worked for an importer of feathers. He too had gone to work sorting and classifying feathers: filthy work that paid two dollars a week. Now, thirty-three years later, the importer was dead, the boy who had brought him into the feather business was Mr. Morgenstern's partner, and the Arnold Importing Company was a well-known dealer in feathers, straws, and other materials for ladies' hats, a tributary of New York's millinery trade. From two dollars a week, Marjorie's father had painfully worked up to about fifteen thousand a year. Every year since his marriage he had spent every dollar he earned on the comfort of his family and the improvement of their station in life. Except for his part ownership of the struggling little corporation and the salary he drew, he was a penniless man. Yet he lived on Central Park West.

"Do you think she'll be all right?" he said, peering at the brown door through which his daughter had vanished.

"Why not? All the kids around here ride. More coffee before it's cleared away?"

"All right."

At Marjorie's vacant place in the dining room was the ruin of the bun she had half bolted, smeared with lipstick. "Why is she suddenly so interested in horseback riding?" said Mr. Morgenstern. "She had one lesson this week."

"Why do you think?" His wife poured coffee from the silver pot she used on Sunday mornings.

"Not that fat fool Billy Ehrmann?"

"There's another boy in the party."

"Who is he?"

"I don't know. Fraternity brother of Billy. He can't be too bad."

The father pulled out the business section of the *Times* and glanced at it, sipping coffee. After a while he said, "What about George?"

"George, I think, is finished. Marjorie doesn't know it yet."

"But you know it, I suppose."

"Yes, I do. It's a long way down here from the Bronx."

"Maybe we shouldn't have moved from the Bronx."

"Now what makes you say that?" The mother looked out of the window, still pleased and thrilled by the view of the park.

"Personally I have no objection to George. A steady boy," the father said. "Could fit in the business."

"A nobody."

"Well, I don't like these Manhattan boys," the father said. "They're too smart. They're cold fish. I talk to them, and suddenly I remember I've got an accent. I can hear it. After thirty years they make me feel like a greenhorn." Marjorie's father had only a slight accent, and the mother had virtually none, yet neither sounded native-born, and they knew they never would. "I don't trust these boys. They look like they'd try any smart trick with a girl they could get away with."

"Marjorie can take care of herself."

"She can, can she?"

Mrs. Morgenstern had been maintaining the opposite viewpoint not less recently than two o'clock that morning while waiting up nervously for Marjorie. This kind of discussion went on all the time between the parents. They could take either side with ease. It all depended on which one started to criticize the daughter. The father stared at his paper and the mother stared out of the window.

After a while the mother shrugged. "She's entitled to the best, isn't she? The West Side is where the good families live. Here she has the best chances of meeting somebody worth while. We went all over that ground."

"She told me all about sex yesterday afternoon," the father said. "Studied it in Hygiene, she says. She knows the whole business like a doctor. She knows a lot more about it than I do. Talked about chromosomes, and tubes, and eggs, and the male this, and the female that. I was embarrassed, I'll tell you the truth, and the strange thing is I felt sorry for her."

"Well, she can't help what they teach her in school. Is it better to know nothing at all, the way we were?"

"Maybe she knows too much. Did she ever tell you the five arguments that prove God exists and five answers that prove He doesn't? She learned them in a course. But she never goes to temple except to a dance, she's forgotten any Hebrew she ever knew, and if she doesn't eat bacon she eats shrimp cocktails, I'll bet a hundred dollars on that."

"This is America."

"We've spoiled her. I'm worried about her, Rose. Her attitudes—— She doesn't know what money is. A wild Indian couldn't know less. I do some magic with a fountain pen and a checkbook and she has a dress or a coat or a riding habit——"

"I saw you going over the checkbook last night. Is that what this fuss is all about? The riding habit? A girl needs clothes."

"I'm talking in general. From a money standpoint this move to Manhattan was crazy. We're eating capital."

"I've told you twenty times you're going to have to give yourself a raise."

The father stood and began to walk back and forth. He was a stout little man with a moon face, curly graying hair, and heavy black eyebrows. "It's a funny thing about a business. You take out more money than comes in and after a while there's no business."

Marjorie's mother had heard nothing but moans from her husband about business through good times and bad. She was not inclined to regard the depression seriously. Her husband's steadily rising income from his feather importing business had seemed miraculous to her in the first years of their marriage, but now she took it quite for granted. "These are the years that count for Marjorie. This new boy she's riding with, whoever he is, he's a Columbia boy, a fraternity boy, isn't he? That means a good family. Would she have met him if we'd stayed in the Bronx?"

"She's only a sophomore. She may not get married for years."

"It won't put us in the poorhouse."

"Then there'll be Seth."

"We'll worry about Seth when the time comes."

"Well, we won't have any problems if she breaks her neck today riding a horse."

"She won't break her neck."

"I heard you arguing with her. She's only had three lessons."

"What is there to riding a horse?"

The father paced to the window. "It's a beautiful day. There go some horses . . . That wouldn't be her, yet. Look, the park is green. Seems like only yesterday it was all covered with purple snow. The snow in the parks looks purple, did you notice that? There must be a scientific explanation." He rubbed his forehead. "I'm worrying about spring hats in November and fall hats in February. A year goes by like a week, it seems."

"She'll be all right, I tell you." The mother came and stood beside him. They were the same height, and she too had a round face. Their expressions were much alike, except that the man's face had sterner lines at the mouth. They might have been brother and sister. He looked about ten years older than his wife, though they were nearly the same age.

"Doesn't it seem strange to you?" said the father. "It does to me. How long ago was she crawling on the floor with wet diapers? What's become of the time? Horseback——"

"We're getting old, Arnold."

"Nowadays they make jokes about the marriage brokers," said the father. "All the same, with the old system she'd be meeting nothing but boys of exactly the right age and background, and no guesswork."

"With that system you wouldn't have the problem of Marjorie at all," said the mother sharply.

The father smiled and looked sly. After more than twenty years it was still a sore point with Mrs. Morgenstern that he had once almost been matched with a rabbi's daughter. "I'm just saying that this is also a strange system. It's going to cost us plenty, putting her near these good families of yours. And one night at one of these dances, what's to stop her from falling for a good-looking fool from a rotten family? And that'll be the end of it. Remember that first one at the camp when she was thirteen? That Bertram?"

The mother grimaced. "She has more sense now."

"She has more education. That's a different thing. She has no more sense. A lot less maybe. And as for—well, religion—the way things are nowadays——" He broke off, looking out of the window.

"All this," said the mother uneasily, "just because the girl goes for a horseback ride? Don't forget one thing. She gets the man she loves. She gets what she wants, not what we pick. That's the right way."

"She gets what she wants?" said the father. "In this world? Not even in America. She'll get what she deserves."

There was a long silence. He finished his coffee, picked up the newspaper and walked into the living room.

Chapter 2. PRINCE CHARMING

"Here you are, miss." The taxi stopped in front of the Chevy Chase Riding Academy, a converted garage with a huge tin horse painted a dirty brown hanging over the entrance. A cloud of horse smell came rolling into the cab. She could hear the beasts stamping. The cab driver, glancing around, took in the stiff new riding habit and the uncertain look. He grinned, baring yellow horselike teeth. "Go ahead, kid. You'll live." Marjorie gave him a haughty look, and tipped him a quarter to prove that she was an aristocrat who loved horses. Handkerchief to nose, she went up the manure-littered ramp, stepping daintily with her toes pointed inward to avoid the unhappy duck-waddling effect which she had noticed in other girls wearing riding clothes.

Rosalind Green, a stocky sallow girl, came waddling to meet her from the gloomy stalls, in a new riding habit of a hideous olive color. "Hello, we were about to give you up. They're getting the horses ready."

"Sorry I'm late." Marjorie followed Rosalind through rows of stalls where horses were snorting, stamping, jingling, and neighing.

The two girls had become acquainted in the El Dorado elevator. Rosalind, a year and a half older, was a consistent A student, but she lacked humor and was dull at dances and parties. Ordinarily she might have hated Marjorie for her small waist, slender ankles, and quicksilver chatter. But she was so sure of her own superiority that she could forgive her. Rosalind had been born on Central Park West; she was a junior at Barnard; and she was engaged to one Phil Boehm, the son of a famous heart specialist. She had nothing to fear from the clever, pretty little climber from the Bronx, a mere sophomore at the free public college, Hunter. Rosalind frankly patronized Marjorie. Marjorie put up with it because of Rosalind's usefulness in introducing her to the Columbia fraternity set. They spent hundreds of hours talking about clothes, hair, paint, movies, and boys. Marjorie had lost touch with her girl friends in the Bronx, and had found no real chums at Hunter. Rosalind at the moment was her best friend.

"Here she is, Jeff," Rosalind called.

At the far end of the stable five horses—very big, eager, and gay—were prancing and pawing under a naked electric bulb. Jeff, a sunburned little groom in shabby breeches and wrinkled boots, stood among the animals, tightening girths and shouting orders at Billy and Sandy, who were saddling their horses. He glanced sourly at Marjorie. "How well can you ride, miss?"

"Not well at all," Marjorie said promptly.

A humane light flickered in the groom's eye. "Well, good for you. Most of them won't admit it, and then—— Whoa, you stupid bastard." He punched the dancing horse in the ribs.

Phil Boehm said, "That's my horse. Don't get him mad." He sat slumped on a dirty bench beside Sandy's girl, Vera Cashman, a handsome blond sophomore from Cornell, who looked sleepy and cross.

"Give her Black Beauty, Jeff," said Sandy, with a smile and a wink at Marjorie. He was deft and quick with his horse's trappings. His breeches were faded, and his boots looked not much better than the groom's. The riding costumes of the rest of the party were almost as new as Marjorie's.

"Give me the gentlest horse you've got," Marjorie said, "and give him a sleeping pill before we start."

Sandy laughed.

Billy Ehrmann, red-faced and perspiring, was heaving at a strap under his horse's belly. At this moment, with a fierce yank, he managed to undo everything, and fell on the floor under the horse, with the saddle and stirrups in a jingling pile on top of him. The groom, looking extremely disgusted, picked up the saddle and pulled Billy to his feet. "I thought you said you could do this, mister."

"Got to learn sometime," panted Billy, brushing manure from his fat face and his jacket.

"Not on a busy Sunday, mister, please." Jeff flipped the saddle on to the horse's back, and Billy shambled toward the bench, saying "Hi, Marge," with a sad grin.

Marjorie smiled at him, thinking what bad luck it was that Billy, of all the fraternity crowd, had attached himself to her. Billy's one claim to distinction was that his father was Supreme Court Justice Ehrmann, whose name seemed to be on most of the letterheads of New York charities. Marjorie had been greatly impressed at first to learn who Billy was, upon meeting half a dozen of the fraternity boys one evening at Rosalind's apartment; but she had soon found out that he was a good-natured dolt with no trace of his father's merit. Still, he was a Columbia boy. He had taken her to the dance last night. So as he walked by, exuding a horse smell which caused her to gasp and fall back a step, she smiled.

Jeff was eying her critically as he saddled Billy's horse. "I got an idea, miss. Give you Prince Charming. . . . Hey Ernest! Let's have Prince Charming."

Marjorie said, "Gentle?"

"Gentlest son of a bitch alive."

A Negro boy in jeans lounged out of a far stall and into another stall. "Prince Charming coming up," he called. After a moment or two he began to lead out a horse; began, that is, because the process took a while to complete. Not that the horse was unwilling. It came out readily enough, but it never seemed to stop coming. The Negro appeared to be unreeling the beast from a large spool inside the stall. It was by far the longest living thing Marjorie had ever seen. At last the rear end came into sight, with a limp straggling tail.

The animal was not only very long, it was a most peculiar mottled red. The Negro boy threw a saddle on its back and led it toward Marjorie. Its long head hung down, nodding. Its face, like every other horse's, seemed to Marjorie to express a weak-willed stupid animosity.

"What do you call that color?" she said to the groom.

"The color don't make no difference," said Jeff, spitting tobacco juice. "That horse is one goddamn gentle son of a bitch."

"I just wondered."

"Well, it's roan."

Roan. The word conjured up wide Western plains and thundering hooves.

"Let's mount, folks," shouted the groom. He held the stirrup for Marjorie, and she tried to get up on the horse, but couldn't. The creature was half again as high as the old mare she had been riding in the armory. She looked around helplessly with one foot in the stirrup, and the seat of her breeches straining. Sandy Goldstone came to her grinning, seized her other leg, and threw her on to the saddle. "Thanks," she gasped.

"Them stirrups the right length?" Jeff said.

"Oh yes, yes, absolutely perfect." The groom went and mounted his horse. Marjorie realized at once that her stirrups were too long. Her toes barely touched them.

"Okay folks, single file now going up the street, and no trotting in traffic."

They went out of the stable into warm blinding sunshine. Marjorie found it nightmarish to be riding along a city street on a horse. The hooves of the seven beasts made a terrible clatter on the asphalt. She kept reaching and clutching for the stirrups with her toes, thinking that a fall on the pavement would certainly fracture her skull. Prince Charming plodded calmly among the honking taxicabs and grinding busses. Every little toss of his head scared her. She clung to the saddle, though she knew it was bad form, though she could see the Cornell blonde grinning at her with contempt. She now cared about nothing except to get through this hour and off this animal undamaged.

When they came to the soft black dirt of the bridle path in the park the horses began to trot. Prince Charming surprised Marjorie with his easy comfortable gait. She found her stirrups and rode to the trot as she had been taught. Her confidence came back and she relaxed a bit. They trotted past the Tavern on the Green. She saw a good-looking boy at a table on the terrace follow her with his eyes as she went by.

Sandy Goldstone rode up beside her, reining in his big coffee-colored horse with a careless gesture. "Was that a joke about not riding well? You're doing nobly."

She gave him a mysterious smile. "You're not bad yourself."

"Spend a couple of months every year in Arizona. Guess I ought to be able to ride a horse . . . Margie, there's no reason for me to hang back and police you, really, is there? This nag's impatient."

"None at all, Sandy. Go ahead."

Sandy streaked away. The riding party passed through a dank muddy tunnel, and came out into a sun-flecked avenue of cherry trees, perfumed and cool. Marjorie was stunned by the charm of it. For the first time she perceived what horseback riding was about. She turned her eyes to the pink blossoms nodding under the blue sky in the breeze, and lost herself in pleasure.

When they emerged into open sunlight she noticed that Prince Charming was falling behind the other horses. The blonde, next to last in the party, was glancing back over the widening gap with amusement. Marjorie clasped the saddle and kicked Prince Charming in the ribs. Nothing happened except that she lost her stirrup and had to clutch for it with her foot. Prince Charming, an old civil servant of a horse, continued to reel off the same number of yards per second.

Far up the path the rest of the riders went round a bend and were hidden from view by green trees. "Giddyap!" Marjorie said. "Aren't you ashamed of yourself? They're beating you. Giddyap!" She made clicking noises and kicked both heels and shook the reins. Prince Charming ground along philosophically. They came to the bend and rounded it. There was a long straight stretch of black path ahead, completely empty except for a settling cloud of dust.

The solitude did not have a good effect on either horse or rider. Marjorie stiffened. Prince Charming, without a rear view of other horses to draw him on, seemed to lose interest in his work. His trot slowed, became bumpy, and subsided into a walk. He began to look here and there. Marjorie said in her fiercest voice, "You going now," and spanked his neck with the reins. Prince Charming yawned. He wandered off the path, stopped and contemplated a clump of yellow forsythia with the look of a nature lover, and began to eat it. Tears of vexation came to Marjorie's eyes. She beat the horse's neck with her fist.

She heard thudding hooves at about the same time Prince Charming did. The horse glanced around, took one more wrench at the forsythia, and ambled back on to the path, chewing. Sandy reined in, wheeled, and came beside her. "Having trouble?"

"Some."

"Kick him."

"I've kicked him."

Sandy surveyed the horse, wrinkling his nose. "Never been out with this one before. Mostly I think kids ride him. Here, try this." He passed his tan leather riding crop to Marjorie.

He should have noticed the terrible flattening of the animal's ears, but he was too busy looking at Marjorie's flushed pretty face.

"Thanks," Marjorie said. She flourished the crop and smacked it clumsily on the horse's flank. Prince Charming jumped, snorted, neighed; then he gathered himself up like a fist, and bounded away in a wild gallop, throwing up a boil of black dust all around Sandy.

After the first crazy moment of the bolt Marjorie found herself clinging to the saddle with no idea of how she had managed to remain on the horse. The reins were dangling free, she had lost her stirrups, and there she was, thundering along the path like a jockey, with trees, grass, and other riders swimming by her in a greenish blur. In a few seconds, hardly aware of what was happening, she overtook Vera, and one after another she passed the rest of the party as though they were standing still. Dimly she heard a shout from Jeff over the tattoo of Prince Charming's hooves and the splatter of flying dirt, " . . . rid of that goddamn *crop!* He's crop-shy! Never . . ." But it meant nothing to her. She went drumming down a clear track with the air whistling in her ears, pulling at her hair, bringing tears to her eyes. Her hat was gone, of course. The stirrups thumped and clanked gaily against the saddle girths. Marjorie noticed that, oddly enough, a maniacal gallop was the easiest of all gaits to sit to. It was like resting in a gently rocking chair, except for the noise of wind and hooves, and the quantities of scenery flying by. She was aware of no fear at all, but rather a silly mildly surprised pleasure. A cold wind on her teeth indicated that she was smiling. On the whole she was idiotically enjoying the fast ride.

Prince Charming came to the reservoir, turned sharp right, and went galloping up the curved path. At the moment that he turned he parted company with Marjorie, for she continued travelling in a straight line, flying off his back, landing on the path, rolling over and over through dirt and puddles, and coming to rest face down, sprawled on sweet-smelling new grass. There she lay, hearing far-off peaceful traffic sounds.

All at once she was surrounded by stamping horses, and girls were screeching and men were shouting and somebody gave her her hat, and a policeman was dismounting and taking out a notebook.

Jeff and Sandy helped her to her feet and set about cleaning her off with handkerchiefs and stray pieces of newspaper. She was smeared with mud and her jacket was ripped at the elbows. One of her ankles was throbbing peculiarly inside the boot, but nothing else seemed to be wrong with her. Exhilarated and quite gay at the center of the fuss, she answered the policeman's questions clearly and calmly. Jeff explained about Prince Charming's fear of crops. Sandy kept apologizing for not noticing the animal's terror. Marjorie said it was all her fault, she should have been able to control the horse anyway. The policeman said he was damned if he knew why more damned Sunday riders weren't killed. He shut up his book and remounted his tremendous brown horse, adding he was damned if he could see why people rode horses for pleasure at all, seeing that saddles were damned uncomfortable, and all horses were damned idiots.

Meantime another policeman appeared leading Prince Charming by the bridle. The animal was streaked black with sweat, and his head drooped meekly. Marjorie at once stepped out of the chattering circle around her, took the reins from the policeman's hands, and with a limber spring that surprised herself got back into the saddle. Her ankle gave her an angry twinge when she jumped.

"Hey," said Jeff, staring at her and scratching his head. The others peered around at her.

Marjorie said, "I'm all right. Let's get going."

"You sure, miss?" Jeff said. "Maybe we better get you a cab, call it a day."

"Didn't you ever fall off a horse?"

"Forty times, miss, but——"

"Well, you're still in one piece. So am I. Just shorten my stirrups, please. Sorry I held up the party."

"Attagirl, Margie," said Billy Ehrmann.

"Well, okay." Jeff sprang to the stirrups. "That's the spirit, miss. You'll be a rider yet. Mr. Goldstone, you better ride with her from here on."

"With pleasure." Sandy reined his horse alongside Prince Charming.

The blonde gave her horse a hard kick in the ribs as she went ahead past Marjorie and Sandy. "Quel cretin," she was heard to murmur.

Marjorie's hands and legs were trembling, and sweat was cold on her forehead. But she was less afraid than she had been at the start of the ride. The worst had happened, and here she was, back on the horse. Without realizing it she was sitting more naturally in the saddle, holding the reins better collected.

"Well, now you're an experienced horsewoman," Sandy said as they rode beside the reservoir, trotting over a golden layer of tree pollen on the black path.

Marjorie laughed. "It'll take more than one fall, I'm afraid. At least I fulfilled my own expectation this morning. I made a fool of myself. I can hardly ride, you know. That's the truth."

"Why did you come, Margie? You didn't have to say yes just to be polite."

She looked him serenely in the eye, smiling. He grew red and stopped talking, and they trotted on in silence.

Paced by Sandy's horse, Prince Charming went along like a machine. Back at the stable Marjorie managed not to limp, though the ankle was bothering her more and more. She didn't intend to be parted from Sandy Goldstone at this point because of a little pain.

When the party came to the Tavern on the Green, Marjorie was very glad she had come along despite the throbbing ankle. How gay it was to sit down to white napery and silver on a sunlit stone terrace under the open sky, in a green park bordered by jagged skyscrapers! Marjorie had never done it before. A stiff brushing at the stable had cleaned all the dried mud from her habit. She didn't mind the ripped elbows; she felt they gave her a raffish Long Island horsy-set touch. She had combed her hair and freshened her makeup. She thought she rather resembled an illustration in a fashion magazine. She was proud of the way she had muddled through the ride and the fall, and pleased at certain small attentions Sandy had been paying her.

"Bacon and scrambled eggs for everybody, I guess?" Sandy said.

"Leave the bacon off mine. Just eggs," Marjorie said, after hesitating a moment.

Vera raised one eyebrow at her. "What's the matter, dear, are you religious?"

"Just habit," Marjorie muttered, embarrassed. She was convinced that the Jewish food prohibitions were mere primitive taboos, but her upbringing was stronger than logic. Once or twice she had tried to eat bacon and had failed; the red and yellow strips made her gorge rise.

"Well, I guess you'll go to heaven and we won't," Vera said. "I couldn't live without my bacon in the morning."

Sandy yawned, "Let her alone. What do you know about it, anyway? Some people think that all the equipment you need to discuss religion is a mouth."

Marjorie blinked at this unexpected support.

"Dear me," Vera said to Marjorie with a grin, "have I stepped on your toes? I'm sorry, I'm sure."

"Live and let live," Sandy said.

Marjorie felt she had been successfully snubbed by the blonde. She resolved, as she had several times before, to practice eating bacon sometime by herself. Some of the fun went out of the brunch for her.

The waitress was just beginning to serve the food when Marjorie's mouth twisted in an involuntary grimace. A thrill of pain had shot up hotly from her ankle to her knee. "What's the matter with you?" Sandy said.

"Nothing, nothing." Everybody looked at her. The waitress was passing Phil's bacon and eggs under her nose. Marjorie couldn't help it; she put her head on her arms on the table, feeling faint and very sick. "I'm sorry, it's my ankle. It hurts like hell. I—I think I'd better go home——"

There was a flurry of sympathy and suggestions. Sandy Goldstone cut it short by tossing his car keys on the table and picking Marjorie up easily in his arms. "She shouldn't walk on it. I'll carry her to a cab and get her to her house, Billy. If I'm not back in half an hour you drive the others home. I'll phone you, Vera, about three o'clock."

"Well, all right. No later," said the blonde.

Marjorie submitted limply to being carried, aware of little besides the stabbing pain. She did notice that Sandy's rough red-checked shirt, against which her cheek rested, smelled strongly of horses. Somehow it was not a bad smell at all in a young man's wool shirt.

It was the pressure of the gradual swelling inside the boot that had caused the agony, the doctor said. He made one tentative effort to pull off the boot. The girl shrieked. Without ceremony he took a sharp instrument from his bag and cut the beautiful new boot to pieces. "There," he said, carefully removing the shredded leather and the rags of stocking, "feels better now, doesn't it?"

"Much."

He squeezed and prodded the red-blue swelling, and made her move the foot and wriggle her toes. She was embarrassed because Sandy could see her bare leg. The doctor began to tape the ankle. "You'll be all right in a few days. Just a sprain."

Mrs. Morgenstern picked up the ruined boot and Marjorie's torn jacket, which lay crumpled on a chair. "You had to go riding in the park after three lessons. You had to wear the new outfit. You had to climb back on the horse with a sprained ankle. Hooray for you."

Sandy said, "It was my fault completely, ma'am. She rides very well. If not for that riding crop——"

"I'm glad she got back on the horse. That's the only good thing about the story," said the father. He was as pale as his daughter. He had not previously uttered a word.

Mrs. Morgenstern gave Sandy a bleak glance. "You said your name is what—Goldstein?"

"Goldstone, ma'am," Sandy said with his easy good-natured smile.

"Goldstone . . . Your mother isn't by any chance Eva Goldstone?"

"She's my aunt, ma'am. My mother is Mary Goldstone."

The mother straightened, smiled, and dropped the torn clothes on a chair. "Well, and a lovely lady, too. Isn't she the vice-president of Manhattan Hadassah?"

"Yes, Mother keeps pretty busy with those things."

"Well, and you didn't have your lunch—I mean your brunch, as Margie calls it. You'll stay and have it with us, of course."

"Well, ma'am, thank you, but I guess I better go and——"

"How long will it take to fix some eggs? After all, you must be starved, and you took such good care of our girl——"

Sandy glanced at Marjorie and raised his eyebrows slightly. She shrugged slightly. "Thanks a lot, I'll be glad to stay if it isn't too much trouble——"

"Trouble!" exclaimed the mother, vanishing. She called them into the dining room in ten minutes. "Just a snack, naturally, there's no time to fix anything." Platters of smoked salmon, smoked whitefish, kippered herrings, lettuce and tomatoes, scrambled eggs, french-fried potatoes, rolls, toast, Danish pastry, and coffee cake covered the table.

"Holy cow," Sandy said. Mr. Morgenstern stared at the table and at his wife.

Sandy, eating continuously and heartily, told them of his comic misadventures with horses in Arizona. It became a very jolly meal. Marjorie's eyes were brightly fixed on Sandy; the mother was enchanted by him; Mr. Morgenstern warmed to him and began laughing. They were having their second cups of coffee when the house phone rang in the kitchen. Mrs. Morgenstern went to answer it. She returned in a moment looking very disturbed, and whispered in Marjorie's ear. The girl seemed startled; then she glanced at Sandy, and her lips curved in a confident smile. "Of course, Mom. George said he might drop by."

"What'll I tell him?" muttered the mother.

"What? Why, tell him to come up of course, Mom dear."

Chapter 3. GEORGE

George Drobes and Marjorie Morgenstern had been keeping steady company for the better part of two years.

George was a victim of the depression. By training and ambition a bacteriologist, he had completed half his studies toward his master's degree before being compelled to go to work in his father's little auto accessories store in the Bronx. George wasn't happy about spending his days in the dusty gloom of Southern Boulevard under the booming rattling El, selling fan belts and hub caps to gray-faced Bronxites, when his mind was full of marvels like amoebas and spirochetes. But there was no help for it. He grimly saved a fragment of his allowance each week (he was getting no salary for helping to keep the large Drobes family alive); for he was resolved to go back and finish his training in bacteriology, even at the age of fifty.

He was by no means the first boy who had dated Marjorie. She had gone to well-chaperoned schoolgirlish dances and parties since her twelfth year. Around her fifteenth birthday, with official if reluctant parental approval, Marjorie had arrayed herself in lipstick, rouge, perfume, eyebrow-black, brassiere, girdle, silk stockings, and stylish clothes, and plunged out once for all into the sea of dating. Mrs. Morgenstern fought off this debut with great energy to the very end. At first, when Marjorie was a little over fourteen, she objected to rouge. Then she gave in on rouge and objected to lipstick. Then she yielded on lipstick and declared war on the eyebrow pencil. She kept up a fierce rear-guard action for a long time against any kind of clothes that looked grown-up, the only kind Marjorie was interested in. But the mother's resistance collapsed when Marjorie reached fifteen. Any further fight was hopeless. Whatever Marjorie's deficiencies in experience and common sense, she looked as womanly as her mother did. Mrs. Morgenstern turned Marjorie loose, hoping for the best. It was the way things were done nowadays.

Marjorie immediately ran into the furtive sex fumbling that all boys her own age considered natural and in fact obligatory. She was upset the first couple of times it happened. But her instinct, backed up by her mother's vague but horrid warnings, made her reject these advances with a strong arm. She found dates disappointing once the first thrill of having them was past. The pleasure lay mostly in the fact that she was doing grown-up things, and in the theatrical fun of dressing and painting herself. Most of the boys she met were pimpled gangling fools. They kept trying to kiss and hug and paw her; and when she fought off these compliments, they sulked. None of them remotely tempted her to try out the sex excitements promised in movies and magazine stories. It often seemed to her, in the first eight months of her fifteenth year, that all males were nasty louts, and that she would have to live and die an old maid for her fastidiousness. She faced the prospect cheerfully. It was during this time of her life that she worked up a number of bright arguments against marriage, and made fun of sex, and declared that instead of becoming some man's dishwasher and cook she was going to be a career woman.

She then met George Drobes.

He came into her life via the Bronx YMHA. Marjorie went there to see an amateur production of *Desire under the Elms,* in the company of a boy whose name was now blotted from memory, but whom she remembered for buck teeth and wet hands. After the play there was dancing. George Drobes cut in on Marjorie. Her first impression of him was that he had pleasantly dry palms. Then she realized, with a little shock, that she was dancing with an adult, not a boy. She had danced with men before—uncles, and aging cousins in their twenties—but this was the first time a grown man had approached her in the open arena of life.

George cut in on her several times, and eventually asked for her telephone number, having danced her out into a quiet corridor. Marjorie was dazzled. She had not yet grown to her full height; George was a head taller than herself. She did not see the glasses and the reddened nose; she did not hear the snuffle. She saw an earnest, well-spoken man of twenty paying court to herself, a girl fifteen and a half, hardly past hanging by her heels in playgrounds, popping bubble gum, and cutting out pictures of stars in movie magazines. George had a narrow bony face, thin lips, and bushy dark hair. His smile was sweet and faintly melancholy. She gave him her telephone number, and for a while they went on with a halting delicious conversation. But he was too big, too powerful, too flopping a fish for her inexpert hands. She could think of nothing but her own age, and at last she blurted it out. George was astounded; he had taken her for eighteen, he said. The conversation died. He took her back to the wet-handed boy and cut in on her no more. Marjorie could hardly sleep that night for thinking of George, and hating herself for mishandling him.

During the next couple of weeks, whenever the telephone rang, crimson rays seemed to shoot out of it, and Marjorie would fling herself at it. But it was never the marvelous twenty-year-old man. Then one rainy evening almost a month later, when she had given up hope, he really did call. He was clumsy and abrupt. Did she remember him? Was she well? Would she come with him to a formal dance at the City College gymnasium? Marjorie answered yes, yes, yes, in painful gasps—and it was over. She stood with the receiver in her hands, numb with joy.

She had to tell her mother, of course. It took Mrs. Morgenstern only a few minutes to extract from the shaky girl everything she knew about George Drobes. The mother was less impressed than Marjorie had been to learn that he was twenty years old, a college man, and a bacteriologist; nor was she quite so thrilled at the girl's being invited to a college formal dance before reaching sixteen. "If this fellow is as marvelous as you say, why should he want to bother with a baby like you?"

"Mom, you'll never look at the good side of anything. Isn't it just possible that he could like me?"

The mother at last gave a grudging consent to the date, and even became a little infected with the girl's exhilaration when they shopped for an evening dress in downtown department stores. Marjorie thought about nothing but the dance for two weeks. There were tremendous debates over hair-dos and makeup and color of shoes and exposure of bosom. The day of the dance was cyclonic in the Morgenstern household, with Marjorie fretting and foaming at the center. Then all at once, an hour before George was supposed to arrive, quiet ensued. The eternity passed, the time came, the doorbell rang; and she tripped to answer it, a shiny-eyed child of fifteen and a half, with a bosom precociously full and panting under the flouncy blue tulle of her dress.

She almost fainted when she saw George. He was in an army officer's uniform, all glittering brass buttons and brown male power and glory. He himself had been too nervous on the telephone to mention that it was a Reserve Officers Training Corps dance.

The military apparition overpowered her family. Mrs. Morgenstern was more polite than she had ever been to one of Marjorie's escorts. The father stared at George with something like awe, and said nothing. Marjorie's younger brother, Seth, a lively urchin of eleven whose face shone from a harsh last-minute scrubbing, kept saluting and prancing in circles, humming *The Stars and Stripes Forever.* As for Marjorie, the only thought that pierced her fog of delight was that the living room was a wretched cramped hole and the furniture terribly dowdy; she couldn't understand why she hadn't noticed it long ago.

There was no end to the wonders of George Drobes. It turned out that he had his father's car for the occasion, an old Chevrolet painted a bright false green, which he drove with practiced ease. Moreover he had a name for the car, Penelope. She thought this was an incredibly clever and whimsical touch. Her father drove a new blue Buick, but nobody had ever had the imagination to give it a name. It was just a machine, nothing like this glamorous lovable Penelope. Sitting beside George in the front seat of Penelope, Marjorie felt twenty-five years old.

The dance was a delirium. The very air in the college gymnasium seemed to be blue and gauzy like her dress, and when she danced she seemed to be standing still, wrapped in George's strong arms, while the great bare walls and the handsome officers and the beautiful girls and the punching bags and monkey bars and wrestling mats and rowing machines wheeled round and round her gently in time to the music.

On the way home, George stopped the car in Bronx Park, in a leafy dark nook filled with smells of springtime; and Marjorie found that there was more to kissing than the pecking wet foolishness of party games, that this touch of mouth to mouth could be sweet. It didn't seem wrong to kiss George. He was gentle and kind. Between kisses he poured out his heart to her. He had tried for weeks to forget her, he said, convinced that she was too young for him. But it had been impossible. He had invited her to the dance to prove to himself that she couldn't fit into his life. Instead he was falling more and more in love with her. Who could deny that she had been the loveliest girl at the dance, the most poised, the most intelligent? What did age matter, when a girl had everything?

"Oh, you've just gone crazy, George."

"Yes. I'll never get over it either. I'll wait five years, Marjorie, ten, whatever you say. You're my girl. There'll never be anyone else."

Hearing such words, Marjorie surrendered herself to the pleasant process of kissing George without further fear. She had never experienced such bliss. How could she deny the evidence of her senses? For her, too, there would never be anyone else.

In the months that followed, George consolidated his position. He lived only a few subway stops from Marjorie. Walks in the park, movie dates, and casual meetings at ice cream parlors or at the neighborhood library were simple to arrange. George soon came to enjoy a great added advantage: Mrs. Morgenstern openly opposed him, saying that Marjorie would do much better one of these days. This would probably have been enough in itself to make the girl adore him. But George did have persisting attractions in his own right. He was—at least by Marjorie's sixteen-year-old standards—adult, witty, gracious, and suave. He had Penelope. And he thrilled Marjorie as she had never been thrilled before. In time their relationship included some rather warm necking sessions. But he was considerate. The advance of intimacy was very slow, and each step seemed natural when it happened. The necking was often preceded by George's reading aloud of some poems of Edna St. Vincent Millay, which he did quite well in a husky voice.

Then Marjorie moved to Central Park West.

She smiled brightly at Sandy when George rang the doorbell, and hobbled to answer it before her mother could stop her.

George stood in the doorway in the usual gray suit with the usual red tie, holding in his hand the battered brown hat, the only one he owned, with the threads coming loose on the band. It still gave Marjorie a thrill to open the door to George, though he no longer quite stunned her with his godlike masculinity. His smile was the same—wide, sweet, a little more melancholy than it had been before he had given up bacteria for auto supplies. She felt a bit ashamed because Sandy Goldstone was in the dining room wearing riding clothes. "Hi, George. Come in."

His eye fell on the taped ankle. "My God, pooch——"

"It's nothing, nothing at all. Sprained it a bit. Come on, you're just in time for coffee and cake." She took his hand and pressed it warmly, trying to tell him with this gesture that the handsome young stranger he was about to meet didn't mean a thing to her; and she led him into the dining room.

Mrs. Morgenstern smiled at George with her mouth muscles. Mr. Morgenstern looked unhappy. Sandy Goldstone rose with an amiable grin. Marjorie introduced the two young men to each other. Sandy poked out a friendly hand. George took it as though it were a telegram containing bad news, and shook it briefly. Marjorie pulled a chair to the table beside her own. "Poor Sandy had the job of bringing me home after I was dumb enough to fall off a horse. Sit down, George." George was still standing, fumbling his brown hat.

"I just had lunch. I'll wait in the living room——"

"Don't be funny." She pulled him into the chair. "Some coffee and cake won't kill you."

"Cake's all gone," said Mrs. Morgenstern.

"Good heavens, he can have mine," said Marjorie. "Pour him some coffee, Mom."

"How are your folks, George?" said Mr. Morgenstern.

"Pop's ulcer is acting up again," George said.

"I thought that new medicine was so good."

"Well, it was for a while. I don't know. He went to a wedding and ate herring."

"Herring? Foolish." Mr. Morgenstern had no ulcers, but feared he was getting them. He often talked with George about his father's ulcer while Marjorie dressed for a date. It cheered him to hear of Mr. Drobes' symptoms, because they were more acute than his own. He had really decided he liked George one evening when George told him of his father being carried off to a hospital in agony. "I hope he isn't in the hospital again?"

"No, but he will be if he doesn't lay off herring, that's for sure."

"I like kippers myself," said Sandy.

"You're just lucky," said Mr. Morgenstern, "that you're too young to worry about ulcers."

"Please!" broke out the mother. "Who brought up ulcers? Do we have to sit around the lunch table talking about ulcers?" She held out a cup of coffee to George. In reaching for it he flipped his hat off his lap, instinctively grabbed for it, hit the coffee with his elbow, and sent it splashing across the table.

"Oh my God, Mrs. Morgenstern, I'm sorry—— Oh, Lord, that's terrible —I beg your pardon——"

"Nothing at all. Coffee stains come out, usually," said the mother, sopping up the brown pool with a napkin. "But that's the last of it, and it'll take a while to heat some more."

"I assure you I don't want any. I was just taking it to be polite——"

"I really have to be going," said Sandy.

"Don't let me drive you away," said George. "Stick around."

"Who drives anybody out of this house?" said the mother. "Please, Sandy, come into the parlor and visit for a minute."

Sandy dropped into the most comfortable armchair in the living room, the one usually occupied by Mr. Morgenstern. George sat on a low bench in front of the artificial fireplace, his legs projecting bonily. He still held his hat, turning it between his legs round and round. Marjorie waited till the others were seated, then perched herself on a peach-colored hassock close to George.

"Marjorie, that's hard on your ankle. Come sit by me," said the mother.

"Oh, Mom, relax. It doesn't bother me at all. I'm perfectly comfortable."

Mr. Morgenstern took a cigar and extended the humidor toward the two young men. They both declined. A silence followed, during which the only activity in the room was Mr. Morgenstern lighting his cigar, and George turning his hat.

"Don't you smoke, Sandy?" said the mother.

"Oh, sure, tons of cigarettes, ma'am. Just don't feel like it at the moment, thanks."

Mr. Morgenstern said, "You're young enough to break the habit. Take my advice and quit."

"That's what my dad says," grinned Sandy. "He smokes twenty cigars a day."

"Mr. Goldstone owns Lamm's department store," said Mrs. Morgenstern to George.

"Oh," said George, reversing the direction of his hat.

"One of these days I'll have to start on cigarettes," said Marjorie. "I love the smell of them."

"Over my dead body," said Mrs. Morgenstern.

"They're not so bad," said Sandy.

"It's not refined for girls to smoke cigarettes," said the mother. "Married women, maybe. Not girls. Get married first, then you can smoke your head off."

"That's right," said George. "I think a cigarette makes a girl look hard."

Mrs. Morgenstern said, "What are you talking about? Nothing could make Marjorie look hard."

"Well, I don't think so either. But if anything could, cigarettes could."

"Nothing could," said the mother.

"George," said Marjorie, "for heaven's sake put down that hat."

"I didn't know I still had it," said George, looking at the hat. It went on turning in his hands. Marjorie snatched it and put it on a table beside her.

"Does your father ride horseback too?" Mrs. Morgenstern said to Sandy.

"Well, Dad's more of a golf player, but when we started going to

Arizona he took up riding. Nothing much to do there but ride. He got pretty good at it. He usually does, whatever he goes in for."

"Your father keeps himself in shape. Smart man," said Mr. Morgenstern, rolling his cigar in his fingers.

"Beats me at everything, pretty near. Won't play tennis with me because I can hold my own at that. Dad doesn't like to lose."

"He sounds like a very fine person," said Mrs. Morgenstern. "A big businessman, but he finds time to play games with his son."

Sandy looked a little less self-assured, almost sheepish. He pulled a cigarette out of his shirt pocket and lit it with a flick of a yellow metal lighter. "Well, Dad says he's going to make a man of me if it kills him. He thinks I'm pretty hopeless."

Mrs. Morgenstern laughed. "I'll bet he doesn't. He's just toughening you up to step into his shoes."

"Well, I know. But I'd rather be a doctor, you see."

George, who was sitting in a mournful slump, looked up with interest. "Are you pre-med?"

"Sort of. Not officially yet, so as to avoid family arguments, but I'm taking all the courses."

Mrs. Morgenstern said, "Well, to be a doctor is a fine thing. But to give up a million-dollar business to study for seven years and then sit around in a dinky office for ten more before you make a decent living——" She shrugged, and smiled. "You'll think better of it when the time comes."

Sandy twisted his mouth. "You're on Dad's side. That's exactly what he says."

"I'm on your side," said George. "I'm a bacteriologist, myself. I'd rather take blood counts in a charity ward than run R. H. Macy's."

"That may be," said Mrs. Morgenstern. "Wait till somebody asks you to run Macy's."

"I would have liked to be a doctor," said Mr. Morgenstern.

"Every man you talk to wanted to be a doctor or a writer," said Mrs. Morgenstern. "It's like a disease. And still half of the doctors are starving, and all of the writers. And why? Because most people are healthy, and hardly anybody reads books. It's that simple. Business is what keeps the world going. And still nobody has a good word for business."

Marjorie said to Sandy with a laugh, "This is an old family fight. Dad wants my brother Seth to be a doctor. Mom wants him to carry on the business."

"And what does Seth want to do?" said Sandy.

"He has a fine ambition," said the mother. "He wants to be the first man to fly to the moon."

Sandy burst out laughing. "I'm all for him." He rose, and offered his hand to George. "Got to go. Nice meeting you. Are you on a hospital staff?"

With a ghost of a grin, George said, "Regard me as a horrible example. I've succumbed. I'm in my father's business. But only temporarily, I hope."

"That's the spirit," said Sandy.

"Take my word for it," George said. "The pressures close in on you as you get older."

"I guess they do," Sandy said, more distantly.

"After all, George," said Mrs. Morgenstern, "an auto supply store in the Bronx isn't Lamm's."

Marjorie said with a cutting edge in her voice, "The principle is exactly the same, Mom."

"Oh, the principle," said Mrs. Morgenstern.

Marjorie limped with Sandy to the door, preventing her mother with a fierce look from accompanying them.

"Thanks for lunch—that is, thank your mom for me," said Sandy.

"Thank you for bringing me home," said Marjorie, opening the door and ringing for the elevator. "I hope Vera won't be too angry with you."

Sandy grinned. "She's boiling, I'm sure." He leaned against the doorpost, fished a cigarette from his shirt pocket and lit it. He looked out of place in an apartment hallway, almost like a cowhand, with his easy powerful gestures, his sunburn, the faint horsy smell from his red shirt, and the slow clear male grin. He had even picked up a trace of a drawl in Arizona, or maybe it was his own way of talking. If so it was very odd in a Manhattan Jewish boy. This was Sandy at his most attractive. He had seemed to dim out in the living room for a while, especially when he spoke of his father.

She rang the bell again. "These elevators."

"I'm in no hurry. You and I can have a nice little chat."

"About what? Vera Cashman?"

He looked at her from under raised eyebrows. He reached out a long arm and mussed her hair.

"Stop that," she said, tossing her head.

"I like your friend George. Kind of old for you, though."

"That's how much you know."

"Let me tell you something about riding a horse," Sandy said. "You must never forget one thing. You're a person, and he's a horse. That means you're better than he is, even though he seems to be four times as smart as you and eight times as big. Now when it's a question of——"

The elevator came jangling up the shaft. "Oh, dear," said Marjorie. "And it was just getting interesting."

Sandy mussed her hair again. "You remind me of my kid sister." He grinned and waved to her from inside the elevator. "Have fun. Stay off that ankle. 'Bye."

Marjorie returned to the living room. "When did he start to vomit?" Mr. Morgenstern was saying to George. "After he went to bed?" The mother had left the room.

"No, right after he got home," said George.

"Was the pain high up, or down low?"

"For heaven's *sake*," said Marjorie. "That ulcer again?"

"Well." The father stood and walked out, saying, "Give my best to him, George. Tell him to stay away from herring."

"That Sandy seems to be a nice kid. Columbia?" said George. Marjorie nodded. "Is he the one who took you to the dance?"

"Heavens, no. I went with a fat fool named Billy Ehrmann. He's the one I went riding with, too. But he just got all panicky when my foot began to hurt. So Sandy took charge and brought me home. Sandy has a knockout of a girl. A rich Cornell blonde from Scarsdale."

"He'd prefer you, if he were smart."

"Everyone isn't as smart as you."

"How's your ankle now?"

"I hardly notice it any more. Once the doctor got the boot off it was fine."

"All the same," George said, regarding the thick white lump of bandage, "I guess the drive in the country is out, isn't it? Too bad. I had plans."

"Did you?"

"All kinds of plans."

Marjorie felt a thrust of combative affection for him. "I don't know why I can't go, George, if you really have plans. My ankle hardly hurts, really——"

George brightened. "Could you? I not only have plans, I've made a reservation, I've——" He stopped short. "But it's all got to be a surprise. Can you come?"

"I'll ask Mama."

The traffic crawled honking under a low orange sun between parallel green lines of trees and gray lines of concrete. Dandelions choked the strips of lawn dividing the auto lanes. Penelope was groaning and clanking over the top of a hill in second gear; they were moving too slowly to travel in high. Far ahead on the winding Long Island parkway

Marjorie could see thousands of cars in two thick black streams, writhing in a dirty blue haze of exhaust fumes.

George hit the horn, and Penelope uttered a jerky noise like the laugh of a sick old man. "Dear, it doesn't help to do that," Marjorie said.

She shifted uncomfortably, crossing the bandaged ankle over the other leg. A loose spring in the seat was pinching her. The decay of Penelope had much advanced in a year. The green paint was cracking off in big patches of rust, the upholstery had popped open in half a dozen places, and the glass in the windshield was held together with surgical tape. Worst of all was the noise from underneath, a queer intermittent rasping groan. George said it was a loose transmission, not worth fixing, and nothing to worry about. But it worried Marjorie.

The whole excursion rather worried her. She was beginning to regret she had allowed her mother's objections to stampede her into going. With a ready-made excuse in the injured ankle, she could easily have avoided this long drive on the first nice Sunday in May, when the parkways were always horrible. But it was almost a matter of honor to insist on doing anything that her mother opposed, the more so when George was concerned. George himself was acting strangely. He was taking her to dinner at the Villa Marlene, he said, the most expensive restaurant on Long Island. How could he afford it, she wondered, and why was he doing it? He had evaded her questions with mysterious winks and grins.

To take her mind from the jam, and her headache, and George's queerness, and Penelope's noise, she suggested a game of Twenty Questions. They played for over an hour, until the traffic thinned beyond Mineola and they began running with more speed through a charming countryside of green rolling estates and brown potato farms. She beat him four times, which irritated him and made her feel better. Twenty Questions had always been their favorite pastime on long rides. At first George had always beaten her; for a while they had played even; now he rarely won. Marjorie's college education was fresher than his, and he had no time to read. He said at last that he was bored with the game, and they rode in silence. The cool fresh country air cleared Marjorie's headache, but her uneasiness deepened as they drove along in a splashing sunset and then in blue twilight. She tried to get George to talk, but he wouldn't; now and then he reached over and fondled her knee and winked. She wasn't pleased by the possessive gesture but she didn't know how to stop it. George had fondled her knee hundreds of times in the past with her enthusiastic approval.

The first view of the famous restaurant was disappointing. Marjorie had expected floodlit vistas of garden, avenues of trees, perhaps a pond with white swans. But it was just a weathered gray wooden house with a faded gilt sign over the doorway, a patchy little lawn, and a few overgrown trees and lilac bushes. The parking lot in the back was full of Cadillacs and Chryslers; Penelope, chugging into a space between two sleek convertibles and dying with a snort and a backfire, looked strikingly out of place. A parking attendant hurried up. With a swift glance at the car, at George's clothes, and at Marjorie's bandaged ankle, he said in a German accent, "Sorry, restaurant all full."

"Thanks," said George, "we have a reservation. Let's go, Marge."

They walked around to the front and mounted the stairs. A big gray-headed man in a tuxedo, with a handful of huge brown menus, opened the door under the gilt sign and blocked their way. "Sorry, restaurant all full."

"I have a reservation. Drobes is the name."

The man glanced at a scribbled list in his hand. "Sorry, sair. No Traub on the list."

"Not Traub. Drobes. This is ridiculous." George raised his voice. "I made the reservation at noon. For six o'clock."

The headwaiter took another look at the list. "Mr. Traub, sair," he said in a tone of heartbroken reproach, "it is quarter past seven."

"That's too bad. We got caught in the parkway jam. We've been driving two and a half hours, and now we're here and we're hungry."

"You have to wait, Mr. Traub. Maybe long wait."

"Okay, we'll wait. Come on in, Marge."

The headwaiter stepped back, shrugging, and showed George and Marjorie through a brightly lit dining room full of cheerful chattering diners into a shadowy parlor that served as a bar, furnished with dingy brown plush armchairs and sofas. Now that beer and wine were legal, restaurants like the Villa Marlene were taking further liberties with the expiring law. In one corner at the bar a group of college boys with shaven heads were making drunken noises. There were about a dozen other couples in the bar, some drinking, some just sitting. They were all very well dressed, and they all had in common an expression of suffering hunger. "Let's have a table as soon as possible, we're famished," said George.

"Sunday night bad, Mr. Traub. Do my best, sair," said the headwaiter, addressing George with the back of his head. He bolted away to greet some newcomers at the door, dropping two of the menus as though by mistake on the arm of George's chair.

After much hand-waving and finger-snapping George caught the attention of a waiter in a red mess jacket hovering by the college boys. The waiter came, flourishing his pad; stared at Marjorie's slippered foot, peered down his nose at George, and said, "What you want, sair?"

"One rye and ginger ale and one Coca-Cola."

The waiter looked revolted, made a note, and walked back to his post by the college boys, where he stood unmoving for perhaps fifteen minutes. George began to fidget. Then he began to wave his hands and snap his fingers. The college boys meanwhile were boisterously ordering another round of drinks. The waiter bowed, smiled, scribbled, and came hurrying past George, who reached out and jabbed him in the side. The waiter halted, looking down at George as though he had meowed.

"How the hell about those drinks?" said George.

"Coming right up, sair."

"Why do we have to wait a quarter of an hour for them?"

"Sunday night is bad, sair."

The frosty Coca-Cola brought little relief to Marjorie's empty stomach. George sipped his drink moodily. The college boys, shepherded by the headwaiter, weaved to a large round table in the dining room, shouting jokes. They could not have looked more uniform—all stringy, bristle-headed, jaunty, long-jawed, with gold rings and cuff links, very white shirts, and baggy brown jackets and gray trousers. Marjorie resented them because George looked so unlike them, because only one of them glanced at her, and because they were going to eat. Sandy Goldstone, she thought, was handsomer than any of them.

One by one couples were called in to dinner, and others arrived to sit around looking hungry. After a while George noticed that some of the newcomers were getting tables. He jumped up and sawed his arms in the air until the headwaiter came. "We were ahead of those people!"

"Sorry, sair, Mr. Taub. They have reservations."

"I had a reservation two hours before they did."

"Right away, sair. Not long now, Mr. Taub."

When the bar was almost empty, and the waiter was yawning and washing the tables, the headwaiter came smiling. "This way, sair." He put them at a flower-decorated table on the glassed porch, next to a large party of elderly people. Marjorie surmised they were rich by their fine clothes, the strange dry twang of their voices, and the champagne buckets flanking their table.

George tried to order filet of sole. But the headwaiter recommended the house specialty, roast Long Island duckling, with such bland patience that George was crushed. "All right then, duck for two. And champagne," he added belligerently.

"Yes, sair. Piper Heidsieck, sair? Mumm's, sair?"

"Just any good champagne."

"Very good sair, Mr. Taub."

Fifteen minutes, twenty minutes, half an hour went by. No food came.

George's lower jaw lolled open, his lip pulled in over the teeth. He said to Marjorie, "I haven't had anything to eat since breakfast. I'm dying." He pounded his glass with a knife and demanded service, glaring like a cornered animal at the headwaiter. With pleasant deference, the man explained that at the Villa Marlene everything was cooked to order. George asked for some rolls and butter, some salad, anything. "Right away now, sair." More time went by. The people at the next table, finishing their dessert and coffee, were having a lively argument as to whether President Roosevelt was a criminal or just a lunatic. "Franklin is a deeply mediocre person, that's all," said one withered little man with a hairy mole on his chin, who was leaning back smoking a long cigar. "He was mediocre when we were working together in the Navy Department, and he's still mediocre." George turned a fork over and over, snuffling, and Marjorie gnawed a knuckle.

Forty-five minutes after they had been seated, the waiter brought two sizzling small ducks, a basket of French bread, salad, and vegetables. While he fussed over the vegetables the headwaiter came with glittering carving instruments and artistically dismembered the fowls. Meantime Marjorie and George wolfed up most of the bread with indecent speed. The headwaiter finished carving the birds and handed the table waiter a platter full of little wings, thighs, breasts, and legs. He then walked off to the kitchen with the two duck carcasses, which were covered with meat; evidently at the Villa Marlene it was bad form to eat the body of a duck. Marjorie groaned, "Good God, make him bring those ducks back. All that meat——" George merely made a gobbling noise, his mouth full of bread, his eyes on the meat that remained.

But almost immediately—the transformation took no longer than the devouring of the food and the drinking of a couple of glasses of champagne—the look of everything changed. The headwaiter, leaning in the doorway with his menus, no longer seemed to Marjorie a bullying snob, but a genuine jolly host, rosy-faced and beaming, an innkeeper out of Dickens. The food was lovely, marvelous, the best she had ever eaten. The Villa Marlene really was charming, after all, with its wallpaper of pink French courtiers dancing a minuet, its dim orange lights, its lilac-scented air. The rich people at the next table were elegant aristocrats of the old school, and it was delightful to be dining so near them. George's spirits came back too. His spine straightened, color returned to his cheek, and liveliness to his eye. He lit a cigar and sipped his champagne, leaning back with one elbow on a chair arm, in the exact pose of the old man who thought that Franklin was deeply mediocre. Marjorie decided that George had a sensitive handsomeness far surpassing the magazine-cover good looks of the college boys (who had left more than an hour ago).

She drank several glasses of champagne, and began to feel mightily exhilarated.

"Everything all right?" said George, squinting through his cigar smoke.

"Everything's divine," said Marjorie. The headwaiter filled their glasses with the last of the champagne and put the bottle neck down in the bucket.

"Thank you, madame." He bowed. "Some brandy, sair, Mr. Taub?"

"Why I daresay, I daresay," said George. "You, Marjorie?"

"I—I'd better not, thanks." Marjorie's teeth felt curiously tight, and she seemed to be hearing her own voice with an echo to it, as though she were shouting down a well.

"Now then," said George, when the waiter had brought coffee and set brandy before him in a shimmering bubble of glass, "are you ready?"

"Sure," said Marjorie. "For what?"

"The surprise."

With a qualm, Marjorie now thought of the hints, the winks, the fondling of her knee. "Why, I guess so. But I'm feeling awfully good as it is, George—I don't need anything more, George——"

Inexorably George's hand went plunging into his jacket pocket. Marjorie knew what was coming, before she saw the little blue leather box in his hand, before he opened it, before the two rings lay winking and glittering at her in a bed of purple velvet.

"Oh, George . . . George!"

"Pretty, aren't they?" His eyeglasses gleamed at her.

"Beautiful, they're beautiful. But—George—really, I'm dumfounded——"

"It doesn't have to be next week or next month," George said eagerly. "Or even next year. We just ought to know where we stand, and let everybody else know——"

Marjorie put her champagne to her mouth and sipped it deliberately, looking at George over the rim of the glass with young scared eyes.

At fifteen, at sixteen, she had daydreamed away a thousand blissful hours picturing this event, panting for the time when it would come. Now here it was. But she had not been panting for it recently. If anything, she had been shutting it from her mind, telling herself that she was too young to be thinking of engagements, ignoring the fact that during the preceding year and a half she had considered herself more than old enough. Defiant of her mother's nagging, she had kissed George, and necked with him, and sworn she could never love anyone else, during all that time; and now here were two rings staring her in the face.

Even now, backed to the wall, Marjorie could not admit to herself that her mother was right, that George was a decent but dull fellow, that she had made a donkey of herself over a girlish infatuation, that she was destined to do much better. She was touched by the offer of the rings, and grateful to George. She was merely irritated with him for his clumsy pressing of the issue. She was only now beginning to grow up a bit, to discover life and her own self. Why was he in such a hurry? Why must he ask her to take herself out of the world at seventeen? It wasn't fair.

She put down the glass. "Wow, this is wicked stuff. I'm floating four feet off the floor."

George said eagerly, waving a finger at the headwaiter, "Let's crack another bottle, really celebrate——"

"Good Lord, no." She looked at her watch. "Darling, do you know it's after ten? We won't get home till morning in all that traffic. Mama will have kittens. Let's go."

"But we've got so much to talk about, pooch. This is an important night in our lives——"

"Dear, we'll have enough time on the road to talk out everything, hours and hours and hours——"

So George asked for the check. The headwaiter brought him the change on a metal platter, and said with a beautiful bow, "Was your dinner satisfactory, Mr. Taub?"

"Perfect, perfect, thank you." George fumbled a five-dollar bill from the plate and gave it to him, and left two dollars on the table for the waiter.

"Thank you, sair. Bon soir, madame. Bon soir, Mr. Taub." He bowed again, George bowed back. They went out into the cool night, and the door closed behind them.

George shook his head and said with a stunned look, "Have I gone crazy? Why did I give that bastard five dollars?"

He tipped the man in the parking lot a dime. The man cursed loudly in German as they drove off.

Penelope's noises seemed worse as they bumped along the dark side road. The groan under the floorboard had changed to a screech like an electric butcher saw on bone. "Dear," said Marjorie in some alarm, "how about that noise?"

George cocked his ear and gnawed his lip. "Well, nothing to be done about it. Can't tear down the transmission now, on the side of the road. I don't know. Sometimes she just works through these noises and purrs like a cat again. We'll see."

Coming to the parkway, they could see strings of white headlights stretched to the horizon in one direction and strings of red tail lights in the other, moving in the moonlight with the slimy slowness of worms. "Oh dear," said Marjorie.

"Well, Sunday night is bad," said George. It took him ten minutes of narrow maneuvering to wedge into the solid westbound line. "Okay," he said with relief, grinning at her, "homeward bound." He reached over and tousled her hair, and she was unpleasantly reminded of Sandy Goldstone. "Don't worry, you'll be in your little brown bed by midnight." He pulled the box of rings out of his pocket. "Take another look at them? I think they're honeys."

"George, they must have cost a fortune." She eyed the rings in the dim yellow light of the parkway lamps. They were a matched pair in white gold, the wedding ring plain, the engagement ring set with a small rose-cut diamond.

"What's the difference? They're yours."

"No, really. After all, I know how hard things have been and——"

"Well, it sometimes helps to have a jeweler in the family." George looked roguish.

"George, did your Uncle Albie give them to you?"

"Marge, it's perfectly all right. It was his own idea. Naturally I'll pay him some day as soon as I'm able." The grinding noise of Penelope was now so loud that George was shouting a little.

"Shouldn't we wait till then?" Marjorie's teeth were shaken by the motion of the car.

"What?"

Marjorie repeated it, louder.

George, clutching the wheel, which was beginning to shimmy, shouted, "What kind of silly remark is that? Good Lord, Marjorie, I'm drudging away in the Bronx, trying to save up enough to finish my M.A. and Ph.D., and you're flitting around downtown meeting new guys every day, going to Columbia dances and what all—how do you suppose that makes me feel? I'm worried. I can't tell what you——"

He broke off, his whole body stiffening, his arms rigid on the wheel. Penelope suddenly was collapsing in a frightful way, shaking and bumping and crashing, with a smell of red-hot iron filling the car and trickles of smoke coming up through the floorboard. George swerved off the parkway; the stricken car went bouncing over soft earth. He shut off the ignition, reached roughly across Marjorie to shove open the door, and pushed her out. "Get clear." Marjorie stumbled away through the grass, soaking her stockings, then turned and watched George cautiously open the hood and shine a flashlight at the engine. He ducked under the chassis and flashed the light here and there. Penelope stood hub-deep in weeds, leaning to one side. On the road cars flowed by with a rich hiss of tires, nobody stopping to look at the wreck or offer help. George stood and waved. "Okay, come back. Stripped a gear, I guess. There's no fire."

Walking back to the car, Marjorie became aware of something bulky in her hand. She held it up, and was astonished to see that she was still clutching the jewel box. "Now what?" she said to George.

"Phone for a tow car. Nothing else to do." He shrugged his bowed shoulders, patted the hood of the car, and peered through the swarm of cars. "There's a police phone, I think, on that lamp post down there. Come with me, or stay here? I'll just be a couple of minutes."

"I—I guess I'd better stay off the ankle, George."

"All right." He opened the car door. "Might as well get in the back where it's comfortable. The front is finished, for a while."

"George," she said as he turned to go.

"Yes?"

"You'd—maybe you'd better hold on to these. I lose things, all the time."

The moonlight made a white blank of his glasses as he took the box. "Right," he said, with no expression in his voice. He carefully stowed the box in his pocket, snuffled, and walked off down the road, swinging the flashlight.

She came home after one. The apartment was dark and quiet. On her bed was a note in her mother's spiky handwriting: *Sandy Goldstone called. Wanted to know how your ankle was. Called three times.*

PART TWO

Marsha

Chapter 4. SANDY AND MARJORIE

Billy Ehrmann was the booby of his fraternity, and being seen with him had done Marjorie little good at Columbia; but once Sandy Goldstone started dating her, the Morgenstern telephone began to ring busily after school hours.

Lively and pretty though she was, she needed Sandy's sponsorship because she was a Hunter girl. That was almost as disqualifying, in the estimation of Sandy's West Side set, as living north of Ninety-sixth Street; which was only a shade less disqualifying than living in the Bronx. Snobbishness, of course, is a relative thing. The older and wealthier Jewish families, who lived on the upper East Side, would have been distressed had the West Side boys dated their daughters. And these families doubtless caused the well-to-do Christian families to wonder what was becoming of Park Avenue and Fifth Avenue. The terracing of caste extended upward into an azure realm of blood, breeding, and property as remote from little Marjorie Morgenstern as the planet Saturn. From her viewpoint, however, her small move upward was skyrocketing. Sandy Goldstone had begun to take her out. It followed that Bill Dryfus could, and Dan Kadane, and Neil Wein, and Norman Fisher, and Allen Orbach. She soon had to buy a little leather-bound notebook to keep track of her dates. The rush of success made her rather dizzy.

It seemed to go to her mother's head too. Mrs. Morgenstern took her on a round of Manhattan shops and bought her a closetful of expensive new clothes. When the father objected to the bills, which were far beyond their means, Mrs. Morgenstern simply said, "A girl of seventeen can't go around in rags." Marjorie had been arguing for two years that girls of fifteen and sixteen couldn't go around in rags (the rags in question being a quite presentable middle-priced wardrobe) but her mother had been deaf to the doctrine until now. Marjorie saw in her conversion a crafty plan to trap Sandy Goldstone, so her gratitude for the clothes was a bit tainted by cynicism. But she did the mother an injustice. Mrs. Morgenstern probably hoped to see her some day catch the department store heir, or a prize like him. Mainly, however, she was carried away by her daughter's flowering beauty—the girl seemed to grow prettier every week in the sunshine of success—and by the mood of springtime, and by the parade of handsome well-dressed boys gathering in Marjorie's wake. Satiric though the mother's attitude was toward Marjorie, her daughter really rather dazzled her. At seventeen Rose Kupperberg had been a Yiddish-speaking immigrant girl toiling in a dirty Brooklyn sweatshop, dressed in real rags. As she watched her daughter burst into bloom on Central Park West, her own lonely miserable adolescence came back to her, and by contrast it seemed to her that Marjorie was living the life of a fairy-tale princess. She envied her, and admired her, and was a bit afraid of her, and drew deep vicarious delight from her growing vogue. The decline of George Drobes that went with it completed the mother's satisfaction.

For after the Villa Marlene disaster George was clearly on the wane. He maintained an aggrieved silence for a couple of weeks, then telephoned Marjorie. She was as sweet to him as ever, and they continued to see each other. But Marjorie's conscience troubled her less and less about dating new boys. George was losing his two great advantages with Marjorie, advantages which often are enough to bring about marriage if nothing interferes. When she was fifteen he had bent down to her from the celestial altitude of twenty; that altitude, however, had dwindled, as Marjorie rapidly matured and George slowed near his final level. And he had been the first man to thrill her with kisses, so the ancient universal spell of sex had in Marjorie's eyes come to halo George Drobes personally. George's one remaining chance lay in nailing the girl down while she was still under that fragile delusion; and a dim sense of this must have been behind his desperate Villa Marlene gamble. Penelope's breakdown lost George much more than a means of transportation. It deprived him of a dark front seat. Since Marjorie was no girl to neck in hallways or on park benches, George was stymied.

The single shred of hope for him was that Marjorie as yet hadn't necked with anyone else. But this was not from want of opportunity or candidates. Evening after evening she was finding herself in dark front seats more luxurious than Penelope's, with the old problem on her hands. It was delightful to be taken to the best dancing places, to be able to chatter knowingly about the Biltmore and the Roosevelt and the St. Regis, about Guy Lombardo and Hal Kemp and Glen Gray; but in the end it all came to the same thing. Central Park West and the Bronx were no different in this respect. Marjorie found the sameness of boys at the end of an evening rather comical—the heavy breathing, the popping eyes, the grasping damp hands, the hoarse unconvincing romantic mumbling—but after innocently laughing at them a couple of times, she realized what a mistake that was. It was too effectively discouraging. They drove her home in a fury and never spoke to her again. The idea was to fend off the advances, not the boys. Moral indignation was hopeless; it was like getting angry at the weather. Every boy tried.

Moreover, Marjorie couldn't help feeling that they had some small right on their side. They were entertaining her lavishly. Were they to have no reward? In theory, she knew, her company for the evening was supposed to be the reward. Theory often required some squaring with facts. Under continual pressure, she soon worked out two rules:

1. No necking at all;
2. No kiss on the first two dates; thereafter, one kiss for good night and maybe one more to cut off prolonged begging.

This policy seemed to work inasmuch as the boys grumbled and complained and whined, but usually called her up again after a few days. However, she acquired a reputation for being "frigid." Sooner or later every boy brought out the word to salve his self-esteem at being fobbed off with one kiss. The diagnosis didn't trouble her. In the Hunter lunchroom she had listened to an enormous amount of conversation about necking. She knew that girls who necked freely were thrown over by boys just as often as those who didn't. Marjorie had about reached the conclusion that boys were on the whole more fascinated by sex withheld than by sex granted; and since this is nearly the sum of wisdom on the subject of young love, she managed for the time being to keep out of trouble.

The one exception in all this, oddly enough, was Sandy Goldstone. Though he took her out more often than the others, he did not even try to kiss her good night. Marjorie was grateful at first for his unusual restraint. Then she began to wonder whether it wasn't a gambit of dark villainy. Then, when he persisted in this genial undemanding conduct, she grew a bit annoyed. The way things were, chivalry seemed to require a man to make some attempt at necking, however brief and formal. However, he was a superb dancer, and obviously he liked her company. His wry sense of humor, mostly directed at himself, amused her very much. She gave over puzzling about his diffidence, leaving the answer to time, and simply enjoyed herself with him.

May drifted into June and examination week came. Marjorie had to break off the lovely whirl to plunge into cramming. Her method was standardized and cold-blooded. The night before each examination she read the textbook through with rapt attention as though it were a detective story; when there were two exams in a day she read both books in one night. Her mind, rather like a boardwalk photographer's camera, took a picture of the subject which stayed pretty clear for twenty-four hours, though it grew blurry in a week and faded to nothing in a month. She drank gallons of coffee, ate tins of aspirin, slept two or three hours a night, and staggered to and from school with red eyes, pale cheeks, and spinning brain. It was a horrible ordeal. But Marjorie had concluded long ago that she got the best marks at the least cost of time and energy this way. She was not much interested in her studies, but self-respect required her to be in the top half of the class. She emerged from the grim week with a high B average as usual; and as usual with a fierce head cold, which developed this time into a grippe. She was in bed for ten days, aching and feverish.

Aches and fever were the least of the troubles caused by this grippe. All the boys telephoned regularly to ask how she was getting on—except Sandy. Rosalind Green, visiting Marjorie on her sickbed, helpfully notified her that Vera Cashman had returned from Cornell, and that Sandy was squiring the blonde around again with great zest. She also volunteered what Sandy had confided to Phil Boehm, and Phil Boehm to her; namely, that Vera Cashman was a remarkably accomplished necker. This was not exactly news to Marjorie. She had observed the blonde's little tricks: taking a cigarette from Sandy's mouth and puffing it, absently running a finger along the back of his hand, dancing too close, and losing her fingers in his hair while they danced. But with a temperature of over 103, she could do little about the information except work up garish nightmares of Sandy kissing, necking, and eventually marrying the blonde.

Helpless in bed, Marjorie consoled herself with long-drawn telephone flirting with the other boys, and with the reflection that she didn't care about Sandy Goldstone anyway, because her future lay in the theatre. The riot of social success had obscured for a while the vision of Marjorie Morningstar. Now in the dragging bedridden hours it brightened. She sent her brother out for volumes of plays, and for the summer catalogues of colleges and drama schools. She read through all of Eugene O'Neill and Noel Coward, and much of Shaw. Her theatrical ambition flared, fed by the heat of fever, and fanned by the delirium of grippe, which dissipated obstacles and multiplied rainbows. The first thing she did when the doctor released her from bed, wan and five pounds lighter, was to enroll in an acting course at New York University and an elementary playwriting course at Columbia; the latter because Shaw somewhere said that the best way to learn about the theatre was to try to write for it. This turn of events greatly annoyed Mrs. Morgenstern, to whom Marjorie's acting plans were the merest vapor. She disliked wasting the forty dollars that the enrollments cost, though she offered to put the money gladly on Marjorie's back in a new dress or suit. After an argument she paid the fees, muttering that Marjorie could probably be cured of any career by actually trying to work at it.

But Marjorie attended both courses faithfully and did well in them, despite an extravagant round of dates, dances, picnics, and parties that went on all summer. She dashed off one short playlet, based on the story of Jael and Sisera transposed to Nazi Germany, which earned an enthusiastic scrawl in red ink from the instructor. Her pleasure in this endorsement—which she happily brandished under her mother's nose—was somewhat lessened by the fact that the seven other student playwrights in the course seemed to be half-witted eccentrics; especially one bright-eyed old maid, who brought two cats meowing in a suitcase to every class session. Her dramatic instructor, an old actor with a shock of perfectly groomed white hair, a hearing aid, and a British accent, said she showed much promise, and gave her the best ingenue parts to act out in class, staring hungrily at her legs while she emoted.

It was a pleasant and diverting summer, but the shadow of Sandy Goldstone's neglect of her lay over it. Mrs. Morgenstern must have suggested twenty ways of getting Sandy to see her again, all of which Marjorie vetoed with growing irritation. She saw Sandy often at parties and night clubs, always with the blonde, who managed more than one poisoned simper at her. He even danced with Marjorie a few times. He seemed as fond of her as ever, behind his smoke screen of ambiguous joking. But he never called her.

Mrs. Morgenstern was not one to float becalmed on an unfavoring drift of events. One steamy morning in mid-August she said to Marjorie at breakfast, "This weather is getting impossible. How would you like to go to the Prado for a week or so?"

"Mom, the *Prado?*"

"If you can spare the time from your dramatic studies, that is——"

"Of course I can, but—why, the Prado's for millionaires——"

"It's not that bad. A lot of my friends are there. They say it's a very nice place. They're not millionaires."

"I'd be mad about it, Mom, but—the Prado——"

"Well, we'll see. I'll talk to Papa."

Next morning they were on a grimy Long Island train, with Marjorie's fancy wardrobe in three trunks in the baggage car. Mr. Morgenstern was remaining in the city; the summer was his busiest season. They had stopped briefly in his office in the garment district to pick up some cash, and Marjorie had all but fainted in the windowless little office smelling so strongly of ink, stale coffee, and the peculiar dust of the feathers and straws lying baled in the shop. Mr. Morgenstern, in a gray tie and coat despite the killing heat, with a face almost as gray as his coat and almost as wet as the dripping water cooler behind his chair, had limply counted out some bills and wished them a pleasant time.

The Prado did not look at all like what it was, a kosher hotel. It had smooth green lawns, a white crushed-stone driveway, broad terraces, red clay tennis courts crisscrossed with new whitewash, and a huge blue swimming pool full of bronzed young people diving, splashing, and laughing. Beyond the hotel and its immense formal gardens lay a white curved beach and the hissing sea. Not long ago it had been a fashionable hotel barred to Jews. But the fashion had changed, the smart set having gone farther out on the Island. A few Christians, mostly politicians and theatre people, still came to the Prado, but it was now a known Jewish resort, and all anybody needed to stay there was enough money to pay the bill. That was sufficient restriction to keep it luxurious and elegant, despite its social decline.

Staring around at the marble pillars, Persian carpets, and fine statuary and paintings of the lobby, Marjorie did not see Sandy Goldstone at the hotel desk until he called, "Hi, Marge!" A white canvas bag of golf clubs was slung over his shoulder, and he was brown as a Mexican. The woman with her arm through his, small and plump, in a smart white sports dress, with streaks of gray in her dark hair, picked up silver-rimmed glasses on a delicate chain around her neck, and peered at Mrs. Morgenstern. "Why, hello, Rose. You here?"

"Hello, Mary," Mrs. Morgenstern said. "Sandy, how are you?"

"Well, what a surprise. Why didn't you let me know you were coming?" said Mrs. Goldstone. "You knew we were here. I'd have arranged lunch——"

Marjorie glanced at her mother, who suddenly appeared sheepish and confused. "Why, I guess—the thing is, Mary, we just decided to come on the spur of the moment. Mr. Morgenstern wouldn't let us stay in the city, it's so awful in there. I don't think you've met Marjorie yet, have you? Marjorie, Mrs. Goldstone."

The silver-rimmed glasses turned and glittered at the girl. "How do you do?" The hand was cool and dry, the handshake brief.

Sandy invited them to come along for a foursome.

"We don't play golf," Marjorie said.

"I'm always willing to learn," said Mrs. Morgenstern. "It would take us a little while to register and change, but——"

"Mom, I do not want to learn to play golf just now," said Marjorie, making the words separate and distinct as pistol shots.

"Maybe we can have lunch together," Mrs. Morgenstern said to Sandy's mother. "What table are you sitting at?"

Mrs. Goldstone smiled. "I'm afraid we won't be back for lunch. We're having a bite at the clubhouse. But I'm sure we'll see a lot of you. Goodbye."

While Mrs. Morgenstern registered, and while they rode up in the elevator, Marjorie held the flesh of her lower lip between her teeth. Mrs. Morgenstern wore an innocent happy smile.

Marjorie slammed the door of their room behind her, and stood with her back to it. "Mother, we're going straight home."

"What? Are you crazy?" said the mother mildly, taking off her hat at the mirror. "We just got here."

"How could you, Mom? How could you?"

"How could I what? Can I help it if the Goldstones like the Prado? Does that mean we're not allowed to come here? It's still a free country, even if Sandy is at the Prado."

Two bellboys in gold-braided scarlet suits wheeled in the trunks. Marjorie strode to the window and stood in a silent rage while Mrs. Morgenstern cheerfully directed the bellboys in placing and opening the luggage, including Marjorie's trunks. As soon as they were gone Marjorie whirled on her. "I said I was going. What's the point of opening everything up?"

"You want to clean up and have a swim, don't you? There's no sense going back into that furnace today."

"I want to leave right now."

Mrs. Morgenstern pulled her dress over her head. "Well, I'm not stopping you. I'm going to have a swim before lunch, myself." She took her bathing suit into the bathroom, dropping Marjorie's new suit on the bed. "Personally, I think you're being very foolish. What's so wrong about having a boy you know at the hotel? It'll be more fun——"

"Good heavens, Mom, how thick is your skin? Didn't you see how his mother looked at us?"

"Mary Goldstone's a lovely person. She looks at everybody that way. She's a little nearsighted."

"She thinks you're sharpening your teeth for Sandy. And that's just what you're doing, and I won't be a party to such——"

"Listen, Marjorie, you can't fool me. You like the boy."

"And what if that's so? This is the very worst thing to do about it— going chasing after him to a hotel——"

"You weren't doing too well by not chasing him, dear."

"Mom . . . *Mom,* that is nobody's business but my own. When will you ever understand that?"

Mrs. Morgenstern came out of the bathroom in flapping slippers and bathing suit, with a towel around her neck. "Sometimes one little push makes all the difference.—Coming for a swim?"

"No, I am not."

Mrs. Morgenstern opened the door. "See you at lunch, then—unless you take the train home, of course. If you do, give my love to Papa."

Marjorie paced the room, fuming. The sun beat straight into the room, white and hot. She was wet through with perspiration. Below the window was the pool, crowded with hilarious young people. There were some especially good-looking boys, she observed, their hair black and disorderly from the water. She stopped in her pacing and fingered her new swim suit. It was the latest style: flesh-colored rubber, perfectly decent, yet at twenty feet giving one the look of total nakedness. The room was really unbearably hot.

There was dancing after dinner on the terrace overlooking the sea. She danced for hours with Sandy. They went for a stroll on the beach in the moonlight afterward; and when they had rounded a bend that hid them from the hotel they sat and talked idly in the gloom, looking at the stars and streaming sand through their fingers, while the white surf at their feet tumbled and roared. After a while Marjorie hesitantly ran her finger across the back of Sandy's hand. The effect was explosive. When they walked back to the hotel half an hour later their relationship was advanced about to the high point that Marjorie had reached with George Drobes. She and Sandy were both dizzy, confused, uncertain, exhilarated, and extremely pleased with themselves.

Chapter 5. SANDY'S AMBITIONS

Sandy's tan Pontiac convertible was quite a change from Penelope: red leather seats, gleaming chrome knobs, and a motor that at sixty miles an hour made less noise than the murmuring tires or the radio pouring clear jazz. The car was his own, not his father's. He drove it as though he owned it, too; negligently, with one arm resting on the window ledge. George always sat up straight, driving like a motorman.

"How do you feel this morning?" Sandy said.

Marjorie, tying a pink kerchief over her tossing hair, said, "Just wonderful. How about you?" She wore a pink cotton frock and tiny gold sandals, with a bathing suit underneath. They were going to swim in a deserted cove some ten miles down the highway from the Prado.

"I'm puzzled," Sandy said. "I can't make you out."

She stared at the long-jawed profile partly masked by sunglasses. His mouth was straight and serious. "You can't make *me* out? Seems to me I've made myself a little too plain for comfort."

"Yes? What was all that, last night?"

"I'm sure I don't know. The moonlight, maybe. Or maybe it's just that I like you a bit more than I should," she said rather sharply.

Grinning, he dropped a strong hand on her knee and gave it a brief squeeze. "That would be nice to believe." She wanted to object to the squeeze, but the hand was gone. She curled in the far corner of the front seat, out of easy reach of him.

If he was puzzled, so was she; extremely puzzled. She had been puzzling, since she woke, over what had happened the night before. Fixed ideas of hers had been shattered. She had thought an instinct of feminine honor prevented a girl from necking with one man when she loved another. George Drobes, even if he no longer filled the world from pole to pole, was still her accepted lover. Evidently no such instinct existed. She had also believed that a surrender to necking marked a dramatic turn in one's emotions. But this morning her attitude toward Sandy remained the same: undefined, but friendly and curious rather than passionate. He seemed more familiar, that was all. It was her own self that was less familiar. Marjorie had surprised herself, and she was waiting with oddly pleasant nervousness to see what strange thing she would do next.

They turned off the highway and went bumping down a lonely dirt road through thick pines. Marjorie's nervousness increased. She was an addict of lending-library novels. Girls were always getting seduced in these books when they went off to a lonely place with a young man to swim; it was almost standard procedure. Sandy Goldstone, big, brown, and powerful, driving in silence with a shadow of a smile around his mouth, looked not unlike the seducers of fiction. Marjorie enjoyed reading about these ravishings, of course, and often dwelled on the vague paragraphs describing the ecstatic feelings of the girls, wondering what sex was really like. But the real thing close at hand wore an aspect of gritty discomfort. Sandy seemed too docile a sort to ravish her, but she rather wished they had stayed at the Prado to swim.

At the beach she slipped behind the car to step out of her frock. The act of taking it off, she thought, might inflame Sandy. She delayed and dawdled behind the car, combing her hair and fixing her makeup. When she came out she saw him lying face down on the sand near the broken remains of an old rowboat, stripped to his bathing trunks, with his head under a ragged yellow newspaper. The sun was blazing, but there was a cool breeze. The cove was about a mile across, fringed by white-gold sand and tangled brush. Marjorie stood by the car for a while, savoring the peaceful silence, the splash of the surf, the smell of pine on the breeze; she was watching him cautiously. He made no move. She went to Sandy and sat beside him, but he did not look up. The sun was almost hot enough to burn her bare skin. Sandy was perspiring in little rivulets.

"Sandy?" She noticed that his breathing was remarkably easy and regular. "Sandy—Sandy Goldstone, damn your hide, have you fallen asleep on me?"

Thoroughly vexed, she kicked him in the ribs; there was such a thing as being too safe from rape. He jerked, grunted, rolled over, and sat up with a guilty grin, rubbing his eyes. "Doggone. Damn near fell asleep, didn't I? Sun always does that to me." He jumped to his feet. "Let's go."

Marjorie knew only public-beach bathing, with its crowds, trash cans, frankfurters, lifeguards, and squalling children. It was all different to walk to the flat clean edge of the land and plunge into the empty sea. They splashed and dived and swam. When she was exhausted she sat on the sand and watched Sandy cavort and snort joyously in the water for another quarter of an hour.

"Do you really want to be a doctor?" she said when he reclined dripping beside her.

"Sure."

"What medical schools have you applied to?"

"Well, I don't know if I will apply, Marge. With my grades it's just about hopeless. I have a high C average."

"But——" She stared at him. "Then you're not going to be a doctor."

"Looks that way."

"Then *what* will you do?"

"Doggone, you sounded just like my father then."

"No, really, Sandy——"

"Know what I'd like to be, more than anything? A forest ranger. No, don't laugh, I mean it. Ever been to Arizona? It's heaven on earth in those national parks. Sky, stones, cactus, desert, the sun and the stars—nothing else. Know what a forest ranger makes? About thirty-five a week. That's all I'd want, for the rest of my life, if I could be a ranger in Arizona."

"That's—well, it's an original ambition, anyway."

"I put in an application last summer. I didn't even want to finish college. My father stopped that. Said I was going to finish college even if I spent the rest of my life digging ditches."

"What's your father like, Sandy?"

"Oh, quite a guy. Quite a dynamo." Sandy sat up, brushing sand from his thick legs. "Slightly disappointed that I'm not the same type. Only son, too. I feel kind of sorry for him sometimes."

"Don't you like the idea of—you know, running Lamm's some day?"

"Sure, I like it—or I would like it, the way you say it. Think it's that simple? I've been in charge of the men's hats section this summer. That's all, just men's hats. He's let me make all the mistakes. He's checked everything in that section every night down to the cash register receipts. Then at dinner he's been climbing all over me. Last week I came to his office and said maybe I'd better quit for a little vacation before going back to school. 'Quit?' he says. 'Didn't you open your mail this morning? You're fired. You're a failure, a complete failure——' Sure enough, I got my mail and he'd written me a three-page memo, in his own handwriting, telling me the store couldn't afford to keep me around any more this summer at the rate I was making mistakes. Then he carefully listed every mistake I'd made since I'd been there. And he ended up with this—I remember every word—'If you don't improve I promise you I'll give this store to a charity foundation rather than leave it in the hands of such a fool.'" Sandy scooped up a fistful of sand and scattered it in the wind. "Oh, he's a wonderful guy. He's right, you know. You've got to be tough to run a big store. You've got to be right on the ball every second." He took her wrists and pulled her to her feet. "Come on, another dip? Let's go up to the point. It's deep enough to dive off that rock."

They were sitting on the rock, panting after a lively swim, when a squat brown fishing boat went wallowing by, leaving a smudgy trail of smoke across the water. "There's something I'd like to do," said Sandy, "run one of those tuna boats out of San Diego down around Lower California. They make fortunes. I can navigate—— What's the matter?"

She was shaking her head and laughing at him. "You're like a nine-year-old kid."

"Oh?" he said, and with an easy sweep of a long bony arm he was holding her and kissing her.

But it was an outdoors, hearty kind of kiss with no menace, so Marjorie yielded to it. While she was kissing Sandy she tried hard to remember how it felt to kiss George, so as to determine which one she really loved. Marjorie believed that the kisses of true love had a unique taste, a vibration which one could never mistake. But the fact was that while Sandy's mouth and manner differed from George's she apparently enjoyed kissing one just about as much as the other. Sandy soon took her by the shoulders and held her a little away from him. "What the devil are you thinking about?"

"Who—me?" she said, blinking. "Why, why dear, I'm not thinking at all, I guess."

"You give me the strangest feeling." He looked at her with his head cocked sidewise. "As though you're adding figures in your head, or something."

"You're crazy. How dare you say such a thing?" She pulled away from him and perched at a distance on the rock. "I shouldn't be kissing you at all. Anyhow, if you expect the kind of kissing you get from Vera Cashman, I'm sorry. I lack her practice."

Sandy scratched his head. "Let's go back to the hotel. I'm dying for a beer."

"Just a moment. How about Vera Cashman, now that the subject has come up?"

"Has it come up?" Sandy said. "How did that ever happen?"

"I just don't understand your pawing me and all the way you do, when you've got a girl."

"Vera's moved to California."

After a moment Marjorie said lightly, "Oh? When did this happen?"

"Couple of weeks ago. Her father went broke, and—Margie, don't look so damned skeptical, it's the truth. He's a Long Island builder. A big development of his went smash. He got out of the state about one jump ahead of the sheriff, my father says."

"Well, well. You must be heartbroken."

"It's all but turned me gray."

"Looking for a replacement, no doubt."

"Margie, honey, I just thought you'd like to come for a swim, and——"

"Well, I won't do. I don't go in for the things Vera goes in for—and wipe that silly grin off your face. Despite last night, it's true. I don't."

"I never said you did, Margie."

Before they left the beach, all the same, she went in for a little more of it.

It was a shock to see George after the week at the Prado. Age seemed to have overtaken him all at once, to make him thinner, paler, shorter, sadder, and more slope-shouldered. He took her to an engagement party of one of his college friends. From the start, everything about the evening depressed Marjorie: the all too familiar Bronx apartment house, one of an unbroken line of gray houses along a dirty narrow street; the dark stairway to the fourth floor, with its memory-wakening smells of immigrant cooking and baby-breeding, of stale paint and fresh wet laundry;

the cramped apartment blazing with electric bulbs, the cheap furniture, the paintings that were copies of copies, the worn best sellers on the shelves (*The Story of Philosophy, Babbitt, The Forsyte Saga, The Bridge of San Luis Rey*); the loud voices, the barbarous pronunciation (awfice, yeah, daaance, lor stoodent, idear, tawk); the singsong cadence which jarred on her the more because she was still trying to free her own speech of it; the unvarying cream soda, sponge cake, and sugary purple wine; the inexorable vanilla ice cream rushed in paper boxes from the drugstore by a small brother to climax the party; the proud fat parents, the proud fat bride in a red evening dress from Klein's, with a bunch of tea roses in a huge silver ribbon on her shoulder; worst of all, the sly giggling jokes that everybody made about George and herself. She pleaded a headache and left, too soon; the silence was very awkward as she and George walked out of the door. Then she felt so sorry for him and so guilty that she kissed him madly when they parked on the Drive (Penelope was repaired at last, after a fashion, and could be driven in a clanking dying way). She found herself responding to George's kisses just as she always had, which further confused and upset her. Alone in her bedroom that night, wretched with self-disgust, she resolved not to neck again with either Sandy or George until she knew what her true feelings were.

She found she could keep the resolve with Sandy but not with George. Sandy reacted good-humoredly to her first repulse. "Well, well. Just a faded summer love, eh?"

She said, "Don't be absurd. There's no sense going on and on with a thing that leads nowhere. Anyway we don't mean that much to each other."

"Marjorie, you know I can't live an hour without you."

"Go hang yourself, you grinning ape."

That was that. But George had enjoyed special privileges for a year and a half, and had come to regard them as his right. She couldn't withdraw to a cooler status without a showdown and possibly a break, for which she was far from ready. She could not bear to hurt George, and she did not want to lose him; not while she was so befuddled. So she dragged on with him as before, though made increasingly miserable by it.

When Marjorie returned to Hunter for the fall term she found that according to general gossip she was all but engaged to the heir apparent of Lamm's department store. Standing on line in the hot jammed basement of the school to draw her textbooks, she was slyly congratulated half a dozen times, and she saw girls pointing at her and whispering. Her denials met with winks, prods, and giggles. She had no idea how the rumor had started, and she didn't much care. The teasing was a welcome diversion from the dreariness of sinking back into the Hunter routine.

Marjorie had never liked the school. Her dearest wish had been to go out of town to college, but her parents had been unwilling to let her leave home so young, and moreover had not been quite able to afford the expense when Marjorie was finishing high school. So, reluctantly, the girl had enrolled in this subway college, which to her was a hell, a nerve-racking place full of the twitters and colors and smells and giggles and screeches of too many unlovely shoving girls. In time she became dulled to it and stopped resenting her fate; but she always moved alone through the perfumed swarm, though she had the usual lunchroom companions and bridge-playing acquaintances. With the move of the family to Central Park West she felt more than ever that her presence in this soprano-buzzing hive was an unlucky mistake. But it was too late to make a change. A bit too pretty, too well dressed, and too cool, she was not popular at Hunter, and she had taken little part until now in any of the activities. But if she heard the school sneered at she would angrily defend it by saying that a girl couldn't get half as good an education anywhere else. This was more or less true; the competition for marks was keen and the girls on the whole brighter than average. She would have traded all the fine education she was getting, however, for a small part of the polishing and the fun that she had once hoped to find in an out-of-town college. In this she was more like the other girls than she quite realized. Hunter was a concentration camp of such displaced girlish dreamers, would-be coeds forced by lack of money into the mold of subway grinds.

It was obvious as the new term got under way that her status at Hunter was changing. Popular girls who had shown no interest in her before were smiling at her, even stopping to chat with her in the corridors. At lunch time she tended to become the center of the conversation circle. A couple of scouts from the formidable Helen Johannsen clique became friendly with her. One day she found herself at lunch with a group that included Helen herself, the sharply clever, beautiful blond senior who was editor of the school paper, leader of the Sing, and exalted general boss of Hunter politics. After lunch Helen took her arm and walked out with her in the sunshine, drawing her on to talk about herself. Marjorie, dazzled and flattered, talked freely. When she shyly disclosed that she wanted to be an actress, Helen advised her to try out at once for the dramatic society's production of *The Mikado*; there wasn't a doubt in the world, Helen said, that she would get a leading part. Then she startled

Marjorie by remarking, "I hear you know my old friend, Sandy Gold-stone."

"Do *you* know Sandy?"

With a little curving smile Helen said, "I've modelled a bit at Lamm's, off and on . . . Dear, I'm no competition for you, don't look so alarmed. I'm a little old for Sandy. Anyway, you don't suppose he'd ever be serious about a Christian girl, do you?" She glanced at Marjorie, a good-humored approving inspection. "I believe you'll do all right."

Marjorie, blushing and feeling all arms and legs, said, "My Lord, I barely know him."

"Sure, dear," Helen said, and they both laughed. Marjorie saw nearby girls, after-lunch strollers like themselves, stare admiringly at the sophomore laughing arm in arm with Helen Johannsen.

Marjorie accepted the jealous stirrings she felt as a sign that she might be in love with Sandy, after all.

Chapter 6. MARSHA ZELENKO

She tried out for *The Mikado,* and to her astonishment landed the title part without any trouble.

From the day rehearsals began the rest of the world became vague to her. She sat in class with the other badly made-up girls in skirts and sweaters, scribbling in her notebook as always; but it was a kind of reflex between her ears and her hand, by-passing her brain. At the end of many an hour she could not have said whether the lecturer had been droning about fruit flies or Anatole France. Sometimes her pen would slow and stop; her eyes would drift to the gray window, to the autumn gale blowing slant streaks of rain on the glass, to the reflected yellow lights that seemed to hang magically in the air over the purplish street; the tune of *My Object All Sublime* would start running in her mind, and she would fall in a trance of imaginary play-acting, adding new comic business to her role. The rehearsal period after classes was like a birthday party that came every day. In a word, she was stage-struck.

One evening rehearsals stopped early for costume fitting. The players came up one by one, giggling and squealing, to be measured under a bright light in the center of the stage, supervised by a fat girl with thick braided black hair. Marjorie had been wondering for days who this girl was. She had seen her sitting by herself in a back row of the auditorium, coming and going as she pleased at these closed rehearsals, sometimes strolling forward to whisper to the director, Miss Kimble, who always listened carefully. Miss Kimble in her youth had sung in the chorus of a real Shubert road company of *Blossom Time;* so although she was now just a skittish old maid in baggy tweeds, teaching music at Hunter, Marjorie was inclined to respect anyone she respected.

When Miss Kimble called, "All right, the Mikado next, please," Marjorie came up the steps of the stage to the stout girl with mixed curiosity and shyness.

"Ah, the star herself." The girl's voice was husky and grown-up. She wore a flaring maroon skirt, a blouse of coarse brown linen with garish embroidery, and a wide tooled-leather belt spiked with copper ornaments. She said to her assistant, a spindly girl with a tape measure, "Chest and hips, that's all. We'll have to hire her costume from Brooks."

Miss Kimble said, or rather whined, "Marsha, we're over the budget already——"

"You can fake a lot with cheesecloth and crepe paper, Dora," said the stout girl, "and I'm doing what I can, but you can't fake a Mikado."

"Well, if you're sure you can't——"

"Thanks," Marjorie muttered in the girl's ear.

Marsha turned her back on Miss Kimble, and said in a tone too low even for the spindly girl to hear, "Don't mention it. You *are* the star, you know, dear." Thereafter she ignored Marjorie.

Next evening she was at the rehearsal again. When it was over she came to Marjorie and made a couple of comments on her performance which were penetrating and useful, more so than any of Miss Kimble's directions. "Let's go out and have a cup of coffee and talk," she said. As they walked arm in arm along Lexington Avenue, bending their heads before the cutting dank wind which swayed signs and flapped scraps of newspaper by, Marsha suddenly said, "Say, I'm starved. Let's have dinner together. I know a wonderful place——"

"I'm expected home for dinner, I'm sorry——"

"Oh. Of course. Well, then, come and have coffee and watch me eat until you have to go home. Yes?"

They went to an old brownstone house on a side street, and up a flight of stairs to a doorway framed by a huge grinning gilt dragon mouth; *Mi Fong's Jade Garden,* the sign over the dragon's ears read. They passed through the fanged jaws into a crimson-lit room smelling of incense and strange cookery. Marjorie was very glad she had not committed herself to eat. She half believed that cats, dogs, and mice were cooked in Chinese restaurants. The pervading odor seemed more or less to confirm the idea. Here and there in the gloom a few diners with odd faces were eating odd-looking things out of oddly shaped dishes. Near the door one fat woman with a mustache was using chopsticks to lift a morsel of meat out of a tureen, from which there protruded a big horribly white bone. Marsha sniffed the air. "God, these places destroy my figure but I'm mad about them—— Hi, Mi Fong. How's your wife? Better?"

"Rittle better, thank you, Missa Masha." A short Chinaman in a white coat bowed them to a latticed booth lit by red paper lanterns. "Same boot? Quiet, peaceful? Rittle drink first, maybe?"

"I guess so. Marjorie, how about trying a Singapore sling? Mi Fong makes the best slings in town."

Marjorie faltered, "I don't know if I want a drink. Coffee——"

"Oh, God, it's a bitter night, you've got to warm your bones. Two, Mi Fong—— He's a marvelous person," Marsha said as they hung up their coats. "His wife paints beautifully. They live in back. I have a screen she did. Gorgeous, and she practically gave it to me. The food is sublime, I tell you, and it costs next to nothing. If you have forty cents on you, you can have a feast. If you haven't I'll lend it to you——"

"Oh no, no, thanks anyway."

With the drinks the Chinaman brought a plate full of fat brown curved things. Marjorie asked what they were, and Marsha exclaimed, "Darling, don't tell me you've never eaten fried shrimps. I'll die."

"I've never eaten any kind of shrimps."

"Bless my soul, haven't you?" Marsha looked at her with a tinge of amusement. "Well—here's to your glorious debut as the Mikado."

Marjorie raised the tall glass, which looked black in the red light. The Singapore sling tasted cool, slightly sweet, not at all strong. She smiled and nodded.

"Nectar," said Marsha. "Don't have more than one, though. Once an evil old man who was trying to make me got me to drink three. Wow."

"Did he make you?" said Marjorie, trying to be as devilish as her companion.

"What do you think?" said Marsha, with an arch air of being offended. She heaved a sigh. "Ah, well. He wasn't really so old, but he sure was evil. Of course that was his chief charm. I'm still mad about him, to tell you the truth." She picked up a plump shrimp and bit it in half with long white teeth. Her face lit up, the dark eyes gleaming. "Ah, Lord, they say it's a vale of tears, Marjorie, and yet there are such things as fried shrimps. Do have one."

"No, thanks."

"Well, you're missing a bit of heaven on earth. But to business. Do you know how much talent you have?"

"Who, me? I'm not sure I have any." Marjorie took a long pull at the

Singapore sling. It went flickering down into her stomach and out along her nerves, it seemed, like little cool flames.

Marsha ate another shrimp, blinking luxuriously. "Well, modesty is becoming. But you're an actress, dear. And I mean an actress. For you to do anything else with your life will be a crime."

"Ko-Ko is ten times as good as I am——"

"My dear, Ko-Ko is a piece of wood. They're all sticks, sticks, I tell you, absolute dummies, except you. Of course they should have given Ko-Ko to you, but Helen had you down for the Mikado. Poor Helen meant well. She likes you in her fashion. I'm afraid she doesn't know her Gilbert and Sullivan. She thought the Mikado part must be the lead."

"Marsha, Miss Kimble did the casting——"

"Dora Kimble, dear, is only the director. Helen Johannsen is business manager of the show, and what's more she'll write the review in the paper. If Miss Kimble wants a show next year she's not going to do anything to offend Helen. The dramatic society is Miss Kimble's one reason for living. She's substituted it for having a man. So she damn well jigs to Helen's tune."

It astounded Marjorie to hear that political influence could touch so sacred a process as the casting of a play. "Is that really how I got the part? I can hardly believe it——"

"Dear, listen, in this school Helen Johannsen can do *anything*." She began to talk about Hunter politics, amazing Marjorie with revelations of the interlocking agreements between the Christian and Jewish sororities, the rigid apportioning of the plums of honor and money.

"Why, it's crooked, it's like Tammany," Marjorie exclaimed.

"Marjorie, really! That's just the way things are, everywhere in the world. School's no different. The girls who do the work are entitled to a little gravy."

"How do you know all this? You make me feel like a blind fool."

"You're just not interested, dear, and I am. I'm ambitious. I tried to buck the system in freshman year. Ran for class president, tried to organize the great unwashed, the non-sorority girls. We outnumber them four to one at Hunter, God knows. Only one trouble. It turns out that the unwashed worship the washed. I got one vote to Helen Johannsen's six. Ah, well." She popped a shrimp into her mouth and drank. "There's something so damn wide-eyed about you. How old are you?"

"I'll be eighteen next month."

"Lawks a mercy me, a child, and an upper sophomore! You're a mental prodigy too. It's too much."

"Prodigy! I barely scrape through every term. It was easy to skip in the Bronx where I grew up, that's all, and I gained a year——"

"You're from the *Bronx?*"

"Lived there all my life until a year and a half ago. Why?"

Marsha squinted at her, the red light making black lines around her eyes. "Well, dear, you *can* act. I'd have taken you for a born and bred Central Park West babe."

"How old are you, Marsha?"

"Dear, I'm a hag. An ancient battered used-up twenty-one."

Marjorie laughed. The drink was taking hold. She was finding Marsha more and more charming, and the Chinese surroundings no longer scared her. "Marsha, will you tell me one thing, and be absolutely honest? It's terribly important to me. What makes you think I have any acting ability? Just from seeing me rehearse a few times——"

Marsha grinned. "Come on, have dinner with me. Call up your folks and tell them you're busy with the show. It's true enough, I have a million things to tell you about your performance."

"Well—look, can you—can you order something for me without pork? I don't eat it."

Marsha smiled. "I can order a whole banquet without pork. Simplicity itself."

Mrs. Morgenstern made no difficulty over the phone, merely asking when Marjorie would be home, and warning her not to work too hard. When she returned to the table Mi Fong was there, ducking his head and smiling. Marsha was saying, "And jasmine tea, of course, and rice cookies and—oh, yes, remember now, no pork. Absolutely no pork."

The Chinaman giggled, glancing at Marjorie. "No polk. Sure thing. Polk too spensive, sure? No polk, missa. Hokay." He went off, laughing.

"Mama says it's all right," Marjorie said, adding, with a rueful look after the Chinaman, "She doesn't know I'm in a chop suey joint."

"You're kosher, aren't you?" said Marsha kindly.

"Well, hardly. My folks are. But pork or shellfish—it's just the idea, it makes no sense——"

"Dear, don't apologize. The power of conditioning is fabulous. Fortunately I've never had the problem."

"Aren't you Jewish?"

"Well now, strangely enough, I don't rightly know. My father's a crusading atheist. My mother doesn't know what she is, she grew up in France as an orphan. I guess Hitler would call me a Jew, all right. But Zelenko, if you don't know it, is the name of one of the noblest old Russian families. How our family comes by it my father doesn't know, or won't say. Maybe my great-grandfather was a noble bastard. For all I know I'm a Russian princess, isn't that a sobering thought?"

"Marsha, did Gertrude Lawrence really come to dinner at your house?"

Marjorie said. The stout girl had casually thrown out this startling fact during their conversation at rehearsal.

"Dear, Gertrude Lawrence has loved my mother for years. But then, everybody does. I don't think there's anybody in the theatre she doesn't know. Damn few I haven't met, in fact. Not that I pretend they're my buddies or anything, it's just through Mama."

Marsha proceeded to tumble out anecdotes about well-known people, all magic names to Marjorie. She knew the funny things Noel Coward did at parties, and where Margaret Sullavan bought her clothes, and which famous actors were conducting adulterous affairs, and with whom, and which celebrated writers and composers were homosexual, and what plays were going to be hits next season, and which producers Marjorie could expect to be assaulted by. She was rattling on in this vein, with Marjorie listening hypnotized, when Mi Fong brought the first course.

As nearly as Marjorie could make out in the crimson gloom, it was a white soup—dirty white. She had an ingrained dislike of white soup. There were things floating in it, some gelatinous, some shredded, some fleshy-looking. She glanced at Mi Fong, who grinned, "No polk, missa."

"Fall to, it's ambrosia," said Marsha, plunging her little china spoon into it greedily.

Marjorie took a few spoonfuls, straining the liquid. The taste was very spicy, not bad. But when she found herself chewing what seemed to be a couple of rubber bands, or possibly worms, she emptied her mouth and pushed away the dish. Then she was ashamed, and afraid she had offended Marsha; but the other girl spooned up her soup obliviously, talking on about the theatre. Marjorie reminded her of Margaret Sullavan, she said, "Not in technique, of course. You couldn't be more raw or awkward, you haven't an atom of experience and it's perfectly obvious you haven't. I'm talking about star quality, about inner magnetism. You walk on stage, Margie, even in a stale old part like the Mikado, and somehow you're alive, and inside the part, and yet you're projecting a peculiar note, your own. That's it, kid, believe me. Everything else is peripheral, it can be learned, it can be taught, it can be bought. *That,* you've either got or you haven't. You've got it."

"Good Lord, I hope you're right——" Marjorie broke off because a steaming heap of food appeared under her nose: a great bed of white rice, and piled on it a number of greasy objects, some vegetable, some animal.

"No polk, missa," said the Chinaman. "Assolutely." Marjorie, however, had smelled pork in restaurants and cafeterias very often. This was pork: if there was such an animal as a pig in the world, this was the remains of a pig.

Marsha said, "You'll love it. It's his masterpiece. Moo yak with almonds." Marjorie nodded and smiled, casting about wildly in her mind for an excuse not to eat it. "They make it with pork in most places," Marsha went on. "Mi Fong makes it with lamb, though." She began shovelling it into her mouth.

"Oh you betcha ram," said Mi Fong, his teeth gleaming redly at Marjorie. "Sure 'nough ram."

"Isn't that meat sort of white for lamb?" said Marjorie, screwing up her eyes and her nose at the dish.

"Assright, missa. White. Chinese ram. Chinese ram alla time white." He poured the tea, which smelled like boiled perfume, in fragile cups, and went away chuckling.

Not wanting to insult Marsha by seeming to call her a liar, Marjorie made a hearty show of enjoying the dish, whatever it was; she scooped the rice from under the meat and ate that. But the light was dim and her instruments greasy for such delicate work. She soon found herself chewing a large piece of rubbery meat. She went into a coughing fit, got rid of it in her handkerchief, and pushed the food around on her plate without eating any more. Partly to distract Marsha from what she was doing, and partly out of the general stimulation of the Singapore sling and Marsha's flattery, Marjorie disclosed to her—for the first time to anybody—the stage name she had invented for herself. Marsha stopped eating, staring at her for several seconds. "Mar-jorie Mor-ningstar, eh?" She lingered over the syllables. "That's you, all right. A silver gleam in the pink sky of dawn. It's an inspiration. It's perfect."

"I don't know—doesn't it sound awkward, sort of forced?"

"Maybe to you it does. You're used to your own name. I tell you it's perfect." Marsha crammed the last scraps on her plate into her mouth and drank tea. "Some day when that name's up in lights over the Music Box, I'll come backstage and remind you of the time we ate in Mi Fong's, and you told it to me, and I insisted that it was exactly right. And you'll turn to your maid and say, 'Give this person a quarter and show her out.' "

They both giggled, and began again on that endless topic, the theatre. Marsha said she was going to be a producer some day after she had made a lot of money in another field. She knew she lacked the talent to be a great designer of costumes or sets. "And I'm not interested in being anything but great, dear." She rejected tolerantly Marjorie's insistence that she was probably a genius. "Wait till you see some of my work. Dull plodding competence, that's all."

"But where are you going to make a pile of money, then, Marsha?"

"That's *my* secret."

"I've told you mine."

"So you have." Marsha looked at her cannily. "Well, it'll do no harm to tell you, at that. I'm going to be a buyer—a big-time buyer of women's clothes for department stores. There's fortunes in it, fortunes! Mother's a good friend of Edna Farbstein, the head buyer at Macy's. Do you know what Edna's worth? Well, dear, the miserable pauper just has one house in Larchmont, another in Palm Beach, a boat, and two Cadillacs, that's all, and both her sons go to Princeton. All I need is a start—one connection, I'll find one somehow—and I'm off to the races. One thing I can do is pick clothes."

Marjorie could not stop a skeptical smile from flickering across her face. Marsha said sharply, "Look, baby, don't say it. This stuff I wear, well, I'm no millionaire yet, and anyway, what can you do for a big fat black-haired slob? Exotic is the word. If you look this way you've got to *lean* on it, and pretend that's exactly what you love to look like."

"I think you dress very attractively," Marjorie said. But she remained a shade skeptical, and they drank their tea in silence for a while. Given Marsha's face and figure, she thought, she would diet away a lot of weight, cut and thin her hair, underplay the makeup, and dress very severely. That way Marsha might achieve a certain theatrical attractiveness, instead of seeming overblown and frowzy. She was afraid to say so, however.

When they came out into the street Marjorie was surprised at the sweet clean smell of the misty air. A Manhattan street seldom smelled this good to her, but after Mi Fong's it was almost like a meadow.

"Which way do you go, Marsha?"

"Ninety-second Street and Central Park West." Marsha pulled her patchy squirrel coat close about her, looking for a cab.

"What! Why, I live in the El Dorado!"

"Gad, next-door neighbors, how lovely. One cab for both——"

"Cab? The cross-town bus is a block from here."

"Oh, the hell with the cross-town bus. This is an occasion." A cab stopped, they got in, and the fat girl snuggled happily into a corner of the seat. "What's the matter with me? Why do I love cabs so? I'm always in hock, just from taking cabs. Anyway, tonight I just had to. After all, my first dinner with Marjorie Morningstar——" She offered Marjorie a cardboard box of cigarettes, and lit one with a practiced cupping of her hands. The smoke was peculiarly aromatic.

"Marsha, you have no idea how queer that name sounds to me when you say it. I haven't told it to a soul before."

"Not even to Sandy Goldstone?"

Marjorie peered at her through the wreathing smoke. "Sandy Goldstone? What about him?"

"Dear, the price of eminence is that you become a goldfish, better get used to it. Everybody at school knows about you and Lamm's, junior."

"Isn't it ridiculous? Marsha, I've just had a few dates with him now and then."

"Well, I hope that's how it is. Don't tie down Marjorie Morningstar at eighteen, kiddo. Not for all the girdles in Lamm's, don't you do it."

"Believe me, nobody's asked me to."

Marsha studied her face. "Well, all right, but don't think it may not happen some day. Lamm's, junior is not above you. The question is whether you're not above him."

Marjorie blushed. "The way you go on——"

"Sugar bun, tell me, are mine really the first mortal ears to hear your stage name? I can't believe it."

"It's the truth. Please don't tell it to anyone either, will you? I mean— it's no state secret, I don't want to seem absurd, but——"

"Darling, I'm a tomb, a silent tomb. Well, history has really been made tonight, hasn't it? Do have a cigarette, they're just Turkish, it's like smoking warm air——"

Marjorie took the cigarette and puffed at it awkwardly. It burned her tongue, and she didn't enjoy it, but she smoked it down.

The cab stopped at a brownstone house midway between Central Park West and Columbus Avenue. Marjorie had walked past it dozens of times, never imagining that anybody who lived in such a house could have any connection with her life. The block was lined with them. Most of them were cheap boardinghouses. The shabby people who came in and out of them looked like small-towners down on their luck and stranded in New York. In the windows the usual sights were fat dusty cats, unhealthy geraniums, and wrinkled old ladies peeking through grimy curtains. "Come on up," Marsha said, "meet my folks. My mother would love to meet you, I know——"

Marjorie glanced at her wristwatch. "Another time. It's after nine, my mom will be wondering what's happened to me."

The girls clasped hands. Marsha said, "We're having lunch at the drugstore tomorrow. I just decided that. Or are we? Is your free hour twelve to one?"

"It is. I'd love to."

Marjorie walked home in something of a daze, not unlike the feeling after first meeting a handsome boy. It took her a long time to fall asleep that night. She tossed and turned, repeating in her mind the things Marsha had said. As she sank into sleep she seemed still to be hearing that energetic, swooping voice talking about the theatre.

What they continued to talk most about, in the days that followed, was the theatre. But the real bond between them was mutual admiration.

Marsha did almost all the talking. She talked and talked and talked, yet it seemed to Marjorie that she could never hear enough of this girl's worldly wisdom, vulgar sharp wit, and intimate gossip about well-known people. Best of all Marjorie liked the long stretches of conversation about herself: her talent, her charm, her promise, with interminable technical discussion of her acting after every rehearsal. The hours flew when they were together; it was very like a romance.

Marjorie was thrust even more into Marsha's company by events at home. Preparations were under way for her brother Seth's bar-mitzva, scheduled for the Saturday before *The Mikado* performance. In Marjorie's view there was no comparing the importance of the two events. Her debut in the college show loomed as large in her mind as an opening night on Broadway; the bar-mitzva was a mere birthday party for a thirteen-year-old boy, with some religious frills. But obviously in the Morgenstern household nobody else thought as she did. Her parents seemed unaware that she was rehearsing at all. It astonished Marjorie to see how her mother's interest in her comings and goings dropped off. Even when she returned from dates with Sandy there were no eager question periods. Usually she found her parents at the dining-room table poring over guest lists or arguing about caterers' estimates. They would greet Marjorie abstractedly and go on with their talk:

"But Rose, Kupman will do it for seventeen hundred. Lowenstein wants two thousand."

"Yes, and maybe that's why every woman in my Federation chapter uses Lowenstein. First class is first class. How many bar-mitzvas are we going to have in this family?"

The girl had always imagined that she hated her mother's inquisitiveness; but she found she actually missed the cross-examinations. They had made the smallest details of her life seem urgent; they had put her in the position of having important secrets. Now suddenly she had no secrets, because her mother had no curiosity. An unfamiliar sensation came over her at times—jealousy of Seth, and of boys in general. Bar-mitzvas were not for girls. Her own birthday, which fell three weeks before Seth's, was going unmentioned. All her life Marjorie had been the darling, the problem, the center of the household; her brother, a healthy even-tempered boy spending all his time at school or in the street, had never before challenged her for the spotlight. So Marsha came along at a fortunate time to flatter Marjorie, make much of her, and restore her good humor.

It seemed to Marjorie that she had never heard so much Hebrew in her life. The house rang with the ancient tongue. Seth was studying for his part in the ceremony as he did everything else nowadays—efficiently, thoroughly, and with ease. He had to learn a number of prayers, and a long reading from a prophetic book in a bizarre chant, and he was constantly practicing aloud. Sometimes a tutor came and chanted with him, sometimes in the evening Mr. Morgenstern chimed in, and all three discordantly bayed the melody. Marjorie heard the chant so often that she came to know it by heart. She was vexed to catch herself chanting as she walked along the street. With an effort of the will she would change over to Gilbert and Sullivan. Marjorie had had desultory Hebrew lessons as a girl, but at twelve, to her great rejoicing, she had been permitted to discontinue them. She had always been bored by the thick black letters that had to be read backward. Her Bible lessons had made her yawn until the tears ran. All of it had seemed an echo of the Stone Age, no more a part of the world of movies, boys, ice cream, and lipstick than the dinosaur skeletons in the museum. Seth, however, had taken to Hebrew from the first and had done well with it, though otherwise he had been a plain street boy, grimy and wild, concerned mainly with ball games, candy, baseball scores, black eyes, and bloody noses.

But lately Seth had been changing. He had gone away to summer camp short and chubby, and had returned a brown elongated stranger, tall as his sister, annoyingly self-possessed. He danced with a smoothness that amazed her, and he actually had dates with prim painted little girls of eleven and twelve. He accepted the vortex of bar-mitzva preparations around him quite calmly, with no trace of stage fright at the prospect of his performance. She told Marsha about these changes, and talked so much of her brother that Marsha asked to meet him. Marjorie had her friend up to tea on Sunday afternoon. Seth talked to Marsha coolly, unperturbed by her ironic teasing; and when he went back to his chant she said that he was an absolute charmer, and that having no brother or sister was the tragedy of her life.

It happened that Mrs. Morgenstern came home before Marsha left, and so met the fat girl for the first time. She evinced a flicker of her old interest in Marjorie's doings, cross-examining Marsha about her background. When Marsha was gone the mother announced that she didn't like her much.

"Why not?" said Marjorie, bristling.

"What kind of people live in those brownstone houses? You've met her parents?"

"No, I haven't, and I think that's the most snobbish remark I've ever heard, Mom."

"All right. I'm a snob. I'm this, I'm that. She doesn't look quite clean, that's all."

"Okay, I'll never bring her up here again!" exclaimed Marjorie, enraged at her mother's unerring hit on Marsha's one unfortunate weakness.

"You'll get tired of her soon enough, the sooner the better."

"That's how much you know. We'll be friends for life."

Helen Johannsen encountered her in a corridor next morning and invited her to lunch. Marjorie hesitated; she had begun meeting Marsha every day in the drugstore for the noon hour. But she was flattered, and she knew the fat girl would understand, so she accepted. Helen took her to a genteel tearoom favored by the faculty. For a while the lunch was very pleasant. They chatted about *The Mikado*, the school newspaper, the sororities, and the yearbook. Helen disclosed no inside information, and seemed unaware of her own great spider web of power, talking of these things as though they were light fun.

Then she said, rather abruptly, "I see you've made friends with Marsha Zelenko."

"Yes."

"She's very clever."

"We have loads of fun."

"You met her at the rehearsals, isn't that right?"

"Yes."

"I want to tell you a couple of things. I know Marsha well. She's all right in some ways. Don't take her too seriously, and don't lend her money." Helen kept her eyes on Marjorie's stiffening face.

Marjorie said dryly, "Marsha is my friend."

"I know." Helen gathered up her purse and gloves. "I'll say no more.— How's Sandy, by the way?"

"Just fine."

"He graduates this June, doesn't he? What's he going to do?"

"Go into his father's business, I guess."

"Oh? He's given up Peru?"

Marjorie said blankly, "Peru?"

"Didn't he tell you? He had it all worked out. He was going to get an agency to sell electrical appliances in Peru. He said there was a fortune in it."

"He's given up Peru," said Marjorie. "Right now he wants to be either a doctor or a forest ranger. He's not sure which."

They both chuckled. "He's nice, though," Helen said.

Marsha Zelenko came out of the drugstore as the two girls were walking past on the street. She waved airily, they both waved back, and she went another way. At the rehearsal that afternoon Marsha sauntered up to Marjorie. "Well, well, lunching with the big shot, hey, instead of poor no-account me?"

"Marsha, she asked me——"

"Darling, by all means, you must never miss any chance to improve your connections. Did she happen to say something about me, maybe?"

"You? Not a thing."

Marsha scanned her face. "Well, just in case she did, dear, just remember one thing. I am the only girl in the class of '34 who has never kowtowed to Helen Johannsen. I am the class cat, full of independence and claws. Doing anything tonight?"

"Just homework, why?"

"How's to walk around the corner after dinner and meet my folks? I've talked so much about you—of course it's not the El Dorado, but we have a lot of fun."

"Sure, Marsha."

When she arrived at Marsha's house that evening, however, the parents had gone out to a concert. The two girls lolled on the divan in Marsha's tiny bedroom, waiting for them to return. Marjorie ate grapes; the fat girl smoked heavy Turkish cigarettes. Marsha asked a lot of questions about the lunch with Helen Johannsen; but Marjorie, an old hand under cross-examination, managed to avoid repeating Helen's criticism.

Marsha said, "Well, now, are you developing a huge crush on Helen, seeing she's so nice to you?"

"A crush? Hardly. But she is terrifically attractive."

"You're more attractive than she is."

"Marsha, how you talk! She's a model——"

"So what? Too much jaw and chin, dear. Strictly not for photographs, and only second class for the cloak-and-suit trade. Oh, I sound like a cat all right, don't I? Look, Helen Johannsen is tops. Clever, pretty, honest, a natural leader, all that. I'll say it to anybody. I'll only add to you, because you're you, that to me she's as exciting as old dishwater."

"Marsha, you're crazy. Men swarm for tall blondes——"

"For dates, sugar bun, for dates. To see how far they can get in one night. Helen won't play. She's intelligent, too, which scares them, and not intelligent enough to make noises like a moron, which would induce them to keep trying. No dear, when the boys want to get married they

skip the big blondes and come looking for little Marjorie Morningstar."
Marsha rolled over on her back, and her skirt slipped up, exposing a patch of downy brown thigh above her stocking. Marjorie would have pulled her own skirt down in such a position, but Marsha merely lit another cigarette and said with a yawn, "I'll bet you've been proposed to already."

Marjorie turned red. Marsha laughed. "More than once, eh? Four times, more likely."

"Good heavens, no. Even counting crazy kids just babbling at a dance" —Marjorie was thinking of Billy Ehrmann, and of a moon-struck boy she had known in the Bronx—"there have only been three. Only one that really mattered."

"Listen to the girl!" Marsha said to the ceiling. She leaned up on an elbow, staring at Marjorie. "You're *eighteen,* punk! You're still in the shell. And *three guys,* no matter how crazy—— I haven't had one, not one. Most girls haven't at your age. Please realize that. By the time you're twenty-one you'll be beating them off with a club. Who was the one that mattered? Sandy Goldstone?"

"Marsha, I told you Sandy's never proposed. Don't you believe me? He's never come within a mile of it. It was someone else." She hesitated. She had until now avoided talking about her love life to Marsha, who seemed too sophisticated to be anything but amused by her problems. But she missed having a confidante. Since her success with the Columbia set she had found it awkward to talk to Rosalind Green; during the summer they had drifted apart. "I can tell you about it, but I'm afraid you'll be bored to death."

"Nothing relating to you could possibly bore me, Morningstar."

Marjorie told her about George, and about Sandy; and she described her early experiences too. Once started, she fairly poured it all out. Marsha listened attentively, hugging her knees, occasionally lighting fresh cigarettes, filling the hot little room with drifting layers of gray strong-smelling smoke. Marjorie talked on for about half an hour, with her eyes mostly fixed on an orange and green Mexican blanket hung on the wall; she never saw the blanket afterward, or one like it, without thinking vaguely of George Drobes.

Marsha said, when Marjorie had finished, "Well. Quite a saga, for an eighteen-year-old."

"It's all a lot of foolishness, no doubt, to you——"

"On the contrary, fascinating, and very revealing, dear. About Sandy, if you want my opinion, you're not in love with him. Of course that may change. George was much nearer the real thing—not that I approve of George, I hasten to say. That was your blind-kitten stage—following the first pair of feet you could smell and hear. It's one of the risks of being attractive, you can get snatched up by some George or other and married while you're still a blind kitten, but in your case——"

"Marsha, he's terribly sweet and fine——"

"Yes, yes, to be sure. You're well out of it, dear. Poor guy. He came close to grabbing himself off a good thing. Kitten-snatching has its points. Except, of course, it's such a horrible humiliation when the snatch fails."

"Well, I'm not sure I agree about George, but—anyway, don't you think I ought to stop seeing Sandy? I do."

Marsha sat upright and glared at her. "Are you INSANE?"

"But—I'm not at all sure I love him—or that he loves me. You're right about that. Besides, his family will never have any part of me. He's just killing time with me, until——"

"LET HIM!" Marsha turned to the ceiling again. "What'll I do with her? Margie, you see the shows with this fellow, you sit in the orchestra, you go to the good night clubs, he doesn't try to make you—what do you want, eggs in your beer? Sweetie, you're like a dumb Indian sitting on oil land, I swear you are. Everything else aside, what a connection he is!"

"Connection for what? I don't want to work as a Lamm's salesgirl——"

The doorbell rang. Marsha glanced at her watch. "Ye gods, the folks already. D'you know we've been jawing for hours?" She rolled off the bed as the bell rang again. "Coming, coming!—Damn them, they forget the key five nights out of six. Come on and meet them, Marge."

Marsha's father was small and white-haired, her mother was big and blond, and they were both carrying brown paper bags. Mr. Zelenko's dull purple suit was not very pressed, nor his flowered red tie very straight. "Well, well," he said with a good-natured grin which completely changed the sad set of his face, "so this is the famous Marjorie Morningstar."

Mrs. Zelenko gave her husband a jolt with an elbow that staggered him. "All right, Big Mouth, that was supposed to be a secret." She smiled graciously at Marjorie. "Hello, dear. You might as well know that in this family there are no secrets. But outside these walls, they could rake the flesh off our bones and we wouldn't talk."

"It doesn't matter," Marjorie said.

"Food?" said Marsha, nosing into the paper bags her parents put down on the sofa.

"Delicatessen," said the mother. "We didn't have dinner. How about you?"

"I had a couple of dogs at Nedick's but I'm starved," said Marsha.

"Fine. Get a few plates, glasses, and a bottle opener," said the mother. "It's all here.—You'll join us, Margie?"

"I had dinner, thank you."

Mr. Zelenko said, "Nonsense. A glass of beer and a corned beef sandwich, what is that? Strictly kosher, by the way, only kind of delicatessen we eat, it's the freshest and the purest, you know." He pulled a fat green pickle out of a paper bag and took a large bite of it.

"Hog, wait for the rest of us," said Mrs. Zelenko, taking a bright green enamel Buddha off a gate-leg table, and unfolding the table.

"Hors d'oeuvre doesn't count," said Mr. Zelenko, dropping into a dilapidated armchair. He brandished the pickle at Marjorie. "Margie, my dear, we're going to have to work over your religious problem. First off, we'll have you read some Ingersoll, I think—then Haeckel, maybe a little Voltaire—and soon you'll be enjoying ham and eggs like any other sensible person."

"Let the girl alone," said Mrs. Zelenko, tying an apron over her billowing red skirt and embroidered peasant blouse. "She has principles, let her stick to them. You could do with a few principles yourself.—Come on, let's eat."

Marjorie was strangely reminded of Mi Fong's restaurant as she sat at the tiny table in the cramped living room with the Zelenkos, eating potato salad, cold cuts, and pickle. The room was dimly lit like the Chinese place, though the prevailing color was orange rather than red. It was decorated with an astonishing variety of foreign materials and objects—among them a metal African mask, a coconut, a bird cage without a bird, a large brass hookah, a small ragged rug hung on the wall, a huge round Mexican copper plate, and the Chinese screen painted by Mrs. Mi Fong, a blurry affair on which the dragons and the ladies in kimonos appeared to have melted and run together before hardening. There was an exotic smell, too, a mixture of old settled-in Turkish tobacco smoke, aging musty upholstery, spicy food, and the pungent furniture polish of the piano. The piano dominated the room; indeed, it took up almost half the floor space, black, shiny, and portentous.

"Principles, she says I have no principles, Margie," said Mr. Zelenko, holding a pastrami sandwich in one hand and a pickle in the other, and biting at them alternately. "People who think they have principles are either fools or hypocrites. Therefore, they're fair game for enlightened people like me, because all hypocrites should be destroyed, and even the Bible tells us not to suffer fools. Of course this gives me an advantage over most people, but I can't help that."

"That's how it happens he's a multimillionaire," said Mrs. Zelenko to Marjorie.

"I thought you didn't believe in the Bible," Marjorie said to the father. She was drinking beer with her cold cuts, and beginning to enjoy herself very much. There was something delightfully fresh and gay about an improvised delicatessen supper at eleven at night. She could not conceive of such a lark in her own home. The hot dinner at seven came as certainly as sunset, and thirty days out of thirty-one her parents were asleep at ten.

"I don't, but it has some bright sayings in it," said Mr. Zelenko. "A book doesn't survive four thousand years without having an occasional gleam of merit. I prefer *The Greek Anthology* for wisdom, and Plato for profundity, and Darwin and Einstein for factual information, of course." Mr. Zelenko while saying this made himself another sandwich containing some six layers of sliced tongue.

Marsha said, "Oh, shut up, Alex, you're shocking Margie. Pass that beer."

Marjorie was more shocked to hear Marsha call her father by his first name than she had been by the fun poked at the Bible. In her own house her parents' first names were sacrosanct; they were Papa and Mama even to each other. When they used "Rose" or "Arnold" it was a sign that a fight was coming on.

Mr. Zelenko passed the beer. "So far as being a multimillionaire goes," he said, "I've been defeated by two things—lack of connections, and scale. Mainly scale. My ideas, executed on the scale of millions, would have made millions. Executed on the scale of a few hundreds, they've lost the hundreds. I'm like a battleship with sixteen-inch guns that can't fight because it only carries buckshot."

"How was the concert?" Marsha said.

"Horrible. Frances is falling apart," said Mrs. Zelenko. "I think she was drunk. She could go to jail for what she did to the Bach Chaconne."

"I liked it," said Mr. Zelenko, taking a long drink of beer.

"Oh, you, Mr. Tin Ear," said his wife angrily.

"Who is Frances?" said Marjorie.

Marsha mentioned the name of a famous concert pianist.

"We went back afterwards," said Mrs. Zelenko. "I'm telling you she was shaking as though she had Parkinson's disease. And her breath! Frances always did like her nip, but it's getting out of hand."

"Maybe you should try her brand of whiskey," said Mr. Zelenko mildly. "Forty-two cities, booked solid through December——"

"I am not a concert pianist," snapped Mrs. Zelenko. "And that's why I can play Bach. When I play, it's as though Bach is listening, Bach himself, not twelve hundred yawning potbellied mink-coated perfumed idiots who don't know a piano from a ukulele."

She threw down her napkin, marched to the piano and struck a chord which startled Marjorie right out of her seat. Mrs. Zelenko crashed ahead into music that was obviously Bach: arid, tremendously powerful, and icily formal. The playing, to Marjorie, seemed masterly. It was unfortunate that the room was so small; the effect was something like sitting inside the piano. The slamming and crashing went on and on, and every time Mrs. Zelenko hit a certain high note the African mask on the wall came alive with a weird brief ping. Marsha and her father continued to eat while they listened to the music. At one point Mr. Zelenko winked at Marjorie, leaned toward her, and shouted, making himself barely audible above the blast-furnace din of the piano, "I knew I'd needle her into playing. Marvelous, isn't it? Ten times as good as Frances, really."

"It's lovely," Marjorie screamed.

"She's an authentic genius," Mr. Zelenko bellowed. "There's no room for playing like that on the concert stage. That's a dirty mountebank's racket."

"Shut up while I'm trying to play," yelled Mrs. Zelenko, not pausing her impassioned pounding.

Evidently it was one of Bach's longer compositions, for after ten minutes it showed no signs of letting up. Marjorie's head began to throb. Marsha and her father had between them disposed of all the food and beer, and now they were lolling on the sofa, smoking Turkish cigarettes, and listening with half-closed eyes. Despite the discomfort of the too-loud piano Marjorie was deriving some enjoyment from the music, to her surprise. She had always considered Bach a composer of mere dry jigging exercises, but she now heard, or thought she heard, moments of passionate melody and traces of a magnificent colonnaded structure of sound. But she half suspected that she was simply trying to appreciate something that was not there. It was hard to be sure of anything except that her ears were ringing and the top of her head evidently trying to open across the middle.

Mrs. Zelenko rose half off the piano stool, raised her hands over her head, and came down to strike a shattering chord. The African mask pinged and fell off the wall. The doorbell rang.

"Oh, God, hold off, Tonia, it's the Angel of Death," said Mr. Zelenko. He went to the door and shouted, "Yes?" From outside came a high-pitched angry cackling in French. He responded with equal irritation in the same tongue, and for a while a Gallic debate yammered back and forth through the closed door. Then the outside voice faded away, still shrieking.

"She sounds hoarse tonight," said Mrs. Zelenko.

Mr. Zelenko smiled at Marjorie. "She lives across the hall. French-woman, probably eighty-five years old, but strong? I saw her carry a leather armchair up the stairs by herself. Lives on oatmeal and skim milk, and reads yesterday's papers that the other tenants throw out. I think she's a millionaire."

"Oh, Alex, don't be dumb, the Angel's no millionaire," said Marsha.

"Look, baby, I once caught her picking the financial page out of our garbage pail and we got to talking stocks. The woman knows every firm that's passed a dividend in the last five years—— I'm in the Street myself," he said in an aside to Marjorie. "I can tell when somebody knows what it's about." He hung the African mask back on the wall and took down a balalaika that hung beside it. "Well, we can still have a little civilized music.—How about some cherry brandy, Tonia?"

When Mrs. Zelenko brought the bottle of cherry brandy out of a back room she also brought a large picture in a leather frame which she handed to Marjorie. "You've seen her on the stage, I suppose," she said casually.

It was a photograph of Gertrude Lawrence inscribed *To Tonia Zelenky, pianist extraordinary.*

"Gosh, that's a wonderful thing to have," said Marjorie.

"It's just a joke, her writing it 'Zelenky,' " said Marsha's mother. "She was always calling me that. She knew how to spell my name."

Mr. Zelenko took a sip of the cherry brandy and began to sing a Russian song, accompanying himself expertly on the balalaika. After a few bars his wife and daughter joined in; they sat on either side of him on the sofa, swaying slightly to the music, and harmonizing with careless sweetness. Marjorie, curled up on an armchair, felt tears rising to her eyes. The song was plaintive, but more than that, there was a strange pathos about the Zelenkos themselves, the little white-headed man with a face curiously expressing cynicism and childishness at once, flanked by the fat bright unattractive daughter and the wife who played the piano better than concert pianists and treasured an autographed picture of Gertrude Lawrence.

Mr. Zelenko began a gay dance melody. Marsha jumped up and clumsily did some steps, arms akimbo, head tossing. Then she broke off and said, "Alex, Alex, stop, I've got a marvelous idea. Tonia, you know *The Mikado* score, don't you?"

"Well, I haven't played it in years, but sure——"

"Come on. Marjorie Morningstar will now do *My Object All Sublime.*"

"Wonderful," said the father, tossing aside the balalaika and pouring himself more cherry brandy.

Marjorie said "No, no," as Marsha tugged her out of the armchair, but Mrs. Zelenko was already at the piano, running through snatches of *The Mikado.*

"Come on!" Marsha said. "A real opening-night performance, now. Do all the things we talked about."

The mother struck up *My Object All Sublime* with grandiose vigor. The space was narrow for capering, but Marjorie went into her number and did her best. When it was over the Zelenkos clapped and cheered.

"Why, she's another Gertrude Lawrence," cried Mrs. Zelenko. "Honestly, it's Gertie all over again, the way she holds her head and uses her eyes——"

"You'll have a million dollars before you're thirty, baby," said Mr. Zelenko. "Come to me and get it invested. Don't be like all the other stars and die broke."

"I *told* you she was marvelous, didn't I?" said Marsha. She seized the brandy. "Come on, we're drinking to the new star." She poured three glasses full, handed them around, and raised her own high. "Here's to Marjorie Morningstar, 1940's toast of New York—discovered by poor little Marsha Zelenko!"

"What are you talking about, 1940?" said the father scornfully. "Why seven years? She'll be on top of the heap in 1938, mark my words! Here's to you, Marjorie!"

Marjorie blushed, smiled, bowed her head. Mrs. Zelenko downed her brandy and said, suddenly looking thoughtful, "Marsha, don't you think Mr. Klabber might be interested in Marjorie?"

"Why, I hadn't—— Say, that's a marvelous idea, absolutely marvelous," Marsha exclaimed. "Gad, he'll go mad over her."

"Who's Mr. Klabber?" said Marjorie.

"Oh—somebody," said Marsha, with a broad wink at her mother.

"A connection," said Mr. Zelenko, looking mysterious.

"I'll just get him to come to *The Mikado*," said Marsha.

"That'll do it. He only has to see her perform once," said Mrs. Zelenko.

"Oh please, this isn't fair, tell me who he is——"

Marsha shook her head. "If nothing came of it you'd only be disappointed. No, sugar bun, forget it. Drink your brandy."

When Marjorie left half an hour later the Zelenkos were in the midst of a violent discussion of modern art. Marsha, even as she accompanied her to the door, was shouting, "Alex, you know perfectly well Rouault is a commercial phony. 'Bye, Margie, it's been heaven, see you at lunch, okay? And how about Picasso's ceramics, Alex, for Christ's sake?" The door closed.

On the dim landing outside the apartment Marjorie paused, buttoning her coat. She was startled in a moment to see a pair of eyes glittering at her from a crack in the door across the hallway. Nervously she headed for the stairs, and as she did so a crone in a shapeless brown garment that was neither a dress nor a slip nor anything else Marjorie could recognize darted at her, shaking a bony finger high in the air. "I am old," she squeaked, "I am seeck person. I vant sleep. Good people all asleep now. You bad people like *them.*" She pointed at the Zelenkos' door. "Stay up late, noise, noise, noise——" This, clearly, was the Angel of Death. Marjorie, her spine prickling, dodged past her and ran down the stairs. The Angel screeched after her, "Bad people! Bad! Bad! BAD!"

The night was chilly, and the moon shone pallidly over Ninety-second Street. Walking home, and riding up in the elevator, Marjorie kept wondering who Mr. Klabber might be; a movie talent scout was her most hopeful guess.

When she came into the apartment she received a smart shock. Uncle Samson-Aaron was in the living room, drinking tea with her parents. It was the first time he had come—had been allowed to come—to visit them at the El Dorado. He was a ghost from the Bronx past.

Chapter 8. THE UNCLE

"Havaya, Modgerie?" said Uncle Samson-Aaron, his fleshy red cheeks shining. "Havaya? Say, our Modgerie has become a something, a lady. Ven ve hear about a vedding, Modgerie?"

"Hello, Uncle, you're looking well," Marjorie said, wondering whether he would pull a Hershey bar out of his pocket and give it to her, as he always had since her babyhood.

"I look vell? Thank you, I look like a cholera. *You* look vell. You look, I don't know, a few years ago I held you on my knee and now you look like a regular wampire from the movies——"

"Sit down, Marjorie, have some tea," said her mother. "Have another piece of cake, Samson-Aaron."

Uncle Samson-Aaron leaned forward and cut himself a vast triangle from the chocolate cake on the coffee table. His paunch, always huge, now appeared to extend out beyond his knees. His blue serge trousers and brown jacket were shiny tight, and the skin on his hands and face was shiny tight. He grinned his sweet foolish scraggly-mustached grin at Marjorie. "Uncle Samson-Aaron, same old gobbage pail, hey Modgerie?" He forked a piece of cake the size of a fist into his mouth.

Marjorie warily accepted a cup of tea from her mother and sat. The presence of Samson-Aaron in the El Dorado was disturbing; she was anxious to find out what it meant.

Samson-Aaron Feder had never been known to her as anything but The Uncle. She had other uncles, but he and he alone was The Uncle. When she and Seth had been tiny children, Samson-Aaron had been the family baby-sitter. He was invited to dinner, gorged himself, and paid for his meal by staying with the children while the parents went out. Usually it was on Friday night. One of her earliest memories was cuddling in Samson-Aaron's lap in the tiny warm kitchen by the soft sad glow of dying Sabbath candles, drowsing while he crooned Jewish lullabies to her. As he crooned Samson-Aaron would gnaw on a chicken leg or wing from the icebox, and nip at the brown bottle of fiery liquid with the strong smell. Even now the smell of rye whiskey could suddenly set her thinking of the Friday nights of her childhood.

She had loved the Uncle then. She was ten or perhaps eleven when she realized that he was considered by her parents, and by all the family, a fool, a failure, and a ridiculous glutton. Before that she had thought his love of food and drink was a charming trait, a source of great lively fun. At the seders, the big family gatherings on Passover eve, it was the annual joke that whatever was left on anybody's plate or in anybody's glass was passed on to Samson-Aaron. Marjorie was fascinated by his gargantuan appetite. Sometimes she would purposely heap her plate and then eat only a little of it just to watch the Uncle gobble up the rest. Perspiration dripping from his forehead, his eyes gleaming, he would shout, "No dishes to vash! Samson-Aaron is here!"—and the plates would go rattling down to his place among the children at the foot of the table. His vitality seemed inexhaustible. When he had eaten and drunk enough for seven men he would lead the singing of the rollicking syncopated hymns, waving his arms and adding wild trills to the happy chorus.

For Marjorie, Samson-Aaron had always been the soul, the visible symbol, of that group of vague people called The Family, whom she had seen often in her childhood, though lately only once or twice a year. They had peculiar Yiddish names—Aunt Shosha, Aunt Dvosha, Uncle Shmulka, Uncle Avromka. One ran a candy store, another was a tailor, another worked in a laundry; the occupations of the rest were equally humble. Her father, by common recognition, was the aristocrat among them, the one who had achieved success in America. He always sat with Marjorie and her mother at the head of the table when the family gathered nowadays; and Samson-Aaron always sat at the foot, among the new crop of children, who loved him and played with him just as Marjorie and her cousins had. There had been some slight question about the Uncle's status when his one son, an English instructor at a small upstate college, had published a novel. In the first impact of the event it had appeared that Samson-Aaron might move as much as halfway up the board. But the novel, a highly grim involved work which Marjorie could not finish, had fallen dead, despite the praise in the tattered clippings which the Uncle carried in his wallet; and Samson-Aaron had stayed at the foot of the table.

"How's Geoffrey, Uncle?" Marjorie said as Samson-Aaron cut himself more cake without being asked.

"Ven do I ever see Geoffrey? Vunce in three years? I suppose he's fine. Geoffrey . . . That name in my mouth still tastes funny. Vy did he have to change it? Milton isn't an American name?"

"Geoffrey is better for a writer of books," said Mrs. Morgenstern.

"For a college teacher Milton is good enough," said Samson-Aaron. "Better he should never have written that book. Do you know how much he made from it, after he vorked two years? Four hundred forty dollars. I said to him, 'Milton, I'm an old nobody, but is it proper to write a story vit a boy and a girl getting into bed ven they're not married? Is it nice?' He says to me, 'Pa, that's true life.' I said, 'Milton, all I know is decent people vunt like it.'—So I'm an old nobody, he starts talking about something else, and sucks on his pipe. So he makes four hundred forty dollars for two years' hard vork. True life. Geoffrey Quill. A cholera."

"That's no way to talk about your boy," said Mr. Morgenstern. "He accomplished something. He's a writer. A book is a book."

"That's right, we're proud of him. The whole family is," said Mrs. Morgenstern.

"An accomplishment? Vot? A mishmash, a person can't make head or tail out of it. Tolstoy I can understand. I told Milton, 'Read Tolstoy!' He says, 'Pop, Tolstoy wrote horizontal, I write vertical.' Did you ever hear of such a thing? I said to him, 'You should only live to write horizontal like Tolstoy.' He makes a face and sucks his pipe. Accomplishment. You know vot I call accomplishment? A home, a good Jewish wife, children——"

"Let's see your wallet. I bet you've still got all the clippings," said Mr. Morgenstern.

The Uncle looked at him with a slow sheepish smile. "Excuse me, he's my son, my only child, I love him. But don't talk to me about accomplishment."

"All the same," said Mrs. Morgenstern, "we're expecting him at the bar-mitzva."

Marjorie now perceived what Uncle Samson-Aaron was doing in the El Dorado. She said to her mother, "Haven't you invited Geoffrey yet?"

"I don't want to send him a printed invitation that he can drop in the wastebasket. I want him to *come*. The Uncle can make sure he comes."

"Vot can I do?" said Samson-Aaron, washing down a huge bite of cake with a slosh of tea. "Get out a court order on my own son he should come to Seth's bar-mitzva? Vot does he care vot I say? If I threaten to come up to Albany and show myself to his friends, maybe that vould scare him enough to come."

"He's not that bad," said Mr. Morgenstern. "Why do you say such things? He sends you money every month like clockwork, and what does he make, after all?"

"He's a good boy, he has a good heart, I have notting against him," said Samson-Aaron. He mopped his pink brow with a large blue handkerchief, regarding the remaining cake longingly (there wasn't much), and leaned back on the sofa with a wheeze. "I don't know, nowadays I have no appetite."

"If nothing else will work on him," said Mrs. Morgenstern, "you might mention who it was who put him through college and kept his father off relief."

Samson-Aaron's cherubic mouth pulled downward into bitter lines. He looked appealingly at Mrs. Morgenstern and nodded slowly and sadly. Then he turned to Marjorie with his old sweet foolish grin. There was a black gap of two teeth missing, the girl noticed with a qualm. "A fine uncle you've got, ha, Modgerie? Not only couldn't support his son, couldn't even support himself. Samson-Aaron the gobbage pail. No dishes to vash."

"Oh, Uncle——" Marjorie said helplessly.

"It's true. And I came to America to become a millionaire. Say, listen, if everybody vas a millionaire, vare vould they get night vatchmen? Notting vould be safe at night." He stood. "It reminds me I've got to go to vork.—But a nickel, Modgerie, a nickel I alvays had, to buy you a Hershey bar ven I came to this house. No Hershey bar, no Samson-Aaron. Right?"

Marjorie threw her arms around the fat old man and kissed his damp shiny cheek. He smelled faintly of the chocolate cake. "Right, Uncle. Where's my Hershey tonight?"

"A Hershey? Vot you vant now is a husband, darling, and that the Uncle can't bring in the pocket." He patted her shoulder and turned to Mrs. Morgenstern. "Vun vay or another, Geoffrey vill come to the bar-mitzva. Satisfied?"

"Is it a promise?"

"It's a promise. From Samson-Aaron a promise."

"I'm satisfied," said Mrs. Morgenstern, regarding him critically. "Tell me this, do you have a suit to wear for the bar-mitzva?"

The Uncle glanced down wryly at himself. "You think I'll come to the Riverside Plaza like a night vatchman? I still have the suit, the good suit you bought me for Milton's graduation. Ven do I vear it except for bar-mitzvas and veddings?"

"Good," said Mrs. Morgenstern. "Make sure it's cleaned and pressed. And get a haircut, and your mustache trimmed, and—*you* know——"

"I know." He ambled to the door and turned around. His paunch was enormous. He grinned at Marjorie. "Next time I vear the good suit—your vedding. Yes? Modgerie's vedding."

"Marjorie has no intentions of getting married just yet——"

"Make it snappy, darling. Samson-Aaron is getting old. I vant you should have a little girl, I can bring her a Hershey bar. A nickel in the pocket I have nowadays. Thanks to my son—Geoffrey Quill, the vertical writer."

When he had gone Marjorie said, "Where does he work, this time of night?"

"Work!" said her father, shrugging his shoulders. "A jobber who owes me some money has a warehouse, and Samson-Aaron sleeps there at night with a time clock in his lap. That's his work—this week. He goes from one place to another."

Mrs. Morgenstern, gathering up the tea things, said, "He'll bring Geoffrey, that's the main thing. He doesn't make promises, but when he does, they're promises."

"Why on earth do you want Geoffrey so badly?" said the girl. "What difference does it make?"

"Because I want him at a certain table with some particularly fine people, that's all."

"The Goldstones," said the father.

"Not only them," said the mother, with a vexed glance at the girl.

"Mom! Mom, have you invited the Goldstones?"

"Why not? They're friends of mine, aren't they?"

"Sandy, too, no doubt?"

"Why should I leave out Sandy? Did you have a fight with him, or something?"

The girl said, "Oh, God," and sank on the window seat with her forehead against the glass. "The Goldstones and the family—well, that fixes everything——"

Mrs. Morgenstern put the dishes down with a sharp clatter.

"The finest people will be at that table. The Goldstones, your father's banker Bill Connelly and his wife, Geoffrey, yourself, and the Robisons from Philadelphia. What's wrong——"

"The Robisons? The parents of Seth's little girl friend at camp?"

"Yes, the Robisons. They like Seth, and they like your father and me, strange as that seems, even though they own twenty office buildings in

Philadelphia. And if you're ashamed of our family, Marjorie, I'm not. Next time we start talking about who's a snob, remember that."

Marjorie worried for days over the prospect of sitting through Seth's bar-mitzva banquet with the Goldstones. She unburdened herself to Marsha. The fat girl was more amused than concerned. "Of course we start from different premises," she said. "I don't care a hang whether you captivate the Goldstones or not. I'm against the match. Maybe when I meet Sandy I'll change my mind, but as of now——"

"Marsha, you know it's not a question of a match, but—look, I do like Sandy and—the family stages such brawls, sometimes, that's all——"

"Sugar bun, the Goldstones have a family too. Everybody does. Actually it's one of the world's mysteries why all relatives are such a gruesome lot of spooks. You'd think mathematically somebody would be related to the human section of the human race, but it doesn't seem to work out that way. Probably it's got something to do with Einstein's theory—relativity, you know——"

Marjorie said, "Very funny."

"I just can't see that it's a problem, dear——"

"God Almighty, don't you think there's something bald about hauling these virtual strangers—millionaires, as it happens—into the bosom of the family along with their handsome son—he *is* handsome, believe me—and plunking me down at a table with them for the evening in full view of all my aunts and uncles? I think's it's the next thing to announcing an engagement, that's all, and I don't think Sandy's folks are going to be amused by such shotgun tactics—let alone Sandy——"

They talked some more, and then Marsha suggested that she invite George. That would baffle the family, she said, and neutralize any suspicion in the Goldstones; George would act so proprietary that Sandy would be lucky to dance twice with her all evening. Marjorie thought this over, and concluded that it was an inspiration. That night she sent him one of the engraved bar-mitzva invitations, adding on the back a prettily worded note begging him to come. She wrote, instead of phoning him, because at the moment matters stood rather awkwardly between her and George. Their last date had ended in a long wrangle in the front seat of Penelope. George had nagged and nagged at her to tell him what he had done wrong, how he had offended her, what she wanted him to do to make things as they had been in the old days. To these classic questions, of course, Marjorie had been unable to invent any good fresh answers.

A week went by; two weeks; three. No response from George. She wondered whether the letter could have gone astray in the mail, and two or three times she almost telephoned him. She was very glad she hadn't when his answer at last arrived. It lay on the desk in her room, an ominously fat envelope, when she came home from rehearsal. She tore it open, and after glancing at the first paragraph she fell on the bed and feverishly skimmed through the letter, so shocking in George's familiar neat script and green ink. He was not coming to the bar-mitzva, he said, and he did not expect to see Marjorie again. It was a dry letter, totally different in tone from anything George had ever said or written to her before. The gist of it was that he had found another girl; and Marjorie could not at all doubt that this was the truth. He spoke with detached clarity of the way she had drifted from him since her move to Manhattan. It was hopeless, he said, to see her any more, and now that he had met this girl—a Bronx girl, much closer to him in background and interests—he had no desire to.

In the last paragraph, which was a short and annoyingly good-humored farewell, half a line had been crossed over and thickly blotted out; it was almost the only mar on the four evenly written sheets. Marjorie stared at the long green blotch and held it up to the light, trying to make out the words, hoping that under the blotch lay a revealing little sentence that would show George's true feelings, cancel the whole letter, and put him back in his place as her adoring suitor. But the blotch was impenetrable, and remained so.

The blow stunned the girl for a week, and she went through agonies of jealousy and remorse, and fantasies of revenge, which amazed her with their violence. But she did nothing. There was really nothing to do. In a heroic last surprise George had stood up from the chopping block, seized the axe, and hit her with it; and that was that.

She braced herself to sit out the bar-mitzva with the terrifying Goldstones and with Sandy.

Chapter 9.   THE BAR-MITZVA

It was strangely impressive, after all, when Seth stood before the Holy Ark draped in his new purple-and-white silk prayer shawl on Saturday morning, chanting his reading from the Book of Malachi.

The temple was full, and hushed. Perversely, perhaps with a touch of injured self-effacement, Marjorie sat far in the back. Her mother had tried to get her to sit on the front bench with the rest of the family, but Marjorie had said no, she would stay in the rear to welcome any late-coming friends or relatives.

Seth's voice rang clear and manly over the massed rows of black skull-caps and white prayer shawls, sprinkled here and there with the frilly hats and rich furs of women. It was a Conservative temple, so the men and women sat together. For years in the Bronx Marjorie had railed at the orthodox practice of separating the sexes; in the twentieth century women weren't second-class citizens, she said. This was one reason why the parents had joined a Conservative temple on moving to Manhattan. Another and more powerful reason was the desire to climb. The wealthiest Jews were Reform, but the Morgensterns were not ready for such a bold leap away from tradition, to praying with uncovered heads, smoking on the Sabbath, and eating pork. The Conservative temple was a pleasant compromise with its organ music, mixed sexes, shortened prayers, long English sermons, and young rabbi in a black robe like a minister's. Mr. Morgenstern, indeed, was a little uncomfortable in the temple. Now and then he would grumble that if Abraham Lincoln could wear a beard, so could an American rabbi. When he had to recite memorial prayers for his father he always slipped into a small old orthodox synagogue on a side street, feeling perhaps that this was the only form of worship that really counted either with God or with his father's ghost. He quieted his conscience by paying the membership fee in both places.

His one reason for putting up with the temple was the hope of instilling some trace of religion in his daughter. But Marjorie had little use for any version of the faith. She regarded it as a body of superstitious foolishness perpetuated, and to some degree invented, by her mother for her harassment. The parents managed to drag her to the temple once in a while on Friday evenings when she had no date, but it was always under protest. She gave her father much pain, unintentionally, with her whispers about the rabbi, a very well-spoken young man with a cultured resonant voice, who talked of current magazines and best-selling novels as well as of the Bible; a style, the father would have thought, perfectly suited to his daughter, if not to him. Marjorie, however, was all satire and disdain.

But today, despite herself, the girl found awe creeping over her as her brother's voice filled the vault of the temple, chanting words thousands of years old, in an eerie melody from a dim lost time. A cloud passed away overhead and morning sunlight came slanting through the dome windows, brilliantly lighting the huge mahogany Ark behind Seth with its arch of Hebrew words in gold over the tablets of the Law: *Know before Whom you stand.* Marjorie had thrilled the first time her father translated the motto for her; and that thrill came back now as the letters blazed up in the sunlight. Seth sang on, husky and calm, and it occurred to Marjorie that after all there might be a powerful propriety in the old way of separating the men and the women. This religion was a masculine thing, whatever it was, and Seth was coming into his own. The very

Hebrew had a rugged male sound to it, all different from the bland English comments of the rabbi; it sounded like some of the rough crashing passages in *Macbeth* which she so loved.

She caught her breath as Seth stumbled over a word and stopped. The silence in the pause was heavy. He squinted at the book, and a murmur began to run through the temple. Seth glanced up, smiled at the bench where his parents sat, and placidly resumed his chanting. Marjorie unclenched her fists; the people around her chuckled and nodded at each other. She heard a woman say, "He's a good boy." She could have kissed him. Her little jealous pique was lost in a rush of love for her baby brother, the prattler with blond curls and huge eyes, fading in the tones of the chant as though he were being borne away by a ship. Time had taken him away long ago, of course, but only in this moment did she quite realize that it was so, and that it was for ever.

Later, at the buffet lunch in the mobbed social hall of the temple, a knot of boys came tumbling past Marjorie through the crowd, yelling and pushing each other, clutching sandwiches and soda bottles. In the middle of them was Seth, flushed and glittering-eyed, his arms full of presents wrapped in tinsel and colored paper. She darted through the boys, threw her arms around her startled brother and kissed his cheek. "You were wonderful, Seth! Wonderful! I was so proud of you!"

Recognition and warmth dawned through the boy's glaze of triumphant excitement. "Did I do all right, Margie? Really?"

"Marvelous, I tell you, perfect."

"I love you," said Seth, in a most incongruous quiet tone, and kissed her on the mouth, leaving a taste of wine. The boys jeered at the lipstick smear on Seth and shoved and bore him away, and Marjorie stood transfixed, alone in the merry crowd, in a turmoil of surprised emotion. Seth had expressed no open affection for her since the day he had learned to talk.

She made her way through the throng to the buffet, but nothing tempted her on the long table crowded with platters of sliced turkey, tongue, and beef, chopped chicken liver, chicken salad, tuna salad, half a dozen kinds of fish, and fruit salad, all manner of vegetables, bread, rolls, and pastries. She was too wrought up to eat. Unnoticed by the busily eating guests, she wandered to the bar and stood sipping a scotch and soda, watching a thousand dollars' worth of food and drink vanish like sand heaps in the tide.

This lunch stemmed from an old-country synagogue custom called a kiddush, or wine-blessing. The parents of a bar-mitzva boy were obliged by long tradition to serve wine to all worshippers. In the United States this custom had evolved—as they say elephants have evolved from one-celled creatures—into a noonday feast hardly less imposing than the main banquet after sundown. Wine-blessing played little or no part in it, though it was still called a kiddush.

The caterers had given the old folkway modern form and variety. There was a five-hundred-dollar kiddush, a thousand-dollar one, and so forth. Mrs. Morgenstern had been miserably tempted by Lowenstein's famous twelve-hundred-dollar extravaganza, which included whole boiled salmons in jelly, a cascade of raspberry soda on a terraced frame of snow, and a Star of David in solid ice bordered by blue neon. But the father, panic-stricken by the mounting expense, had frozen at the thousand-dollar kiddush. The Morgensterns did not have enough friends and relatives at the temple to eat up all the food, but that was no problem. On many another Sabbath there might be only four or five rows of worshippers, lonesome in a barren stretch of purple cushions and brown wood; but when a bar-mitzva was scheduled the house of God was seldom less than full. Marjorie had noticed the same phenomenon in the old synagogues of the Bronx.

A gay commotion started up on the far side of the hall—handclapping, singing, stamping. She finished her drink, worked across the room, and found all the aunts, uncles, and cousins of the family clustered in a corner, chorusing a wild Yiddish tune full of childhood echoes, and beating out the rhythm with feet and hands. In a small clear space ringed by laughing faces and pounding palms, Uncle Samson-Aaron was cavorting with Uncle Shmulka. Shmulka was bald, slightly under five feet in height, and emaciated by a lifetime of sweating in the furnace room of a steam laundry, therefore quite a frail partner for Samson-Aaron. The two uncles stomped here and there, cutting pigeon wings and various other capers, with Shmulka sometimes swinging precariously in the crook of the Uncle's massive elbow, his feet clear off the floor. Samson-Aaron held a bottle of rye whiskey in one hand and a brown turkey leg in the other. As he came bounding and roaring past Marjorie, his face blazed up with delight. "Modgerie! Hollo, Modgerie! Shmulka, go vay, who needs you?" Shmulka went rolling to the sidelines, grinning with relief, and Samson-Aaron seized her hand with two fat fingers of the hand that held the bottle. "So? Vun dance in honor of Seth, no, Modgerie?" The family laughed and cheered; he was irresistible; without coyness Marjorie let him pull her into the ring. Samson-Aaron did not fling her about as he had Shmulka. All at once he was precise and courtly, and Marjorie remembered that he was supposed to have been a slim dandy in the old days, in the old country. She could almost see the thin gay youth inside the fleshy envelope of the old man with teeth missing in front and shaking red jowls. Marjorie had learned the steps of the dance at family celebrations in her childhood; she followed the Uncle easily. Samson-Aaron's eyes shone. "Next time at your vedding, ha, Modgerie?" He exaggerated the elegant gestures of an old-world beau, crooking his arms and swinging his huge rear and huger paunch in an amazingly funny burlesque. Marjorie burst out laughing as she danced. The Uncle laughed too, and before she knew what had happened she was holding the turkey leg; he had placed it neatly in her hand as they cut a figure. The family cheered again. Marjorie, warming to the joke, brandished the leg and did a spirited little jig; and it was several seconds before she realized that she was waving the turkey leg perhaps ten inches from Mrs. Mary Goldstone's nose. Sandy's mother stood at the rim of the circle, staring at her through silver-rimmed glasses, somewhat as though she were a dancing horse.

Marjorie tried to smile at her with aristocratic good humor, but it was a rather hard effect to bring off with a turkey leg in her hand and the immense old man bobbing and bellowing around her.

Mrs. Goldstone returned a smile that was pleasant enough in the circumstances, slipped backward into the crowd, and disappeared.

The banquet that night did not start off badly at all. Mr. Connelly, the Irish bank manager, picked up the skullcap that lay by his place card, and put it uncertainly on top of his pink bald head. "This way?" he said to Mr. Goldstone. "First time I've ever worn one."

"More like this," said Mr. Goldstone, snugging his cap flat at the back of his head. "Me, I wore one every day of my life till I came to America, couple of years after that." Sandy awkwardly put a cap on, imitating his father. Marjorie thought it looked almost as odd on him as on the Irishman.

"Well, it's all very interesting, very interesting." Mr. Connelly looked around the ballroom. "The whole thing has certainly been done beautifully."

"Oh, leave it to Lowenstein," said Mrs. Goldstone. "It's always perfect." Diamonds sparkled at her throat and wrists. Despite her graying hair, she looked hardly forty in a black Paris dress that Marjorie guessed cost more than her own mother's entire wardrobe. Only the glasses on the silver chain gave her a touch of gravity. She had greeted Marjorie cordially, not mentioning the dance with the turkey leg.

Marjorie was feeling optimistic, now that the banquet was upon her, and she had had a couple of glasses of champagne. She was even hoping that it might turn out to be fun. She had pictured the Goldstones as an island of pained superiority at one of the old-time family gatherings in the Bronx. But the flower-decked ballroom, the spacious dance floor, the waiters in blue mess jackets, the murmuring orchestra behind potted palms, the fine linen and silver on the tables, the camellias by each lady's plate, left nothing even for the Goldstones to desire. Her mother had arranged the seating perhaps cold-bloodedly, but with wisdom. Marjorie's table was on the favored side of the dance floor, where one saw nothing but stiff shirt fronts, black ties, pearl studs, and evening dresses. Here were her father's business associates, her mother's friends from fashionable charity organizations, and a number of acquaintances gathered over a lifetime who had done well. On the other side of the dance floor were acquaintances who had not done so well; also her father's employees, and Bronx neighbors who were entitled to invitations for old times' sake, and the aunts, uncles, and cousins. Some of the guests on that side wore evening dress too, but most of them were in street clothes. On the dais at the long rear wall of the ballroom, on either side of three vacant seats in the center, were several rabbis with their wives, and Assemblyman Feuer, Mr. Morgenstern's highest connection in the world, a red-faced little man with pince-nez glasses on a black ribbon. There was also Seth's one living grandparent, Mr. Morgenstern's mother, a tiny old lady who lived in New Jersey with Aunt Shosha, and who now looked bewildered and lost in a big gilt armchair.

Mr. Goldstone pointed to empty chairs between himself and Sandy. "Who's missing in our party, Marjorie?"

"The Robisons, and my cousin Geoffrey Quill," said Marjorie. "They're all from out of town."

"Well, what do you say, should we start on the grapefruit?" Mr. Goldstone's voice was harsh and his manner direct. He had a thin-lipped wide smile and bright satiric brown eyes, which seemed to take on crinkles of kindliness when he looked at Marjorie. She instinctively liked him and suspected—at least hoped—that he had taken to her. Yet she could well understand the fear with which Sandy usually spoke of his father. Mr. Goldstone had a long face like Sandy's: browner, leaner, and very seamed. When he wasn't talking or smiling he looked rather like an oak carving of an Indian.

She said timidly, "I think we're supposed to wait for the grand entrance. Mother and Dad with Seth, you know. But please go ahead if you——"

"Of course we'll wait," said Mr. Goldstone.

"Is that the novelist you told me about, Geoffrey Quill?" said Sandy, peering at Geoffrey's place card.

"Yes, he's my cousin—our cousin."

"You have a cousin writes books?" said Mr. Goldstone.

"He wrote *The Gilded Ghetto*," said Marjorie. "It got wonderful reviews."

"I had a son writes books, I'd shoot him," said Mr. Goldstone. "Put him out of his misery."

The ballroom lights went out and a pink spotlight cut through the darkness and struck the doorway. The musicians began to play *Pomp and Circumstance*. The doors swung open; the headwaiter appeared, a tall gray man in tails, wheeling in a table on which a hissing copper cauldron was shooting up orange-blue flames. Behind him marched the parents, each with an arm linked through an elbow of the stiff unhappy boy. All the guests stood and applauded.

"What's burning in that copper pot, I wonder?" said Sandy.

"Money," said Mr. Goldstone.

"It's the brandy sauce for the grapefruit," said Mrs. Goldstone. "Haven't you been to a Lowenstein dinner before?"

"Brandy before dinner?" said Mr. Goldstone. "Say, it's an idea. Maybe some ice cream too?"

"It's just for the effect, and stop being so clever, Leon."

While the boy and his parents went to the dais, followed by the spotlight, the waiter in the center of the floor stirred the cauldron, making the flames leap and whirl. "Caterers, restaurants, great angle they got," said Mr. Goldstone. "Anything they can set fire to they charge ten times as much. Set fire to a twenty-cent flapjack, crêpes suzette for two dollars. Maybe we could use it in our store, Mary. Sell a flaming pair of shoes, fifty dollars instead of five dollars. A flaming corset——"

"All right, Leon. It's very pretty and you know it. Quiet——"

"Maybe we set fire to Sandy, make him worth something," said Mr. Goldstone.

The lights came on, the flames went out, the music stopped. The oldest rabbi, a little gray-bearded man in a long black coat, blessed the bread. Waiters brought bowls of sauce from the cauldron and doled it out at the tables, grapefruit by grapefruit. "This is fine," said Mr. Goldstone. "Get drunk on a grapefruit. Maybe I ask for a second portion, you got to carry me home."

Mrs. Goldstone turned to Marjorie. "He doesn't mean anything, it's just his way. He goes on much worse at home."

Marjorie had been gnawing her lip to keep from laughing. She allowed herself one chuckle. "I think he's terribly funny." Mr. Goldstone shot her a keen look, his face puckered like a comic mask.

"Don't encourage him," said Mrs. Goldstone.

The tall headwaiter touched Marjorie's elbow. "Pardon me, miss. Your mother sent over this telegram. Asks you to make the apologies." The wire was from the Robisons. Their girl had developed mumps that morning, and so they were not coming.

"Robisons from Philadelphia?" said Mr. Goldstone. "Real estate man? One daughter? I know him. Fine man. Very well-to-do. Sorry to miss them."

Mrs. Goldstone glanced at Marjorie with new respect, and again the girl was reluctantly impressed by her mother's shrewdness. The Robisons had done their work without even putting in an appearance.

"Hello, Marjorie."

Geoffrey Quill, rather more pudgy than in the picture on his book jacket, and thinner of hair, but wearing the same tweed suit and holding the same pipe, stood beside her. His smile was the old crooked mixture of bashfulness and furtive superiority. "Sorry I'm late. I can never remember how snarled up New York traffic is."

"You're just in time."

She introduced him and he sat. He picked up the menu, a booklet with Seth's picture on the cover, and glanced at the food list engraved in fine italics. "*Pamplemousse royal*," he read in a wondering tone. "*Foie de volaille Lowenstein, consommé Madrilène, langue de boeuf en sauce piquante*—— Ye gods, Marjorie, isn't this banquet kosher? I'll get right up and leave."

"Kosher as *you* want it, surely," Marjorie said, looking across to the other side of the ballroom, where Samson-Aaron was roistering from table to table, waving a bottle and pouring drinks. Accompanying him was Aunt Dvosha, the vegetarian fanatic, who wore a very strange shiny green evening dress decorated with dyed yellow feathers.

"You don't have to worry, Mr. Quill," said Mrs. Goldstone politely. "Rabbi Jung himself eats at Lowenstein dinners."

"I assure you, Mrs. Goldstone, these things worry me very little. I had a ham sandwich on the train.—I trust that doesn't offend anybody."

"Not us surely," said the bank manager with a chortle. "We're Irish, you know."

"Of course we respect other folks' customs," said Mrs. Connelly. "We're very strict about meat on Friday ourselves. I think it's nice to keep up these customs."

Marjorie saw Samson-Aaron tug at Aunt Dvosha's elbow, point with the bottle across the ballroom at Geoffrey, and lumber through the tables toward the dance floor, dragging the old spinster with him.

Mr. Goldstone squinted at Geoffrey. "Me, I have a strict kosher home. On the outside I eat anything. But home is home."

"Isn't that slightly inconsistent?" said Geoffrey, clicking his pipe in his teeth. His back was to his oncoming father.

"Sure. It means I'm only half no good," said Mr. Goldstone.

Geoffrey smiled and murmured, "Of course, these folkways remain valid for anybody who gets solace from them . . ."

Samson-Aaron and Aunt Dvosha were crossing the dance floor. Marjorie looked toward her mother on the dais. Mrs. Morgenstern made a gesture which she at once understood. "Geoffrey!" she exclaimed, jumping up and taking his hand. "There's your dad. Let's go over and say hello to him——"

Geoffrey rose slowly, confused. "Well, there's no hurry, but if——"

"Stay vare you are!" roared Samson-Aaron from the middle of the floor. "Ve come over to you! Ve come to the fency side!"

As the Uncle drew near, his boisterous laugh faded. He took his son's outstretched hand hesitantly, as though conscious that his own was grimy or wet. "So, Geoffrey, you came, just to please an old father. You're a good boy."

"How are you, Papa?" said Geoffrey in a tone of embarrassed kindliness.

"Thank God, as you see me. Health is everything, the rest is mud."

Aunt Dvosha seized Geoffrey's hand. "Geoffrey, your book! I read it. I was so proud. Marvelous! Geoffrey, with your great gift you can bring important messages to the world." She had a high chirping voice and very bright eyes.

"Thank you, Auntie——"

"I would like to talk to you for just five minutes on a very important subject." She moved toward the empty chair beside him.

"Sure, Aunt, but not during dinner," laughed Geoffrey, warding her off with his hand. "Later, maybe."

"Of course, I wouldn't impose on you," said Aunt Dvosha, hurt. "I've never imposed on anybody and I never will."

The Connellys and the Goldstones were frankly staring at the visitors.

"Geoffrey, you're getting a little fat," said his father.

"I've got somebody to take after, Papa."

Samson-Aaron threw back his head and laughed. He looked at the bottle in his hand and said with sudden resolve, "Vell, ve all drink to the bar-mitzva boy, yes? Then ve go back to our side." He began pouring whiskey in small glasses that stood at each place. Fat and clumsy as he was, he poured with speedy deftness, spilling not a drop on the stiff white cloth.

Mr. Goldstone said, "Whom do we have the pleasure of drinking with?"

Marjorie introduced the Aunt and Uncle. Samson-Aaron said, "Pleased to meet you, pleased to meet you," and held his glass high. "Vell, the old Yiddish toast, yes? God should bless the boy and the parents—and he should grow up to the Law, to marriage, and to good deeds."

"Best toast I ever heard," said the Irish bank manager, drinking off his glass with relish.

"It takes God to fill such an order nowadays." Mr. Goldstone looked quizzically at the Uncle. "You're Mr. Quill's father, Mr. Feder?"

Samson-Aaron grinned his forlorn gap-toothed grin at Geoffrey, who said quickly, "I thought Quill seemed a more acceptable name for a book jacket, you see, not that——"

Mr. Goldstone said to Samson-Aaron, "You don't see him often?"

The Uncle shrugged. "He lives in Albany, and I'm here——"

"Then what the devil are you sitting on the other side of the room for? We've got two empty places here. Sit down. Sit down, Mrs. Raphaelson. You'll have dinner with us."

Samson-Aaron glanced timorously at his son and at Marjorie. "No, ve go back to our own side—I have no tuxedo——"

"Sit down." It was a command. Marjorie glanced toward her mother, but she had left the dais. "Why—it's a wonderful idea. Please join us, Uncle—Aunt Dvosha."

"For Modgerie, anything!" Samson-Aaron fell into a chair beside his son, and planted the bottle firmly before him on the cloth, an explorer's banner in Arctic snow.

Aunt Dvosha said, "Thank God. We were sitting right next to the radiator. Ninety per cent of t.b. comes from radiator heat."

The waiter was replacing the grapefruit with chopped chicken liver. Marjorie had never seen chicken liver served like this before: at each place a mound the size of a cantaloupe in a silver-plated bowl of ice. "For pity's sake, how are we supposed to eat anything after this?"

"My dear," said Mrs. Goldstone, "you may as well resign yourself to not eating for a week. Lowenstein is fantastic." She began eating the liver heartily, and so did everyone else except Aunt Dvosha, who sat looking around with a bright smile. Mrs. Goldstone was trying hard not to stare at Aunt Dvosha, but her gaze was repeatedly drawn by the shining eyes, the bobbing yellow feathers across the aunt's shoulders, and the twinkling rosette of green sequins. Aunt Dvosha caught her eye, and her smile became twice as bright. Mrs. Goldstone said, "You aren't eating, Mrs. Raphaelson?"

"Chicken liver is concentrated poison," said Aunt Dvosha pleasantly.

Sandy choked and everyone looked extremely startled. "My aunt is a strict vegetarian," Marjorie hastily said.

"Oh." Mrs. Goldstone resumed eating with less gusto.

"That's interesting," said Mrs. Connelly. "I have—ah——" She broke off and blinked as Samson-Aaron finished his liver, took Aunt Dvosha's, and went on eating with hardly a skipped beat of his fork. "We—that is, Mr. Connelly has a brother-in-law who is also a vegetarian——"

Samson-Aaron poured himself a large shot of whiskey and waved the bottle around. "Somebody else?"

The bank manager cleared his throat. "Why, I believe I will, thanks."

"Me too," said Mr. Goldstone.

"Leon, there's all kinds of wine coming——"

"Let it come." The men drank, with little convivial gestures. Samson-Aaron then ate his soup and the aunt's. He also ate two portions of tongue in sweet-and-sour sauce, and three of sweetbreads in a pastry crust. He kept pouring whiskey for himself and the other two men, and they kept drinking it despite mutters from their wives. Mrs. Connelly, who was extremely thin and ate very little, was watching the Uncle with morbid fascination. Sandy's mother was more troubled by Aunt Dvosha. She kept watching the vegetarian out of the corner of her eye. When the sweetbreads were served and she was about to eat them, Aunt Dvosha laid a hand on her arm and Mrs. Goldstone jumped as though pinched.

"Excuse me," said Aunt Dvosha, "but don't."

"Pardon me?"

"Excuse me, I know it's not my business. But you're an asthenic type. Like me. For an asthenic type to eat a gland—you may as well cut your throat and be done with it."

"Aunt Dvosha, *please!*" exclaimed Marjorie. "You have no right to——"

"No, no, it's most interesting," said Mrs. Goldstone faintly. "I never thought of sweetbreads as a gland—it's rather a horrible word, but——"

"Of course it's a gland. What else is the pancreas but a gland? One huge gland, the biggest gland," said Aunt Dvosha. "For other types a gland is bad enough, but for you to eat a gland——"

"I believe you're quite right," said Mrs. Goldstone, pushing the sweetbreads far away. "I definitely will not eat that gland.—Leon, don't you think you've had enough whiskey?"

Samson-Aaron was refilling the magnate's glass. Geoffrey laid hold of the bottle. "Papa, go easy for a while——"

"Miltie, it's a bar-mitzva!" cried Samson-Aaron, twisting the bottle out of his son's hand.

"By God, you're right. Here's to Arnold Morgenstern and his family," exclaimed Mr. Connelly, who was now quite rosy-faced. He tilted his skullcap rakishly forward and raised his glass. "Jew or Christian, a man's a man, I say, and Arnold's as good a man as I know, and I know lots of them. I'm proud to be at this bar-mitzva and here's to Arnold, and to his wife, and to his fine son and"—he swung his glass toward Marjorie—"to his beautiful and charming daughter, the elegant hostess at our table, by God, and if I were twenty years younger and single I'd propose to her on the spot!"

Mr. Goldstone and Mr. Connelly discovered that they were both golfers; they exchanged one anecdote after another, leaning back and shaking with laughter, in which Samson-Aaron joined with happy bellows.

Aunt Dvosha, meantime, talked across Samson-Aaron to Geoffrey, explaining to him all the characters and incidents in his novel, and urging him to insert something about diet and health in his next book. Geoffrey gnawed his pipe and slumped in his chair, nodding, his eyes dull. Mrs. Connelly and Mrs. Goldstone talked about the problems of charity theatre parties, watching their husbands anxiously as the brown bottle went around.

The headwaiter wheeled up a table bearing four rib roasts sizzling on a steel grill over a spirit flame. An assistant in dazzling white began slicing slabs of rare meat, and another assistant dished out immense baked potatoes and thick brilliant green asparagus.

"Glory be," said Mrs. Connelly. "Nothing for me, please, nothing. I declare I can't eat another bite. I've never seen anything like this!"

"Give her, give her," Samson-Aaron said to the waiter, "somebody vill eat it." He threw Mrs. Connelly a sly wink. She shuddered and smiled.

Mr. and Mrs. Morgenstern came to the table, beaming, arm in arm. "Having enough to eat, folks?" said the father. He glowed at the chorus of gay answers.

The mother said, "Somebody rearranged the seating plan, I see." Aunt Dvosha fingered her feathers. The Uncle, with a side glance at Marjorie, bent over his plate, eating busily. "Well, it's only right, after all, a father with his son. I'm sorry the Robisons couldn't come, lovely people——"

"Couldn't be any more lovely than the company we've got," declared Mr. Connelly. "Salt of the earth, Mrs. Raphaelson. Great fellow, Mr. Feder."

"Time of our lives," said Mr. Goldstone. "Marvelous party. Worth every penny, Morgenstern. Fine boy you've got there."

"You've got a fine one there yourself." Sandy looked embarrassed and adjusted his skullcap.

Mrs. Morgenstern said with a laugh, "Well, we won't keep you from your food. Come on, Arnold. Hearty appetite, folks. Take care of things, Marjorie," she added, pressing the girl's shoulder.

"I'll do my best, Mother."

Samson-Aaron, eating faster than usual to avoid Mrs. Morgenstern's eye, had cleaned his plate. He took Aunt Dvosha's, which had on it an unusually thick piece of meat and an oversized potato. Mrs. Connelly's eyes widened. There was silence while everybody attacked the food except the bank manager's wife, who sat drumming her fingers, staring at the Uncle like a rabbit at oncoming headlights. He heaved a great sigh as he finished Aunt Dvosha's roast beef and potato; laid down his knife and fork, leaned back, and mopped his brow. He heaved another sigh, picked up his knife and fork, and turned to Mrs. Connelly with his harmless grin. "Vell," he said, indicating her piled-up plate with his fork, "if you're sure you don't vant it, no sense it should go to vaste, so——"

"No, no!" shrieked Mrs. Connelly, recoiling in her chair.

The bank manager said, "Good heavens, Katherine, what's the matter?"

"He can't, he can't. Don't let him. It isn't human." She passed a fluttering hand over her face.

Samson-Aaron looked at Geoffrey, then at Marjorie in astonishment. "Vot's the matter, the lady don't feel good? Vy is that? She didn't eat so much."

"She's another asthenic type," said Aunt Dvosha. "She ate enough chicken liver to kill an army of asthenics."

"Kate dear, what is it?" Mr. Connelly seized her hand and patted it.

"Darling, I'm sorry, it's terribly rude of me, but——" She returned her horrified glance to the Uncle. "Didn't you see how much Mr. Feder has eaten? It's incredible. I don't believe four tigers could have eaten what he has. And now he wants my roast beef. I'm afraid he'll die, right here. I—it's unbelievable——"

Samson-Aaron looked at Marjorie, smiling uncertainly. He laid down his knife and fork. "I eat too much? I make a shame for you? Good food, a pity to vaste it——"

"It's all right, Uncle." Marjorie turned to Mrs. Connelly and laughed. "Really, we're so used to the Uncle in the family, nobody thinks anything of it. He's our champion eater, that's all."

"I've been envying him his appetite," said Sandy. "I thought I was an eater, until tonight."

"It's about time you stopped, Papa," said Geoffrey. "You've eaten more than enough—even for a bar-mitzva."

Samson-Aaron turned his palms outward, picked up the bottle, and said to the Irish lady, "Missus, I upset you, I'm sorry. Take a drink, please. You feel better, make me feel better."

Mrs. Connelly accepted the whiskey, drank it, and did feel better almost at once. She said with a giggle, taking hold of her plate, "I believe I would like to see him eat it, at that."

She passed the plate to Samson-Aaron, who contemplated the meat without enthusiasm. "I don't know vy, but I haven't got the appetite no more—but still——"

"Thank heaven, Papa, let it alone," said Geoffrey, who had grown very red. "It's no entertainment for anyone to watch a human boa constrictor in action."

Samson-Aaron swung his head heavily and regarded his son with mournful eyes. "Vot's a boa constructor?"

"A snake that can swallow its own weight in one meal," said Geoffrey, chewing his pipe.

"Miltie darling, that's your old father, it's an old story," said the Uncle, with a placating shrug. "It's a bar-mitzva after all, no? A man shouldn't eat because he sits on the fency side?"

Mr. Goldstone emptied his whiskey glass and set it on the table with a thump. "Tell me, Mr. Quill, you got something like that in your book? A son who calls his own father a snake?"

There was a moment's silence. Geoffrey looked at Mr. Goldstone with a half-smile, holding the pipe awkwardly in his teeth, like a boy of twelve caught smoking. The musicians struck up the tune to which Marjorie and the Uncle had danced that afternoon. She said brightly, "Oh, really, Mr. Goldstone, Geoffrey meant no harm——"

"Let him answer for himself," said Mr. Goldstone, looking steadily at Geoffrey.

"Vot's to answer?" said the Uncle. "My son Geoffrey makes a little joke, so vot's wrong? In our family who doesn't make jokes vit me? Mr. Goldstone, you should never need nothing from your son, but if you do, he should treat you no vorse than my son. My son is a good son. He calls me a boa constructor, say listen, he could call me much vorse, it still vouldn't be no lie, you know?" He laughed and picked up the bottle. "Come on, everybody have a drink vit the boa constructor! Listen, it's a bar-mitzva, isn't it? The son of Arnold Morgenstern, the big success in the family, ve all proud of him."

He offered the bottle around, but nobody pushed forward a glass. Geoffrey said, with an anguished twist of the head, "Pa, everybody's had enough. So have you—put the bottle away——"

Mr. Connelly said, "Why, I'll join Mr. Feder. He's right, these things come once in a lifetime."

Samson-Aaron gratefully filled the bank manager's glass. "Mr. Connelly, you're a gentleman. Vit Irishers I alvays got along, God bless them. I'll tell you something, it's thanks to an Irisher, nobody else, I could come here tonight, I could see my son, have a good time——"

"An Irishman? Really?" Mr. Connelly said with a little smile. "Who?"

"I should live so. My boss, Mr. Gogarty, an Irisher vit a Jewish heart"—

Mr. Goldstone, who was folding his napkin, looked up—"I told him it vas a bar-mitzva, he hired a substitute vatchman from his own pocket, it's strictly against the rules vare I vork. So here's to Mr. Gogarty, no? He should live and be vell. You too, Mr. Connelly——"

"Pardon me, Mr. Feder," said Sandy's father. "Where do you work?"

"It's a new job," said the Uncle, "temporary, for the Christmas rush season, but listen, a job is a job, no? I vork in the downtown storehouse of Lamm's department store."

Mr. Goldstone, his mouth an upcurving line of grim amusement, looked at his wife. Mrs. Goldstone raised her eyebrows and glanced from Marjorie to Sandy. The bank manager drank his whiskey and made a great thing of taking cellophane off a cigar. Sandy grinned halfheartedly at Marjorie, who laughed and stammered, "Well, really, that's—talk about a small world! Isn't that something? That's a real joke——"

"Vot's the joke?" said Samson-Aaron, looking as though he would very much like to laugh if he could.

"You only think that this Mr. Gogarty is your boss," Marjorie said, trying to keep bubbly amusement in her voice. "Your real boss is sitting right across from you."

"Vot?"

"He owns Lamm's," said the girl, pointing.

Geoffrey Quill blurted to Mr. Goldstone, "You really do? *Lamm's?*"

Mr. Goldstone nodded. "You want to write a book about a department store, pay me a visit. Only don't call me a snake in the book."

Samson-Aaron stared at Mr. Goldstone, opened his mouth, closed it, and smiled foolishly, showing the black gap in his teeth. He pushed back his chair with a heavy scrape and stood. "Come, Dvosha, ve go to the other side——"

Marjorie said, laying a hand on his arm, "Uncle, don't be silly——"

"If I know you're the owner of Lamm's," the Uncle said to Mr. Goldstone, "I vouldn't sit down at the table in the first place. Respect is respect, the boss and the night vatchman don't eat at the same table." He pulled at Aunt Dvosha's hand.

Mr. Goldstone said, "Sit down and don't embarrass the whole table." Samson-Aaron, responding like a child, sank back into his chair. The magnate went on more pleasantly, "It's a family occasion, those things don't count here. You're very good company and we're having a fine time. So forget about it, and——"

He broke off because the young rabbi of the temple was rapping a fork on his glass at the dais. When the room quieted the rabbi led the after-grace. He then made a speech; then another rabbi made a speech; then a third rabbi made a speech; all elaborate and repetitious tributes to the

Morgenstern family, ornamented with Biblical and Talmudic allusions, and in the young rabbi's case with quotations from Aristotle and Santayana. The grandmother on the dais curled up in her chair, asleep. Mr. and Mrs. Morgenstern listened eagerly and proudly. Seth sat slumped on one elbow, listlessly mouthing a banana.

Marjorie could not follow any of the speeches, preoccupied as she was by the restlessness and boredom of the guests at her table. Tears were standing in Sandy's eyes from swallowing yawns. Mr. Goldstone made no effort to swallow his. Once Marjorie saw him make an impatient sidewise gesture of the head to his wife, who answered with a weary negative shake. The Connellys alone kept up a resolute air of smiling attention.

Worst of all was the effect on Samson-Aaron. The glaze of his glance, the frozen creases of his smile, the viscous settling of his body like warm putty, were ominous. The applause for the third rabbi startled him into looking here and there and clapping wildly. But then the assemblyman began to speak; and his prose acted on the Uncle like a rolling cloud of chloroform. Poked from left and right by Aunt Dvosha and his son, he absorbed the blows like a feather bolster, and kept settling. His eyes drooped, his smile faded, his head fell forward on his chest. Samson-Aaron was asleep, and there was obviously nothing anybody could do about it.

Geoffrey said to the others in a strained light tone, "I must apologize for my father. A man of extremes, I'm afraid . . ."

"A natural man," said Sandy. "When he eats he eats, when he drinks he drinks, when he sleeps he sleeps. I envy him."

"I believe you do," said Mr. Goldstone.

Sandy shrank under the cutting tone and sardonic look of his father. "Well, all I mean—we'd all fall asleep if we dared."

"Let's go, Mary, or I will fall asleep," Mr. Goldstone said. "Marjorie will excuse us, I'm sure——"

"Not while he's talking, Leon. He's an assemblyman."

"So? Don't I know him? A police-court lawyer, hung around the Democratic Club thirty years. What is that? Let's go——"

"Be quiet," said Mrs. Goldstone, with a naked note of authority, and Mr. Goldstone subsided, growling.

When the assemblyman finished, about a quarter of an hour later, Mr. Goldstone jumped up. Dance music started at the same time. "Come on, Mary, Sandy, let's go."

The mother rose. Couples were coming out on the dance floor. Sandy said, "I don't know, Dad—thought maybe I'd stay and have a dance or two——"

"I want you to drive. I don't see so good at night. You know that." Mr.

Goldstone held out his hand to Marjorie. "You give your mother and father our thanks and excuses, Margie, okay? Lovely party, and you're a lovely girl——"

"Thank you. Must—must you go?"

Mr. Goldstone's eyes rested on the sleeping Uncle for a long moment. As through his eyes, Marjorie saw with painful clarity the split seams of the dangling vest, the stains on the blue jacket, the buttons of the striped silk shirt straining over the huge paunch, the gray stubble on the slack chin. "Tell your uncle not to worry about Gogarty, it's perfectly all right— quite a fellow, your uncle——"

Mrs. Goldstone said with an amiable smile, shaking the girl's hand, "Too bad we're not staying. I'd like to see you repeat that dance with him you did this afternoon. I think Sandy would have enjoyed it."

"Turkey leg and all, I sure would," Sandy said. He grinned affectionately at her and, Marjorie was sure, just a shade sadly. "You'll have to show it to me sometime."

In a moment they were gone, with the Connellys in their wake, all murmuring thanks and farewells. Left at the table were Marjorie, Geoffrey, Aunt Dvosha, the gently snoring Samson-Aaron, and five pushed-aside empty chairs.

Marjorie suffered over this debacle for six terrible days. On the seventh all was forgotten, and her young spirit soared higher than ever. For her life turned a great corner; Marjorie Morningstar was triumphantly born.

Chapter 10. MR. KLABBER

The girl playing Ko-Ko, prancing on stage at the start of *The Mikado*, dropped her executioner's axe with a silly plop of hollow cardboard. The squeals from the audience so demoralized her that she never recovered. She forgot her lines, scrambled the action, and panicked the other players. As the show struggled feebly on, the dialogue began to be drowned out by the coughing, whispering, and shuffling of feet in the audience. All was confusion, shrieks, and lamenting backstage between the acts; and it was in this climate of fiasco that Marjorie went out to face the audience for her first appearance, with *My Object All Sublime*.

She felt it was up to her to save the show. And she was carelessly, senselessly confident that she would do it, that she could not fail, that she was Marjorie Morningstar, the one glittering professional among these poor frightened painted-up college girls in red and yellow cheesecloth.

Sandy was in the audience, and so were her parents and Seth; but awareness of them dropped away as she stepped from the gloom of the wings into the glare of the stage. The dim mass of faces beyond the footlights was as one face, one presence, something like a new vast collective Boy she intended to captivate.

She came out with a flourish, striking an imperial pose, and there was scattered applause. Her scarlet and gold silk costume was the most spectacular in the show, and Marsha had painted her strikingly, in the traditional fashion: flour-white face, huge black eyebrows and mustaches, crimson mouth. When she began her song, the audience grew still. In this rattled company her mere self-confidence gave her some of the authority of a star. She performed as she had rehearsed, with a little extra vibrancy brought out by having an audience, and after a few seconds her grotesquely dignified gambols began to bring laughs from the darkness.

My object all sublime
I shall achieve in time . . .

The chorus, taking heart, responded in unison for the first time, and with something like verve:

His object all sublime
He shall achieve in time . . .

Marjorie picked up the song, rapping out the sharp Gilbert words so that they rang through the hall; then it was the turn of the chorus, sounding better and better as she capered to stronger laughter. She finished squarely in mid-stage in a pompous attitude, and bared her teeth at the audience with comic ferocity. There was dead silence perhaps for one heartbeat. Then came an electrifying solid CRACK! of applause.

She swung into her rehearsed encore. Now the chorus and even the orchestra, catching fire from her success, seemed to acquire precision, wit; the air of the audience began to sparkle, as it were, with the true radiance of Gilbert and Sullivan.

My object all sublime
I shall achieve in time . . .

Marjorie felt bodiless, floating free; she had no thought of making a mistake; she could not; she was inventing this song like a bird. The handclapping when she finished was stronger than before. The conductor signalled to the actors to go on with the show. They tried to speak lines, but the handclapping drowned them; and now came a few shouts, cleaving through the air like thrown roses, "More! More! More!"

Marjorie, frozen in mid-stage in her regal pose, felt shuddering thrills along her spine; the hairs on her head prickled like warm needles. The conductor looked at her, shrugged, and nodded for another encore. She had stopped the show.

She glanced around at the chorus, all staring at her with shining-eyed admiration. She allowed herself a bashful, grateful smile at the audience, her first break out of character, and strutted forward to sing again, her face contorted in the fierce Mikado frown.

My object all sublime
I shall achieve in time . . .

Her mind cooled and became detached while she paced through this encore. She was back in the school auditorium. She saw individual faces in the audience, friends sawing at fiddles in the orchestra, the chorus capering clumsily in wretched costumes, the smeared rickety set. She thought, "It's just a ratty college show, after all. But it's the beginning. Now I know I can do it. And I will, I will!"

With secret personal meaning, tossing her head and waving both clenched fists in the air, defying the audience and the gods, she sang from an exulting heart:

My object all sublime
I shall achieve in time!

The evening was hers. "Mikado! Mikado!" the audience called when the principals stepped forward for their collective bow. The curtain dropped. The shouts continued. Miss Kimble came darting out of the wings, clutching the prompter's script, her hair flying, her eyes and nose red, her glasses falling off as she ran. She threw her arms around Marjorie. "You're a star! A star! You made the show!" She ran off again, picking up her glasses. "Curtain! Curtain! Solo bow for the Mikado!" And when Marjorie stepped forward the noise was louder, and the cast applauded too; and somebody dragged Miss Kimble on stage squeaking protests and fumbling at her hair, and all theatrical discipline collapsed, and the curtain came down on an orgy of weeping, giggling, hugging, kissing, and jumping up and down by the entire cast.

Ko-Ko slunk off the stage unnoticed (she married a bald young dentist two weeks later and dropped out of school). Marjorie was set upon by the cast, and by Miss Kimble, and by the stagehands and the musicians, all pounding her back, pumping her hands, kissing her, and shouting congratulations. "Thank you, thank you, thank you." Her face stiff from smiling, her costume soaked with sweat, she was pulled this way and that. "Please, please, there are my folks, let them through!" Mrs. Morgenstern's eyes were glittering with pride. The father, quite pale, was holding a handkerchief, smiling weakly, and it was obvious that he had been crying. She threw herself at him. "Papa, Papa!" Then she embraced her mother, and Seth.

"I'm beginning to think you're somebody after all," said her mother. "You were fine, really fine."

Seth said, "The show was lousy, but you were okay."

Miss Kimble pounced on the Morgensterns and began to gabble about their daughter's great gifts. Sandy came edging through the crowd, trying not to jostle the girls; as she watched him come, Marjorie found herself wondering whether his blue serge suit was unbecoming or his hair needed cutting, or whether something less obvious was wrong with him. He looked, all at once, like an overgrown and not very bright boy. He clasped her hand. "Hi, kid. Nice going."

"Did you really like it, Sandy?"

"Well, you know, these things are always so fierce. You were the only one that didn't blow up."

Marjorie said, frigidly, "Oh, sure. What can you expect from a college show?"

"How about getting that stuff off your face? We'll take your folks out for a soda, and then maybe go dancing."

"Sure, Sandy. Love it."

She made her way with difficulty out of the ecstatic crowd around her. Marsha fell on her when she opened the dressing-room door. "*Where* have you been? God, Morningstar, what a triumph! Unbelievable! Hurry, hurry, hurry! Mr. Klabber has been going stark mad. He's waiting for you." She pushed and pulled Marjorie about, removing her costume and paint. "You've *got* the job, sugar bun, it's a lead-pipe cinch, and believe me, it's——"

Marjorie grabbed the fat girl's hands, which were sloshing cold cream on her face and neck. "Marsha, for heaven's sake, *who is Mr. Klabber?*"

"Why, dear, haven't I told you? He's the owner of Camp Tamarack, where I do arts-and-crafts. He needs a dramatic counselor next summer, the one he had got married. You're *it!* Okay, rub it all off with the towel, now, I'll get at your ears and——"

Outrage and disappointment clanged in Marjorie's voice. "He runs a *camp? A children's* camp?"

"Don't be a little idiot, I tell you it's marvelous. A free vacation, the food is terrific—go over your lips again—what's more, the dramatic counselor does nothing, nothing but put on a half-hour show every week, it's a cinch, and you get *paid,* dear, two hundred dollars for the season—there's still a lot of black in your eyebrows——"

"Look, Marsha, I'm not——"

"*Will* you let me get in one word? I haven't told you the main thing. Tamarack's on the same lake as South Wind! It's ten minutes by canoe, two minutes by car, a fifteen-minute walk on the road, and——" She stopped rubbing Marjorie's ears and looked at her blank face. "Now don't—don't tell me you haven't heard of South Wind. I'll absolutely shoot you to put you out of your misery."

"Go ahead and shoot," Marjorie said crossly. "I haven't. Wait—that's just a camp too, isn't it?"

"Monkey face, it's the adult camp, the most famous in the world. It's unbelievably beautiful, grounds like Windsor Castle, the social hall is like the Waldorf grand ballroom. They put on fantastic revues there every single weekend, regular Broadway shows. The talent they have on the social staff! The connections you can make! Why, the head of the staff is Noel Airman, he's written dozens of big song hits like *It's Raining Kisses,* and the set designer is Carlos Ringel, he's done ten Broadway shows, and he happens to be a dear friend of mine, the evil old wretch. The dances, the parties! Not only that, you'll learn more about the real professional theatre than——"

There was a knock at the door. Marjorie, in her underwear, shrank behind a dressing screen. Marsha went out and came back in a moment, grinning broadly, a little white card in her hand. "Honestly, if old man Klabber isn't a riot. Standing with his back to the door, so he wouldn't catch a fast peek by mistake! Real religious, I swear. He had to run along, Margie. You're to phone him tomorrow."

Marjorie glanced at the card. "What's all this? Jewish Educational Association?"

"That's what he does winters. Solidest citizen you ever saw——"

"Look, Marsha, haven't you gone way off the deep end here? How can I be a dramatic counselor? I don't know beans about sets, or lighting, or——"

"Sweetie, you can bone up on all that in a week. It's child's play. You can imagine, if Dora Kimble can do it——"

"Herding around a lot of snivelling kids—I don't know, Marsha . . ."

"Marjorie, sweetheart, I tell you the dramatic counselor's the queen of the camp, does absolutely nothing, lives in lone grandeur in a cabin on top of the hill, contemplating her art—and South Wind, kitten, *South Wind,* which she can see plain as day, smack across the lake, the Promised Land. I tell you we'll be spending the whole *summer* at South Wind. It's heaven on earth. You're going to discover a new world, I swear to you."

The after-theatre crowd at Schrafft's was very noisy; so when her parents and Seth began eating their sundaes, Marjorie ventured to say in a low voice to Sandy, "Ever hear of a place called South Wind?"

"Hear of it? I've been there. Mighty gay. Why?"

"South Wind?" said Mrs. Morgenstern, not looking up from her chocolate sundae. "What do you want to know about South Wind? I'll tell you about South Wind. It's Sodom. That's South Wind."

"Mom, I didn't ask you——"

"She's not far wrong," said Sandy.

"Why are you suddenly interested in South Wind?" said Mrs. Morgenstern, peering at her daughter. "If you think you're going there this summer, start thinking again. My daughter is not going to South Wind."

"Oh Lord, I'm sorry I started the subject. Let's talk about something else."

Later, when she and Sandy were dancing at the Biltmore, he described a couple of weekends he had spent at South Wind. From what he said, and from what Marsha had told her, she began to picture the adult camp as a coruscating evil wonderland bathed in a reddish glow.

She let a week go by. Then one evening after dinner she casually mentioned that her *Mikado* performance had brought her the offer of a job at a children's camp teaching dramatics. Mrs. Morgenstern was pleased at first, saying it was high time Marjorie found out what it felt like to earn a dollar. But when she put her daughter through the question grinder and Marsha's name came out, her face changed. "It doesn't sound good."

"Mom, Mr. Klabber is the president of the Jewish Educational Association. Why, he's like a rabbi, Marsha says——"

Her mother was staring at her. "Tell me, what has all this got to do with South Wind?"

"South Wind?" said Marjorie, with a merry little laugh. "Why, whatever makes you ask about South Wind?"

"I don't know," said Mrs. Morgenstern. "First you start asking questions about South Wind, and next thing you have a job at a girls' camp——"

"Mom, we were talking about South Wind *weeks* ago."

"Well, I don't know, it's one thing right after the other. Is there a connection or isn't there?"

Marjorie, thoroughly exasperated at her mother's clairvoyance, calculated that a lie would break down. "It happens," she said lightly, "that South Wind is on the same lake, that's how I happened to hear of it. If you call that a connection. It has nothing to do with Mr. Klabber's camp——"

"That's where the dog is buried," said Mrs. Morgenstern. "You think you'll have a good time for nothing at South Wind all summer. Don't you know you can't get in there at night if you aren't a paying guest? They have guards with guns, and dogs——"

"How do you know so much about it, if it's such an awful place?"

"It's just by accident, I assure you. Papa's lawyer, Mr. Pfeffer, was suing the place, they didn't pay a big linen supply bill. He drove up there and took us with him. It was all free, the owner was trying to be nice to him. That owner. A devil. The right owner for Sodom."

The upshot was that the mother agreed, with many skeptical reservations, to go with Marjorie to Mr. Klabber's office later in the week. She was most happily surprised when she met the camp owner, and he seemed equally gladdened at the sight of her. He was a small old man with a large bald head, thick greenish glasses, and very hairy ears. The hand he held out to Marjorie had a dry papery feel. The walls of his tiny office were lined with diplomas, plaques, and certificates hailing his work in Jewish education.

He began with elaborate compliments about Marjorie's talent. Mrs. Morgenstern wasted little time on these preliminaries. "First of all, Mr. Klabber, I'd like to ask you about South Wind."

Mr. Klabber managed the feat of looking sad through an unchanged smile. "Ah, yes. South Wind——"

"It's near your camp, isn't it?"

"Unfortunately, yes. I say unfortunately. It's a most attractively laid-out place, but——"

"It's Sodom."

"That's a strong term, madam. I grant you it's more than a little bohemian——" The camp owner turned hurt eyes upon Marjorie. "But surely, my dear, you told your mother our rule about South Wind? No? But surely Marsha told you." He turned back to the mother. "Why, we have an iron rule, Mrs. Morgenstern, a cast-iron rule. Any Tamarack counselor seen at South Wind at any time during the summer is summarily dismissed. She packs and leaves on the next train, be it by day or be it by night."

Mrs. Morgenstern cast a pleased glance at Marjorie, who could not help looking stunned. "Good for you!" This news seemed to settle the matter for the mother. Haggling ensued over Marjorie's salary, in which the girl took very little part. Mr. Klabber, citing Marjorie's youth, tried to get her for fifty dollars. Mrs. Morgenstern, pointing to her genius as displayed in *The Mikado,* asked for at least three hundred. After extended arguing the mother allowed herself to be beaten down to the usual price of two hundred dollars, and handshakes all around closed the deal.

That night at the Zelenko apartment Marsha assured her that Mr. Klabber's cast-iron rule was the joke of Tamarack. "Darling, the counselors all *live* over at South Wind." She brought down tattered paint-stained play booklets from her closet shelf. "Here's some of the stuff we've put on. He doesn't care if you repeat. We've still got most of the sets up there. We can lay out the whole season tonight. Nine weeks, nine shows —God, sugar bun, what marvelous fun we're going to have . . ."

During the next weeks Marjorie spent more and more time with Marsha and her parents, and less and less with Sandy Goldstone. On the West Side she still formally held the title of Sandy Goldstone's girl, and only she knew how hollow the title was. Thus glamorized, she could go out as many nights a week as she wished. Dates were so frequent and so commonplace that they were losing charm. Nobody could ever have made Marjorie believe, when she was seventeen, that there could be anything finer than going out every night in the week with boys from Columbia and the out-of-town colleges. But now, one year later, a date with a wealthy boy like Norman Fish, who went on droning about jazz bands, Haig & Haig pinchbottle, and convertibles, began to seem like a ridiculous waste of time when she could be with Marsha Zelenko.

She was in the dark cluttered Zelenko flat four or five nights each week, talking about summer plans, or about the Broadway theatre, or about painting and music. By silent mutual consent Marsha seldom visited the Morgenstern apartment. The mother's open dislike of Marsha fell little short of rudeness. The disorder at the Zelenkos', the balalaika music, the cherry brandy, the wreathing Turkish tobacco smoke, all made a congenial, a sort of tropic climate for the luxuriantly unfolding friendship. It tended to droop and curl among the cool modern furnishings, the heavy cream satin floor-to-ceiling drapes, and the big spaces of the El Dorado apartment, always hospital-clean under the fanatical housekeeping of Mrs. Morgenstern.

The girls went often to concerts and art galleries. Marsha seemed to know all the free ones, and also how to get passes to the ones that cost money. Marjorie began to find some honest pleasure in classical music and in painting, for the first time in her life. She also discovered in herself, rather to her surprise, real ability to work and to learn, once her interest was caught. She bought books on stage direction, makeup, lights, and sets, and she mastered them rapidly. Marsha was taken aback at her technical comments on the Broadway productions they saw together. "Baby, you're giving old Klabber too much for his money," she jeered.

It gradually became clear to Marjorie that the Zelenkos were really living on Mrs. Zelenko's earnings as a piano teacher. There was a prevailing genteel fiction in the household that the teaching was a lark whereby she picked up a little pin money, while Mr. Zelenko earned the family's bread through his operations in the Street. Marjorie gathered, however, from fragments of spats she heard, that the net effect of Mr. Zelenko's wily dealings in the Street was to wipe out, each week, about half the income from Mrs. Zelenko's piano lessons.

Marjorie also realized after a while that Marsha culled her intimate gossip about celebrities from theatre magazines, *Variety*, and *The Hollywood Reporter*. Indeed, before the two girls went away together for the summer, Marjorie was well aware that her friend was in certain respects a phony.

Yet she was not much alienated. If Marsha's Broadway intimacies were only pretended, her love and knowledge of the theatre were real. She did have a lively natural gusto for the arts. She was full of bounce, quick to be offended but quicker to forgive. Above all, she was the first person Marjorie had ever encountered who seemed to value her for the right reasons. The boys in Marjorie's life had been dazzled by her small waist, her charming bosom, her fine legs, her quick good-natured coquetry. She was very glad she had these assets, but she had always felt a slight contempt for those who liked her merely for them.

As Helen Johannsen had predicted, Marsha began borrowing in the third or fourth week of their acquaintance. She made sporadic repayments. But they fell more and more steeply behind her borrowings, and the account became embarrassingly confused. One day, after a half-hour attempt to straighten out the debits and credits, Marsha said, "Oh, look, baby, this is awful. You may as well know that I'm a complete featherhead about small change. It's meaningless to me, it's like cigarettes or matches or something. I know it shouldn't be, Lord knows I'm not that rich, and I know it isn't to others. Will you do me a big fat favor and keep a little book on me?"

Marjorie said uneasily, "Oh, that's ridiculous. Let's forget all about it, a dollar *thirty*-five or *forty*-five, what does it all matter——"

"No, no. Please. Keep an account, you're damn methodical when you want to be. When we get paid at the end of the summer we'll settle up. I'm just helpless about little money. Big money I can keep track of like a CPA." She caught a satiric wisp of a smile on Marjorie's face and flared, "I'll *tell* you where I've handled big money, kiddo. On the Street I was Pop's assistant one summer when things were so good we were living at the Peter Stuyvesant, not in that hole on Ninety-second Street. And believe me, I was never off one cent in ten thousand dollars."

Marjorie agreed to keep the book, but quickly saw it was not a good idea. It released Marsha of all compunction about borrowing. "Just mark it in the little black book, dear," she would say, thus managing to relieve Marjorie of some money and patronize her at the same time. When they went off to Tamarack the account had grown to twelve dollars and change, and Marjorie, increasingly irked, was really keeping the black book with dogged accuracy.

Chapter 11. NOEL AIRMAN

With a small hissing ripple at the bow, the canoe slipped over the black water toward the winking lights and distant music of South Wind.

It was a windless, moonless night ablaze with stars. Marjorie sat in the bow with her suitcase between her knees, chilled through despite the sweater thrown over her shoulders. The thin cotton of her orange blouse and green bloomers, prescribed dress for counselors at Camp Tamarack, gave little warmth. She hugged her bare knees and crouched, trying not to shiver.

Marsha paddled expertly, with hardly a splash.

"What music is that?" Marjorie hoarsely whispered, breaking silence for the first time when they were a few hundred yards from the Tamarack shore.

Marsha laughed, a thin far sound in the open air. "You don't have to whisper, baby. Mr. Klabber is fast asleep behind us, you know. That's the orchestra. Steak roast tonight. The guests sit around the campfire, and sing, and stuff themselves, and get swozzled on beer, and the band plays for them."

"I thought there'd be dancing."

"Oh, all the dancing you want, afterward. They have the dress rehearsal of the show while the guests are at the roast out of the way. You'll really see something."

A shudder made Marjorie's teeth grate. "I'm freezing, do you know that? It's a wonder you don't catch pneumonia, doing this night after night."

"Why, honey bunch, it's warm tonight. Sometimes it's really frigid on this lake, when the wind starts cutting up. You're having beginner's luck."

"I see." Another racking shiver passed through her. "Maybe I'm just scared."

Marsha laughed again. "That's something you'll get over, too. This is a cinch. I've been doing it for three years, and here I am, fat and sassy as ever."

"Yes, I know," Marjorie said in no very amicable tone, and the conversation lapsed.

Marjorie strained her eyes toward South Wind, wondering whether the adult camp was going to prove another disappointment, another of Marsha's lies that would blow up in her hands. In the first four weeks of the summer, her attitude toward her friend had drastically changed. If she was not wholly disenchanted, she now regarded everything Marsha said with caution or downright disbelief. For she had gradually found out that Marsha had induced her to come to Camp Tamarack with lies, bald outrageous lies; and even at the camp she had tried to cover her first lies with more and more falsehoods, progressively lamer.

It was true enough, as Marsha had said, that the dramatic counselor lived in comfort in a cabin atop a hill overlooking the lake, and that she didn't have to herd children. It was also true that from the cabin Marjorie could see, three miles away on the far shore of the lake, the grounds and buildings of South Wind—a charming panorama, like a land in a child's picture book, all rolling green lawns, sculptured darker green clumps of trees, and fantastically shaped white and golden towers.

The rest was fabrication, cynical and deliberate. Mr. Klabber's "cast-iron rule" against visits by the counselors to South Wind, far from being a joke, was observed with terrified strictness by every girl on the staff—except Marsha. Indeed, they avoided talking about the adult camp, as though it were a leper colony in the neighborhood. Marsha's story at first was that it took a week or so for the counselors to warm to each other and start arranging sneak excursions to South Wind. But as time passed it became clear that Marsha alone regularly visited the adult camp, at a risk none of the others would even discuss taking. Her method was to paddle across the lake after dark in a canoe, tie it to a diving raft anchored beyond the floodlights, and swim to shore. There she borrowed towels, clothes, and makeup. She couldn't beach the canoe because the owner of South Wind, Mr. Greech, always chopped up with his own hands and burned on the shore any unfamiliar rowboats or canoes he came on at night, in order to discourage non-paying visitors.

The other counselors, mostly scrubbed dumpy girls with muscular bodies, regarded Marsha as an eccentric, and her canoe excursions—which they knew about but never reported—as unwholesome and dangerous foolishness. Marjorie had at last forced Marsha to admit all this in an acrimonious quarrel, late one night in the second week. Even then, Marsha had tried to cover herself by calling the other counselors cowardly lumps, sexless clods, and so forth. Marjorie had walked out on her in disgust while she was talking, and the two girls had hardly spoken for a week.

But the sun was bright and warm at Tamarack, the smell of the pine needles delightful, the sleep in the mountain air sweet, and Mr. Klabber's meals excellent and huge. Moreover, Marjorie had scored an instant great success with her shows, and was admired and popular, so her spirits were good. She worked hard, and handled her little actresses with natural good humor and grace. Mr. Klabber frankly said she was the best dramatic counselor he had ever had. She was unavoidably thrown together backstage with Marsha, who painted the scenery and sewed the costumes with a squad of stage-struck girls. Her grudge melted in the workaday joking backstage, though her attitude toward the fat girl remained tinged with distrust.

Marsha had importuned her day after day to try a canoe excursion to South Wind with her, swearing by all the gods that it was the simplest, safest, gayest kind of escapade imaginable. Marjorie had resisted for weeks. But tonight, at last, she had given in. After four weeks of twittering little girls, of orange blouses and green bloomers, of the dull elephantine small talk of the other counselors, and of Mr. Klabber's prosy piety, she was famished for a little fun. Marsha had promised to get her safely to the other shore without the necessity of swimming in the dark. Carlos Ringel, the set designer of the South Wind shows, would meet them at the raft, she said.

Marsha paddled in silence for perhaps a quarter of an hour before Marjorie saw the low flat black streak on the water. "There's the raft," she said, "and no sign of Carlos Ringel."

"Now, dear, don't fret. Carlos will be there."

After another long pause filled with discreet rhythmic plashing, Marjorie said, "What do we do, exactly, if we run into this—this Mr. Greech?"

"Why, honey, you're just another guest. There's a thousand of them. He doesn't know all their faces. Course, the sooner we get out of these horrible duds the better. We go from the cove straight to the singers' cottage, where we dress. It isn't a hundred feet and it's all bushes and shadows."

"What does he look like?"

"Who, Greech? Satan."

"Oh, really."

"I mean it. Satan with a potbelly and white knickers. You'll see."

Marjorie uttered a small involuntary groan, pulling the sweater more closely around her. Marsha said, "For Pete's sake, sugar bun, why are you so nervous? What's the worst that can happen to you? Do you think he'll eat you? Or that Klabber will? Stop being a child. We're going to have a hell of a marvelous time tonight, and don't you forget it."

"Marsha, I'd rather not get kicked off the first job I've ever held for moral turpitude, that's all."

The fat girl giggled. "Moral turpitude. Baby doll, your idea of moral turpitude is having two helpings of pie after dinner. But I love you just the same. Now you relax, do you hear?"

As the canoe drew nearer the raft, the adult camp began to come alive with little lights, like a lawn full of fireflies. Voices and women's laughter came floating over the water with the music. The floodlights showed a mass of red canoes—there seemed to be hundreds of them—beached bottoms up in serried lines along the shore. The social hall was floodlit too, a snowy modernistic building with a huge gilded round shell at the back. Above the entrance a broad white shaft towered up through the trees, with enormous letters on it in slender gilded script, SOUTH WIND MUSIC HALL. The swimming dock reached far out into the lake, a sweeping arc lit by red and green lanterns.

Marsha pointed with her paddle at a canoe emerging from a shadowy part of the shore. "There comes Carlos, Old Faithful himself—grumbling like anything, I bet, but there he is."

They came alongside the bobbing, clanking wooden raft which was built on oil drums, and Marjorie's hand was clasped by a thickset black figure. "Easy does it," said a rasping voice, and she stepped first on a dripping drum and then on the burlap-covered raft. Marsha climbed out of the canoe with Marjorie's suitcase.

"Carlos, this is Marjorie——"

"Hi. Hurry, kiddies, rehearsal's started already." He helped them into his canoe, and impelled it toward the shore with powerful plunging strokes. Marjorie, hunched in the bottom at his feet, was embarrassed by his silence. "Sorry to put you to all this trouble, Mr. Ringel."

"No trouble. Quiet now, we're getting in close, never know when he's skulking in the bushes."

The canoe crushed through sweet-smelling branches wet with dew and scraped on the beach. "Take your friend on ahead, Marsha, I'll get rid of the canoe." A quick fearful scurrying through brush and briars, and they were panting inside a brightly lit cottage, the rafters of which were festooned with girls' underwear, stockings, and bathing suits. Sitting up on a bed reading *The Saturday Evening Post* was a beautiful tall blond girl, stark naked. "Hullo," she said to Marsha. "Brought a friend this time, hey? You're early."

"It's a quarter past nine."

The blonde glanced at her watch and yawned. "Damn, so it is. I'm due on stage in ten minutes." She rose and strolled around picking up clothes, not at all troubled by the absence of blinds on the windows.

Marsha said, "This is Marjorie Morgenstern—Karen Blair."

"Hi," said Karen, waving a brassiere at Marjorie and then putting it on. "Help yourself to anything—combs, powder—need underwear?"

"Thanks, I brought everything."

"Well. Glad you aren't all moochers on the other side of the lake."

"What are you complaining about? I can't get into any of your things, you beanpole," Marsha said.

Karen zipped shut a pair of green shorts and a white shirtwaist, and slid her feet into moccasins. "See you, kiddies." With a wave of long limp fingers she was gone.

"Noel Airman's current flame," Marsha said, taking clothes out of a closet.

"She's stunning," Marjorie said. "Are they going to be married?"

"What, her? Strictly a bed partner for the summer. She's thirty-one, and dumb as a post. Been married and divorced three times."

"Good heavens, she doesn't seem much more than twenty——"

"Look close around her eyes and mouth next time, honey. She sure does."

"How old is he?"

"Noel? Twenty-seven, twenty-eight, maybe."

"He'll be at the rehearsal, won't he?"

"He's directing it, dear," said Marsha, a shade impatiently. She went into the bathroom with an armful of clothes.

Marjorie knew that Noel Airman was the head of the entertainment staff at South Wind, the social director who wrote and staged the shows. In the city Marsha had played and sung at the piano many of his tunes from the camp revues. Airman sounded like an extraordinary person indeed. Some of his musical skits had been performed in Broadway revues. He had had a number of songs published; two of them, *Barefoot in Heaven* and *It's Raining Kisses,* were current hits. Marjorie was much excited at the prospect of meeting such a celebrity. As she dressed she was thinking that the blond girl was the first honest-to-goodness mistress she had ever seen, though she had been reading books and seeing movies and plays about them all her life. Karen Blair did not look the part, somehow. There was a disappointing absence of any air of sin or guilt about her. Perhaps, thought Marjorie, it was just another of Marsha's lies.

Marsha came out of the bathroom painted and slimmed, in the brown Mexican blouse and copper-spiked leather belt of the city days. Marjorie was used to the sight of her in the baggy orange and green uniform. "Gad, look at you!"

"Human, eh?" Marsha said, mincing. She slipped her arm through Marjorie's, and they stood before the mirror together. "The two sirens from across the water. Not bad."

"Bet you could beat that blonde's time," Marjorie said. "You ought to try flirting with Noel Airman."

"What, and have Carlos strangle me and leave my body in the bushes?"

"Oh, nonsense. What claim has he got on you?"

"Why, none in the world, the old slob—let's go." Marsha turned out the lights. "Now remember, if we meet Greech ignore him. You're just a guest. He knows me, so that's no problem."

"He—he does know you?"

"Well, good grief, honey girl, I'm here three nights a week, I couldn't go dodging him forever. Carlos has told him some kind of cock-and-bull story. Greech makes an exception for me. I'm supposed to have a summer cottage around here. Come on."

The air in the dim lane was heavy with the sweet smell of mountain laurel. Marsha walked confidently into the darkness. "This way, Marge. —So far as flirting with Noel Airman goes, he's not for the likes of us, baby. He's another Moss Hart or Cole Porter. He'll probably marry someone like Maggie Sullavan when he gets around to it."

"He's not Jewish, is he?"

"I don't know. Probably."

"But—'Noel'——"

"Oh hell. I've known Jews named St. John."

The lane turned and widened, and they walked out on a deserted open lawn, queerly yellow-green under floodlights, like the grass of a stage setting. In the center of the lawn a white concrete fountain lit by red, blue, and yellow spotlights cascaded a foam of changing color. Rustic benches and summerhouses dotted the grass. Here and there on the lawn were tall noble old oaks, ringed with whitewashed stones, in which the floodlights hung. Beyond the lawn lay the lines of canoes, the red-and-green arc of the swimming dock, and the black lake. "Good God," murmured Marjorie, "it's so quiet."

"Saturday afternoon this lawn is like Times Square." Marsha struck across the grass toward the social hall and Marjorie hurried at her side. "They're all at the steak roast now."

"Where does everybody sleep? In those big buildings?" Instinctively she hushed her voice. She felt a little as though she were treading on a village green in Nazi Germany.

"No, in cottages back up among the trees. The men over to the left, the girls behind us. That large building with the glass front is the dining hall. Good food only on weekends for the big rush of guests, otherwise garbage. The other is the administration building where——"

A piercing whine filled the air. In unison all the oak trees croaked, "Bernice Flamm—long-distance call in the office. Bernice Flamm." Another whine, a click, and silence.

"Goddamn loudspeakers," said Marsha. "They go all day and all night. Drive you crazy."

"What separates the men and the girls? A fence or something?"

"Just foliage, dear, and upbringing," Marsha said dryly. "They're big boys and big girls, you know."

"Must make for some wild times——"

Marsha gripped her arm. "Oh, Christ. Just our luck. Greech. Coming out of the social hall. Straight at us."

Marjorie saw a little man in white knee pants descending the steps of the social hall. Her legs became weak. "What do we do, turn and run?"

"Don't be a jackass. Keep right on walking. Don't look at him. Just walk. And for God's sake don't look guilty."

Marjorie became aware of her hands dangling at the ends of her arms, and suddenly it seemed to her that there was no guiltless way to hold one's hands. She slipped them behind her back, each clutching an elbow. The figure in white knee pants drew nearer, walking with an odd side-to-side motion, half swagger and half wobble. Marjorie tried to avert her eyes; but like a child irresistibly drawn to peek at the monster in a horror movie through spreading fingers, she kept glancing at Mr. Greech. He was staring at the canoes as he walked, counting them, it seemed. In his left hand he swung a flashlight as long as a club. Suddenly his head turned and he was looking right at Marjorie. She thought she would faint. His eyes paused a moment, then flickered to Marsha; his mouth drooped a little, and he walked past them without a word.

After a few seconds Marsha said, in a tone of forced gaiety, "Well, dear, see? The bad dragon didn't eat us."

Her throat constricted, Marjorie said, "I thought you said he knows you."

"He does, very well."

"But he looked straight at you. Through you. He didn't say hello. He didn't say anything."

"Sugar bun, do you talk to the dogs you pass?"

"He—you know, he *does* look like Satan? He really does. It's amazing."

"He would be offended if he heard you, dear. Satan looks like Max Greech."

The high square doorway of the South Wind Music Hall was bordered in bronze with geometrical patterns. Over the entrance was a flat bronze female nude with streaming hair, puffed cheeks, and pursed lips. "Lady South Wind," said Marsha, pointing. "The staff has another name for her. Not fit for your innocent little ears." She went up the steps, pushed open the redwood door, and beckoned to Marjorie. "What's the matter with you? Come on." Marjorie could not have said why she was hesitating. She ran up the steps and through the door.

The lobby was decorated with posters of past shows—*South Wind Vanities, Wonderful Times, South Wind Moon, I'll Be Seeing You, South Wind Scandals.* She followed Marsha into a brightly lit auditorium where hundreds of yellow folding chairs were racked around a bare dance floor. On the stage was a very fake-looking setting of palm trees, with a red cardboard moon hanging in the background. Karen Blair, wearing a jungle costume, was swaying her hips and her upraised arms as she sang, in a sultry beguine rhythm,

Moon madness
Now at the flood
Moon madness
Burns in my blood. . . .

The rehearsal pianist, a fat man chewing a cigar, began to pound louder. A pair of dancers in jungle costume came stamping out and did an angular dance full of sexy gestures. Marsha waved to Carlos Ringel, sitting in back of the auditorium beside a thin man in a black turtle-neck sweater. "There he is," she said, "with Carlos."

"Noel Airman?"

"Himself. When the number's over I'll introduce you."

The dancers wriggled off, locked in a desperate embrace, and the blonde repeated the song.

"All right, Karen, stand by," called the man in the black sweater. "We'll try the lights before we strike it." He rose and came forward.

Marjorie stared, stupidly fascinated; she had never seen a handsomer man. He was amazingly tall and slender. If there was one flaw in his features, it was that his jaw was too long and curved too far forward. But what did that matter? The straight nose, broad brow, deep-set eyes, long bones, and shock of reddish-golden slightly curling hair gave him the look of a Greek god, she thought. She had heard the phrase often; about Airman it was true.

"Is he really as thin as he seems, or is it that black sweater?"

"Oh, Noel's a rail. The girls keep him trained down."

"I can well imagine."

"Come on over and say hello."

"No, no," Marjorie said in panic. "They're busy."

"Nonsense, we can't hang around the rehearsal without his permission." As Marjorie still held back Marsha snapped, "My God, act your age," and propelled her out on the floor by an elbow. With her free arm Marjorie frantically felt at her hair. Carlos Ringel, whom she was seeing for the first time in the light, looked very old indeed: quite bald, except for a fringe of gray-sprinkled red hair, with a seamed and pitted fat face, and gnarled veins on his hands. He nodded at the girls. "Ah, the spies from overseas."

Airman turned. His eyes, deep in their sockets, were an extraordinarily bright blue. He needed a shave; the thick stubble along his jaw was redder than his hair. His arms were hugged together, and he was rubbing his left elbow with a palm. "Hi, Marsha."

"Hi, Noel. Can we watch for a while? This is a friend of mine, Marjorie Morgenstern."

"Of course." He was uninterested.

"Margie's the dramatic counselor at my camp."

Noel Airman smiled at Marjorie, and his somewhat forbidding ironic air softened. "Well, well, a colleague. You're entitled to the courtesies of the profession.—Wally! Couple of chairs."

A pimply boy in black glasses looked out of a wing of the stage. "Right, Noel."

Marjorie said, "You embarrass me. I don't know anything about the stage." He was so terribly tall, she was thinking. She had packed low-heeled shoes in her hurry, and that made it worse. She felt like a little girl.

"Marjorie, to tell the truth, I don't know very much myself.—Thanks, Wally." The pimply boy came running with two folding chairs, which he opened and placed before the girls, looking hard and hungrily at Marjorie. It was the familiar look of a smitten sophomore at a dance. She judged him to be perhaps seventeen.

Airman called out an order to the electricians as she sat. Suddenly bathed in colored light, the stage took on a new look. The moon seemed less like cardboard, more like a moon. The palm trees, the monkeys in the tops, the lions peeping through the trunks, lost some of their smeary flatness. "Oh, I like that lighting," Marjorie blurted.

Airman looked down at her absently, lit a cigarette, and began talking to Ringel in a rapid jargon: phrases like bringing up the ambers, killing number three, flying the scrim. Marjorie cursed herself for speaking too soon and with such asinine enthusiasm. As Ringel and Airman called out orders, the lights kept modulating, and at each change the stage picture took on depth and prettiness. The boy called Wally went clambering up an iron ladder in the back of the auditorium to a catwalk cluttered with spotlights, where he shifted the colored slides. Airman walked back and forth, hugging his elbow, suggesting changes to Ringel in a calm, pleasant tone. At last he said, "All right, let's see how she really looks. Kill the house." The auditorium was thrown into darkness. The setting glowed forth, brilliant and exciting. The eyes of the monkeys and the lions gleamed; the painted sea on the backdrop rippled and glittered; the moon shone dull-red beams through the palm trees. "Oh, it's just beautiful," Marjorie exclaimed.

There was a silence during which her voice seemed to echo in the air, squeaky and childish. "What do we do about that hot spot next to number four, Carlos?" Airman said. There were more changes, and then he called out two or three swift final orders. The lights altered subtly, a transparent curtain came down before the set, and a shimmer of magic life seemed to pass over the stage. "Well, that'll have to do," he said.

Marjorie was crushed. She had been earnestly studying a book on lighting for weeks, and had fancied her effects in *Peter Pan* were professional. "Come on out, Karen, Bert, Helen," Airman called. The singer and the dancers looked unpleasantly, weakly white under the lights. Airman, pacing past Marjorie, unexpectedly stopped and said to her, "They'll be in brown body makeup, of course."

"Oh yes, sure, naturally," Marjorie babbled.

"Cigarette?"

"Why, yes, yes, thanks." Her hand shook as she took the cigarette, and her puffing at the flame of his lighter was sickeningly long and inexpert.

"Strike the set," Airman said to Ringel, as she puffed. "It's okay."

The lights came on again. He went to the piano and called Karen to the apron of the stage. "Couple of things, dear, in the chorus—listen." The rehearsal pianist leaned against the footlights, stolidly puffing his pipe. Airman's long black-clad arms and arching thin fingers danced back and forth on the keyboard; he threw his head back, nodding and shaking it vigorously as he sang. He was a far more exciting singer than Karen, thought Marjorie, and he obviously played better than the pianist. She whispered, "What else can he do, for heaven's sake?"

Marsha said, "Well, let's see. Plays better chess than Carlos, and Carlos is a club player. Sings and plays whole operas by heart: Mozart, Verdi, in Italian. Knows about seven languages. Knows more philosophy than any prof alive. That's what he really wanted to be, a philosophy prof, or so he says. You never can tell when he's serious. History, literature, art, it's all at his fingertips. But you'd never know it until some phony highbrow starts up with him. Then he shrivels them like a flame-thrower. Oh, just incidentally, he's the best dancer alive."

"For heaven's sake," Marjorie said, "there's no such person."

The cigarette was embarrassing her. She was afraid to inhale because it made her dizzy, and afraid to puff smoke out of her mouth because she felt that looked adolescent unless it came gray from the lungs. So she exhaled through her nostrils, but it stung her nose terribly. As soon as the cigarette was burned halfway down she crushed it out with her toe.

The boy Wally appeared at her side, holding out a gold case. Marjorie had seen him on the spotlight catwalk a second or two before. The apparition so startled her that she accepted another cigarette. He grinned happily as he lit it for her. Lank black hair hung to his eyes when he leaned over. He had a high bulging brow, hollow cheeks, and a big nose, and his eyes gleamed with a peculiar mournful keenness behind the glasses. But the most striking thing about him was immaturity. It seemed to be fuzzed all over him like a chick's down. Every gesture was awkward, every expression too eager. Marjorie had stopped bothering with this sort of smudge-eyed pimpled lad more than a year ago. "Your first visit to South Wind?" he said.

"Mm," said Marjorie, looking at the stage. She drew on the cigarette and grimaced. It tasted like a cough drop.

"Mentholated. Hope you don't mind," said Wally.

"Not at all." He made her feel as calm and superior as Noel Airman made her feel small and flustered. She looked him full in the face, smiling. His Adam's apple jerked. He muttered, "Well, they'll be screaming for me backstage," and ran off.

Musicians in white coats and black ties began to straggle into the hall with their instruments, mounting the bandstand in a far corner. Airman left the piano and came to Carlos, who was sitting cross-legged on the floor beside Marsha. "Carl, the thundering herd will be here in a few minutes. We're in good shape. Let's call it and have a few beers."

"With pleasure." Carlos rose, taking Marsha's hand.

Airman smiled at Marjorie. It was a wonderfully warm, intimate smile; it seemed to say that Noel Airman and the person he was smiling at were equals, rather better than most people, and sharers of some secret knowledge that was at once ironically amusing and a little melancholy. "Won't you join us, Marjorie?"

She was enchanted with the Sirocco Bar, as with everything at South Wind. It was a narrow room running along the lakeward side of the social hall, decorated with fish netting, coconuts, seashells, and paper palm trees, and lit with murky amber light from tortoise-shell lanterns. Broad plate-glass windows looked out on the rainbow fountain and the lake. A late orange moon was rising, and on the black water the lights of the swimming dock were reflected in long rippling red and green streamers.

Airman took his beer to a little red-lacquered piano and played Broadway show tunes and old South Wind songs. Marjorie sat among the show people in a crowded cubicle, listening to Airman, and at the same time, despite herself, eavesdropping on the salty South Wind gossip. The guests were swarming across the lawn toward the social hall. She could hardly keep from laughing at the epithets the staff used in referring to the guests: the cattle, the peasants, the thundering herd, the lynch mob, the locusts, the Jukes and Kallikaks. For the women guests there were special names: the dogs, the beasts, the witches, the sacks, the pigs. Contempt is such a contagious feeling that within an hour Marjorie was also regarding the guests with scorn, though at first they had seemed to her a rather attractive crowd of young adults.

She was thinking that she had probably never had a better time in her life—Airman at the moment was playing and singing his hit song, *It's Raining Kisses*—when Marsha tapped her arm and pointed through the window. "Cheese it." The little man in white knickers was wobbling across the lawn directly toward the bar, swinging his flashlight.

"Oh God," Marjorie said.

"Come with me." Marsha led her out through the social hall, where dancing couples filled the floor, to a dark porch in back overlooking the lake. "All we have to do is lay low here for a few minutes. He never stays long in the bar, he has an ulcer."

Marjorie was surprised at the brisk wind whipping across the lake, and the black clouds tumbling in front of the moon. She glanced at her watch; it was ten past twelve. "Maybe we'd better go back—look at the weather——"

"Are you nuts?"

"It's late——"

"It's barely midnight, puss. We're here for some fun."

"I've had enough for one night. It's been wonderful. Come on, before the lake gets too rough."

"No." Marsha's lip was lifted and she looked very unpleasant, all at once.

Marjorie said with a qualm of loneliness, "Well, *when* do we go back?"

"Oh, later." Marsha glanced toward the bar. "Okay, I think the coast is clear."

"But if Greech——"

"Good grief, are you fourteen? I'm not going to dodge around the whole damned night, you know. Can't you handle yourself with an old baloney like him? Just tell him he's a good dancer or has a nice tan, and he'll swoon with pleasure. Or else do as you damn please. I'm going to the bar." Marjorie followed, of course; she was in Marsha's hands.

Wally was playing the piano now, his lips pursed, his brow wrinkled in concentration, a cigarette dangling from his mouth. The sounds he made were thin, heavy-handed, and tinkly after Airman's expert jazz. Nobody was paying attention to him. Greech wasn't in sight. Ringel quickly pulled up two chairs for the girls.

Noel Airman, at the head of the table, was sipping a highball and arguing with good-natured authority, against everybody else, that Cole Porter was the best living songwriter. The girl who had done the jungle dance objected that Porter was precious.

"Precious!" Airman said. "Of course he is. Who was more precious than Gilbert, the best of the best for all time? My dear girl, popular songs are light verse. Light verse is a precious form. Before it can flourish there must be a leisure class to support it, refined, easily bored, with a taste for nuance, and——"

"Hell, Noel, the leisure class in this country doesn't support popular songs," Ringel said. "What do the capitalists care about jazz?"

"Capitalists! Carlos, you're haunted by Marx. The capitalists have no leisure whatever. They all kill themselves with scheming and worrying to make more money. No, the leisure class that supports popular songs is the high school and college kids. It's a transient class but a solid one, several million strong. It lives off the sweat of parents just as callously as the French aristocracy lived off the sweat of peasants. Eventually they marry and they're gone, but the new crop keeps coming along. And so——"

"Precious and popular are contradictory words," said the dancer. She had a pale face and black bangs. "We're talking about popular songs."

"True," said Airman, with his peculiarly gracious and winning smile, "but we're also talking about excellence. The most popular verse in English, so far as I know, is

A man's ambition must be small,
To write his name on a privy wall.

It's much more popular than

What is love? 'Tis not hereafter;
Present mirth hath present laughter . . .

Nevertheless it's not as good. It's doggerel, honey, not light verse, you see. Most popular songs are doggerel—vulgar or stupid or pleasant or ingenious, as the case may be. Porter writes light verse."

"What would you call *Moon Madness?*" the dancer said.

"Why doggerel, of course, trash of the worst sort. But please remember

I wrote it in about three minutes when you and Bert showed up with that jungle dance. I can do slightly better."

He slouched very low in his chair, with one arm hung over the back, making his points with short graceful gestures of a lean hand. He spoke with conviction, yet with a gentlemanly lightness, almost a negligence, as though to cancel any tone of dogmatism or intentional smartness in his words. His pronunciation was free of New York tones. If anything, it had a slight British fall of pitch and slur of r's, but it seemed entirely unaffected.

The dancer said, "What exactly is the difference between light verse and doggerel?"

"The difference between a real apple and a wax one," said Airman. "Or the difference between art and craft, if you will, or the difference between an actress playing Juliet on stage and yanking her girdle off in the dressing room. I'm being very fuzzy, I know. When a man spouts metaphors it's usually because he's having trouble with plain English. —Listen." He sauntered to the piano. "Wally, stop abusing that instrument and let me at it."

The boy slid off the stool without a word and shambled to the table, hands in pockets. Airman played *Love for Sale*. Then he went over it again line by line, pointing out the values of vowels and consonants at each turn of the song, showing the structure of the imagery, underlining the irony of the phrases. After that he began to play the most popular song of the time, a jigging ballad about a brokenhearted lover. He seemed to render it with all seriousness, yet soon everybody around the table was laughing. He emphasized the wrongly placed vowels, the cheap words, the grammatical errors, with faint elegance, and the contrast was killingly funny.

Marjorie laughed louder than anyone. She was transported with pleasure at her own acuteness in understanding Airman. She felt she had come into the circle of wit and charm in the world that she had always dreamed of. Airman was a fantastic being in her eyes. She found it hard to believe that she was sitting in the same room with this man, breathing the same air. She perfectly understood why women were as insane about him as Marsha said. She had no thought of flirting with him, of ever being any more to him than a blurry adolescent visitor. She would as soon have thought of flirting with a cardinal.

Wally got out of his chair and dropped into the one beside Marjorie. "Care to dance, Miss Morgenstern?"

"Well—a little later, do you mind? I love the way he plays."

"Sure," said the boy with deep gloom. "Plays like a streak, doesn't he? I'm taking lessons."

"You'll get there, I'm sure. Say, have you seen Marsha and Carlos Ringel? Know where they are?"

"Gosh, no." Wally hugged his elbow in a ludicrous unconscious caricature of Airman's gesture. He held his head a little to one side like Airman too, but with an entirely different, ungainly effect, because his head was big and his shoulders narrow. "Maybe they're dancing. If we took a turn on the dance floor we'd see——"

"All right," Marjorie said with a weary sigh.

"Do you go to Columbia?" she said when they were shuffling among the tanned brightly dressed couples. Marsha was not in sight.

"Yes," he said, surprised. "How——"

"You dance that way." She did not add that his dancing was a stumbling parody of Sandy Goldstone's style.

Airman was no longer at the piano when they came back to the bar. Two guests, a man and a woman, were on the piano bench together, playing *Chopsticks*. "Looks like everybody's taken off," said Wally. "Care for a drink?"

Marjorie's watch read quarter past one. "Well—I guess I'd better, till Marsha shows up. Thanks."

They sat at a table by a window. The floodlights were off; the night looked very black; the moon was gone. She noticed that the glass was smeary. "Lord, is it raining?"

"Sure looks it."

At a quarter to two she was sleepy, angry, and full of loathsome suspicion of Marsha. Wally's answers to her questions were growing feeble. "Another beer?" he said, in a lull of their makeshift talk about Broadway shows.

"No, no, thanks. Look, could you show me the way to Karen Blair's cottage?"

"Sure."

"Let's go." She was out of the chair and slipping through the door before the boy stood. Wet grass brushed her ankles, soaking her stockings. The air was full of an unpleasant drizzle, blown slanting by a strong wind.

Wally said in the darkness at her elbow, "You need a raincoat."

"No, don't bother." But he led her around through the foyer to the gloomy empty auditorium, ran up into the stage, and returned in a moment with a yellow slicker. They walked out into the drizzling night, and her feet made slushing noises in her shoes. "I don't envy you the canoe trip back," Wally said. He stopped when they came to the trees. "You go about fifty feet and turn sharp left——"

"Well, come along."

"I—well, I'd better not. It's the girls' side, they walk around with nothing on in those cottages."

Marjorie smiled and held out her hand. "Thanks for being so helpful."

"Helpful? I——" He seemed to choke. "Suppose you don't find Marsha? Would you like me to take you back in a canoe? I'll be glad to."

"But Marsha's bound to show up."

He lit a cigarette with an odd furtive gesture, hunching over the flame to protect it from the drizzle. "Well, listen, you're going to change, aren't you? I'll wait here. If Marsha hasn't come by the time you're ready I'll take you back."

"You'll get soaked——"

"I am soaked. It's warm. It's very pleasant. Go ahead."

The singers' cottage was empty. To put on the orange and green uniform again gave Marjorie a turn of disgust, but she did so quickly. She was closing her bag when Marsha came in, streaming rain, her hair in streaks, a man's tan raincoat over her shoulders. "Well, well, beat me back, hey? I looked for you in the bar."

Marjorie busied herself over the clasps of the bag. She knew, though, that Marsha was standing still and staring at her. After a moment the fat girl threw off the coat, stretched and yawned. "Well, time to go back to Devil's Island. This is the part I hate. Seems it rains half the time when I'm going back.—But it's worth it, don't you think?"

Marjorie swung her bag to the floor and walked to the doorway. "I'll be back in a moment."

"Where are you going?" Marsha stepped out of her skirt.

"Oh, not far. Wally Wronken is waiting in the rain to paddle me across the lake in a canoe. He wasn't sure you'd show up at all."

Marsha laughed lightly. "So, you wound up with Wally. Sugar bun, really, you can do better than that. Almost at random. Poor little Wally."

"What's wrong with Wally?"

"Oh, really, pet. That sad imitation of Noel he does, like a monkey with glasses. And he's just a little young, don't you think?"

"It's sometimes an advantage to have a young date. They expect less." She opened the door.

Marsha strode at her. "Just a minute, dear. In a bit of a temper, aren't you?" Her tan flesh bulged like dough around the tight edges of her pink brassiere and girdle and over the tops of her stockings.

Marjorie said, "Am I supposed to ignore the fact that you vanished for hours?"

"Look, pet, I owe you no accounting for my time and you owe me none for yours. I don't know what you've been doing with little Wally. I couldn't care less. I brought you here to have yourself some fun. What you did with your time is no——"

"You and I were supposed to be here together—I thought."

"I didn't undertake to wet-nurse you through the evening, girl. Or believe me, I wouldn't have asked you to come."

How ugly this fat girl was in her straining underwear, with her lip lifted in the strange mirthless grin, Marjorie thought. "Where have you been, Marsha?"

"Are you sure you'd like to know?"

Marjorie felt a little panicky at the shiny staring look of Marsha. "I daresay I wouldn't—let's go back to camp."

She turned toward the door, when Marsha's hand grasped her elbow and spun her around. "No, just you wait a bit, sugar bun." The fat girl was grinning openly. "What you're apparently thinking is that I've been in bed with Carlos all this time."

"Look, Marsha, I don't want to——"

"Sweetie, when you grow up just a bit you'll learn that it doesn't take hours. I've been in bed with Carlos, all right, but just for the last half hour or so. Fun, too. Do you mind so terribly much?" She stared at Marjorie's blank face impudently, yet there was something sad, something wistful in her expression. "The rest of the time we were at a drunken brawl in one of the staff bunks. I knew it would offend your tender sensibilities, that's why I didn't drag you along. Is it all clear now?— No comment? Well, dear, I'll tell you one thing more and we'll consider the subject closed. His wife is a monster, see, a psychotic white-haired hag. He'd marry me in a second if his wife would die or get a brainstorm and let him go. I cried myself to sleep for months on end because the hag wouldn't divorce him. And now, d'you want to know something, I'm beginning to be glad. Carlos is all right, but I'm not at all sure I want to marry him."

Marjorie could hardly look at the other girl. The conversation was weirdly dreamlike—Marsha in her underwear in the bright light in the strange room, rain clattering on the roof, herself in Klabber's green bloomers and orange blouse, her eyes smarting for sleep, her whole body trembling. "Marsha," she said with difficulty, "I'm not sophisticated, I know, but it's wrong, isn't it? I mean, he's a married man, and——"

Marsha uttered a foul obscenity. Then she laughed in a surprisingly good-humored way. "Oh Lord, now you will think I'm depraved." She dropped on to a bed, and her look was quite friendly. "I've been so careful with my language around you, too, haven't I, now? Honey, all I can tell you is, you've got so much to learn that I pity you. Really, your folks have given you a terrible upbringing. You seem to live in some pink-and-white dreamworld where all the men are Galahads and all the girls are lily maids of Astolat except they eat kosher food. Margie, you're an infant. The world is all like South Wind, just a lot of eating, maneuvering, guzzling, and fornicating, and everybody is like me and Carlos, loused up, grabbing what fun we can. Nothing matters as much as it seems to, sugar bun, believe me—nothing shakes the world, it just goes on and on in the old ways."

There was a heavy rush of rain on the roof. Marjorie said, "Wally'll drown. I have to go chase him off——"

"Sure, do that. Carlos is waiting for us in the boathouse." She added as Marjorie opened the door, "I hated to shock you, baby, but really, it had to come sooner or later, and I think it'll do you good." She had wriggled swiftly into the camp costume. She stood now under the electric bulb in her baggy blouse and bloomers, her arms akimbo, a forlorn puckish smile on her face.

She looked like an overgrown schoolgirl, Marjorie thought. It was impossible to connect her with the grand conception of adultery. Marjorie's irritation melted in an impulse of pity. She said, "I'm shocked, yes. It's all new to me. And he's—he's old, Marsha, you know. But it's none of my business, and—come on, aren't you about ready? I'll wait."

They arrived back at Tamarack soaking wet, and nauseous from the tossing of the wind-whipped water. Marjorie climbed the hill to her cabin with lead-heavy limbs, dried herself, fell into bed, and slept till noon. The sun blazing in her face woke her. She sat up, blinked at the light, and peered out of the window; and she saw, on the far shore of the azure lake, the lawns and towers of South Wind, green and golden in the sunshine.

PART THREE

Sodom

Chapter 12. WALLY WRONKEN

Maxwell Greech sat in his New York office on a gloomy afternoon of the following March, going through his accumulated mail, mostly bills. Scrawled on his calendar of appointments were two names:

Wally Wronken
Marjorie Morningstar

Though a noisy steam radiator kept the narrow room roasting hot, his neck was wrapped in a worn brown muffler. Outside the rattling window snow whirled, seagulls screeched, and steamships slipped past the Statue of Liberty with melancholy howls. Greech had leased this office in a tall old building overlooking New York Bay in his early years as a lawyer. He had drifted into the managing of South Wind as a result of the bankruptcy of its first owners; now he had all but abandoned the law, and the camp was his career, his passion, his life. Everybody at South Wind hated him, but he loved South Wind.

Bored by the mail, he glanced at his calendar for the afternoon, and grunted with glum pleasure. Greech had encountered some tough opponents during the morning—a wholesale butcher, a delegate from the waiters' union, the mortgage manager of a bank—and he looked forward to the relaxation of breaking a couple of butterflies. He flipped a switch on his desk. "Anybody out there yet?"

The speaker answered tinnily, "Wally Wronken just came, sir."

"Send him in."

In a blue overcoat flecked with melting snow, clutching a pigskin briefcase, Wally looked older than he had in the summer; but not old enough, Greech decided at a glance, to give any trouble. The boy said he wanted to be a writer this year, not a mere stagehand. Eagerly he pulled his new credentials from the briefcase. There was a clipping from the Columbia *Spectator*:

Wronken Varsity Show
Chosen by Judges

also a program of the show, with a full-page picture of Wally, pale and owlish and seeming about fifteen years old. Some of the comic songs he had written were reprinted in the program. Greech looked them over; they were surprisingly smooth and clever. "Well, well, this is all fine, but a college show isn't a South Wind show——"

"I realize that, Mr. Greech, but honestly, I wrote this whole show, book and lyrics, in three weeks. Noel will probably have to throw out a lot of my stuff, but I'll write tons, tons!"

Greech pursed his lips and shook his head. "Now, Wally, I don't doubt that, but trouble is, I need an assistant stage manager on the lights and props and all, same as last year, and I don't need a writer. I'm up to my belly button in writers."

"Why, I'll do the lighting, Mr. Greech, and all the rest too, that won't bother me, providing it's understood that primarily I'm working as a writer——"

While he spoke Greech was pleasurably calculating that he could now do without the sarcastic sketch writer, Milt Quint, who cost him two hundred dollars a year. Wally obviously had enough talent to write skits. He said sorrowfully, "Well, no, Wally, I'm afraid it's impossible." He waited a moment to let the dejection deepen on the boy's face. "Fact is, have to let you in on a little confidential secret, I'm not even hiring Quint this year. I'm planning to use old show material. I can't pay a writer this year, that's the point."

"Oh." Wally paced, hugging his elbow. His look became very sad. "You can't pay anything at all?"

"Nothing."

"But—well, frankly, I knew I wouldn't get as much as Quint, but—I don't know, can't you even pay fifty dollars?"

"I can't pay fifty cents, Wally."

The boy sighed, picked up his briefcase, and put the papers back into it. Greech had a moment of worry. At fifty dollars Wally was a bargain. He said, "It isn't that I don't admire your progress, Wally. Those songs are fine. Looks to me that we have a big South Wind writer coming along in you, maybe a big Broadway writer." Gratitude and delight shone on Wally's face. "For all I know, if things get better next year and you have the experience of one season under your belt, you may be worth two hundred to me easily. Or three hundred or a thousand. After all,

Noel isn't going to direct South Wind shows forever. In fact I'm lucky to have him this year. He's outgrowing us. Grooming the next social director is what I'm mainly interested in——"

Wally burst out, "Look, I'll work for nothing. Provided that my official title is writer, and that I sleep in the writers' cabin this year, not with the caddies."

Greech picked the big flashlight off the desk—it was his trademark at the camp, his mace, and he kept it in the city office half as a joke and half as a token of his majesty—and slapped it against his palm, staring out of the window at the whirling snow. The radiator hissed and the windows rattled. "You'll do everything you did last year around the stage—lights, props, and such?"

"Yes. Can I—will you pay my railroad fare this year? Seeing I'll be doing all this writing, too——"

Greech smiled and held out his hand. "Well, Wally, we won't quibble about details. You're in the writers' cabin. If you work out as a writer, why, come in and see me at the end of the season about the fare."

Wally smiled uncertainly, shook hands, and left. Greech put the flashlight down with satisfaction. Not a bad interview; at the price of a cot in a staff bungalow he had a writer for the season. It was not even going to cost railroad fare.

Coming out of Greech's office, Wally was amazed to see Marjorie in the waiting room, sitting bundled in a beaver coat. She was much prettier now than she had been in the summer, and he had thought her then the prettiest girl alive. "Gosh, hello! Aren't you Marjorie—Marsha's friend?"

She smiled, a little nervously. "I'm Marjorie. How are you, Wally?"

"Fine! Glad you remember my name—— Say, what brings you to the gates of hell?" He dropped his voice, glancing at Greech's stenographer.

"I'm trying for a job as an actress."

"Why, that's great—that's marvelous! Hope you make it. I'm going back this year. I'm going to be a writer." He said it with exaggerated nonchalance.

"I thought Noel Airman wrote the shows——"

"He writes the songs, mainly. Also occasional skits. There's always been at least one skit writer. Sometimes other songwriters, too——"

"Is—ah, is Noel coming back this year?"

"Noel? I guess so. He has this musical comedy, *Princess Jones*, that may get produced—but not this summer, I don't think. Say, can't I see you some evening? Are you in the phone book?"

Marjorie hesitated. "I'm busy almost every evening, Wally. I'm with a theatre group, the Vagabond Players, at the Ninety-second Street Y. We're rehearsing *Pygmalion*."

"Really? I'm in the theatre too, now, you might say. I'm the author of the Varsity Show this year at Columbia."

"Well, congratulations! That's a great honor——"

There was a buzz at the stenographer's desk. She called, "Miss Morningstar——"

Marjorie jumped up. "My father is Arnold Morgenstern, Wally, first Morgenstern in the Manhattan phone book. That Central Park West address is wrong, we've moved."

"Okay." Wally seized her hand, dropped it as though it were hot, and went stumbling out.

Greech looked much less like Satan than he had on the grounds of South Wind, Marjorie thought. In the flat yellow light of a Manhattan office, with snow falling past the window behind him, with a brown muffler around his neck, he was just another drab little businessman like her father. The big flashlight seemed a bit silly, lying on a desk in New York. "Take off your coat, my dear. I keep this room too hot, I know—confounded draft from the window on my neck all the time——"

"Thank you, Mr. Greech." She slipped out of the coat, glad she had worn her tailored gray-blue tweed, the best outfit she owned.

Greech was astonished at the way the girl had matured. She had seemed hardly more than a child last summer, trailing in the wake of the unsavory Marsha, and then coming to his office by herself at the end of the season with her stammered inquiry about working as an actress. "How's Marsha?" he said.

"All right, I guess, I haven't seen her for months. She's working in Lamm's department store."

"Oh? Doing what?"

"Corset department, I think."

"Well, now," said the camp owner, "it seems you're still determined to work at South Wind, eh?"

"It's what I want to do more than anything in the world."

"But you still can't sing and dance, can you?"

"Well, I can be in a chorus, I think. But I'm a dramatic actress, mainly——"

"I told you, though, my dear, that we only do one dramatic show every couple of weeks, and so we don't have much use for——"

"I remember everything you told me, Mr. Greech. I've learned shorthand and typing."

Greech sat forward with a squeak of the swivel chair. "You have!"

"Well, you said that sometimes if a girl could make herself useful around the office, you took her on as a dramatic actress."

"Why, that's so, but——" He stared at her. It was much more than he usually expected or hoped for. His practice was to staff his office with would-be actresses. They cost him nothing, and they filled out the dancing chorus in the revues; and around the office they did unskilled chores like tending the front desk and the switchboard, keeping the files, and running errands. For stenographic work he had the wives of the headwaiter and the golf instructor, both trained secretaries who worked for nothing in order to spend the summer with their husbands. Greech had never before encountered an actress who had taken the trouble to learn stenography.

He said after a moment, "Well, of course, we expect that. But you understand that we can't afford to pay our secretaries, it's a question of whether the dramatic experience is worth it to you——"

"Oh, certainly. I didn't expect you'd pay me."

Her clothes, he saw, were not only fetching, they were expensive; and he began to scent possibilities in the situation. "How about taking a letter right now, to show what you can do?"

"Well——" He did not miss the fleeting consternation on the lovely young face. "I'll try. I'm pretty raw, you know, Mr. Greech, but I'm still studying, you see. The course doesn't end till June."

He gave her a pencil and pad, and dictated a little faster than his usual rate. She tried desperately, became more and more flurried, and stopped. "I'm horribly sorry, Mr. Greech, I can't—I know it's not too fast—I just need practice, I'm taking two hours of dictation a week, I'll be much better——"

He shook his head sadly. "Well, my dear, at the moment you're not a professional stenographer, and not a professional actress, and still—of course you're a very bright and pretty girl, but I'm in business here."

She was groping in her wide black purse. She pulled two letters out and gave them to him. One was from Miss Kimble at Hunter and the other from the director of the Vagabond Players, a Mr. Graub. Both stated that Marjorie Morgenstern had a brilliant future as an actress. "Very nice, my dear, but this is all amateur stuff."

"The Vagabonds charge admission," the girl said faintly.

Greech smiled, and handed the letters back to her. "Now, Margie, I admire your spirit. But you have to consider that a three-month vacation at South Wind, which is what you'd be getting, costs something like eight hundred dollars. Sometimes in unusual cases we do work out a sort of compromise arrangement. Sort of split the difference, you see. Now if you could pay four hundred dollars for the summer, why I think, seeing that you do have a lot of promise for the future, we might—— What's the matter?"

The girl put her hand to her face for a moment, bowing her head, and when she looked up and tried to smile her eyes were wet. "I—nothing's the matter, I'm a little disappointed. I appreciate what you say. But I haven't got four hundred dollars. I haven't got any money." She stood and picked up her coat, wilted, awkward.

He said in a fatherly tone, "Well, of course, you're a little young to have much money, but surely your parents are interested enough in your acting career to help out——"

"My parents!"

"Conceivably we could work something out for two hundred fifty, three hundred, something like that——"

"Mr. Greech, my parents don't want me to act. They don't want me to go to South Wind." She put on her coat, adding in a shaky voice, "Thanks anyway. Maybe next year."

Greech stood. He had a divining-rod instinct for small sums of money, and he was certain that at least a hundred dollars could be wrung out of this girl. But her charm had softened him, and anyway, even with her limited shorthand ability, she was a better bargain than most of his office actresses. "Marjorie, if you promise to keep it confidential between us," he said, "I'm going to gamble on my intuition. I think you'll be a fine actress some day. I'm just not a businessman, I guess. I'm going to give you the job."

The girl peered at him mistily. "I don't have to—to pay?"

"Well, just your own railroad fare, naturally, but that's a mere trifle, some thirty dollars round trip—is it a deal?"

She grasped his outstretched hand tightly. "You'll never be sorry! God, I can't believe it——"

He patted her hand and released it. "Now then. I thought your name was Morgenstern. What's all this Morningstar business?"

She smiled shyly at him. "Well, that's my stage name. Might as well start with it now, I thought. Is it all right?"

Greech shrugged; she was a child, after all. "Yes, dear, it's very pretty."

She went out, leaving in the hot yellow-walled office a faint fresh scent like lilac; quite different from the heavy theatrical perfumes of the usual actress applicants.

Actually, his instinct had been right. Marjorie did have a hundred seventeen dollars in the bank, the remains of Klabber's pay. She had been on the verge of offering it to him when he cracked.

Marjorie went home in a cloud of joy which even the cramped dark West End Avenue apartment could not dispel. She shut herself in the little bedroom, hardly as large as the maid's room had been in the El Dorado, and spent the rest of the afternoon curled on her bed with a novel, often dropping the book on her lap and drifting into dreams of the coming summer.

They had been in the new apartment for half a year. The Morgensterns had been forced out of the El Dorado the previous October by a catastrophe in the millinery market, a sudden wild seesawing in the prices of felt and straw which had all but wiped out the Arnold Importing Company in a month. The details of the collapse were vague to Marjorie, although her fourteen-year-old brother seemed to understand it, and tried to explain it to her at the time with a grasp that seemed highly precocious. All the girl really knew was that the golden days at the El Dorado came to a stop in funereal family conferences, an extraordinary rush of telephoning, and then a horrid invasion of grunting furniture movers with grimy slings and barrels, their brutal voices echoing through the stripped, gutted apartment.

It seemed to her at first that this was the end of all her hopes, that she could never face any of her friends again, that she was cut off from decent society. But a week after the family was installed in the small back apartment on West End Avenue she was quite used to it and thinking of other things. Making beds and washing dishes came naturally to her after a Bronx childhood; she did not particularly miss the maid-servant. Mrs. Morgenstern declared that she was happy with the decreased housekeeping, and had never really liked having a stranger in the kitchen. She also insisted that Marjorie had a lovely view of the Hudson. It really was possible to see a blue patch of river from the girl's bedroom by leaning out far enough to risk falling ten floors to a concrete yard. Otherwise the view was the usual New York one: window shades, bedrooms, and dirty bricks. But Marjorie decided it didn't matter much what one saw out of the windows. The lobby of the building did have marble pillars, plenty of gilding, and Persian rugs in good repair. They were still far from the Bronx.

In fact, the net effect of the shock was bracing. Marjorie felt that she was in a Spartan time of life, that her grasshopper days were over. Her parents were amazed and delighted by her announcement that she had added stenography to her program at Hunter. "My God," said Mrs. Morgenstern, "watch out or you'll wind up useful." Marjorie did not mention that her goal was South Wind, of course, and she was very casual about the dramatic group at the Y which she joined.

The Vagabonds were a hard-working group, putting on a new play every three or four weeks, and Marjorie rose rapidly to be a minor leading lady. She loved the rehearsals, the theatre talk, the late sandwiches and coffee; and though none of the men in the company interested her, she was kept buoyant by the attention they paid her, and by the consequent coolness and sarcasm of the girls. The men were mostly college graduates struggling for a foothold in business, teaching, or the law. A couple of them, handsomer than the rest and with long well-oiled hair, called themselves professional actors, and accepted parts in each new play with the express understanding that they might be called off at any instant to Broadway or to Hollywood. Such an emergency never arose, however, during Marjorie's entire association with the Vagabonds.

What she particularly valued was the freedom the theatricals gave her. "I'm going to rehearsal" was a simple unchallengeable password out of her home in the evening. Mrs. Morgenstern's opinion of her daughter had risen sharply when she saw her at her shorthand homework, actually making pothooks on a pad. Perhaps the disappearance of Marsha from Marjorie's life, though it was never discussed, also made a difference. Anyway, the mother discontinued her cross-examinations almost entirely. For the first time in her existence the girl tasted privacy, and she relished it.

One evening in November Marsha telephoned her, and after a cold exchange of greetings she said, "I know you have no use for me and that's okay, but I'd like to see you for just a few minutes tomorrow. I'll meet you anywhere. It's very important to me." Marjorie couldn't quickly think of a gracious phrasing for a refusal, and so she made the appointment.

She had not seen Marsha since the end of the summer; the friendship of the two girls had been quenched by the uncovering of Marsha's affair with Carlos Ringel. Marjorie's first amazement had soon worn off, and she had been pleasant in her dealings with the fat girl for the rest of their stay at Camp Tamarack. But in New York, Marsha having graduated from Hunter, their paths did not cross; and they did not seek each other out. Marjorie knew it was mainly her fault. She spent a great many hours thinking about Marsha, often regretting the end of the friendship, which had left a painful hole in her life. Sometimes she tried to condemn her own attitude as old-fashioned, prudish. There was no such thing as an adulteress any more, she told herself. People had affairs if they wanted to, observed a few precautions and decencies, and that was all there was to it. But her attitude was not a matter of reason. It was as instinctive as the humping-up of a cat at a dog, and she could not change it.

Marsha walked into the drugstore near Hunter looking puffy and pale, with marked shadows under her eyes. There were bald patches in her old squirrel coat and the seams in her blue kid gloves were split. She said cheerily, dropping into the booth where Marjorie sat, "Gad, this brings back memories. I'll be conjugating Latin verbs any second. Let's get some coffee fast."

The first thing she did was to press fourteen dollars and twelve cents on Marjorie, the exact sum she had owed her at the end of the summer. Marjorie tried hard to demur, but at last took the coins and the crumpled bills. Next Marsha asked about the change of address and expressed sympathy at the reverses. "I guess things are tough all over," she said. "Compared to my folks, yours are still millionaires. We're really getting it this year. Pop's so sick of it he hardly goes down to the Street any more, and Mom can't even get the piano lessons these days. I've got to find work, Margie." She paused and gulped her coffee. "And not just work for me. I want enough money to take care of my folks. They broke their backs getting me through college, God knows. They're wonderful and I love them, but neither of them all their lives ever learned how to hang on to a dollar long enough to see whose picture was on it, and they'll never learn now. It's up to me. I just want one thing now, money, money for my folks and for me, and I'm going to get it."

Marjorie said, fumbling at her purse, "Why did you give me this money then? I told you I don't need it."

Marsha sharply pushed her hand away from the purse. "Sugar bun, develop some antennae some day, will you? That was my great symbolic act—for myself—Marsha taking the vows and the veil. I don't want your pity, kid, I want help. Do you see Sandy Goldstone much these days?"

"Hardly ever. Just once this fall."

"But you're still friends."

"Well, we never had any fight, but——"

"Give me a letter of introduction to him." She grinned at Marjorie's astonished look. "It's just a handle, baby, a shoehorn, you always need something like that to get started. Once I'm in his office as a friend of yours I'll get me a job at Lamm's, don't you worry."

"Marsha, a letter from me—I'd feel so silly writing it—it wouldn't mean a thing——"

"It'll get me past doors."

Marjorie agreed to write it.

When they were out on the street, and about to part, Marjorie said, "Did you and Carlos see Noel Airman after the summer?"

Marsha said, with an amused narrowing of the eyes, "What makes you ask?"

"Just curious."

"Why yes." Marsha thrust her hands in her coat pockets in a coquettish pose. "We saw quite a bit of him. He lives at 11 Bank Street, you know, real cosy Villagey kind of apartment. Lot of fun. Matter of fact I still see him now and then. Maybe you'd like to come one afternoon and——"

"Oh no, no, my God," Marjorie said. "It's just that—well, you can't help being interested in a celebrity you've met."

"What are you doing for a love life if you don't see Sandy?"

"I haven't any."

"What? Aren't you dying of boredom?"

Marjorie told her about the Vagabonds. The fat girl nodded approvingly. "Good practice for you. I still think you're going to be a great actress, Margie. So do my folks. They talk about you all the time. They miss you. . . . And none of the guys in that acting crowd mean anything to you?"

"Well, I run around with them, but they're bores."

Marsha said briskly, "You know what, sugar bun? I think you've got a case on Noel Airman."

"That's ridiculous." But Marjorie's heart began slamming and her face became hot.

"Oh, stop blushing and looking as though you'd dropped a garter. It's perfectly all right. In fact something might come of it."

"Marsha, he's thirty——"

"What if he were? It happens he's twenty-eight."

"A man who sleeps around with everybody——"

"Oh yes, you and your Old Testament upbringing. Well, he does nothing of the kind. One at a time, and choice." Marsha cocked her head, looking Marjorie over. "It's hard for me not to think of you as a baby, but really, honey, you look older and prettier by the month. Maybe you could handle Noel at that. I've seen queerer matches, God knows. What can a girl lose by trying? It would be the easiest thing in the world for me to get you two together in an accidental way——"

"Good heavens, Marsha, will you forget it? You're spinning something out of thin air. I haven't the faintest interest in Noel Airman."

"Okay, okay." Marsha laid her hand on Marjorie's arm in the old gesture of patronizing good humor. "When do you think I can have the letter?"

Marjorie was so flustered that it took her a few seconds to realize what Marsha meant. "Oh, the letter. I'll write it as soon as I get home."

Before starting her homework that night Marjorie mailed the letter off. Then she found she couldn't concentrate on her textbooks. Marsha's remarks about Noel haunted her. The plain fact was—though strangely she had not faced it until now—that from the start she had been unfavorably comparing all the men in the Vagabond Players to the social director of South Wind. She could recollect doing so. Airman had somehow become for her the image of an ideal man; and it had happened so quietly, so naturally, that he now seemed always to have been the measure. To Marjorie, indeed, he was still more than half an abstraction. She had seen him in all for less than two hours. She dimly remembered a tall man with red-blond hair and crackling blue eyes; a man whose conversation was all wisdom, whose tones and gestures were all gentlemanly grace, and who could do anything in the world better than anybody else. Even at the height of her worship of George Drobes, her glamorizing of Sandy Goldstone, she had remained aware that they both fell rather short of perfection. Noel Airman actually did seem a perfect man.

During the next few days, in a whirl of shifting moods touched off by Marsha's casual words, "You've got a case on Noel Airman," she gave way to a desire to think about Airman, and thought about nobody and nothing else. She went over and over every moment of the evening at South Wind, piecing together his words, his actions. She daydreamed about him through her classes, her meals at home, her Vagabond rehearsals at night.

Marsha gratefully phoned the next week to tell her that she had a job in the corset department at Lamm's. "My specialty, sugar bun, I've been studying for years how to squeeze a mass of living putty into the shape of a woman. Won't bother you again till I work up to corset buyer, then I'll phone you the good news. Give me two years."

Marjorie, whose heart leaped when she heard Marsha's voice, asked a lot of questions to keep the conversation going, hoping fiercely that Marsha would in some way come to talk of Noel again. But Marsha said at last, " 'Bye, sugar bun, enjoy life," and hung up. Marjorie fought against telephoning her in the days that followed, the way a man who has quit smoking fights against taking a cigarette. Once, late at night, she actually dialled the number; but when she heard Mr. Zelenko's voice she crashed the receiver on to the hook.

Gradually her emotional turmoil subsided, though she never entirely stopped thinking about Airman. On her nineteenth birthday, a bitter snowy day, she did a very queer thing. She went downtown to Bank Street after school hours, and for twenty minutes stood across the street from the shabby red brick house where he lived, staring at the windows, while snow caked on her beaver coat and caught in her eyelashes. It occurred to her, as she stood there in the blizzard with her breath smoking, that she was hardly better than the squealing simpletons who gathered in fan clubs to worship an actor. Noel Airman was as remote from her as Clark Gable, and as unaware of her existence. But though surprised at herself, and ironically amused, she somehow was not really ashamed. She went home half frozen but obscurely satisfied, and she did not do it again.

The best result of this strange period was that she discovered in herself a capacity for keeping silent and holding a cheery appearance no matter what her mood was. She was on gossipy terms with some of the Vagabond girls, who picked over their love tangles by the hour, but she said not a word about her own. As for her family, the man who was occupying her thoughts did not even exist for them. All during the winter, and into the spring—while she dreamed of him, and wrote letters she never intended to mail and tore them up, and scribbled *Mrs. Noel Airman* on loose-leaf sheets which she instantly shredded into a wastebasket, and planned and plotted to make her way to South Wind, and finally made the appointment with Greech and won the job—all that time, for anything her parents or her brother knew, Marjorie was a girl without an aim or a care in the world.

Into this same reservoir of silence she dropped the tremendous news that Greech had hired her to work at South Wind. That very evening at dinner, as it happened, a discussion of summer plans came up. Mrs. Morgenstern dismally observed that, while the rest of them might have to sweat it out in the city, Marjorie at least was assured of fresh air and sunshine at Klabber's camp. The girl let it pass. She knew that in June she would have to fight a wild battle with her mother, and saw no point in starting hostilities in March.

The phone rang in the middle of the discussion. It was Wally Wronken. He said breathlessly, "Marjorie, my Varsity Show has its opening night at the Waldorf next Thursday. Will you come with me?"

"What! My gosh, Wally, you take my breath away. It's awfully sweet of you, but—no, ask someone else—that's an important evening for you, you hardly know me——" But he would not be argued out of it. Astonished and flattered, she finally agreed to come; then his joy made her uneasy.

When she arrived home from school on the evening of the show there was a massive white orchid nesting in green tissue paper in a box on the kitchen table. Mrs. Morgenstern, peeling potatoes at the sink, said, "Who is this Wally Wronken, a gangster?"

Marjorie was smiling over the card: *Only four more hours until I see you. I may live.* She said, "Oh, a crazy kid," and she told her mother about the Varsity Show.

Mrs. Morgenstern said, "He must be talented. And from the looks of that flower, not badly off."

"Unfortunately, Mom, he's an infant. Put away the wedding invitations."

Wally appeared at her door at seven-thirty in a skyscraping opera hat, a flowing white silk muffler, white kid gloves, and a coat with a black velvet collar; he carried a black cane with a white ivory handle. Marjorie managed with a great effort to keep from laughing. His words of greeting when he saw her rather stark halter-neckline evening dress were, "Holy cats." In the taxi he sat gnawing the head of his cane, smiling foolishly at her. Walking into the buzzing Waldorf ballroom, hailed and congratulated on every side, he stumbled and grinned like a drunkard.

His family, already seated in the box, looked Marjorie over very critically. One glance at the dresses of the mother and sister told Marjorie that the Wronkens were well-to-do. "I feel very odd," Marjorie said to the mother and father. "I told Wally he ought to give this great honor to a girl who knew him better——"

"I don't see how he could have picked a prettier partner," the father said.

Mrs. Wronken merely smiled.

Marjorie was a little surprised by some of the wit in the show. The actors were ungainly and smirking, and she was not amused by the knobby knees and hairy legs of the dancing chorus, which constituted the main charm of the evening for the audience. She had seen too many Varsity Shows. But the songs rhymed well, and there were excellent jokes sprinkled in the book, an otherwise foolish business about dictators, Greek gods, and Hollywood. From time to time she glanced at Wally beside her, his face a dim white triangle in the shadows of the box, his glasses glittering toward the stage, and wondered where he buried the sense and sophistication these lines showed.

When the lights went up at the end of the first act Mrs. Wronken, her eyes agleam, took her son's hand. "It's brilliant, brilliant, Wally. Where did you ever learn to write like that?"

"Pretty off-color, some of that humor, son," said his father.

Marjorie said, "Really, Wally, it's awfully good——"

A fat young man in a tuxedo came through the curtains of the box. "Well, Wally, it's going great, don't you think?" It took Marjorie a moment to realize that this was Billy Ehrmann. She had stopped making dates with him, as with the other West Side boys, in her preoccupation with Marsha. He was heavier, especially in the face, and looked much older.

Wally said, "I think it's coming off all right." He introduced Ehrmann to his family as the manager of the show. "Billy, I guess you know Marjorie Morgenstern——"

Billy turned. "For crying out loud! *Marge!*"

"Hello, Billy——"

"Say, you look *marvelous*. Gosh, it's been a year, hasn't it? Why, if I'd dreamed you felt like seeing this show, why, I——" He became aware of his babbling tone and looked around sheepishly. "Margie and I are old friends—— Say, Wally, I didn't mean to crash your party, the thing is my brother Saul came after all. He doesn't want to just barge in on your box, but if you feel like——"

Wally was on his feet, seizing Marjorie's hand. "He did come? Let's go, Marge. I've got to hear what he thinks."

Half dragged, Marjorie followed him out of the box. Leaning against the wall in the corridor, hugging his elbow and smoking a cigarette, was Noel Airman. Marjorie actually staggered; she had to hang on to Wally's arm. There wasn't the slightest doubt that it was Airman. In a rather worn greenish tweed suit and a tan sweater, pale and a little tired, he appeared among the chattering pimply collegians in tuxedos like an eagle among sparrows. "Wally, it's good to see you. Congratulations." He held out his hand and came forward with the charming smile that Marjorie had been seeing for months in her visions. "You're not a college boy after tonight. Welcome to the ranks of unemployed writers."

Wally said, "It's all a lot of kid stuff, isn't it, Noel?"

"Wally, this is your first piece. Nobody's looking for *Of Thee I Sing*. It's all right, and you're going to be all right." His look wandered to Marjorie, and rested on her without recognition. Marjorie could not imagine what was keeping her from fainting. She was quite numb, quite stunned.

"This is Margie Morgenstern, Noel," Wally said. "Don't you remember her? She came over from the kids' camp with Marsha one night——"

Noel's face livened. "Why, sure. The girl in the purple dress. The dramatic counselor. Hello."

"Hello."

"How's Marsha? Haven't seen her in a long while."

"Neither have I." He didn't seem quite so fantastically tall, she was thinking, when she wore high heels.

Billy Ehrmann said, "Saul, I told you about Marjorie long ago."

Noel turned and smiled at him. "What, Billy, is this *Marjorie*?"

"That's Marjorie," said Billy with a sad shrug.

"Well. I see. I can hardly blame you."

Marjorie blurted, unable to help herself, "Is your name Saul, or Noel? Or am I being very stupid?"

"Surely Billy told you about his black-sheep brother, one time or another?" Noel said with a laugh. "He told me all about you, God knows."

Marjorie recalled now, as one recalls pieces of an old dream, that Billy when drunk had once spoken of an older brother who had flunked out of law school, changed his name, and become a writer. He was saying to

Wally, "That patter song of Mars and Aphrodite is funny, Wally. Let's use it in the Decoration Day show."

Wally beamed. "Really? Is it that good? Say, you'll stay around for the second act, won't you, Noel? There's another pretty good number next to closing."

"Wouldn't miss it, Wally. See you later."

Marjorie could not have recounted afterward a single detail of the second act of Wally's musical comedy. She sat in the dark box, digesting in a daze the startling news that Noel Airman was Saul Ehrmann, Billy Ehrmann's rascally older brother. She concentrated on trying to recall exactly what Billy had said about his brother, but she could dredge up few additional facts from her memory. He had talked about him only once, in a conversation on the sofa of the fraternity house, at the weary end of a Thanksgiving dance two years ago. She had been arguing with him about popular songs, and to bolster his authority he had drunkenly declared that he knew more than she because he had a brother in the business. He had then poured out an incoherent tale of a brilliant scapegrace who had deliberately failed at school, revelled around Europe for years, and drifted at last into Tin Pan Alley. She remembered that another time when she asked Billy to tell her more about his brother he became ill at ease and changed the subject.

She was struggling with the impression that there was something odd in Airman's appearance tonight, something abnormal, which she had not noticed at South Wind. He was as handsome as ever; and in city clothes he looked, if anything, more elegant than he had at the camp. What was wrong? She began scrutinizing the audience, and saw him sitting on the far side of the ballroom, slouched low in his seat, his arms folded, watching the play with his head aslant. From then on she mainly watched him.

After the show the ballroom floor was cleared for dancing. Noel was waiting at the foot of the mezzanine stairs, topcoat over his arm, to congratulate Wally. In a moment, giddily, she found herself in his arms, dancing; for Wally took his mother out on the floor, and Noel at once tossed his coat on a chair and held out his hand to Marjorie.

They danced in silence for a while. Marjorie lacked the strength to utter a word. She had danced with a great many young men, but never before had she felt so weightless, so skimming. He was, as Marsha had said, a perfect dancer. After a while Airman said, "You've been rather hard on my brother Billy, haven't you?"

"Why, not at all."

"He was shattered last year. And he's all shaky again tonight, just from seeing you. He says so."

"Oh, he just likes to talk that way," she said. "I'm very fond of Billy."

Noel leaned away and looked down at her. "Fond, eh? Sounds fatal."

"Well, I'm not picking and choosing words. You know what I mean." The blood was tingling in her face.

"I certainly do. If you'd said that you hated him, that he was a swine, a cad, I'd advise him to persevere. But if you're really fond of him——"

"Don't tell him to persevere, please." After another silence she said, "How did you like Wally's show?"

"Very inventive and gay."

"Marsha used to play and sing your South Wind numbers all the time. I loved them. Wally's a long way from writing things like that."

He cocked his head at her wryly. "I'm a little older, you know."

"Are you going back to South Wind this summer?"

"It looks that way."

"I guess you'll be my boss, then. I've got a job on the social staff."

"Have you now?" He held her away from him, and his look was detached and amused. "That's fine. Going to be one of Greech's office slaves?"

"Also do a little acting, I hope. It seems like a perfect place to learn."

"You can learn a lot at South Wind. I'm not sure about learning to act, but—— Well, Wally must be in heaven, eh? He went over to your camp half a dozen times last summer to try to see you, and always got thrown out."

"I never knew that."

"I suppose he's too shy to tell you." He held her close again and they danced. There was nothing in his dancing but easy politeness. The music was ending, and sadness came flowing over her. What a botch it was turning out! He classed her as a girl for Wally or Billy. The way he held her, the way he talked to her, told her that. Nothing, nothing she could decently say or do would change it.

Wally was waiting for them at the ballroom door beside the chair where Noel's coat lay. As Noel bowed, his arms at his sides, saying good-bye, Marjorie suddenly saw what it was that had seemed odd to her before. It was his left arm, the one he usually held bent, hugging the elbow. When it hung straight down it appeared a little shorter than the other arm; and unless she was mistaken, it was a little crooked.

Chapter 13. A KISS UNDER THE LILACS

Billy Ehrmann telephoned her a few evenings later, saying plaintively, "As long as you seem to be in circulation again, I thought I'd try my luck."

When he came he looked around at the elaborate furnishings from the El Dorado, crammed and jumbled in the new apartment, and said politely that it was a very nice place. He made her more self-conscious about her family's comedown than she had ever been before. "Don't take off your coat," she said. "We'll go somewhere. Maybe Old Casablanca."

Billy protested, begging her to let him take her to the Stork Club. But she felt guilty about going out with him, and was quieting her conscience by suggesting the cheapest place she knew, so to Old Casablanca they went. It was a decayed restaurant on Broadway, only a couple of blocks from her home, where three shabby musicians ground out gloomy music every night for collegians short of funds. The walls, irregular and jagged plaster simulating a grotto, were painted dead blue, and the lights were blue. The dance floor was full of skinny boys in threadbare jackets and dirty white shoes, clutching dowdy girls with sagging hemlines, all shuffling and swaying in the sepulchral light. Marjorie and Billy chatted over beer and rubbery hamburgers, and she casually mentioned that she was going to spend the summer at South Wind.

"South Wind? My brother Saul's the social director there!"

Marjorie nodded. "I knew Noel Airman was. I didn't know he was your brother Saul until the other night."

Billy smiled crookedly, grunted, and tossed his head to one side. In that fugitive moment Marjorie saw the brotherly resemblance. "Noel Airman. Great name, isn't it?" He began to play with the ketchup bottle.

"You hardly ever mentioned him."

"He's kind of a sore point in the family, Marge, with one thing and another."

"What's the matter with his arm?"

"Oh, you noticed that? He covers it pretty well. It's a thing they call Erb's palsy. He's had it from birth. Comes from a forceps delivery. Lots of people have it. You've seen 'em with arms all short and bent. Well, Saul's wasn't too bad, and he exercised like a fiend and got it corrected more or less. That's another thing he blames on my father. Claims Dad got in this doctor who was no good just because he was an old school pal——"

"He and your father don't get along?"

"Well, you know, Dad being a judge and all, he wanted Saul to study law. Saul wanted to be a philosophy teacher, or so he says now, but I think he wanted to be anything but a lawyer just to spite Dad—— Well, the hell with Noel Airman, do you mind? Take an old friend's advice and just steer clear of him this summer, that's all."

"Have no fear."

"Look, I'll say this for Saul, it's not that he's a bum or anything. If women fell down right and left wherever I walked I'd take advantage of it the same way, I'm sure—— Come on, there's a rumba, let's dance."

Billy telephoned her two or three times after that. She was as pleasant as possible, but she had a legitimate excuse in the Vagabond rehearsals, and he soon became discouraged.

It was different with Walter Wronken; he was persistent and disarming. "Look," he said once over the telephone, "let us assume I'm too young for you, and too funny-looking. It doesn't follow that you should cut me off. We're still interested in the same things, and I'm not disgusting company. You can't imagine what capital you're accumulating in heaven by seeing me occasionally. You're keeping me alive. You'd give a pint of blood to me if I were dying, wouldn't you?"

And she would laugh at such extravagance and agree to see him. For a while he could banter only over the telephone, and would dry up in her presence; but he became a little freer after spending several evenings with her. Once he embarrassed her by coming uninvited to a Vagabond rehearsal; he might have been the son of the director, so young did he look in that group. She scolded him, but allowed him to come out for coffee with her afterward, and she was struck by the shrewdness of his comments, especially on her own playing. He completely grasped what she was trying to do with her part.

"You have lots of sense—about some things," she said, raising her voice over the clatter of cutlery. They were in an Automat. She had insisted on paying for her own coffee, and there was a little soreness between them.

"I'm brilliant." He bit a doughnut in half as though he were angry at it.

"Or very conceited."

"Both. One trait doesn't exclude the other. Look at Shaw."

"Well, don't be so obvious about it, my boy, at least till you've got a beard like Shaw's. It's not attractive in you."

"Don't you call me 'my boy.' Do you know the exact difference in our ages? One year, three weeks, and five days."

"That might as well be ten years, Wally, when the girl's the older one."

He slumped over his coffee, a picture of gloom. "It's true. But it shouldn't be, Marge. It's a miserable trick of time, a mistake in simple arithmetic by the gods. It shouldn't mean anything at all."

"If you behave we can be very good friends. I like you. Don't look so tragic."

"Well, all right, I'm willing to play Marchbanks to your Candida— for the time being."

"No, thanks. Candida at nineteen, indeed! You'd have to be four years old, at that rate. Sometimes you act four. Just be yourself and let me be myself. Don't get silly ideas about me, that's the main thing. I'm just another girl."

He looked at her, his head tilted in Noel's way. "Okay," he said, "you're just another girl. I'll have to remember that."

The Vagabonds did their last show early in April, and after that Marjorie had nothing to do with herself but go to school and wait for life to begin again at South Wind.

College was beginning to seem a worn-out game to her. She was bored, bored in her very soul, with the overheated classrooms, the scarred chairs with one bloated arm for writing, the gongs ringing at the dragging end of dragging hours, the smell of chalk dust, the cramping weight of textbooks under an arm, the corridors full of giggling freshmen with smeary lipstick, the frumpy teachers nagging forever about numbers and words. She had been going to school since she was six. In the dismal routine of the free city colleges, which squeezed out graduating classes like sausages every six months, she would graduate next February. Several of her classmates were getting married, and did not intend to return after the summer for the last half year. She would have done the same gladly, had she had someone to marry.

She was invited to a few of the weddings. Each time it was a shock to see a Hunter senior transformed into a bride floating in a white brilliant mist, on the arm of an awkward trapped-looking young man in formal clothes. It made Marjorie feel that time was closing a vise on her. She could not help comparing the bridegrooms to Noel Airman, and the comparison made them seem pretty poor prizes; but what consolation was that? She meant nothing to Airman.

Several of the Vagabonds kept calling her for dates, but it was so dull to be with them that she could hardly stay awake; she much preferred to sit at home reading. She went through all the novels at the nearest lending library and then began reading old novels, just to have something to read; and she was rather astonished to find that books like *Anna Karenina* and *Madame Bovary* were spellbinding. Perversely, perhaps to prove to herself that the indifferent marks in her college work had been a matter of choice and not of ability, she worked hard at her studies, though she had never been less interested in them. She took a grouchy satisfaction in accumulating a number of A's.

She went for long walks on Riverside Drive. The soft April air blowing across the blue river, the smell of the blossoming cherry and crab-apple trees, the swaying of their bunched pink branches, filled her with bittersweet melancholy. Often she would slip a book of poetry in her pocket, and would drop on a bench, after walking far, to read Byron or Shelley or Keats. Her yearning for Noel had opened her heart to the magic in these old words, which had been so dryly chopped up and rammed down her throat all her life by the inhuman hags who taught English.

Sometimes she walked over to Central Park. Every yellow splash of forsythia reminded her of Marsha, and the wonderful first months of their friendship. The horseback riders splattering by on the muddy bridle paths brought back the picture of herself, a scared and foolhardy seventeen, bumping along on Prince Charming, and then falling off. She could remember how wise and mature and desirable a man Sandy Goldstone had seemed; she could remember just as clearly how he had dwindled to an ineffectual fool. She would stare up at the windows of her old apartment in the El Dorado, and wonder if some bright-eyed girl of seventeen was standing behind the white curtains in a nightgown, gloating over the golden look of the world.

Wally telephoned one May morning after a long silence. "Ever been to the Cloisters?"

"No. What's the Cloisters?"

"The Cloisters is heaven on earth. Let's drive up there tomorrow morning. The lilacs are in bloom. I want you to see the lilacs."

Tomorrow was Saturday. She felt that Wally should be discouraged, but this was hardly a date, a Saturday-morning drive to look at lilacs. "Well, sure, Wally. It's nice of you to think of me."

Next morning it was pouring rain. She perched on the window seat of her bedroom in a lounging robe, reading a new novel greedily. It was a very agreeable way to pass the time, with rain clattering on the panes and the blue-gray light of a storm falling across the page. The hero of the novel looked like Noel Airman, even to the red-blond hair, and he was the same kind of dashing reprobate. When the doorbell rang she paid no attention to it. In a moment her mother poked her head into the room. "That boy Wally is here. Says you have a date to go driving. Is he crazy, coming out in this rain?"

"Oh, Lord. Tell him to wait a minute, Mom." She glanced at herself in the full-length mirror on the closet door. Her hair was combed, but her face was wanly empty of makeup, and the robe was simply a maroon wool thing, not quite covering the frilly bottom of her nightgown. To show herself in this condition to a date was impossible; but she hated to get all dressed and painted just to tell Wally to go home and stop being an idiot. She decided that Wally wasn't a date, exactly, more like a younger brother; and she went out into the living room tying the belt of her robe more closely. He was sitting at the piano in his yellow raincoat, gaily playing one of Noel's songs. "Wally, sometimes I think you have no sense. D'you expect me to go driving in this weather?"

"Why, sure, Marge. This rain is a break. We'll have the Cloisters all to ourselves."

"You'll have it all to yourself, boy. I know enough to stay in out of the wet if you don't."

The narrow shoulders sagged; the big head drooped; the long nose seemed to grow longer. She had seen dogs make this instant change from frisky joy to deep gloom, but never a human being. "Oh, look, Wally, I'm glad you came, just give me a minute to put on some clothes. We'll sit around and drink coffee and talk about the summer."

"Okay," he said mournfully.

When she came out again, hastily dressed as for a school day, he was slouched in an armchair, still wearing the raincoat. "What's the matter with you?" she said.

"Marge, I guess you haven't ever lived in the country. The best time to look at flowers is in the rain."

"I don't think you'll ever smile again," she said, laughing, "if we don't go to see those lilacs."

"Well, I do believe you'll like them."

"What the devil. I've done stupider things. Let's go."

As often happens, Marjorie was glad Wally had dragged her out, once they were driving along the river. She had forgotten how snug and exciting it was to roll through a rainstorm in a car, especially a new powerful one like Wally's father's Buick; to be dry, and cushioned at one's ease, while the storm whistled at the windows and beat on the roof, and the windshield wipers danced to and fro, wiping patches of clarity in a blurred gray world. She accepted a mentholated cigarette and curled on the seat. She did not have the habit of smoking yet, but mentholated cigarettes always seemed less sinful to her, almost medicine or candy. "This is fun," she said. "Sorry I was a slug about it."

"This is nothing," Wally said happily. "Wait."

They passed under the colossal piers of the bridge, turned away from the bubbling black river, and drove through an arch and up a steep rocky road. "See?" he said, as they pulled into a deserted parking space. "Saturday morning, but we have it to ourselves."

The medieval museum on the bluff overlooking the Hudson was new to Marjorie. Strolling through the Gothic corridors, she said, "How on earth did you discover this?"

"Fine arts course."

Their steps echoed in the dank stone galleries. The gorgeous tapestries, the great wooden saints and madonnas, the jeweled swords and suits of armor, the vaulted halls, all woke in her mind the atmosphere of the novel she had been reading; she could picture turning a corner in one of these empty corridors and coming on the tall blond hero. Wally, shambling along in his flat-footed way, with his hands in the pockets of his yellow raincoat, and the straight black hair falling over his eyes, was a comic misfit in this setting. But she was feeling very kindly toward him, all the same. He was giving her the kind of explorer's pleasure Marsha had first opened to her when they had gone to concerts and art galleries together.

They had coffee in a bleak empty dining room. "Game for a walk in the gardens?" Wally said. "I think the rain's letting up."

"Sure, I'm game."

The trees were dripping copiously, so that it still seemed to be raining; but when they walked into an open space among the flower beds they saw that the storm was over. White clouds tumbling and rolling overhead were uncovering patches of blue. Rich perfume rose on the damp air from purple banks of iris, and across the river a shaft of sunlight was whitening the great cables of the bridge. A quiet breeze stirred the flowers, shaking raindrops from them. "Ah, Lord, it's beautiful, Wally," Marjorie said. He took her hand and she allowed him to hold it; if a palm could feel remote and respectful, Wally's did. He led her around a corner of thick bushes into a curving shadowy path filled with a curious watery lavender light.

It was an avenue solidly arched and walled with blooming lilacs. The smell, sweet and poignant beyond imagining, saturated the air; it struck her senses with the thrill of music. Water dripped from the massed blooms on Marjorie's upturned face as she walked along the lane hand in hand with Wally. She was not sure what was rain and what was tears on her face. She wanted to look up at lilacs and rolling white clouds and patchy blue sky forever, breathing this sweet air. It seemed to her that, whatever ugly illusions existed outside this lane of lilacs, there must be a God, after all, and that He must be good.

She heard Wally say, "I kind of thought you would like it." The voice brought her out of a near-trance. She stopped, turned, and looked at him. He was ugly, and young, and pathetic. He was looking at her with shining eyes.

"Wally, thank you." She put her arms around his neck—he was taller than she, but not much—and kissed him on the mouth. The pleasure of the kiss lay all in expressing her gratitude, and that it did fully and satisfyingly. It meant nothing else. He held her close while she kissed him, and loosed her the moment she stepped away. He peered at her, his mouth slightly open. He seemed about to say something, but no words came. They were holding each other's hands, and raindrops were dripping on them from the lilacs.

After a moment she uttered a low laugh. "Well, why do you look at me like that? Do I seem so wicked? You've been kissed by a girl before."

Wally said, putting the back of his hand to his forehead, "It doesn't seem so now." He shook his head and laughed. "I'm going to plant lilac lanes all over town." His voice was very hoarse.

"It won't help," she said firmly, putting her arm through his, and starting to walk again, "that was the first one and the last, my lad."

He said nothing. When they reached the end of the lane they turned back, and paced the length of it slowly. Rain dripped on the path with a whispering sound. "It's no use," she said after a while.

"What?"

"It's fading. I guess your nerves can't go on vibrating that way. It's becoming just a lane full of lilacs."

"Then let's leave." Wally quickened his steps, and they were out of the lane and in the bright open air again.

They drove downtown in sunlight along a drying roadway, with the windows open and warm fragrant air eddying into the Buick. "Come up and have lunch," she said when he stopped at her house.

"I have to go straight to the library, Marge. Term paper due Monday. Thanks anyway."

"Thanks for the lilacs, Wally. It was pure heaven."

She opened the door. Suddenly his hand was on her arm. "Maybe not," he said.

She looked at him. "Maybe not what?"

"Maybe it wasn't the last. The kiss."

With a light laugh, she said, "Wally, darling, don't lose sleep over it. I don't know. Maybe when we find such lilacs again."

He nodded, and drove off.

She walked into an explosion when she entered the apartment. Her mother, sitting on the edge of a chair in the living room, stood as Marjorie came in. "Hello. I hope you had a nice time."

"Very nice," said Marjorie, kicking off her overshoes. A battle alarm rang in her mind at her mother's tone and manner.

"You generally manage to have a nice time," said Mrs. Morgenstern, approaching with her arms folded.

Folded arms were serious. Marjorie searched vainly in her mind for the provocation. She had really been unusually passive and sinless in recent weeks. "I try," she said as she hung up her coat.

"Try. I'll say you try. You'll try anything. You'll even try to go to Sodom if I'll let you, which I will over my dead body."

Now Marjorie saw on the foyer table the ripped-open envelope with the South Wind emblem in the return-address corner. She sighed. "Mom, I thought we settled long ago that you weren't to read my mail." She picked up the letter and walked into the living room. It was a mimeographed notice, signed by Greech, of a meeting of the social staff.

"I opened it by mistake. I thought it was a circular. How should I know you're getting letters from Sodom?"

"Well, as long as you opened it by mistake, why not pretend you didn't open it, and we'll all be happy? I'm hungry——"

"Is it true or isn't it?"

"Is what true, Mom?"

"Are you or aren't you on the social staff of Sodom?"

"Isn't that my business?"

"Excuse me, it's my business if my daughter decides to go to the dogs. At least I should be notified."

"Nobody's going to the dogs."

"If you intend to go work in Sodom you're going to the dogs."

Marjorie faced her mother. She was a couple of inches the taller of the two. Mrs. Morgenstern was looking up at her with her nose wrinkled, arms stiff at her sides. "Please, Mom, won't you come out of the Middle Ages? South Wind is not Sodom. It's a perfectly respectable summer place, much more respectable than the Prado, if you want to know. You were perfectly willing to take me to the Prado, where more damn necking goes on night and day, and those divorcees in tight corsets are always flirting with the damn musicians, kosher or not kosher——"

"Where does all this language come from, Marjorie? Damn, damn. Did you pick that up at Sodom? Or from Marsha?"

Very wearily Marjorie said, "I haven't seen Marsha in nearly a year and you know it."

"Yes, and when I said you'd get tired of her, what did you say? She would be your dear bosom pal for the rest of your life, I was an old fool from the Middle Ages, I was this, and I was that. Well, who was the fool? I was right about Marsha and I'm right about South Wind. It's no place for you, Marjorie. All right, some decent people may go there—older people, people who know how to handle themselves—you'll be a babe in the woods, you're only nineteen——"

"Nineteen and a half and I'll be nearer twenty in July. You were married at eighteen."

All the lines in her mother's face pulled down satirically. "You're comparing us? I was on my own at fifteen, earning a living. When I was eighteen my hands were rougher than yours will be when you're fifty. I went bleeding and yelling in a taxi, from a sweatshop on Spring Street to the hospital, when you were born—a sweatshop where I broke my back sixteen hours a day and made three dollars a week——"

"What's all this? Would you rather I hadn't gone to college? Plenty of girls I knew in high school are working now. I've done what I thought you wanted, nothing else——"

"Darling, of course we wanted you to go to college. Papa and I want you children to be everything we couldn't be. That's why I don't want you to be broken to pieces at nineteen in Sodom."

Marjorie passionately launched the argument that to become an actress she needed the training she would get at South Wind. But Mrs. Morgenstern was at her most irritating. "Actress, my eye. A good husband and children is what you'll want in a year or two, darling, once you've had a taste of dragging like a tramp around Broadway." Seeing her daughter's angered look, she added hastily, "Maybe I'm wrong, maybe you're another Ethel Barrymore. All right. Let's say so. Did Ethel Barrymore have to go to a place like South Wind? When she was nineteen there were no such places. She still became a great actress."

After running into a couple of more roadblocks like this, which Mrs. Morgenstern could throw up in an argument with unending ingenuity, Marjorie said, "Well, I don't exactly know what you can do about it. I'm going, that's the long and the short of it."

"Suppose I forbid you?"

"It makes no sense. I have a career to think of. I can't give it up because you have a wild prejudice against adult camps."

Mrs. Morgenstern regarded her with silent surprise and a tinge of grudging respect. She was accustomed to much noise and flailing about by Marjorie in such disputes. Relatively calm determination was something else, something new. She said cautiously, "Papa will feel exactly as I do."

Marjorie answered with the same caution, "I think I can talk to him. I can't to you."

"And if he says no?"

"I'm going to South Wind."

"Anyway?"

"Anyway."

"I see. And afterward?"

"What about afterward?"

"You still have to finish school."

"I know."

"You expect to come home, eat our food, have us buy your clothes, as though nothing had happened?"

"Now, Mama, are you suggesting that you'll tell me never to darken your door again?"

After a short hesitation Mrs. Morgenstern said, "Well, you say yourself you're an independent woman, with a career of your own to think of. You don't need our advice, our guidance. You shouldn't need our support."

Marjorie looked at her mother for a long time, her face very pale. She said nothing, but slowly she began to smile.

"What are you smiling at? Let me in on the joke." There was the faintest faltering in Mrs. Morgenstern's tone.

Marjorie felt like a prisoner who, leaning against a cell door, tumbles unexpectedly into sunlight and freedom. "I don't, Mom," she said. "I don't need your support. Remember, you said if I weren't careful I'd turn out useful? I am useful. I type. I take shorthand. And I'm not bad-looking. I'm worth fifteen dollars a week on the open market. It's no fortune, but girls are living on it, heaven knows, all over town. Let me know when you want me to move, Mom."

The mother stared. Marjorie gave her a minute to think of an answer. There was none. She patted her affectionately on the arm. "I'm hungry, Mom dear," she said. "Guess I'll wash up."

She walked out of the living room, as off a stage, in a gentle queenly way, hearing phantom cheers and applause from her many vanished selves.

Chapter 14. MARJORIE AT SOUTH WIND

Marjorie came to South Wind on a lovely June afternoon.

There was no sheriff waiting with a subpoena to take her back to

New York; and when in her bungalow (the same one Karen Blair had occupied) she opened her trunk, Mrs. Morgenstern did not pop out at her. Neither occurrence would have entirely startled the girl. The mother's defeat in the first skirmish over South Wind had been temporary; she had rallied her forces for a month of energetic nagging, snipping, fault-finding, and obstructing, only to surrender with queer docile suddenness a week before Marjorie's departure. She had seen the girl off at the train in excellent humor, even calling out her standard parting joke as Marjorie went up the steps of the coach car, "Don't do anything I wouldn't do." Marjorie had made the standard reply, "Thanks, that gives me plenty of rope," only halfheartedly, wondering what devilment her mother was up to. Mrs. Morgenstern was a last-ditch fighter by nature, and her philosophic resignation struck the girl as extremely suspicious.

Nevertheless, though Marjorie could hardly believe it, here she was in South Wind. She unpacked, still expecting the telegram, the telephone call, the sudden turn of events that would send her home. Nothing happened. She walked down to the social hall with a book under her arm, feeling more secure and more triumphant with each passing quarter hour; and at the bar she bought a pack of cigarettes for the first time in her life. She still did not enjoy smoking, so she chose Wally's mentholated brand; and strolling out on the lawn, puffing a cigarette, she felt quite grand and grown up.

Her elation was somewhat spoiled by the seediness of the camp. Seen by daylight in June, after a winter of neglect and hard weather, South Wind radiated little of the glamor it had had a year ago by moonlight. The fountain in the center of the overgrown lawn was dry. The spout, a rusty iron pipe, stood out a foot above the cracked concrete cascade, which was splotched with sickly green moss. All the buildings needed paint. The white had gone to dirty rust-streaked gray, and the gilding had mostly peeled off, showing tin or wood underneath. The dock was being torn, sawed, and hammered at by workmen. Three tan boys in sweaters and bathing trunks were slapping red paint on the mottled canoes. Everything seemed smaller—buildings, lawn, fountain, lake, oak trees—everything. In her winter visions the lawn had been a public park, the oaks towering old monarchs, the social hall a great building marvelously transplanted from Radio City; she had honestly remembered them that way. But the lawn was just a good-sized hotel lawn, the trees were just trees; and the social hall was not much more than a big barn topped by a phony modernistic shaft, which badly needed replastering.

But there was Airman himself, coming out of the camp office! Weedy, golden-haired, long-striding, in the black turtle-neck sweater that seemed to be his badge of office, he at least, of all the attractions of South Wind, retained his first lustre. He saw her, and turned his steps across the lawn. "Hi, Marjorie. Got here at last?"

"About half an hour ago, Noel."

"Good. Welcome."

"Thanks." Her face was stiff in a smile. "How about the show this weekend? Can I help?"

"No, it's all set. Just a scratch revue, old stuff—there won't be two hundred people here. Got another cigarette?" But when she held out the pack, he fended it off. "Good God, you too? You and Wally. The younger generation certainly has depraved tastes." He pointed to the book. "What are you reading?"

She handed him Plato's *Republic* at once, glad of the chance to cover her cursed mistake of buying Wally's brand of cigarettes.

She really was reading the *Republic*. Shortly after Billy Ehrmann had informed her that his brother was interested in philosophy, she had found herself taking philosophy books out of the library. It had seemed natural to do so, just as, when George Drobes had been her god, it had seemed natural, in fact inevitable, to elect biology as her major subject in college. Biology had now become stupefyingly dull to her; Plato and John Dewey, on the other hand, seemed full of good things, and amazingly easy to read.

Airman wrinkled his nose at the book and at her. "What are you doing, catching up on next fall's homework?"

"No, I'm just reading it."

"Just reading Plato?"

"That's right."

"You're silly. Why don't you get hold of a decent mystery?" He gave back the book.

"I wish I could. I think I've read 'em all."

He rubbed his elbow, smiling at her with a trace of interest. "Seen my brother Billy lately?"

"I don't see your brother Billy." It sounded too sharp; but his kindly tone flicked her nerves. "I mean, years ago when I was a freshman we ran around in the same crowd. That's all."

He ran a knuckle over his upper lip, inspecting her. "Maybe we can use you in the show at that. Come along."

Most of the staff people were the same. Carlos Ringel, fatter and very pasty-faced, was waddling around the stage, shouting to someone in the wings, who was shouting back. The performers sat here and there on the floor of the hall, dressed in sweaters and slacks; several of the girls were knitting. The couple who had done the jungle dance last year were stomping near the piano, doing a Hindu dance. The rehearsal pianist was the same, and he seemed to be chewing the same cigar, and to need the same shave. Noel introduced her to everyone as Marjorie Morgenstern; she lacked the courage to correct him. Then he turned her over to a little plump man with tiny fluttering hands, Puddles Podell, a comedian who had exchanged some horribly coarse jokes with Marsha in the bar last year. Puddles took Marjorie out on the back porch of the hall and taught her a burlesque sketch called *Fifty Pounds of Plaster*.

"It's strictly the hotel bit, sweetheart," he said, acting out the scene with a thousand little hand gestures. "Just say whatever comes into your head. We're honeymooners, see—affa-scaffa, wasn't it a beautiful wedding, abba-dabba, at last we can be alone, abba-dabba——" The point lay in two lines at the end. The honeymooners rushed indignantly on stage, supposedly out of the bridal suite, to complain to the desk clerk.

"What's the matter with this hotel?" Marjorie had to say. "The ceiling in our room is coming down. Fifty pounds of plaster just fell on my chest." Whereupon Puddles said, "Damn right—and if it had fallen two minutes sooner, it would have broken my back."

When the joke emerged, Marjorie turned scarlet and burst out laughing. The comedian paused and stared at her. "Are you laughing at the *bit?*"

They played the skit on the dance floor for Noel, who slouched low in a folding chair. "I guess she'll be okay," Puddles said to Noel. "What do you think?"

Noel nodded. "Marjorie, it's a longish road from *Fifty Pounds of Plaster* to *Candida*—but nobody can say you're not on your way. Try it on stage, Puddles."

Wally Wronken came into the social hall just as the sketch was starting, and squatted on the floor beside Noel's chair. Almost at once he began talking earnestly to Noel, who listened, shrugged, and raised his hand. "Hold everything—— Margie, do you object to acting in this skit?"

"Object? Why, no."

"That's not the point, Noel," Wally said. "It isn't funny with her in it, *that's* the point. She looks too pretty on stage, too wholesome."

Puddles came to the footlights. "That's what's bothering me, Noel. We always used one of the strippers in this bit. Margie looks like my baby sister or something, it kills the gag."

Glaring at Wally, Marjorie exclaimed, "Look, I'm *delighted* to do it, please let's get on with it."

Noel shook his head, yawning. "I'm not very sharp today. Thanks, Wally. You're out, Margie, sorry. We'll get someone else to do this immortal scene."

She stalked off the stage and out of the social hall, humiliated, furious. When Wally tried to talk to her, she cut him dead.

It was only four o'clock; two hours before dinnertime, and nothing to do. She went up to the camp office, hoping to make herself useful there. But it was an utter chaos of tumbled furniture, strewn papers, stained cloths, and paint cans and ladders; it was being repainted a very fishy-smelling green. Greech ran here and there in his shirt sleeves, his face streaked green, snatching up a ringing telephone, bawling at the painters. He shouted when he saw her, "Get out, get out. No time for you, no use for you. Clear out. See me Sunday. Don't come in here again."

Marjorie wandered down a curving road behind the dining hall toward the tennis courts, thinking that her first day at South Wind could not have been worse if her mother had planned every detail. She was a bit of female clutter on the landscape; moreover, she was Marjorie Morgenstern—stamped, branded with the name for good, all in a few seconds. Her irritation and anger focused on Wally Wronken; she felt quite capable of not speaking to him all summer. She lit another cigarette, but it reminded her of Wally, and it tasted awful anyway. She threw it away after one puff.

At that moment she saw the Uncle.

He was carrying a tin tub of garbage down wooden steps from the back door of the kitchen. She recognized him instantly, though he wore a kitchen uniform: small white hat, white undershirt and trousers, and an amazingly dirty apron. There couldn't be two men in the world with such a paunch; besides, as she stood frozen in surprise, watching him empty the garbage, she faintly heard him singing the song to which they had danced with the turkey leg. "Uncle! Uncle, for heaven's sake! Hello!" She ran up a slope through daisies and long grass. "What on *earth* are you doing here, Uncle?"

"Havaya, Modgerie! Vait, I come to you! Up here it don't smell so fency. Vait, vait, I come down." She halted midway on the slope. He approached, grinning broadly, mopping his streaming red face with a handkerchief. "Is a surprise, no?"

"Surprise? I'm stunned——"

"Modgerie, ve keep it a secret, no? By Modgerie and the Uncle a little secret. Better ve don't tell your mama, she'll only make a big hoo-hah. I tell you, darling, by the golf course vas too lonesome. Here is more fun, nice fellers, plenty to eat—hard vork, but vot is vork? I make plenty money, too—not like by the golf course——"

"The golf course?" she said, more and more bewildered. "What's the golf course got to do with it? Why are you here?"

The Uncle smiled in a placating way, showing the black gap in his teeth. "You vent to find me by the golf course, no? Your mama thinks I'm still there. Ve von't tell her notting different, vy does she have to know I'm a dishvasher?"

After Marjorie asked a good many questions, it came out that Mrs. Morgenstern had arranged a caretaker's job at South Wind for the Uncle, a week or so before Marjorie's departure. This explained her sudden mysterious good cheer, of course. She had succeeded in placing a chaperon of sorts over her daughter at "Sodom," after all. Greech had taken the Uncle on without salary (and with Mrs. Morgenstern paying the railroad fare) as a kind of janitor and watchman for the lodge on the golf course. But then two dishwashers had quit. Greech had offered him the kitchen job at twenty-five dollars a week, and he had accepted it gladly.

It penetrated the old man's mind very slowly that Marjorie was amazed to find him at the camp at all. "Vot? She didn't tell you notting? How is it possible?"

"She didn't, Uncle. Not a word. I swear I thought I was seeing a ghost for a minute."

"A nice fat ghost, hah?" He shook his head. "So! For you it's some disappointment, no? A fat old uncle you need around your neck, hah? Like a cholera, you need it. It's too bad, Modgerie, I'm sorry—your mama is a smart vun——"

"Uncle, it doesn't matter, really——"

"Listen, Modgerie, a mama remains a mama, she can't help it. By her it's still Friday night in the Bronx, the Uncle has to keep an eye on the baby. So vot? You think I spoil your fun, Modgerie? Have a good time, darling, vot do I know? I'm busy in the kitchen."

She had been looking at his hands uneasily. Now she caught one as he made a gesture. "Uncle, what's the matter? What are these?" There were several gaping little red wounds on his fat fingers. They were neither bleeding nor healing. They were like mouths, open, dry, and red.

With a laugh, Samson-Aaron pulled his hand away. "You vash dishes you get cut. Dishes break. Soap keeps vashing in the cuts, so they don't heal, so vot? You lay off from vashing dishes they heal up."

"I don't like the look of them. Did you see the doctor?" Marjorie stared at the red gaps.

"Modgerie please, it's notting." He put both hands behind his back. "Don't be like your mama, alvays questions."

"I just don't know if you ought to be doing this, Uncle."

"Vot, I'll disgrace you? Modgerie's uncle is Sam the dishvasher? I von't say a vord to nobody, depend on the Uncle."

She threw her arm around his neck. "It's not that. You're—— It's hard, dirty work, you know——"

"So? I never vashed dishes? I vashed dishes in the Catskills, Modgerie, before you vere born. Vot is it? Caretaker, vatchman, that's the jobs I don't like. Jobs for old men, for cripples. I'm strong like a horse—— Vait, I show you something." He fumbled under his apron, brought out a tattered sweat-blackened wallet, and pulled a snapshot from it. "Did you see yet a picture of Geoffrey's vife? Here, look at a doll, a sveetheart——"

Geoffrey had been married for six months. The picture showed him standing on the porch of a tiny house, in shirtsleeves, with his arm around a thin girl in flat shoes and a house dress. She was squinting into the sun, and her hair was pulled flat in a plain knot, so Marjorie could form no notion of her looks. Geoffrey, fatter and with much less hair, was grinning foolishly, his chest thrust out, a beer bottle in his hand.

"She's lovely, Uncle. What's her name?"

"Sylvia. Her father is a doctor in Albany, a big specialist. You know vot? She calls him Milton. Says it sounds more like him than Geoffrey, God bless her. A doll, hah?" He showed the black gap again in a happy grin, curiously like Geoffrey's, and lowered his voice. "Modgerie, in October they have a baby already."

"That's wonderful."

"You see vy I vash dishes maybe, Modgerie? Vy should I take money from Geoffrey ven he needs it? I send it back! Comes October I send *him* money. For the baby, a present. The baby should sleep in the finest crib money could buy. A crib from Samson-Aaron the gobbage pail. A good idea, hah?"

A voice roared from the rear of the dining hall. "Hey *Sam*, you fat old bastard, you drop dead or something?"

"Okay, okay——" yelled the Uncle. He chuckled. "That's Paul, the other dishvasher. A good feller, a Hungarian, plays good chess. So?" He caressed Marjorie's cheek lightly. "I see you sometimes, Modgerie, hah? I got a secret, you don't tell Mama, I don't tell her your secrets. It's a bargain? I see you sometimes ven nobody's looking, I give you maybe a Hershey bar." He ambled toward the kitchen, shouting, "Vot's the matter, Paul, you vash a dish good and break your back?" He toiled up the stairs, his paunch shaking, waved at Marjorie from the top stair, and disappeared.

Marjorie marched straight to the public telephone booths in the main building across the hall from the office, and put in a call to her mother. The fishy fumes of the office paint brought tears to her eyes. In the next booth Mr. Greech was alternately growling and howling incomprehensibly at his secretary in New York. The operator told her that the circuits to New York were busy. She went out on the porch to escape the fumes while she waited. The afternoon had clouded over; a dank wind was lashing the oak trees, and there was a smell of rain in the air. Marjorie dropped dejectedly on the porch steps, her chin resting on her hands.

All magic was leaking out of South Wind, like air out of a punctured tire. She liked Samson-Aaron; no, she loved him, shabby old glutton though he was. But the injection into South Wind of a family face soured the very light of day. South Wind had been, in Marjorie's visions, a new clear world, a world where a grimy Bronx childhood and a fumbling Hunter adolescence were forgotten dreams, a world where she could at last find herself and be herself—clean, fresh, alone, untrammelled by parents. In a word, it had been the world of Marjorie Morningstar. The shrinking of the camp's glamor, her own lowly status, the mischance with the name, were bad enough. And here came the Uncle, dragging behind him the long chain of all the old rusty realities. She could feel the weight of that chain; she could feel the clamp, cold on her ankle, fixed there by the invisible far-stretching hand of her mother. It was unendurable.

"Rain again, for Christ's sake!" grated Mr. Greech, making her jump. He stood directly behind her, scowling at the black sky, slapping the flashlight on his palm, looking fully as satanic as he had last year. Being on South Wind soil did something to Mr. Greech. "When in the name of hell am I going to get these buildings painted? Do you realize we've had rain for fourteen straight days?" He bellowed this last observation directly at Marjorie.

"I'm sorry," she said.

He looked at her with a blink, as though a stone had spoken. "What? What did you say?"

"Mr. Greech—pardon me, I hate to trouble you—it's a small matter——"

"What, what?"

"My uncle—he's washing dishes, I see."

"Who? Oh yes, old Sam. Well, sure, he'd rather make twenty-five a week than nothing a week. So would I, by God, and it doesn't look as though I will this season."

"It's just—well, it's hard work."

"Of course it is. That's why I pay him."

"He's—well, he's an old man——"

"What's all this, now? See here, your mother told me he's stronger than I am. He's not chained in the kitchen. He jumped at the job. He seems to be thriving. In fact, the cook tells me he's eating like ten men. I'm going to talk to him about that, by the way, I'm not running a hog-fattening farm in that kitchen. Now, what exactly are *you* fussing about? What's eating *you?*" He thrust at her with the flashlight on each *you.*

She withered under his tone and his stare. "Well, I just thought—I don't know—I suppose if it was his own idea . . ." She trailed off. Greech was walking away from her into the office.

In a few minutes the telephone call went through. As Marjorie waited, receiver in hand, to hear her mother's voice, this thought flashed through her mind: *When I object to her sending the Uncle here without my knowledge she'll say, "What's the matter, are you planning to do something up there you don't want us to know about?"* She was trying to think of a crushing answer when her mother came on the line. After assuring her that she was well and the camp was splendid, Marjorie said, "Quite a surprise you prepared for me!"

"What surprise?" said Mrs. Morgenstern blandly.

"Samson-Aaron."

"Oh. The Uncle. Well, how is he?"

"Just fine."

"That's good. Give him my regards."

After a little pause Marjorie said, "Don't you think you might have told me he'd be here?"

"Didn't I?"

"Of course you didn't."

"Well, that's right, I guess it was the week when you were so busy with exams. Well, you have no objections to his being there, do you?"

"It's a little late to be asking me that, I would say."

"What's the matter," said Mrs. Morgenstern, "are you planning to do something up there that you wouldn't want us to know about?"

"I've already done it," said Marjorie. "I've been having an affair with Mr. Greech since March. How do you suppose I got the job?"

"Don't be smart."

"He's washing dishes."

"Who?"

"The Uncle."

"What! No, he isn't. He's a caretaker."

"Not any more. He makes money washing dishes. Wants to buy a nice present for his grandchild."

There was a silence. Mrs. Morgenstern said, "Well, I can see that's not too nice. Your uncle washing dishes. I'll write him to go back to caretaker."

"Let him alone! You're hopeless, Mom."

"What are you so touchy about? One of these days you'll be glad the Uncle is there."

"I'm sure that's why you did it, Mom—to accommodate me."

"What do you want of me, Marjorie? Why did you call? Do you want me to write him to come home? Say so, and I'll do it, that's all."

Several seconds went by, while Marjorie weighed the neat impasse. It would have been hard for her under any circumstances to force the Uncle out of South Wind, once he was there. Now that she had seen his pride and pleasure in earning money, it was impossible. "Thank you, Mama, I don't want anything. I thought you might be interested to know that he's all right, and that I'm all right, and that everything couldn't be lovelier."

"It fills me with joy, dear."

"Fine. Give my love to Papa."

"I will. Goodbye. Don't do anything I wouldn't do."

"Thanks, Mom, that gives me plenty of rope. 'Bye."

Another round lost.

But once Marjorie became used to two unpleasant and very unwelcome facts: that she was still Marjorie Morgenstern, and that she was not likely to fascinate Noel Airman (at least not straight off), she perked up and began to enjoy South Wind. She hardly ever saw the Uncle; and if they did come on each other by accident they smiled and exchanged a few quick pleasant words, and that was all. It was still gratifying to look across the lake to Klabber's camp on a fresh sunny morning, and to realize how far she had come in a year. It was fun rehearsing in the shows, even if she did nothing but kick her legs in a chorus of office girls. She began to find a certain arid pleasure in the office work. Keeping her desk clean and severe, getting her work done on time, drawing a grunt of praise from Greech for letters typed up swiftly and without errors—however petty, these things were satisfying.

Every day the look of the camp improved. The weather turned fine, too. By the first of July, after a week of continual sunshine, the fountain was flowing, the grass was velvet-neat, the buildings were dazzling white and gold, and the grounds were alive with noisy merry people in summer clothes of carnival colors. They were a helter-skelter group of ordinary young New Yorkers; a few girls spoke with comic Brooklyn and Bronx grotesqueness, and a few of the men were excessively crude, but most of them were just like the young people she had known all her life. They ate, danced, drank, and played at all the sports with great gusto. Gaiety and freedom were in the air. The food Greech fed them was a curious mélange of traditional Jewish delicacies—gefilte fish, stuffed neck, chopped chicken liver—and traditional Jewish abominations, like shellfish, bacon, and ham; the guests devoured the delicacies and the abominations with equal relish. Marjorie had to comb the bacon off her eggs for the first week or so, until the waiter became used to her old-fashioned ways.

If South Wind was Sodom, it seemed to be a cheerful, outdoors sort of Sodom, where tennis, golf, steak roasts, and rumbas had replaced more classic and scandalous debaucheries. Marjorie did notice a lot of necking in canoes and on the moonlit porch outside the social hall, but there was nothing startling in that. Perhaps terrible sins were being committed on the grounds; but so far as her eyes could pierce there was nothing really wrong at South Wind. All was jocund and fair to see. She lost her curiosity about the guests after the first week or so. They were a blur of similar faces; part of the background—like the lake, the trees, the clouds—to the real life that went on among the people of the staff.

For the Fourth of July weekend, a crooner named Perry Baron came to South Wind to add glitter to the entertainment. He was a sort of second-class celebrity, good-looking but flabby, about thirty-five, with a yellow Cadillac convertible, a voluminous camel's hair coat with white pearl buttons, and rather strikingly limited intelligence. For some reason Baron took a strong fancy to Marjorie, from the first moment he saw her at the registry desk in the camp office. All weekend long he paid court to her, dancing with her, canoeing with her, driving her here and there in his yellow Cadillac, and requisitioning her from Airman as a girl to sing to when he performed. His most spectacular gesture was sending to New York for two dozen roses, which were delivered to Marjorie Friday evening by a truck which drove more than a hundred miles. If she had not been so desperately infatuated with Airman, Marjorie might have been overcome by all this; as it was, though flattered, she was bored. But since Baron treated her courteously, and since it was obvious that her stock in the camp was rising by the hour, she was pleasant to him, and put up with his extravagant antics as gracefully as possible.

Wally Wronken was the real sufferer in this turn of events. He mooned, he gloomed, he glared, he glowered, he got drunk, he stopped writing, he left rehearsals. Embarrassed by this display, Marjorie tried to make it up to Wally by praising his writing, asking him to dance with her, and so forth; but he snubbed her with proud Byronic agony.

At the end of the Saturday afternoon rehearsal, Airman came strolling up to her as she was pulling a sweater over her head. "Rushing off to dinner? How about a drink first?"

"Love a drink." She was glad that the sweater hid her face and muffled the excited tones of her voice. Until this moment he had paid no attention to her whatever, even at rehearsals, beyond moving her around the stage like a chair, or giving her directions prefaced with the meaningless "darling" which he used in addressing all the office-girl actresses.

They sat in a booth by the window. The sun was setting in immense smears of red and yellow on the purple lake. The floodlights had not yet been turned on, and a violet haze darkened the lawn and the white buildings. "Best time of the day," he murmured after a long pull at his highball. He was silent for a while, looking at her with his characteristic ironic smile. He was so far above her, she thought; yet his deformed elbow, resting awkwardly on the table, warmed her with pity and tenderness.

He seemed to notice her eyes on his elbow. He leaned back, folding his arms, ghost-thin in the black sweater. "I suppose you know that Wally's eating his heart out." She said nothing. He added, "I live next door to him. He comes shambling in and I have to listen to his moans. It's kind of repetitious, after brother Billy."

Marjorie pulled a cigarette out of his pack on the table and lit it with a moment's yellow glare in the gloom.

"Not talking, Marjorie?"

She puffed at the cigarette, looking straight at him.

"You will admit," he said, "that a yellow Cadillac and roses from Trepel's sent a hundred miles are crushing competition for a college boy. But it's all wrong, you know. Wally's worth ten Perry Barons. Baron's a faded carbon copy of Crosby. Wally has talent. You mustn't be dazzled because that oaf throws around the few dollars he earns. Singers are like that."

"Noel, pardon me, but what business is it of yours?"

His eyes widened and gleamed. "Question of staff morale. I like Wally. Furthermore, he's writing some fine material and making my life much easier. I don't want him demoralized."

"I see." After another silence she said, "It would probably help if I set you right on a notion that seems fixed in your mind somehow." She took a slow drag on her cigarette. He did not unnerve her any more; he stimulated her. She felt that she had come to a tight turn in life, and that she was going to round it smoothly and well. "I like Wally too. I also know that he has a crush on me. It's too bad, but I've gotten over many a crush in my time, and I'm sure Wally will get over his. What puzzles me is your impression that there's some kind of romance between him and me. It's a bit annoying. I'm more than a year older than Wally, Noel. He's eighteen and a half and I'm nearly twenty. Now as for Perry Baron, he has nothing but the nicest things to say about you. That being the case, I'm not quite sure which of you is the oaf."

He looked surprised; then he laughed, a low, pleasant laugh. "Okay. Wally's eighteen and a half and you're nearly twenty. From your viewpoint I suppose you and he belong to different generations. But look here, you were at the opening of Wally's show with him——"

"Certainly. He asked me, and I was proud to go. I admire him just as you do, he's extremely clever. I've seen him a few times since. I can envy the girl he'll really fall in love with and marry some day, but I know perfectly well it isn't me. So will he, one of these days. Maybe next week, for all I know. I've snapped out of crushes faster than that."

He nodded approvingly, hanging his elbow over the back of the chair, and running a knuckle along his upper lip. "Good, Marjorie, I'm glad I talked to you. I'll be less sympathetic now when Wally starts languishing. In fairness to him, though, you've grown up terrifically in the past year, you know, while he's still pecking his way out of the egg. Girls do hit this time when they grow like mad. I won't annoy you any more by bracketing you with Wally, and I apologize for the comments on Perry Baron. Okay? Let's go to dinner."

"Okay."

As they stood he said, "I can't help hoping, all the same, that you won't decide, in the mature insight of nearly twenty, that Baron is the storm god come to earth. Such things happen, Lord knows, only too often. He really is just a slimy slug, you know, an overgrown jellyfish that shaves and sings. I hate to see a nice girl run over by a rented yellow Cadillac."

They were walking past the bar piano. He stopped at the keyboard and rippled a chord; then he sat on the stool and moved his fingers idly, making soft chiming waves of sound. "I'll tell you something, Margie—the prettiest and cleverest girl I ever knew threw herself away on an imbecile, a four-footed animal posing in human clothes, because he could do two things—rumba well, and treat her badly. Every other man she'd ever met had fallen at her feet. His indifference was a piquant novelty. He was so dull, and his tastes were so gross, that he actually didn't think much of her. So she pursued him, and forced him to marry her, and now his father supports them both, ostensibly by letting his son manage a few dry-cleaning stores. She might have been the wife of an ambassador, a playwright, a senator, with elegance and distinction. She did this in the wisdom of nearly nineteen. The wisdom of nearly twenty is another matter, to be sure."

He struck a clashing dissonance; then, after a silent instant, he began to play one of his own waltzes, a sentimental tune that Marjorie loved. She stood behind him for a few moments, listening. Then she said softly, "She must have been someone you liked pretty well."

"Oh yes, she was," Noel said, playing on and not looking up, "in fact I still like her pretty well. My older sister, Monica. She's thirty-two now and has three children. She's as pretty as you, and looks as young."

When Marjorie glanced back, from the doorway of the bar, Noel was stooped over the piano, playing on in the amber gloom. He did not seem to know that she was leaving. But just as she was stepping through the door he said, "Wait." He broke off his playing, came to her, and leaned against the doorway. "Am I wrong, or when you were here last summer did you utter several bright sayings about my lighting effects?"

"Well, I remember saying they were brilliant and marvelous, and so forth."

"I see. No wonder I retained the impression that you showed precocious good judgment. Well, come clean, do you really know anything about lights?"

"I—well, you know, kid-camp stuff. But I did read up on it a lot."

"Wally wants to do some directing, and he's carrying a big writing load. That may be one reason he's overwrought. I'd like to take him off the switchboard, and it occurred to me that you might help——"

Marjorie broke in, "I accept the job. I'll do anything you say. Look, I can't pretend to be blasé. I'm crazy about lighting, I love this idea——"

"You still have to do your office work. And dance in the chorus. This is just extra labor without extra pay."

"When do I start?"

He hesitated, smiling a little at her eager tone. "Well, Marjorie, let's say we'll try you out Sunday evening after the storm god leaves, okay? That is, if he doesn't carry you off to the cave of the winds, forever and a day."

During the dancing on Sunday evening he came to her. "Ready? Let's go backstage."

She had been restraining herself with some difficulty from speaking to him first. "Why, sure. As you see, I'm not off to the cave of the winds."

He nodded, with a small grin.

They went through the stage door and were alone together in total darkness. "Give me your hand," Noel said. His touch in the dark thrilled her. "Damn, my orders are to leave one light burning at all times. Greech keeps sneaking back here and turning it out——" He groped along, tugging her cautiously. A rope roughly brushed Marjorie's face. "Watch out, don't get hung in these damned lines—here's the board. If I touch the wrong switch send my body to brother Billy." Light drenched the stage, streaming through the curtains on them. "Ah, that's better." He released her hand, but his grasp remained palpable on her skin for a while like a warm soft glove. He began to demonstrate the switches and rheostats for her, and he let her execute some black-outs, dim-outs, and fade-ins.

He told her to improvise a morning effect and a night effect, using the labelled color switches. "Well! Not bad at all."

The stage door slammed. "Who the hell is fooling with that switchboard?" called Wally, and his steps came running across the stage.

Noel grinned conspiratorially at Marjorie. "Take it easy, Wally. Just training up your replacement."

"Oh. Sorry. You pulled the wrong switch or something, Noel. One of the pink spots on the catwalk came on——" He appeared through the curtain. His mouth opened when he saw them, and he stood holding an edge of the dusty black drape, staring.

"Hi, Wally," Marjorie said.

"My replacement?" Wally's voice was thick and queer.

"You'd be amazed. She knows plenty about lights."

Wally came to her and touched her arm. His big head shook heavily. "Look, Marge, please don't. Please. I never thought he'd ask *you*. I can do it. It's a dirty messy job, you have to go climbing around on catwalks, staying up till all hours——"

"I love it," Marjorie said. "There's nothing I'd rather do."

Wally said to Noel, "Forget it, forget I ever asked for a replacement. I'll do the writing, I'll do the lights, and I'll pick up the directing when I can——"

Marjorie said curtly, "Wally, can't you understand that I want to do this? I'm here at South Wind to learn, just as you are."

Noel said, "You're being silly, Wally. There's no chivalry backstage. Lighting is dull hackwork for you now. Let her take it over. You have more important things to do."

The boy looked from one to the other. Marjorie and Noel stood side by side at the board. Noel's arm was around behind her, resting lightly on a switch. "Please. I'll do the lights," Wally said in a terribly melancholy tone.

Marjorie said sharply, "I'll do them. It's all arranged!"

"All arranged," Wally said. He swung his head around like an animal and went out through the curtains.

Chapter 15. SHIRLEY

The sight of her own uncovered breasts in the lamplight shocked Marjorie out of the sleepy sweet delirium that was paralyzing her. She sat up. "God in heaven, what am I doing? What are you doing? Turn away, please, I want to dress."

"I'll do better than that. I'll leave," Noel said. He stood and strode out.

The drawing board and the lighting-plan sketches lay on the floor where they had fallen. A log had caved in on the fire, and a flaming chunk which had rolled against the screen was smoking into the room. As soon as she had buttoned her shirtwaist she pushed the ember back with the poker, thinking the while that she must have succumbed to the spell of Noel's room; it was the most beguiling place on earth. The rough-plastered stone fireplace, the crude wooden walls crammed with books, the wagon-wheel chandelier in the high dusky ceiling, the smell of to-bacco, books, green trees, and wood fires, all blended into a comfortable warm lulling maleness. The brass red-shaded reading lamp by which they had been working cast a round of yellow light on the Indian blanket covering the couch; the rest of the room was gloomy. Blue cold moonlight falling through the windows only made the lighted place by the couch and the fire seem cosier.

She had thought she was weeks away from having to plan for the possibility that Noel might want to neck with her. It had happened like a short circuit between live wires. She had abandoned herself to shocking freedoms unknown to her before; and the worst of it was that she did not even feel conscience-stricken. The sensible thing was to get out at once, of course. But she wasn't angry at him, though she was scared, exquisitely and pleasantly scared in her remotest nerves. She thought she had better wait just long enough to tell him she wasn't angry at him. She curled up in the armchair by the fire. The excitement which had made her fingers almost too unsteady to button her blouse died away, leaving a warm languor in her limbs as after a bath. Five minutes went by.

The door opened. "Good Lord, you still here?" he said. "I thought you'd have run off shrieking into the night. By now, you should be coming back with a policeman." He dropped on his back on the couch, with his head propped against a cushion. His face was sombre and tired. "Go away, Marjorie."

"Policeman? Why?"

"Impairing the morals of a minor would be the charge, no doubt."

"Oh, cut it out, Noel."

He reached for cigarettes, glancing wryly at the dump of papers on the floor. "Big mistake, obviously, asking you to come here to work."

"May I have a cigarette, please?"

He came to her, lit her cigarette, and walked away, making nothing of the brief touch of her hand on his. Flinging himself on the couch, he said, "No, no. Not Shirley. Not again. I won't have any part of it. I'm too old. I know better. I don't even enjoy it . . ."

"Shirley? My name's Marjorie, my friend——"

"Your name is Shirley." He sat up stoop-shouldered, his hands hanging between his knees, and stared at her. The firelight and the lamplight shadowed his face; the lines were deeply creased along his bony cheeks. "Look, kid, just remember this, and remember I said it very early in the game, too, the first time I so much as made the mistake of touching you. I'm not going to marry you or anybody like you. Nothing can ever make me do it, *nothing*, is that clear——"

"Who in heaven's name is talking about marriage?" She was alarmed, dizzied, delighted. "I don't even like you particularly."

"Oh, damn that bloody nonsense. Look"—he stood and walked toward her—"I trust you believe that when I asked you last Sunday to help with the lights I wasn't subtly and fiendishly leading up to this. I'm not a college boy. Necking disgusts me. I can have all the sex I want, when I want it, with the pleasantest of partners——"

"Not with me you can't," she broke in without thinking.

"I haven't the remotest desire for it with you," Noel said. "I doubt that you could force me. In time you'll probably try."

She jumped out of the chair, tears storming to her eyes. "I stayed to tell you that I wasn't angry, but I'm getting angry fast. I'll do your lights and act in your shows and for the rest you can go to hell. Good night."

His hand was on her shoulder before she had taken two steps. He held her away from him with his long arms, looking earnestly at her face. "How would you like to go for a nice walk? I think we ought to talk a little bit, maybe."

"You think I'm just a stupid kid, don't you, with a crush on you, the way Wally has a crush on me. Well, what if it's true? Why should you insult me like a beast? What do you want of me? You won't get me to do anything bad. I know all the women are dying to sleep with you. All right. *All right!* Let me alone then! Don't ever kiss me again. Keep your hands off me, don't talk to me, don't dance with me, don't ask me to have drinks with you, don't torture me, that's all I ask! I've wanted to kiss you ever since I saw you a year ago. I admit it. Now I've done it and that's that. Let me go. I don't want to walk with you."

He dropped his hands. She walked to the chair where her leather jacket was lying, and put it on.

"Marjorie," he said. He was smiling now, the warm and faintly sad smile about the ironic secret. "This won't work. Willy-nilly we're together for the summer. We have to talk a bit. Here, or walking, it doesn't matter."

Her hands were thrust in her jacket pockets. "Let's walk, then. Let's get out of here."

At the end of the swimming dock there were benches. Marjorie and Noel walked out on the echoing boards in the moonlight, their faces red and green and red as they walked past the lamps. They sat on a bench, the grainy wood of which was dank in the night air, and lit cigarettes. Wavelets slapped at the dock, and from the golf course, far off, came floating the music of the band playing *Love's Old Sweet Song*, accompanied by raucous beery group singing.

"We should have gone to the steak roast," Noel said.

"Yes, indeed," Marjorie said.

"I was eighteen," Noel said—the moon was behind him, and his face was invisible except in red puffs of his cigarette—"when I first slept with a woman. I was dramatic counselor at a kid's camp, and she was the mother of one of the kids. Most harmless-looking woman you ever saw, dark, demure—— Gad! An education. Makes me feel dirty when I think back on her, which I try never to do——"

"Look, Noel, I don't want to hear about your past. You're nothing to me."

"Take my advice, and listen. You'd better know all this. . . . Up till then I had been all tied up in knots of shyness with women, but Mrs. Dearing, that was her name, made it contemptibly simple, once for all. I turned into something of a young rake. My father sensed the change in me pretty quickly. *Got to get you married, Saul, it's the only thing that will straighten you out, give you some backbone.* Seems I wasn't getting good marks in college. This was after getting pretty near the highest high school average in New York State, and cracking IQ tests all my life with marks that showed me right up there with Einstein and Shakespeare. You see, my father wanted me to go to law school, and—well, you'd have to know my mother and my sister to appreciate my side of the story. Let's take it as understood that I was a dissolute worthless loafer, on the verge of disgracing the great Judge Ehrmann by getting kicked out of Cornell. My father, Marjorie, and I say it with regret, is the stuffed shirt of the world, and has succeeded in overbearing everybody all his life, except me —though that's his chief aim in life——

"But that's neither here nor there. I was perfectly willing to do as he wished. I wanted to get some backbone and straighten out, if possible. I didn't much like being a loafer. I didn't understand myself at all then. So I dutifully began making the rounds of the West Side among the eligible girls. I must have had dates with nine tenths of them. That's how I became such a connoisseur of Shirley. I went out with Shirley after Shirley. It was uncanny. She was everywhere. I would hear about some wonderful new girl—Susan Fain, Helen Kaplan, Judy Morris, the name didn't matter. I'd telephone her, make a date, go up to the apartment, she'd open the door—and there would stand Shirley. In a different dress, a different body, looking at me out of different eyes, but with that one unchanging look, the look of Shirley. The respectable girl, the mother of the next generation, all tricked out to appear gay and girlish and carefree, but with a terrible threatening solid dullness jutting through, like the gray rocks under the spring grass in Central Park. Behind her, half the time, would loom her mother, the frightful giveaway, with the same face as Helen's or Susan's, only coarsened, wrinkled, fattened, with the deceiving bloom of girlhood all stripped away, showing naked the grim horrid respectable determined *dullness,* oh God." Noel stood and walked back and forth, his heels making the hollow dock boom. "Oh God, Marjorie, the dullness of the mothers! Smug self-righteousness mixed with climbing eagerness, and a district attorney's inquisitive suspicion—*Judge Ehrmann's oldest boy, they say he's brilliant but I don't know, not solid, wants to be a composer, something crazy like that, also I hear he's been mixed up with women, doesn't do his work at school*—Marjorie, it's amazing, absolutely amazing, how the grapevine works among the mothers. I was feared. The word was out that I was a fascinating loafer. It was quite true. The peculiar thing was that I affected Shirley the way whiskey hits an Indian. She knew I was bad for her, but I drove her crazy. Marjorie, I have my conceit, but it doesn't extend to my romantic career on the West Side. I tell you soberly I was like a man with a cane walking down a lane of hyacinths, smashing flowers right and left. They all recovered, mind you. Shirley is indestructible. They're all married now—to dentists, doctors, woolen manufacturers, lawyers, whatever you please—but I assure you they remember Saul Ehrmann. And it wasn't always one-sided. I remember a couple of them. I've been ragingly in love with Shirley, you see. That's the worst torment of all."

Marjorie was astonished when a shudder broke through her frame. She realized that she was hugging herself, that the damp of the bench seemed to be going into her bones. "Noel, I'm cold."

He stopped in his pacing and looked down at her. The moonlight made black hollows in his long face. His hair was still unruly from the thrusts of her fingers. "I'm boring you senseless."

"No, no, no. But it's so damp here——"

"You're right. We need brandy. I'm damned near shivering myself." He did not say another word until they were sitting in the dimmest booth of the empty Sirocco Bar. Then, after drinking off half his double brandy at a gulp, he said, "Shirley doesn't play fair, you see. What she wants is what a woman should want, always has and always will—big diamond engagement ring, house in a good neighborhood, furniture, children, well-made clothes, furs—but she'll never say so. Because in our time those things are supposed to be stuffy and dull. She knows that. She reads novels. So, half believing what she says, she'll tell you the hell with that domestic dullness, never for her. She's going to paint, that's what—or be a social worker, or a psychiatrist, or an interior decorator, or an actress, always an actress if she's got any real looks—but the idea is she's going to *be* somebody. Not just a wife. Perish the thought! She's Lady Brett Ashley, with witty devil-may-care whimsey and shocking looseness all over the place. A dismal caricature, you understand, and nothing but talk. Shirley's a good girl, while Lady Brett was a very ready hand at taking her pants off. To simulate Lady Brett, however, as long as she's in fashion, Shirley talks free and necks on a rigidly graduated scale, which varies from Shirley to Shirley, but not such a hell of a lot——"

"You're so damned smart, aren't you?" Marjorie said, increasingly uneasy at every word he was saying.

"Darling, let me make one thing very plain, I'm not blaming Shirley for anything. I admire her. She has one hell of a job. She's turned loose at fourteen in a black woods. She can find no guidance anywhere. Her parents pretend she has no problem. Religion gives her milksoppy advice that nobody she knows pays any attention to. In literature her problem doesn't exist. The old novels are all about Jane Austen and Dickens heroines who'd as soon put bullets through their heads as let a man kiss them. And the new novels are all more or less about Brett Ashley, who sleeps with any guy who really insists, but is a poetic pure tortured soul at heart. This leaves Shirley squarely in the middle. What can she do? She talks Lady Brett and acts Shirley, handling the situation on the whole with remarkable willpower——"

"It doesn't take too much willpower," Marjorie burst out, almost snarling, "with most of the boys, who are plain animals, and just need slapping down. And it doesn't take much willpower either with the conceited intellectuals who try to disarm you by telling you that you're frigid. They're just amusing. I daresay that was your approach, hey?"

Noel blinked at her and slowly smiled. "Glory be, my sweet, are you taking any of this personally? It's just abstract talk——"

"Well, blast you, you've called me Shirley fourteen times. You're a damned intellectual snob, that's what you are. You're also a ratty bohemian and, if you want to know, a bit of an anti-Semite!"

"Indeed?" said Noel.

"Furthermore, I'm *going to be an actress,* not a fat dull housewife with a big engagement ring, whatever you say. And I'll tell you something else. I could turn this thing around and tell you all about—about *Sidney,* who wants to be a writer or a forest ranger or a composer or anything except what his father is, because he's ashamed of his father being a Jew, or because he thinks he's too sensitive for business or law, whatever the damned Freudian reason may be—and he ends up in his father's business just the same. I've opened my apartment door to enough of those."

Noel crooked his head and hugged his elbow. For the first time since she had known him his face was discomposed. His eyes gleamed angrily, his mouth was open and smiling, and the lines were curiously erased from his cheeks. She had a flashing glimpse of what he must have looked like as a college boy; whiskey for the Indian, indeed! He said in an unusually slow easy tone, "Good shot. But you see, I really am a composer. Making cash and a name, bit by bit, year by year. And having been thrown out of Cornell Law School with the lowest first-year grades of all time, it's not likely I'll end up in my father's business. But let's see. Intellectual snob? Certainly, it's the breath of my life. Bohemian? Yes, sure. Anti-Semite? Not any more. I had a spell of it. But I broke out of the West Side, you see. I found that Shirley existed everywhere. It's a general problem, not a Jewish one, the flux of the sex code. Shirley Jones has the same nature as Shirley Cohn and the same milieu, and is in the same jam. So she evolves into the same creature, essentially. Some time ago I stopped identifying all the evils in life with my father and therefore with being a Jew." He signalled to the bartender for drinks. "Of course by that time I was Noel Airman, legally. It seemed pointless to change back. I wish now I'd yearned a little less obviously toward Noel Coward. I was not yet twenty-two. It's rather ridiculous for a Jew to be named Noel. At this point of course I'm a Jew by birth only, but that seems enough, say, for Hitler——"

"Being a Jew doesn't mean anything to me, either," Marjorie said. "But still I don't make fun of them the way you do, and I try to——"

"Marjorie, your lack of self-knowledge is fabulous. Being a Jew is your whole life. Good Lord, you don't eat bacon. I've seen you shove it off your plate as though it were a dead mouse."

"Well, I can't help that, it's habit."

Noel shook his head, regarding her affectionately, and leaned back slouching, his arms crossed. "Ye gods, Marjorie, dearest Marjorie, you are such a sweet beautiful girl . . ."

"But a Shirley," Marjorie growled, glaring at him.

"A Shirley. A complete, final, Raphaelesque, golden-haloed Shirley." A shadow of sadness was on his face.

The bartender set the drinks on the table. "What's the matter, Mr. Airman, losing your taste for steak?" Noel laughed. The bartender said,

"Well, I guess there's better things than steak in life, hey folks?" He leered at Marjorie, and went off wiping his hands on his apron.

She said, "I guess I'll be known far and wide by tomorrow as your new mistress."

"No. In this one case I think your reputation for stuffiness will outrun mine for vice. You're still the wonder of South Wind, you know, for the way you held off Perry Baron. Everyone thinks you're a religious fanatic or something."

"How do they know I held him off?"

"Darling, at South Wind they know these things. If you and I start spending time together it's going to arouse great interest. The battle of the Titans. Evil versus good. The irresistible force and the immovable object. Ormuzd, spirit of light, and Ahriman, prince of darkness. They'll be placing bets."

"Noel Ahriman," Marjorie said.

He burst out laughing. "Gad, you make jokes, too."

She was extremely pleased with herself. "I'll tell you this much, old Prince of Darkness, if there's going to be such a battle you'll lose. There's that much of Shirley in me and I don't care who knows it. I'll never have an affair with you, never. If I'm unlucky enough to fall in love with a hound like you, you'll still have to marry me. If I'll have you, that is. I don't know if I ever could. There are some awful things about you."

"Well, Sweetness and Light, you frighten me too, a little bit."

"I'm sure I do."

He regarded her in silence for a little while, his head to one side. "What does the name Muriel mean to you?"

"Offhand I think of a fat girl in my last Latin class. Who's she, another Shirley?"

"Oh no. Muriel was all too real." He took a deep drink of his brandy. "Muriel was the only reason I stayed on at Cornell. I did just enough work to keep from getting kicked out because she was in my class. A year or so older than I was." He peered speculatively at Marjorie. "She wasn't quite as pretty as you. Nor half as bright. She couldn't have thought of that Noel Ahriman joke to save her life."

"Oh, pooh, that sad pun," said Marjorie, feeling very kindly toward Noel.

"But she had her own special charm. Tall. Very thin. Black-haired. Her name was Muriel Weissfreid. I'm sure half of Muriel's fascination for me lay in this blue-eyed black-haired Irish look she had. Well, to synopsize, and without conceit I say it, she was as mad about me as I was about her. The necking we did was historic, it was cataclysmic, she wanted it and I was her slave, of course. For months I was a nervous wreck. I swear, much as I loved her, I grew to hate it. But necking it was and necking it remained. Anything was all right except natural sex. And one other thing. We necked in absolute silence, never discussed it, and never admitted, not to the last hour, that we were doing it or ever had done it. Those were the rules. I tried once or twice to make a joke about it but, Gad, she got angry as a tiger, and I knew if I said three more words I'd lose her. So I shut up. She was my queen, my star, what else could I do?" He drank.

"She sounds horrible," Marjorie said.

"I organized a dance band just to make money to spend on her. I wrote term papers for her in our courses—papers that got her A's, when my own papers got low C's. It seemed the most natural thing in the world to do. Writing a good paper for her was like giving her a corsage.—Well. Came the Junior Prom. Naturally Saul and Muriel were to go together. The other fellows at school didn't even bother to ask her. But Saul didn't go with Muriel. Saul went stag. Muriel, you see, had met a young man during Christmas vacation, and had improved the acquaintance on weekends in New York, while our fantastic necking continued at Ithaca on week nights. It continued, so help me, until two days before the Prom, when she informed me she had invited this fellow as her escort. Marjorie, she wore blue velvet to the Prom, and the biggest diamond you have ever seen or are ever likely to see outside a museum. If she'd fallen in a river wearing that diamond she'd have been pulled down and drowned. He was a pleasant little fellow with a round head and pink cheeks, a little shorter than Muriel. His father owned a big woolen mill.

"Honestly, Marge, in my life I have never done a better imitation of Noel Coward than I did that night. I wished them joy with the most astringent elegance, and begged the favor of a last dance with her. He was really a very nice little fellow. And what the devil, he had her. They were going to be in bed together in the bridal suite of the *Mauretania* in two weeks, she was quitting school to marry him. He handed her over with a good-hearted, and, so help me, apologetic grin. And Muriel and Saul danced their last dance."

"Lord," murmured Marjorie.

"Blue velvet," said Noel in a light amused tone, "and Muriel's arms so thin and white, and the spring-flower smell of her hair the same as always —and that damned Rock of Gibraltar winking on my right shoulder where her left hand rested, as it always had, with a finger lightly flicking my hair." He finished his drink and slouched back, smiling at her. "So you see, in my epic duel with Shirley she has gotten in a solid blow or two. I'm well ahead, however, and I mean to stay ahead."

Marjorie said, "It's a nasty picture. I recognize parts of it, I have to admit. Only parts. She was a miserable girl——"

"I know. My generic girl is named Shirley, not Muriel."

"I'm not anything like her. You can believe me or not, as you please."

"You mean you wouldn't marry the fat little son of the woolen mill? Maybe not. I hope you're never tempted." Marjorie thought of Sandy Goldstone, and looked down at her drink. "I daresay you don't go in for obsessive necking, at least I hope not."

"Certainly not! As for tonight, I——" she stammered and stopped, blushing.

"Don't elaborate, Margie, it was perfectly obvious how astounded you were. You made me feel ashamed of myself, for the first time in maybe ten years. Amazing. I thought my conscience had atrophied."

"Oh, you're not as black as you paint yourself."

"I'm exactly that black. Whatever you do, don't fool yourself about that."

She said, "You don't scare me. Not any more."

"Feet of clay."

"No, that's all right. I'm just beginning to understand you."

"And to feel the urge to make me worthy of myself, perhaps."

"No. I don't give a hang what becomes of you, why should I?"

Noel lit a cigarette, and looked out at the lake. "I had a sweet revenge, by the way, given to few in this life. When I had my first song hit, Muriel wrote me a letter saying how proud she was of me. Then, when *Raining Kisses* got to be such a success, here came an invitation to a party at her home in Rye, New York, an Italian Renaissance palace the woolen man had given his son for a birthday present. I went. I'd driven past the place several times, long ago, gnashing my teeth. I had no trouble finding it. Seven years had gone by. Well, Margie, it was a hell of a party. You never saw so many expensive dresses. Ah, but they were so much the young married set, so thirtyish, so fearfully hair-thinning hip-spreading loud-laughing wide-grinning thirtyish! Here a real estate man, there a chain grocery man, here a lawyer, there a doctor, here a woolen man, there a cotton man, all sleek and plump and connubial. The wives, a couple of dozen aging Shirleys. Muriel's chin had sharpened. All the sweetness was out of the curves of her face. She was stiff and tight— tight smile, tight clothes, tight desperate gay eyes. I came there with the most beautiful girl in New York, an imbecile named Imogene something, eighteen, a raging redheaded beauty. Later married an oil man. Darling lovely Marjorie, I tell you we two bohemians walked among those thirty- ish respectable people like gods. We dazzled them. Those well-fed com- muting husbands hungered for Imogene and hated me. Their wives hated

Imogene and hungered for the romantic-looking composer in tweeds. Oh, it was rare. Muriel took me for a walk in the garden. I would not have made a pass at her, Margie, for twenty million dollars in gold, payable in advance. I was Noel Coward again, being distantly cordial to a sweet old aunt. She batted her eyes a bit in the old way, and said she was very happy and only hoped I would settle down some day with some fine girl and prove worthy of myself. She was implying that Imogene was a tramp. Which was entirely true. And—one thing that makes me feel kindly toward her, I must say—she apologized with clumsy sincerity for her somewhat crude parting words to me at the Prom seven years before.—Well. That was that. I'll tell you, I'd been getting pretty tired of Imogene—she was a moron, truly—but the hot eyes of those husbands sort of Simonized her for me, you might say, and we were great pals for another month or so after that marvelous party. Never seen Muriel since, and don't expect to." The bartender brought brandy. Noel drank. "Sam's brandy is beginning to taste pleasant. Incredible."

Marjorie was looking coldly at him. "You really are a devil in some ways—vindictive, petty, arrogant, smug——"

He glanced toward the windows and pointed at the guests streaming across the lawn. "Here come the Jukes and Kallikaks, full of steak and beer. Let's get the hell out when I finish this."

"What did she say to you?"

"Who? When?"

"Muriel. At the Prom. Her parting words."

"Oh, that. I forget." He drank.

"What did she say, Noel?"

"Interests you that much, this dead yarn of a dead time?"

"Yes, it interests me."

"Well, okay. Please understand, it was mainly my doing. I danced her into a corner, sat her down, and in a few sparkling and rather nasty sentences described her marriage to her as only Saul Ehrmann could. She began getting that furious cat look, but what the hell did I care? When I was all through she said something like this: 'You've always been able to talk rings around me and to hurt me. You've hurt me now, all right. I feel sick. What you say about my marriage is all true. I'll say one thing for Marty, though. He isn't a cripple.' With that, away went the blue velvet, the white arms, and the diamond." He finished the brandy and stood. "Let's go."

They walked in silence up the lawn, hand in hand. When they came to the path through the bushes to the women's cottages, she faced him. "I'm very stupid, I know, but——"

He brushed his hand gently on her cheek. "Enough talking for one night, darling. There's the whole summer."

"I can't tell you how strange I feel. Dizzy, unreal—it wasn't the brandy, I didn't have enough——"

"Marjorie, my sweet, we've fallen in love with each other, that's all. You love me. I love you. Don't lose any sleep over it."

Electric stings ran through her arms and legs. She put out her hand with spread fingers toward him, half reaching for him, half warding him off, a peculiar blind little gesture. He took her hand. She pulled him into the shadow of the path, and kissed him.

Chapter 16. THE RED GLASSES

Within the next couple of weeks it became a settled thing at South Wind that Marjorie was Noel Airman's girl. During rehearsals she sat at his side, when she wasn't working the lights or acting; she informally came to be a sort of assistant stage manager. She spent her free time with him, canoeing, dancing, playing tennis, talking endlessly.

It was a new era for Marjorie, a sunburst of love, and fun, and glory. Noel put on *Pygmalion* and there were no open complaints when Marjorie drew the part of Eliza. The staff people all assumed Marjorie was sleeping with the social director, and quite understood that he would want to treat her well, at least in the first few weeks of their affair.

To everybody's surprise, she scored a hit in the show. Really failing in a part like Eliza would have been hard, but it was obvious that Marjorie's success was not just the success of Shaw's lines. The audience liked her. Their warm response seemed to fill her with power and sparkle, almost to add inches to her stature; after a hesitant start she sailed through the evening bravely, and at the last curtain she received an ovation very like the one after *The Mikado.*

It turned into a memorable night, a staff revel lasting until dawn. Greech invited them all to his charming rustic bungalow on the lake, and was moved after a while to send up to the kitchen for a case of domestic champagne. About two o'clock in the morning, when everyone was quite drunk and full of eagerness for the party to go on and on, somebody suggested that Noel play the score of his new musical comedy, *Princess Jones.* He tried to beg off, but there was a great clamor for it, and at last he sat at the piano and began. The noise died down; for they were theatre people, and the unfolding of a new creative work was a solemnity. They sat here and there, on the furniture and on the floor, drinking quietly as they listened. After a while their respect changed to enthusiasm, and then to excitement. Several times they broke into applause. When Noel finished—playing and singing the score took him over an hour—there was a tumult of congratulations. Marjorie thought *Princess Jones* was unmistakably brilliant; but, being Noel's girl, she sat quietly, enjoying the rush of praise as much as he did, saying nothing. Wally Wronken reeled up to Noel with a highball in his hand, and actually got down on his hands and knees before him. "Salaam. You are the master, Noel. It'll be produced in a year. It's a sure smash. You'll be rich and famous. I kneel to the master. Salaam." He touched his forehead to the floor, spilling his drink.

From that night onward, she was accepted by the staff people as one of them. The sarcastic nickname she had been tagged with, "Sweetness and Light," fell into disuse. The redheaded singer Adele, with whom Marjorie shared her bungalow, dropped her patronizing air, offered her scotch from the bottle in her suitcase, and began confiding to her all the daily twists and turns in her affair with a waiter. The office-girl actresses, now that she was sleeping with Noel (as they thought), talked more freely about their love problems in her presence, as well as about the romances of other staff members. Marjorie was astounded at the scope and complication of South Wind sex activity thus uncovered, and dismayed to think how blind she had been.

Her eyes thus opened, she began to notice among the guests, too, the clues that indicated affairs—a good-looking man continuously with a mousy or ugly girl; a woman guest dancing night after night with the same waiter or caddy; a middle-aged man and a young woman in steady company, both looking composed and making no effort to amuse each other. She pointed these things out to Noel.

"Well, goodbye to your innocence," he said. "It was charming while it lasted. Of course you're not really good at this yet. Eventually you can tell by the way a man's paddling a canoe while the girl lounges, or by the way two people play a hand of bridge, or by the way they dance, or how they act on a golf course or a tennis court, or how a girl's lipstick looks at breakfast time. I could win fortunes if anybody would bet me on such things."

"Why, this place is alive with sex," Marjorie said. "It seethes with it. It crawls with it. It pullulates with it. It's horrible. It's like Dante's Inferno. A lot of nasty squirming writhing naked bodies."

"Oh, come," said Noel. They were on the porch of the social hall, sunning themselves in deck chairs. "Have another beer."

"I mean it. My mother calls it Sodom. She's right."

"You're reacting too violently, dear. There isn't nearly as much sex here as you think. Among the staff, I grant you, being cooped up together all summer, it does get to be a bit of a barnyard. But the guests are entirely different." He gestured at the crowds frisking on the lawn and the bathing beach, the girls in vivid swim suits, the men in brief trunks, all tanned, smiling, making a lot of noise. "The fellows do come here, of course, with the usual bachelor's dream of seducing a pretty girl, in between tennis, golf, and sunbathing. But they don't have much luck. The nice girls, the Shirleys, come with their tight bathing suits and bright flimsy dresses, intent on trapping a husband, and not inclined to settle for less. It's the pigs who mainly benefit by the tension that ensues. Their hopes are low and humble. They only want some attention, and they'll pay with their messy bodies for it. A few of the men really do break down and get interested in some nice girl. A few more, the less fussy ones, end up coupling with the pigs. That's about it."

"You're much too callous and contemptuous about the whole thing."

"Look, Margie, there's one fact you'd better face. Sex exists. People not only eat, drink, and breathe, they mate. That's how it happens that there are always more people when the old ones die off. Your viewpoint —evidently you got it from your parents—is as queer today as an Australian bushman's. The wonder is not that there's so much sex at South Wind, but that there's so little of it. Most of these people get nothing more in the way of sex than a few fumbled kisses and hugs, and the handful who do go farther with it skulk and crawl in the dark as though they were committing a crime. That's Moses for you. At a remove of forty centuries he still has these poor young Jews under control. It's absolutely incredible."

"What do you advocate?" Marjorie said. "Complete promiscuity?"

"I don't advocate anything, my dear. I just go along, living my way, and not trying to make generalizations. I have a very good time. There are certain girls, Marjorie, easygoing heathens like myself, to whom sex is as simple and accessible a pleasure as a highball. They ask only that it be good, and enjoyed in good company. You'll never understand that state of mind, so don't try."

After a silence she said, "I don't know anything about your gay heathens. I don't think a girl can go to bed with a man and forget about it. It's against human nature——"

"It's against your nature, Marjorie. Don't generalize. The Eskimos exchange wives as a matter of course. A Polynesian girl your age——"

"Oh, sure enough, the Eskimos and the Polynesians," Marjorie said. "That was bound to come up, wasn't it? Well, you don't live in an igloo and I'm not wearing a grass skirt, and we're not discussing people who do, but people like ourselves."

"Try to be consistent, old girl. Though I appreciate that it's an effort. You said human nature. They're human."

Marjorie said, "I believe I will have another beer, thank you." She watched the guests at their gambols while Noel went to the bar. "You know what all this reminds me of?" she said when he handed her the tall foaming glass. "A set of French postcards some idiot once brought out at a fraternity dance. They were colored pictures, you know, and perfectly harmless to look at—even pretty—just people dancing, and walking in the park, and what not. But then he gave you some red glasses to look at them with, and you suddenly saw the most disgusting obscenities. That's what I've been feeling like, here at South Wind, this last week or two. I feel as though I'd put on the red glasses."

Noel said with a grin, as she drank deeply of the frosty beer, "The red glasses are your Mosaic morality. What you're looking at is everyday life."

Marjorie said, brushing foam from her lips, "You know what? I think everything you say about sex is a lot of glib lies. You say it because you enjoy amazing me, and because it's a game for you to turn my ideas inside out."

Noel's expression was frankly mocking. "Of course that is what you'd prefer to believe."

"Otherwise you're trying to seduce me, after all."

He puffed his cigarette, narrowing his eyes at her through the smoke. "Well, you keep growing up right under my eyes. I'm beginning to think it might be very good for you."

"I hope you'll let me decide that."

"By all means."

She shook her head, looking at him with wonder. "Your conceit—or your frankness, I'm not sure which—passes all bounds. I don't know how to talk to you."

"You're not doing badly."

"I sometimes think you're the devil himself."

"That's your red glasses again. I'm just a fellow you happen to find attractive. You're supplying the horns and the tail."

"I wonder," she said softly. After a pause she said, "Noel, what's going to become of us?"

"Who knows? Who cares? Summer romances are queer things. Like shipboard romances. Just enjoy it while it lasts. Have fun, and don't get yourself into knots of Jewish conscience. Either of us may fall for someone else next Tuesday, and that'll be that."

"Oh, sure," she said. They looked into each other's eyes, both smiling, yet with expressions half-hostile.

She did not know how long Wally Wronken had been watching them when she finally became aware of his gaze. He was perched on the rustic rail of the porch, his big head slumped below his narrow, wanly tanned shoulders, smoking and staring at them. His expression was masked by the glitter of his glasses in the sunlight. She waved, miserably embarrassed, feeling that she and Noel had been gawking at each other with silly lovesick grins. "Hi, Wally. Got a cigarette?"

He came off the rail. "Just a Kool."

"Thanks." He held a match for her. The cold roll of menthol across her tongue brought back the day at the Cloisters, the lilacs in the rain. "Long time since I've had one of these, Wally. They're nice for a change."

"Any time you want a change, just ask me."

Noel said, "How'd the sketch go?"

"Pretty good. I'm going to run them through it again a few times."

Marjorie said, "Do you enjoy directing, Wally?"

"Well, I think it's worth learning, like most everything else. I'm learning and learning." He flipped his cigarette over the fence and went into the social hall.

After a pause, the menthol strong in her nostrils, Marjorie said, "What does one do about things like that?"

Noel said, "Nothing. All freshmen must get paddled. That's the law. Let's swim."

Since her fifteenth year Marjorie had believed firmly that sex was the most important and perilous concern of her life; that she would be a damned fool to lose her virginity before her wedding night; and that a serious affair before marriage would be the worst catastrophe that could happen to her. Now, for the first time in her life, her certainty on these points began to break down.

Compared to Noel, both George and Sandy had been mere furtive boys about sex; ready and eager, like all boys, to take any favor she would grant. Noel's scathing frank humor about sex was something new. He really didn't want to neck; she precipitated it, like as not, when it happened, and it was he who stopped it with a swift joke and the offer of a cigarette. He seemed to want to protect her from her worse self, from her maddening infatuation with him, instead of taking advantage of it as she imagined any other living man or boy would do. She could not help admiring him for this. Therefore, when he said, in his light way but with apparent sincerity, that it might be a good idea for her to have an affair with him, she was shaken.

She had to press him in several talks to tell her why he thought an affair would be good for her; he kept putting her off with jokes.

At last he said, "Well, all right. It would give you a yardstick, that's all, an emotional measuring rod that would last you a lifetime. We really love each other. From everything you've told me it's the real thing for the first time, for you. It isn't for me, darling—and don't bare your teeth at me, I can't help being twenty-nine—well, you see, I know what I'm experiencing. But you, you're as ignorant as a codfish. In your present state of heavy book learning and Mosaic prejudice and emotional illiteracy you're apt to take off and marry heaven knows what kind of horrible yahoo for all the wrong reasons. Like my sister. Honestly, I sometimes think of you as Monica, given a second chance."

"Would you rather have seen your sister have an affair with a man who'd leave her flat—as you would me?"

"A thousand times yes, if it would have taught her enough about love to prevent her marrying that lump of pig fat she calls a husband."

The environment made Noel's ideas all the more plausible. At South Wind there seemed to be no other sensible way of looking at life. The guests at their everlasting coy game—the flirtatious Shirleys, the eager-eyed bachelors, the pigs hovering on the sidelines for garbage scraps of desire—Noel had made them figures of fun, quaint people with quaint customs, almost like the Japanese. Yet a few months earlier her ways and her values had not much differed from theirs. Now it was the people of the staff who seemed wise and normal, the dancers, singers, musicians, actors, with their free-and-easy morals, their tolerant joking about all the solemn things of life. The married couples among them were no more staid than the rest. There were half a dozen flourishing adulteries Marjorie knew about and several others that were generally suspected. Among the unmarried ones, the drift in and out of random affairs was rapid and apparently almost painless.

Though Marjorie had been accepted among them, traces still remained of reticence and amusement in their attitude toward her. It was a running joke that certain subjects must be avoided so as not to shock poor Marjorie. Playing at anagrams, for instance, the women took delight in forming obscene words and covering them from Marjorie's sight with winks and giggles. This kind of good-humored teasing was not without its effect. Marjorie was the stodgy one, the outsider, the bumpkin; naturally she wanted to be more acceptable to the inner circle, more like them. In these theatrical folk Marjorie had found for the first time people who really talked and acted somewhat like the characters in lending-library novels. This added to their smartness, glamor, and authority. She submitted to their joking with the best grace she could, and day by day grew more used to the premise on which it rested—that she was warped by a ludicrous out-of-date upbringing.

One of her old ideas was crumbling more swiftly than the rest—the notion that an illicit love affair ruined a girl's life. She had always pictured the effect as no less damaging, obvious, and permanent than that of being thrown through a windshield. When she had learned last summer of Marsha's affair with Carlos Ringel, she had seemed to see horrid scars and scabs all over the fat girl. But this was clearly nonsense. There wasn't a virgin on the staff, to Marjorie's best knowledge, except herself. Most of the dancers and actresses talked frankly of past and present affairs. They were normal in appearance, polite in their ways, and not one of them was insane with grief or prostrate with shame. On the whole they didn't differ much from the virgins of Hunter and the West Side, except in being more shopworn. They had all stooped to folly and found too late that men betray, but they hadn't died; here they were, alive, tanned, laughing, and like as not in some new intrigue with a waiter or a musician. If they were coarsened and tough, if their new affairs seemed to be a grasping for cheap pleasures, if their lives were on the whole quite unenviable, it still remained a fact that they weren't fallen women—not if the phrase retained any meaning. Either women didn't fall any more nowadays, or it took a lot more than an illicit love affair or two to constitute a fall.

But the strongest assault on her old convictions came from a most unexpected quarter: her own body. It was becoming impossible to allow herself to be alone with Noel. More than once he had had to shake her roughly by the shoulders and put a cigarette between her lips; she would wake as though out of hypnosis with her hair in wild disorder and her face hot and sweating, with almost no memory of what had been happening, but with a sense of shame and a black terror at this utter loss of self that could come over her. It was like insanity.

And it was a wholly new kind of conduct for Marjorie. It had nothing to do with her personal preferences, her tastes, her ideas, her inclinations. It was like another identity, a strange will that proceeded outward from the fleshly recesses of her body. It was a more insidious arguer than Noel. It was taking on more and more the sound of her normal inner voice, the familiar vigilant friend of a lifetime whose job it was to suggest that it was time to eat, or that the yellow dress would be more becoming than the green, or that she had better freshen her lipstick. In the same comradely tones this new voice kept suggesting ways and means of being alone with Noel. At eleven o'clock at night, when she was undressing for bed, she would suddenly think that she would love to read a new novel. It would then occur to her that she had seen the latest best seller in Noel's room. She would have to fight with herself, exactly as with another person, to keep herself from going to visit him.

She was getting used to the thought of having an affair. It no longer was something that couldn't possibly happen to Marjorie Morgenstern, like becoming a drug fiend, or killing herself. She pictured what it would be like. She imagined her frame of mind afterward.

She was in a distracted and highly nervous state. Twice she packed her bags late at night, only to unpack them sheepishly in the morning. She sought out Samson-Aaron and spent long evenings with him reminiscing about her childhood, trying to make her slipping anchor catch and hold in the old realities. Marjorie had long ago told everybody that Sam the dishwasher was her uncle, having become thoroughly ashamed of her first hostile reaction to finding him at South Wind. Nobody thought the less of her for it. The Uncle was, in fact, rather popular as a "character," a legendary eater and spicy Yiddish philosopher. Often she thought she would confess her heart to Samson-Aaron. But the gulf of years and language and background was too wide; he was only the Uncle, after all, coarse and comical, fat and old. There was something too humiliating in appealing to the dishwasher for help in her love affair. She couldn't do it.

Samson-Aaron seemed to sense trouble. He was very patient and tactful with her. Only once did he try in a clumsy way to open the subject. "So, vot is vit Mr. Airman? Maybe ve have a vedding yet? All the time you are together, no?" Marjorie laughed and said she was just having fun with Noel; he wasn't the marrying kind. "Dot's vot I think, Marjorie. A gentleman, I think he is. A serious fella, I don't think he is. You're a good girl, you know vot you're doing, so vot's the difference? So long you know vot's vot, so have fun. Listen to me, giving advice to a college girl."

"There are some things they don't teach us at college, Uncle."

"Your mama writes is Modgerie got a steady fella? I answer nothing. I say is good veather in South Vind. I say I catch plenty fish on my day off."

"You're a sweetheart."

"Vot do I know? I'm in the kitchen vashing dishes.—So, but next veek Mama and Papa come here, no? Then vot?"

"Well, let them come."

Marjorie had been thrusting the impending visit of her parents out of her mind. They were going to arrive Saturday evening and leave Sunday afternoon to drive on to Seth's camp, a hundred miles farther north in the Adirondacks. Somehow, she thought, she would slide and stumble and dodge through those twenty-odd hours, and hide from her parents what was happening.

Chapter 17. THE ROWBOAT

The night her parents were watching the show Marjorie stumbled and fell, dancing out on the stage with the chorus. It was the first time it had ever happened to her. Before the laughter in the audience could spread she was on her feet again, kicking nimbly and smiling. When she came prancing off into the wing Noel was there, lounging with a hand on the curtain rope. "Are you all right? You must have scared your folks."

"Oh, I'm fine. My big feet suddenly got all tangled up, that's all."

He smiled. "Not according to Papa Freud. That fall was heavy with meaning."

"No doubt. Why don't you write a book about it? Excuse me, I've got to change."

As the show went along she was embarrassed at the spate of sex and bathroom jokes. It had not seemed to her at rehearsals that the show was particularly coarse. But tonight Puddles Podell's skits made her blush, and it struck her that Wally's lyrics and sketches were especially vulgar. The hit of the evening was Wally's number in which three actors representing Hitler, Stalin, and Mussolini, wearing nurses' uniforms and carrying prop babies, sang of the methods they were using to increase the birth rate. She had laughed till the tears came the first time she heard it at rehearsal; but now she realized how dirty the jokes were.

She removed her makeup and dressed in great haste after the show, oddly eager to talk to her parents. She found them sitting on the sideline of the dance floor on folding chairs, watching the couples. They looked old, after a month of not seeing them. The father was almost all gray, and Mrs. Morgenstern had deep wrinkles that her daughter had never before been aware of, her neck in particular showing the corded look of age. Of course, they were both past fifty, Marjorie reflected. She couldn't expect them to go on looking forever as they had in her childhood.

The father said, "I never knew till now what a beautiful daughter I had. You looked better on that stage than any movie star I ever saw. All the fellows here must be in love with you."

Marjorie laughed. "They're committing suicide right and left, Papa."

"Did you hurt yourself when you fell?" said Mrs. Morgenstern.

"No. That stage is hollow, makes a big boom. It was nothing. Hot night, isn't it? How about something to drink?"

They settled in a small booth of the bar. She saw her parents exchange a look when she ordered ale. Her father asked for the same. Mrs. Morgenstern hemmed and hesitated and at last ordered lemonade. They exchanged another look when she pulled out a pack of cigarettes and lit one. "Ale, cigarettes," said the mother. "All grown up, aren't you?"

"We may as well face it, Mom, I've gone to the dogs, just as you predicted." Marjorie blew a smoke ring, and was annoyed that it came out ragged. She blew another one, a smooth one.

"That's not what the Uncle tells us," Mrs. Morgenstern said. "He says everyone thinks you're the only good girl on the social staff."

"Oh well, Mom, I put up a good front. I'm an actress, you know."

"You're our daughter, so you're good, that's all," said the father. "It doesn't surprise me, and don't be ashamed of it. People may make fun of you, but they'll respect you."

The drinks came, and Marjorie drank off half her ale at once, glad to observe that this startled her mother. "Ah! Could anything be better on a hot night?" She dragged at her cigarette, squinting like a man.

The father said, "Tell me, Margie, don't you feel a little—I don't know, a little funny—acting in such a show? I mean, I'm not so fussy, I've heard a lot of dirty jokes in my time, but——"

"What do you expect in Sodom?" the mother said. "Hamlet? That's what the crowd wants, so they give it to them."

"Mom's right, Dad. I think tonight it was a little worse than usual, but after all, with this crowd—— Hello, Noel, come over and meet my folks." He was walking past with a highball, wearing a rust-colored corduroy jacket over the black turtle-neck sweater, and she was glad to see that he was freshly shaved and his hair well groomed. On Saturday night he often looked like a skinny tired tramp. Noel said, with a faint lift of the eyebrows, "Hi! Sure, Margie, love to."

"Mother—Dad—this is the social director—you know, he writes the shows and puts them on—Noel Airman."

Noel was gracious and easy in the exchange of greetings. "I hope you weren't scared when Marjorie fell. That wasn't part of the dance, she thought of it herself."

"We enjoyed your show," said the father. "A little bit on the rough side, but naturally you expect that here."

"I'm afraid so."

"Do you think our daughter has any talent, Mr. Airman?" said the father.

Noel looked down at her and smiled. "That's hard to say, Mr. Morgenstern. Frankly, when an actress is as attractive as Marjorie, the question of talent isn't easy to decide. Good looks are a camouflage. But I think she has talent."

"Why, thank you, dear." Marjorie patted his arm and smiled at her parents. "Well, I'm glad you came. That's the first time he's been forced out into the open on the subject. Ordinarily he won't pay me a compliment to save his soul."

"It's a compliment to say you're attractive," said Mrs. Morgenstern, sipping her lemonade and regarding Noel over the rim of the glass.

"Not when I'm trying to find out if I can act, Mom. It's like saying a doctor is attractive when you want to know if he can take out an appendix."

"Are you from New York, Mr. Airman?" said the mother.

"Yes, ma'am."

"Manhattan?"

"Yes. The Village, at the moment." Noel lit a cigarette. His eyes flickered to Marjorie's for a second. He slouched back, his arms folded, looking at the mother with his head aslant.

"Oh, the Village. Do you put on shows in the winter also?"

"I'm a songwriter, Mrs. Morgenstern."

"Oh, a songwriter."

Marjorie said, "Noel's had skits in Broadway shows, and he's had dozens of songs published, Mom. You remember *It's Raining Kisses,* that big hit."

"I'm afraid I don't."

"Well, I don't know how on earth you could have missed it. It was the biggest smash hit of 1933."

Noel said, "Well, not quite."

Marjorie said, "Dad, you heard it. It was always on the radio, all the orchestras everywhere played it——"

The father said, "I guess the days when Mama and I followed the popular songs are far behind us."

"Well, what's the difference?" said the mother. "A hit song is something. Listen, Irving Berlin isn't poor."

Noel grinned. "One hit song doesn't quite make me Irving Berlin."

"You've had lots of hits," Marjorie said.

"Well, I'll have to start looking for your songs," Mrs. Morgenstern said. "How do you spell your name again?"

Noel spelled it.

"Noel Airman, eh? That's an interesting name. I didn't catch it before. Well, so you're not Jewish. I didn't think you were."

Marjorie said, "Good Lord, Mom, what difference does that make? It happens he is Jewish, but for that matter most of the staff isn't, and——"

"But *Noel,*" said the mother, peering at him. "Noel means Christmas, doesn't it? Nobody calls a Jewish boy Noel. You might as well call a Catholic boy Passover."

Noel threw back his head and laughed. Marjorie gnawed her lips. He said, "Mrs. Morgenstern, I couldn't agree with you more, but I'm stuck with Noel." He waved at the waiter. "I must buy you a drink."

"Thanks, I've had all the lemonade I want," said Mrs. Morgenstern.

But Noel ordered another round for everybody. Then he explained that he had given himself the name when his first song was published.

"Oh, then it's a pen name, that's what it is," said the father. "Like Mark Twain, or Sholem Aleichem."

"Well, I wish the resemblance were closer, but that's the idea, Mr. Morgenstern."

The mother said, "What is your other name then, if I may ask, your real name?"

After a tiny pause Noel said, "Saul Ehrmann. Not so very much of a change, you see."

"No, not at all," said Mrs. Morgenstern. "Ehrmann . . . I know a Judge Ehrmann. But he spells it with two *n*'s."

Noel expelled a sigh, and shrugged. "So did I, Mrs. Morgenstern. He's my father."

"What? Judge Ehrmann is your father?" She turned on Marjorie. "He's Billy's brother! Really? For heaven's sake, why didn't you say so?"

"Mother, you've been so busy asking questions nobody could possibly have gotten a word in."

"Don't be ridiculous. Well! Judge Ehrmann's son!" Mrs. Morgenstern looked at Noel with more friendliness. "Of all the coincidences! Why, we have a great many acquaintances in common. I know your mother quite well from the Federation, and—don't you have a sister Monica? Married to the older Sigelman boy? The Sigelmans of the Snow Maiden Dry Cleaners?"

"That's my sister."

"Of course. Well, Mrs. Sigelman, that's your sister's mother-in-law, happens to be the best friend of one of my oldest friends, Belle Kline. I know them well. Lovely family, the Sigelmans. What's your sister's husband's name? Horace, isn't it?"

"Horace," said Noel.

"Very good-looking boy. Very bright. He's in business with his father, isn't he?"

"He's in business with his father."

Marjorie said, "I think I'd like to dance."

"Well, and you a songwriter!" said Mrs. Morgenstern. "Come to think of it, Belle did tell me once about the older Ehrmann boy writing songs

—I just never connected your name—with your father a judge I should think you'd be in the law."

"Well, you see, Mrs. Morgenstern, I flunked out of law school with the lowest marks in the history of Cornell University." Noel was sitting up straighter, hugging his elbow.

Mrs. Morgenstern laughed, then looked uncertainly at Marjorie and back at Noel. "Don't tell me that. Not in your family. Too much brains——"

Marjorie slid out of the booth. "If you won't dance with me, Noel, I'll find someone who will."

Noel said pleasantly to the parents, "Will you excuse us?"

"Go ahead," said the father. "Have a good time. Don't sit around talking with a couple of old fogies."

"But I've thoroughly enjoyed it." Noel stood. His smile was warm and candid. "Maybe later we can chat some more about the Sigelmans, and all."

She clung to him in the dance, fearing a chilliness in the way he held her. She waited a long time for him to speak. One dance ended and another began. She said, "You can certainly be poisonous, can't you?"

"I beg your pardon?"

" 'We'll chat some more about the Sigelmans.' Just dripping with venom."

"It was a small joke for your benefit. Sorry if it seemed anything else."

She looked up at him. He pressed her waist slightly, his face in the habitual cast of satiric good humor. "What are you looking at, Margie? You'll get a crick in your neck."

"Trying to figure you out."

"Oh, that dreary game. Well, the face is no help. Look, I'm not upset, or surprised, or mad, or anything, if that's what's worrying you."

"I have a memory, you know," Marjorie said. "I remember what you said about the mothers. The frightful giveaways, the same face as the daughter twenty years later, with all the beauty gone and just the horrible dullness left."

"I like your mother."

"Oh yes! The way you were bristling at her . . ."

"Well, that's a reflex. The mouse and the cat. I haven't been through that business in eight or nine years, I'd almost forgotten how it went."

"Mom's being particularly left-footed tonight."

"Now look, Marjorie, don't start apologizing for your mother. She's fine. In fact she's perfect. Had she been any different I'd have been disappointed. She has a Shakespearean exactness and intensity of character. All is as it should be. I don't know, I guess I'm irresistibly drawn by the authentic. I like you both."

"Oh fine. Lumping me with my mother. I'm really lost."

"I love you," Noel said in a different voice. She looked once quickly into his eyes and stopped talking. They danced. After a while she saw her parents sitting on the folding chairs, watching her. When the music ended Noel said, "You'd better make up your mind what the script is, my darling, and then stick to it. Do you want to dance with other guys, or sit with your folks, or what? Don't get into knots, don't worry about my feelings, just do exactly what you want to do. Your folks are sitting over there, right behind you, following all your moves."

"I know where they are. I want to dance with you."

"You're sure."

"Yes."

"And the inquisition?"

"Let me handle that."

The next number began. He took her in his arms. "All right, then."

Shattering blasts of Mexican music brought her awake the next morning; she half started out of the blankets and then fell back with a groan, glancing at her wristwatch and covering her ears. The loudspeaker for the women's area hung in a tree directly over Marjorie's bungalow. It was Fiesta Day. It was exactly eight o'clock. Mercilessly the office had started the music on the dot.

Her temples were throbbing. In her irritation and tension last night she had drunk several highballs after the ale. The fingers in her ears were of no avail whatever in shutting out the *Mexican Hat Dance* raging and crashing overhead. The loudspeaker seemed to be inside her head, leaping about with excess power. She staggered to the medicine chest and swallowed two aspirins, noting unhappily that the air felt warm through her flimsy nightgown. A white bar of light thrust through the trees and the screened window of the bathroom, hurting her eyes. She moaned. Cavorting about the camp all day, in greasy brown makeup and a heavy Mexican costume, promised to be hot nasty work, not suited to her state of nerves.

She had invited her parents to come on the fiesta weekend, calculating that the excitement and fuss would distract their attention from herself and Noel, especially since Samson-Aaron had been recruited to play the toreador in the bullfight. The first Sunday in August was Fiesta Day at South Wind, and the annual custom was to give the bullfighter role to the fattest man in the camp. The Uncle had had no competition. The toreador's costume, outsize though it was, had had to be enlarged to fit him. He was the vastest of all the toreadors, and—Noel had told Marjorie—with his natural bent for foolery he promised to be the funniest.

She was wriggling into the green flouncy skirt of her costume when she remembered that she had Greech's permission to go rowing with her father before getting to work as a señorita. "I'm losing my mind," she muttered. She put on her bathing suit and went to the bar for a cup of coffee, feeling no desire for breakfast. Workmen out on the lawn were hammering bright decorations on the little booths for dispensing tamales, enchiladas, and rum drinks, and over the noise of the hammers the loudspeakers merrily blared a cascading rumba. The coffee and the aspirins lifted and soothed Marjorie's spirits. Seeing her father come out on the boat dock in a bathing suit and a sombrero (sombreros were distributed free by the management on Fiesta Day), she finished her second cup and hurried to meet him.

"Señor Morgenstern at your service, my dear," the father said with a bow. The sombrero was set on the back of his head, showing his gray hair.

"Buenos días, señor," she said. "I've got to get to work in an hour, so let's hurry. How's Mama?"

"Fine. She's watching the Uncle rehearse the bullfight. Such foolishness——"

Marjorie had not been in a rowboat all summer. It moved over the water much more sluggishly and heavily than a canoe. The brim of the sombrero flapped as Mr. Morgenstern pulled at the oars. The sun was very hot, though it was not yet nine. She thought her father must be uncomfortable in his one-piece bathing suit, a black baggy woolen garment which accentuated the dead office white of his thin arms and legs. She wanted to suggest that he roll the suit down to his waist, but an awkward shyness stopped her.

When they were well away from the shore he slid the dripping oars back into the boat and pressed his hand over the middle of his chest. "Whew. Getting old. I used to love rowing more than anything. We would come down from the Bronx every Sunday, your mother and I, and row in Central Park. I would row for hours. It was before you were born. I used to point at the big houses on Fifth Avenue and say, 'See, that's where we'll live some day.' Listen, we came pretty close, after all—Central Park West." He sighed deeply and smiled at her in a defensive sad way. She was thinking how marked her father's accent really was. When she lived at home she was too used to it to take notice. "Twenty-three years ago. Seems like a lifetime to you, doesn't it, my darling? It goes by fast, I warn you. I'll tell you something strange, I'm not much different from what I was then. I don't feel like a different person. It's just that the machine is wearing out. Twenty-three years. Twenty-three years ago I was twenty-eight. Probably your friend Noel's age."

The mention of Noel's name gave her a little nervous throb. "He's twenty-nine."

"Hm. Of course I was an old married man, not a bachelor."

She lit a cigarette and lounged sideways on the thwart, her back against one gunwale and her legs dangling over the other, wondering tensely whether her father would dare discuss Noel. He had never once talked about any of her romances with her; the subject seemed to paralyze him with bashfulness. He was looking at her with his eyes crinkled in a half-smile. "Did you put on a little weight? Or is it just the bathing suit?"

"It's me. I'm getting big as a hippo. It's horrible."

"Don't be foolish. You're a beautiful girl. Except—well, girl isn't the word any more, Marjorie, you're a woman. When did it happen? It seems to me like last year you were running around the house calling your toy elephant a 'helfanet.' You probably don't even remember."

Marjorie smiled. "You and Mom have talked about that 'helfanet' so often, I think I do remember."

Mr. Morgenstern shook his head and took off the sombrero. "The sun is good. A little sun on my face won't hurt me."

"Dad, why don't you take a vacation? You look so tired. And you're so white."

"That's what your mother keeps saying. You're both right." He leaned forward, his elbows on his knees, turning the sombrero slowly in his hands. Marjorie suddenly thought of George Drobes and the brown hat. George seemed to be as remote in time as the "helfanet." The father said, "Tell you the truth, Margie, two, three days away from the business I get terribly restless."

"You should learn to delegate the responsibility, Dad. For your own sake you've got to."

He gave a mournful little laugh. "Well, it looks like Seth is too lazy to be a doctor after all. Another seven years, he'll be in the business, then I can take it easy. What's seven years?"

"Good Lord, Dad, in seven years I'll be twenty-seven. An antique."

"Well, you'll see. It goes by before you can turn around. I hope by then you'll have a couple of children. The younger you have them the better. The more you have the better. Marjorie, if I had breath before I died to tell you one thing, I'd say to you, 'Have children!' "

She laughed. "That's because you have such nice ones."

"No, because it's the truth. Nothing else in life stands up, in the long run."

"Well, then it's all pointless, isn't it? You raise children, so that *they* can raise children, who will *also* raise children—what is it all getting at?"

"Yes, yes, darling, I once said that too. When you have your first child, you'll know."

She said impatiently, "If what you say is so, then why can't you explain it to me right now? So far as I'm concerned, children would be a nuisance before I'm thirty. By then I ought to be about ready to retire from the human race and become a breeding machine." (This was a phrase she had picked up from Noel—an apt one, she thought.) "But before that, I want to have everything else in life worth having. Any moron can have children. They all do, regularly as rabbits."

"I see." The father nodded slowly. He perched the sombrero on top of his head. He made her feel obscurely ashamed, sitting there in the silly long black bathing suit and the silly hat, with his sagging belly, thin limbs, and dull white skin. Only his face was familiar. It was a little like coming on him in the bath. Her instinct was to avert her eyes. "Tell me, Marjorie, what is it in life that's so worth having?"

"All right, I'll tell you. Fun is worth having. And love. And beauty. And travel. And success—— My God, there is so much worth having, Dad!" It felt very queer to be talking to her father about herself in earnest, as though he were Noel Airman or Marsha Zelenko. It was like blurting confidences to a new friend whom she wasn't sure she could trust. But she was enjoying it. "The finest foods are worth having, the finest wines, the loveliest places, the best music, the best books, the best art. Amounting to something. Being well known, being myself, being distinguished, being important, using all my abilities, instead of becoming just one more of the millions of human cows! Children, sure, when I've had my life and I'm not fit for anything else any more. Oh, don't misunderstand me, Dad." Her tone softened as he seemed to flinch. "I'm sure I'll love them once I have them, and all my values will change, and I'll be content to settle down to nag my daughter to be a good girl and wash her ears and not use the telephone so much, just like Mom. But Dad, *think* about it. Is that the best I can ever be? Look at me! I'm just beginning. Am I so unfit for anything else? Must I turn into Mom overnight?"

"Your mother has been a pretty happy woman, I think," said Mr. Morgenstern, clearing his throat. "Despite all you think she missed. Talk to her."

"Oh, Dad. *Me* talk to her? You know it's hopeless."

"She's a smart woman. You may not like some of her ways, but——"

"Listen, I love her, Dad. But I can't talk to her. I've never been able to, and I never will be able to. We're two cats in a sack, that's all."

"It's too bad. There's a lot she could tell you, a lot." He pushed the hat back on his head. "Should I row some more?"

"Why? It's nice, just drifting."

"How do you intend to get all these fine things, darling?"

"Acting. You know that."

"It's a very uncertain trade. Most theatre people starve." He smiled. "A rich husband is a better bet."

"Maybe I'll be one of the exceptional actresses. I can try."

After a silence he said, "Well, it's very interesting. We should talk to each other like this more often."

"Yes, we should, Dad."

"I'll tell you, Margie, most of those things you say are worth having, I don't know about. You have a better education than I did. Music, books, wine, art, all that—I'll tell you, I think if you're happy they must be nice to have, but if you're unhappy they don't help much. The main thing is happiness. Love, sure, I agree with you. But love means children, just as I said."

"Not necessarily, Dad, except for Catholics." She was mischievously amused and also a little sorry when he turned red.

"Yes, Marjorie, you know an awful lot, I realize that. I'm glad you're so well educated. Only when you're really in love, you want them, that's the point."

"Well, there we don't agree, Dad. There are different ways of being in love."

He pushed the oars out through the locks and began to row slowly. He was looking at his moving hands when he spoke again. "About travel, though, you have something there. Once you have children you don't travel. No." He paused. "Strangely enough, your mother and I were talking about that very thing last night. We couldn't sleep. We—well, you know, we were talking. We were saying that after all, going to Hunter, you've—well, you've never been anywhere. And it being a free school, you've saved us maybe a thousand dollars or so by not going out of town. So—well, the idea is, would you like to travel? I think we could arrange it. We're not that poor."

He had turned the boat so that the white sun was directly in her eyes. She squinted at him, shading her brow. "What's all this? Would I like to travel? I'd give an arm to travel."

"Well, if you want to travel, why don't you?" he said rapidly. "Take yourself six, seven hundred dollars. Make a trip out West. California,

Yellowstone Park, the Grand Canyon. You're old enough to travel by yourself. You'll meet all kinds of interesting people."

"Dad, I——" she stammered and laughed. "This is too marvelous to believe—out of the blue sky—why, thank you. Maybe I ought to get it in writing——"

"Don't worry. It's nothing more than you're entitled to. Mom says there's six, seven weeks before you have to go back to school. You could have a fine trip, and still——"

"What!" She peered at him. He kept his eyes on the oars. "You don't mean travel *this summer?*"

"Darling, the time to travel is whenever you've got the chance."

"But I'm working, Dad, I have a job here—why, I assumed you meant next spring when I'm through with college."

"According to your mother, Greech isn't paying you."

"Yes, but—well, I like it here. Just to pick up and start travelling now, when I—it's such a crazy idea, somehow."

"Well, as I say, we got to talking, and this question of travelling came up, and as long as you mentioned it yourself . . ." His voice trailed down.

She swerved around and sat up straight, staring at her father. He kept his eyes on the leather-covered oar handles, and rowed in even unsplashing strokes. After a while she said frigidly, "Couldn't Mom tell me this herself? Why did she have to put you up to it?"

He looked at her from under his graying eyebrows. There were heavy reddish shadows under his eyes. "What's the difference who thought of it?"

"She must really hate Noel to want to part with seven hundred dollars."

"Marjorie, please don't think that we're trying to——"

"What's the matter? He's Judge Ehrmann's son, isn't he? How high does she want to fly? I should think she'd be jumping for joy. Not that those things mean anything to Noel or to me, but——"

"I think he's a very clever good-looking man, so does your mother."

"Oh, Papa, please tell me what it's all about. Mom will anyway, sooner or later, she has the diplomacy of a steamroller. What's she got against him? The name Noel? He hates it too, he'll probably get rid of it one of these days."

"She remembered some things, Marjorie, that—this is very hard, darling . . ."

"Go ahead."

". . . Things Belle Kline told her, that she heard from the Sigelmans. I have nothing against the man, but if all this is true—I'm sure it is—

he's—well, he's not your kind. He's a—you know—a Village kind of fellow, he's been mixed up with God knows how many girls, married women too. He isn't no good, I don't want to say that, but he's—he's lazy, with all kinds of talent and opportunities he's accomplished nothing. He sleeps all day in the city, writes a song only when he's ready to starve. He doesn't talk to his father. And they say he's an atheist."

"He isn't an atheist. He believes in God. He told me so."

"Marjorie, you're not going to tell me a religious man would lead such a life."

"I didn't say he was religious in your terms. He is in his own way. What right have you got to be intolerant of his religion, whatever it is? Just because he doesn't believe he'll be struck by lightning if he eats a ham sandwich does that make him a fiend, a criminal, an axe murderer? *You* try eating a ham sandwich sometime. See if you're struck dead. Maybe Noel's religion is a little more enlightened than yours. It's just a faint possibility, isn't it?"

The father rested on his oars, breathing heavily, and looked up at her, his brow deeply furrowed. "He loves you?"

"Yes."

"He said so?"

"Yes."

"You're going to get married?"

"No."

"You're not?"

"Of course not. People in love don't necessarily have to get married."

"They don't? What do they do, then?"

"They have a glorious time and enjoy each other's company as long as it lasts. The longer the better."

"I see. They enjoy each other's company."

"Exactly. I enjoy Noel's company more than I have anything in my life."

"I believe you." The father sighed, slid the oars into the water, and twisted the bow of the boat toward the shore. "Time we went back."

She sat stiff and angry, her thighs numb from the hard seat, and smoked another cigarette while he pulled toward the shore. His head was down as he worked the oars, and the sombrero hid his face. After a while the sombrero fell off and rolled in the muddy bilge water. He rowed on, apparently not noticing the loss of the hat. The pink of his scalp showed through the gray wavy hair at the top of his head. Marjorie picked up the sombrero and shook dirty drops off the yellow straw. "Dad, your hat."

He let go of the oars. They swung forward and rattled downward in the oarlocks until stopped by the leather handles. He covered his eyes with one hand and leaned on a knee.

"Dad——"

Tears spilled through his fingers and dripped into the sloshing water at his feet. He made no sound.

"Oh, Papa, don't! For God's sake don't cry, there's nothing to cry about, I swear to God Almighty there isn't." Her throat swelled. Dry sobs broke from her, sounding like laughter. "Papa, please, don't let's have a crying spree out here on the lake, people are out canoeing, they'll see us." She fought with all her will to keep her eyes dry. "It's so absurd, nothing's happened to me——"

"I'm sorry," he said. "It's all right, give me my hat." He put the sombrero on backward and drew his forearm across his eyes. "All right." He pulled the oars up through the locks, and rested them on his knees. His face was dry when he looked at her, and white. "You say nothing has happened."

"No, no, nothing."

He blew out a long breath. "All right. That's one thing." Slowly he began to row again.

She said, "You don't think much of me, do you?" The father looked at her with a suffering face. "Mind you, as long as we're being so frank, Dad, I'm not sure there'd be anything wrong about it. You and Mom have inculcated me with your prejudices, and apparently I've got them for good. Noel is too decent and fine a person to make me do anything I don't want to do, for whatever reason. We have the most marvelous time together and it's never been a problem."

"Our prejudices." The father nodded. "How long have you known him, a month?"

"Well, we met a year ago—but yes, a month, really."

"Marjorie, I should have talked to you more, I know, I should have taken more interest in you, I've been a neglectful father. The business, the business, the time slips by——"

"I'm not complaining, Papa, for heaven's sake. I'm all right——"

"I asked your mother over and over, is everything all right with Marjorie? I begged her to go easy on you, to talk with you, not to insist on her own way all the time. I told her a girl needs guidance, not to be pushed, pushed, pushed all the time. Marjorie, your mother knows it, she can't help herself. She says you're stubborn and you shout her down, the least thing she says, and it's true, I've seen it. A girl needs her mother. You've got to be tolerant. Both of you. You've got a better education than her but she knows life, she's very smart, even if you don't like some of her ways."

"I know all this, Papa, but——"

"Look, darling, I don't want to fool you, this trip is your mother's idea. But I beg of you, do what she says. Go away from South Wind tomorrow. Take this trip."

"You don't trust me. It's interesting to know."

"Oh, my God in heaven, trust you? Don't you know what an ignorant baby you are?" He raised his voice for the first time in the harsh powerful tone she had often heard him use in business talks on the telephone. It scared her a little. He glanced around self-consciously at a red canoe sliding by not far away with two sunburned girls in it. He said in a lower tone, "If you go away on the trip will he disappear, will he marry somebody else? You'll be back in September, you can see him all you want, if you're still interested in each other."

Ordinarily the chance to travel out West by herself would have sent Marjorie wild with joy. It was characteristic of her mother, she thought bitterly, to make the offer with such a big black hook sticking nakedly out of the bait that it was impossible for her to take it. "Well, Papa, the argument works both ways. If I don't go West till the spring will the Rockies disappear? I don't want to leave South Wind. I'm having the best time of my life, and I've learned more in a month here than I learned in four years at Hunter."

"Well, I don't want you to learn too much. Is that plain enough for you?" His voice was harsh again. He looked her straight in the face. "What's the matter with you? I'm over fifty, Marjorie, and you're not ten years old, nobody's getting fooled here. At least talk straight, for God's sake. Don't you know what your situation is here, what a risk you're running? Your whole future is in it. You can break yourself in pieces in a month, in a week——"

"Oh, those are just your damned old-fashioned ideas, yours and Mom's! This isn't a melodrama, Papa, and Noel isn't the villain with a big black mustache, and sex isn't so world-shaking as you think it is, and I wouldn't break in pieces if I had an affair, you're living in a dreamworld, Papa! I'd be just the same as before, maybe a little wiser and sadder. But I'm not going to, I tell you, I'm not going to, do you hear? You can believe me or not, as you please. And I'm not going out West, either. You can tell Mom to keep her seven hundred dollars. *I'm not going to leave South Wind.*"

The father bared his teeth as though in pain. "Marjorie, what have we done that was so wrong? Where have we missed out? What's happening to you?"

"Oh God, Papa, it's just that it's 1935 and we're in the United States, that's all." The tears were streaming down her face and her cheeks were dripping. "Don't sound so pathetic about me, please, I'm not a lost soul—— Oh God, look at me, now I'm bawling." She dashed her hands across her face and smiled mechanically. "Please, Dad, let's drop it, shall we? We'll all live. And hurry, I'm late for work."

He pulled hard for the shore, his lower lip between his teeth, his thin white legs braced against the floorboard, the sombrero flapping with each stroke.

Chapter 18. THE TOREADOR

At the end of the elaborate Sunday dinner in the dining hall, around two in the afternoon, the musicians in their hot nest over the kitchen broke off a languid Victor Herbert medley, clapped sombreros on their heads, threw garish serapes over their sweat-stained shirts, and began a lively paso doble. Into the center of the dance floor there leaped a tall figure in yellow, cracking a bull whip. It was Noel Airman, amazingly Mexican-looking in sideburns, mustache, and brown paint; only the deep-set glittering blue eyes identified him. His suit was trimmed, his boots studded with silver; he wore a silver-tasselled sombrero and silver-worked pistols; a belt of bullets slanted across his chest. "Buenos días, señoritas, señoras y señores!" Flashing a wild white-toothed grin, he lashed out again with the whip, and women guests yelped as the end of it flicked near them. With a laugh and a swift rattling announcement in Spanish, he disappeared. Half a dozen couples in gaudy Mexican costumes came swirling out of the kitchen door, where the waiters usually passed in and out with trays.

The last of the girls to emerge was Marjorie Morgenstern, almost asphyxiated by the food smells and furnace heat of the kitchen. The dancers had been held up for ten minutes between a stove and a steam table, waiting for the roast beef to be cleared away in the dining hall. But they stamped lustily and shouted "Ole!" and the girls threw roses at the guests with roguish sweaty smiles. Marjorie went through the fake folk dance in a vertiginous stupor, stumbled off to the kitchen, stumbled on again for the clamorously demanded encore and stamped some more, wondering when this bank of grinning New York faces would stop swooping and whirling about her.

Then she sat with her parents at a table bordering the dance floor, mopping her brow. The waiters rolled forward a scratched dusty upright piano. Noel came out of the kitchen, cracking the whip. With another flood of Spanish, gesturing flamboyantly, he dropped the whip on top of the piano, and began to play and sing Mexican songs.

Noel had originated the fiesta four years ago in his first summer as social director, after six months of itinerant loafing in Mexico. He enjoyed it; his energetic preparations in the past week had contrasted markedly with his bored workaday attitude toward the revues. Greech granted him a good budget for costumes and decorations and put the entire working force of the camp at his disposal, for the Mexican fiesta at South Wind on the first Sunday in August was becoming almost as popular as the July 4 and Labor Day weekends.

Marjorie forgot her resurgent headache, her tiredness, and the discomfort of her sweat-soaked costume, listening to Noel sing. It was better, in a way, that his voice was untrained and his breathing faulty. He really sounded like a Mexican. In the plaintive slow songs the melancholy shaking of his head, the reedy quaver of his high notes, made a melting effect that she loved. She did not applaud, but was dreamily grateful when waves of handclapping kept him at the piano.

Her mother startled her by murmuring in the middle of a love song, "He's wonderful." Marjorie looked at her. Mrs. Morgenstern was watching Noel with glistening eyes, smiling slightly and tapping the table in a slow rhythm with one finger. "Why didn't they have more of this last night in the show instead of those stupid jokes?"

"He would be better," said Mr. Morgenstern, "if you knew what the words meant. He ought to sing in English."

"Sh," somebody said from the next table.

After several encores Noel broke into English to thank them; then he announced the fiesta program. In the afternoon there would be folk dancing and singing on the lawn and after that the bullfight. In the evening a Mexican supper would be served in the open by torchlight, followed by a masked carnival and a display of fireworks over the lake. He urged them to put on costumes, and to come to the social hall for free sombreros, Spanish combs, mantillas, and shawls. Buzzes of laughter and excited talk filled the dining hall as he cracked the whip once more, shouted "Adiós! Hasta la fiesta!" and went bounding out the front door to a burst of music.

"I don't know," Mrs. Morgenstern said to the father. "Maybe we ought to stay for a while."

"Why don't you? It'll be fun," Marjorie said.

The father said, "Rose, I don't want to drive at night." His manner was listless. He was avoiding Marjorie's eye.

Mrs. Morgenstern said, "Well, when will the bullfight be over, four o'clock? It's only a two-hour drive to Seth's camp. We'll stay for the bullfight. Wait till you see Samson-Aaron. You'll die laughing."

"Is it something so new to see the Uncle make a fool of himself? I can do without it," said the father.

Marjorie stood. Her mother's word always prevailed in these disputes. "Fine, I'll see you later. Come to the lawn early and get good seats."

"Where are you going?" said the mother.

"My bungalow. I have to change costume."

"I'll go with you." The mother pushed back her chair. "I'd like to see where you live."

They left the father sitting at the table gloomily rolling his cigar between his lips.

"That Noel is certainly talented," said Mrs. Morgenstern, walking by her daughter's side across the lawn. "Where did he learn to sing like that?"

"Oh, he doesn't really sing well." The sun was baking hot on Marjorie's head, but a breeze plastered her clothes, chilly and clammy, against her skin. Her legs were strangely light as she moved them. Under the strain of fatigue and headache, and the emotional tension of the weekend, Marjorie's sense of reality was giving way. Things seemed to be happening about her in a brightly colored noisy dream. "It's just that he's unaffected, which makes him more refreshing than most singers."

"But his piano playing is certainly unusual. Why, he could make a living just doing that, I'm sure," said Mrs. Morgenstern.

"He organized his own band when he was nineteen," said Marjorie.

"You don't say. It's amazing. The man can do everything, can't he? You should have seen him at the rehearsal this morning with the Uncle and the bull. He's very clever, the things he thinks of." They passed into the shady path through the trees. Marjorie glanced sidelong at her mother, wondering what all this was leading to. "I'll tell you though, Marjorie, it worries me the way the Uncle carries on. It's like he behaves at a wedding, you know, jumping, dancing, in this heat. The man is over sixty and he weighs a ton and he acts like I don't know what, a college boy, a crazy man."

"Mom, you can't do anything with Samson-Aaron. That's just how he is."

"I got him to do something. He's lying down now, resting before the show. I told that Greech what I thought of him. 'You should be ashamed of yourself, making an old man do strenuous monkey business like that,' I said. That Greech, he looked at me with that face like a devil, but he didn't say a word. He knew I was right."

"He didn't make Samson-Aaron do anything," Marjorie said. "The Uncle wanted to be the toreador. It's an honor. And it's fun."

"That's how much you know. They're paying him a hundred dollars to do it."

Marjorie was astounded. "Who told you that?"

"It's so. When they asked him to do it he said no, and finally Greech offered him a hundred dollars. So then he said yes, the old fool, because he wants money to buy things for Geoffrey's baby."

"Mom, they're not paying him. Greech never would. The Uncle is doing it for the fun of it. He told me that himself."

"He told *you*. Me he can't put off with such stories——"

"Here's my bungalow."

Marjorie took a quick shower. Turning off the water, she heard her mother humming *It's Raining Kisses*. She wrapped a towel around herself and dashed dripping out of the bathroom. "*That's* the song. Noel's song. The one you said you never heard of."

"I know." Mrs. Morgenstern was lounging on one elbow, on her daughter's bed. "He played it for me this morning. Of course I knew it. I just didn't remember the name or the words."

Marjorie said warily, "You became real chummy, didn't you?"

"Don't stand there soaking wet in a draft, dry yourself and put on your clothes."

Marjorie took fresh underwear and the new costume into the bathroom. She said through the open door, "How did he happen to play the song for you?"

"We got to talking after the rehearsal. He's very charming, that Noel. I don't blame you for falling for him. If I were a few years younger I might try to give you some competition." Mrs. Morgenstern laughed.

Marjorie came to the door, holding the towel around her, to look at her mother's face. "Mom, do you really like Noel Airman?"

"Listen, he could charm a cigar-store Indian. Of course I like him, I can't help it."

"But you don't approve of him."

"I didn't say that either. Go put on your clothes." When Marjorie was out of sight the mother said casually, "What's the matter with his arm?"

A thrill of alarm ran from Marjorie's scalp to her heels. "There's nothing wrong with his arm."

"He holds it funny. His left arm."

"He does not."

"Well, it's marvelous the way he's learned to use it and hold it and everything, but it's a little crippled, isn't it?"

The daughter was in the doorway in her underwear, her face blazing, her eyeballs white-ringed, her teeth bared. She said in a thick voice, "If you're going to object to Noel because of something that happened to him at birth, something that he couldn't help, something that he's overcome with the most incredible willpower I've ever seen, I warn you I——"

"Why do you keep saying I object to him?"

"You do, you do, you do!"

"I don't."

"You *don't?*"

"No. I said I like him and I do. What's the matter? Should I swear to it on the Bible? Why are you staring at me? Am I such a stupid idiot that I can't possibly appreciate a remarkable young man?"

"It would be the first time," said Marjorie, peering like a frightened animal at her mother.

"This is the first time you've showed up with one. Sandy Goldstone I said was a nice boy and a good catch, and he was. I never said he was a genius. This fellow Saul Ehrmann—I'm sorry, I can't stand that 'Noel' business—is somebody. I would be a fool to tell you otherwise."

Marjorie steadied herself with a hand on the doorway. She had taken two more aspirins, and was feeling more and more disembodied and tranced. She combed her mind for the gritty contradiction that was haunting her, perceived it, and pounced on it. "So. He's just dandy, is he? That's why you sent Pop out this morning to bribe me with a western trip to leave South Wind tomorrow. Because you like Noel so much."

"Yes. It's exactly the right thing for you to do," the mother said calmly. "Don't I know how you feel about me? You're still looking at me as though you're waiting for me to pull out a knife, or something. That's why I told Papa to suggest it, I thought he might have better luck with you. He did fine, didn't he, the great diplomat! I have to laugh. It's an easy thing to say, be diplomatic. For years he's been saying I'm not diplomatic. Darling, wait till you have to be diplomatic with a daughter in love with some good-for-nothing, or with her mind made up to do something stupid. You'll see. Get dressed." The mother stood and came to the doorway of the bathroom. "Do you remember when you showed up with George Drobes? Do you remember?"

"I remember." Marjorie began to put on her costume.

"Do you remember how you hated me, do you remember the things you called me, for so much as suggesting that George Drobes wasn't Clark Gable and President Roosevelt and Einstein and Julius Caesar all rolled into one Bronx college boy with a red nose? Do you remember?"

"I was fifteen——"

"It went on till you were seventeen, till two and a half very short years ago, my darling Marjorie. All right! Now then, was I right or was I wrong? Should I have gone out and danced in the street when you brought home George Drobes? Was I such a monster after all, such a devil, such a cold heartless killjoy to picture, to dare even to imagine for a minute, that somewhere in the world there might be a fellow—a Noel Airman, let's say—walking around, who might conceivably be a tiny bit more promising, a tiny bit more talented, more good-looking, more everything, than the wonderful George Drobes?"

"All right," Marjorie flared, "what do you want me to do, lick your shoes because you're an adult and can see more clearly than a girl of fifteen? I'm not ashamed that I liked George. I never will be. He was good and sweet and bright, and if he was unlucky enough to——"

"How does he compare to Noel Airman, darling? Because if not for me, remember, you never would have met your Mr. Airman. You'd be Mrs. George Drobes of Southern Boulevard, right this minute."

"Mom, you're not being fair. It isn't in you to be fair," Marjorie said chokingly.

"No, I'm not fair, I'm not diplomatic, but I just ask you to remember this stupid habit I have of being right sometimes. Because I'm going to argue with you some more now for your own good, just as I did then. You told Papa you don't want to marry Noel. Don't tell *me* such stories. You're putting the best face on it, so as not to look like a fool. Marjorie, if you're not honest with anyone else, at least be honest with yourself. You think you're going to get this fellow to marry you, and steady down, and use his talents, and become somebody big. That's what you really think. Listen, it's a very tough job, but it's possible. After all, how far does the apple fall from the tree? Judge Ehrmann is a very big man."

"I'm not planning to marry him. I'm not planning anything. I'm just *enjoying* myself. That's what you and Dad can't seem to understand. I don't have to calculate my every move, Mom, I'm not fifty-five, I'm twenty, for heaven's sake. Noel amuses me, he's brilliant, he's charming, as you say—except you don't know how charming and brilliant he is, you can't begin to imagine—— Naturally it's fun to be around such a person."

"All right. Marjorie remains Marjorie. Say what you please," said the mother. "I'm not blind. All I've got to see is the way you look at him and the way he looks at you. He's in love with you, too."

"I never heard such nonsense," Marjorie said, and in the wave of gladness that swept her she thought that her mother was really changing with advancing age and becoming more likable. Fluffing out her skirt, she walked to the door. "Mom, I'm sorry to break up this fascinating con-versation, but I have to get to work——"

"If you're a minute late, Greech won't fire you, for the money he's paying you. Listen to me, it's important. Your friend Noel is so used to girls that he can't take a new one too seriously, not even the great Marjorie Morgenstern. Your problem is to make him be serious. And believe me, the way to do it is to get out from under his thumb. This way you're at a disadvantage. You're always around, you're working for him. Any time of the day or night you're handy if he just snaps his fingers. It's too easy. Let him miss you a little bit. That's the first thing you have to do."

It was amazing, Marjorie thought, how sometimes her mother could crash to the heart of a matter. The fact was she had been feeling neglected and piqued during the past week. Exactly the same ideas had been going through her mind. She had ventured once to complain to Noel of his inattention. He had laughed heartily at her; he was simply preoccupied with the fiesta, he said. The explanation was a reasonable one, and she had accepted it. But she had not forgotten the mood of chilliness, the fear of being despised and discarded by Noel, that had overwhelmed her for a couple of days.

She said with a laugh that wasn't very successful, "Well, he'd probably just be glad to get rid of me if I went out West, and that would be the end of it."

"Marjorie, if that's the case, isn't this the time to find it out?"

"Dad doesn't like him, I know that. He hates him."

"He doesn't hate him. Papa is jealous, that's all. He doesn't think any man in the world is good enough for you. Listen, Marjorie, I won't fool you. I'm not overflowing with happiness. A man who changes his name, a songwriter, Greenwich Village—but listen, you're in love, you're almost out of college. His background is fine. He's strange, but you're strange too. My actress!" The mother smiled at her, half fondly, half satirically.

"You really—you do really like Noel, though?"

Mrs. Morgenstern shook her head. "I'm not saying he's the right man for you. I don't know. I did my best for twenty years. Now, it's up to God."

"We'll talk about the trip, Mom. Later. Let me think about it."

"Think all you want."

Every seat was taken for the bullfight, and a heavy overflow of spectators sat on cushions on the grass. The bull ring was a huge three-quarter circle of yellow folding chairs, five deep on the lawn. At the open end of the circle, near the social hall, the band in sombreros and charro outfits and eyeglasses sat in a huddle, their music sheets flapping in the breeze on rickety stands.

Marjorie made her entrance with the other dancers from behind the social hall, laughing, shouting Spanish, and throwing roses. She was extraordinarily gay. Her mother's astounding friendliness to Noel had given her hope that all was going to be well. She swished her skirt so flirtatiously, and cast such brilliant smiles at the circle of guests, that many of the men watched her to the neglect of the other dancers.

It was so strange and so pleasant to be dancing on the grass in the summer sunlight! The ring of guests made a bright show. Earlier in the day they had struck her as a grotesque lot, skylarking about the lawn in Greech's cheap sombreros and pink cheesecloth mantillas, singing snatches of *Rancho Grande* and *Cielito Lindo,* calling each other Pedro and Carmen, affecting Mexican accents, often as not in the flat singsongs of the Bronx and Brooklyn. It had occurred to her that they were material for a *New Yorker* story. But now, looking around at them as she twirled and smiled, she thought that they were exactly like herself, youngsters snatching at fun while they chased the dream of a happy marriage; chased it through a world that became more of a maze, and more slippery underfoot, each year. She even had compassionate thoughts for the bulbous pigs scattered through the crowd, wearing rakishly cocked sombreros.

The afternoon was cooler and the shadows were growing long when the dances ended and she joined her parents to watch the bullfight. Mrs. Morgenstern had kept a vacant chair for her, fending off the guests ruthlessly. "It's not fair, you know," Marjorie panted, sinking gratefully into the chair despite the glares of guests squatting on the grass. "I'm just hired help."

"Let him fire you, that devil," said Mrs. Morgenstern. "For what he pays you, you can sit in a chair."

The bullfight began.

The annual South Wind corrida, though colorful in its fashion, bore only a remote resemblance to the sombre and gallant ritual described in the works of Ernest Hemingway. First the band lined up at the open end of the ring and marched in, playing the entrance music raggedly and thinly. Next came a procession of assorted waiters, caddies, and bellboys, grinning stupidly in motley bullfighter costumes, which were tight in the seat, and ran heavily to red cheesecloth and gold spangles. Some of them were mounted on horses from the camp stables. The horses, too, were decked out in loud-colored cloth, feathers, and paper streamers. There was scattered applause, together with some laughter and jeers, as the burlesque parade filed around the ring. "It's pretty, though," Mrs.

Morgenstern said, when the marchers halted in a semicircular array facing the entrance. "They've gone to a lot of trouble."

"Noel's done it all," Marjorie said. "He even designed the costumes."

The music stopped. The giggling and the shouting died away. A cool breeze fluttered the streamers on the horses. Everybody looked toward the entrance. The band crashed into the toreador song from *Carmen;* the bullfighters began to sing, in raucous chorus; and from behind the social hall Samson-Aaron appeared, riding a spindly old white horse.

He was wearing an unbelievably vast pair of lavender tights that extended from his knees to his armpits; also white silk stockings, purple pumps, a purple silver-trimmed jacket that barely covered his shoulders, and a tiny flat matador's hat with two purple pompons. Fastened to his side on a belt in place of a sword was a gigantic meat cleaver. As he came trotting into the ring, his great paunch bobbed and flopped in the straining tights, which threatened to pop like an overblown lavender balloon. He was so broad-bottomed that he appeared to hang over in lavender bags on either side of his bony mount. He was grinning his black-gapped grin, bowing this way and that with blubbery precarious majesty, as he bobbed in the saddle. Marjorie and Mrs. Morgenstern were shrieking with laughter at the fantastically ridiculous sight from the moment he appeared; and even the father, after a reluctant grunt or two, threw back his head and laughed as Marjorie had seldom heard him laugh. The whole lawn echoed with cheers and guffaws. Samson-Aaron jogged once around the ring, doffing the little hat to the cheers, and rode out, leaving the crowd still laughing. The musicians marched out behind him and took their former seats. The bullfighters scattered about the ring, and stood with their cardboard weapons poised.

A bugle brayed, and the "bull" catapulted snorting into the ring.

It was a remarkably lifelike fake. Puddles Podell was in the front end; the rear was occupied by a grumpy little stagehand who was jealously proud of this assignment. In four years the pair had worked up a supple, scary imitation of a bull's gait and stance. The head had ghastly staring eyes that could roll and blink. The ragged-toothed mouth opened and closed on a string, with a monstrous red tongue licking in and out. After pawing the ground and snorting in mid-ring for a while, the bull let out a fearful bellow, and came charging down directly at the part of the ring where the Morgensterns were sitting, its eyes staring, its sharp curved horns poised to gore, its mouth flapping open as it roared, a terrible red cavern. The bullfighters scattered out of its way, yelling, and as it bore down on the seats Marjorie was a bit frightened, despite herself. In front of her some guests ducked, and one fat girl ran squealing from her seat. Inches from the chairs, the bull stopped short with a sound of screeching brakes. As the fat girl returned sheepishly to her seat, to the laughter of the crowd, the tongue poked out of the bull's mouth and licked her hand; then the bull nosed her behind, and rolled its eyes, and clicked its rear legs in the air.

Ten minutes of extravagant monkeyshines with the bullfighters followed, at the end of which several of them lay scattered on the grass, presumably gored to death. The bull, bristling all over with crepe-paper banderillas, stood in the center of the ring, panting, its tongue hanging down nearly three feet. The band struck up the toreador song, and Samson-Aaron came waddling into the ring, sharpening the cleaver on a razor strop.

The foolishness that ensued was indescribable. Marjorie laughed so hard that at one point she sank off her chair and sat on the grass with her head in her hands, moaning and weeping feebly. All the spectators were howling and writhing with laughter. The Uncle chased the bull; the bull chased the Uncle; they boxed; they butted each other; the bull got on its knees and begged for mercy; it seized the cleaver in its teeth and beat the Uncle over the head with it; there were a hundred other crazy antics. Noel had used all the gags of previous years and had invented some new ones; and Puddles and the Uncle had worked out a few more. Marjorie had never laughed so loud or so long in her life. At the finish, as Samson-Aaron with upraised cleaver was about to despatch the bull, he pronounced over the drooping staring animal the first words of the Jewish prayer for the dead. The bull raised its head and bellowed the correct response. The Uncle dropped the cleaver, amazed, and asked the bull in Yiddish where it came from. In a rapid Yiddish exchange the bull and the toreador discovered they were both from the same small town near Odessa. Samson-Aaron threw his arms around the bull and kissed it. The band started up a lively Russian dance. The Uncle began to bound and twirl, then he squatted and kicked out his legs, his belly shaking fearfully. The bull stared at him for a moment, then it too squatted and kicked out its four legs, Russian style. It was at this incredibly ludicrous sight—the gargantuan toreador in lavender and the bull with the hanging tongue squatting and dancing Russian-fashion, and shouting "Hey! Hey!"—that Marjorie fell off her chair. Samson-Aaron and the bull danced out of the ring side by side, and all the guests rose and cheered, and threw sombreros in the air.

They kept applauding and cheering. They would not be satisfied with bows. Even when the bull took off its head and Puddles tried to beg off with a grateful speech, wiping his purple face, they would not listen. The bull had to go back to the middle of the ring, and Samson-Aaron had to come on again stropping the meat cleaver; and they repeated the entire act. This time at the end Samson-Aaron did not dance, but sat on the ground, crossed his arms and kicked his legs as though he were dancing, and then staggered off with his arm around the bull's neck, pantomiming exhaustion. The audience laughed at this variation, but Mrs. Morgenstern all at once grew serious and stood. "What's the matter with him? Why's he doing that?"

"Don't be silly, Mom," Marjorie said, "it's his idea of clowning, that's all." But the mother was already working her way out of the seats.

They found the Uncle behind the social hall, sitting on a folding chair, surrounded by the cast of the bullfight. Marjorie was terrified for a moment when she saw the cluster of people around the fat lavender-clad figure, but relief warmed her when she heard them laughing.

"Hello, Modgerie!" he boomed. His face was pale and the tights were streaked black with sweat, but his eyes gleamed with triumph and fun. "Vell, you and me, ve go on the stage and make lots of money, ha? The Uncle is a regular Chollie Choplin! If I only find it out a few years earlier I vould be a millionaire, not a dishvasher, ha? Whoosh! Such a vorkout. Good for me, I lose twenty pounds."

The father said, "You feel all right, Uncle?"

"Vy not? A little exercise hurts a man?"

Puddles, standing in the bull skin with the head under his arm, said, "What's everybody worried about him for? What about me? I nearly died inside this damn head."

"You!" said Mrs. Morgenstern. "You're a young man." She tried to get Samson-Aaron to go back to the kitchen workers' barracks at once, but he insisted on accompanying the Morgensterns to their car to see them off. "Vot, I vouldn't come and say goodbye? I'm crippled or something?"

As they crossed the crowded lawn, from which the ring of chairs was being removed, some guests cheered and applauded the Uncle, and he had to take off his matador's hat repeatedly. "A dishvasher should be so popular, ha?" he said. "Milton should see it." The old man's face beamed and perspired under the absurd purple pompons. The usual high color had flowed back into his puffy cheeks, and he hummed an old Yiddish song as he walked springily along.

The parents' luggage was already piled in the car in the cinder-strewn parking space behind the camp office. "Well, I guess it's goodbye," the mother said. She tossed the father's sombrero into the back seat.

Mr. Morgenstern embraced Marjorie in a quick nervous hug, not looking at her. "Take good care of my daughter," he said. He slapped Samson-Aaron on the back and got into the driver's seat.

The mother peered at Marjorie, wrinkling up her eyes. "So? Any decision?"

"Mom, I really—I appreciate it, believe me, I do. You may be right. When will you be home, Wednesday? I'll call you."

"Don't wait till Wednesday. If you make up your mind tonight, tomorrow, whenever it is, call me at Seth's camp. I'll call Papa's office and they'll make everything ready for you." She gave her the camp telephone number. "Marjorie, do it."

"Maybe I will. I really may, Mom."

"Good." Mrs. Morgenstern turned to the Uncle. Her face clouded. "So, Samson-Aaron? You want to listen to me? Enough foolishness. Quit this job. Come home. We'll find you something better."

"Vy? I make a dollar, it's nice, I fish, I see Modgerie——"

"You're an old man. Why must you keep up the foolish tricks? Look at you, sweating like a horse, dancing like a crazy man. Look at your hands, all chewed up from broken dishes." The Uncle guiltily put his red-notched hands behind him. "What's going to be the end, Uncle? Are you going to be Samson-Aaron for always?"

The Uncle smiled. "Who else should I be if not Samson-Aaron? Goodbye, Rose, you're good, you're like a sister."

The mother expelled a long sigh, puffing out her cheeks. She looked from the girl to the old man. "I keep trying to fix everything. Why? It's God's world." She kissed them both. "Take care of yourselves. And . . . and grow up, both of you." With a little laugh and a shrug of her shoulders, she got into the car. It drove off with a rattle of cinders. Looking after it, Marjorie felt the scarred damp hand of the Uncle softly clasp hers.

She leaned on the Uncle's shoulder and kissed his bristly cheek. "Let's both go and lie down. I'm dead. You don't have to wash dishes tonight, do you?"

"Me? I sit at the table vit Mr. Airman for dinner. Big shot."

"Good. See you later. You go and rest now, the way Mom said."

"Vot you think," the Uncle said, "I play a game tennis?" They went separate ways. She could see him for a while laboring up the hill toward the kitchen barracks, a monstrous waddling figure in lavender tights and a purple matador's hat.

Marjorie made for her bungalow, almost staggering under a sudden wave of fatigue, and fell in a disorderly heap on a bed.

Chapter 19. THE SOUTH WIND WALTZ

A kiss awakened her—a kiss strongly flavored with rum. It was still daylight. Wally Wronken was stooped over her, swaying. He wore a yellow polo shirt and gray flannel trousers; there was no fiesta touch about him except the drink in his hand. "Ah, the princess wakes," he said.

"Say, where do you get your nerve?" She made instinctive sleepy gestures at her bodice and skirt. "You get out of here. You're not allowed on these grounds. And what do you mean, kissing me when I'm asleep? I ought to sock you."

"Why, it's the classic way of arousing the sleeping beauty," said Wally. "I've broken the hundred-year spell, princess. The clocks are ticking again in the castle. The cooks and the grooms are gaping and stretching. The king has resumed counting his tarnished money, and the spider is finishing the web that has hung incomplete and dusty for a century——"

"You're drunk," Marjorie said, yawning. "And it isn't even dark. You're disgusting."

"Yes, I know, princess. I am disgusting. But I was not always thus." He spoke with a slow, slightly thick precision, making elegant gestures with the drink, spilling it a little. "Now that I have broken your spell, will you break mine? A wicked witch, princess, has put me into this form of a loathsome bespectacled toad. One kiss from your virgin lips, and before your eyes I shall spring erect, a tall handsome golden-haired social director in a black sweater. We shall marry and live happily ever after, on kisses, hamburgers, and Automat coffee."

"Don't be so funny." She glanced at her watch. "Oh, Lord, six-thirty already."

"You're wanted in the social hall," said Wally, "by the great I Am."

"Noel?"

"Christmas himself. Tell me, would you like me any better if I called myself Ash Wednesday Wronken?"

"Get out of here. I'll be down there in a minute. What does he want?"

"Your fair white body. As who does not?"

"Good Lord, how many have you had?"

He drained the glass, tossed it aside, walked stiffly to the door, and turned. "No lilacs." He pointed overhead. "Look. No lilacs."

"What?"

"She doesn't remember," he said to the ceiling. "And the words are graven on my heart. 'You'll get another kiss,' you said, 'when we find such lilacs again.'—I got it, kiddo. No lilacs. Fooled you."

"Well, I hope the thrill lasts," Marjorie said. "Lilacs or no lilacs, I'm not going to have much more to do with you, if you don't stop behaving like an infant."

"She does not know the secret in the poet's heart. Exit Marchbanks," said Wally. He stepped out of the door and fell head first down the stairs of the bungalow, with tremendous thumping and banging. When Marjorie came to the door in alarm, he was on his hands and knees, brushing dead leaves and dirt off himself. "No harm done. Mere nothing. Tell me, by the way, how did your folks like Noel?"

"Get up and get out of here, you loon, before I report you as a Peeping Tom."

He got to his feet, blinking and peering around. His face looked oddly bare and defenseless. "If the indictment is to stand I need my glasses. I can't peep at my own hand without them."

"They're right behind your heel. Don't step on them."

He put them on and squinted at her. "Ah. That's better. Dr. Livingstone, I presume?"

"Go away." She went inside and quickly showered. Though she had slept two hours, she felt unrefreshed and heavy. This day was the longest, or at least the slowest-moving, of her life. A week seemed to have passed since her talk with her father in the rowboat. She put on a green cotton print dress and ran down the path toward the social hall.

"Let us maintain our dignity, please, Miss Morningstar," she heard Wally say as she came out on the lawn. "Does Katharine Cornell scamper? Did Bernhardt?"

"You again?"

He came and walked beside her. "Really, what did your folks say? Did they like our man of a thousand perfections?"

"They liked him a lot better than they'd like you in your present state, I'll tell you that. You should be ashamed. A kid like you, getting drunk in the middle of the day."

"I have several answers to that. Six-thirty is not the middle of the day, but the last of its declining slope. I am not drunk, I am fuddled, in the best tradition of an English gentleman. I am not a kid, but a marvelously talented young writer. As such I demand your respect, and I strongly advise you to consider whether your choice of——"

"That's something I'm going to talk to you about, Wally, when you're a little more sober. Your writing. You need a straightening-out, my boy."

"Oh, indeed?" He pointed to a booth. "Excuse me while I pick up a drink. Won't be a moment. You too?"

"No, thanks. You're excused for the evening. Go ahead, make a hog of yourself. Only stay away from me."

"Not a hog. A frog. Frog prince. Please don't desert me. There isn't another virgin within a thousand miles."

Marjorie made a face at him and walked off to the social hall. Noel was at the piano, still in his yellow charro outfit, teaching a Mexican song to performers clustered around him. The silver-ornamented sombrero lay on the piano top. He looked extremely singular, with a dark brown complexion and thick wavy blond hair. "Hi, Marge, enjoying the fiesta?"

"It's wonderful. Except I'm half dead."

"It has gone pretty well, hasn't it?" He left the piano. His eyes and his teeth, set off with peculiar brilliance by the brown grease paint, flashed in a virile grin. "No other camp has anything like it. It's just a lot of trivial foolishness, of course, but it is gay."

"Very gay."

"Did your folks enjoy it?"

"Yes. They've gone. They had a marvelous time."

"I hope so. They're very likable, really. Your mother and I got quite friendly this morning."

"So she said."

"Your chores are all done, aren't they? There's no more dancing scheduled."

"That's right. Unless there's something you want me to do."

"No, no, I was just wondering—why don't you eat at my table at the torchlight supper? With me and your uncle? I have a feeling that I haven't seen you for a year."

"Oh?" She laughed with relief. "Is that why you sent for me? I've been having somewhat the same feeling. I'd love to, Noel, thanks. I'll go and dress up."

"Wait, there's one more thing."

Wally was at Marjorie's elbow, thrusting a drink at her. "Here, Morningstar. Drink, for once dead you never shall return."

Marjorie reluctantly took the drink and said to Noel, "This fool, look at him. He came and woke me up with a big wet rum-soaked kiss."

Noel laughed, glancing at Wally with friendly curiosity. "Well, what's happening to you, Young Sobersides? South Wind's finally gotten to you, hey?"

"I have gone native," Wally said. "And when I fall, I fall like Lucifer. It will interest you to know that I am seriously looking over the pig situation."

"Get away from me," Marjorie said, "I'll never talk to you again."

"Nonsense," Noel said amiably. "He's such a starry-eyed snob, if he does take up with a pig he'll spend the evening reading T. S. Eliot to her."

"That shows how much you know. I shall reveal my plan of action to you," Wally said. "At precisely midnight I shall, after making a suitable announcement over the loudspeakers and turning on the floodlights, ravish said pig in the middle of the lawn. Away with this Victorian skulking, I say. Sex is beautiful."

"You're in bad shape," Noel said. "Look, Marge, the other thing is, the fiesta pretty well bogs down at night, usually. Half the people have gone home, the novelty of the costumes is played out—even the fireworks don't help much. We've had a lot of requests for a repeat of the bullfight at supper, just the part with the bull and your uncle. He was a terrific hit, and——"

"Gosh, Noel, I honestly think he's done enough for one day, don't you?"

"Well, that's why I wanted to ask you."

"Why? Is it so important?" She was disturbed at the sudden fall in his buoyant manner. "I mean—well, the thing is just about over anyway, Noel, and—I know he's looking forward to eating at your table, it's such a great honor in his eyes——"

"Why, he'd still do that, Marjorie. It's just that he was so perfect—Greech wouldn't pay him anything more, I know. Blood from a turnip and all that. But I'd pay him another fifty out of my own pocket."

"Look, Noel, why don't you ask him?" It was exceedingly distasteful to talk about money with Noel, and to hear him confirm that the Uncle had been paid.

"Well, I will, if you don't mind."

"But he'll eat with us? It would be awful if he had to give that up."

"Of course he will. Before the show starts."

"And then perform those didos on a full stomach," Wally interposed. "Fun."

"Wally, just shut up, won't you?" Noel said in a startling tone of ragged irritation. Then he smiled, slapped Wally's back, and said with his usual pleasant warmth, "Sorry. Temperament. Nerves. Overwork." He turned and shouted to the singers, who were arguing at the piano, "Back in five minutes, kids!" He put his arm around Marjorie's neck in a brief hug. "Look very beautiful tonight." He hurried out.

Marjorie glanced at Wally, then took a deep gulp of the drink. "Say, this tastes marvelous. There's pineapple in it."

"Come," Wally said, taking her elbow.

"Where?"

"You'll give me that talking-to."

"Oh no. When you know what I'm saying, I will."

"Believe me, Morningstar, every word you ever say sinks into me."

Marjorie took another deep drink, nearly emptying the glass. "Why, it isn't strong at all, it's like a fruit drink. However did you get in such shape?"

"Like another one?"

"Sure."

"Come along."

The gray rock behind the social hall was called Lover's Point. They sat with drinks in the cool breeze, under a pale green clear sky; the sun, dipping huge and orange to the trees, threw a long rippling orange path on the lake. Wally turned his glittering glasses toward her. "Go ahead. Drop the guillotine."

"What?"

"The talking-to."

"Forget it. Let's just enjoy the sunset." She sipped the drink.

"No, please. Lay it on. It will probably be good for me."

"Well, all right, Wally." The drink was beginning to warm her. "Somebody's got to tell you. I like you, you know that, and I say this only because I like you, and want you to have a great future. You're—well, you're prostituting your talent."

"Oh? Exactly how?" he said, blinking.

"You know very well how. By writing a lot of dirty jokes and double-meaning rhymes to get cheap laughs."

He stared. "But, Marge——"

"I know what you're going to say. South Wind shows don't matter. The audience is vulgar and stupid, you've got to pander to them, and so forth. Well, that's just where you're wrong. If you start by pandering here, you'll do it the rest of your life, and you'll end up a hack. Now is the time to start having principles about your work. And—well, that's all I wanted to say, really." His face was still turned expectantly to her. There was a short silence. "That wasn't too bad, was it?" she said lightly, feeling the weight of the quiet. "But it's true, and I hope you'll take it to heart. You have talent, and you should use it properly." She drank. "Lord, look at that sun. It's flattening like a pumpkin."

"Marge, I appreciate what you say, I truly do." His tone was low and unexpectedly sober. "You may well be right."

"Good for you, Wally. I'm glad I spoke up. Laughs aren't everything, that's all. You should study Noel's writing. There are such things as charm, taste——"

"Oh my God." He stood, and said slowly, "Let's get this on the record now. You just said I should study Noel's writing. Correct?"

"I certainly did, and if you——"

"All right. Thank you." He finished his drink. Suddenly he threw his glass at the nearest tree. It struck and shattered, and the pieces made little orange sparkles as they tinkled to the ground. "Marjorie, you've asked for this. Now you listen to me." He stalked up to her and stood before her, stoop-shouldered and weaving. He was on a lower shelf of the rock, his eyes level with hers. He poked a finger out at her and spoke with precise slowness. "For the past three weeks you have been making such a colossal overbearing goddamned fool of yourself around Noel that you haven't a friend left at South Wind except me. There's nobody, I tell you, nobody on the staff who doesn't regard you as a prime jackass, nobody who doesn't laugh themselves sick over your antics. You couldn't have tortured this out of me, Margie, but when you have the gall to tell me I ought to study what *Noel* writes——"

"Why, Wally, how dare you start reviling me just because I criticize your work? You asked me, remember, you *asked* me——"

"Look, my work is crude, I know that very well, but in the name of heaven, I'm nineteen years old. I'm still in college. Noel is practically thirty, Marjorie—he's THIRTY, don't you realize that? And right now my work is better than his, *better*——"

"You're pretty drunk, my boy——"

"Good Lord, how blind can love make a girl?" His full lower lip was trembling. "Can't you see that he's hit his level, that he hit it years ago, and has never gone above it, and never will? That he does a little of this and a little of that, a tune, a lyric, a piano solo, an orchestra arrangement, a skit, a chess game"—he threw his shoulders rhythmically from side to side, making sneering little gestures—"a conversation in French, a conversation in Spanish, an argument about Freud or Spengler, and that's Noel Airman, the beginning and the end of him? Marjorie, take it from me, and don't ever forget that I told you this on the first Sunday in August, 1935—Noel Airman is NOTHING. He will never get anywhere, never. By the time I'm thirty, Noel's present age, mind you, ten years from now, I'll be FAMOUS, do you hear?"

He was leaning far forward, passionately shaking his fist at her. He actually reminded her of a Marchbanks she had once seen in an amateur show, shrill, eager, ugly, short, who had leaned so far forward in a tirade at Candida that she had wondered whether he wore trick shoes fastened to the floor. The thought made her smile.

"All right, Wally. You're a great unappreciated genius. It'll be our little secret. Let me have a cigarette."

"Don't you patronize me! I won't stand for it!" He jerked the pack of mentholated cigarettes from his trousers, knocked one out, and lit it for her in angry little gestures. "Talent really doesn't matter, though, does it? It wouldn't matter if I'd already written *Once in a Lifetime* and *Private Lives*. I'm not Noel. That's all that counts. He is Noel. Therefore he's Shaw and Coward and Richard Rodgers and——"

Her tone was quiet, though clear, as she said, "Wally, how about *Princess Jones?*"

He stopped short in his pacing, and squinted at her. "Eh?"

"*Princess Jones,* dear." He blinked and stared. "Come, Wally, you remember that little piece Noel played for us the other night? The complete musical comedy he wrote, book, lyrics, music, everything? You said yourself it was a masterpiece. How about that?"

His jaw hung slightly open. He said after a moment, "*Princess Jones?*"

"Why, yes. *Princess Jones.*"

Wally dropped down on the rock and put his head in his hand. "I'm drunker than I thought. I'm dizzy." He said nothing for several moments.

The sun was gone. The lake had turned purple, and the breeze, cooler and stronger, smelled of laurel. Wally said in an altered tone, his face still in his hand, "I don't exactly know about *Princess Jones.* I was drunk when I heard it. But I admit—I mean, it's certainly got charm, but as far as a Broadway production goes—anyhow, nobody can tell about those things. I mean, maybe I've been laying it on a little, but you know damned well he hasn't done a thing here this year that can compare with my Hitler number——"

She put her hand on his shoulder. "Dear, he's bored by this place, can't you see that much? He's told me himself that his work has been much too routine. He's delighted with your skits because they're fresh. You're nineteen, Wally, South Wind is a challenge to you——"

"But it's beneath Noel Airman, eh? Okay. You'll find an answer for everything. I might have known better than to argue about him with you." He jerked away from under her hand. "I hope you realize that everyone on the staff except me is certain you're sleeping with him."

"Yes, we've had plenty of laughs over that. I can't help the kind of minds people have."

"You've given them no cause to think so, is that right?"

"I've been dancing a lot with Noel and—well, going with him, the way I have with several other fellows in my time, but among my kind of people that doesn't mean having an affair——"

"It's incredible." He shook his head at the sky. "I'll never forget this as long as I live. The blindness, the complete loss of self-criticism—— Marjorie, I know you. You're bright as the devil, you have a sense of humor, you're alert to everything around you. Don't you realize that you've been acting like a wife, and a very bossy wife, at rehearsals the past few weeks? Telling Noel how he should do this and that, criticizing people's performances to him while they're standing on the stage listening, practically directing some scenes, or trying to? Haven't you noticed at all how he's had to smooth people's feelings, how he's diplomatically told you to shut up twenty times? You've been impossible, in your charming little way. Mrs. Fixit herself, blooming overnight out of an office girl. How dumb do you think people are? Or how obtuse are you, actually?"

This attack threw Marjorie into a muddy scared turmoil. "It's untrue, absolutely untrue, you're just saying it to upset me, you're a cruel little wretch." But her mind was racing across the past weeks, and Wally's accusation shone out like a phosphorescent thread connecting a number of puzzling incidents and remarks. "I've made some suggestions about lighting, yes. I'm in charge of the lights. But——"

"Marjorie, I used to be in charge of the lights. Did you ever hear me open my face at rehearsals? You haven't just offered your opinion on lights, you've been moving in on everything——"

Her eyes stinging and moistening, she said, "Well then, if I've made such an idiotic spectacle of myself how is it you don't think I'm having an affair with him? What's your doubt?"

"I'll believe it when you tell me. Nothing else will ever make me believe it. As he says, I'm starry-eyed. About you, anyway."

She stamped her foot. "I don't want you to be *anything* about me, do you hear? I hope you write your hit at twenty-five and make seven billion dollars and win the Pulitzer Prize. I'm sure you'll make some girl very happy. Don't talk to me about your colossal talents any more. And don't come running down Noel to me. Nothing you say matters. It isn't because love has made me an imbecile, either. It's because you're nineteen, and don't know what anything's about. You do have talent, but you're pitifully ignorant of the first principles of taste. My crime is simply that I had the ghastly nerve to tell you to your face that you were being vulgar in your writing, and so you were! I don't take back a word of it, Wally. Some day you'll thank me. You may even apologize, if you grow up that much."

He put his hands out to her, supplicating. "Margie, please, *please* believe that what you said about my work isn't the reason I——"

"Let me tell you this, now!" She raised her voice. "Noel has always treated you wonderfully, and you know it. He's given you every encouragement. He's praised you to the skies. He's given you new responsibilities as fast as you could take them on. He doesn't fear you or envy you—— Nobody would be happier than Noel if you turned out to be his successor at South Wind. But you—you can only see him through a fog of ambition and jealousy. And you're so unbalanced with your little success last night that a few drinks brings it all out of you. Listen, Wally, I'm not as blind as you think. Noel has been spoiled by his own good looks and charm. He's sowed too damned many wild oats. I'm perfectly aware of that. And yet, just offhand, with his fingertips, without trying, he's had hit songs, he's put on wonderful South Wind shows, he's mastered everything he's ever put his hand to. Even my mother, who has a mind like a bank manager where I'm concerned, likes Noel. And she doesn't know about *Princess Jones*. If *Princess Jones* isn't a smash—and I think it's going to be—the next one he writes will. Nothing can stop Noel Airman, if he ever really tries to do what——"

Wally interrupted shakily, "Your mother—your mother likes Noel? Is that true?"

"I wouldn't bother to lie to you, believe me."

Wally lit another cigarette with his hunched-over furtive quick motion, like a boy sneaking a smoke. He sank down on the rock; his shoulders curved and drooped; his big head dropped forward on his chest, and the black hair fell over his forehead. "God knows it could all be true, Margie—that I'm eaten alive by envy, that I'm a heavy-handed vulgarian, that I start sneering at Noel, and bawling insults at you, because I'm full of rum. Surest way to win your fair hand that I could devise, isn't it? Oh, God." He dropped his head on his arms, resting them on his drawn-up knees.

She felt she owed him some gratitude. He had exaggerated her helpfulness at rehearsals into a horrible false picture of herself as a domineering harpy; but the wagging tongues of the staff, she knew, were quite good at such malicious caricature, and now she was warned. "Wally, please don't be so miserable. You have no idea what a day I've had." She put her hand on his shoulder. "You were pretty rough on me, you know. I still like you, I admire your work—nothing's changed."

He put his hand on hers. "Margie——"

She bent, kissed him lightly on the mouth, and laughed. "There. See? No lilacs. Well, Mr. Frog Prince? Why don't you change? You said you would."

He stood wearily. "I lied to you, you see. I can't change. I'm a frog, that's all. Never was, never will be, anything else."

"That's not so. You're going to change slowly but surely, in about ten years, into a fine prince——"

"I've got to go help put up the torches," he said. "Thanks for the talking-to. I won't forget."

At the torchlight supper, Samson-Aaron was himself again. He ate enormously of the chile and rice and enchiladas, laughing at Marjorie's objections. His hand rested on the whiskey bottle, and he replenished his own glass and Noel's the instant they were empty. "Vot, little queen, you gonna be like Milton?" he roared, his face ruddy and shining in the flaring yellow light, when she tried to move the bottle out of his reach. "A fiesta is a fiesta, hey, Mr. Airman?" He kept Noel laughing with a stream of Yiddish jokes and aphorisms—Marjorie was surprised at how well Noel understood them—and laughed just as hard at them himself. He joined in the Mexican songs, shouting "Da diddly da" instead of the words, showing a quick ear for the melodies. After a while Marjorie stopped worrying, and gave herself over to enjoying the strange party of three. Noel's small table was placed near the fountain, at the highest point of the sloping lawn, so that he could watch the progress of the supper. The loud splashing of the multicolored streams of water made the air damp and fresh, and forced them to raise their voices when they talked.

The feeling that she was in a dream now almost overwhelmed her. With rushing cataracts of changing red, green, gold, blue, and white water on one side of her; with an array of tables stretching away from her on the other side, lit by wobbling yellow flames; eating queer-tasting food, under a black sky ablaze with stars; Noel at her left in his sombrero, yellow suit, and brown paint, the Uncle at her right in his unbelievable lavender drawers and purple pompon hat; with a queerly mingled aching and lightness all through her body, and a recurrent tingling in her arms and ringing in her ears; with a feeling of exhaustion, emotional and physical, and yet a defiant hilarious sense of being ready to go on and on with ever madder nonsense; with all these feelings and sensations whirling in her brain, Marjorie was nervously enjoying the phantasmagoria, and wishing—at one and the same time—that it would continue for hours, and that she were already awake tomorrow in a gray sensible Monday morning, with nothing seriously gone wrong.

The bullfighting act fell flat. It was hard to see, despite the floodlights, and the tables interfered with it, and most of the guests were lethargic in the backwash of the day's excitement and stuporous with food and drink; and anyway, it was the third repetition of the same joke. The Uncle returned to the table panting, dripping, grinning palely. "Vas good?" Marjorie and Noel urged him to go to the barracks to shower and change, and rather to her surprise the Uncle agreed. "Vun drink. To keep varm." He swallowed a stiff shot of whiskey. Noel told him to be sure to come to the staff party backstage after midnight. "Such an honor for a

dishvasher?" he panted. "Thanks, Mr. Airman, vy not? I come vit bells."
He disappeared into the gloom beyond the fountain.

Marjorie and Noel looked at each other. Noel said, "I guess we could
have done without it. But it did help. It really did."

"Of course it did," Marjorie said.

The fireworks began to bang and burst over the black lake, in colored
showers.

Summertime has passed,
This night is our last,
Listen! It's the South Wind Waltz.
Once before we part,
Heart to loving heart,
Come, we'll dance the South Wind Waltz. . . .

In the black turtle-neck sweater, with the brown makeup gone, Noel
looked extraordinarily young, pale, and attractive at the piano. Marjorie,
her arm around the Uncle's waist, a glass of champagne in her hand,
swayed sentimentally to the music, enchanted with this party amid stacks
of painted scenery, cardboard rocks and trees, and all the tangle of ropes,
spotlights, and electric cables. It was two in the morning. The staff, re-
vived from the exhaustion of the fiesta by raw cheap California champagne supplied by Greech, was clustered around the rehearsal piano, a
decayed upright, with cigarette-scorched keyboard, no front panel, and
dirty hammers visible and creaking. The tinny tones added somehow to
the pleasant melancholy of Noel's new waltz.

Time may change us, estrange us,
Chance may turn true love to false—
But years and worlds apart,
We'll still be heart to heart,
Each time we hear the South Wind Waltz.

There were approving murmurs, and a little applause. "It's lovely,
Noel," Adele said.

"It's a cheap organ-grinderish kind of thing," Noel said, rippling
chords. "It's the Labor Day finale. I think it'll bring a few tears, which is
all it's designed for." He played it again. The tinkling plaintive melody
moved Marjorie deeply. She didn't think it was cheap. Some of the singers hummed with the piano, swaying their heads.

"Is sveet," the Uncle said to Marjorie. "Is a little too sad. I like better

223

happy songs." He had shaved in haste just before coming to the party, and the powder was thick and streaked on his fat face.

"Tired, Uncle?"

"A little vile I stay, then I go, yes. Is nice, a party, young people——"

"Are you sure you won't have more champagne?"

He smiled. "Excuse me, by me it's yellow seltzer, it only makes me thirsty. Thanks."

Adele, her head resting on the broad chest of her waiter lover, said dreamily, "Let's hear the words again, Noel. They're pretty."

The others joined in haltingly as Noel sang,

Summertime has passed,
This night is our last,
Listen! It's the South Wind Waltz.
Once, before we part . . .

"Valtz," Samson-Aaron said. "My vife, she vas the valtzer in the family. Your mama's sister. You vouldn't believe, I was skinny like a toothpick then." He crinkled his eyes at Marjorie. "She looked like you, you know? Different hair, different-style clothes, sure. She looked like you, a little bit."

Marjorie turned to him and held out her arms. "Uncle, let's waltz."

"Vot?" he laughed wearily. "Vas thirty, forty years ago I valtzed."

Greech, who was standing beside Marjorie, beating time with his flashlight against his palm, said, "That's a good idea. Come on, Sam. Go ahead, Marjorie."

The others took it up: "Come on, the toreador! Sam, Marjorie! A waltz! Let's go!"

Samson-Aaron looked around, his face showing something of his customary merriment. "An old elephant like me? Anyway, in the old country is a different valtz, not like here——" But Greech, with a little push of the flashlight in the small of Marjorie's back, sent her into her uncle's arms. He clasped her waist. "So, all right, vunce the Uncle has a dance vit you, Modgerie?" He held out her arm in formal awkward straightness, took one dipping little hesitant hop, then launched out on the bare stage in a grave rotating waltz.

The old fat man in the crumpled yellow Palm Beach suit and the girl in the bare-shouldered blue frock moved in perfect time once around the stage. Applause and cries of approval broke out. "Attaboy, Sam. Shake a leg, Sam." As they twirled through the precise old-fashioned steps, with the stage, the people, the piano going slowly around and around them, Samson-Aaron was looking at his niece with forlorn gratitude and pleasure. She said, "Why, you dance beautifully, Uncle. We should have waltzed together before."

"Ve should have? Vot ve should do in life and vot ve do—— My vife, she—vell, ve dance, ve don't talk."

Once before we part,
Heart to loving heart,
Come, we'll dance the South Wind Waltz.
Time may change us, estrange us . . .

Marjorie was dancing with her eyes closed, pleasantly giddy, close to tears, thinking what a rare moment this was, so simple and yet so hard to come by, just a waltz with the Uncle, to a tinkling tune that would always remind her of him.

"Whoosh!" He stopped. She opened her eyes. He was looking around, smiling wanly. "People, I tell you, at my age give me instead dishes to vash. Is easier." He waddled to a chair, sat amid handclapping and laughter, and comically fanned himself with his hands. Leaping from the piano, Noel pulled a bottle of champagne from the tin tub of ice, swiftly wiped it, and placed it in Samson-Aaron's lap. "First prize! To the winner of the waltz contest—Sam Feder—dishwasher, bullfighter, good sport extraordinary, with the affectionate thanks of the staff of South Wind."

The applause was swift and loud. Even Greech slapped his flashlight noisily. The Uncle looked here and there with glistening eyes, his mustache spread and straggling over a wide grin, his hands fumbling at the bottle. "Vell, so now the young people valtz, no? I showed you how."

The rehearsal pianist sat at the stool, banged a few chords, and swung smoothly into the song. Waltzing couples filled the stage. Noel took Marjorie's hand without a word, and they danced. She saw Wally leaning on the piano, watching her expressionlessly, then she shut her eyes. The magic warmth came streaming as always from Noel's hands into her body. "It's a beautiful song, Noel," she murmured. "Really, it is."

"The words are nothing," she heard him say. Her face was against the rough black wool. "Wrote them as fast as I could move the pencil. The tune has a bit of feeling, I hope. It's for you."

She pressed his hand, and he held her a little closer. Her heart was full of a happy warm ache. It was only because another couple bumped them that she opened her eyes, and saw Samson-Aaron quietly drop the champagne bottle back in the ice tub and walk toward the stage door. She broke out of the dance and, holding Noel by one hand, ran after him. "Uncle, wait, wait."

He turned, flabbily stooped, and his fatigue-shadowed eyes had a somewhat startled look. Before she could say a word he straightened, and life

225

and good humor flowed into his face. He said, "Enough for the old man. I go to sleep. You drink my champagne from the valtz, you and Mr. Airman. I'm very thirsty. I get a glass real cold vater in the kitchen. Then I go to sleep."

Noel said, "We'll have sandwiches in fifteen minutes, Sam. You're not going to pass up a chance to eat?"

"Mr. Airman, I ate enough tonight. For a good glass cold vater I vould give a hundred dollars, lucky it's for free. That yellow stuff, it's like salt. Good night. Dance, dance, have a good time."

Marjorie said, "I'm going to walk with you to the kitchen. I feel like having some air anyway, and——"

He pushed her shoulder so rudely that she lurched against Noel. "Vot's the matter, I'm a baby? Don't be like your mama. I go by myself. Thanks." Then his tone softened. "Good night, my darling. The Uncle is going to sleep, so vot? You dance. Dance vit her, Mr. Airman." He went down the gloomy steps, and out the stage door.

A few minutes later Noel and Marjorie were out on the terrace, alone in a far corner in blue moonlight, kissing. She had completely forgotten the Uncle. Noel said after a while, "I regret to tell you that I've decided I really like you. Really." He was very ardent. His eyes shone.

"Wally says I've made a big pest of myself at rehearsals. That you're embarrassed by me, and would like nothing better than to get rid of me."

"Forget Wally, please. Come here." She was bending back in his arms, avoiding his kiss. "What's this, mutiny?"

"Don't you want to get rid of me?"

"Clearly not."

"Well, it's too bad then, because you're going to."

"Going to what?"

"Get rid of me."

"Really?"

"I'm leaving South Wind. Probably tomorrow. I'm going for a trip out West."

His hold loosened. "Out West?"

"Yes."

He looked at her in silence, his mouth beginning to curl with amusement. She said, meeting his eyes defiantly, "I've always wanted to see the Grand Canyon."

"I know. You've talked of nothing else all summer."

"Don't be sarcastic. I do want to see it, and now I've got a chance, and I'm going."

"Are you serious?"

"Perfectly."

He nodded slowly, smiling. "Of course. Inevitable, at that. You're being snatched out of the fell clutches of Saul Ehrmann, aren't you?"

"Don't be silly. I'll see you in the fall."

"Queer, though. I could have sworn your mother liked me."

"She does like you. Look, she's not sending me out West. Nobody sends me anywhere. I'm going."

"You want to go?"

"Yes."

He took her by the arms and studied her face. "What is this, now? Are you feeling neglected, or something? I know I've been too wrapped up in the fiesta, but——"

"Noel, believe me, I simply want to go out West. What's so hard to believe about that? Wouldn't you go, if you could?"

"Margie, for heaven's sake, don't play games with me, will you? You're up against the Masked Marvel. I eat little girls like you. This western trip comes out of nowhere, a few hours after your folks have been here and gone, so don't give me those wide eyes and tell me you've been planning it since you were fifteen. What did your mother say? Does she know my family very well?"

"Oh, what are you going on and on about it for? It's just for a few weeks, Noel, it's August already. Don't you want me to go? Do you care at all?"

He pulled her into his arms and kissed her. She said, taking her mouth from his, "That isn't enough."

"Marjorie, why are you being so small, so obvious? What words are you trying to wring out of me?"

"I don't want to wring anything from you. Don't say anything, just let me alone—let go of me——"

"Marjorie, I love you. If you want to be really clever, don't be clever. Give me time. Give me rope, that's all you have to do——"

They were twined in each other's arms. "Oh, God, Noel, why did I ever meet you? Why did I come with Marsha that night across the lake? I ruined myself."

"Don't go out West, sweet. Don't go."

"Oh, damn you!" Her hands curved up behind him and she thrust them into his hair. She sighed and shuddered. "Do you think I can refuse you anything? You may be lying when you say you love me. I'll probably never know. But I love you so much I don't know what I'm eating, what I'm wearing, what I'm doing, what I'm thinking. It's all been a fog, all summer. The only thing I'm afraid of is waking up. It seems to me I would die."

"Marjorie, darling, listen to me. You know—God knows—you're not the first girl in my life nor the second, but I swear to you this is new. The reason you're so crazily in love is that I am, too. There's no other reason. It happens once in a lifetime to everyone, and I swear to God I'm beginning to think it's happened for us."

"You called it a shipboard romance——"

"I know, I've been so damned clever and superior and sure-footed about it, haven't I? Don't press me, Margie darling, don't try to pin me down, whatever you do. That doesn't work with me." He was leaning against the rail of the porch, holding her close.

She felt her will dissolving. "I won't go out West. I'll stay here. I'll do anything you want me to do. I don't care about anything except being with you. You know that. You've known it ever since the first time you kissed me."

A small part of her mind stood apart and watched curiously while they kissed again, with new passion. The rest of her was drowning. She realized dimly that Noel had never tried to woo her before, and now was doing it. She could not protest. She did not want to. The sweetness of his lips on hers, the sweetness flooding her body, passed all her experience. Her innocence vanished. In a moment, in a blink of an eye, the barrier was gone, and she was seeking adult satisfaction of an adult desire.

"All right," Noel muttered. "This won't do at all, you see. Let's go." He had to push her away, tenderly and firmly, laughing a little in a hoarse low tone.

"Where?"

"My place."

"They'll be missing us."

Noel laughed.

She said, "Not your place."

"Why not?"

"Someplace else."

"Why? Don't be childish."

"Wally. He—it's just a partition. He's on the other side, under the same roof."

"He's drunk, and anyway he sleeps like a stone."

She yielded to the tug of his hand and came a few steps. "Noel." She stopped. Her senses had been narrowed to their two selves. Now she saw the moon and the stars and the blue moonlit mirror of the lake, heard the lapping of the water under the terrace and, faintly, the music of the backstage party. "Noel, I love you. I don't care about anything else. My whole life will go by and nothing will change it. I love you, Noel."

They kissed quietly, apart, bending toward each other like a couple in a public place. Arm in arm, they walked down the terrace steps and across the lawn.

The floodlights and the colored spotlights of the fountain had been turned off since midnight. The gloom of the lawn was relieved here and there by a lamp on a rough log post, in a mist of darting insects. It was very quiet. The plashing of the fountain sounded loud and musical, like a waterfall.

They were halfway across the lawn, not speaking, moving in one rhythm, quietly happy. Marjorie never knew what it was that she saw, out of the corner of her eye, that made her glance toward the fountain. Even looking straight at it, she saw nothing: a patch of white, or yellowish white, a little different from the foaming white of the water, in the dim lamplight. Then she saw that the surface of the water in the fountain was tumbling irregularly. She said, "There's something in the fountain. Some fool dropped something big in the—— Oh God." She dug her nails into Noel's hand. The yellow was the yellow of an old Palm Beach suit, and she thought she saw a hump of that yellow under a swirl of water.

"What is it?" Noel said. He looked where she was looking, and said, in a sudden frightful shout that tore through the stillness, *"MY GOD!"*

She ran, and he ran.

Samson-Aaron lay in the long wide shallow basin of the fountain, face up. His mouth and eyes were open. Water was cascading across his face so that the features were blurry. His body was slightly out of the water, for it was only a couple of feet deep, but his head was submerged. Noel seized him by the shoulders and dragged him into a sitting position in the water, his back against the rim. Samson-Aaron's head lolled. His eyes rolled opaquely.

"Uncle! Uncle! Oh my God, Uncle!" Her arms were around him, feeling into his streaming clothes. Her mouth was on the wet face. "Noel, he's cold, he's terribly cold."

"I'll get the doctor." Noel bounded away, dripping. Marjorie crumpled over the fat wet slumped form, soaking her dress. "Uncle, Uncle. Oh my God, Samson-Aaron! Uncle! Uncle!" She rocked his head on her breast. "Uncle, it's Marjorie." She was crying bitterly. "Come back, Uncle! Uncle!"

Chapter 20. NO DISHES TO VASH

He did not respond. She felt for his pulse. She had a moment of serious panic at the deadness of his wrist, but then she thought she felt dim throbs. She could not tell whether he was breathing. There was no rise and fall of his huge chest or perhaps a very, very slight motion. His lips, she noticed, were warm, warmer than the rest of his face. Though tears kept pouring down her cheeks, her first shock passed rapidly. She was fairly calm when the commotion started up in the gloom of the men's side: voices, the running of feet, the glow of lights, the lancing of flashlight beams. She was sharply aware of everything about her—the smell of the trampled grass, the half-moon glittering almost overhead, the stars, the moonlit glassy lake, and the loud splashing of the fountain. Everything was very normal and familiar, except that Samson-Aaron was sitting up to his waist in water in the bowl of the fountain, slumped in her arms, soaking wet.

The doctor, a plump almost bald young man, came running in his pajamas, carrying a black bag. Two waiters, naked except for underwear shorts, ran with him. The hair of all three was mussed, and they looked sleepy and scared. "Let's get him out of the water," the doctor said, seizing the Uncle's arm.

One of the waiters jumped splashing into the fountain and took the feet, the other took an arm. They lifted him out on the grass and laid him on his back. The doctor pushed up Samson-Aaron's eyelid and shone a flashlight into it. He shone the light on his lips, pulled open his mouth and flashed the light inside. He felt his pulse and listened to the heart with a stethoscope.

"Is he going to be all right?" Marjorie said. She watched the doctor's face closely.

"How long ago did it happen, do you know?" he said, rapidly and carefully preparing a hypodermic needle.

"How about artificial respiration?" said a waiter.

"Yes, go ahead," said the doctor.

Marjorie, searching her mind for the time sequence, tried to remember how long she and Noel had been on the terrace. "Maybe twenty minutes ago he left the party, more or less—no, no more, it isn't even twenty minutes."

The doctor pushed up the Uncle's left sleeve and injected the arm with the needle. Noel came with Greech and the people of the staff while the waiters were pumping the Uncle's arms and pressing his sides. The doctor kneeled beside Samson-Aaron's face, which was turned to a side, expressionless, eyes closed, mouth slightly open, water trickling from his hair. Nobody said anything. After a little time, the doctor said, "Quit it. There's no water coming out and there's a free passage of air. He isn't drowned."

"Doctor, how is he? What is it? What can we do?" Marjorie said.

The doctor looked at her, and the absorbed expression of a mechanic at his trade passed from his face. He was a staring fat young man. "Marjorie, it's very bad."

With a throb of astonishment, she said, "Is he dead?"

"I can try a shot of adrenalin directly in his heart. He has no heart action, you see."

"Doctor, do whatever you can, please." She was speaking calmly, and she was aware of being the center of the sombre circle, the dramatic figure in the scene. She was also beginning to feel a ghastly nauseous dread.

He set about the injection. The tension was out of his movements. Marjorie turned away as the waiters rolled the Uncle over and bared his chest. She covered her eyes and slumped against Noel. He held her with one stiff arm.

She heard Greech say, "Is there anything else we can do, Doctor? Shall we phone the Tetersville Hospital? They'll do anything I say——"

"Well, if he should come out of it he'd need an oxygen tent at the least, he'd need—— I think it's pretty bad. I can tell better in a minute."

"Meantime we can call," Greech said, "and tell them to get ready."

"All right, Mr. Greech," the doctor said.

Greech told one of the girls to telephone the hospital.

"Marjorie," the doctor said. She looked at him. He was getting up from beside the Uncle, replacing the hypodermic in his bag. "Has he been complaining of pains in the chest? Dizziness? Any history of heart trouble?"

She answered a series of questions dully. The Uncle lay as before, wet and relaxed on the grass. She was beginning to understand that he must be dead, after all.

"He was very thirsty. That was almost the last thing he said. He was terribly thirsty," Marjorie said.

The doctor looked at Greech. He knelt and examined the Uncle again. He stood and took off the stethoscope. "Marjorie, I'm sorry, your uncle is dead. By all odds it was a heart attack. He didn't drown."

She nodded. "I see. Thank you, Doctor." She said to Noel, "I'm afraid I have a lot of telephoning to do." Then she looked again at the body of the Uncle. Tears filled her stinging dry eyes. With a feeling that it was a melodramatic thing to do, but unable to stop herself, she fell beside the Uncle and threw her arms around his chest. "Uncle, Uncle, oh God, oh my God. Samson-Aaron is gone. What happened, Doctor? How did it happen?"

The doctor looked down at her, and she was surprised to see that he was crying. "Margie, I don't know. Nobody will ever know. He's the only one who could have told us, Margie, don't you see? And he never will." She peered up at him, tears rolling down her face, her arms still around the Uncle. The doctor said, "Maybe he—he could have felt the attack coming on when he was crossing the lawn, don't you see, and sat on the edge of the fountain to catch his breath. Or maybe, if you say he was so thirsty, maybe he tried to take a drink in his palm and got dizzy and toppled in. We can't tell, don't you see? Once he'd fallen in, for whatever reason, there'd be fright, panic, violent agitation—he must have died in seconds, or he could have pulled himself out. He was a strong man. That's a comfort, Marjorie. It was only seconds, whatever it was. He never really knew. He was alive, and then he was dead——"

"In the fountain. Oh God, in the fountain," Marjorie said, and she bowed her head on the Uncle's chest, on the cool skin and the wet curly hair, and sobbed.

The needle hardly stung. The doctor promised her that the sedative would not put her to sleep, and it did not. After a few minutes a strange warm loose feeling trickled into her arms and legs. Her trembling died away. Noel was sitting at the foot of the bed, watching her, smoking. "Let me have a cigarette," she said. She sat up and held it to the match. "I'm sorry."

"Good God," Noel said, "you've been remarkable, don't apologize. This thing is hell."

"Where have they put him?"

"He's here in the infirmary."

"Well, I want to see him. Then I have to phone."

"Look, why don't you lie down for a while? The phoning can be done for you. It'll be better that way."

"No. Let's go." She stood, straightening her wrinkled wet dress.

The long sheeted figure on the bed looked like something in a movie. Greech stood beside the doctor, who sat by the dead man, rapidly scrawling with a fountain pen on a long printed form. The yellow plasterboard room was lit by one white bulb hanging on a black cord. It had the usual strong medicine smell, and there was another smell completely new to Marjorie, a rather pleasant one, yet scary because she believed this was what the books called the smell of death. The doctor glanced up at her. She said, "I'd like to see him."

"It isn't a good idea, Margie," Greech said.

"It's all right," the doctor said, standing and pulling back the edge of the sheet.

Now Marjorie saw that the Uncle had died. His face was not a living face. It was smiling and greenish. His hands rested loosely on each other on the front of the wet Palm Beach suit, and the many open cuts were not red but nearer purple. In a powerful momentary hallucination she heard his voice, as though he were alive. The voice said, "*No dishes to vash.*" She shook her head and said to the doctor, "He's dead."

"Oh yes," the doctor said sadly. "He's dead."

She remembered a fragment of her religious training. She took one rough cool hand of the body in hers and said in Hebrew, "*Hear O Israel, the Lord Our God is One God.*" She turned to the others, still holding the hand. "That's the last thing you're supposed to say when you die. I don't suppose he had a chance to say it." She put the hand back, and covered the Uncle with the sheet.

Greech was wiping his eyes. "Marjorie, anything I can do for you——"

"Thanks, Mr. Greech, right now I have to call my mother."

Noel went with her to the camp office. The loud-ticking wall clock read three-forty. It took the sleepy country operators fifteen minutes to get through to her mother. She sat with Noel by the light of one desk lamp, smoking, talking about a new novel he had loaned her. The warmth and calm of the sedative possessed her body. She felt quite equal to the ordeal of the next day or two. She thought over the dresses in her closet back home to select the darkest and plainest for the funeral.

Her mother's voice sounded shrill and scared, "Yes, yes, operator—I tell you this is Mrs. Morgenstern, hello, hello, who's calling me, who is it?"

"Mom, hello, it's me."

"Marjorie! Hello, Marjorie! What is it, darling, for heaven's sake, four o'clock in the morning?"

"Mom, I'm sorry, I hate to tell you, it's the Uncle."

"What?"

"It's the Uncle, Mom."

There was a pause. Then, a hoarse cold tone, "How bad is it?"

"It's over, Mom."

She heard a gasp, and a sob. Then, crying, Mrs. Morgenstern said in Hebrew, "*Blessed be the true Judge.*" After another pause, "What was it? What happened?"

"Heart."

"Heart?"

"Yes."

"When? How? My God."

"Just now, Mom. It just happened. Mom, come. Come here."

"Did you call Geoffrey?"

"I don't know his number."

"I'll call Geoffrey. I'll call the family. How are you? Are you all right? My God, Samson-Aaron! I told him—Samson-Aaron—— Marjorie, are you all right?"

"I'm all right."

"Marjorie, don't let them touch him or do anything, do you hear? Nothing. Sit by him. We'll have to take him home."

"All right, Mom. I won't let them do anything."

"That's right, nothing. We'll be there in a couple of hours. *Samson-Aaron!* Goodbye, Marjorie, I'll call Geoffrey."

Marjorie hung up, feeling with some shame that the conversation had been too trivial, too matter-of-fact, for the awful grandeur of the subject, the death of Samson-Aaron. It had been shorter than many telephone talks with her mother about having dinner at a friend's home.

"How did she take it?" Noel said. "Sounded all right at this end."

"You don't have to worry about my mother. I have to go sit with him, she says. Let me have another cigarette, please." Noel followed her outside. She was quite uninterested in Noel now, except as an intelligent acquaintance, useful to have at hand until her mother arrived and took over the responsibility. She was abstractedly aware that they had been making love on the terrace when Samson-Aaron had fallen in the fountain and died. But it was something that had happened on the other side of a break in time. She was numb to all the past before the death of Samson-Aaron. The present was the death, and only the death. A few people were clustered chattering at the fountain, and a few more moved shadowily here and there on the lawn. When they saw her they dropped their voices and stared, and murmured to each other. The darkness, the moonlight, the sweet odor of mountain laurel in the breeze off the lake, were all exactly as they had been on twenty other nights when she had walked very late with Noel across the lawn. The strangest part of this new side of time was how unchanged everything was. The death of the Uncle made no more difference in the natural world than the death of a slapped mosquito.

In the one lamplit room of the dark infirmary, the death smell was now pervasive. The camp nurse sat beside the sheeted form, her face creased with sleep, her eyes puffy, her uniform partly unbuttoned. A bed lamp threw an amber glow on part of the sheet, leaving the rest in shadow.

The nurse put her magazine aside guiltily. "Marjorie, I'm terribly sorry about your uncle——"

"Thanks, I'll sit with him now."

"But the doctor told me to."

"No, I will."

The nurse looked at Noel, obviously glad of the chance to be rid of the assignment. "Well, I don't want to interfere with the wishes of a relative. But it is a strain——"

"She's all right," Noel said.

"I'll be in the doctor's office," said the nurse, escaping, "if there's anything you want."

"All right." Marjorie sat in the chair.

Noel whispered, "I'll get a chair and sit with you."

"You don't have to, Noel." She spoke in a natural offhand way. "Why don't you get some sleep? You must be absolutely dead, after that fiesta and all. Gosh, it seems long ago, doesn't it? And it's only been a few hours."

Noel glanced uneasily at the body. "I can't leave you alone in here."

"Don't you understand?" she said wearily. "It's over. It's just that my mother wants me to be sure they don't do anything to him that isn't according to our religion."

Noel took her hand and pressed it to his lips and then against his cheek. Her own was limp and warmly numb. The gesture made no impression on her. He stared at her face, and went out.

She resisted a temptation to lift the sheet. At this point, she thought, it would be morbid thrill-seeking; Samson-Aaron was dead, and he was entitled to the privacy of being dead. Marjorie was conscious that, for all the horror and the dread, the death was a marvelously exciting and dramatic experience; she felt, with a little shame, that she was taking too much pleasure in it, despite her real grief and pain. It was all too complex and new for her, and not in the least what she had ever expected of a death. It was, in a strange wretched way, fun; this was true, though she would never be able to explain it, nor would she even dare to mention it to anybody for the rest of her life. Wherever Samson-Aaron was—she felt that his spirit was somewhere around, not very far from his vacated body —he would not be angry with her for her queer and undignified reaction. Maybe it was due to the sedative; maybe she was no longer responsible for her thoughts.

Her nerves suddenly tightened, and she felt scared and sick. She picked up the magazine and flung it open in her lap.

"This won't work, Marjorie." Greech stood in the doorway, slapping his flashlight on his palm. "Somebody else has got to do this, not you. Where's the nurse? I woke her up myself——"

She explained about her mother's instructions.

"That's all right," Greech said. "I'll give orders that nothing's to be done till your mother comes."

"I'd better be sure, Mr. Greech. I'd never forgive myself if—— Really, I don't mind——"

"Get out of that chair," Greech said. Marjorie automatically obeyed, dropping the magazine. Greech sat, and put the flashlight on the bed table. "Nobody has done anything on these grounds without my permission in fifteen years, and nobody ever will. That means constables or anybody else. I swear that. I'll sit with him till your mother comes. Now do exactly as I say. Get the nurse. Both of you go into one of these empty rooms, and you lie down."

She hesitated, glanced once more at the covered dead Uncle, and left him with the little fat man in white knee pants.

But then it was all a dream, after all, because there was Samson-Aaron in lavender tights out on the grass in the sunlight in the middle of the cheering circle of guests on yellow chairs, capering with the bull, and her mother was saying to her, "What was all that foolishness about Samson-Aaron being sick or dead or what? He's perfectly fine."

"Mom, it must have been a dream, but honestly it was so real, so vivid, I couldn't help telephoning you——"

A hand was laid on her shoulder. She turned her head to look up, and all her nerves shrank with horror. Marsha stood behind her, with streaming greasy hair, wild eyes, and a pustular face. She held a sharp kitchen knife in her hand, and she plunged it straight at Marjorie's throat, giggling.

Marjorie forced her eyes open. The hand was her mother's. The window behind her was a dim rainy daylight blue. Mrs. Morgenstern said, "I'm sorry, darling, you'd better get up. Geoffrey just came."

"Oh my Lord, did I fall asleep? What time is it?" She sat up, throwing aside the rough brown blanket, her spine still crawling from the nightmare, the recollection of the death flooding in on her.

"It's seven-thirty. I'm glad you could sleep a little. You'll need it."

"How is Geoffrey?"

"Pretty good, considering."

"Did you bring Seth?"

"No. Time enough for him to face these things later in life."

Marjorie stumbled to the mirror of the cheap bureau and straightened her hair. Her evening dress, ridiculously inappropriate for the morning and for the grim occasion, was crumpled and stained. Her face was a smear of ruined cosmetics. She had long silver rings in her ears. It was impossible to be seen like this, a picture of wrecked frivolity, like a torn paper hat in a trash can. "Mom, look at me. Can't I have five minutes to go to my cabin and fix myself up?"

"It's raining."

"I don't care." She turned away from the mirror. Her mother's eyes were a little red, but otherwise she looked exactly as before, wearing the brown coat in which she had driven off yesterday afternoon. "Oh, Mom, it was so awful." She embraced her mother.

Mrs. Morgenstern held her close, patting her shoulder. "Well, never mind now, Greech told me all about it."

"Mom, he seemed perfectly all right when he left the party. A little tired but—I wanted to walk with him, he wouldn't let me——"

"Darling, are you going to argue with God? It happened because his time came." She cleared her throat. "Now there's lots to do. I've got the undertaker coming, and the family knows about it. The funeral is in New York at eleven-thirty, so there's not much time——"

"Eleven-thirty this *morning?*"

"The law is to bury them at the first possible moment."

"Mom, I'll be back in five minutes, I swear I will."

As she ran past the room where the Uncle lay, she heard voices, and scuffling noises like the moving of furniture. Outside, the drizzle was so thick that she could see only the near trees. The social hall was a dim shape in the mist. She was running past the fountain unthinkingly when she noticed that it was drained and muddy; then she remembered, and turned her face away, horrified.

As she hastily washed and dressed, putting on a dull gray cotton dress, she was planning how best to have her luggage packed and sent home. She would have no time, she realized, to do it herself. She did not make a decision to leave South Wind. She simply knew that she was not coming back. For a moment she hesitated at the mirror. Her face looked yellowish without makeup, actually ugly, she thought. The dry pale lips were impossible. She touched them faintly with red.

A long black automobile materialized out of the mist as she ran back to the infirmary. It was standing in front of the camp office, and a man in black was sitting at the wheel.

"Oh God, it's all going so fast," she murmured.

Her first thought when she saw Geoffrey was that he must have put on sixty pounds since getting married. His face was puffed out, and his bulging lines were beginning to suggest the shape of the Uncle. He stood in the hall of the infirmary, talking in a knot of people, wiping his eyes with a handkerchief. The door of the room where Samson-Aaron lay was shut, and Geoffrey's back was against it. He nodded mournfully when he saw Marjorie. She went through the others to him and embraced him. His tweed jacket was damp, and he wore no tie. "Geoffrey, I'm so sorry——"

"Thanks, Marjorie, I know you are. You loved him. I'm sorry you had to bear the brunt of it. Thank you for——"

"Oh, God in heaven, Geoffrey, don't thank me!"

"This is my wife—Sylvia, this is Marjorie."

The wife looked like her snapshots, a stranger, a blond thin-faced girl in a grossly distended maroon maternity dress, leaning against the wall with her hands behind her. She said, "Hello, Marjorie," and Marjorie remembered not to smile, and returned a solemn-faced nod.

Her father and mother, with Greech and the doctor, were talking to the undertaker, a black-haired man in striped pants, gray spats, and wing collar. He looked rather like a shoe salesman in a Fifth Avenue department store, at once eager and grave. He was saying, "Naturally, Mrs. Morgenstern, I brought the plain box. We always defer to the relatives' wishes. But really, it's gone out, the plain box, really it has. And for the ceremony itself, if I may merely suggest it, a nice silver-trim mahogany casket should be substituted——"

"What's gone out?" Mrs. Morgenstern said. "The law? The law doesn't go out. The law says the plainest possible box. It's not a question of expense. That's the whole Jewish idea, a plain box. Dust to dust."

"I assure you, madam, I've conducted several hundred Jewish funerals with the finest caskets, and only the most old-fashioned——"

Mr. Morgenstern took Marjorie's arm, and led her a few steps away. His face was white and frightened. "Are you all right?"

"Certainly, Dad."

"You don't look good."

"It was quite a night."

"You'll drive in with us."

"Yes, Dad."

"What'll be afterward?"

"I'm not coming back here."

"Good. Good."

The undertaker was saying, "In the last analysis, madam, the son, rather than the sister-in-law, should decide. Really, Mr. Quill, I appreciate this isn't the best time to talk of such things, but I'm sure you'll want a casket. We're using the box temporarily, but——"

"Do what my aunt says," Geoffrey said tiredly, wiping his eyes.

The undertaker stared at him. "Very well, sir. Naturally your wish is ours, but the casket is really not costly when you consider——"

"A plain box," said Mrs. Morgenstern.

Greech, dressed in a gray business suit, still holding the flashlight, was leaning against the other wall. Now he said, "And when it's all done, send the bill here."

The undertaker said doubtfully, "Here?"

"South Wind, Incorporated," Greech said. "Maxwell Greech."

Mrs. Morgenstern regarded him with astonishment. "Mr. Greech, that's very decent of you, but we can very well take care of our own——"

"My grounds. My employee," Greech said harshly, slapping the flashlight. "First death ever at South Wind. He was working for me. Send the bill to me."

The undertaker brightened. "Well, sir, I think that's admirable. A crisis brings out the finest in people. I'm in a position to observe that. Now, so long as South Wind is paying, why, perhaps the casket may be——"

"A plain box," said Greech. "Everything exactly as Mrs. Morgenstern says."

The undertaker now looked, for the first time, as sad as Marjorie had thought undertakers should look. "Very well, a plain box," he said.

The door opened behind Geoffrey, and there emerged from the room a large long box of coarse yellow wood nailed together roughly, very like a crate except for the coffin shape. It was maneuvered into the hallway by a couple of strangers in undertaker garb, the doctor, two men from the kitchen staff, and—of all people—Wally Wronken. The box seemed to have nothing to do with Samson-Aaron, though Marjorie knew his body was inside it. The raw death, the real thing, so strange and horrifying and exciting, was over. This was a funeral. Greech, Mr. Morgenstern, and Geoffrey put their hands to the burden. It went by Marjorie, and she could see fresh saw marks on the boards. Wally looked her in the face sombrely as he trudged by. The women followed the coffin outside.

The drizzle was breaking up. The sky was dazzling white. The far trees and the still lake were visible, and the air was much warmer. There were thirty or forty people in summer clothes gathered on the lawn near the hearse. They fell back and watched as the box was slid inside the automobile.

Noel Airman stepped out of the crowd, dressed as always in his black turtle-neck sweater, his blond hair gleaming in the morning light. She walked to him automatically, and he took her hand. "Marge, tell me anything I can do."

"Thanks, it's all over, I guess, Noel. We're going."

The pallbearers and mourners were in a group behind her, and the guests and staff were massed several paces behind him. She and Noel were alone in an empty middle space, like parleyers of opposed armies. She felt conspicuous; people were watching them, she knew, with inquisitive awareness of their romance. She said in a quiet voice, "I'm not coming back."

He looked very surprised; then he nodded. "I can understand your feeling that way, Marge. But in a week or two, maybe——"

She shook her head. "I won't come back."

"I'll come in to see you then, maybe Thursday—more likely Sunday——"

"Thanks. I hope you will."

"I wanted to come along into town for the funeral, Marge, but it just isn't possible. The show . . . I can't get anyone to take over."

"Of course you can't leave, I know that. Excuse me, Noel." She beckoned to her roommate Adele, who stood not far behind him. The singer came to her, white-faced except for a gash of lipstick, the sun showing her hair black at the roots under the red dye. Marjorie quickly arranged to have her things packed up and sent home. While they talked, cars were rattling the gravel of the driveway, rolling and backing to form a cortege: the hearse, then a black limousine, Geoffrey's rusty little gray Chevrolet, a South Wind station wagon, and the old Morgenstern Buick.

Wally was at her elbow. "Your mother says come along, Margie. Just a couple of minutes more. She says you'll need a coat——"

Adele said, "I'll get it, Marge. Which one?"

"I don't know—I guess my blue raincoat——"

"*I'll* get it." Wally ran down the lawn.

The sun broke through as Marjorie walked to the cortege, making the fenders and windows of the cars gleam, and warming her back. She paused with her hand on the Buick's door, and looked back for the last time at the grounds of South Wind. The Buick stood in front of the camp office, so that she had a clear wide view down to the beach and the social hall. The lake glittered white. The tower of the social hall was a glare of white. On the lawn the rain-soaked grass twinkled in myriads of tiny rainbow sparklings, and the trees dripped in little glitters. In the middle of the scene, dry and squat, its black iron pipe thrusting up through the gray plaster cascade, was the dry fountain. She shuddered, climbed into the car, and sat alone in the rear seat.

Wally appeared at the window, holding up her crumpled coat. "Margie, I'll help Adele," he panted. "You'll get everything in perfect shape."

"Thanks, Wally."

"He was a wonderful guy."

"Yes. Goodbye, Wally."

Honking, the cortege started, and moved down the road. The public-address horn over the camp office blared, "Breakfast now being served in the main dining room." The crowd on the lawn was already melting, straggling to the doors of the dining hall. It occurred to Marjorie that she was very hungry; but it was too late to do anything about it. Looking through the rear window, she saw Wally and Noel standing side by side on the porch of the camp office, watching the procession depart.

The cars bumped slowly along the rough muddy camp road, splashing brown water high in the air; then they went out through the entrance arch, and glided down the main highway. Marjorie looked back at the glinting coppery image of Lady South Wind atop the arch, remembering the elation and triumph with which she had passed under it in June. It was a little startling when her mother said, "A lot different coming out than going in, hey?" Mrs. Morgenstern, twisted round in the front seat, was regarding her daughter wryly.

"Yes, Mom. A lot different."

"Well, it's still more different for the Uncle."

"I know."

After a silence Mrs. Morgenstern said, "Tell the truth, Marjorie. It's Sodom, isn't it?"

Marjorie hesitated. Then she said, "Oh, more or less, Mom, more or less, I suppose it is. Now you tell me this. Why is it so beautiful?"

The mother grimaced. "That's an old question." She faced the front.

The cortege rolled smoothly down the highway to New York.

Only many hours later—when the funeral was over, and the cars were leaving the cemetery on Long Island where the Uncle had been lowered into the brown earth—did the thought at last strike Marjorie, through all the fog of shock and fatigue, that the death of Samson-Aaron had stopped her from having an affair with Noel Airman; and that nothing else in the world could have stopped it.

PART FOUR

Noel

Chapter 21. RETURN OF MARSHA

Not many girls get an offer of a star part in a Broadway production the day after they graduate from college; but Marjorie Morgenstern did.

Just before the commencement exercises began—when she was joking and skylarking with the other senior girls in a dressing room at Carnegie Hall, putting on her cap and gown—the dramatic coach, Miss Kimble, came darting in all red-eyed and red-nosed. She pressed on the bewildered Marjorie a damp kiss, a hug redolent of pine soap, and a letter to the Broadway producer, Guy Flamm. "It's no open sesame to the pearly gates, Lord knows. But believe me, dear, any contact is important when you're starting on Broadway. You're on your way to a glorious destiny. I know it. Give my love to Guy, and God bless you." With this, and another kiss, and another pine-scented hug, Miss Kimble disappeared.

Marching into the crowded concert hall, to the strains of *Pomp and Circumstance* played loudly but uncertainly by the college orchestra, Marjorie stared straight ahead, face rigid, shoulders thrown back, seeing nothing but the bunched red curls of Agnes Monahan in front of her; and, out of the corner of her eye, a stretch of blurred staring faces, and hands holding white programs. The rented coarse black gown she was wearing gave out a musty smell, as though it had been lying long disused in a loft. She was extremely conscious of the black square cap on her head and the tassel dangling near her eye. In the dressing room she had joked with the other girls about the absurdity of the costume and the hollowness of this commencement in a hired hall, with its sad farewell to ivy-covered subways and hallowed carbon monoxide. But as she marched down the aisle her eyes misted, and she forgot for the moment that she had been despising her schoolwork for years, and that she had hated Hunter because it wasn't Cornell or Barnard.

Her mind was in a turmoil of sentimental regret and excited anticipation. She had read Guy Flamm's name often in the theatre columns; he wasn't one of the famous producers, but a producer he most certainly was. The unexpected letter from Miss Kimble in her pocket meant more to her than the diploma she was about to receive. It was the real accolade for whatever she had done at school; more than any diploma, it might light the way to the future.

She was wondering, too, whether Noel was in the audience, and, if so, how she would manage matters after the ceremony. Her mother, she knew, would inevitably want to go to Schrafft's; and Noel, who could eat with pleasure in the noisiest, dirtiest cafeterias, had once said that the middle-class miasma at Schrafft's gave him the black horrors.

After some remarkably uninteresting speeches, the roll call of the graduates began. Rank on rank, seven hundred girls marched to the stage, and as their names were called, they each received from the dean a handshake and a white cylinder tied with lavender ribbon. It went as regularly and swiftly as bottle-capping. Little lonely handclaps rose here and there in the hall for each girl. Only the prize winners and a few expert politicians in the class evoked any real applause. Marjorie tensed as her turn drew near, and her regret became acute at not having worked hard enough to lift herself out of this black line of nobodies.

"Felice Mendelsohn . . ."

"Agnes Monahan . . ."

"Marjorie Morgenstern . . ."

A bit dizzily, she walked across the open space to the dean. To her amazement there was a general outbreak of handclaps. She glanced to her left at the banks of faces. Even some of her classmates were applauding. The dean's eyes relaxed from a formal grinning glitter to friendliness; her hand was hot, moist, and strong. "Good luck, Eliza." It was over. Marjorie Morgenstern, bachelor of science, was leaving the huge stage of Carnegie Hall with a diploma in her hand. "Katherine Mott . . . Rosa Muccio . . . Florence Nolan . . ." Evidently her production of *Pygmalion* in November—she had organized and staged it herself, after the dramatic club had rejected the idea as too ambitious—had won her a trace of distinction, after all.

She wept a few minutes later, as did many girls about her, when the graduating class closed the ceremony with the alma mater hymn:

Fame throughout the wide world is the wish
Of every Hunter daughter true . . .

She had always considered it a silly song—"fame throughout the wide world" indeed, for this sad crop of subway riders!—and it seemed silly now, too. But it was the end, and so she wept.

The lobby, jammed and steamy, was pervaded by the smell of rain and wet overcoats. Marjorie shouldered her way through, clutching the diploma, went outside, and saw her parents at the outer edge of the crowd under the marquee, talking to Noel. It was raining very hard, slantwise; the wind on her ankles was icy. She pushed through to her parents and hugged them, then briefly clasped Noel's hand. "Quite an ovation you got," he said. He wore an old brown hat with a shapeless brim, and a brown herringbone topcoat slightly frayed at one elbow. Fists jammed in his pockets, shoulders stooped, a vague smile on his face, he looked ill at ease and almost seedy. His white lean face fully showed his thirty years.

"That was probably you and my folks," she said, "clapping hard enough to raise echoes."

All at once arms were flung around her, and her face was momentarily buried in wet gray squirrel fur. "Sugar bun, congratulations! Welcome to freedom!"

"Marsha! Hello——"

"Honey, you don't mind, do you?" Marsha's face had the old eager look, but she seemed to be much thinner. "Saw the commencement announced in the *Times* this morning, *had* to beg out of the corset department long enough to see la Morningstar graduate. Darling, you looked sublime, but the rest of the class—gargoyles, my dear, where does Hunter collect them?" She turned to the parents. "Look at your folks, will you? How do they manage to get younger and younger?" She glanced roguishly at Noel. "And if it isn't the great Mr. Airman!"

"Hello, Marsha," Noel said with a smile, his tone faintly weary.

Marsha said, linking her arm with Marjorie's, "Did you hear that claque in the balcony when they called your name? That was me. I damn near split my gloves getting it started——"

The wind veered and spattered cold rain over them. Mrs. Morgenstern said, wiping her face, "Well, it's silly to stand here in the wet. Schrafft's is just a few doors down——"

Marjorie was troubled by Noel's demeanor in the restaurant. He slumped very low in his chair, smoking, and glancing around at the brown-panelled walls and the parties of middle-aged women in big hats eating ice cream and shrilling at each other. Automatically, not watching his fingers, he was tearing apart the paper doily at his place. Marsha kept chattering about the graduates. When the waitress came the parents ordered ice cream and the girls cocktails. Noel scanned the menu with drooping eyes. "I'll have a cottage cheese and Bartlett pear salad with watercress."

Marjorie peered at him. "Good heavens, you never eat such junk. Have a drink."

"It's a penance. This is like going up a holy staircase on my knees," Noel said. "I may as well do it all the way."

Marsha's eyes gleamed at Marjorie. "What have you done to him? He's a broken man."

"Broken," Noel said. "Saddled, bridled, bitted, and tamed. Children ride me in Central Park for a dime."

The parents smiled uncomfortably. Mrs. Morgenstern said, "Listen, don't complain, Noel. That's steady work."

Noel laughed and said without rancor, "Mrs. Morgenstern, how would you like to see me make twenty-five thousand a year?"

"I think Marjorie might like it," the mother said.

"Would you?" Noel said to Marjorie.

"Look, Noel, what do I care? Do whatever you think will make you happy." It was an impossible situation, Marjorie thought, especially with Marsha grinningly absorbing every word.

Talk started up of what Marjorie was going to do with herself now. Mrs. Morgenstern said she ought to go to work as a secretary in the father's office. "Just to find out what it feels like to make a dollar," she said. "The whole world looks different once you've made a dollar."

"That's absolutely true," Marsha said.

Marjorie turned on her. "You, of all people!"

Marsha, tossing her head, took a cigarette and a silver lighter from her purse. "Honey, if the Theatre Guild is holding a part open for you, that's another matter." She flicked a flame to the end of the cigarette. Marjorie had an impulse to drop the Guy Flamm bombshell into the discussion. But she suppressed it; time enough to talk about that when she knew what the outcome would be. Marsha went on, "I've always believed in you, and I still do. But it's just true, you're only half alive, you're only a child, really, until you've earned money. You might as well pile up a reserve for the pavement-pounding next fall. And find out, incidentally, how most of the world lives. It's a big gap in your education."

"On that theory," Noel said, "she also should go out and get an arm torn off in the subway or something. One way or another, most of the world lives maimed."

"What kind of talk is that?" the father said with unusual harshness, and there was silence until the waitress returned.

Marsha lifted her manhattan and said cheerily, "Well, here's to the star about to dawn on the world."

Noel lifted a forkful of cottage cheese toward Marjorie and ate it.

Mr. Morgenstern pushed his ice cream aside after a few spoonfuls.

"You'll excuse me, people. We'll celebrate a little better tonight at dinner. The office is in a bad mess."

Noel stretched out a long arm, seized the check from the waitress, and put on his dingy hat and coat. "Well, rising star, talk to you tonight. I have to go, too. Have to see about that twenty-five thousand a year."

Mrs. Morgenstern chatted for a while with the girls, questioning Marsha about her department store job with more kindliness than she had shown in the old days. When she left, the two girls glanced at each other and burst out laughing. "How about another drink?" Marsha said.

"Why not? I have no homework tomorrow."

Marsha caught the waitress' attention, and made a swift circle with her forefinger over the two drinks. "Sublime feeling, isn't it?"

"Marsha, how much weight have you lost, forty pounds? You look splendid." Marsha simpered and put her hand to her hair, which was cropped, thinned, and curled close to the head. The thick paint and purple lipstick were gone; she wore only a little light makeup. The loss of weight had brought the outlines of bones into her face. Her frame was still bulky, but the black suit and plain white silk shirtwaist made it less noticeable. Gone, too, were the gaudy earrings. Her one ornament was a large curious gold crab pinned to a shoulder.

Marsha said, obviously enjoying Marjorie's scrutiny, "Oh well, dear, I've done as well as I can by the old hulk, I guess. Lamm's has been an education, it beats Hunter seven ways. I'm not assistant corset buyer yet, so I suppose I shouldn't have gotten in touch with you, but——"

"Don't be an idiot, Marsha, I'm very glad you came."

"Well, honey, you know you regarded me more or less as a leper not even two years ago. Maybe after a summer at South Wind you feel a little kindlier toward me. At least you'll agree I didn't invent sex."

"I was kind of young, you know, Marsha."

"Oh, darling, I wish to God you'd been right, instead of just young. It's a nasty pigsty of a world, and that's the truth. But I broke with Carlos way back when I went to work, in case you're interested—and I've been a good girl ever since, honestly. Not through choice, I won't claim that much saintliness. I've had no chances worth speaking of. But the hell with all that. Bless you, you little devil, you've harpooned Moby Dick! Who would have thought it? Noel Airman, brought low by little Marjorie! I'm proud of you, honey, and if you remember, I *told* you you could probably do it.—Well, don't sit there with a face like a boiled lobster, tell me everything."

"I haven't harpooned him, don't be absurd." Marjorie drank to cover her delighted confusion.

"Oh, please, baby. I never saw a man so thoroughly and hopelessly gaffed. How did you do it? What's your secret? Spare no details."

"Oh, Marsha, it's awful. I'm in terrible trouble, if you want to know."

"Poor baby. Are you pregnant? It's nothing to worry about——"

Marjorie choked over her drink, sputtered into her napkin, and coughed and coughed. It was some seconds before she could gasp hoarsely, "Ye gods, Marsha. You'll never change, will you?"

With a hugely amused grin Marsha said, "Sorry, honey, I've never been able to resist shocking you. You always react like a Roman candle."

"Oh, shut up and give me a cigarette." Marjorie began to laugh. "No, I'm not pregnant. As a matter of fact I think I'll shock you now. I'm not having an affair with Noel."

Marsha looked searchingly at her face. "I believe you."

"Well, thank you——"

"Don't be sarcastic," Marsha said. "Have you any idea what a feat you're pulling off? Men like Noel don't put up with your West Side brand of inconclusive mush. What's been happening?"

Marjorie still felt her old mistrust of Marsha, but the need to unburden herself overcame it. "Well, Marsha, it's all so weird I wouldn't know where to begin."

"Are you engaged?"

"Far from it." She began to describe the summer at South Wind, and soon was pouring out the story. Marsha listened like a child, her eyes glowing, sometimes holding her cigarette unregarded until ash fell on her suit. When Marjorie narrated the death of Samson-Aaron she stammered and her voice became shaky. Marsha shook her head. "You poor kid."

Marjorie was silent for a little while. Then she said, "I had the strongest possible feeling that I'd never see Noel again. I didn't want to. He wrote and I didn't answer. He phoned and I pretended not to be in."

"Did you go out West?"

"No. Mom took me to one of those hotels in the mountains where you meet nice young men. She never said she was against Noel. She hasn't, to this day. Well, I met nice young men, hordes of them. Doctors and lawyers with mustaches, half of them. They come out in force in the mountains in August, like goldenrod. I was the belle of the place, if I do say so. The other mamas would gladly have poisoned my noodle soup if they'd dared. Well, when I came home there was a big rush of dates, and—this all sounds pretty boastful, doesn't it?"

"Darling, we're old friends," Marsha said. "Curse your pretty face, I know every word of it's true."

"All I'm getting at is, I was twice as bored as if I'd been a wallflower.

All those fellows seemed so dreary, after Noel! Marsha, I hold no brief for him, but he's—well, you know, he's somebody——"

"Somebody? You may as well know it, kid, Noel Airman is the end of the trail. I hope you marry him—of course you will, for better or worse, otherwise he'll haunt you to your grave. They don't come like Noel. Men, that is."

"Now we come to the strange part. It's a little hard to talk about." She looked away from Marsha's inquisitive eyes, out into the street. The table was near the window. Rain was showering down, breaking in little gray stars on the pavement. Since her infancy she had loved to watch those little leaping stars. "It's a cloudburst, do you know? Happy day, Marjorie graduates—I think I might have refused to see him when he finally did phone again, Marsha, late in September, if not for all those dull dates. But it was such a blessed relief to hear his voice, an intelligent voice. He *sounds* intelligent, you know. So—I did it, I said all right, I'd meet him for a drink. We went on to dinner, naturally. And there were more dates, and—I don't know, I hate getting clinical about these things——"

Marsha said, "Dear, I'm an old woman."

Looking out at the dancing gray bubbles on the sidewalk, Marjorie said, "I didn't enjoy kissing him any more. Or—or any of that, you know. It was like kissing Wally. That was five months ago, and it's still more or less true. Now you know. That's the gist of it. In every other way I still admire him and like him, in fact he fascinates me, I guess, but—the romancing, shall we say, just doesn't work any more."

"Not at all?" Marsha said, staring. "Never?"

"Well, to be honest—confession is good for the soul and so forth—a couple of times, when I've had a few drinks, there's been a sort of glimmering. But so feeble, compared to what it used to be, that he just gets disgusted and quits. I don't fight, you see, or anything. I just don't care."

"No response," Marsha said.

"Exactly. No response." Marjorie laughed self-consciously. "Could anything be queerer?"

"And how does he feel about you? Or say he feels?"

"Oh, him. Exactly as always or more so, he claims. Under the circumstances he's been remarkably patient and kind. He talks about it a lot, of course."

Marsha's lips curved. "What's his theory, dear?"

"Oh, very complicated. I'm a horrible emotional mess—Judaism, and sex guilt, and father-love, and mother-hate, and a desire to torture Seth, and all that, all tangled up in the background. What it all boils down to is that I still love him madly, but my uncle's death was a horrible shock and brought out the guilt feelings and all the complications, and I've got a bad case of emotional paralysis or amnesia. There's some name for it. He says the books are full of it, it's the commonest thing in the world, and I'll get over it. He's just going to wait it out."

"And then what? Marry you?"

Marjorie hesitated. "No, not necessarily."

"What, then?"

"Oh, you can imagine, can't you? When two people are in love the way we are, it's too precious to be ignored or wasted—and so forth, and so on."

Marsha lit a cigarette from a burning butt. "He hasn't written any new songs lately, has he?"

"He's done nothing since he left South Wind. Or virtually nothing. It's absolutely incredible how lazy he can be, Marsha. It worries me. He'll sleep eighteen hours at a stretch. He'll go to one of these chess clubs and just play chess day after day. He's a whiz. Then again he can do a staggering amount of work, staggering, in no time at all. During Christmas week, a producer named Alfred Kogel said he'd take an option on Noel's musical comedy if he'd make certain changes. Well, in nine days Noel wrote a whole new show. So help me. Including a lot of new music, beautiful music. I mean, it's the same basic idea—it's a script called *Princess Jones*—but he improved it terrifically. I'm sure it'll be produced some day, and it'll make Noel. It's brilliant. But it's off the beaten track in every way, and——"

"What happened with Kogel? He's a damn good producer."

"It was heart-rending. Noel came to his office with the revised script, and found out Kogel had nearly died of a heart attack on New Year's Eve, and has to stay in a sanatorium for a year. So, back he went to sleeping and chess. That's what he's still doing."

Marsha shook her head. "Well, I can understand that. Nasty blow." She sipped her cocktail, then stirred it for a long time, with her eyes on the moving stick. "But never fear, Golden Boy will recover. You can't down a man like that. There are other producers, and he'll write other shows. As for this emotional numbness of yours, why, it's nothing, it's bound to wear off. It's the luckiest thing that could have happened, in a way. You've challenged the man to his soul. The one thing Noel does with both arms tied behind him is arouse women. He'll wake you up again, or die trying. Male vanity. You've *got* him, baby. I foresee nothing but a happy ending for both of you. Orange blossoms, fame, fortune, and a huge house with a swimming pool in Beverly Hills."

Marjorie couldn't help smiling at Marsha's unchanging glibness. "And what's been happening with you, Marsha? Good Lord, you just let me talk on and on about myself."

"Honey, you're the interesting one. What can happen to me? I'd love to meet a guy. I've done everything I can, you see—starved myself to death for a year, and so forth——"

"You look stunning now."

With a wry smile Marsha said, "It was really my mother's fault, you know, the old exotic effect. Russian intelligentsia's idea of high fashion. Gawd. By the way, she has a fur coat now. A beautiful Persian lamb. She really looks grand in it. When she flounces into Town Hall in that coat, you'd swear she was Wanda Landowska. I bought my father some decent clothes, too——" Marjorie's eyes wandered to the damp squirrel coat on a rack by the table, which Marsha had worn years ago to *The Mikado* rehearsals. Marsha followed her look and quickly said, "Hell, what's a coat? Something to wear in the cold and the wet. It's just that my mom had built up this fur-coat idea in her mind. Wanted one for ten years, ever since her old one fell to rags. But what with my dad's brilliant operations in the Street—— Don't you worry, kid, I'll have a mink one of these days, and so will Mama, but first things first. Had to get some decent furniture for the apartment—— I've bought everything on time, and heaven knows I'm in hock up to my eyebrows, but I'm a fanatic on prompt payments, baby. You wouldn't know me. I think it was the money that split you and me, as much as anything. I never forgot it."

"Oh, Marsha, I swear I never thought about it——"

"You thought plenty." Marsha drank. "My folks talk about you all the time, you know. And I—well, I've never stopped thinking about you. You're one of the household gods. You just flashed through, like a rocket on the way up—you see, you're so pretty, and fortunate, and so damned respectable. My folks have wanted to be respectable since they got off the boat, and they've never made it. Until now. But they're respectable, kid, you wouldn't know them. Petty bourgeois, pure and simple, sitting in the sun in the park—they'll be spending their winters in Florida in another year or two, I'll see to that. They've never had much. But at least they've got me, by God, now that I'm a big girl."

Marjorie said in a subdued tone, "You're worth ten of me, Marsha. I'm still a burden to my parents."

"Oh, Prince Charming will relieve them pretty soon. Or if not, you'll be raking in the dough on Broadway. That little red carpet is going to go right on unrolling in front of you, sweetie." She laughed. "I'll give you one teeny bit of advice, though. If you promise not to sock me."

"Go ahead."

"Well, it's nothing much. Just this—if Noel ever does corner you in that Bank Street love nest of his one evening, with a mad gleam in his eye, don't bite and scratch too hard or too long, will you? He's not used to such struggling—— Oh, come, don't look so cross-eyed at me. What do you think it is, a fate worse than death? Take a poll among your graduating class ten years from now, sugar bun, about their marriages, and find out how many of them clinched the deal by giving out a few free samples —if you can get them to tell the truth—— Okay, here I go again, the corrupter of youth. Welladay. Pay no attention to me."

"I don't," Marjorie said. "I never did, really, and I never will." She shook her head, smiling.

"Stick to your ideas, sweetheart," Marsha said, putting on her coat. "Lord knows mine have got me exactly nowhere, though I don't think they're the reason. We'll compare notes when we're old and gray and see who came nearer the mark." As they walked to the front of the restaurant she added, "But let's not wait till then to see each other again. This has been fun." The change from stagnant steam-heated air to cold wet wind made Marjorie sneeze. They hesitated outside the door, shrinking from the rain, buttoning their coats. Marsha said, "Me for the bus. You?"

"Oh, it's graduation day. I'll take a cab."

Marsha looked into her eyes. "Do you have fun, Margie? Do you have many friends?"

"Not to speak of. Noel, mostly. You know how that is."

"Sure." Marsha held out her hand. "We had some wonderful times, didn't we? This was like the old days. Happy graduation, Marjorie Morningstar."

Marsha ran off into the rain toward the bus stop. It was the old clumsy run; hips swaying, heels kicking outward.

Chapter 22.   GUY FLAMM

Marjorie kept waiting for Noel to telephone all evening. She tried to seem gay and grateful during the elaborate dinner her mother had prepared to celebrate her graduation, but her mind was so far away that Seth finally said, "Your ear is going to fall off, Margie."

"Eh?"

"The one that's stretching toward the telephone."

The parents guffawed, and she turned a little red. Seth sat imperturbably enjoying the success of his joke. He was fifteen, six feet tall, with huge dangling bony hands, and an absurdly smooth childish face topping his lanky frame. He was president of his class, his marks were good, and he held a number of school honors and posts. He was enormously favored by fourteen- and fifteen-year-old girls, painted children wobbling on high heels in too-mature dresses. It was hard for Marjorie to realize that they were the same age she had been at the start of the great dim George era.

Marjorie was not much annoyed by Seth's gibe. Noel was an old story by now in the family; the time of surreptitious dates in the Forty-second Street library was long past. It had ended abruptly one night in October when she had said, for the third time in a week, "Well, I have to go down to the library again," and her mother had answered, "Look, call up that book and tell him to come here for a change. I like him." Mrs. Morgenstern was unfailingly cordial to Noel, though the father was inclined to short formal growls with him. Noel avoided coming to the Morgenstern apartment as much as he could. He said it was nobody's fault, but he felt trapped there.

Mr. Morgenstern said, rubbing his eyes, "It seems to me we ought to do something tonight. Go to a show——"

"Thanks, Papa, but I think maybe I'll turn in," Marjorie said. "Get up bright and early to face the cruel world."

"Are you really going to look for an acting job?" the mother said.

"I'm going to get one."

Mrs. Morgenstern said, "Well, to me it's like fishing for nickels in subway gratings. A crazy way to make a living, but you'll be out in the open air a lot. Listen, it's your life. Good luck to you."

Mr. Morgenstern said through an immense yawn, "She was fine in that school play. Maybe she'll surprise us all."

Marjorie was lounging in a housecoat on her bed, reading a lending-library novel, when there was a tap at her door. "Are you dressed?"

"Come in."

Seth wore a loud gray tweed overcoat with the collar turned up, and a new red-and-yellow tie. His blond hair gleamed wetly. "Well, I just wanted to say congratulations and all that, from me to you personally."

"Thanks, Seth."

"Sorry I missed the commencement. I'd have liked to see you in a cap and gown. Bet you looked silly."

"Idiotic."

"How does it feel, Marge? To be out of school, all finished and done with it?"

Marjorie paused. "Well, it's a great relief. But also a little empty."

"I think I'd be scared. I don't want to finish school."

"You'll change your mind about that. Of course right now you love it. You're king of the school. And all your little dates seem so precious and fascinating——"

"Oh well, so far as that goes——" Looking at his moving shoe, he said, "Not that you're any great shakes, but I've never come across a girl anywhere near you. Shows you how sad the female half of the human race is."

Marjorie went to him and kissed his cheek. It still felt queer to look up to her towering baby brother. "Thanks, despite the reservations."

Briefly, and with astonishing rough force, he hugged her, and let her go. "Margie, all the luck in the world. I think—well, hell—I'm sorry I kidded you about Noel—he's all right, I guess." Seth went out in a stumbling tangle of arms, legs, and tweed.

Guy Flamm's office was in a narrow old building in the West Forties, between two theatres. It was a thrill just to read his name on the grimy directory board. Once again she felt in her purse for the letter; then she rang for the elevator, hands perspiring and stomach fluttery.

She opened the glass door marked in gold leaf *Guy Flamm Enterprises* with a feeling of stepping into the future.

A fat girl with greasy hair and thick greenish glasses sat inside, boxed between an old switchboard, an older filing cabinet, and a card table piled high with scripts bound in many colors. "Yes?" she said in an offended tone, sipping coffee from a paper cup, and biting a semicircle out of a bun.

"I'd like to see Mr. Flamm."

"What about?"

"An acting job."

"No."

"I beg your pardon?"

The girl chewed the bun for a few seconds. "He's not casting."

"I have an appointment."

"Well, say so then. Name?"

"Marjorie Morningstar."

"Wait." The girl announced the name into the switchboard, and after a pause repeated, "Wait." She resumed reading a script in her lap, peering and frowning through the greenish glasses.

Marjorie stood awkwardly in the middle of the little anteroom, uncomfortably warm in her beaver coat, but unwilling to take it off. Half of the effect of the new red dress lay in unveiling it; she wanted Guy Flamm to see that effect. There was a chair behind her heaped with scripts. "Miss, do you mind if I use this chair?"

"Yes."

"Eh?"

"Don't use it. I've got those scripts in a certain order."

So Marjorie stood there in silence. It was eerie to be in a space the size of two telephone booths with another human being and not to exchange a word. She kept shifting from foot to foot. Ten minutes drifted by. Marjorie was working up her nerve to protest, when the switchboard buzzed. "Go on in," the girl said, jerking her thumb over her shoulder.

The first noticeable feature of Guy Flamm was a pair of popping eyes, one of which was red and streaming. He held a handkerchief to it. He stood up behind his desk, a red-faced little man with thick well-groomed white hair, a trim white mustache, a tan tweed jacket, a shirt with faint green lines in it, and a green bow tie. "Come in, come in, my dear." He gestured at a chair. Marjorie couldn't help wondering what he had been doing while she had waited. The office was absolutely empty except for a desk, two chairs, and Guy Flamm. No telephone calls had gone through the switchboard. There was nothing on the desk but an ashtray containing two dead cigars and some ashes. On a shelf over Flamm's head was a row of play volumes which looked as though they had been undisturbed for some years. "Well, well, so you're Dora Kimble's favorite pupil. And you're going to set Broadway on fire. Sit down, sit down."

Marjorie took the letter out of her purse and handed it to him. "Miss Kimble's been awfully sweet to me."

"Wonderful girl, Dora. Never cut out for show business, but——" Mr. Flamm glanced at the letter, mopping his bad eye. "You've done Eliza in *Pygmalion,* eh? Quite a challenge. Staged it yourself! Interesting." He looked at her kindly. "That's a very pretty coat. Not many young actresses can afford a coat like that. Aren't you hot in it, though?"

Marjorie nodded and took off the coat. Since Mr. Flamm's eyes popped anyway, she could not be sure of the impact of the red dress. She thought the eyes popped a bit more. "Marjorie Morningstar, eh? Very euphonious. Is that your real name, dear?"

"No. It's Morgenstern."

"Ah. Jewish?"

"Why—yes."

Flamm nodded and mopped his eyes. "My first wife was Jewish. Lovely person. Where do you live?"

Marjorie told him.

"Ah. With your parents?"

"Yes."

"What does your father do?"

"He's an importer." Puzzlement crept into her tone.

Flamm smiled. "There's method in my madness, dear. I'm watching everything you do and say. You'd be surprised how you've characterized yourself already." He fell silent, staring at her. "Interesting." He reached to the shelf, took down a book, blew the dust off it, and held it out to Marjorie. "Are you a trouper? Right now, let's hear Julie Cavendish's big speech in *The Royal Family*."

Startled, Marjorie said, "Give me a couple of minutes."

"All the time you want." Flamm smoked and mopped his eye.

She read over the scene; stood, book in hand, collected herself, and burst forth into the speech. Flamm's eyes seemed to bulge further, and he stopped mopping. He began to nod, slowly at first, then more emphatically.

When she sat, trembling, he nodded for a long time, his eyes on her. "My dear, this is a little too good to be true. Girls just don't walk out of college and read lines like that." He stood and turned his back to her, looking out of the window at a brick wall. He whirled, smiling. "Look, I'm sorry, I should be more self-controlled, at my age. It's a one-in-a-billion shot. I've been looking for a Clarice for eight months, and you've walked into my office, straight from Hunter and poor little old Dora Kimble. It's incredible, but——" He yanked open his top drawer and flung a script bound in red on his desk. "*If* you can read Clarice the way you read Julie . . . Mind, it's not the lead. It's one smash scene in the second act. I've had every girl in town read Clarice—— What's the matter, dear?"

Marjorie was gasping, holding her hand over her pounding chest. "Mr. Flamm—is there a part—a chance for a part?"

He thrust the script into her hands. "I don't want to be cruel and say there's even a chance. Read the play, that's all." His voice was shaking a little. "This is the theatre, so anything can happen, even a break like this. But I'm promising nothing. You may be terrible as Clarice. Now this play, remember, isn't Shaw. Forget about your college dramatics, dear. This is Broadway, and this play is money, plain old commercial money. How quick a study are you? Are you willing to come back tomorrow and risk a reading? All or nothing, your one chance at Clarice? Tomorrow at this time?"

"Yes, yes! Oh, God, Mr. Flamm, I'll be here."

She stumbled out of the dank building into the sunshine with the script under her arm. The feeling of unreality was as strong as it had been on the night of her uncle's death; but this was a dream as sweet and beautiful as that had been horrible. She tried to read the first page on the sidewalk, but sunlight glaring on the white paper blinded her. She ran to a sandwich shop across the street, ordered coffee and cake, and began to read the play. The pages looked pink after the sun glare. It was hard to concentrate at first, there was so much excitement in holding a professionally typed and bound script, with its character names in upper-case letters. (*JOHN walks in. HE is a young man of thirty, dressed for tennis. HE crosses to the mirror, L.*) The cover of the script was a peculiarly tough rippled paper, bright scarlet, bound to the pages with brass fasteners. The title of the play was *Down Two Doubled.*

The first few pages made little sense. She could not get her mind calmed. Bolting her coffee and cake, and lighting a cigarette, she read on. She had read perhaps forty pages when she began to suspect that the fault might not lie in her agitation. The play seemed to be unspeakably stupid trash. The dialogue was silly, the characters vague, the action feebly meandering. She forced herself to read on, trying desperately to concentrate. The further she read, the worse it got.

After a while she decided that it was simply not possible to read *Down Two Doubled.* It was worse than a legal document. She flipped the pages until she came to a stage direction reading (*Enter CLARICE. SHE is a beautiful dark-haired girl aged 18. AMANDA and TONY jump up from the couch in amazement at HER appearance*).

Clarice was as nebulous as the other characters. Her lines were weak facetious echoes of a style of college slang ten years outmoded. The play was about two young couples, rival tournament bridge teams, who went through complex bedroom intrigues in order to get at each other's bidding signals. Clarice was the younger sister of one of the wives. She came from college for the weekend, exposed the intrigues, and outplayed all the experts in a bridge game on stage. This was as much as Marjorie could extract from the tangled fog of words called *Down Two Doubled.*

The disappointment was sickening. Had Guy Flamm decayed into a harmless old lunatic? Yet she had seen his name in the *Times* theatre gossip quite recently. Had he written this gibberish himself? Or was her judgment so worthless, so warped by collegiate idealism, that she couldn't perceive the possibilities in a commercial script? She had a frantic impulse to telephone Noel; he could read this play in half an hour, and give her an unerring estimate. She went to the phone booth, dropped in the nickel, and then balked. Her dear wish was to surprise him, knock him over, with the news that she had a part in a Broadway play. She got back the nickel, looked up the number of Hunter College, and called Miss Kimble.

The music teacher became almost hysterical when Marjorie said Flamm had given her a script. Marjorie interrupted the foam of congratulations. "I'd like to see you about it, right away, if I can." Miss Kimble fluttered and stammered about all the work she had to do, and finally told Marjorie to come at once by all means; she would put every-thing else aside even if it meant losing her job.

It was queer to arrive at the college at eleven-thirty in the morning. Miss Kimble fell on Marjorie's neck, and kissed her, and blew her nose, and looked red-eyed, and locked her door. She stared at the script with frightening eagerness. "Is that—is that it?"

"I'd like you to read it. Not necessarily all of it. One act ought to be enough, Miss Kimble. But right away——"

"Of course I will, Marjorie. I'm at your service, dear. I'm the stepping-stone, the ladder, and proud of it. And call me Dora, for heaven's sake, everybody in the theatre does." Her fingers worked toward the script. Marjorie hastily handed it to her. "*Down Two Doubled*. Exciting title. Oh, my! Isn't Guy a dear? And he's brilliant——"

"Miss—Dora, suppose I take a walk or something? I've got to have your opinion. Suppose I come back in an hour?"

"Perfect. Perfect. Run along, dear." Eyes agleam, Miss Kimble was already immersed in the play.

When Marjorie returned, having smoked so many cigarettes and drunk so much drugstore coffee that she was shaking, she found Miss Kimble less excited. "Sit down, dear," the teacher said, pursing her lips and smoothing her brown tweed skirt. The script lay closed on her desk.

"How much did you read—Dora?"

"I finished it."

"What do you think?"

"Well—it has definite possibilities."

"Really? Is that your honest opinion?"

"Marjorie, Guy Flamm is an awfully shrewd man. He's been in the theatre a long time. If he likes a script it must have values——"

"But did *you* like it?"

"Well, frankly, it's slightly confusing at a first reading, and of course I just raced through it."

"Dora, isn't it utter and hopeless garbage?"

The music teacher looked offended. "Marjorie, the first thing you'll have to learn in the theatre is not to make snap judgments. It's a com-mercial comedy. That kind of script is full of hidden values, very often. Look at *Abie's Irish Rose*. You can't see them, and I can't see them, but Guy Flamm sees them. Tell me, did he remember me at all?"

"Oh yes. Spoke very highly of you."

The music teacher blushed and fumbled at the glasses on her desk. "We had a lot of fun that summer with *Blossom Time*—— Well. What role is he considering you for?"

"Clarice."

"Why, that's the best part."

"I can't make head or tail of it, Dora. It's just words. She has no character. She doesn't talk like a person. She's just the result of some imbecile pecking at a typewriter for a while. I'm sorry, Dora, that's how it strikes me."

Miss Kimble put on her glasses, and with them her classroom authority and severity. "I think you lack a sense of proportion, possibly, a teeny bit, Marjorie. What did you expect? You've been out of college one day. Did you expect to be cast as Juliet or Candida today by the Theatre Guild?"

"No, but I——"

"Guy Flamm is offering you a chance to act. To walk out on a Broadway stage, for God's sake! You should go down on your knees in gratitude to him. And to me, although that doesn't matter in the least. If he gave you just a walk-on, just two lines as a maid in a dismal flop——"

"Dora, I'm terribly grateful to you, it isn't that——"

"You've had the most fantastic luck I've ever heard of. *Grab* it, you fool. You're supposed to be an actress. *Make* something of Clarice, even if she is just a lot of words from a typewriter. *Get out on the stage.*"

Marjorie took the script from the desk. "Well, you've certainly made me feel like a worm."

Miss Kimble was upon her, hugging her, diffusing pine fragrance. "Marjorie, no. Don't take it to heart. Or rather, do! It was just a pep talk, but I mean it. Dear, it's a chance, don't you see, it's a *start*."

Marjorie went home and studied the script all afternoon and all evening. She turned out her bed lamp at midnight, and tossed for hours, with Clarice's vapid lines tumbling fragmented in her mind.

Flamm's fat secretary, still drinking coffee and still chewing on a bun, greeted Marjorie next morning with an astoundingly pleasant smile, and told her to go right in.

Another red script lay before Flamm on his desk. He was still mopping the eye, which looked worse. Today he wore a blue checked shirt, a blue bow tie, and a blue sports jacket. "Not a word," he said, as Marjorie started to greet him. "Take off your coat. Forget that Marjorie Morgenstern ever lived. You're Clarice Talley." She sat in the chair, clutching her script. "One question. Do you think you understand the play?"

"I—yes, Mr. Flamm."

"Which adjective would you say best describes it—sentimental, romantic, raffish, brittle, gay?"

"Well—gay, and slightly raffish."

Flamm's eyes bulged like a lobster's, and he smiled. Then, looking stern, he flipped open the script. "Act 2, page 41," he said. "Let's go."

It took twenty minutes to read through Clarice's scene. Marjorie was damp with perspiration when it was over. She could not tell whether she had read the drivelling lines well or badly. She had tried to convey innocence and mischievous charm with her voice and her face.

Flamm deliberately closed the script, turned his back on her, and looked out of the window. Three or four minutes went by. He whirled as he had yesterday, his whole face alight. "I'm sorry. I should send you home, let you stew for a few days—here it is, between the eyes. I'm in business, after an eight-month search. You're Clarice! Bless your heart. We start rehearsals a week from Monday. We open in New Haven March 15."

Marjorie broke down and cried. He stood over her, patting her shoulder. She said, "I'm sorry, it's silly——"

"Not at all, Marjorie. I feel like crying myself." He gave her a cigarette and she calmed. He talked a while about wonderfully exciting details: costumes, rehearsal schedules, hotel rooms in New Haven. She could hardly follow, so stunned with delight was she. She said, "Yes, yes, Mr. Flamm," and kept nodding, thinking deliriously of how she would break the news to her parents and to Noel.

Somehow, after ten minutes or so, Flamm was on the subject of his brother, a Colorado mining engineer, for whom he had countersigned a note in connection with some mining equipment. The story was extremely complicated, but the upshot of it was that he had had to pay ten thousand dollars, which his brother would unquestionably repay in six months, since his contract was with Anaconda Copper, a client more reliable than the U. S. Government.

"Meantime, of course, it's a devilish nuisance," Flamm said. "In fact, that's the only possible snag here. It happens that Broadway money is the tightest it's been in all my experience. Why, Kaufman and Hart are having trouble raising money for their new play. Had I known—— Well, we'll just have to raise the money somehow."

He paused, and not knowing what to say, she nodded brightly. He talked some more about New Haven arrangements. Then he said, "Of course, if you know someone who has ten thousand to invest in a sure-fire comedy and who wants to see you get ahead—the return on a hit is a thousand cents on the dollar, you know, easily, and now that I've got my Clarice I've got a hit for sure——"

"Golly, Mr. Flamm, I don't know a soul with that kind of money. Ten thousand! I wish I did."

"Well, of course, in the theatre we usually parcel these things out—five thousand here, five thousand there."

She shook her head, smiling. He said, "Well, silly as it sounds, at the moment this may make the difference between our going into rehearsal or not. Six months from now brother Bart will give me the money, of course. In fact, I'll gladly secure any investor with a personal guarantee against loss, countersigned by my brother. That's how sure I am of this play. But you see, six months from now my cast may be dispersed, you may be sick, I may be sick——" He mopped his eye.

"I'm sorry, I wish I did know somebody—gosh——"

"Well, actually, the plan I've worked out is four equal shares, twenty-five hundred each—don't you think your father, for instance, I'm sure he's anxious to see you get launched in a part like Clarice—after all, an importer—he'd probably never miss twenty-five hundred dollars, and then there's the fun of watching rehearsals, and all——"

At the words "your father," a wave of sickness went over Marjorie. Staring at Flamm and shaking her head, she put the script on his desk.

"How about a thousand dollars, then? Surely a thousand, for an importer——"

"Mr. Flamm," she said huskily, "my father hates the theatre. He doesn't believe in it. My father won't invest in your play. I'm sorry. It's impossible."

He mopped his eye. The friendliness and excitement were gone from his face. He said, wearily and dryly, "Well, Marjorie, as I say, you're a talented girl, but let's face it, you're a complete newcomer. If I'm to stake my reputation on launching you, it seems to me it's not asking much of your father to show his confidence in you to the extent of five hundred or a thousand dollars."

She was blindly putting on her coat. "Goodbye, Mr. Flamm." Her hand was on the doorknob.

He said, "I mean, for five hundred or a thousand I can't give you Clarice, but the maid's part would be yours. Well, goodbye. As I say, you have talent, though it's raw——"

Dazed, wretched, she went home on the subway. She was lying on her bed face down, unmindful of the way she was crumpling the red dress, when the telephone rang. "Marjorie? Hi!" Noel's voice had a striking lift in it. "Missed me? How about having lunch with me at the Ritz-Carlton?"

She sat up. "The—the Ritz-Carlton? Noel, you can't afford it—"

"Who can't? You're talking to a twenty-five-thousand-a-year man. Now hurry!"

"Hello!" she said. "Good Lord, look at you."

The change in him was startling. He wore a new pin-stripe black suit, black shoes, a white shirt with a short pinned collar, and a gray silk tie. His hair was trimmed close, and the color in his face was remarkably fresh. "Come along, I've ordered the lunch already." The headwaiter bowed them to a conspicuously empty table in the middle of the crowded wood-panelled room.

Marjorie was very ill at ease. All the women in the room looked bitingly smart: Paris hats, tailored suits, elegant hair-dos were everywhere. She wore no hat, her hair fell loosely to her shoulders (this had been an effort to look like Clarice), and the red dress was a truly horrible blunder. She had been too prostrated by the Flamm fiasco to think of changing when she left the house. The glances of the men were the usual thing, but the glances of the women, which really mattered in such a place, were disdainful and slightly amused. "I look like a streetwalker in here," she muttered to Noel as they sat.

"Hardly," he said. "As it happens, several of the town's most eminent streetwalkers are around us, and as you see, they look quite different."

"That headwaiter treats you like a long-lost friend."

"I've been here often, dear."

"Not since I've known you."

"That's right. It's been a lean stretch, too. You don't have the price." He laughed at her vexed look. "Gad, it's fun to torment you. It's true, though, that on occasion the lady's paid. Usually some lady I've gone broke for, first."

"Don't you find it humiliating?"

"Not in the least. I sit and calculate how many Automat meals I'm saving, by not paying the check."

"You're a hoodlum. I hope you're not counting on my paying this time."

"*You,* dear?"

"Well, what's going on here, then? Why the prosperous getup? Why are you looking seventeen years old? What's all this about twenty-five thousand a year?"

"I went to work this morning."

"Where? What kind of job?"

"Paramount Pictures." The waiter set two champagne cocktails on the table. "Ah, here we are. You'll drink to the new Noel, won't you? He's your creation, as much as anybody's."

Marjorie picked up her glass, looking at him suspiciously. "Paramount! Are you serious?" He nodded. "As a writer? Are you going to Hollywood?"

His lips were compressed in amusement. "No, dear. You're not losing me, don't be tragic. Drink up. Here's death to the old Noel, that seedy bum, and long life to the new, eh?"

She smiled, in a half-disbelieving way, and drank.

Noel said, "Why are you so amazed? I've told you about Sam Rothmore, one time or another, haven't I?"

"The rich old man you play chess with?"

"That's the one. Didn't I mention that he's with Paramount?"

"I don't think so——"

"Well he is. And he loves me, the sad old bastard. He must be the lonesomest man in town. No children, and his wife's a year-round invalid in Florida. He's one of the heads of the New York office. Puts on a tough-guy act, but he's really pretty softhearted. Practically supports the chess club I play at, and a couple of Jewish old folks' homes in the Bronx, that kind of thing. Fine taste in painting and music, very good Mozart collection and—well, I've told you about the paintings, I'm sure. I've spent hundreds of hours in his library with him, listening to music and playing chess, and drinking the best brandy on earth. Frankly, and this is probably not nice of me, he gets to be an awful bore after a while. I can't say why. I guess all lonesome people are pathetic and boring, no matter who they are. So damn grateful for your company, you know, so reluctant to let you go. Anyway, Sam's clapped a harness on me at last. I'm breaking in as assistant story editor at a hundred twenty a week, and then——"

Marjorie blurted, "What? A hundred twenty a week, right off the bat?"

Noel grinned, and ran a knuckle along his upper lip. "You don't flatter me, dear. The idea is to shift me around through the departments for training, and eventually land me in a sort of chief-of-staff capacity under him, if I work out. Sam's been suggesting this off and on for a couple of years. I used to laugh at him. I didn't see myself as a wage slave. But I started talking seriously about it a week or so ago. He's sure I'm a misguided genius, and he's going to discover me and make me into a major executive. He says I can be making twenty-five thousand a year or more in a few years. I think he's more excited about my coming to work than I am. . . . Well, that's the story. Doesn't it please you?"

"Why, I'm breathless. Gosh, there's no end to you, is there? Just to walk out and get a job at a hundred twenty a week—in the middle of what everyone else calls a depression——"

"I'm getting an odd kick out of it so far, to tell you the truth. How do you like my junior-executive costume?"

"Perfect. Brooks Brothers?"

"Feinberg's, on Delancey Street. I've been outfitting myself there for years. One size too small in the extra longs gives me a fairly acceptable fit. However, I'll put a real tailor to work, one of these days. Haven't done it since *Raining Kisses*. Fun, but costly. I don't really care whether I fling money around or squirrel it, Margie, life's interesting either way, but I've had a long squirrel siege, and I must say I've been getting rather tired of it."

Marjorie had observed Noel's peculiar skill at managing his money. He had stretched the thousand-dollar fee from Greech through the fall and most of the winter. He knew an amazing number of cheap restaurants. He was good at cooking, too, much better than she was, but lazy. He would make a vast pot of excellent spaghetti, and eat at it for a week. "You'd just about run out, hadn't you?"

"Oh, I could have gone along for a few more months. I'd have gotten a little thin and irritable, maybe, like a hibernating bear. In Paris they make an art of this kind of living. You pick it up. I swear I'd just as lief be poor as rich. It's sport, nibbling away at a store of money, and scheming to make it last."

The lunch was superb: hors d'oeuvres which Noel selected from a huge wheeled cart, veal delicately sliced and cooked with mushrooms and rice, a side dish of curiously prepared eggplant, and a salad with eggs and anchovies which he dressed himself. The white wine had an exquisite glowing clean taste. Marjorie forgot her self-consciousness, eating with great relish.

Noel said, pouring wine, "Why kid ourselves, Marjorie? The best things in life cost like the devil. Every time I poke my nose back into the upper-crust atmosphere, I realize why people kill themselves for money. Oh, hell, there's a case for impoverished freedom, but——" He drank. "You know, there are some charming perquisites to this job. Where do you suppose I go from here, this afternoon? Newark Airport. To meet Janice Gray, if you please, and escort her to the Waldorf."

"Janice Gray?" Marjorie did her best to keep the note of alarm out of her voice. "Well, that should be nice. She's beautiful."

"Yes indeed. Usually Sam meets her. This is high policy. She's been a bad girl at the studio, showing up late for shooting, balking at stories, and so forth. I'm an insult to her, you see, a mere hireling greeting her, instead of the boss."

"Well, I hope she'll be properly offended." Marjorie's appetite was suddenly gone. She put a cigarette in her mouth, and the waiter startled her by springing at her with a lit match.

Noel said, busily eating, "She's a dull creature, no doubt, in person. She's on her third or fourth divorce, and I hear she's utterly dissolute. Probably arrive drunk as a goat."

"No doubt. And you'll probably be in bed with her before the day is out. I hope you enjoy it."

He put down his knife and fork and laughed at her, his eyes brilliant.

She said, "All right, laugh. You've always lived like a pig, and there's no reason for you not to go on that way. I swear I don't care what you do. Only one thing puzzles me. Why do you keep coming around to me? Why is it me you call up when you've got the new job? And why have you taken the job? What are you trying to prove to me? I'm just a West End Avenue girl, dumb, untalented——"

"Beautiful——"

"Not like Janice Gray——"

"Fresh, sweet, blue-eyed, a sprig of lilac in the morning sun. Darling, I shouldn't bait you, but I can't help it. Why do you always bite? Janice Gray's a revolting old bag. When she walks in front of the camera to play a scene, I see nothing but her agent just off camera, blotting the new clause in the contract. She's odious."

"Oh, sure," Marjorie growled, but she felt better. "Well, you still haven't answered me. Why have you taken this job?"

Noel shrugged. "Isn't it pleasanter to eat at the Ritz than at Mama Mantucci's on Eleventh Street?"

"Why, of course, but you seem to like it the other way——"

"I like life almost any way it comes—except—well, I was going to say, except the respectable way, but I'm not sure that's so. I'm beginning to think I might love being bourgeois, with a difference. With an inward grin, you might say. Hell, Marjorie, I like good things. I like the thought of being able to afford them. I like shirts that fit well, and ties that knot attractively because the material is good, and suits made of fine stuff instead of Feinberg's wrought iron." He fingered his sleeve. "I like gold cuff links, but I'm damned if I'll wear plated ones. I'm more and more attracted to the notion of affording these things all over again, as I did in the *Raining Kisses* days. It was a golden time. All the good things in my wardrobe date from then. I like ocean trips, too—first class. It's a deep pleasure just to know I can go if I want to. And then of course there's that luxury of luxuries, a bourgeois wife. Love knows no logic. Suppose I should one day be unfortunate enough to want to marry such a creature?"

She avoided his look, and said with a great effort at lightness, "Here's hoping you don't. You'd make her acutely miserable for life."

"Possibly. Then again, if I knew exactly what I was doing, I might make her happy as a fairy princess."

She couldn't help it; she faced him. His unsmiling passionate glance agitated her. She murmured after a few seconds, "Don't look at me like that, you fool."

"I'll look as I damn please."

"Don't, I say. Let me ask you this, what's suddenly brought on such a radical change of front? Have you given up your writing ambitions?"

Noel sipped at his wine, his expression thoughtful. "Not in the least. There's been a conspiracy of events forcing me into Sam's office lately. That disaster with Kogel and *Princess Jones,* for one thing. The theatre is nothing but a machine for breaking spirits, Margie—that is, so long as you try to make a living from it. Cole Porter's a millionaire. So's Coward. Light music, light verse, comedy, are products of leisure, of a debonair existence. I've been living like a Chicago slum novelist. It's all wrong. The theatre's exactly like a silly girl. Pursue, beg, coax, be willing and assiduous, and you get kicked in the face. The careless confident gesture is what conquers. I fully believe now I'll crack Broadway the day I don't give a damn whether I do or not. That's reason number one for taking Sam's money. To break out of my stagnant poverty-stricken rut and live well—until I crack through with *Princess Jones,* or write a new show. Maybe I'll stay on with Sam even then. Maybe the pattern will prove a stable one. It all depends on whether I can effectively split my time between breadwinning and writing, over the long haul. We'll see."

"Well, that makes sense, God knows."

"I think it does. I feel full of beans today. And I'm grateful to you. Do you know, I believe it was your graduation that pushed me over the edge. I actually went from Schrafft's and phoned Sam. The graduation was such a great divide of time for you . . . and somehow, I felt myself passing over it, too. I saw myself all too clearly. Thirty, and nowhere, and disgusting your parents, your ratty down-at-the-heels admirer from Greenwich Village. Maybe if it hadn't been so gray and rainy, and I hadn't been wearing my oldest coat and my greasiest hat—— And then Marsha showing up, grinning at the pair of us like an itchy old maid . . . I don't know, everything closed in on me, all at once, and I went and called Sam. I'd been fearfully low for days, you see. Last Sunday I found out that my brother Billy was engaged to be married."

Marjorie looked startled. "Billy!"

"Twenty-two. In his second year at law school. She's the daughter of a

268

big corporation lawyer, a heavyweight in the Democratic party in Brooklyn. Another Marjorie, by the way, Marjorie Sundheimer——"

"Marjorie Sundheimer? Good Lord, Billy's marrying *her?*"

"You know her, then?"

"Oh, for years at fraternity dances—and all that—— Well, well, Billy Ehrmann and Marjorie Sundheimer. Honestly, truth is stranger than fiction."

"Marjorie, ugly girls get married, too."

"I never said she was ugly."

"Your tones, dear, are implying that you'd be less surprised if Billy'd become engaged to a red-bottomed baboon."

"That's absurd. She's a lovely girl. It's just—well, they're both so young."

"Sweetheart, this sets Billy up for life. He'll be a judge at forty. Nothing can stop it. What the devil, I'm happy for him, he's a decent egg."

"Billy's grand."

"He dropped in with this girl unexpectedly at my apartment, the night of your graduation. That's why I didn't call you. I couldn't have been more depressed. They're such children! I'm barely used to the idea that he shaves. She's had her nose fixed, by the way, and she's really quite pleasant-looking. And for such a rich girl, she's touchingly humble. Like Billy. They're a nice couple. I think they're going to be happy."

"No doubt she knows all about us."

"The last thing she said at the door was, 'Love to Marjorie,' in a quavering voice, after nobody'd referred to you for two hours. I think coming below Fourteenth Street was a scary adventure for her. She kept staring around, you know, at the books, and the carpet, and the pictures, and the dust on the molding, and at me. She laughed hysterically at everything I said, including half a dozen remarks that were perfectly serious. Obviously she thought I was a highly decadent monster, like Baudelaire. I think she was looking around for hypodermic needles. I was sorry I didn't at least have a gorgeous drunken blonde to fall naked out of the closet at one point. She seemed to be waiting for something like that."

"What she was waiting for, more likely," Marjorie said, "was for me to come out from under the bed in a transparent negligee."

Noel burst out laughing. "I swear I think that was it."

Marjorie said, "Well, what do I care? My reputation's gone, anyway, from associating with you."

He said with sudden earnestness, "Honestly, the uptown idea of Village life is preposterous, isn't it? Believe me, the main charm of the Village is the cheap rent. For me, anyway. I find overgrown hair and dirty necks as offensive as you do. As for the celebrated Village sex life, which had Billy's girl's eyes popping out of her head looking for evidence—what is it, after all, once you're over the college boy's glee at finding it available? Most of the time it's a mean dirty chore. Unattractive people snuffling and wrestling together because they're bored, or lonesome, or sick in the head. You say I've lived the life of a pig. Well, it's not true. I've always been fastidious by any standard, I claim. But I'll tell you this, and I don't say it to score a point. Since the day you left South Wind, there's been nothing like that for me. Nothing at all."

This question had been plaguing Marjorie for months. Her heart swelled to have the answer, but how like Noel to drop it casually into a conversation, as a fact of no importance! She looked him in the face. "I'm not sorry to hear that."

"Understand this, I have no more scruples or morals than before. I've simply decided it's the better part of self-indulgence to have love or nothing."

She couldn't repress a grin. "Noel dear, I think you're slowly but surely reverting to your origins."

He shook his head at her. "You'll make me over, come hell or high water, won't you? Or you'll tell yourself you're doing it, anyhow. Your voice just then had the timbre of your mother's. Let's get out of this oak-panelled vault."

"All right, but I must say I love it here."

"What tastes you're acquiring! You'll keep your husband broke, and working nights in his dress business." He paid the check.

"I'm not marrying anybody in the dress business."

"Of course. I forgot. A doctor. A specialist."

"Yes, with a big black mustache, named Shapiro. We've been all through that."

"Ah, you see, our relationship's exhausted. I'm repeating my jokes."

They walked up the side street to Fifth Avenue. It was cold and windy, but clear, and the sunshine was almost blinding. He said, "Come, walk up Fifth with me. I have to pick up Sam's car at Sixty-third."

"Sure.—Ever heard of a producer named Guy Flamm?"

"Of course. The fringe of the fringe. What about him?"

She told him the story while they strolled uptown past the shopwindows, amid a scurrying crowd. He was amused and sympathetic. "You poor baby."

"Oh, I don't much care. It didn't last long enough to mean anything. And anyway, the play was such balderdash—at least I thought it was."

"Of course it was. All the same, he'll probably produce Down Two Doubled one of these days, when a Clarice walks into his office with a richer or dumber father than yours. It can happen tomorrow, there are so many Clarices drifting around Broadway. The desire to be an actress, in middle-class American girls of a certain IQ—say around 115—isn't even a conscious decision, Margie. It's a tropism, an organic thing that comes out of the nature of their lives. . . . All right, all right——" She was gnawing her lips, scowling at him. "I thought we'd agreed that no generalizations whatever applied to you."

"Noel, does Flamm know *Down Two Doubled* is rubbish? Or does he really think it's good?"

"Who knows? For a career like his what you need is an infinite capacity for self-deception."

"How does he live, pay his rent? His name gets in the theatre columns——"

"Why, dear, he's a real producer. He probably has scratched up some money with *Down Two Doubled* already, small amounts from idiotic amateur backers. The theatre is so cockeyed, he may even produce a smash some day. Those scripts you saw his girl reading were the flotsam that drifts around the producers' offices forever, one abomination more frightful than the last. I was a playreader for a few months once. I nearly went crazy. Undoubtedly he pulled *Down Two Doubled* out of that rancid flood. Maybe he likes it. Maybe he's had the author rewrite it ten times. Maybe he's charged him for his advice. There's no end to the follies that go on in the theatre."

She said, "I take it you've decided I have no talent. You were still dodging the issue, last time we talked about it."

His face wrinkled. "I'm really not sure. Anyone can see you're bright and pretty and full of nineteenish charm. You walk on stage endowed by nature with half the effects a skilled actress has to work to create. But such incandescence doesn't last. What you'll be left with when it goes, I can't say. My guess is that you'll be snagged into a fine fat marriage long before that, so you'll never really find out. One thing I'll tell you, though. If you're going at this seriously, you ought to get rid of that Marjorie Morningstar name. It has a fake ring."

"Shows how much you know. It's in the New York phone book."

"I don't care. You'd be better off calling yourself Marjorie Morgan."

"That's drab and commonplace."

"Well? The idea of a name change is to make you more like other people, not less."

"I suppose Noel Airman is commonplace."

"I was in just about the stage you are now when I thought of that. If I had it to do over again, I'd call myself something like Charlie Robinson. If you want to pretend you're not a Jew, you may as well do it right."

"That's not why I'm doing it."

"Then what's wrong with Morgenstern?"

"It's too ordinary."

"I see. You want an unusual name, like Maggie Sullavan."

"Well, that's different. Morgenstern sounds so . . . I don't know——"

"So Jewish, girlie, so Jewish. Those overtones of potato pancakes, Friday-night candles, gefilte fish—that's what you don't like."

She said, irritated, "Of course, everybody's motives have to be as wretched as yours. All the same, Noel, I'm going to call myself Marjorie Morningstar, and I'm going to become an actress, in spite of Guy Flamm, and my mother, and you, and all the odds."

He put his arm around her waist and briefly squeezed it. "That's the old college fight." They walked in silence for a while. He said, "But I can't picture it, and you know why, Margie? Every real actress I've ever known has had a—I don't know, a sort of iron core. When you talk to them—even romantically—you get a metallic ring in response. I'm not putting this well. I don't mean insincerity, d'you see, or phoniness, or frigidity. It's—well, they're more like men, in a fixity of purpose, and a hard alertness to the business at hand. Most of them make a hash of their love lives. It's as though the price of having talent is the loss of the womanish instinct for sniffing along the right path of life. Well, you—you're such a female, such a cat picking your way with dainty paws——"

"I often wonder where you get your ideas about me. Of all my graduating class, I think I should have been voted the girl most likely to hash up her life."

"You like to romanticize yourself. You're pure cat, sniffing nervously but surely toward a house in New Rochelle, and a husband making a minimum of fifteen thousand a year."

"Go climb a tree. Lord, you're a bore sometimes."

He laughed. They were walking along the eastern side of the plaza. The breath of the hansom-cab horses across the street smoked in the sunshine. "D'you know, you've had an effect on me? I respect cat wisdom. I think now I might very well enjoy that kind of life, myself—and buying in these shops, and staying weekends at the Pierre or the Plaza, and all that—always providing one thing. Providing that my wife and I both regarded such a life as a pleasant comic mask, put on like Mexican living or Fiji Island living, because at the moment it pleased us—but in itself unreal, empty, of no importance, and discardable overnight." With a sharp turn, he pulled her into a florist's shop.

"What on earth——"

"Violets, in February! Didn't you see them in the window? Must buy you a bunch."

"You're a madman."

Noel scribbled a card while the florist prepared the violets. He handed the little purple nosegay and the card to her with a flourish:

Violets in winter,
Sweetness in ice—
Not that you need, dear,
This wily advice.

She blushed, laughed huskily, and dropped the card in the purse. "Very witty. I think I'll carry the flowers."

Sam Rothmore's black Cadillac stood in front of a lean gray stone house which had rococo black iron grillwork on the windows and the massive doors. The chauffeur, a neat gray-haired man in black, greeted Noel respectfully and held the door of the limousine open. "Say, come on, I'll drop you off at home first," Noel said.

"Oh no, Noel, the car is for business."

"Nonsense. There's all kinds of time. Get in and stop arguing. Seven-forty West End Avenue, Philip."

"Certainly, Mr. Airman."

Rolling through Central Park in the Cadillac, Marjorie sniffed the violets, and looked out at the muddy brown-green lawns with patches of ice on the rocks, and thought that it might not be bad to die at this instant. She turned to Noel. "You're ruining my life. I wonder if you're doing it deliberately."

"I'm in love with you," Noel said.

She glanced at the chauffeur's back, then reached up and kissed him lightly on the lips. "I'm in love with you, too."

"One of us must crack," Noel said.

"Not me," Marjorie said.

Chapter 24. THE ENGAGEMENT PARTY

Noel did not telephone during the next three weeks, and a very dreary three weeks they were. She spent the time exploring the theatre district, and what she found out mainly was that there were a large number of girls like her—droves of them, indeed—marching doggedly and without much hope from one producer's office to another, through February snow and slush, under unchanging black skies that seemed to hang a few feet above the tops of the buildings.

When Sandy Goldstone called, inviting her to come with him to Billy Ehrmann's engagement reception, Marjorie accepted eagerly. She was only mildly curious to see Sandy, or for that matter Billy and his bride-to-be; but she figured that Noel would probably appear at the party. A melancholy, quenched Sandy called for her that Sunday. He seemed to be a foot or so shorter than she remembered him; round-shouldered, listless, dull. But he said bravely that he loved working at Lamm's, and that everything couldn't be better. He confided to Marjorie that he had found a way to make a fortune. He owned twenty per cent of a race horse; and while twenty per cent of the horse's weekly hay consumption cost him most of his salary, he had high hopes of making a killing soon in one of the big stake races.

The ballroom at the Sherry-Netherland was too crowded, when they arrived at the party, for Marjorie to be able to see whether or not Noel was there. Perhaps four hundred people, most of them young, all of them well dressed, were strolling about the smoky flower-decked room and chattering, with highballs or glasses of champagne in their hands.

"Usual brawl," Sandy said. They were standing inside the door, on the reception line. The engaged couple and their parents were hidden by shuffling handshakers.

"It's such a waste," Marjorie said. "I swear I'll never have a big party. I'll save the money."

"You'll have the big party," Sandy said. "Why do you keep looking at the door?"

"I wasn't looking at the door at all."

The handshakers ahead gave way, there was an open space, and Marjorie was face to face with Marjorie Sundheimer. Immediately she glanced at the ring. It was a very large oblong diamond, but not the largest Marjorie had ever seen; and she felt more kindly toward the girl. Marjorie Sundheimer said, "Margie, I'm so glad you could come!" Her face was flushed, her eyes wide and sparkling, and she looked more nearly pretty than Marjorie would have thought possible. She wore a striking floor-length green and orange gown, with curiously draped shawl sleeves. Marjorie was glad, after all, that her blue dress was insignificant. Her only safe note today was cheerful dowdiness.

Billy Ehrmann grasped her hand eagerly. He was perspiring, his shirt was bunched up, and his gray suit was too new. His blond hair hung straight down on his forehead. "Margie!"

She said demurely, "The other Margie. All the luck in the world, Billy."

He spluttered, "Well, gosh—Margie—say, did you ever meet my folks? Mother, this is her, this is Marjorie Morgenstern."

Mrs. Ehrmann's mechanical smile dissolved, as she glanced at Marjorie, into a look of intense alert friendliness. "Well, Marjorie *Morgen-*

stern! My dear, I'm very glad to see you. Dad!" She pulled at the elbow of a tall bald man beside her who was talking to another couple. "Dad, here's Marjorie Morgenstern."

He looked around quickly. A long face, a curved long jaw, deep-set blue eyes, scrawny cords in his cheeks and neck; he was Noel grown old. His voice was deep and slow. "Well, my dear, this is a privilege. How do you do?"

"How do you do, Judge Ehrmann?"

"You'll stay a while, won't you, Marjorie?" the mother said. "I really want to talk to you."

"Yes, of course."

Sandy went off to get her a scotch and soda. She was pushed here and there by people hurrying past. She began to make her way toward the wall, peering around for Noel.

"Hi, Margie. Thought you'd be here." Wally Wronken came plowing through the crowd, holding by the hand an amazingly young-looking girl with a very pretty face, and the puzzled happy eyes of a baby animal.

"Hello, Wally."

"Marjorie Morgenstern, I'd like you to meet Marjorie Pechter."

"Great day!" Marjorie said. "How many Marjories are there in this Godforsaken town?"

"Not many where I come from," said the girl in a high little voice. "I'm from Harrison, New York."

"Marjorie's a freshman at Barnard," Wally said. "You look wonderful."

"I live in the dorms," the girl said.

"Where's Noel?" Wally said.

"I don't know. I'm here with Sandy Goldstone." Marjorie plunged away toward the wall.

She landed near the musicians, and sank on a red and gilt chair. Sandy brought her the drink and went off again. Marjorie sat watching the blathering crowd with the detachment of a Hindu. A third or more of the faces were familiar, the same faces she had seen all through college at school dances, at parties, and at the hotel grills. The boys' faces were heavier, the girls' warier and less fresh. Those who had paired off and married seemed to be making more noise and drinking more than the others.

"Hey there, Margie! Where's Noel?" The saxophonist was waving at her. She recognized him—a South Wind musician; then she realized that all four players were from the camp band. She went and talked to them. "Noel recommended us," the saxophonist said. "We play these dates all winter, Marge." The musicians raised their eyebrows at each other when she said she hadn't come with Noel. Wally Wronken reappeared without the Barnard girl, and asked her to dance. His flat-footed style had not much improved.

"Where's your date, Wally?"

He tossed his head, with the look of concentration he always wore dancing. "Over there, somewhere."

Marjorie saw the girl, talking to three of the younger boys, laughing and turning bright eyes from one to the other. "She reminds me of me—a few ages ago."

"I wish she reminded me of you," Wally said gloomily. "Good kid, but very vanilla-flavored."

"What's my flavor? Red pepper?"

"Samian wine in a cup of gold."

"Very pretty. I'll bet you never drank Samian wine in your life."

"It's in some Byron poem. It sounds right for you."

"Samian wine! That's your whole trouble, Wally Wronken. You'll probably find out some day it's a horrible Greek vinegar that puts fur on your teeth."

"You sound like Noel."

"What of it? You've always sounded like Noel. It's just something that happens to people who've been around him."

"I know. How is he?"

"Haven't seen him lately."

Wally leaned back and looked at her. "How lately?"

"None of your business."

"Are you two going to get married?"

"Not that I know of."

"My new Varsity Show's been accepted."

"Congratulations."

"Will you come to the opening with me?"

"Now listen, don't go dragging your grandmother to that again, it looks very odd, Wally. You take Marjorie Pechter. She's charming."

"She's unconscious. I don't know how she finds her way around the streets."

"Don't be such a snob. You'd better get used to the idea that there aren't many girls as bright as you, my lad, or you'll die a mean old bachelor."

Sandy cut in. His smooth dancing was a relief. But for the moment she missed Wally's worship, his tender constrained hold on her waist. She and Sandy were as easy together as two girls. She started glancing toward the door again.

At the bar they encountered Phil Boehm and Rosalind, both half drunk. Since Rosalind was obviously pregnant, Marjorie was shocked, and said something about it. Rosalind wagged her head. "Don't you worry, Margie, I'm a baby-making machine, that's all, just a baby-making machine. Nothing interferes. Turn 'em out like Fords, don't I, Phil?"

"Like doughnuts," said Phil Boehm.

"Good Lord," Marjorie said to Sandy, as the Boehms waltzed unsteadily away with their highballs splashing in their hands, "what comes over the married ones at engagement parties? I sometimes think——"

There he was.

He stood in the doorway, far down the room, tall, blond, dressed in black, looking around with the casual majesty of a big cat. She wasn't the only one who noticed him. Lines converging on him might have been drawn through eyes everywhere in the room. There were four girls at the party, to Marjorie's knowledge, who had had romances with him; all were now married. There were others, without a doubt. He was a legend to many men, too, who were staring just as hard. He strolled into the room, ignoring the reception line. A girl darted at him, seized his hand, and began chattering. Two couples stopped dancing and went to him. In a moment he was surrounded and hidden.

Now for the first time Marjorie became aware that lines of eyes were converging on her, too, and that Sandy was regarding her with dejected amusement. She realized she had been stretching her neck and staring. She became dreadfully confused, almost dropped her highball, and spilled it slightly, taking a hurried sip.

"Getting crowded, isn't it?" Sandy said.

She smiled piteously at him, and took another sip. He said, "Well, he's good-looking. I hope you can handle him. They say he's quite a boy."

"He is, Sandy."

"What's the matter with his arm?"

She was startled. She had not thought of the deformity since the summer, nor indeed consciously seen it. "Why, nothing much. I'm surprised you noticed it at this distance. Let's dance, shall we?"

It wasn't long before she saw the long tapered hand in the black sleeve touch Sandy's shoulder. "Cut?"

"Sure. Take good care of her, she's fragile," Sandy said, handing the girl over.

"I know," Noel said. "Fragile as chrome steel."

They danced in silence for a few seconds. "Thanks for nothing," Marjorie said. "Chrome steel, indeed."

"How've you been?"

"Oh, just deliriously happy. And you?"

"Busy, sort of. Is Max here?"

She peered up at him. "Max?"

"Dr. Shapiro, the stomach man."

"Go to hell."

"I mean it. That's what engagement parties are really for, you know. You confront the unattached ones with the terror of passing time, and they start pairing off in panic, then and there. Half the marriages in the world are started up at engagement parties. I thought for sure you'd find Max here today."

"Well, he hasn't showed, so you're still stuck with me, Noel Airman."

"Who, me? I never heard of you."

The saxophonist shouted, "Hi, Noel." Noel nodded, grinning. The musicians finished the number and swung without a pause into *It's Raining Kisses*.

Marjorie noticed that people were watching them. A thin irregular line of spectators now bordered the dance space, and there were fewer couples on the floor. "Are you still working for Sam Rothmore?"

"Sure. It's no picnic, either. Sam gets a day's work out of you for his money, believe me. None of that brandy-and-chess charm in working hours. In fact he's a pretty coarse bully. I don't mind. He amuses me. But he keeps me jumping."

"Keeps you too busy to call me, I take it."

"Oh no, no. Don't blame Sam."

"Well, who, then?"

"Why, nobody."

"Look, I don't care if you never call me again."

"I'm sure of that."

The music changed, and the tempo. A chill passed through Marjorie's body. They were beginning the *South Wind Waltz*. "Wouldn't you know. Damn their hides," she murmured.

Noel was holding her close. "Pleasant little tune," he said. "Not very original, but sweet."

Marjorie was flooded with painful feelings: memories of Samson-Aaron, of the smell of the South Wind trees at night in the moonlight, of fierce knee-weakening kisses, of the grease-paint odors backstage . . . There were only two other couples still dancing. The ring of staring, whispering onlookers had thickened. "I've had enough," she muttered. She broke away, still holding Noel's hand, and dragged him off the floor.

"What's the matter?" he said.

She pressed through the spectators, pulling him along. "I don't know, I suddenly felt as though I were doing the dance of the seven veils. It's so smoky in here! Let's walk in the hall. Let's get out of this room——"

"Noel! Wait!" A middle-sized woman wearing a caracul coat and a Russian-style cap of the same fur came hurrying through the crowd, followed by a thickset man in a swinging topcoat of camel's hair. Both carried highballs. "So! His Majesty favors us with his presence, after all," she said, looking keenly at Noel and then at Marjorie. Her face was that of a girl in her twenties, but there was much gray in her brown hair. "Horace and I had about given you up. We were escaping from this rat race. Quite a dancing partner you've gotten yourself, brother dear."

"Marjorie, this is my sister Monica. And this is Horace Sigelman." Noel's manner all at once was strangely graceless.

"Hello, Marjorie." The woman clasped her hand and looked into her face, conveying sweetness and good humor in a glance. "I've heard about you. You're prettier than anybody said."

Horace Sigelman, who had handsome tanned features and thick black hair, patted Noel on the back. His voice was hoarse and loud. "Boy, you've got yourself a real girl this time. How about hanging on to this one?"

Noel said, "I'll tell you, Horace, I lack the necessary charm. How about giving me lessons?"

"Shut up and dance with me," the sister said, putting her arm through Noel's. "You don't mind, do you, Margie dear? This is a once-in-ten-years proposition, you see. In fact if I hadn't had five scotch and waters, or is it six, Horace——"

"Seven——"

"—seven, I wouldn't dare approach him even now. He despises his dumb sister, though I love the big wolf."

"I don't despise you, my love, we just disagree on a few little things."

"Well come on, dance then."

"You and Horace are the dancers. Why don't you give us a rumba?"

Monica's huge blue eyes seemed to be tearful, though she was smiling gaily. She was extraordinarily attractive, with a magnetic presence not unlike Noel's, and Marjorie realized that she must have cut down a hundred boys in her time. Her all-fur outfit was a slightly false note, strained and flashy. "Please, Saul, dance with your drunken sister, just once. To celebrate Billy's great day." She finished the drink and handed the glass to her husband.

"And hurry, Noel. The next train to Portchester is at five," Horace said. "I'll be glad to take Marjorie off your hands. I'll keep her happy, boy."

Noel's glance at Horace and Marjorie was bleak. "By all means." He followed his sister to the dance floor, and they started to glide automatically, like a married couple, the wide black fur skirt of Monica's coat swirling outward.

"Now she'll get overheated," Horace said, "and catch cold, getting in and out of those lousy trains. She's always catching cold."

"She's lovely," Marjorie said.

Horace's face filled with pleasure; he watched Monica proudly. "You don't know her. Hope you pay us a visit real soon. There's nobody like her. Say, would you like to dance? I can get rid of this coat."

"Oh, no, thanks, Mr. Sigelman, I've been dancing and dancing."

"Horace. We might as well be informal. Something tells me we might be seeing a little more of you." He gave her a heavy slow roguish grin. "That Noel, he's one hell of a guy, isn't he? I swear I think he's the most brilliant person I've ever met. Monica about worships the ground he walks on. Though we never see him. I've always said if he ever married some nice down-to-earth girl, who'd steady him up, you know, why he'd be famous in short order. He's an awful wild man. You know, the kind other fellows envy, until they stop to think about it. I don't envy him any more. I used to, in a way. But I don't now, he's seemed sort of sad the last few years, lonely, you know, and not getting much of anywhere."

Monica said when they returned, "It's all set, Margie. He's going to bring you out for the day to our place as soon as the weather gets better. My brood'll climb all over you, and drip ice cream on your dress, and it'll be fun."

"Wonderful."

Noel said, "Providing Margie's still talking to me."

The sister took her hand and suddenly kissed her. " 'Bye, dear, you're sweet. Pay no attention to me, I'm a sentimental drunk. Take me home, Norace. Horace—listen to me—'Norace.' " She reached up, pulled her brother's head forward and kissed him swiftly on the cheek. "Goodbye, you scoundrel. Follow Billy's example, real soon."

"Gad," Noel said, looking after her, "she's ossified. Ordinarily she'd as soon give me an arm as a kiss."

"Well, I don't like to kiss my brother, either, it's silly. No wonder you're so fond of her, she's charming."

"Who said I was fond of her? She's a bore, a suburban slattern with a house boiling with kids."

"You told me so yourself, at camp. You also said Horace was a lump of pig fat. I think you're wrong there. He's very likable."

"Did I call Horace that? That's rather neat. Weren't we going outside?"

Some of the couches in the mirrored corridor were screened by fake palms in green tubs, and on these there were couples talking earnestly, holding hands, kissing. "Here, you see?" Noel said. "The pairing-off process is well advanced already. A pity Max, the doctor, didn't show up. You two are star-crossed lovers. Why, to miss such an opportunity——"

Marjorie said, "I must have no sense of humor, after all. I don't think Max, the doctor, is funny any more."

"You're getting sensitive."

"Well, it's the drop of water on the stone, you know."

"I erase that joke from my repertoire. You will never hear it again."

"Thank heaven."

"I'll miss Max, though. I was getting fond of him."

They were strolling past the ladies' lounge. Phil Boehm leaned against the wall beside the door, his hair rumpled, a droopy-eyed grin on his face. Marjorie said, "Hi. Is Roz all right?"

"Guess so, guess so. Li'l sick, she says."

"Shall I go in and help?"

"No, no, no. Four gals with her now."

Marjorie said as they walked away, "Maybe you can tell me why the married ones cut up so horribly at these things."

"Good Lord, is that a question? To forget, of course," Noel said. "To forget their own high hopes, and their sad mornings after. To forget the budgets that don't balance, the friends with bigger cars, the baby's sore throats, the sleepless nights, the bloody miscarriages, the procession of quitting maids, the flatness of routine sex, the neurotic mother-in-law poisoning their lives——"

"You make marriage sound like a nightmare."

"Do I? I don't mean to. No, time passes and the path narrows and narrows, and after a while there's nothing to do but marry. But marrying doesn't help, you've just got to do it anyway, and after you're married life just goes on being a series of decreasingly pleasant choices. And you wonder why the married ones get drunk——"

"Well, I'll say this, a girl would be absolutely crazy to marry a man who thinks the way you do."

He turned on her, and his look was so scornful that she started back a little. "Aren't we past those devious female noises yet? You'd marry me in two seconds if I asked you."

"You're the most unbearably conceited man I've ever met."

"Listen, Marjorie, you've been lying awake nights thinking of me. Those rings under your eyes! You look awful."

"You fiend, of course I've been thinking of you! Haven't you been making love to me for a year?"

"Well, why the devil didn't you telephone me then?"

"Telephone *you?* You said you'd call me."

His laugh was a short bitter burst. "Christ, that was really it, wasn't it?

Margie, ever hear of the French king who roasted to death rather than move his chair back from the fireplace with his own hands? You've got him beat hands down. The heavens can fall, but Shirley's protocol must be observed, isn't that the idea?"

She faced him. "You said you were starting work and might be busy for a while. You know you did. The way you left it, no girl with any self-respect would have called a devil like you. It would have been nagging, crawling——"

"You're all wrong. Girls call up devils like me every day in the week, Margie, girls with all kinds of pride and self-respect. Why, the land rings from coast to coast with such calls. Only they never call for a date, don't you see? They call about a book they meant to borrow, or because they heard you were sick, or they dialled the wrong number by mistake, or some old thing like that. Naturally." He put his arm around her waist. They were at the end of the corridor, looking out of the window at a crimson sunset over the bluish downtown buildings. He said after a moment, "I'm sorry. I should have called you, I know. But it was better not to. I've been in a foul mood, and still am, and that's the truth. Going straight, keeping nine-to-five hours—the old Adam dies hard, Margie. And of course, in my lowest moments it's always you I blame. However——" He kissed her temple lightly. "Come, one dance and then I must leave you."

"Where are you going?"

"I have a date."

"Anybody I know?"

He grinned. "Janice Gray." He grinned wider at the fall of her countenance. "Listen, she's a lonesome old bat. She's the mistress of a sweater manufacturer who's on his way home from Europe to meet her, and she's dying of boredom. She doesn't know anybody in New York. *She's* not bashful, she phones me all the time. She doesn't like me at all, but I'm sort of a neutral presentable dancing partner. She pays all the checks, so I'm not wasting my hard-earned funds."

Marjorie said angrily, "No doubt you're standing in for the sportswear manufacturer in bed, too."

He looked her in the eye. "No."

"No?"

"No. She isn't interested, and anyway, she's inches deep in makeup. It would be like trying to make love to a greased pig."

With a nervous giggle Marjorie said, "That's some way to talk about a movie star. You're lying to make me feel good."

In the ballroom the musicians had stopped playing. Noel said, "Well, guess I'll pay my disrespects." He went up to the exhausted Sundheimers, with Marjorie on his arm, and urbanely congratulated them. Marjorie Sundheimer looked a little frightened, shaking his hand. He slapped Billy on the back. "My boy, read your Genesis again. The younger ones aren't supposed to marry first."

Judge Ehrmann said heavily, "You'd better read *your* Genesis again, Saul. That applied only to the daughters."

"Well, all the same," Noel said to Marjorie Sundheimer, "don't be surprised if you wake up on your wedding morn and find yourself married to me. It's an old Biblical custom."

Marjorie Sundheimer said, "I'm afraid I'd never stop running."

The judge laughed hoarsely.

"So long, Mother," Noel said. He bent and kissed her pink wrinkled cheek.

"Are you going already? You just came." She accompanied them out to the elevator, saying to Noel, "Why don't you come up to dinner, say next Friday, and bring your little friend here, Marjorie? It's been so long——"

Noel said, "Why, I barely know this girl."

"Stop your nonsense." As the elevator door slid open, Marjorie suddenly said, "Mister, this is your last date with Janice Gray."

"Who says so?"

"I do."

"Goodbye, girls. Have a nice chat, now."

At midnight Marjorie telephoned Noel. There was no answer. She sat in bed reading her novel until one, and called again. No answer. She dropped the book and thought about the engagement party. She was still appalled at the wretched incident that had ended the afternoon. One of Noel's former girls, married for five years, the mother of two children, had staggered up to her and, with distorted features and thick speech, had begun gabbling disconnectedly about Noel. Completely out of control, the woman had shrugged off her husband's embarrassed efforts to stop her, and her voice had become louder and her smile queerer. Sandy at last had hurried Marjorie out of the room, with the woman shouting after her, "Come back, come back! There's lots more you'd better know about Saul Ehrmann——"

When the minute hand stood at exactly two, she called his apartment again.

"Hello?" He sounded sleepy.

"Hello. It's Shirley."

"Holy smoke!" His voice rose with pleasure. "Calling a man at two in the morning——"

"I know. I'm totally depraved. You've ruined me."

"Well, it's nice to hear from you, ruined or not——"

"I hope I'm not disturbing you. Is Janice Gray there?"

"Oh, don't be a jackass. I dropped her at the Waldorf an hour ago. How about coming down here? We'll neck."

"Not a chance."

"Well, then, come down here and fight me off."

"No. I had enough trouble fighting off Susan Hoffen this afternoon."

"Oh my Lord." His voice grew cautious. "Don't tell me—was she drunk?"

"She was mighty strange. All about how nice you are and how pretty I am, on and on, with her hand gripping my arm, and her eyes popping. It gave me the creeps."

"Susan can give you the creeps, all right. She hates her husband, and she takes it out on the world."

"Just one of the broken blossoms along your path, Mr. Airman."

"Oh, sure. They litter the West Side. Only Susan victimized me, as it happens. Turned around and got married because we'd had a fight, and left me stunned for months. Now it's all my fault, obviously, and will be till she dies."

"Obviously. And you're still brokenhearted about her. Or is it Betty Frank, or Irene Goren, or Ruth Mendelsohn, or Marilyn Lubin? You ought to write a book."

He laughed. "Well, what can I do for you?"

"Not a thing."

"You called me."

"I know. Just because you made such a silly fuss about it. Also, I want to borrow a book."

"Now you're talking. What book?"

"Oh, I don't know, any book. Plato's *Republic*."

"That's a honey. Hell of a trick ending. I'll give it to you when I see you again."

"Fine. When will that be?"

"Marjorie Morgenstern, are you asking me for a date?"

"Sure, why not?"

"Well, bless my soul. Let's have a date right now. I'll get dressed and come get you."

She chuckled. "Noel, don't be insane."

"Why not? Damn it, the only good hour is the present one. We'll have hamburgers, and ride back and forth all night on the ferry, like Edna Millay says——"

"I'm no Edna Millay, mister. And I'm in bed, and my face is all cold cream, and my hair is a mess, and I wouldn't get up and eat hamburgers with Clark Gable."

"You definitely lack romance," he said in a disappointed tone. "Come on, our future may hinge on this. In fact it does. Have a hamburger with me, and I'll marry you."

"Not even for that."

"Well, all right. I'm not sensitive. How about lunch tomorrow? Sardi's at one?"

"Sure."

"Gad, you've actually called me for a date, do you realize that? Shirley is dead. Long live Marjorie! I swear there's hope. Good night, my darling."

Chapter 25. MURIEL

Noel cheered up strikingly after that. They called each other several times a day. It was a rare week in which they did not meet at least half a dozen times for lunch, cocktails, or dinner. They saw all the best shows and movies, went to the best concerts, and ate at the best restaurants; for Noel now had a continuing plentiful supply of money from his Paramount job. It seemed to Marjorie that she was discovering New York City. Her college set had stayed rigidly in a zigzag path through the town, traversing a few hotel bars, night clubs, and eating-places which they considered smart. The rest of downtown New York had been an unmapped jungle of boredom, left to the inferior animals called older people. Now Marjorie, moving toward her twenty-first birthday, and imperceptibly becoming one of those older people, saw that the collegians' tastes had been as naïve, in their way, as those of small-town visitors. Her brief explorations with Marsha had been limited by lack of money. But Noel suffered from no such lack; and he loved New York.

Equally with the expensive fairyland between Fifty-ninth Street and Forty-second Street—which he knew from river to river like a guide—he loved all the sights and sounds and smells, wherever they were, provided only that they were poignant and sharp. They would go in one night from the Club Ferrara, from costly food and wine, murmuring music, and the aura of celebrities and beautifully dressed women, to the stinking fish market at the foot of Fulton Street, where, under the glare of big electric bulbs, bright fish lay in bloody heaps, and trucks ground, and hairy men in ragged sweaters cursed and yelled. Or they would ride a ferry for a nickel, hugging each other to keep warm in the icy river breeze, watching the jagged line of black skyscrapers slide past in the moonlight; and they would laugh at the sluggish roll of the boat, the foul oil-and-garbage whiffs from the river; then they would go to a big night club for out-of-towners, a vulgar whirl of colored feathers and naked kicking legs and bad food and wine, where thirty dollars would melt in an hour. Noel had an insatiable enthusiasm for this rounding. When Marjorie was ready to drop, he would have some eager inspiration. "God, this is such wonderful fun, Margie. Let's keep going. The night's young."

"Noel, you maniac, it's after four. I can't put one leg in front of another. And my eyes, they're absolutely red. Take me home. Harlem, indeed, at this hour!" But she would laugh.

"What the devil, Marge, I have to be in an office at nine. You don't. I tell you this joint only gets going at four, and this Ken Watt and his Kilowatts make the greatest jazz in the United States. Benny Goodman's a fraud next to them."

"Well, for one drink. Then we go home. Promise?"

"Of course—— Taxi! Ah, Margie, money's the only thing."

She often slept till noon. She read *Variety* and *Billboard* regularly, and spent a lot of time at the Broadway drugstore where young actors and actresses gathered. She was pursued quite a bit by the actors, especially when her indifference to them became noticed. But their good profiles, large eyes, long hair, and knowing manners were wasted on her. There was only one male human in the world, and his name was Noel Airman. Indefatigably she made the rounds of the producers' offices, when she wasn't with Noel; and indefatigably, like all the other young actresses, she was turned away by yawning office boys. But she was not discouraged. Life bubbled with promise.

Marjorie's parents were extraordinarily tolerant of the life she was leading. There were no questions, no objections, not even worried hints or looks. She surmised after a while that they had been talking with the Ehrmanns, and that both sets of parents had decided to keep hands off and pray for a happy outcome. Mr. Morgenstern, while continuing to exhibit fretful gloom, seemed resigned; when he met Noel he tried hard to be pleasantly paternal.

It was the most intoxicating time in Marjorie's life; sweeter and gayer even than her first weeks with Noel at South Wind, because now there was nothing surprising or scaring about him. Above all, the gradual pressing out to the limits of sex, which had so excited and terrorized her before, was absent. They joked about it. Noel said he didn't mind, and he really seemed not to care. "You're growing up," he said once. "That's fine. It was you who were doing all that, really, you know. I was a helpless bystander." And when she hooted, he said earnestly, "It's true. And it's true most of the time, for that matter, with nearly every couple. Of course the guy makes the first pass. It's the code. It's like tipping his hat, or holding the door open. The girl takes it from there, and sets exactly the pace she pleases, but *exactly*, unless she's been dumb enough to get involved with some gutter brute. Why, hell's bells, that's what you're doing right now. I've kissed you good night forty times lately. Why hasn't it gone into one of our old necking sessions? Simply because you haven't started swarming over me like an octopus."

Marjorie tried to look annoyed; but she couldn't help it, she burst out laughing. They were riding around the park in a hansom cab on a frigid sunny March afternoon, their cheeks red and frostbitten, their hands warmly clinging under a huge mangy fur lap robe. Noel was hatless, and his hair was rumpled by the wind. He looked like a boy. His joy of life was infectious. One glance of his laughing brilliant blue eyes could make Marjorie as dizzy and happy as if she were on a roller coaster.

That was the day he persuaded her to eat a lobster. They went from the hansom cab to the Plaza and drank martinis, and all at once it was dinnertime, although they hadn't planned to dine together. He said, "We're both going to have broiled lobster, with a very delicate white burgundy. It's the only thing, when two people are feeling so good and so foolish."

"Oh no, Noel—not lobster, sorry——"

"Come, it's the twentieth century."

"Oh, I know, it's a ridiculous prejudice. Conditioning. I just don't think I could go it, dear."

"Sure, honey. Have something else. Although from what little I know of those queer laws, isn't it just as bad to eat anything at all here? Nothing's kosher."

"Well, you're right, at that. I couldn't be less consistent. Does it—is lobster really good?"

"Why, it's the most exquisite food there is."

Marjorie said, "Somehow it doesn't seem as bad as ham, does it? I don't think I could eat ham if you put a pistol to my head."

"Well, ham's the symbol, the universal joke about Jews. Pride makes you take a stand on that point, and actually I think you're right. I'm just a sybarite. Next to lobster, there's nothing I love like good Polish ham. Anyhow, what'll it be—want to try the chicken curry? They have a marvelous Indian sauce here——"

"Oh, what the devil. You're perfectly right, even the chicken isn't kosher. What's the difference? I'll try a lobster."

But when it came she gazed askance at its scarlet feelers and hairs, its numerous jointed legs, its dead eyes on stalks, its ragged pincers. "Noel, it's—doesn't it look like a big red dead bug?"

"Why sure. Crustaceans and arachnids are about the same thing, as a matter of fact." He was expertly lifting out the tail meat with a fork. "Good, though. Sweeter than the roses in May."

She took up her fork gingerly, watching how he went at it. "Well, I never thought I'd live to eat a big old water bug."

"Why, honey, there's all kinds of Biblical precedent for that. Didn't the prophets all live on locusts, or something?"

"I guess so. I wonder if locusts turn this ghastly red when you cook them. These things are so *red.*" The tail was coming out of the shell easily. She cut it, and, following his example, dipped a piece in the little bowl of melted butter, sighed, and put it in her mouth. It tasted very much like ordinary fresh fish, except that it was sweetish, and took more chewing. Not wanting to spoil the occasion, she widened her eyes and said, "Mm, exquisite."

Noel said, "Observe that no forked lightnings have come through the window to destroy you."

"Well, I didn't expect that, really. Those Bible laws were just for hot countries in the old days." She took another bite. It was quite pleasant, especially with all the butter on it. "I wonder, though, if it would taste so good if there were no law against it."

He laughed, pouring the wine. "Very likely not. They say hunger is the best cook, but they're wrong. Prohibition is. There isn't a living Christian who can enjoy ham and eggs the way a renegade Jew like me does."

"Don't call yourself that."

"I'm kidding, you know. It's all a question of upbringing. I've had nothing to renege from. In my home we always ate everything—pork, oysters——"

"Really? That's a little surprising."

"Why?"

"Your folks are so active in Jewish causes."

"Marjorie, my father's a politician. He'd be active in Moslem causes, if his district had enough Arabs in it."

Marjorie had finished the three or four bites of white fishy meat that made up the lobster's tail. Still very hungry, she stared at the creature, wondering what else there was to eat on it. It seemed quite whole and impregnable. She said, eying Noel's lobster, "What is that part you're eating now? It looks perfectly revolting."

"This green soft stuff? Why, that's the liver of the beast. It's the best part of it."

"Is it edible, really? I'd say it was poisonous."

"Well, a lot of people are fool enough not to eat it because of its looks. But I assure you it's marvelous. Try it."

Marjorie dug her fork into the green mass. It squashily yielded, oozing a thin fluid. "No, no." She dropped the fork. "I'm not that sophisticated, not yet." She hurriedly drank off her wine; then, following his example, she applied a little device like a nutcracker to one of the lobster's claws. It did not yield. She squeezed with both hands. There was an echoing crack, and the claw flew across the table into Noel's lap.

"I'll crack them for you," Noel said to the blushing girl.

"Honestly, the damned creatures are like a Chinese puzzle, Noel. They're not worth the bother."

"Practice and patience, my dear." He deftly extracted two morsels of meat from the claws, laid them on her plate, and poured more wine. "What do you think of this wine? Isn't it good?"

"Lovely, as always."

"Let's go see the new French movie at the Fifty-fifth after this."

"Sure. Aren't you writing any songs, or anything? You seem to have nothing but free time these days."

"Ah, well, I can always write songs when I'm a little creakier. As a matter of fact I did a new first-act finale for *Princess Jones* the other night, and I like it. Have to play it for you."

"How are you getting along at Paramount?"

"Oh, fine, fine. Not rising as meteorically as I'd hoped. But then, what fair prospect ever looks so fair once you're in it? It's all right."

"What's the matter?"

"Sam and I not seeing eye to eye again, the old thing."

"Well, you'd better stop disagreeing with him. He's the boss."

Noel looked annoyed. "Suppose he's wrong and I'm right, just once? It's conceivable. I'd match IQ's with him for a thousand dollars."

"He has the experience, Noel, don't forget that."

"Darling, experience nine times out of ten is merely stupidity hardened into habit.—Well, the hell with Sam. Let's enjoy ourselves. I like his money, I'll say that for him. . . . What's the trouble now?"

Marjorie was glaring and poking at the lobster. "I'm famished. And I don't know how to get at this miserable thing."

"Look, you haven't even touched the legs. They're loaded with meat." He held the body of his lobster, and pulled a leg out with a little twist. A chunk of white meat clung to the scarlet stump. "See?" He gnawed the meat.

"Well, that seems simple." Marjorie did exactly the same thing, she thought. But instead of the leg pulling loose, the whole center of the lobster came lifting out of the shell, and there she was, holding an oval white thing with many trembling red legs, for all the world like a spider six inches across, warm and horridly alive. With a grunt of disgust she threw it splashing into the melted butter.

"I quit," Marjorie said. "I'll order ham next time. Damn red bug."

Noel choked with laughter over his wine.

His dissatisfaction with the Paramount job was the one discordant note of this happy time. She heard it again in the weeks that followed, more frequently and louder. Sometimes Noel would be deep in gloom when they met, and it would take an hour or more of drinking and banter to bring him to his usual gaiety.

In his first weeks at Paramount Noel had shrugged off his work as a trivial necessary evil, and had refused to talk about it with Marjorie, but by the end of March he was discussing it freely and at length. It relieved him to set Marjorie laughing with his caricature of Rothmore. He marvelously simulated a stooped heavy old man with half-closed eyes, talking through thick tired lips while biting on a cigar. There were two main sources of trouble. Sam Rothmore thought Noel's taste in stories for the screen was too literary and high-flown, and he was displeased by his irregular hours, though the disapproval took no stronger form than crude sarcasm. It seemed to Marjorie, even though Noel was describing the arguments, that Sam Rothmore was right at least part of the time. Noel looked black when she ventured to say so. On the whole, naturally, she sided with Noel. There seemed little doubt that Sam Rothmore, beneath his surface of weary benevolence, was just a brutal businessman, and that his taste in movies reflected the juvenile vulgarity of Hollywood at its worst. All the more, then, did she want to give him his due in the petty instances when he seemed right.

But Noel, usually so graceful and so amusingly self-critical, was peculiarly obdurate in this. He persisted in coming late to the office and leaving early, and would not admit there was anything wrong in it. "I'm beginning to regard myself as a test case," he said to Marjorie, "a milestone in the education of Sam Rothmore, and the whole Hollywood machine."

"Don't try to change the world, Noel. Paramount's a business. Businesses have to run on a system."

"True, dear, and exceedingly profound, but this is a unique business. It employs creative talent and original insight. Therefore, time and motion studies become slightly absurd. As for instance, working in the office with me is one Morris Mead, also an assistant story editor, a good fellow, a drudge, been there fifteen years. I've been there a month. I'm reading four stories to his one, and writing four reports to his one, and Sam concedes that my reports are clearer, better, and more useful. Morris arrives at nine and leaves at five. So much for system."

One rainy evening late in March Noel took her to the opening night of a musical comedy. When they came into the lobby for a smoke after the first act, Marjorie saw familiar signs of depression in Noel; he was avoiding her glance, and repeatedly rubbing one hand over his eyes. His tone remained level and light. "It's a sure hit. I know the boys who wrote it. They've been doing the summer shows at Camp Paradise for years. Maybe one of these decades I'll write a show."

"You'll have a show on Broadway one of these months, and it'll be a lot better than this one."

He smiled at her. "Keep saying those things."

A woman at his elbow said, "Noel! Of course it's Noel! Isn't it?"

Surprise came over his face, then he smiled. "Why, hello, Muriel. How are you? You look wonderful, as always."

The woman said, "Good Lord, how many years is it now?" Her dress was a billowing swath of rust-colored taffeta and she wore many diamonds. She had a tiny nose, a sharp chin, and pinched cheeks, and her black hair seemed varnished in place. She held a cigarette high in two straight fingers.

"Don't start reckoning them up," Noel said. "You won't enjoy the second act. How are you? And the kids, and the hubby?"

"We're all just wonderful." She peered around at the crowd. "I'll have to tell Marty you're here—he'll get a kick out of it."

Noel said, "Marjorie Morgenstern, Mrs. Hartz."

They nodded at each other. Mrs. Hartz with an eye-blink looked Marjorie over and turned back to Noel. "What is your secret? Are you really Peter Pan? You just don't change."

"Dorian Gray."

"I'll bet. Well! Noel Airman. You keep turning up like a bad penny, don't you?" She laughed. "I'm always looking for your name in the theatre columns, Noel, and I don't see it."

"Well, the truth is, I've become a Trappist monk, Muriel," Noel said. "It happens I'm in the world of vanity tonight, as an extreme penance. I was late for vespers."

"Ha, you a monk, that's a good one." The woman glanced at Marjorie, laughing nervously. "That'll be the day. Say, maybe we can all go out and have a drink afterward. We're here with a crowd from Rye, but you can join us, they're lots of fun. They'd love to meet you."

"Don't you have to catch a train?"

"We drove in." She laid her hand on his arm. "Please do look for us.

It's nice to see you. It's amazing. You just don't change." She smiled at Marjorie, and moved off into the crush, puffing at her cigarette.

Noel said softly to Marjorie, "You gather who that was, no doubt."

"It can't be the Muriel you told me about. She's over thirty-five."

"She is Muriel, though. Muriel Weissfreid. Muriel Weissfreid of the blue velvet and white arms. And she's thirty-three." He dropped his cigarette and trod on it. "Let's go in."

Marjorie said when they were in their seats, "She's really not bad-looking, you know—I mean, for thirty-three. It's just that you described her as such a beauty, and—well, she's just another one of those dressed-up mamas from the suburbs."

He stared at her. "Just another one of those dressed-up mamas from the suburbs . . ."

"What's wrong now?"

"Didn't you feel a chill? You've just spoken your own epitaph."

"Oh, shut up. I'll die before I'll live anywhere but in Manhattan."

"Promise?"

"Of course. I can't stand the suburbs."

"You wouldn't change your mind, and drag a husband out there after having a baby or two, would you, because all your friends were doing it, and the grass and fresh air were wonderful for kids?"

"No, I wouldn't."

"All right. . . . You noticed that glittering boulder on her finger, I suppose?"

"Well, actually, no. I kept looking at her face, trying to see what you saw in her."

"Believe me, it was all there once, Marjorie. She had the face of an angel." The music started and the lights dimmed. He slouched in his seat. "I feel tired."

When the show was over Noel cocked his head, listening to the applause. "Hit. Sure hit." He gathered up his overcoat. "Let's duck, shall we, and see if we can avoid Muriel?"

The audience was still applauding as they slipped out through a side door. The sidewalks were wet and black, with fiery streaks reflected from the electric signs, but the rain had stopped. They walked to the corner of Broadway, and stood undecided. "What would you say to some deafening jazz in a small dark cellar?" Noel said.

"Anything you feel like doing."

"All right." He gazed around at the blazing dancing advertisements, and then up at the sky. "Look. Over all this spectacular foolishness, there's the black sky and the misty moon."

"The sky looks more like pink here," Marjorie said, glancing up. "I never noticed that."

"All these people are going to die," Noel said. "All of them. They have just a few years, and they'll be gone like leaves. But after the last one of them's dead, the crowds hurrying along this pavement under an unnoticed moon will be just as big, and the faces will all look the same."

"Don't be so morbid. The light's green for us. Let's cross."

Noel said as they hurried in front of the massed taxicabs, "Can you imagine the moon as an eye, the eye of God, looking down into this lighted square in the darkness? This must look like some great religious pageant. Hordes, hordes marching everywhere, and over them in great letters of fire the thundering words, *Smoke Camels*."

Marjorie said, "Everything seems silly, in view of the fact that you're going to die, but what do you want everybody to do, cut their throats? You're just in a bad mood. Muriel, or something. Take my advice and don't think about death."

He laced her fingers in his. "You have a way of summing up the world's wisdom in a couple of banal sentences. The effect isn't to make you seem wise, but to reduce all the philosophers to the level of twenty-one-year-old girls. How do you explain this curious phenomenon?"

"The philosophers are a pretty sad lot, if they can't make any better sense of the world than I do."

"Believe me, they don't."

They sat at a tiny table directly in front of four blasting Negro musicians in a club called, for no visible reason, the Tibet Room. Noel drank off half his scotch and soda, clinked down the glass, and said, "Would it upset you very much if we made this our farewell night, and never saw each other again?"

"Don't be a fool."

"I'm absolutely serious. Listen carefully." He spoke with peculiar clarity over the gales of jazz. "I'm never going to amount to anything. I'm all surface. Everything I have goes up in charm and conversation. I have a fatal lack of central organizing energy. Furthermore, I'm past my peak. I was wittier and more energetic four years ago. I'm very tired. At the moment I feel sorry for you, for being in my toils. There's such a horrible gap between you and Muriel! I've spanned a generation. I'm like a vaudevillian playing the same little act forever. Give it up, Marjorie. The game isn't worth the candle, I assure you. Go find Dr. Max Shapiro, he won't wait forever.—I'm sorry, I wasn't going to mention him again, was I?"

She put her hand on his and said loudly, with a trumpet blaring in her face, "I love you, and you're better than you ever were, and your peak is still to come. The songs you wrote in your last revision of *Princess Jones* were a terrific improvement over anything you've ever played for me, including *It's Raining Kisses*."

He said, "Yes, that was a good burst, wasn't it? It really was. Last flare of a dying fire——"

"What do you expect Muriel to do, remain looking like your college sweetheart? It's an old story that women age faster than men. A woman at thirty-three is finished, just playing out the hand. A man at thirty-one is lucky if his career is even started. You know these things better than I do. You've said them. Why are you so childish tonight? It isn't like you at all."

He smiled at her and clasped her hand. The music was so tumultuous he couldn't speak for a few seconds. Then he said, "You're really wonderful for me. I'm an ass to suggest parting with you. At least I can wait till you kick me out."

"You'll wait a long time."

"I am low, fearfully low. Another big row with Sam, and then seeing Muriel—I don't know, the bottom fell out."

After a few drinks they went to his apartment and necked more than they had at any time since the summer. She leaned back in his arms after a while, and said with a low laugh, "Well, you're not quite the washed-up old man after all, are you?"

He released her and looked at her in the dim light with no great friendliness, smoothing his mussed hair. "Why, you calculating little cat. You're doing this to cheer me up."

"Not at all. I liked it."

"You liked it." He lit a cigarette and strode around the room. "You can't imagine, you can't have the faintest idea, of how completely exasperating you are. And I used to think you were passionate. Why, you're about as passionate as an adding machine."

"Oh, don't start on that again, Noel——"

He stood over her, and for a moment she thought he might hit her. Then he said, "Well, it's a fitting end for me, indeed. Trapped in a platonic relationship with Marjorie Morgenstern, of 740 West End Avenue. 'Vengeance is mine, saith the Lord, I will repay.'" He stroked her hair. "Come on, let's have some hot dogs."

They roasted frankfurters on long forks over embers in the littered fireplace, and drank beer, and played symphonies on his huge phonograph, the only valuable thing in the shabby room. Gradually he cheered up. It was past three when she left, and he was quite himself again. He took her downstairs and put her in a cab. Kissing her good night, he said, "You haven't the faintest idea of how much good you do me. You're adrenalin. You saved my life tonight. One of these days I may repay you, darling."

Chapter 26. SAM ROTHMORE

The telephone woke her. She blinked at her clock; it was half-past nine. "Hello?" she said hoarsely.

"Are you dressed? We're going for an airplane ride."

"What, are you crazy, Noel? I'm fast asleep. What are you doing up so early? Airplane? I've never been in an airplane——"

"Well, you're going in one. I have to run an errand for Sam up to Albany, and I'm going in a taxi plane. You too. We leave at eleven, so get ready."

"Eleven? Noel, I can't *possibly* make it. Aren't you exhausted? I am——"

"Haven't been to sleep. Wrote a song after you left. Best yet. Wait till you hear it. I feel absolutely marvelous."

She dressed in a rush, and left without telling her mother where she was going. There was no time to argue, and she would have overridden her mother's protests anyway. The gay timbre of his voice had set her tingling despite the weariness weighing down her limbs. She met him at the Paramount Building and they rode out to the airport in Sam Rothmore's Cadillac. Noel wore a new loose gray tweed topcoat with the collar turned up, and carried a thick sealed brown envelope. "What's it all about, Noel?"

"Oh, high intrigue. An assemblyman's making a speech today about the movie admissions tax situation. Needs these papers by one o'clock. Sam gave me no details, just asked me if I was afraid to fly, and then handed me the envelope. Can't use a regular messenger, it's all hush-hush, for some reason. I feel like the Scarlet Pimpernel." It was incredible, Marjorie was thinking, how this man changed with the days and the hours. Today he was the gaunt blond god of South Wind again, full of force and dash, his eyes sparkling. "I haven't slept a wink, do you know? Wait till you hear *Old Moon Face*. It's a real crack-through. I feel it in my bones. We'll be rich. Came to me walking around in the rain last night after you left——"

"I'm dying to hear it."

When the airplane soared up, narrowly clearing the telephone wires, she thought she would faint from choking joyous alarm. It was a four-seater, single-motor plane, piloted by a morose man in a worn leather windbreaker. The windows rattled and whistled, the wings flapped, and the sides and the seat shook as in a very old Ford. But she didn't care. She was terribly afraid, but even more exhilarated, and it seemed like a good way to die if her time were at hand (which she didn't believe). The plane thrashed its way up the Hudson River valley, and Marjorie and Noel held hands and looked down through empty space at towns, fields, hills, and the river, a brilliant storybook picture in glaring sunlight. A car was waiting at the Albany airport, with an emissary from the assemblyman. Ten minutes after they landed they were in the air again, flying south, straight into the white blaze of the sun. Marjorie was drunk with the speed, the scare, the sunlight, the unexpected giddy novelty of the trip. Noel was inexhaustible, she thought. He threw off surprises and thrills like a pinwheel; it was his nature, his pattern. She would never find a man like him again. There weren't two in the world. She leaned over and kissed him passionately on the mouth, straining at her safety belt. He looked at her in astonishment, and roared in her ear, "Well, if that's all it takes, I'll charter a plane and we'll fly to Albany every day."

They glided down over Manhattan in clear afternoon light, making a lazy circle above the towers, the bridges, the Statue of Liberty, the steamships, the glittering harbors. The thud of the landing gear on the turf of the airport was a gloomy sound. He said, unstrapping his belt, "You're coming with me to the office."

"Nothing doing."

"Sam's got a piano in his inner office. Must play you *Old Moon Face*."

"Noel, don't mix your social and business life. I shouldn't even have gone in the plane——"

"You're a hopeless prig. Sam knew I was taking you, and told me to bring you to the office. He wants to meet you. Satisfied?"

She was awe-stricken by the Paramount offices. The panelled walls were lined with huge ikon-like portraits of stars; and the Paramount trade-mark, which she had been seeing on movie screens all her life, was carved, printed, or painted on the glass doors, on the posters, on the portraits, over the archways, filling the offices with the Arabian Nights magic of Hollywood. Noel returned the receptionist's smiling nod, and led Marjorie through a door marked *Private. No Entrance,* into a little blue-painted library room lined with leather-bound books, with a movable bar in it, and a spinet piano. "Cosy, eh?"

"It doesn't look like a business office at all."

"That's right. This is where the really cutthroat deals are made. The outer office is for routine skulduggery. I'd offer you a drink, but Sam foams at anybody drinking during working hours."

"Well, thanks, I don't want one. Are you sure this is all right, our being in here?"

"All Sam can do is fire me, which I rather wish he would." He tossed his coat on a small sofa and sat at the piano. "It's amazing, songwriting, when you think about it," he said, rippling chords. "The right little combination of notes, the lucky little pattern of words, all of it lasting no more than a minute or two, and the man who writes it suddenly owns, in effect, an office building or an oil well. It's like a contest. Write the magic jingle, and win the grand prize. Well, here's the magic jingle of 1936, kid. Noel Airman's *Old Moon Face.*"

Marjorie felt the gooseflesh rise as he sang it. The song was built on the notion of the moon seen as a wistful old bachelor peering down at the lovers on the street, following them to their apartment, staring in at the bedroom window, envying them their joy. The suggestiveness of the lyric was masked by the last touch, the wedding ring of the girl glittering in the moonlight, as she pulled down the shade to shut out lonely Old Moon Face.

She threw her arms around Noel's neck. "Bless you, it is a hit."

"I know it is," Noel said. "I'm dickering for a villa on the Riviera. The melody's really got something, hasn't it?"

He began to play it again. The door to the outer office opened and Sam Rothmore came in, complete as Marjorie had pictured him to the cigar in his teeth. His clothes were dark, correct, elegant, his pink wrinkled hands were manicured, and there was a touch of majesty in his bearing despite the stoop, or perhaps because of it. "What's all the music-making?" he said in the throaty voice that Noel had caricatured so well.

Noel jumped up. "Sam, the envelope's been delivered. Assemblyman Morton's secretary was——"

Rothmore nodded. "I talked to Morton on the phone an hour ago. Thanks." He was looking at Marjorie. "Hello, I'm Rothmore. And you're Marjorie Morgenstern, and you're a friend of this low-life."

"I hope I'm not intruding——"

"Not a bit. You're a breath of fresh air in the old factory. Well, how'd you like the plane ride?"

"Marvelous. I just wanted to go on flying forever."

His glance flickered ironically to Noel, and back to her, and she noticed the terrible blue shadows under his eyes. "Well, go ahead, Noel, finish what you were playing."

"It's a new song he just wrote," Marjorie said. "I think it's superb."

"Oh, you wrote a new song? Interesting. Have you read any movie properties lately?"

Noel said, in a manner curiously mingling fear and arrogance, "Sam,

I turned in three reports before I left. Your secretary has them, and I told you——"

"I read your reports."

"Oh. Are they all right?"

"Let's hear your song." He sat heavily in an armchair and looked at Noel. "Well, play the song."

"Are you really interested?" Noel stood awkwardly beside the piano stool.

"I like to know all about my staff's talents. Go ahead. What's the title?"

Noel told him. Rothmore nodded slowly, leaning on an elbow in the armchair. Noel played and his employer sat slumped, holding the cigar, his eyes on the wall. Marjorie noticed that he breathed through his mouth in shallow little gulps. When the song was over, he said after a moment, "It's all right."

"I think it'll be a hit. A hell of a hit," Noel said.

"So do I," Marjorie said.

Rothmore sighed. "What got you started writing songs again? Aren't we keeping you busy?"

"Sam, the thing just popped into my head and I wrote it out. At five this morning, if you want to know. On my own time."

Rothmore glanced at his wristwatch. "I guess I'll have a scotch and soda. Usually it makes me sleepy in the daytime, but I had too much coffee for lunch." He started to get up, but Noel sprang to the bar. "I'll get it, Sam." Rothmore sank back in his chair, saying, "Make drinks for everybody." He turned to Marjorie. "See? That's what we do to ourselves. We keep tightening up our nerves with tobacco and coffee, then loosening them with alcohol. We do it all our lives. Then we blame God when we die young."

"I'd rather die ten years younger and smoke and drink all I please," Noel said, clinking glass and ice.

"You're talking through your hat. Wait till you're clipping the last few coupons like me."

"I'm glad you like *Old Moon Face*, Sam."

Rothmore shrugged. "It's a good song. So what?"

"So lots and lots of money," Noel said. "Acres of cash."

"Grow up," Rothmore said. "How much money does a hit song make, five thousand dollars? Ten is a lot."

"Why, some of them make a hundred thousand."

Rothmore screwed up his face and thrust the cigar in his teeth, and Marjorie could hardly keep herself from laughing, he so exactly resembled Noel's imitation of him. "What are you talking about, the freaks? *Bananas* and *Silver Threads*? Are you figuring on writing a freak?

Why don't you just buy yourself a sweepstakes ticket? It's less work, and a much surer thing. What did you make on *It's Raining Kisses?* Eighty-five hundred?"

Noel narrowed his eyes at Rothmore, handing him a drink. "To a hair. Been checking with my publisher?"

"I know the business, a little bit. Once I owned a piece of a publishing house. Songwriting's for kids. Set aside your handful of geniuses, your Gershwins, Porters, Berlins, Rodgers, and there's nothing in it. Get yourself a small producer's job and you can hire and fire songwriters, good ones, all day like messenger boys."

"What does that prove? A creative man doesn't care which chair-warmer is hiring or firing him," Noel said. "It's just the stupid book-keeping of his career, which any fool can do."

"That sounds good," Rothmore said, "except that all the songwriters out there are breaking their necks, trying to warm chairs and do some stupid bookkeeping. Scribbling isn't all there is to creation. That's lesson number one of this business. Though I can see that you choke over it." Rothmore pushed himself painfully out of his chair. "Well, we're boring Marjorie."

"No, no," the girl said, curled on the couch, watching the two men.

Rothmore's look, resting on her, became kindly. He drank off his high-ball. "Let me take both of you to dinner tonight."

Noel glanced at Marjorie, who said, "Don't we have tickets for a show?"

"Never mind tickets," Rothmore said. "If you have any, change them for another night."

Noel said to the girl, "You don't argue with Sam. Thanks, Sam, it'll be grand."

Rothmore walked slowly out, leaving behind a gray haze of rich-smelling cigar smoke.

She knew from the gossip columns that it was the most expensive restaurant in New York. The furnishings were old-fashioned, even dowdy, but the food was unbelievable, and the wines better than any Noel had ever ordered. It was food such as Marjorie had read about in French novels; she had never believed that such marvels of the cooking art really existed. The caviar, the soup, the steaks, were all sauced and seasoned to a creamy perfection of taste that was almost humiliating; she felt a bit like a barbarian encountering civilization. So numbed was she by the pleasant assault on her senses that she began following the argument between Noel and Rothmore only when their voices rose. Noel apparently wanted the company to buy an obscure Italian novel, twenty years old, which could be had for fifteen hundred dollars. Rothmore said it wasn't worth fifteen cents to the company. "It's for Europeans. It's adultery among the poor, and the foreign poor at that, and she dies. What do you want to do, empty the theatres?"

Noel said, "You assume the American people are too dumb to recognize a good thing. It's an anti-democratic notion, did you ever stop to think of that? They're not too dumb to elect the right president. Or so we all believe."

"Why, you fool, do you think we opened our doors yesterday? We don't have to assume a damn thing. We *know*. Will you ever get it through your head that a movie house is a candy store? The people are not dumb at all. They're a hell of a lot too smart for the likes of you. You try to sell them bread and spinach in your candy store, and they'll go to the candy store around the corner. You get the reputation for being a stupid bastard, and after a while your store closes. Look, Noel, the Europeans keep making the kind of pictures you like. In their own countries, the people line up for our pictures, and their art plays to half-empty houses. The people have decided what movies should be, not us. That's the democracy you're talking about. We'll make anything they want. You can't ram what you like down their throats. You're not in Russia."

"You're just hiding behind a false analogy," Noel said. "A movie house isn't a candy store at all, it's more like a library. You've filled the library with pap and prurience, catering to the lowest instincts of the people, instead of meeting your cultural responsibility——"

"Cultural responsibility." Rothmore buried his head in his hands. "Oh God." He looked at Marjorie. "Don't give 'em what they want. Hell, no. They got low instincts. Give 'em what's good for them—what *you* think is good for them. That's your red-hot democrat talking. Isn't that the whole damned communist idea, Noel? Stick a gun in their ribs, and make 'em eat strawberries and cream?"

"Oh, sure, see my whiskers and my bomb? The old story, epithets when you have no arguments."

"No arguments?" Rothmore turned to Marjorie. "I'm glad I had no children. If I'd had a son, he'd have turned out like this specimen. That's all the colleges seem to be producing these days, either rah-rah morons or this kind of souped-up snob who despises the American people——"

"A beautiful instance," Noel said, "of the abusive non sequitur. If you don't like Paramount movies, you're a traitor to your country."

"All right, do you think the American people are a lot of goddamn fools, Noel, or don't you? And try to be honest for a change instead of cute. Maybe it's important."

Noel paused, his face more serious than usual, then said slowly, "The answer is yes, but no bigger fools than any other people. God made humanity with an average IQ of 100, Sam, and you'll admit that's about twenty points too low——"

"What the hell do you know about God, and what the hell is an IQ?" Rothmore rasped. "Do you think an IQ is something real, like a nose? It's a goddamn number dreamed up by goddamn psychologists, and all it proves is that farmers aren't as smart as psychologists. If the farmers had enough time to waste to make up an IQ system, the psychologists would all come out morons and the farmers geniuses. Because they'd give a big credit for being able to grab a cow's teat right, and nothing at all for counting the number of triangles in some goddamn meaningless diagram."

"You're an anti-intellectual from way back, Sam, that's no news."

Rothmore turned belligerently to Marjorie. "And I'm the epithet man! Marjorie, who's right?"

"Oh, Lord, leave me out of it. This rice pudding is sublime, Mr. Rothmore. I've never tasted anything so good."

"Put down the spoon and talk. Let's see what kind of girl he's got."

"Well"—she glanced sidelong at Noel—"I've always thought the way Noel does about—I mean, I prefer the foreign movies, to be honest, Mr. Rothmore. But I must say you put things in a little different light. If the people—after all, maybe they've decided that they want heavy stuff in books, and light stuff on movie screens—candy, as you put it. That's what I never thought of." She said to Noel, who was regarding her very sourly, "Well, it's true, isn't it? Candy isn't good for you, and all that, but people eat tons of it, they like it. He says the Europeans keep making serious movies, and their own people keep going for the American candy. Maybe that means the movie as an art form is really candy making. That's what never occurred to me before."

Rothmore beamed on her, taking small gulps of air. "Bless your little heart. You at least listen to the old bastard." He said to Noel, "She's one in a thousand. Marry her."

Noel said, "Why, because she's taken in by a trivial sophistry that you don't even believe yourself? Do you call that a triumph? She's twenty-one years old."

"She's smarter than you are, my boy." Rothmore chuckled, deep in his chest. "If you only knew." With a gloating grin, he lit a cigar.

"Look, why don't you fire me, Sam? I completely disagree with you on practically everything that matters. I'll go on recommending the *Smoke over Etna* kind of book till hell freezes over, because I believe in it, and nothing you say——"

Rothmore jabbed him in the chest with two fingers. "Now listen to me, junior. I was trying to talk the front office into *Smoke over Etna* books when you were wetting your diapers. There's room for both kinds of pictures, that's the whole truth of this matter. If you keep the budget low, and spot your releases in the right big-city spots, you can come out all right on a small-audience movie, and we've done it, and we do it. But that's a very small part of our business in life." He pounded the table. *"We've got to supply the neighborhood houses and small towns with three hundred movies a year, will you ever grasp that?* That's our job. What country ever produced three hundred good books a year, or three hundred good plays, or three hundred good *anything?* God damn it, your job as a story editor is to find grist for the mill, usable entertainment, usable trash, if you want to be sniffy about it! Do I need you to tell me that *Smoke over Etna* is a good book? Don't you think I can read? When you grasp this elementary point, maybe you can start fitting into the organization. Maybe you'll wind up producing art pictures. What the hell do I care what you do? But you've got to understand what business you're in first."

Noel answered acidly, "Getting me into this business was your idea, Sam, not mine, and you still have to prove it was a good one. You're not going to make me over in your image. If I'm useful to you on my own terms, that's a different matter."

Rothmore said to Marjorie, "D'you see? This is it. You run into some kind of neurotic stone wall with this boy at a certain point. All his intellect blanks out, and you——"

"Naturally, disagreeing with you constitutes a neurosis," Noel said.

"Why do you bother with him?" Marjorie said. "I'm in love with him. I'm stuck with him."

Rothmore puffed on his cigar, his lids heavy, staring at Marjorie. "Margie, there's damn little talent in the world, and when you see it, you want something to come of it, that's all. I've seen a lot of young men come and go. Noel's got something, and he's a charming low-life somehow, and if he could be straightened out, why, he'd be an asset to Paramount, and to me. But at the present rate——"

"You see the picture, I trust," Noel said to Marjorie. "Sam's joined the Save-Noel-from-Himself Club."

Rothmore looked at Noel, shook his head, and signalled for the check. "Sometimes I wonder," he muttered.

He tried to persuade them to come into his limousine, saying that they could have the car and chauffeur for the evening after dropping him at his home. But Noel wouldn't hear of it. The old man lumbered into the long black car. Just as the chauffeur was about to close the door

Rothmore jammed his cigar in his teeth, leaned forward, and said to Noel, "Your report on the *Redbook* serial was all right. I phoned it out to the Coast. They've put in a bid. Twelve thousand."

Noel's rather glum look vanished in an eager grin. "Why didn't you say so a little sooner, you old sadist?"

"Your other two reports weren't bad, but those I want to think about a bit more. You're learning slowly, slowly." He glanced from Marjorie to Noel, and the tough downward lines around his mouth softened in a smile of grudging approval. "Maybe you'll be all right. Good night. Good night, Margie."

Chapter 27. THE SEDER

When Mrs. Morgenstern first suggested inviting Noel and his parents to the family's Passover dinner, the seder, Marjorie thought it was an appalling idea. On reflection, however, she decided that there was some hard good sense in it.

With Noel doing well at Paramount, with their relationship becoming each week more intimate and hopeful, it did seem to her that the time had come for his parents and her own to confront each other. She also thought Noel had better see the Family and glimpse her religious background. At fourteen and fifteen she had hated seders, bar-mitzvas, and all the rest, and she had taken pleasure in shocking her parents with atheistic talk. In recent years, however, she had found the seder oddly appealing, and she wanted to see how he would react. The complex rituals and symbols of the Passover feast—the matzo, the horseradish, the four cups of wine, the pounded nuts and apples, the hard-boiled eggs in salt water, the great goblet of wine for Elijah—these things, with the old family songs and the annual jokes at the same points in the Hebrew service, had attractive bitter-sweet nostalgia for her. It was fun in a way, too, to see the Family once a year, and find out which of the cousins had married, and see the new babies, and marvel at the rapid growth of the old babies. There was a risk, of course, that Noel and his parents would be dismayed and put off by the seder; but she didn't think it was much of a risk, and anyway she was prepared to take it.

She was rather afraid to bring the subject up with Noel. But to her astonishment he agreed very readily to come. He knew nothing whatever about seders, except that matzo was eaten; but when she described the ceremonies to him he said, "Why, it sounds very colorful and alive. My father will undoubtedly make a bloody ass of himself, as usual, but that might prove amusing, too."

"I should warn you that all the relatives from miles around get together at this thing, and the children, and the grandchildren, and it's a pretty noisy mess."

"Oh." Noel looked thoughtful, then he brightened. "Well, don't you think that may be a good thing? I may well go unnoticed in the crush. Of course, all your relatives will gossip about us, but if you don't mind I don't."

"Honestly, Noel, you're a chameleon. If there was ever anything I dreaded, it was mentioning this thing to you. And here you are, being just as nice as pie about it."

"Darling, you really do me an injustice. I have a heart of gold. My only faults are that I'm totally selfish and immoral. Tell your mother it's okay —my folks and all."

He arrived late. The seder guests were already crowded in the smoky living room, with children darting between their legs and around the furniture, laughing and squealing. Four babies in baskets and portable cribs were howling in Marjorie's bedroom, and their young mothers, wild-haired and with blouses coming out of their skirts, were rushing to and fro through the foyer, brandishing bottles, diapers, pots, and rattles. Noel grinned at Marjorie, cocking his ear to the noise, as he slipped out of his coat. She said, "Well, didn't I warn you?"

"Why, it sounds very exuberant. My father here?"

"Yes, and your mother, and they're both in evening clothes. They go from here to a Democratic banquet."

The doorbell rang, and Marjorie's cousins, Morris and Mildred Sapersteen, came in with their son, Neville. Marjorie was amazed to see how the child had grown. She remembered him as a particularly loud-bawling blond infant, but he was now a large redheaded boy. "Gosh, how old is Neville, anyway?" she said to the father, who was carrying a black suitcase. Neville's mother began taking off his coat, which was no simple thing to do, since he was rearing and tearing to get at the children in the living room, shouting, "Hi, Suzy Capoozy! Hi, Walter Capalter!"

"He's five, just turned five," Morris Sapersteen said. He was Uncle Shmulka's oldest son, a writer of advertising copy, a sad-faced young man not much bigger than his father. He set down the suitcase with a sigh. "Gosh, you'd never believe how heavy those things can be."

"What have you got there?" Marjorie said.

"Airplanes."

"Airplanes?"

"Forty-seven airplanes. Neville won't go anywhere without them."

Neville, disentangling his arms from the sleeves of his coat, was off into the living room like a rocket. Marjorie introduced Noel to the Sapersteens. Morris's wife, Mildred, a thin freckled girl with very large front teeth, and black straight hair cut like an inverted bowl, was a piano teacher of sorts, and sometimes played at family gatherings. She looked very tired.

Morris opened the suitcase. It was really crammed to the top with toy airplanes of every shape, color, and size, all tumbled in a tangle of wheels and wings. "Where can I put this, Margie? Just so he can get at them when he feels the need for them. I don't want it to be in the way——"

Marjorie indicated a corner in the hallway. "It's a nuisance," Mildred Sapersteen said, "but we've tried taking him places without them, and it sets up all kinds of traumas. The planes have become a sort of security symbol for him."

Noel said gravely, "A substitute for the father image, would you say?"

"Well possibly," Mildred said, "but we think it's a compensatory mechanism for a rather small sex organ. It's well within the normal range, but—— Morris, leave the lid up, he goes into a frenzy if he sees it down——"

"I'm leaving it up, I'm leaving it up," Morris said. "I say it's a surrogate for masturbation, myself, but whatever it is, he won't go anywhere without these damn planes, that's for sure. Whew! There we are." He stood and peered into the clamorous living room. "Well, I see the panic is on. Let's go, Mildred. Where is he, anyway?"

When they were out of sight Noel collapsed against the closet door, shaking with laughter. "That's right," Marjorie muttered, "laugh at my crazy cousins——"

"Crazy!" Noel gasped. "Honey, nearly every young married couple I know talks that way. I bait them for hours sometimes, and they never tumble. Morris, leave the lid up, or he'll get a trauma——" He choked, his shoulders quivering. "Now you know why I won't get married. . . . Forty-seven airplanes——"

Mrs. Morgenstern, flushed, and with an apron over a fine new purple dress, poked her head into the foyer. "What are you two billing and cooing about in a corner? We're starting the seder. Come in."

The flower-festooned glittering table, extended with all its leaves and eked out with a card table, stretched from the windows to the far wall of the long narrow dining room, under a blaze of bright white electric bulbs. An auxiliary table had been improvised in the living room, visible through the opened French doors, and the children were shepherded out there by Mildred Sapersteen, who volunteered to stay with them, so as to keep an eye on Neville. The children objected raucously to being steered away from the adults' table, and Neville, in the course of his objections, put his foot through a pane in the French doors. But the glass was cleared away, the children pacified with a round of Pepsi-Cola; and against a background of rich lively noise, mingled with the quarrelsome chattering of the children and the muffled but powerful howls of the babies in the bedrooms, the seder began.

The liveliness did not extend to the table of the adults. Here, as the ceremonies proceeded, there gradually fell a strained queer quiet, unlike the atmosphere of other years. The little people of the Family, old gray tailors, candy-store keepers, mechanics, and their wives, were terrorized by the presence of a judge and his lady; and their grown-up sons and daughters, usually a joking and irreverent band of ordinary young Americans, wore awkward company airs. The fact that the Ehrmanns were in evening clothes did not help matters. Tiny Uncle Shmulka, the laundry sorter, jammed in his cheap frayed brown suit against the resplendent judge, kept trying in vain to shrink away, and not contaminate the great man with the rub of poverty. Seth, too, sat clumsy and glum beside Mr. Morgenstern, supporting his father's opening chants over the wine and the matzo with his uncertain baritone voice, and shooting occasional suspicious looks at Noel.

Noel, though his behavior was faultless, seemed to make the Family even more uneasy than his parents did. A chill radiated from him, causing much of the lameness of the singing, the stumbling of the Hebrew responses, and the embarrassed side glances among the relatives. The skullcap perched on his thick blond hair somehow looked as incongruous as it would have on an animal's head. His bearing was sober, his comments courteous; Marjorie could not accuse him of deliberately trying to appear out of place and trapped. Nor was there anything intentionally offensive in the way he kept looking around. But the effect was to make the Family, including Marjorie, feel increasingly like painted Africans performing a voodoo rite. Mrs. Morgenstern didn't improve things by trying to explain the ceremonies to Noel. She would get all tangled up in theology, and dead silence would drop over the table while she painfully bumbled her way through; and Noel all the while would nod brightly, saying that it was really terribly interesting. This happened over and over.

Worst of all, however, was the absence of the Uncle.

Until this year, Marjorie had not realized how central Samson-Aaron had been to the seder. Her father always had sat at the head of the table, as he sat now, conducting the service out of the beautifully illustrated Hagada printed in England. Samson-Aaron had seemed merely the funmaker, the heckler, of the feast. Now Marjorie saw that he had been nothing less than the soul of it; and he was gone. He had warmed the air. Single-handed, he had dispelled the stiffness of a year's separation, and the frost of all the permanent quarrels, of all the sad unchangeable differences in income. His bubbling jokes, his bellowing of the songs, his pounding of the rhythms with fist and foot, his cavorting, his fabulous eating and drinking, had gradually wakened the spirits of the Family, brought the old ties of blood to life, and welded the scattered estranged group, at least for the evening, into something like the close-knit tribal Family of the old country. Without him, the seder was but a moribund semblance; and it was enacted with less and less heart as the evening went on, under the fixed smiles of Judge and Mrs. Ehrmann, and the cool observant eyes of their son.

If anyone promised to save the seder as an institution, it was Neville Sapersteen. He was giving the occasion what liveliness it had. The children's table was a vortex of noise and motion, all of it churning around Neville. Snatching the other children's Pepsi-Cola, breaking matzos over their heads, drinking off the salt water, throwing plates, forks, pepper, flowers, hard-boiled eggs, Neville was exhibiting enough vivacity for ten children. His mother stayed one step behind him, as it were, catching the plates before they broke, putting back the flowers, wiping up the wine, comforting the other children while Neville drank their Pepsi-Cola, and persuading them not to break matzos over Neville's head, on the grounds that revenge was an unworthy motive. Marjorie's back was to the living room, so that she missed much of the byplay; but at every sudden burst of noise she would look around fearfully, to make sure that nothing jagged or wet was sailing her way.

Matters broke out of control very suddenly in the living room, just as Mr. Morgenstern was putting down the three wrapped matzos after reciting *This bread of affliction*. There was an explosion of laughter and yammering, with Neville's voice rising in infuriated soprano shrieks over the din. His mother yelled, "Morris, Morris, come quick! The airplanes! They're into the airplanes!" While Morris struggled frantically to get out of the seat where he was wedged between two fat aunts, half a dozen children came giggling and shrieking into the dining room, swooping toy airplanes in their hands and making noises like airplane motors—"*Braah! Braah!*" After them charged Neville, his face dark purple, waving his fists and uttering hideous choked sounds. The children dived under the table and under chairs; they flew between the legs of their pursuing parents, in and out of the clutching arms of Mildred and Morris Sapersteen, into the bedrooms and round and round the living room, all the time roaring "Braah! Braah!" Neville did a remarkable simulation of running in fourteen directions at once, whimpering, screeching, and snapping his teeth. The seder stopped dead for ten minutes, while all the parents joined the chase. The airplanes were at last rounded up, and the children herded back to their chairs; it was a difficult business, because they kept snatching new airplanes from the suitcase after being deprived of the ones they had, and galloping around again.

Morris Sapersteen stood at bay in the middle of the living room, clutching the suitcase, while Mildred attempted to quiet Neville, who was lying on his back, kicking the floor with both heels, and yelling. Morris said, "I'll just have to lock the lid, I guess."

"No, no," Neville screamed. "I want the box open!"

His mother said, "There's only one answer. These kids are impossible. You'll have to hold the suitcase open on your lap."

"Gosh, Millie, how will I eat?"

"Look, Morris, it wasn't my idea to come to this thing, it was yours. I warned you." She led Neville off, and Morris stumbled back into his chair, and sat with the suitcase on his lap.

Peace ensued; but not for long.

The next part of the seder was the reciting of the Four Questions. Essentially the seder was a sort of pageant, or religious drama, performed at home. The youngest child who could memorize Hebrew delivered four queries about the table symbols: the horseradish, the matzo, the salt water, and so forth: and the adults in reply chanted the tale of the Exodus from Egypt, explaining the symbols as the story unfolded. Marjorie had scored great triumphs with the Four Questions from her fourth to her eighth year. The Family had all said even then that she was a born little actress.

This year the Questions were admirably performed in a sweet piping voice, in flawless parroted Hebrew, by Susan Morgenstern, a chubby six-year-old from the Newark branch of the family. She retired to the children's table, after curtsying to the applause. The adults had hardly begun the concerted chant of the response when the most horrible imaginable scream rang out from the living room, and Neville's mother was heard exclaiming, "Neville, that was cruel! You're not supposed to be cruel!"

Neville, it developed, had sneaked up in back of Susan Morgenstern and bitten her with all his might on the behind.

Again the seder stopped while the four parents hurriedly unscrambled the children; for Susan was rolling with Neville on the floor, trying to strangle him, and making fair headway.

It happened that there was bad blood anyway between the Newark branch and the Far Rockaway branch, which was Neville's, and a nasty argument sprang up when Neville's father tried to say that the bite had actually been a good thing. He said that Neville had gotten rid of the hostility naturally created by Susan's spell in the limelight, and so in reality the bite had drawn the cousins closer. "Holy cow, Morris!" exclaimed the father of Susan, a heavy good-natured young butcher named Harry. "If he bit her he bit her. But I'll be goddamned if I'll let you say it was a good thing, too. Why, for crying out loud, suppose all the other kids had —what'd you call it?—gotten rid of their goddamn hostility like him? My girl would have been chewed to death."

"Harry, please, don't curse at the seder table," said Mrs. Morgenstern, smiling pathetically at the judge and his wife.

"Perfectly natural, nothing to get excited about," the judge said, craning his neck and watching the flailing Neville in the other room with some alarm.

"Neville's exceptionally aggressive," his father said. "It's the normal pattern of the only child, especially the insecure male."

"It's not that at all," his mother shouted angrily. She was squatting, trying to hold Neville still while she straightened his clothing. "It's all this primitive magic and symbolism and Hebrew he's being exposed to. It upsets his nerves. He's been brought up rationally, and he's at a stage where all this poppycock disturbs him deeply!"

Morris Sapersteen, fumbling at the open suitcase on his lap, glanced around at Mr. and Mrs. Morgenstern. "All right, Millie, there are other people here besides us, who think a little differently——"

"Oh, it's all right. He's got to be exposed to all these folkways sooner or later, I guess, but we might have waited a couple of years, that's all."

The Family meantime, with all the excitement, had become a little livelier. There was chatter around the table, instead of stiff gloom. Harry Morgenstern, Susan's brawny father, sneaked himself a couple of drinks of the Palestinian plum brandy to calm his nerves. He immediately became very red in the face, and began to pound the table with his fists. "What the hell, people, is this a seder or a funeral? Come on, put some life into it! The judge here is going to think he's in an old folks' home!" And he started to bawl a song, and several of the Family joined in.

Judge Ehrmann waved at him and laughed. "Don't worry about me. I'm thoroughly enjoying myself, I assure you."

"This is nothing, Your Honor," Harry shouted. "We warm up a little, we'll show you what a seder is all about! Come on, Dora, come on, Leon —sing!"

Mr. Morgenstern said, "That's the spirit, Harry, that's what we need. You sound like the Uncle." He beat time on a glass with a fork, and after a moment broke into the song himself. Everybody sang. Mr. Morgenstern returned to the Hebrew chanting with more zest and heart, and the Family's responses became stronger, too.

Noel turned to Marjorie, his eyes lively. "Well, I begin to get the idea."

"Oh, this is nothing," Marjorie said. Her spirits were rising. "This is a ghost of what it used to be. We used to have Samson-Aaron."

"I can imagine," Noel said. "I'm really beginning to understand him, a little bit—and you too, for that matter."

The seder continued to pick up momentum and gaiety, and soon it was more or less in the old swing. Harry the butcher showed some promise of leadership, bellowing and pounding with energy equal to the Uncle's, if with less charm and flavor. Marjorie felt the familiar old warmth enveloping her. The sweet grape taste of the wine woke childhood recollections. She began to care less what Noel and his parents were thinking, and she joined in the songs with abandon. She noticed that both Noel and his father had taken to reading the English translations in their Hagadas, watching the others to see when pages were turned. Noel looked to her at one point and said, "Do you understand all this Hebrew?"

"Well, fortunately, yes, we've gone over and over it for so many years —otherwise my Hebrew is pretty rusty——"

Noel said, "The English is absolutely atrocious, at least this translation furnished by the matzo company is. But I do get a dim idea of what it's all about. It has terrific charm and pathos, actually—and power, too. I rather envy you."

The ritual had arrived at another song, and as the family burst into it with gusto, Judge Ehrmann glanced up from the book, his high bald brow wrinkled. "Why, I believe I know that one," he said to Uncle Shmulka. He hummed a few bars with the others, and Shmulka nodded with delight. "Well!" the judge said. "I guess that's one that percolated through to the German Jews. My mother used to hum it to me when I was a baby. I remember it distinctly, though I haven't heard it in fifty years." Waving a stiff extended finger high in the air, Judge Ehrmann joined in the song. The effect on the Family was tremendous. When the song ended Harry bawled, "Three cheers for the Judge!" And the Family cheered, and gave him a round of applause. He bowed here and there with pleased dignity, his long face flushed, his gray fringe of hair a little disordered, a pulse throbbing in his neck.

A crash of crockery from the living room now indicated that Neville Sapersteen was emerging from his doldrums. Marjorie looked over her shoulder, and saw Mildred Sapersteen on her hands and knees, picking up the pieces. Mildred caught her look and said angrily, "Well, there's just so much I can do. Susan is impossible. She keeps calling Neville 'Neville the Devil.' No child with any brains would stand for that——"

Harry Morgenstern shouted into the living room, "Susan, you stop that, do you hear? No more calling Neville 'Neville the Devil.' Understand me?"

"Yes, Daddy," piped Susan, and added, "Just one last time, all right, Daddy? Neville the Devil!"

Now that it was officially forbidden, all the children took up the cry and bayed rhythmically, "Ne-ville the De-vil! Ne-ville the De-vil! Ne-ville the De-vil!"

Neville left his chair and catapulted into the dining room, yelling, "Daddy, I want my airplanes! Give me my airplanes!"

Morris jumped up, forgetting that the suitcase was open on his lap; the suitcase slipped, he clutched at it and upset it, and the forty-seven airplanes went clanking and tinkling all over the floor under the table. There was a moment of silence after the crash; even Neville shut up, staring pop-eyed at his father.

"All right," Mildred Sapersteen said in an icy tone. "Nice going, Morris. Now pick them all up."

"No, no," screeched Neville, "I don't want them picked up. Leave them there. I've got to make a parade!" He dived under the table and could be heard crawling, and sliding airplanes along the floor.

"What's he going to make?" Mrs. Morgenstern said nervously to Mildred. "Get him out from under the table, please."

"A parade," Mildred said. "He won't harm anything. He just lines them up three abreast. In perfect formation."

"Mildred dear," said Mrs. Morgenstern, "not under the table, please, with people's feet and everything——"

Morris said, "Aunt Rose, if you want some peace and quiet, believe me this is the best idea. A parade absolutely absorbs him. You won't know he's there. Take my word for it. Just ignore him and——"

At that moment Judge Ehrmann leaped to his feet with an incredibly loud snarl, upsetting his chair, clutching at his leg. "Aaarh! MY GOD!"

"My parade! You kicked my parade!" Neville squealed from under the table.

"Good heavens," the judge choked, "the little monster has really bitten my ankle to the bone!" He pulled up his trouser leg, peering anxiously at his thin bluish shank.

Morris Sapersteen plunged under the table and pulled Neville out, thrashing and howling. "My airplanes! My parade! I want my parade!"

The whole table was in an uproar. The judge said to Morris, "Good Lord, man, forgive me for being blunt, but what that child needs is the whipping of his life. He needs it desperately."

"Morris!" shrilled Mildred, glaring at the judge. "Let's go home."

"Take it easy, Mildred, for God's sake," Morris said.

"We're going home, I say! Pick up the airplanes!"

"I've got *him,* Millie," Morris panted, still struggling with Neville, as with a large live salmon.

Uncle Shmulka said, "Mildred, dolling, don't go home, it's a seder. You didn't eat nothing yet." He held out his arms to Neville. "Come to Grandpa, sweetheart." Neville with astonishing readiness stopped writhing, slid from his father's arms into little Shmulka's lap, and nestled. The judge edged slightly away. "There, Mildred, everything's fine," Shmulka said. "He'll sit vit me and be good. For Grandpa, he's alvays good."

"Oh no, I'm not going to have that again." Mildred's mouth was a black line, her brows were pulled in a scowl. "That lulling is all wrong, and that grandfather-fixation business is really sick, and I'm not having it in my family. *Get* the airplanes, Morris, and let's go." She folded her arms and leaned in the doorway. The children behind her were still.

Morris looked around with a smile, his eyes big and sad. "Sorry, folks, I think it's best, maybe." He dropped on his hands and knees, and knocked and shuffled under the table.

Mildred was standing almost directly behind Marjorie. Impulsively getting out of her chair, Marjorie put her arm around Mildred's waist. "Millie, you're right to be upset. But I think you'll be more upset, and Morris certainly will be, if you walk out now. It's only another hour——" she faltered. Mildred Sapersteen's eyes, curiously flat and shiny as they looked into hers, horrified her.

Mildred said, "Marjorie dear, you're very sweet and pretty, and you've got everything in the world, I know, but I've just got a son, and I've got to do what's best for him."

Harry said to Marjorie, "Give up. She's just a goddamned pill. She's enjoying this."

Mildred whirled, glared at Harry, then looked around at the table. "Well! Thank God we live in a time when you can pick and choose your own culture. Nobody can say I haven't tried to cooperate, but this mumbo-jumbo is impossible, and Neville senses it, and I've always said so. If I have anything to say, we'll wind up joining the Unitarian Church. They have all the answers, anyway." There was a horrid silence. "All right, Morris. Get the baby and let's go."

Uncle Shmulka said in a small tired voice, "He fell asleep." Neville indeed, the storm center of the wrangle, was curled in a ball in his grandfather's lap, eyes closed, breathing peacefully.

The last thing Morris said after fumbling goodbyes, as he carried the slumbering boy out of the room, was, "Papa, she didn't mean that about the church. We're not joining any church."

"I know, Morris, I know you're not. She's a good girl, she's upset. Be vell," said Uncle Shmulka.

As Morris trudged out of sight one of the children called out half-heartedly, "Neville the Devil."

Mrs. Morgenstern said to the Ehrmanns, "I don't know what you must think of us."

Judge Ehrmann smiled, and his voice was deep and soothing. "You should see our family get-togethers, Rose. When blood doesn't flow, it's considered dull. Now I know you've got a big happy family."

He had not used her first name before. Mrs. Morgenstern glowed, and the drawn countenances all around the table relaxed. Harry Morgenstern said, "By God, Judge, you're right. We do have a big happy family. There's one of those in every family, and to hell with her. Come on, Aunt Rose, we're through with the Hagada, aren't we? Where's the eats?"

It was a heavy delicious feast: chopped chicken liver, stuffed fish, fat beet soup, matzo balls, chicken fricassee, potato pancakes, fried chicken and fried steaks. Judge Ehrmann went at the food with startling enthusiasm, saying there was nothing in the world that he loved like Jewish cooking. The relatives, who had been fearing that they would have to eat daintily in the judge's presence, fell to joyously. Soon everybody was very merry except Aunt Dvosha, who sat nibbling at a platter of dry chopped-up carrots, lettuce, tomatoes, raw potatoes, and apples. She had recently given up cooked vegetables, on the grounds that vitamins were destroyed by heat. As she looked around at seventeen people stuffing themselves with vast quantities of fried meat, her face became long and gloomy, and she grumbled to herself, and to whoever would listen to her, about stomach linings, amino acids, protein poisoning, and sudden death.

The judge began glancing at his watch when the dessert came. After finishing his second cup of tea, he deliberately removed his skullcap, folded it on top of his napkin, and cleared his throat. The gesture and the single sound were enough to make all the guests stop eating and drinking, and turn their faces toward him.

"My dear Rose and Arnold, Mrs. Ehrmann and I certainly regret that we have to leave this warm and lovely family circle, and these beautiful ceremonies, and this marvelous food, and go to a dull political dinner, the kind of thing I have to do almost every night in the week, but I can't——"

"It's perfectly all right, Judge," Mrs. Morgenstern said, not quite realizing that this was a preamble rather than conversation.

The judge rolled over her smoothly with a smile, "—but I can't, I say, leave this sumptuous, and may I say sacred, table without a word of appreciation." Noel slumped. His eyes dulled, and his face was so morose that Marjorie was afraid others would notice. But all eyes were on the judge. "Come what may tonight," Judge Ehrmann said, "I've eaten Rose Morgenstern's food. And I'm even more grateful for the spiritual food I've received tonight. Mrs. Ehrmann and I aren't religious people in any formal sense, I'm afraid, but I trust in all our actions we've always showed ourselves good Jews at heart. You see, we're both descended from the old German families who have pretty well dropped all that. Sitting here tonight, I asked myself, were my grandfathers really so wise? Twentieth-century psychology has some very complimentary things to say, you know, about the power of symbol and ceremony over the conduct of men. And I wonder whether it isn't going to turn out that these old-time rabbis knew best. The marvelous warmth and intimacy of your ceremonies tonight! Even the little family quarrel only made things more lively. It gave the evening—well, tang. I was going to say bite, but I'd better not." He paused skillfully for the laugh. "The little Hagada, with its awkward English and quaint old woodcuts, has been a revelation to me. I've suddenly realized, all over again, that I'm part of a tradition and culture that go back four thousand years. I've realized that it was we Jews, after all, with the immortal story of the Exodus from Egypt, who gave the world the concept of the holiness of freedom——"

"Oh lawks a mercy me," Noel muttered.

"Shut up," Marjorie whispered angrily.

"But somehow," the judge said, "your seder has done more than even that for me. Somehow I've almost seen the Exodus come alive tonight. While you've chanted the Hebrew, which regrettably I don't understand, I've closed my eyes and seen the great hordes of Israel, with the majestic gray-bearded giant, Moses, at their head, marching forth from the granite gates of Rameses into desert sands by the light of the full moon. . . ." Judge Ehrmann proceeded in this vein for perhaps ten minutes, drawing a vivid picture of the Exodus and then the revelation on Sinai. The relatives sat spellbound. Marjorie, for all of Noel's sarcastic mutterings, was thrilled and amazed. Noel had described his father as a ridiculous windbag; but actually, though his language was flowery and his manner magisterial, the judge had eloquence and humor. Describing the Israelites heaping their ornaments before Aaron for the making of the golden calf, he said, "Earrings, finger rings, ankle rings, nose rings, gold, gold, in a clinking, tumbling, mounting pile! Just picture it! They stripped themselves bare! They gave away their last treasures for this folly, this golden calf, these impoverished Israelites with the light of Sinai still on their faces!—And to this day, my friends, a Jew, no matter how poor, will always dig up ten dollars for a pinochle game." The relatives roared, and the older men nudged each other and winked. The judge sat quietly, waiting for the laugh to die, his eyes alert, his face serious, the pulse in his neck throbbing, and Marjorie was forcibly struck by his resemblance to his son. Noel, too, never laughed at his own jokes, but sat solemnly, timing his pauses to the laughter of his hearers. The deep-set clever blue eyes were identical in the two men, now that the judge's were roused into vigor. The gap of age, and Noel's smooth handsomeness and mass of blond hair, could not hide the fact that he was, after all, his father's son.

And as Noel sat sunk low in his chair, staring at a wine stain on the tablecloth, and slowly crumbling a hill of matzo crumbs over it while his father talked, Marjorie could see him sitting so at his father's table from perhaps his thirteenth year onward, sullenly enduring eclipse. One thing was obvious: at a table where Judge Ehrmann dominated, there were no other attractions.

When he rose to go, after finishing his talk with, "—and now goodbye, God bless you, and happy Pesakh," everybody at the table stood, crowding toward him, offering their hands, chorusing compliments. He had a handshake and a word for everybody. He remembered which children belonged to which parents, and mentioned them by name in making his farewells, a feat which stunned all with delight. Mr. and Mrs. Morgenstern accompanied the Ehrmanns to the foyer, and several of the guests followed, still exchanging jokes with the judge. Noel's mother, a richly dressed small wraith of a woman, with makeup a little too pink, stopped to kiss Noel on the forehead, and then she kissed Marjorie. "You have a lovely family, Marjorie dear, really lovely. You're a girl to be envied. Good night. I wish we could stay."

Marjorie said, when she was gone, "I think your mother's a darling. And your father's charming, too. Why did you paint him to me as such an idiot?"

He glanced briefly at her with a dip of the head, and a smile that was not pleasant. "Did you believe any of that speech, by some chance?"

"I thought it was moving, I don't care what you say."

"Really? Just remember, dear, he's a politician, and your house is in his district. When will this thing be over? Can I take this off?" He reached for the skullcap.

"Well, the ceremony starts up again now, Noel, and some of the best songs come——"

"How much longer?"

"Oh, not much, not even an hour. I appreciate that you've been very patient——"

"Well, it's been interesting, but frankly I do have the idea now."

She said at once, "Noel, it's perfectly all right if you want to leave now. Everybody will understand."

"I'll settle for some more of that Palestine brandy." He poured a stiff drink—he had been drinking brandy steadily since the dessert—swallowed half of it, and stared at the amber liquid. "Curious taste. Rough, not quite civilized. Primitive, potent, exotic. Well suited to the occasion."

The change in tone was marked when the seder resumed. The glory was departed. The guests were all stuffed with food, and sleepy with wine and brandy, and more interested in talking about the wonderful judge than in following the ceremony. Mr. Morgenstern had to rap for quiet several times.

There soon ensued a lot of glancing toward Noel and Marjorie among the Family, with winks, and nods, and whispers. Marjorie began to be uneasy. The rite that came next was the traditional occasion for teasing sweethearts and engaged couples. Noel, oblivious, was leafing through the Hagada in a bored way, sipping plum brandy. Even Aunt Dvosha became lively and gay, whispering across the two vacant chairs to Uncle Shmulka. The arch faces she made at Marjorie would have frightened an alligator. In the expectant quiet that settled over the table, Uncle Harry said, "Okay, who opens the door this year?"

The relatives giggled, pointing at Marjorie. Noel looked up. "What on earth——?" he said mildly.

"This is it, Noel," Harry said. "The door's got to be opened, you know." There was more laughter.

Noel said, "For whom?"

"Elijah, the prophet Elijah. Don't you know? Elijah comes in now and drinks his cup of wine."

Noel said, "Well, he's no friend of mine, but I'll be glad to open the door." At the howls of mirth that followed, he turned to Marjorie. "Was that funnier than I thought?"

"Margie and Noel open the door," squealed Aunt Dvosha, and collapsed on the table, laughing.

Noel said, "I begin to understand. . . . Well, let's go." He took her hand and stood amid ribald guffaws.

Marjorie, completely scarlet-faced, said, "It means nothing at all, nothing." They went out to jocular shouts. "Just some nonsense about making a wish, but a boy and a girl are supposed to go together."

"Well," Noel said, as she halted in the hallway. "Do we open it now?"

"No. One moment." A chant began in the dining room. "Now. Go ahead, open the door."

With a wry smile, Noel did so. The empty tiled outside hall, and the rows of doors, looked strange. He glanced at her. "Damned if I didn't feel a cool wind on my cheek. The power of suggestion——"

"I've felt that wind every year since I was four," Marjorie said.

"How long does Elijah stay?"

"Just for a minute."

"Am I supposed to kiss you, really?"

"Not at all. Skip it, by all means."

He kissed her lightly. He had drunk a lot of brandy; he smelled of it. In a swift motion he had his coat out of the closet, draped over his arm. "Margie, make my excuses to your folks, will you? I'm going out on the town with the prophet Elijah." She stared at him. He said, "Really, it's best. They're sweet people, and I've had a wonderful time, the judge's oration notwithstanding. It's been a revelation to me, really it has. But I think at this point I'd better run along."

She said faintly, "It's probably an excellent idea. Goodbye."

"I'll call you," he said. He looked at the empty air in the hall. "Elijah, wait for baby!"

The door closed.

Chapter 28. IMOGENE

She didn't become uneasy until three days had gone by without a call from him. It wasn't possible this time, somehow, to telephone him in the free-and-easy way she was growing used to; not after his abrupt departure from the seder. She wasn't really angry about it; he had on the whole behaved well during a very trying evening, she thought, and the outcome might have been far worse; still, his manner of leaving had been a rebuff of a sort, and the next move had to come from him.

It was only on the fourth morning that she woke wondering whether she had misjudged him, after all; whether he was actually a shallow snob, capable of thinking less of her because she had poor relatives, and a few strange ones like Aunt Dvosha and the Sapersteens.

It was a relief when the phone rang at ten after eleven, the time he almost always, for some reason, chose to call her from the office. "Miss Morgenstern? One moment, please." It was the cold correct voice of the Paramount switchboard operator.

"Hello? Marjorie? How are you?"

"Why—why hello, Mr. Rothmore . . . Sam . . . I'm fine, thank you—gosh, what a surprise!"

"Hope I didn't wake you up——"

"Oh no, good Lord, what do you think of me? I've been up for hours——"

"Thought you might have acquired the habits of our no-good friend, a little bit. Where is he, by the way, do you know?"

"Isn't he at the office?"

"Hasn't been here for three days, and his phone doesn't answer."

Marjorie said with impulsive alarm, "He must be sick."

"Have you seen him or heard from him in the past three days?"

"Monday night was the last I saw him."

"Is that so? Well, Tuesday morning he didn't show up. I don't think he's sick. I sent a messenger down to his apartment yesterday. Place was dark. No answer to the bell. He's off somewhere, nobody knows where."

"Why Sam, it's—it's very strange that he'd just go off, without telling your office."

"Goddamn strange," Rothmore said sadly. "Goddamn strange. Margie, what are you doing for lunch? Come down and have lunch with me."

"Why——" She thought frantically for a moment about clothes. "Why, of course. I'd love to, Sam."

She immediately called Noel and let the telephone ring and ring. He had a trick, when he didn't want to be disturbed, of unscrewing the base of the phone and wadding up the bell with paper. He had fixed it that way during the two weeks he had rewritten *Princess Jones*, and she had sat in his apartment laughing at the dull little angry buzz it made. The noise was irritating, and if it went on long enough he would occasionally take the receiver off the hook. But this time the ringing continued until it got on her nerves, and she slammed down the receiver. She dressed quickly in an old blue suit, making several last-minute changes of hats and costume jewelry.

She had not seen Rothmore before at his desk, in his huge main office. The desk was immense, the wainscoting very dark, the carpeting very thick underfoot, and there were many modern paintings richly framed on the wall. He got up slowly, holding out his hand. The severe look he had darted from under his brows at the opening door faded to a pleasant tired smile. "Hello. Heard from our vanished friend since I talked to you?"

"No."

"Messenger boy just went down and tried to kick the door in. No luck. Come with me. I'd like to show you something."

He led her to a small office facing out on Times Square, with two desks in it. "Noel shares this office with another man. Here's his desk. He left it open Monday. I had to dig into it this morning for some correspondence that's overdue." One after another he pulled out the drawers. They were overflowing with jumbled papers, books, letters, printers' galleys, copies of *The Hollywood Reporter* and other trade papers, office memoranda, and the rest of the debris of a desk job, all in an unbelievably slovenly chaos. There were some half-eaten stale sandwiches and a few empty Coca-Cola bottles. Marjorie stared, speechless. Rothmore said, "I don't know how he did it. Except maybe by emptying his wastebasket into the desk every day since he's been here—or all the wastebaskets of Paramount, more likely." He shut the drawers with contemptuous backhand thrusts. "Well, I'm glad he's been doing something to earn his keep. The wastebaskets should be emptied, though not necessarily by story editors."

Marjorie faltered, "I thought he was doing pretty well. . . ."

Rothmore looked at her over his thick glasses. "Let's go get some coffee."

Over exquisite cold salmon in a small French restaurant, he told her the story of Noel's career at Paramount. She was at once fascinated and repelled by the disclosures, and her nerves were shaken. Rothmore was not bitter, but he was not kind, either. This was the other side of Noel's sarcastic anecdotes. After the glimpse of the desk drawers, Marjorie could hardly hide from herself where the truth probably lay. According to Rothmore, Noel had been lazy and insolent from the first day. He had been rebellious before there was anything to rebel against; and his resentment had been directed not at anything in his own job, but at the entire process of business. "I mean, Margie, the man would say things like, 'Naturally, we've got to make sure our pictures show a profit,' in a sneering tone. As though it were some goddamn guilty secret that a business has to make a profit. Childish, you know, unless a person's a communist, and he's no communist, I managed to make pretty sure of that. But I'm damned if I know what's eating the man. I mean, *why?* Why the petty lies? Why the inefficiency? He's one of the cleverest fellows I've ever met, but he couldn't hold a job as a twelve-dollar-a-week file clerk, his methods are so disorderly. He'd lie about the most trivial things, get me in silly jams—you know, saying he'd answered a letter, or sent back a set of galleys, when he hadn't. When it caught up with him, he'd say in the airiest way that the thing had slipped his mind, or some stupid answer like that. Totally irresponsible. Why, today I found in his desk letters, important letters, he should have showed me, weeks old. It isn't normal, Marjorie. No man is that lousy. He had to work at it, to be that bad. Now, why?"

Marjorie said miserably, "Maybe he isn't cut out for business, that's all. He was very efficient at South Wind, staging shows. A lot of creative people just can't stand business."

"Well, my answer to that ought to be, why did he take Paramount's money? But I'll skip that. Margie, he's very valuable when he wants to be. He's got a fine grasp of pictures, and I mean a business grasp. For some perverse reason he kept taking the high artistic tone, I guess because that made it easy to insult me, but I'd put him up against anybody to analyze a story property—a musical, a novel, a farce, anything—for its basic values. Why, he pulled a story out of an obscure magazine that we bought for twelve hundred, and I'm bound to tell you if he didn't do anything else all year he earned his keep with it. We're making a big A picture of it. And I told him so, and gave him a bonus. Maybe that was my mistake. But I was trying everything, you see. I tried being tough. I tried being nice. I tried giving him his head. I tried riding him. Hell, all I was after was to straighten him out. Nothing helped. From the day he came to the day he left he was the same mess. Pouting one minute, charming the next, smart as a whip today, stupider than the most idiotic clerk tomorrow, fast as a snake, slow as molasses, blow hot, blow cold, the most aggravating man I've ever encountered. I'm a pretty stubborn customer, Marjorie, and I don't as a rule start anything I can't finish, but this has beaten me. I'm all through with Noel Airman." Rothmore sipped his coffee, lit a cigar, and sat staring at her from under his brows, taking little gulps of air. He seemed to be waiting for her to plead Noel's case. She found nothing to say. There was a panicky undercurrent to the speed and hunger with which she went on devouring her food, shaking her head gloomily at Rothmore's story. He said after a while, "Well what do you think? You must know him better than anybody."

"Sam, he's a total enigma to me, a black mystery. He has been, since the first day I met him."

"It's none of my business, but have you been giving him a bad time? A girl can mess up a man's work, like nothing else."

She faced him. "That's not it. Take my word for it."

"Well, maybe he's just no good, as he keeps saying. I can't say he hasn't pretty well proved his point."

"What do you think of his songs, Sam, really?"

"His songs?"

"That's what he's really interested in, after all."

Rothmore said, "There's no comparison, none at all, between where he could go as an executive and as a songwriter."

"But obviously he doesn't care about being an executive."

Rothmore puffed at his cigar. "Look, he's past thirty. He's a competent songwriter, pretty competent, but frankly they're a dime a dozen. And they're not like Noel, you know, the Brill Building crowd. They're ignoramuses, lowbrows, neurotic bums, these fellows who write an occasional hit song. I'm not talking about a Johnny Mercer, a Cole Porter. He isn't that, or he would have shown the form long ago. If you ask me, he writes songs with his fingertips, the way he does everything else. I don't know what the trouble is. I'm no psychoanalyst. Maybe he's so afraid of being a failure he won't put his back into anything, so he can always tell himself that he's never really tried. I have a brother like that. I started him in four different businesses. He was always my mother's darling, but he's never earned an honest dollar. He can whistle all the themes from Beethoven's quartets. My brother Leo. Never married. Hangs around with the Philharmonic musicians." Rothmore motioned to the waiter for the check. "More coffee?—I'll tell you, I think he's got a hit in that *Old Moon Face*. What ruins him, probably, is these occasional hits. If he'd only fail completely at it, he'd concentrate on something with a future. But your friend's curse, Margie, I'm afraid, is that he never fails completely at anything. He's got too much ability for that."

"I've told him over and over he's got to concentrate on one thing." Marjorie could not keep the heartsickness out of her voice. "Has he showed you his musical comedy, *Princess Jones?*"

"No."

"Well, I think it's brilliant, Sam, I really do. He's had awful luck. I'm not trying to excuse him, but——" She told Rothmore of the misfortune with the producer Kogel.

He moved a shoulder disparagingly. "That's the theatre business. You've got to be able to take such knocks. Still, if you say this show's good, maybe it is. He has remarkable ability, I know that." Rothmore's eyes flickered at her. "He talks a lot about you. Pretends to laugh at you, but—he's damned selfish, but I do think he's in love with you. You're his hope, if he has any."

"I can't imagine what's happened to him, Sam. I'm going to find him, one way or another."

Rothmore helped her from her chair. "Margie, I said I'm stubborn, and I am. If you can get him to promise you that he'll start afresh, and really try, I'll forget about this little vacation, and take him back. It's got to be a promise to *you*. Otherwise——" He shrugged. "He's an attractive young man, God knows, but there's just so much time you can waste trying to straighten out one bent pin."

When they parted on the street, Rothmore said, "He owes me money. Not much, but he was supposed to pay it back this week. If that's what's bothering him, tell him to come back and stop being such a damned baby. We'll work out an easy way to pay it off, five dollars a week deducted from his check, or something."

This upset her more than anything else he had told her.

Noel's window was open slightly at the bottom, and the Venetian blind was drawn up. This was as much as Marjorie could see from the street. She rang the outer bell. Surprisingly, there was an immediate answering buzz, and the hallway door yielded to a push. She went up the dimly lit stairs, full of an indefinable fear. She seemed to be seeing the torn blue linoleum on the steps, and smelling the incense odors from the ground-floor apartment, for the first time. Every detail of the staircase stood out—the old-fashioned molding along the wall, the dirty Victorian balustrade, the extinct gas jet near the top, below the single dim light bulb. She rounded the top of the stairs with a slight effort, dreading what might confront her, but his door at the end of the hallway was shut. She walked to it and rang the bell.

The girl was taller than Marjorie, and dressed in a blue housecoat. She seemed pretty, but it was hard to tell because the light of the window was directly behind her. She said, "Oh!" and then, "I was expecting a boy with groceries."

The two girls looked at each other. Marjorie could hear water drumming in the bathroom. She said in a pleasant calm tone, "Is Noel Airman here?"

The girl said, "Are you Marjorie?"

"Yes. I'm Marjorie."

"Well, come in. He's taking a shower. He'll be right out."

The bed was neatly made, and the room looked as it always did, except for the new calfskin suitcase open in the corner, overflowing with pretty white and pink lingerie. The girl went to the bathroom, pounded a fist on the door, and shouted, "Hey! Your friend Marjorie's here." She smiled at Marjorie with easy good humor. She was redheaded, and lusciously attractive. The water stopped running, and Noel's voice called, "What?" The girl said, "Marjorie's here, I tell you."

There was a silence. Then Noel shouted cheerily, "Fine. Give her some coffee. I'll be right out." The water gushed again.

"Sit down, honey, and take your coat off. Coffee's just hotting up. I'm Imogene Normand."

The girl stood with her hands in her housecoat pockets, smiling down at Marjorie, who was tensed in the armchair, her coat flung back from her shoulders. "Don't start throwing things at Noel when he comes out. I landed in New York without five dollars to my name, and Noel let me park here. He's been staying on the fourth floor with his painter friend, the fellow with the beard, Van something. He comes down to shower because all his things are here."

Imogene said this with such offhand pleasant sincerity, with such utter absence of embarrassment or guile, that Marjorie's muscles relaxed slightly, and she even smiled. "Well, I'm glad you told me. I was going to stab him with the bread knife. You're awfully pretty."

Imogene threw her head back and laughed. "Thanks, but you're one girl who has nothing to fear." She glanced appreciatively, professionally, at Marjorie. "Well, he has good reason. You're terribly sweet." The boiling over of the coffee interrupted Marjorie's answer. Imogene called from behind the screen that hid Noel's tiny pantry and gas burner, "Cream? Sugar?"

"Black."

"Ah, a coffee lover, like me." She brought out two steaming cups.

Marjorie noticed that there were no rings on the girl's bony hands. "Are you—are you the Imogene Noel told me about? The one who married an oil man?"

Imogene's lips twisted cynically. "Oil man, of sorts. We've busted up. I'm back looking for work."

"Oh. I'm sorry."

"Nothing to be sorry about. One of those things. Fun while it lasted, and all that," Imogene said gaily. She sipped, crouching over the cup. She had slant eyes and a charming slow smile; one of those lucky girls, Marjorie thought, who walked around inside a body like jewelers' work, every detail perfect, and none of it her own doing. It was like being born rich. Her legs through the slit in the housecoat were dazzlingly long and lovely. She had minimized her one defect, a big jaw, by piling the beautiful red hair full on the head, rouging the cheeks high, and broadening the mouth a bit beyond the natural line. There was a faint coarseness about Imogene. Perhaps it lay in the very excellence of makeup, the shrewdness of hair arrangement. Marjorie's eyes kept moving to the open suitcase full of underwear. Imogene said, "I'm getting out of here tomorrow, so friend Noel won't be dispossessed any more. I didn't want to get involved in hotel bills, you know, before I was sure I had work."

"I suppose you do modelling."

"Well, I'm more a singer, really, but the modelling pays the bills, you might say. Gosh, things are *awful* in this town. I thought Roosevelt was supposed to fix the depression. Why, I've never seen it so dead. Will you excuse me, honey, while I finish dressing? I'm late."

"Go right ahead."

Imogene's slip, her shoes, her stockings, were all expensive and smart. Nothing could have been more conservative, yet more designed to set off her voluptuous figure, than the hand-tailored black suit and the mannish black hat. She put on her clothes with little waste motion, chattering about her singing career, the unreliability of coaches, the high price of vocal arrangements, and the miserable state of the night-club trade.

Dressed, she somehow looked coarser than before. She rapped at the bathroom door. "Hey, have you drowned? I'm off."

The door opened and Noel looked out, unshaven and pale, dressed in moccasins, corduroy pants, and his old black turtle-neck sweater. He said, "What are you going to do about breakfast? Hi, Marge."

"Oh, I'll get a bite uptown. I'm late. That kid never did come with the butter and eggs. I thought that's who Marjorie was, but it wasn't."

"Had I known, I'd have brought some," Marjorie said. She was watching them like a detective, trying to guess from inflections, gestures, and looks what had really been happening in this apartment for four days. She was sick with tension. Her arms tingled; her fingers were cold as a dead man's.

"It's just as well," Noel said, yawning. "I don't feel the least bit like eggs, and I know exactly what I do want. I want some whiskey and oysters."

Imogene laughed. "You! I thought you'd gotten over those habits. Whiskey and oysters!" She turned to Marjorie. "How about that for a breakfast?—By the way, Noel, I've already explained to Margie that you're sleeping upstairs with Van Renheim while I use your place. So she won't be breaking the crockery over your head."

Noel grinned, glancing at Marjorie. "Why did you do that? You should have let her stew. Jealousy's good for some girls."

"Well, I've got my reputation to think about now, you know, being an old married woman with a kid, and all. Though I must say, now that I'm back, it all seems like a dream. Well——" She opened the door. "Nice meeting you, Margie. 'Bye, Noel, hope you enjoy your whiskey and oysters. You might shave, at least, seeing you've got company, you bum. See you tonight, maybe. Let's see, have I got the key? Yes. 'Bye."

The door closed. Noel and Marjorie confronted each other across the familiar room. The scent of Imogene's hyacinth perfume drifted in the air between them. Noel leaned in the doorway of the bathroom with a yawn and a smile. "Well, how are you? Can I offer you a matzo?"

"Don't be so clever."

"I mean it. I have them." He brought a box of matzos from behind the screen, and rattled it at her. "I've been eating 'em, fried with eggs and sausages, all week. Developed a great yen for them at your house. How about some more coffee and a matzo? Damn kid never did come with the butter."

"No, thanks. I see what you meant about Imogene. She's really beautiful."

"You should have seen her when she was eighteen. Three years in Oklahoma have made her pretty leathery, to my taste, and duller than ever. But she's a good kid." He yawned again, and slumped on the bed. "I'm really falling apart. Even a cold shower does nothing to me, just makes my lips blue and leaves me sleepy."

"Haven't you had enough sleep?"

"Very little, past four days. Been on a reading and writing jag. These things happen to me."

"Is that why you haven't been at Paramount? I thought you must be sick."

He looked amused. "Has Sam been after you?"

"I've just come from lunch with him."

"Gad! The Save-Noel-from-Himself Club in emergency session. Well, what's the diagnosis? Rigor mortis of the conscience? I'm hungry as hell. Come on, let's go out and eat. Oh, you just had lunch. Well, watch me eat, then." He got up, put on the threadbare brown overcoat, and regarded himself wryly in the mirror. "Are you sure you want to be seen with such a tramp?"

"You've looked better, I'll say that——"

The telephone buzzed at that moment, a faint frustrated noise. They glanced at each other. It buzzed again and again. Marjorie, putting on her coat, said, "Aren't you going to answer it?"

"There's nobody I want to hear from—now that you're with me, my love. Who can it be? Sam, or my folks. Let it ring."

"Funny," she said, staring at the buzzing phone.

"What now?"

"If Imogene's using the apartment, what's the point of muffling the bell?"

His wide-eyed blank look lasted only a second. He burst out laughing. "Skip it, will you? If Imogene and I were living in sin, she'd tell you or I would, it means nothing to either of us. She's out all day and half the night on her rounds, or whatever queer things she does. I still work down here. I've been working like a dog, eighteen hours a day."

"Doing what?"

"Writing something that will shake the world. Come along, I'll tell you about it."

Marjorie felt absurdly like a movie character snooping for clues at a murder scene. There were ashtrays on the night tables at either side of the bed. They had not recently been emptied. In the ashtray on the side near the window, the butts were all red with lipstick. In the other ashtray the butts were white. Both trays were equally full.

"Do you know you're standing there like a sleepwalker?" Noel said. "Come on, I'm starving."

It was impossible to ask him about the ashtrays. It was too low, too humiliating; it was comical. She could grin, thinking about it. And yet she was in such pain she could hardly breathe. She followed him out, and down the stairs.

Chapter 29. BRIEF CAREER OF AN EVANGELIST

"Gad, smell this air!" Noel stood at the top of the street steps, breathing deeply. "Who's growing jonquils on Eleventh Street? Why didn't you tell me it was so warm? I don't need a coat."

"I don't think it's warm," Marjorie said. "I'm cold."

"Another April," Noel said. He took her arm and they walked down the steps. "You know, there's nothing to do in New York, really, when the year turns like this. People just let it happen, and go about their business, in and out of the turnstiles. In Paris, or even in Mexico City, it would be a kind of holiday. Everybody'd be out strolling, young couples kissing on street corners, pushcarts with flowers everywhere——"

"I think I prefer the New York style," Marjorie said. "I like to do my kissing in private."

"You don't much like the whole process, public or private," Noel said. "If you could back God into an argument in a restaurant—as you're about to back me—you'd want to know why He couldn't think of a less messy way to keep the race going."

"I'm not eager for any arguments, Noel. In fact why don't you just have breakfast somewhere by yourself? I'll go home. I came down here because I thought you might be sick."

"Okay, you go on home. That's a good idea. I've got a lot of thinking to do."

"About us?"

"No, indeed. About my work."

"What are you working on, more songs?"

"No, something else."

"Look, whatever it is, if it's so important that you have to take time off from work, don't you think out of common courtesy you ought to let Sam Rothmore know?"

"I'm uncommonly uncourteous, sweetie. That's an old story." He paused in front of a little French restaurant in the cellar of a brownstone house. "They make fine onion omelets, and the bread is real bread . . . But I want those oysters. Come on."

She said after walking in silence, "You should know better than anybody in the world that I don't regard sex as something messy. That's a vile thing to say to me."

"Don't let it rankle. It was just a bum joke."

"You're being very strange."

"Am I? I wasn't aware of it. This breeze, this April breeze . . . it has the edge of a scythe in it. Time's passing, baby, did you know that? You're a big girl. Little Marjorie's all gone. Dr. Shapiro, where art thou? Here's where I'm having breakfast. Are you going home?"

"Why—it's just a saloon. What can you eat in a saloon?"

"They have very good oysters." The wan sunlight on his face showed a few gray bristles in the blond stubble on his cheek. She had never noticed them before. He needed a haircut. He grinned at her scrutiny, stoop-shouldered, his thick long hair stirring in the breeze. "Debating whether to sit down in public with this panhandler, hey?"

"Maybe I'll come in for a little while."

"Well, what a pleasant surprise." He led her through the saloon, where a couple of morose men in overalls were drinking beer, to a back room, and sat on a bench under the window at a little table covered by a soiled red and white checked cloth. "Couldn't ask for more privacy, could you, for giving me a going-over?"

"What is this place?" Marjorie looked around with distaste at the bare brown-painted walls, the disorderly tables and chairs, the naked lamps, and the cardboard beer advertisements in the window. The sour smell of beer was very strong. "I thought I knew all your haunts——"

An old fat woman came from the barroom, wiping her hands on her apron. Noel ordered oysters and a double Canadian whiskey, and the woman waddled out.

"Good Lord, I thought you were fooling. You can't have that for breakfast," Marjorie said. "You'll kill yourself. Have some cornflakes or something."

"Best breakfast in the world," Noel said. "Cornflakes, if you want to know, are what's poisoning America, and causing the rise in mental disorders. You know what cornflakes are, don't you? Didn't I ever tell you how cornflakes got started?"

She was not in the mood for one of his crazy improvisations, though usually she found them very funny. "No, but I wish you'd order some cornflakes right now, if you can get them in this hole, instead of whiskey and oysters."

"Well, dear, it was a cold March evening in 1899 in Chicago, outside one of the big flour mills. There was this pile of refuse big as a mountain in the yard of that mill, the waste products of years, and years, and *years*, of milling. Well, there came a knock on the door of the president of this mill's office. When he went to open it, there was this little ragged old man outside. He had a long bushy beard stained with tobacco juice, and a tattered old burlap sack over his shoulder. And this old man whined, all scrunched over, 'Mister, can I please have some of that junk off that pile in your back yard?' The president said, 'I don't know what you want it for. Hogs refuse to eat it. But sure, you're welcome to it, all you want.' The old man said, 'Okay, mister, I sure thank you. That's all I wanted to hear.' He straightened up and walked into the yard, tearing off the beard as he went—he was really only eighteen years old—and he took out a whistle and blew it. In about five seconds a fleet of a hundred and forty-seven wagons drawn by dray horses came galloping into that yard. Margie, they cleared away that mountain of rubbish before you could have smoked a cigarette. They didn't leave a grain. That eighteen-year-old boy became the cornflakes king. When he died he owned that flour mill and four more besides. He left seven billion dollars in cash to his wife. In fact, he was the finest example of the hard-fisted young American industrialist anybody has ever seen. We all ought to be more like him, especially me, instead of coming late to work, and eating whiskey and oysters for breakfast. Nevertheless, and you can stand me up against a wall and shoot me if you want, I don't give a good goddamn for corn-flakes, and I never will." The woman had returned and was setting the whiskey and oysters in front of him. "Ah, these look fine, Mrs. Klein-schmidt. Well, Margie, that's how it happened that Imogene Normand opened my door this morning, instead of me. I feel you're entitled to this explanation."

"What's the matter with you?" Marjorie said. Noel was drinking the rye neat. "I'm beginning to think that isn't your first drink today."

"No indeed," Noel said, "but I trust I'm coherent."

"Well, yes, very much so, only a little too gay or something, all things considered."

Noel dipped two oysters at once in horseradish and tomato sauce, and ate them. "Exquisite. I was dying for these."

"Lord, you must be hungry." He was cramming a handful of oyster crackers into his mouth. "That cornflakes story is very interesting, dear, but I don't quite see how it explains everything about Imogene."

"Don't you?"

"No. Not that it matters. I think it's nice of you to give her the room and put yourself out like that, but I'm not surprised. You're always painting yourself blacker than you are."

He stopped wolfing the oysters, and looked narrowly at her. "You know, you're always saying I'm a mystery, but you're twice as mysterious to me. You absolutely baffle me. I've known you intimately for a year, and I'm still not sure whether you're incredibly naïve or as smart as a snake."

"What have you been working on, Noel? Or don't you want to talk about it?"

He lit a cigarette and idly picked up a greasy box from the bench. It was full of chess pieces. He pulled out a black knight and the white king, and placed them in the red and white squares on the tablecloth so that the knight was attacking the king. "I like this place. Most evenings and some afternoons you can pick up a chess game with one Village character or another—a boozed-up poet, a communist, a book critic, a painter, or just a plain precious nobody with an avant-garde magazine under his arm. The talk is more interesting than the chess. I bait them. You'd swear I was all worked up over Kafka, or John Strachey, or Alfred Adler, or whatever, and all the time I'm fighting to keep from rolling off the bench laughing. It's a great diversion when you're dull."

"You enjoy that kind of thing because you're such a horrible intellectual snob," Marjorie said. "You like to see the little creatures crawling at your feet."

"Do you really want to know what I've been working on?"

"I'm dying to know."

He put his hand on the back of her neck, and caressed her briefly. His eyes were very bright. "I wish—well, no use wishing, is there?" He picked up the whiskey. "You're responsible for the whole thing, you know, this tangent I'm off on. Next time you talk to Sam Rothmore admit your guilt, at least. You touched it all off by dragging me to that seder." He drank off the contents of the glass. Marjorie had never seen him drink this way. It appalled her to watch raw spirits disappear into him like water. He did not cough or even blink. His speech was quite precise, if anything, slightly more so than when he was sober, and he was holding himself very erect. He was silent, moving the white king idly from square to square in the tablecloth, and pursuing it with the black horse. Then he said with sudden gloom, "I don't know, this involves considerable baring of the soul, which offends the only modesty I have. But, what the hell! We'll all be dead in a few years. I don't know why I take myself so seriously."

"Noel, what's it all about?" He had worked Marjorie into a fever of inquisitiveness.

"If you laugh I'll sock you. I came away from that evening at your home—you know, the seder—with the perfectly sober idea that I might become a rabbi." He grinned at her amazed look. "It's true. That is, I didn't have the idea when I left your house. I walked the streets all night, going from one bar to another, drinking and walking on. I walked down to the Village from your house. It's about five miles, you know. Working from saloon to saloon, it took me until dawn. Kid, it was a nerve crisis the like of which I've never known. Something exploded in my subconscious. It'll be a long time before I hoot down the idea of ancestral memory again, and all that—— You're looking at me like a fish. Does all this strike you as insane?"

"I guess I look like a fish when I'm enthralled," Marjorie said. "For God's sake, go on."

"It's hard to describe how it was. For a while half my mind was holding back, you might say, watching the development of this fantasy in my own brain with cool amusement, but little by little it took over my whole spirit, and by dawn I was panting over the idea as I haven't panted about anything—including a girl—since I was eighteen.

"It all started, Margie, with that charming Sapersteen woman, and her precious little Neville the Devil. What she said about your Passover, when she blew up, was pretty much what I'd been thinking—folk legends, primitive totemism, and so forth. It occurred to me that anything that woman said must be wrong. She sounded exactly like one of these characters I play chess with here, a dreary ass with a headful of Modern Library Giants. That's when I started to pay attention to the seder. I started to read your prayer book and listen to the melodies. My mind began to catch fire. You know what offended me most about my father's after-dinner speech? The fact that I actually was beginning to feel what he said he was feeling—the power of the whole Exodus yarn, the terrific charm of an observance practiced by Jews who crumbled to powder a thousand years before Shakespeare was born, and observed in exactly the same way by your father in 1936 on West End Avenue. It's electrifying, when you think about it——"

"Maybe your father really felt it, too, Noel. Why not?" She was very excited.

"Darling, take my word for it, the man's a phonograph. Now, please understand me, Marjorie, I don't *believe* your Exodus story or anything else about your religion. But what I suddenly realized that night was, *what does that matter?* Suppose it isn't literally true? Suppose it's emotionally true, poetically true? Does that count for nothing? Is *Macbeth* true? It's a childish ghost story, but nothing truer has ever been written. Well, all this is old stuff, it's straight Santayana, but it came alive for me the other night, wildly alive. And I thought to myself, why must this thing dry up and die? How much literal truth is there in this lousy world? How much truth of any kind is there? This religion is full of fire and comfort, it's beautiful, it's a way of life far wiser and better than random scrambling for dough. . . .

"And then—I remember distinctly I was in a bar on Broadway in the Forties, and the man beside me, with a scraggy pink face, was ogling a fat whore in blue satin two stools down—it hit me: I'd go to some theological seminary, study day and night, master Hebrew, give myself two years of the most fanatic work, or at most three——

"Margie, I've wandered into temples, you know, just for the hell of it, to hear young rabbis preach. I really think they must all be subnormal. It's inevitable, when you think about it. What man with any kind of brains and will power goes in for the pulpit in a commercial society? You get the bunnies, the misfits, the mama's darlings, and so forth——

"And I thought, why, glory be, I'd have the field to myself. I'd be a national sensation. I'd start a whole trend of talented intellectuals back into this field. It would spread to the Christian denominations—I'm sure they have the same problems—oh, I tell you, by the time dawn came I was the biggest thing since Moses, and better, because I was going to cross that old Jordan myself, and be first man into the Promised Land. I was also somewhat fried. But not feeling it, believe me."

Noel put aside the two chess pieces, which he had been jumping incessantly from square to square. He bolted several more oysters. Marjorie said, "Is this what you've been working on for the last four days? I think Sam Rothmore's likely to forgive you——"

"When I got home I took down the Bible and got into bed and started to read. You'd think I'd have fallen asleep. Not at all. I was so stimulated, my nerves were strung so tight, that I read the Old Testament straight through in about eighteen hours, not skipping anything. It's not so long, you know. I'll bet *The Brothers Karamazov* is longer. I didn't eat. All I did was drink coffee. But as soon as I finished the last page, I did fall asleep. I don't know to this hour how long I slept. It was blazing day when I woke up. I staggered out and went to Fourth Avenue, and hunted up a history of the Jews, and a book on the customs and ceremonies. Then I took those home and read them straight through. That only took a few hours. Now maybe I should have stopped at some point and called Sam Rothmore, and explained that I'd suddenly gotten religion and he'd have to excuse me for a few days. But I tell you, Margie, Sam Rothmore might have been on Mars for all I knew or cared.

"So there I was, still reading, it must have been late afternoon, four or five. I hadn't talked to anybody or eaten for two days. My head was swirling with Moses and Isaiah, with phylacteries and Talmud sages, with the Spanish Inquisition and the separation of milk and meat dishes, the whole picturesque mass tumbling in my brain—when the bell rang, and in walked Imogene with a suitcase." Noel chuckled at Marjorie's groan. "She was dog-tired, famished, thirsty, covered with grime. She'd just come on a bus from Tulsa, Oklahoma, to New York—walked out on her husband after a bloody fight, and hocked nearly all her clothes for the bus fare. This so-called oil man she married turned out to be just a shady hick promoter. But she was really in love with the guy, so she stuck it out for three years, and then quit. All this she told me sort of weeping into a few scotch and sodas. Which rather surprised me, as I never figured Imogene to have any more feelings than a buffalo. Why she picked my place to come to, I'm not sure. Probably because out of all that dizzy crowd we ran with I'm the only one whose name's still in the phone book.

"Well, so I told her to take a shower and change her underwear and so forth, and I took her out and bought her a steak, and she perked up amazingly. We got to talking of old times, and the crazy things we'd done in that crowd, and we laughed and got pretty drunk and all that, and then her fatigue caught up with her, and she went to sleep in my bed. And I was out walking the streets again, trying to pick up the threads where I'd left off.

"Margie, this may strike you as the strangest part yet. It had all vanished—vanished, faded like a dream. I didn't have anything left. Well, no, I had something. Sorry, cigarette?" He was lighting one.

She took it, hardly aware of what she was doing, her gaze fixed on his drawn stubbly face and gleaming eyes. "What did you have left?"

"Revulsion," Noel said, "fearful depressed revulsion, luckily relieved with amusement at myself, the most colossal jackass in the whole Village full of jackasses. I was back in the twentieth century. I was Noel Airman, and there were autos and neon signs all along the street, and a plane going by overhead in the night sky, with its red and green lights blinking. And the notion that I might become a rabbi was about as silly as the thought of my climbing Mount Everest some summer afternoon in sneakers. My mind had exploded in a crazy fantasy, that's all. The whole incident would make me fear for my mental health, if I didn't have a good idea of what caused it. Imogene pulled me back from the brink. I'll always be grateful to the dull cow."

Marjorie shook her head slowly, sadly. "I sometimes wonder if you are quite sane. What living man ever tried to absorb a religion in a couple of days, starting from total ignorance? It was lunacy. The marvel is that you actually went through all that reading. No wonder you had such a violent reaction, it was absolutely inevitable—but it proves nothing. Heaven knows I don't want you to become a rabbi, that part was wild, but some of the things you've just said make sense, Noel——"

He laid his hand on her arm and patted it. "Marjorie, my dear, please give it up, you're wasting breath. This fantasy was the last gasp of my resolve to try to become respectable, which really went glimmering after I'd been at your seder an hour. I saw what you were, and what I was. I shut the realization out of my mind with this whole burst of sickly enthusiasm because I'm in love with you, and because I know in your case love means marriage. Back of this whole dream was the delicious figure of the young would-be actress Marjorie Morningstar, a reformed, sedate, utterly charming spouse with downcast eyes. Oh, you were in it, all right, but incidental, casual, in true daydream fashion, the real motive masked."

Something in his tone when speaking of her frightened Marjorie. She said hurriedly, "Well, but you say you're working on something——"

"Yes." He drummed on the table with the fingers of both hands. "I'm suddenly ravenously hungry. I've got to have a steak or I'll kill myself. You, too?"

"Noel, I just had lunch."

"I keep forgetting." He rapped loudly with a chess piece, and when the woman came he said, "How about a steak, rare, just off purple, and some home fries? And rolls, huh?"

The woman beamed. "Good. You need some meat on your bones, Mister Airman. Iss better than oysters." She hurried out.

"I feel like having a cigar, too, right this second," Noel said. "I'm full of queer yens. Can it be that I'm pregnant? Intellectually, maybe. Stop me if I start eating chalk. I'll be right back." She could see him buying a cigar from the bartender. He came back smoking it. "You know, I don't smoke half a dozen cigars a year. But this one tastes ambrosial." He dropped down beside her and puffed.

"Margie, out of all this turmoil, this queer and rather shattering crisis I've been through, I think I've gotten a tremendous idea. One advantage of such a shaking-up is that you see things new and clear again for a while—the way everything tastes good and looks good, you know, when you're recovering from a grippe. You see, I had to ask myself this question: granted that religion is a pathetic dream, what isn't? What do you really believe? What do you want? What's good?

"Well, it's a hell of a thing, I tell you, when all the old philosophic puzzlers come at you suddenly, with the same urgency as—for instance— 'What restaurant shall I eat at tonight? How can I get this girl into bed? Where can I get hold of some more money?'—the questions people really spend their time trying to answer. I believe I've hit on a fresh answer, a serious and original idea, that is going to make a bit of a noise.

"I'm still struggling to reduce it to words. Whether I'll ever be able to get it right, I don't know. It could be a book—rather short, but rather difficult—or a long Socratic dialogue, or a series of connected essays. I'm just writing it out raw, now. Maybe it'll never be anything but this white-hot fragment as it stands, a *pensée,* but I don't think so, I'm certain the form is going to hit me all at once, like a revelation, the way the idea itself did.

"I'm a philosophy major from way back, you know, and even when I was having this religious seizure, as you might call it, I could ticket it in my mind. Santayana slightly tinctured with James, taking on a sudden feverish personal color. And my revulsion wasn't against your religion, but all religions. They're all more or less alike. You can't blame the human race for preferring some bright storyteller's dream or other to the black cold meaningless dark of the real universe. And if one has to make a choice among the durable fantasies, I don't know that your religion is worse than any. But I have an incurable temperamental preference for facts, however cold and nasty. That disposes of Reverend Airman, twentieth-century evangelist extraordinary.

"But I honestly can't ticket this new idea of mine. And believe me, Margie, I know the classic answers, I've read all the philosophers, soaked them up. You see, they all suffer from one fatal defect. They're philosophers. *That,* they can't help. That's the cage they can't get out of. They love words. Thinking is pleasant to them. They can't help conceiving the highest good in terms of intelligence and morality. They can't avoid it, that's their nature, they think in those terms the way a cat meows. Whereas the plain people in God's green world have little morality and less intelligence. People let the butterfly fanciers catch all the butterflies they want, and they let philosophers make up all the philosophies they want. It isn't as though the philosophers were thereby making sizable sums of money and sleeping with the prettiest women, which would be a serious matter. Philosophy seems to the world a highly involved form of sour grapes, by which very clever men prove to themselves that it really isn't worth while to make lots of money and get the pretty women. But the world's absolutely sincere in respecting and praising philosophers, Margie. Its attitude can best be summed up as follows: 'Philosophy is the real stuff all right. Everybody in the world ought to be a philosopher, except me.'

"Okay. Religion's an old worn-out comedy. Philosophy's the sour grapes of ineffectual geniuses. What's left? Anything? A great deal, obviously. The world moves, it's well organized, people rush around like mad, work hard, laugh—there's no chaos, no mass suicide. There must be *something* under the activity, some guiding sustaining idea, some driving belief we all have that keeps us going. What is it?

"You'll say Marxism contains the answer to all my questions. That is, you won't, but everybody else who's ever warmed the bench where your pretty behind is now resting would say that. But it's no answer at all.

Even granting that Karl with the Smith Brothers' beard really did figure out a better way to make the world's goods and pass them around—I don't grant it, and I can argue for a week against it, very effectively—but all right, let's say Marxism's absolutely true. The big question remains, why should anybody *bother* to be a communist? Why the dedication? Why the drudgery? Why improve society? Why do *anything*? What do we really want? What keeps us all moving—communists, capitalists, songwriters, little Marjorie Morgenstern too, for that matter, from West End Avenue, with a dream of an electric sign on West Forty-fourth Street blazing out *Marjorie Morningstar?*" He paused, looking intently into her face.

Marjorie said, "Well, I'll tell you this, if you've really answered the questions you've raised, you'll be the most famous man in the world."

"I've answered them."

"Well, come on. It's almost like a murder mystery by now, this big idea of yours."

Noel nodded, his eyes wide and gleaming, his fingers drumming on the table. "Can't wait to find out who's the Bat, hey? Well, it isn't Moses or Jesus, or any religious figure—and it isn't Marx, and it isn't Freud——"

"There's nobody left nowadays, is there?"

"There's the butler," Noel said. "The inconspicuous little character who really did it."

"What's his name, for heaven's sake?"

Chapter 30. NOEL'S THEORY

At that moment Mrs. Kleinschmidt set the steak before Noel on a thick cracked white plate, brown and sizzling, oozing red juice around a heap of potatoes. He seized knife and fork, cut the steak across the middle, and peered into the purple gash. "Very good. Perfect. Thank you. And a bottle of Guinness, please." He crushed out his cigar. "Margie, I propose to enjoy this steak more than I have any food in my life. Please eat something."

"No, thank you."

He ate a bite of steak. "Superb. Now then, listen carefully. If I were to get technical about what I'm writing, I'd say it reintroduces teleology as a major concept in dialectical analysis, which in itself is mighty startling, or would be in a professional journal, or I'm very much mistaken. But I'll spare you the academic verbiage. I think I can put it clearly and simply, and still be fair to it. I'm developing the concept, briefly, that the force that moves the world is a desire for Hits. *Hits.*"

"Hits?" Marjorie said, vaguely disappointed.

"Now wait, don't get that dumb stunned look. All important ideas sound trivial or wild the first time you hear them. Let me spell it out a bit. The central truth about human nature and conduct, I say, is hidden inside a fortress of four rings, four walls of illusion, Margie—remember that, and remember Noel Airman said it. Those four walls of illusion are: religion, philosophy, sex, and money. What worldly wisdom does is punch through those two mushy outer walls, and come upon the big thick bastions of pretty girls and dough. Whereupon it cries, with French gestures, 'Voilà! Zut alors! Parbleu! Here's the truth! The real inside story! We've found it!' It stops there. It never learns that the truth is further inside yet, and that you've still got to blast.

"No, ten million dollars in the bank, and all the pretty girls in bed with you, that's the final wisdom of the world. People talk religion, but they pursue sex and cash—that's the big secret of life. It's the entire point of French literature, for instance, the glory of which is supposed to be that it's wise and matter-of-fact and ironically honest, and lays bare the secrets of the human heart. Well, honey, no man is more saturated with this ironic view than I am. I've lived with it for a dozen years. In fact I've *lived* it, the way a monk lives a creed. I've found out the hard way that that's all it is—another creed, another hopeful story, another dreamy lie.

"The pretty girls break down first, once you try to grasp the dream. They're hard to get at, sure, but not nearly as hard as lots of money. Oh, I suppose if I'd been a little humpbacked spider I'd have tried to become a millionaire, and then gone out to buy women. But as it was, I simply worked myself into the circle of the pretty girls, the wolf in the fold. They really do herd like sheep, you know, in New York. They do the same things, go to the same parties, talk the same talk, all of them. I actually lived the dream life of the college boys and the bald businessmen. I had models, show girls, all I wanted, 'the real stuff,' as they would say, for years. There's nothing anybody can tell me about that answer—— I'm not annoying you, I hope?"

Marjorie with an effort took the frown off her face, and unclenched her fists on the table. "Well, you needn't elaborate the point, that's all."

With the shadow of a crooked grin he said, "But what I'm getting at should comfort you, if you're irritated. The pretty girls turn out to be as phony an answer as philosophy.

"Pretty girls are just girls, Margie, you see. That's what finally emerges. The most immoral slut among them, even a dumb roundheels like

Imogene, at heart just wants a fellow and a nest and clothes and furniture. What's more, they tend to be stupider than other girls, because being pretty makes life too easy for them. The day they sprout those charming breasts, they usually turn off their brains, and just bob along on the tide of attention and fun that starts up. Then after a while they're twenty-five and have to start thinking again. Because by that time the breasts are beginning to droop and the fuss is dying down. Of course by then it's too late, like as not. They're empty-headed fools, they can't read, they can't talk, they can't think, their emotions have been gutted by random sleeping around, and their lives are a shambles——"

Marjorie said, "You're a cruel hound, do you know? A cruel hound."

"Well, I don't want to offend you, Margie, truly I don't, but we're coming to the heart of the matter. The poor slobs in restaurants and theatres who used to goggle at me when I'd walk in with one of those girls were suffering for nothing, if they'd only known. They were thinking, 'Wowie! There goes the lucky guy, the guy with the answer.' But there's nothing special about a pretty girl, and that's God's truth. Once you're in bed with a girl, it hardly matters a damn what she looks like. Because you're too close to her, don't you see? She's just a pink warm expanse and a blurry face. The rest is all imagination. No matter who a man's bedmate is—his old boring wife, or the glamorous new model he's inveigled or bought—when he gets right down to it sex is just the same old clumsy business, Marjorie, that the birds and the bees and the dogs do. If he's in love, or thinks he's in love, then it's charming. If he's not in love, if he's just doing it to be doing it—Margie, I swear to you, with the prettiest living girl it's nothing. A man makes it something only by telling himself over and over, 'Look at me, look at me, I've got myself a model, a show girl,' whipping up his imagination to remind himself that he's achieved the world's desire. Because it's so ordinary in fact, so paltry, so trivial. If he has a shred of affection for his sagging old wife, or the homely girl next door he grew up with, he's better off in bed with her than with all the M-G-M starlets, one after another. That is the fact of the matter. Few people have a chance to find it out. And those who do, like me, usually shut up about it. Because they don't want to knock down their own achievements in their minds, they can't afford to. Happily, my self-esteem doesn't happen to rest on my box score with girls.

"Now you'll say that certain men spend their lifetime wallowing with one pretty girl after another—rich lechers, gangsters, Hollywood wolves. 'How come,' you'll say, 'these men never find out they're living a lie, chasing an empty delusion, if it's so obvious?'

"And now we're getting really warm. For them, it's no lie, no delusion at all. For them, you see, a model isn't a model, a show girl isn't a show girl. Sex is the least of their preoccupations, though they do nothing but talk and think about it. For a certain low-grade or immature or sick mind, a pretty girl is a Hit."

"Noel, I hate to interrupt you, but your steak's getting cold. Take a few bites."

She was scared by the flash of anger across his face. He struck the table with his fist. "I'll eat when I'm *bloody* good and ready. What's the matter, is this too hard for you? I don't think I've used a single three-syllable word. Hell, I'd be better off telling all this to a turtle." He splashed Guinness into the empty glass and drank thirstily.

Marjorie now decided that there was something seriously wrong with Noel. She had frightening forebodings that he might be on the verge of a mental collapse. He looked sick. He fell on the steak and began devouring it with unhealthy voracity. She said, "Dear, I'm fascinated, but you said you were starving, and you *look* starved, that's all——"

He ate in silence for a while, washing down the meat with Guinness. "Okay, don't apologize. I shouldn't have flared. I'm tense and tired, just don't interrupt me again. And don't go blank on me. This takes some telling and some listening.

"All this evolved, obviously, from a process of self-searching. I was asking myself, All right, let's get down to it, just once in this life. What do you honestly and truly want? Do you want to marry Marjorie Morgenstern, for instance? You're in love with her——" (Marjorie's breath caught, and she listened to what followed with a throbbing ache in her breast.) "She may not be the most beautiful girl in the world, but she is in your silly eyes, and that's all that counts. . . . Well, after some hard thinking the answer was no, I don't want to marry Marjorie Morgenstern—certainly not with my whole heart. Okay, next question, do you want to sleep with her? Answer, yes and no—the chains and the mess would be the same as if I married her. Maybe more so."

"Well, thanks for that, anyway." Marjorie's gay tone broke to hoarseness in the middle of the sentence.

Noel went on, "Is there some other woman you really want, then? Miss America? Hedy Lamarr, maybe? No, we've been through all that. Professional beauties are dull people, and actresses are hard-boiled guys inside lovely bodies. Well, then, down comes bastion three, sex.—You understand, we've already levelled religion and philosophy."

"I understand, dear."

"Good. We proceed to the last bastion. Money. Cash. *L'argent,* the great French secret of secrets, which God knows the French actually do revere like religious fanatics, as though it were the last inner mystery of a creed. Now, I asked myself, is that the ultimate answer, really? Is

Balzac the last word? And after a few minutes I burst out laughing to realize how completely I *myself* refuted that idea. Margie, you know that the path to money, all the money I can ever use, is open to me in Sam Rothmore's office. Sam, sad old bastard, wants a son. I can have the job by simply showing up on time and answering the mail. In time I can be a millionaire like him, own paintings and black Cadillacs. But I hate the whole prospect so, I've been fighting it by being a sloven and a washout. I didn't start working in his office because I wanted money, but because I thought maybe you wanted it. And not even because *you* want it so much. But because your mother estimates men by their earning power, and I was just piqued enough by this whole thing to want to show her I could beat old steady Dr. Shapiro at raking in the shekels, as well as in all the more important ways——"

"I thought we were going to forget Dr. Shapiro——"

"And the real motive under it all probably was that I suspected, as I still suspect, that you have the same ideas as your mother deep down. And that they'll emerge like rocks at low tide, when the dream of being Marjorie Morningstar ebbs."

"You're drawing a lovely picture of me, I must say."

"Please don't be idiotic enough to take this personally, Margie, will you? I'm following the thread of an idea."

"Oh, I see. Following the thread of an idea."

"Yes. Shut up, please. I thought of all the clichés. 'It's not money, but what you can buy with it. Money is power. Money is security. Money is freedom.' And so forth. Well, then, whatever the last bastion is, evidently it's not money, is it? It's freedom, or power, or security, or whatever money really represents. We haven't come to the prime mover, the uncaused cause, of human nature. As for the French and all their ironic wisdom about sex and cash—well, they're not only erotic lunatics, as Tolstoy said long ago, they're pecuniary lunatics, that's the long and short of it, and so to hell with Balzac. I don't particularly want money—or, rather yes, sure, I want it, the way I want a dinner tonight, so that I can go on being Noel Airman, comfortably and pleasantly. But what does *Noel Airman* really want? In common with everybody else? That is the question.

"When the answer suddenly broke over me, Margie, I got up and danced. I swear I danced around on the steps of the Forty-second Street Library, where I'd gotten to with all my walking, hours and hours. I'd been sitting there on a stone bench by the lions, all alone in a black mist—you could barely see the street lamps, just little yellow blurs, it was so foggy—it must have been four in the morning. Well, I got up, and danced and capered between those two lions, Marjorie, like the devil on Bald Mountain.

"You see, by great good luck I'd had the crucial clue that same afternoon.

"Imogene brought me down to earth, you know, out of that religious seizure I was having, and I remembered that my publishers had had *Old Moon Face* for a couple of weeks, and I hadn't heard anything. I phoned them. They said they'd been trying to get in touch with me for days. Well, baby, the song's a dead-sure hit. Crosby is going to record it. Benny Goodman, too. It'll be played everywhere. My publisher says it's bigger than *Raining Kisses*——"

"Noel! How marvelous!"

He squeezed briefly the hand she put on his. "I can't make less than ten thousand. Margie, it isn't the money, I swear. I know that by being a good boy I can make more in the Paramount hierarchy than I ever will writing songs and shows. But—and this is where the French are so cock-eyed—five thousand earned by a hit song makes me feel richer than fifty thousand earned at a Paramount desk. At the thought of having a hit again after four years, I tell you I'm filled with a happiness that's sweet and pure and total. That's the inspiration that came to me, Marjorie. What makes Noel Airman purely and wholly happy? Answer: a Hit. Nothing else. A Hit is beauty bare. And if you ask me what I really want out of life after this, I have to tell you I want nothing, really, but another Hit. And after that, another Hit. And for the rest of my life, Hits. I'm being honest. This is the filthy bottom truth that people will never say about themselves, and half of them won't even believe. But that's the fire that will never burn out, Margie, it's the worm that never dies.

"Don't you see that that's all money means to the old mumbling billionaires? Why do they keep working and scheming? Why do they lie awake nights figuring out new mergers? They can't measure their own security and power, it's so colossal. They could roll in golden excess for fifty years—champagne baths, diamond dog collars, harems of blondes, they could paper their walls with Rembrandts—it wouldn't begin to dent their pile. Yet they go on making more, and more, and more. Why? Because every time the total of their net worth jumps up, it's a Hit. And *THAT* is the prime mover, the uncaused cause, the center of human nature and conduct, Margie.

"I tell you, with this piece once in your hand, the whole puzzle of life falls apart. It's like calculus, or the theory of evolution, this one idea—it absolutely opens up the secrets of the universe. Not the physical, the social universe. Freud's sex drive is foolishness compared to it. This thing only grows stronger and stronger and stronger with the years. It's strongest in old age. Look at a politician, eighty years old, making a speech to a crowd in the rain. What's driving him? Not ambition. He's been a senator for forty years. He can never be anything more. But by winning this election he can have one more Hit. He'd rather die of pneumonia than risk missing the Hit. Take a minister with a white head, preaching humility and selflessness and meekness—why is he rolling his voice so beautifully? Why is the sermon typed up in extra-large type, so he won't have to squint, while he preaches forgetfulness of self? He wants his sermon to be a Hit. Don't you suppose the selfless mother, scrimping and starving to send her pretty daughter through college, regards this girl as the great Hit of her life? Don't you suppose a communist is making himself part of the great Hit of history? Take a dried-up old skeptic like Santayana. If life's really meaningless and valueless, just a pretty dream, why bother to write about it? Why say life is meaningless in twenty volumes full of exquisite meaning? Obviously because every volume means another Hit for old Santayana—no other reason is possible. Turn wherever you will on the human scene, this thing governs. It's as universal as gravitation, it's as all-pervading as Spinoza's God. . . ." He fell silent, staring wildly at her, and she felt terribly nervous. "Well? I could go on and on, but why should I? That's it. Rough, hurried, told all wrong. Does it mean anything to you? Does it convey one thousandth of the light to you that it does to me?"

"Noel, it's absolutely brilliant——"

His face shone. "It really does get over to you. It really does? It does sound like something?"

"Oh yes, yes indeed."

"Thank God." He looked at the knife and fork clutched forgotten in his hands, grease hardening on them in little bubbles. He cut into the steak, then threw down the knife and fork and pushed the plate away. "What on earth is this great bloody hunk of a dead cow doing under my nose? It's the most repulsive thing I've ever seen." He pounded on the table with his fist and yelled, "Mrs. Kleinschmidt! Take this away! Bring me a drink."

Marjorie said, "Noel, eat something, please do, you need it."

"Marge, if I eat another bite of that purple horror, I'll go mad. I'd as soon eat a boiled child. How can people eat meat, anyway? I swear, I'm going to turn vegetarian."

The woman started to mutter when she saw the uneaten steak, but after one glance at Noel's face she subsided, carried it off, and brought him a double drink of rye. He drank half of it. "Tell me more about how good my idea is, Marge. You can't imagine how I need to hear it. I feel like Galileo the first time he saw Jupiter's moons. The man must have run around like a scared rat, to find someone else to look through his telescope and tell him he wasn't crazy."

"Noel, what you're saying isn't crazy in the least. It's absolutely true. You're proving that what really drives people is nothing but egotism. Everybody knows that's so, actually. And the way you put it, it's even——"

Some of the gladness went out of Noel's expression. "Egotism? Who said anything about egotism? I never mentioned the word egotism, not once."

"Well no, but this hunger for hits, what is it but just plain egotism? You're completely right, Noel. The more I study people, the more I realize——" She broke off. He was covering his face with his hands, groaning. "Now what's wrong, for heaven's sake, darling?"

He took his hands away and looked at her for a long time, his face dead gray. "Margie—Margie, my dear good girl—to say that people are driven by egotism is probably the dullest and most obvious banality that the human mind can ever achieve. Don't tell me that what I've been working on for four hysterical days and telling you for twenty solid minutes amounts to no more than that. Don't . . ."

"Noel, I don't think it's a banal idea at all. It's a very shrewd observation."

His staring sunken black-shadowed eyes were making her more and more uneasy.

He said, "I daresay I skimmed over it, left out all the fine points, ruined it in the telling, but still—Margie, you should have gotten more out of it than that. This idea has absolutely nothing to do with egotism, nothing at all, I swear. Why, the difference between the passion for Hits and egotism—egotism is solipsist, don't you see, Hits are externalized, that's the whole point—maybe I should have made that a hell of a lot clearer—I'm sure I have in my writing——" His voice was fading. He seemed to be talking to himself. "But you're right, by God, the thing actually does skirt the most ghastly and empty banality, doesn't it? If I don't make that one difference crystal-clear the whole thing is nothing but the vapidest college-boy philosophizing and—how fundamental *is* that difference? Isn't it just a question of projection, isn't the externalizing just a secondary mechanism?—No, no." He glared and hit the table with both fists. "It's my punishment for being so damn eager, that's all, for talking technical philosophy to a girl. Margie, it's not your fault. I don't mean to scare you. Maybe you've let all the air out with your hatpin, but I don't think so. I'll still get this thing down on paper and show it to somebody who *knows*——"

"Noel, I didn't mean to discourage you. On the contrary, I really think you've hit on something extraordinary, I really do, dear——"

He smiled at her and drank off the rye. He coughed a little and slumped back on the bench. "Whew."

"I think you should go home and get some sleep, a whole lot of sleep, Noel, before you do any more work. It'll come out better, you know it will, in the end. You're just burning up your last resources of nervous energy, and living on alcohol, and that's no way to write anything really good."

"I have been in quite a state," he said, and his voice was low, weary, and relaxed. "That must be fairly obvious. I couldn't have slept these past few days if I'd wanted to—— Marjorie, have you ever thought of a joke in your dreams that seemed the funniest and smartest joke in the world? And then awakened and realized that it was absolutely silly, made no sense at all?"

"Lots of times, but——"

"It's barely possible that this whole idea, this rigmarole about Hits, is just another manic fantasy, after all, a mishmash of Adler, Nietzsche, La Rochefoucauld, and who knows what else—just another lulling hallucination to keep my nerves from going PAING! like a thousand breaking piano wires——"

"It isn't, Noel, don't believe that——"

"I won't, don't worry, not yet. But if it turns out that way—well, hell, I wouldn't be surprised if the earth goes on turning. On the whole, I'm glad I got to tell it to you, before I left. The feminine reaction always has its cold-water validity, tempering if nothing else——"

"Before you left? Where are you going?"

He sat up and took her hand, looking at her with a sad smile. She said after a terrible moment or two, "Noel, what is it? Where are you going?"

"Marjorie Morgenstern, love of my life, we're through. Isn't that obvious to you? We're not going to see each other after today. We wouldn't have seen each other today if you hadn't come barging down to my apartment, and if Imogene hadn't thought you were a grocery boy. I'm going to Mexico, probably Sunday morning, driving down with a sculptor friend of mine, Phil Yates. Just as soon as I finish a draft of what I'm writing, and get an advance from my publisher to buy us a jalopy. Bye-bye Rothmore, bye-bye Marjorie, bye-bye the whole bourgeois dream. It was great fun, as the fellow says, but it was just one of those things." His glance was kind, melancholy. "Are you desolate?"

She felt very little pain and, strangely, not much surprise. "No. In fact, it's quite all right, Noel. It's probably for the best."

"You do think so?"

"I suppose so. I hope so. It's a little sudden, but that's all right, too."

"Kill or cure, Marjorie. Clean break. It's the only way."

"I'm sure you know all about how to do these things."

"You're going to be bitter?"

"No. Really not."

"Don't. Some of it's been harrowing, I know, but we've had a marvelous time, on the whole, and we haven't maimed each other for life—and we're at an absolute impasse, really, there's nothing else to do——"

"Noel, it's all right. I'll live. It's far from unexpected." She was astonished to find herself putting a handkerchief to her eyes, and she stopped it. "I've thought of making this break myself often, believe me. I sort of wish I'd done it first, that's all. No girl likes to be kicked out. You can understand that."

"Marjorie, you're kicking me out. You know you are."

"Am I? I guess I've got this conversation turned around in my mind."

"I've never been through a battle like this in my life. You've beaten me." He looked haggard, almost forty, she thought, slumped with his hands jammed in the pockets of his shabby overcoat, his long hair disorderly, thick blond bristles all along his jaw. "You never gave an inch. It had to be on your terms or none at all. Well, no, that isn't quite so. At South Wind you started out like any other girl. But ever since your uncle died, it's been this way. No girl ever thrust terms on me before. You've made me try to conform, you've actually done that. But it's hopeless, Marjorie. It's been driving me slowly out of my head. I'm still a little panicky at the narrowness of my escape. I've been in a panic ever since that seder at your house. Going through black depressions and golden exaltations like a real nut. It's got to end, it's got to." His voice trembled.

"That seder. My mother's bright idea——"

"Brighter than you think, maybe. Ask your mother what her real motive was, some day. Some day when this is all long in the past, Margie, and she's dandling her third grandson on her knee, on your lawn in New Rochelle—little Ronald Shapiro—you ask her——"

"All right, shut up!" Marjorie said. "One blessing at least is that I'll hear no more now of that damned Dr. Shapiro."

Noel said, "You're right. I keep harping like a stupid boor on one old dull joke. I beg your pardon."

"Just remember this, Noel, I never told you to go to work for Sam Rothmore. You did it all by yourself. All I said was that while you worked for him it was only fair that you do a decent job. I think going to work at Paramount may have been a terrible mistake. That's what's been depressing you. You should have stuck to your composing, and not lost faith in yourself. I never lost faith in you. I still haven't. I told you that song was going to be a big hit. And I'll tell you something else. *Princess Jones* is going to materialize, and it's going to be glorious. You're going to be tremendously successful on Broadway, probably in a year or two, if only you work at it. You're on the verge." His face was coming to life again. He sat up and his eyes brightened. She began to put on her coat. "Only you'd better stick to your writing, and not go off on any more wild-goose chases like being a rabbi, or inventing new philosophies about Hits, or whatever. I wish you the best of luck, I swear to God I do. I'll never regret knowing you. It's been an education. I've got to get home. Goodbye."

"Wait." He stopped her as she moved to get up.

"Really, I've got to go, Noel. Mom's in bed with a cold——"

"You sit."

She did not fight hard against the push. "What is it? I can only stay another minute. It's all over——"

"There's a few more things we'd better get straight. So long as we're being frank with each other, and you're regarding this as part of your education. Which is an astonishingly sensible way to look at it. But you're a sensible girl, unusually sensible. Your advice to me is very acute. Thanks for it, and here's some in return. If I were you, I'd forget Marjorie Morningstar. I've been rough and mean with you about that, purposely. The fact is, you do have some talent. You really do. You make a sweet exciting figure on the stage. Your voice is weak and thin, but that can be corrected. For someone without any training, you have a surprising flair for projecting a character. Only——"

Her eyes were moistening. "Dog, you might have said this long ago——"

"Marjorie, my sweet, you're not an actress. You're not built to take the strain and smut and general rattiness of a stage life. You're a good little Jewish beauty, with a gift for amateur theatricals. Take my advice, direct all the temple plays in New Rochelle, and be the star in them, and let it go at that——"

"You supercilious son of a bitch, *I'm not going to live in New Rochelle.*"

He could not have looked more comically astounded if she had flipped up her skirts in his face. "Dear me, Marjorie! Such language."

"Any other advice for me, Father Time?"

"You're angry."

"Oh, not in the least. I'm just swimming in pleasure at being jilted and patronized and called a stupid bourgeois Jewess seven different ways all in a few breaths——"

She stopped because he caught her wrists in a bony cold very painful grasp. He said gruffly, "I love you. Don't you understand, you little torturer? You've executed the vengeance of your non-existent God on me. I've never loved or wanted any girl in my life as I do you. But I'm not going to commit suicide to have you, nor put myself in a booby hatch, nor turn myself into a nice tame stepson of Sam Rothmore. You're an absolute infant. You don't know what you've done to me. You've damn near destroyed me. I ache with pleasure right now, just touching your skin. What does it mean to you? Nothing. You're ten years away from understanding passion, and nothing can hurry you into fathoming it, absolutely nothing. It'll all come in time. Your passion will force itself up out of the stony soil of your Jewish prejudices, like a tree, and some unknown dolt of a steady-earning doctor or lawyer will pluck the fruit. And I'll be old or dead, or for all I know rich and famous, as you say, but I'll never never have Marjorie Morgenstern, and she's all I want."

She was crying, and she could see Mrs. Kleinschmidt watching them from the barroom, but she didn't care. "Why did you ever come back to me? It was all over after South Wind. Why are you whining? You know you started it all up again. You did it."

"Sure I did. And I made the one frightful blunder that's all but driven me insane. I resolved to play the game by your asinine rules—to be faithful to you, can you imagine that? Not to touch a girl. That's been at the root of this whole series of aberrations. I've been in a state of unnatural tension for months. It's served to halo you with a ridiculous glamor, and it's made all kinds of idiotic behavior seem normal and even spectacularly clever, like going to work for Rothmore. It's been nothing but collegiate sex hunger, turning a grown man inside out. I doubt I'd have had the courage to this moment to call it quits with you if Imogene hadn't come along and broken that spell. Now at least I can think and analyze without a rosy haze of sex yearning to discolor all the values—— What's the matter? What are you staring at?" He pushed her down as she started to rise stiffly, like a machine. "Good Lord, don't tell me you believed Imogene! Don't tell me you really thought for five seconds that I've been sleeping upstairs!"

"I did—I did——"

He made a despairing sound. "I thought you were being really subtle, pretending to ignore it, letting me sweat. Marjorie, how childish and unrealistic can you be? Imogene and I have been on a racketing sex binge for days. I've never been through anything like it. She's learned things in Oklahoma that I——"

His teeth felt hard and sharp against her palm as she slapped him with all her strength. She stood. "I'm in love with you, you rotten tramp," she said. "That's why I believed her. Get your feet out of my way. I'm going home."

He was looking at her with a lopsided grin as she slipped past him. "Fair enough. Goodbye, my love."

She turned on him. "You're a disgrace. To your father, to yourself, to the Jews, to anybody who has any part in you. I'll never stop thanking God for being free of you. Even if you become the most famous man in the world. Goodbye, Noel."

He slumped grinning on the bench, dishevelled, dingy, looking as desirable as ever. Her hands wanted to touch his hair. She ran out of the saloon. It had begun to snow, in a queer bluish twilight. With snow-flakes whirling about her, stinging her hot cheeks and making her eyes blink, she ran two blocks to the subway. She rode uptown for fifteen minutes before realizing, when a colored woman came into the car with snow clinging to her rabbit fur collar, that it was strange to be having snow in April.

Chapter 31. DR. SHAPIRO

Noel's first letter, lying at the door in the morning mail a couple of weeks later, gave her a frightening throb of gladness.

She had been dragging through the days, waking to mental misery, walking with it, and lying down with it; seeing him in crowds and in magazine illustrations, picturing him as the hero in the novels from the lending library; telling herself she was well out of it, and believing it, and yet no less miserable for this belief. She hurried with the letter into her bedroom, like a cat with a stolen fish head; closed the door, and stood staring at the envelope, passing her fingers over the thin air-mail paper and the gaudy green and yellow Mexican stamp. Then she read it. It was a long breezy typewritten account of his automobile trip, with enthusiastic descriptions of Mexican scenery and food. She skipped through the paragraphs, searching for a line about herself and himself. But there was nothing. It was headed "Hi, darling," and signed "Love, Noel." She flung the letter on the bed. Later she read it over and over. She tore it up after a few days without having answered it or noted his address in Mexico City; nevertheless, she knew the address.

For weeks thereafter she kept watching the mail. She knew it was irrational to hope for mail from him without answering his letter, but her conduct had little to do with logic.

She haunted the producers' offices and the drugstore more assiduously than ever, and with as little result as ever. But she had learned by now that discouragement was the bread of Broadway, and she kept at her rounds; if nothing else, the pain of being ignored by the theatre distracted her from the pain of having been dropped by Noel.

During this time Marjorie's evenings filled with dates, once the "kids" (as the young unemployed actors and actresses at the drugstore called each other) found out that she was free. She tried necking once or twice, to get her mind off Noel, but it was disheartening flat foolishness, and she gave it up. She went docilely to temple dances, crowding her date calendar still further with young lawyers, businessmen, and doctors. The contrast between her temple friends and the "kids" made for what slight amusement she could find in the days. Marjorie didn't encourage any of them. She accepted their invitations calmly, and dined or danced with them placidly, and yielded a kiss at her door, after some formal reluctance, in a way that made it seem an old-fashioned courtesy.

Oddly enough, the one person among all her new dates who woke a stir of interest in her was a man named Dr. Morris Shapiro. She met him at a Zionist lecture to which she was more or less dragged by her parents. When he was introduced to her, she inadvertently burst out laughing on hearing the name. Then to cover her embarrassment at this startling rudeness, she went out of her way to be pleasant to him; and he soon was taking her out every week or so. He turned out to be not a bad fellow, about thirty-two, with an excellent sense of humor and a sharp mind. After a while she began to enjoy his company, in a fashion, and to overlook his scanty hair, black-ringed eyes, and puffy pallor. He was obviously and frankly smitten with her. Eventually she told him why she had laughed at him at their first meeting; he pleased her by being genuinely amused. He said that he was grateful to Noel for his clairvoyance, and stood ready to fulfill Marjorie's destiny any time she said the word.

"I might believe you were my destiny if your name were Max," Marjorie answered. "That's the big discrepancy."

"The importance of being Max," he said. "Why didn't you tell me? I'll go to court and get it changed, if that's all you want."

She laughed at him.

Noel's second letter came when she had almost given up looking at the mail. There it was at last, the bright Mexican stamp poking through the usual trash of bills, charity requests, and circulars. It was another brisk typewritten travelogue. There was one faint personal touch in the last line: "Be civilized and write a guy a postcard, won't you? Don't be melodramatic. Nobody loves me. Noel."

She didn't tear up this one.

Noel's song had been published, and it was a great success; she was hearing it at night clubs and restaurants and on the radio. Inevitably, whenever the tune started up, she would see Noel at the piano in Sam Rothmore's inner office, with his long blond hair falling on his forehead, the blue eyes blazing. She fought off the temptation to write him for two weeks. Late one night, coming home from an evening of dancing with Morris Shapiro, in a lively mood (she had landed a summer-stock job that day), with the strains of *Old Moon Face* running in her head, she sat at her desk and dashed off this note:

Dear Noel:

Nobody loves you indeed. I pity you. I suppose the two señoritas sitting on your lap as you read this don't count. Give them my best.

Your Mexican trip sounds fascinating, and I wish I could figure out some respectable way to join you, but I can't. So you'll have to be satisfied with your sculptor and the señoritas. And, of course, your memories. By the way, they're playing *Moon Face* all over town, and it sounds just as good as it did that day in Sam Rothmore's office. Congratulations. I guess you're rolling in royalties.

I've moved up a bit in the world too. All the pavement-pounding has at last paid off, after a fashion. I'm going to the Rip Van Winkle Theatre for the summer. I guess you know all about the place. Katharine Hepburn graduated from there, so why not Marjorie Morningstar? All the kids say it's the best of the summer theatres. I'm the new heroine of the drugstore. Seems I practically broke into Cliff Rymer's office, took him by the throat, and made him listen to me read *Pygmalion*. I really did. Desperation makes one do strange things. I'm only an apprentice actress, so I won't get paid, but at least I'll get my room and board. I'll be off my parents' backs, thank God. Most important, I'll be *acting* at last.

Yes, I'm still chasing that dream, or tropism, or whatever you called it, and I still say you'll live to apologize to me backstage on my opening night.

However, it may amuse you to know that my love life now includes a Dr. Shapiro. There would be something eerie about it, except that his name isn't Max, it's Morris. I told him about your standard joke, and he offered to change his name to Max, the fool. But don't worry, your predictions aren't coming true. Dr. S. is great fun (we've just been dancing) but it's still Marjorie Morningstar for me, I'm afraid, unless our medical friend acquires a white horse somewhere and carries me off. Which he may be capable of, at that.

Well, you rascal, have yourself a time. Don't drink too much tequila, or you might wake up married to a tubby little señorita with thick ankles one bright morning. And wouldn't that be a sad end to the Masked Marvel!

In signing it, she paused a long time. At last she wrote *Sincerely*; but once on paper, it looked too stiff and had a hint of hurt pride in it. So she recopied the second sheet of the letter, just to be able to sign it *Best*.

She left the letter on the desk and went to bed. In the morning she hesitated over mailing it. She knew that the only sensible course was to throw away Noel's letters, and never write to him. But the digs about Dr. Shapiro seemed pretty neat, even by daylight. She sent the letter.

The same day a printed invitation to Wally Wronken's college graduation exercises came in the mail, together with a note on scratch-pad paper: *I'm not asking you to be my date. Just come. Please.*

Slightly curious to see poor Wally in his cap and gown, she went to the commencement. To her surprise, he was the salutatorian, and he received a minor prize for French studies. On the platform he looked pallid, terribly earnest, and not nearly as young as before. After the exercises she went up to him, as his sister was unfolding a small Kodak, and shook his hand. The parents and sister looked amazed. "I was very proud of you, Wally. I'm sure your family was, too."

Wally said, "Ruth, take a picture of me and Margie. Just one, Marge. All right?" Before she could say anything he had her by the waist, and was turning her toward the camera. The sister, with a grudging glance, snapped the picture. "There, you're compromised forever," Wally said.

"Send me a print. I'll probably show it proudly to my grandchildren," Marjorie said.

The print came in the mail just before she went to Sleepy Hollow. On the back was written, *World renowned actress, just before her rise to fame. Exhaustive research fails to reveal identity of strange man in cap and gown with glasses and long nose.* She laughed and dropped it in the rosewood box where she kept favored souvenirs. She meant to write a note thanking him, but it slipped her mind.

About the middle of June, she received a mimeographed instruction pamphlet from the Rip Van Winkle Theatre which contained an unpleasant surprise. There was a page and a half of cloudy verbiage on the subject of money, but what it boiled down to was that Marjorie had to pay fifteen dollars a week for room and board. At the end of the summer, if box-office receipts were normal, all this subsistence money would be paid back to her, with a bonus, the size of which would depend on work performed. Katharine Hepburn, the pamphlet pointed out, had earned a bonus of seven hundred dollars, when she was utterly unknown.

Marjorie was appalled at having to ask her parents for fifteen dollars a week. But somehow she choked it out at dinner that night. The father and mother looked grave; then Mr. Morgenstern, with one of his infrequent wistful smiles, reached over and patted Marjorie's hand. "My God, don't look so guilty. It won't kill us."

"Oh, I feel so useless, Pop, such an overgrown parasite——"

"It'll be all right."

"I'll earn it all back, I swear I will. I'll bring back a bonus."

"Say, you'll probably bring back seven hundred dollars, like Katharine Hepburn."

"If she lasts out the summer," said Mrs. Morgenstern.

So Marjorie went off to the Rip Van Winkle Theatre. Six weeks later, on an extremely muggy August afternoon, she appeared bag and baggage at the Morgenstern apartment, looking flushed, tired, and dirty. She vanished into her room with hardly a word of greeting to her mother. At the dinner table she showed up fresh and elegant, but full of mysterious wrath, and coughing violently from time to time. Her answers to questions about her work at the summer theatre and her reasons for coming home were short and uninformative. She kept up this lowering silence for a couple of days, and spent most of the time on her bed in a housecoat, reading and coughing. The cough gradually improved, but her mood didn't seem to.

It was Wally Wronken to whom she finally unburdened herself. He came in from South Wind to see his parents off to Europe. With an evening to spend alone in town, he forlornly called Marjorie's parents to ask how she was, and found himself talking to her. She readily accepted his happy stammered invitation to dinner.

"I'm still furious," she said to him. "I can hardly bring myself to discuss it." They were at a small expensive steak house in the theatre district. "I know what you probably think and what my parents *certainly* think—that I ran blubbering home because the work was too hard and I wasn't getting all the star parts——"

Wally said solemnly, "Marge, I know you better than that."

After a dangerous glance at him she went on, "Well, I don't much care what anybody thinks. But believe me, I stayed on for weeks after I saw I ought to quit, simply because I didn't want to have that said about me. I was going to stick the season out no matter what. But then Morris came up last Saturday and when——"

"Morris? That's a new name. Who's Morris?"

"Don't you know about Morris? Well, he's a very nice guy, a doctor— but never mind pulling such a long face, Wally, it's nothing like that. And it's about time you stopped all that phony languishing, anyway. You're getting too old for Marchbanks."

"Curious, isn't it? And you're getting too young for Candida."

"Thank you. I'm beginning to need such compliments—— Anyway— listen, Wally, I worked like a dog at the Rip Van Winkle. You can ask any of the kids who were there. I was up late, night after night, sewing costumes, carpentering—I turned out to be surprisingly handy with a hammer and saw. You never know what you can do till you try——"

Wally wrinkled his long nose at her. "Hammer and saw? *You?*"

"Dear, mostly what I did at Rip Van Winkle was build scenery. Oh, and nail up double-decker bunks, and repair the roof when it rained in on us, and such things——"

"Marge, don't they have men up there?"

"Don't talk to me about men, Wally. That is, actor-men. They're an aberration of Nature. I swear to you, Wally, compared to the average actor, a peacock is a beast of burden. I think they exhaust themselves with all that running a comb through their hair. You'd think they'd gouge tracks in their scalps with those combs. And a girl is supposed to fall down curling with ecstasy if one of them so much as asks her what time it is. You see, there are four girls for every man at the Rip. Maybe it's that way at all summer theatres. I don't know—— Anyway, where was I?—Well, I found myself working like a slave, that's all, my hands all blisters, no sleep—and mind you, I *like* working on scenery and costumes, I like anything remotely connected with the theatre, but there's such a thing as enough——"

"There were other girls, weren't there? How did you get so loaded with work?"

"It wasn't me alone. Me and a couple of others. That's Cliff Rymer's fiendishly clever system. Oh, I tell you he's got it down pat. He'll work the last drop of blood out of a girl, a girl with any real desire to act, that is. He hardly bothers the boys. Obviously he hates girls. He used to stand around and watch us hammering flats together in the broiling sun, a couple of girls in filthy old jeans and halters, pouring sweat, hair hanging, looking like witches—and he'd just stand there, with a look on his face like a kid pulling wings off a butterfly. He dangles a star part under your nose, see? A star part in one of the September shows. Like for me, Eliza in *Pygmalion,* my old standby, which they're doing on Labor Day. Another girl was on the hook the same way for Anna in *Anna Christie.* Naturally, if you think there's a chance, you want to please and impress Cliff Rymer. You're about ready to *die* to impress him. So, you work, you smile, chin up, you take walk-ons, you kill yourself building sets, you smile sweetly selling tickets or working as an usher—and it gets mighty cold at night in an evening dress in that barn in Sleepy Hollow, let me tell you. I caught the most horrible cough. It kept me out of shows, but not out of carpentering, of course. You can hammer and saw between coughs. And Mr. Rymer is pleased and drops another word about Eliza and you're happy——"

The waiter set steaks before them. Marjorie said, "This is something they don't serve at the Rip. Gad, the food! A herd of pigs would have gone on strike, but the apprentice actresses didn't dare—we practically lived on peanuts and Hershey bars . . . Mm! These rolls! Aren't they exquisite? Our breakfast rolls seemed to come out of a quarry—cold, hard, jagged. You'd tear your gums eating them. I'm not exaggerating, Wally. You'd bite at a roll and there'd be blood on it. Oh well. This is a good steak."

"Did you get to play any parts?"

"A few bits, yes——" She put her napkin over her mouth and had a paroxysm of coughing. "Gad, I thought I was over this. I haven't coughed all day. Morris had a real fit when he heard me coughing. He's a doctor, you know. It was Saturday afternoon, and I was staying in bed trying to shake the thing off so I wouldn't cough during the show. I was supposed to be an usher. Morris said if I left the bed to be an usher that night he'd never talk to me again. When he saw me come into the theatre in a bare-back evening dress he just turned purple. So we had this big battle afterward. He called me an imbecile, said I was just being victimized, and so forth. Well, my back was up, you know, so I called him a Philistine. But he was absolutely right. You see, I'd found out just a couple of days before that I couldn't possibly play Eliza. The part had been promised way back in June to a girl named Sally Trent—you know, the blonde who did that wonderful drunk scene in the last Kaufman play—— I didn't have a prayer. I never had had a prayer. Oh, I hated, really really hated, Wally, to leave my dad's money in Cliff Rymer's little fat paws. No refunds, of course, if you quit. But I've figured that out. I'll get a job, if it's scrubbing floors, and pay Dad back."

Wally said, "Rymer has a fine thing there. He'll never run out of slave labor, will he? No matter how many he disillusions, there's always a new crop of girls every year dying to go on the stage."

"There sure is. Noel calls it a tropism of middle-class girls. He seems to be right. I think ninety per cent of the kids at the Rip were exactly that, creatures obeying a tropism. For all I know, I'm one too. By the way, I was Marjorie Morningstar at long last——"

"Congratulations——"

"Thanks. I have six playbills to prove it. Though I'm an usher on three of them."

"How is Noel?" Wally said, carefully pouring the coffee.

"Oh, fine."

"In Mexico, isn't he?"

"Yes."

"Heard from him?"

"Sure."

"How long is he going to be there?"

"Haven't the vaguest idea. Until his royalties on *Old Moon Face* run out, I guess."

After a moment's pause Wally said, "What's all this about his going to Hollywood?"

With a pang of astonishment, which she did her best to hide, she said, "Hollywood? That's news to me."

"He wrote Greech that he's got a Hollywood offer. He's going there when he gets tired of Mexico."

"Well, how nice."

"Strange he didn't write you about it."

"Strange? How so?"

"Margie, have you and Noel broken up?"

Marjorie sipped coffee. "There was nothing to break up, Wally. Noel Airman's just a pleasant ghost. Now you see him, now you don't. I had a marvelous time with him, and I wouldn't have missed it for worlds. But he's melted into thin air now, so far as I'm concerned, and a good thing too, no doubt——" She broke off in surprise, seeing Wally pull a pack of Lucky Strikes from his pocket. "What happened to the Kools?"

"I don't know. Guess I've graduated." His little furtive hunched gesture of lighting was gone; he struck a match and puffed. She had noticed too that he looked directly at her, instead of at the ceiling or the tablecloth. "Margie, why don't you come back to South Wind for the rest of the summer?"

"Me? South Wind?"

"Greech would take you back in a minute. He talks about you a lot."

"I'll never go back there, Wally."

His large brown eyes, looking straight at her, were clever, almost girlishly soft, behind the glasses. "Why?"

"I never will."

"Well, of course, it would be too good to be true, having you to myself up there."

"Haven't you graduated from me, as well as Kools? I'm sure you have. You just like to make these melancholy sounds."

Wally said, "Maybe you're a symbol of some kind. I admit it's gone on too long. I seem to be evolving from Marchbanks to Major Dobbin. The funny part of it is, Margie—and this is where the books are so wrong —Major Dobbin can turn around and be Heathcliff to some other girl."

"Well, well. How are you doing as Heathcliff?"

"Not complaining."

"Good for you," Marjorie said.

"I'm also writing a brilliant farce. Greech mistakenly thinks I'm coming back next year. Next year I'll be famous, and rich, and independent. In fact, can't I beat you into insensibility with my prowess and my prospects, and drag you off by the hair to my cave?"

"You almost sound like Noel."

"Let's go home."

"Wouldn't you like to take me dancing? I'm having fun."

"Why, of course. I'll take you anywhere you say, till dawn, you know that."

"The thing about you is, Wally, you probably don't want to get married. You use me as an excuse to the little girls who are beginning to try to trap you. The great lost love, and all that."

He stared for several seconds before smiling awkwardly. "Now *you* sound like Noel."

"Oh, sure. The Masked Marvel, he used to call himself. He was an education, all right." She pulled over her shoulders the cerise shawl Noel had sent her from Mexico. "Seems to be haunting the conversation, doesn't he? Old trick of his. Let's go."

The first thing she said in the taxi was, "Remember telling me last year that Noel wasn't going to amount to anything? How about *Old Moon Face?*"

"I remember being very drunk on rum and pineapple juice, and I remember an orange sun about six times normal size setting behind the trees," Wally said. "I don't remember much else except wanting to choke you, or beat you with a rock. *Old Moon Face* is a superb song. I'd be an ass to deny it. When Noel is in stride, he's terrific."

"He's rewritten *Princess Jones*. It's bound to get produced one of these days," Marjorie said. "It'll be a sensation. Then I guess we'll all be boasting we knew him when."

"Could be," Wally said, with less good nature.

His dancing had much improved, too. She said to him during a slow fox trot, leaning back in his arms, "I think you've got a girl."

"Thousands, if you want to know."

"No. One. Somebody's been working on you."

"How do you like the result?"

"Just don't get too smooth. You wouldn't be yourself any more."

Later she asked him what his farce was about. He told her the plot rather reluctantly. It seemed to her a wild and unfunny business. "It reads much funnier than it sounds," Wally said.

"Is there a part in it for me?"

Wally grinned. "If you'll agree to a fate worse than death I'll write one in."

"Sorry, I can't see you as the seducer of hopeful actresses, Wally. That's Noel's side of the street."

Wally glanced sidewise at her, twisting the glass stick of his highball in his hands. "Some day you'll have to tell me how you fended Noel Airman off. It's one of the marvelous achievements of the twentieth century, like Lindbergh's flight to Paris."

"You're assuming I succeeded in fending him off."

"I think I'd know if you hadn't."

There was another silence. For the first time since she had known him he caused her a stir of enjoyable discomfort. "I think you would. I'm getting bored with all these clever writers. I think I'll marry a doctor and get it over with, just as Noel prophesied. No use fighting it."

"Dr. Morris?"

"Morris Shapiro is the name. Maybe, who knows? He's really a great guy, once you get to know him."

"He has a discardable sound."

"Just for that, I will marry him."

"Marjorie Shapiro," Wally said meditatively. "No. I don't feel the cold clutch at my heart. There's no fate in it."

"That's exactly the name Noel predicted for me, strangely enough. Marjorie Shapiro."

In a totally different voice, hard and a little shrill, Wally said, "Would it be too great a strain on you, Marjorie, if neither of us said anything more this evening about Noel Airman?"

"Why, it's you who keep talking about him, isn't it?"

"Let's dance." He stood and pulled at her hand.

When the taxi drew up in front of her home at half-past one in the morning, she held her face up to him unthinkingly for a kiss. "Nothing doing," Wally said.

It startled her. She was rather sleepy. She peered at him, dropping her chin. "Huh?"

He took her hand. "You won't really marry Dr. Shapiro yet, will you? I mean, there's another couple of years yet."

"Oh, you fool." She put her hand to his face for a moment. "If it gives you pleasure to carry on like that, I'm sure I don't mind. I'll warn you before I marry Dr. Shapiro."

"Promise?"

"Okay. I promise." She laughed. "Small danger, since you insist on worming it out of me."

With the humiliation of the summer-theatre fiasco—of having wasted ninety dollars and six weeks, of having crawled home defeated and bilked, exactly as her mother had predicted—Marjorie struck bottom in her own soul. She told herself that unless she was paid real money for acting—the amount didn't matter, a dollar would be enough to start with, symbolically—but unless she earned that dollar, and fairly soon, she had better face the fact that she was living a childish fantasy.

So she set out on an earnest and grim quest for the dollar. She fanatically studied all the theatrical trade papers, and listened hungrily to every scrap of gossip at the drugstore about new plays. Again she trudged to the producers' offices to try out for any part that seemed in any way suited to her. Again she could never get past the contemptuous office boys and telephone girls. Her amateurishness seemed written on her forehead, a mark of Cain. The same thing happened when she decided to try for radio jobs. The advertising agencies, unimpressed by her condescension, turned her away at the outer railings of their offices. So did the networks.

She made the round of the semi-professional groups on the fringe of Broadway, including two communist enterprises and a little company that sent out shows to tour churches and Kiwanis clubs. She answered every advertisement for actresses that she saw; she followed up every lead that came to her ears in the drugstore, however unpromising. It became clear after a couple of months that she could get all the theatrical work she wanted—of a certain kind. There were radio groups and experimental theatre groups, university groups and temple groups, charity groups and educational groups; an almost infinite number of groups, diverse as they could be in origin, and similar in two characteristics: a willingness to use actresses, and an unwillingness to pay them.

At any place where money was to be made by an actress, Marjorie was shut out as though she were black.

Only the fact that this had been the experience of all the kids in the drugstore consoled her. Some of the girls were beautiful, and in her opinion strikingly talented. Evidently this preliminary discouragement was a part of the game. The kids had a folklore of reassuring stories. Helen Hayes had gone through years of rejection. The new star of the new hit comedy had hung around these very booths in despair only two years ago, ready to go home to Nebraska for good. With such tales went a litany of cheering phrases. "One of us is going to make it. . . . There's always room at the top. . . . All it takes is one break. . . ."

Marjorie began to pay more attention to the talk at the drugstore about other ways of earning money. Some of the kids supported themselves by working as movie ushers or salesclerks. They tried to get part-time or evening jobs, so as to be free in the afternoon when the drugstore buzzed with life. A few of the prettiest girls and handsomest boys worked as photographers' models. There were less savory recourses. A couple of girls, it was whispered, were posing in the nude, or at least with bared chests, for painters and photographers; and some resorted to posing for lingerie and stocking advertisements, which was considered not much better. One emaciated redhead defiantly admitted working as a taxi dancer. A tall shabby southern boy with a shock of wheat-colored hair was supposed to be keeping body and soul together by writing pornography, though this seemed incredible to Marjorie, because he was so sweet-natured, and so familiar with Ibsen's plays.

Marjorie finally decided to ease her conscience by trying any kind of paying work. She asked a starved blonde from Canada, who had just gone to work in Gorman's department store, to help her get a job. The girl was skeptical; Marjorie, sleek and furred, comfortably nested with her parents on West End Avenue, didn't seem to be salesgirl material. But Marjorie convinced her that she meant it. The girl took her to the personnel office, and Marjorie was readily inducted into the working class with a punch card.

She was placed in the women's underwear section, substituting for a girl who had mumps. For the first hour or so of the first day she worked at Gorman's, Marjorie really enjoyed it. There was an exciting novelty about standing at her ease in the black dress of a salesgirl on the wrong side of a counter, while women in hats and coats thronged by noisily, looking preoccupied and mean. It was gay to make change, to chirp brightly about nightgowns and panties to customers, to crouch and search around in the stacks of boxes, to fill out sales slips with a sharp fresh-smelling pencil. She was, in fact, Katharine Hepburn, playing a store clerk in the first reel of a smart comedy. The trouble was that the young millionaire played by Gary Cooper didn't show up. Instead a stringy rouged woman in an old squirrel coat lost patience with Marjorie's ignorance and began squawking insults at her, and Marjorie answered angrily, and the woman yelled for the section manager, and Mr. Meredith descended with a smile on his mouth and a glare in his eyes. Marjorie got a sharp hissed reprimand. Mr. Meredith apologized to the hag, while Marjorie sulked at the other end of the counter, feeling spat upon.

So much for Katharine Hepburn. Thereafter, through that day and the next and the next, and all the days she served in the store, the job was nothing but exasperating drudgery through a long day under a paralyzed clock; daily it gave her a tired spine, aching feet, rubbed nerves, and a growing hatred of women.

Mr. Meredith, her section manager, began keeping her after hours to teach her about the bewildering stockpiles of underwear. He was a tall mustached man of about fifty with waxy pink good looks, a fetid breath vainly masked by wintergreen drops, and a continual false smile. Marjorie found it decidedly queer to go rummaging through piles of frilly lingerie with Mr. Meredith, and to listen while he fingered brassieres and slips and talked about them. But she put up with it. The reward at the end of the week for all this slavery was twelve dollars. Her father had been giving her half that much each week just for being his daughter. But she brought the pay envelope home with some pride.

Mr. and Mrs. Morgenstern, however, took a disappointing attitude toward their daughter's new self-reliance. The father seemed saddened. "Does my daughter," he said, "have to work as a clerk selling underwear? Are things that bad in this house?" Mrs. Morgenstern said that Marjorie was a fool to drudge in a department store when she could make more money with less effort working for her father. Marjorie couldn't very well explain to her parents that the Arnold Importing Company seemed to her a black pit which would swallow her forever, once she fell in.

She said, "I thought you wanted me to be useful, earn my own keep——"

"I don't know what's the matter with you," the mother said. "You do everything backwards and sideways. You're a stenographer. Papa needs another girl in the place. Twenty dollars a week. So you work like a horse for twelve dollars a week in Gorman's behind a counter."

"Don't you see that working for Dad wouldn't count, wouldn't mean anything?" Marjorie said.

Mrs. Morgenstern rolled her eyes toward the ceiling. "If I had a college education maybe I would follow you. When I went to school, twenty was eight more than twelve."

It was a heavy effort to get herself to answer the alarm clock and go down to the store, and the fact that her virtue went unrecognized made it harder. She arrived at Gorman's the following Monday already on edge from a breakfast wrangle with her mother, wherein she had finally been driven to exclaim that becoming a stenographer in the Arnold firm was the fate she most feared. Mr. Meredith, who had an eerie way of popping at Marjorie around pillars and corners, flashing his false smile, especially when she was being rude to some unbearable customer, chose this morning to do an extraordinary amount of popping. Also, the girl who had had the mumps returned to work, and showed instant jealousy, fear, and hatred of Marjorie. She sneered at her mistakes, snarled at her when she leaned on the counter to rest, and kept whining and snivelling that somebody had mixed up the stock so that it would never get straight again. She was a fat girl named Viola, with a short upper lip and two large front teeth. The lunch in the clerks' cafeteria, greasy meatballs and spaghetti, disagreed with Marjorie, shaky as she was. After lunch Mr.

Meredith, with an odd change of manner, came fawning around, and started to talk to her about yoga exercises. He recommended a couple of books, and suggested that Marjorie might like to come with him to a meeting of his yoga group. He talked on and on, at very short range, overwhelming Marjorie with bad breath and wintergreen. Her head ached as though a tomahawk were sunk in it. Far down the counter the fat girl glared and glared; at last she came up with a look of fixed hate, and broke in to whine to Mr. Meredith about a mess in the stock which Marjorie had made. They both went out of sight around the corner of the counter. That was the last Marjorie saw of either of them. She left the floor, went to her locker, got her coat, and walked out into the sunshine. She never even shopped in Gorman's again. But she remembered Mr. Meredith and Viola for years afterward, with extreme vividness, as though she had worked with them half a lifetime.

Morris Shapiro said to Marjorie that night, strolling home with her from a movie, "The point is you don't need the money. When you need it, the Violas and the Mr. Merediths just become acceptable details of life."

"I need money," Marjorie said. "Badly."

"Not as badly as somebody does who has her stomach to fill," Morris said. "And that's the only kind that makes a good salesclerk."

"Well, I'm not beaten. I'm not going to work for my father yet. There must be some other answer——"

"Margie, how good a stenographer are you?"

"Fair typist. My shorthand never was much."

"How would you like a job at a hospital? There's a vacancy in the admitting office at my hospital. I'm pretty sure they'd take you on—you're presentable, that's important——"

Marjorie glanced at Shapiro walking beside her in a baggy tweed suit, hatless, in the parti-colored neon light of the Broadway sidewalk. This pale plump middle-sized doctor was certainly no Noel for looks or conversation. But he had his own charm. He was masculine, self-confident, and kind. Had Noel not anticipated Morris with such prophetic caricature, things might well be different now between them, she thought. How could the fiend have foreseen a doctor named Shapiro with a mustache?

"It would be very odd, working at the same place with you. You'd probably get all disillusioned with me in a week."

"I won't be disillusioned if your work's no good. You'll get fired, that's all."

She walked beside him in silence for a while. "All right, I'm willing to try," she said.

The hospital job turned out to be perfect for her. It ran from eight in the morning to two in the afternoon and there was nothing to it but typing, keeping files, and now and then relieving the switchboard operator. The pay was only ten dollars a week, but her afternoons were free for haunting the drugstore, which seemed a decisive advantage.

In point of fact, however, her passion for the drugstore somewhat declined as her interest in Morris Shapiro increased. In his white rumpled coat, with his stubby hands scrubbed bright pink, and the smell of tobacco smoke and medicine about him, he was an authentic doctor, not a mere date; and he had new charm. Often when her work was through, she would have lunch with him; they would sit drinking coffee and talking, and the latest theatre gossip would seem a less urgent matter, safely to be left to tomorrow.

He was a Research Fellow. In the hospital, where long hard work was a matter of course, Morris Shapiro was regarded as an almost maniacal worker. She became curious about his work. But she had to badger him for a long time before he would believe that she really wanted to know about it. Once he started talking he talked copiously, half forgetting her, his face alive and his eyes bright. It was current practice, he told her, in cases of fractures that wouldn't heal, to put pieces of bone from another part of the patient's own body into the breach. Morris was doing original work in clinic cases, using bone from other people's bodies in the same way. He had had some striking successes, and hoped eventually to write a monograph that would modify surgical practice in the field.

Marjorie stared at the tired, puffy-faced slouching young man in the creased white coat, forgetting that he was almost bald and hardly taller than herself. "I had no idea that you were doing anything as important as that."

He shrugged and lit a cigarette from a burning butt. "It's just like a Ph.D. thesis. You have to think of some trivial new angle and work it up, that's all. If I write a good monograph I might wind up with an appointment on some hospital staff. It's just part of the game."

He would never concede that he was doing anything but maneuvering for promotion. She grew used to this pose and made no effort to argue against it, while she admired his masked passion for his work.

In due time they got around to necking. She told herself for a while that it was every bit as exciting as it had been with Noel. Then she gave up the effort to maintain that illusion, because it was making her irritable, and spoiling her pleasure in Morris's company. It wasn't true. Noel was gone. The special charged and frightening excitement of her first love was gone too, no doubt forever. But she liked and admired Morris Shapiro. She couldn't pretend to herself that Morris's conversation had any of the color and sparkle of Noel's rainbow cascades of words, but he was clever, good-humored, and refreshingly honest.

The greatest enemy of the slowly, shyly burgeoning romance was her mother. Mrs. Morgenstern could not contain her enthusiasm for Dr. Shapiro. She kept extolling Morris and pointing out how superior he was to unreliable nervous types, such as, for instance, songwriters. Morris's father was a textile manufacturer and a trustee of the temple; he attended services every Saturday in a frock coat and a high hat. Marjorie's mother and Mrs. Shapiro were old acquaintances. Mrs. Morgenstern let slip at one point that the girl's meeting with the young doctor at the Zionist lecture had been far from accidental; the fruit of a plot, indeed, contrived by the two mothers for over a year. Morris had been dragged to the lecture as Marjorie had been dragged. His mother had pointed the girl out, and the young doctor's disgruntled skepticism had changed at once to hot attention. Mrs. Morgenstern thought this was a good joke, perfectly safe to divulge, after Marjorie had been at the hospital a month or so. She had no idea what a horrible yellow blight it threw over the doctor in Marjorie's eyes. Suddenly Morris seemed to her once more the comic caricature husband predicted by Noel. She hated his pudginess and his mustache, his scanty hair and plodding good nature, and the unlucky name Shapiro. It took her a week or so to get over it. But she finally decided that she was twenty-one, after all, and that it was time to stop being influenced by her mother's likes and dislikes. It was as childish to reject a man because her mother was trying to push him down her throat, as it would be to accept him. She began to be pleasant to him again.

There were evenings during the month that followed when she almost believed that she had come to the happy end of the long rough road; there were times when she sat at her desk in the admitting office, idly scrawling on a pad, *Mrs. Morris Shapiro*.

Chapter 32. DINNER AT THE WALDORF

Noel seemed to spring up out of the pavement.

This time it was Noel, all right. She had seen him coming at her in crowds a thousand times in the past months, but he had always melted into a tall stranger as he came close. This was Noel. He stood on the corner opposite her, waiting for the green light, looking back and forth at the traffic. His hands were thrust in the pockets of a camel's hair topcoat;

his blond hair stirred in the wind. The lift of his long jaw, the imperious turn of his shoulders, were unmistakable. He was very brown.

The light changed. He came striding toward her. His unconcerned eyes fell on her, and the abstracted look blazed into recognition and excitement. He seemed to lunge. The long arm swept around her waist and he pulled her up on the sidewalk. "Don't get killed, please, in the middle of Lexington Avenue. You're still precious to me."

"I'm trying to get a cab. I've just come from the hairdresser. My hair's damp," Marjorie said idiotically.

"Right now you're going to get a drink. With me."

"Noel, it's impossible, I swear it is. I haven't got a minute to spare, not a second. Help me get a cab, if you want to make yourself useful."

He looked around and waved an arm, and there was a cab. He bundled her in and dropped beside her. "Waldorf, driver."

"If you're going to the Waldorf that's perfectly all right, Noel. I'm taking this cab on from there, straight home."

"Of course." Noel sat back comfortably. His eyes shone at her, brilliant and seeming more blue than ever in his tanned face. "Ye gods, it's no illusion, it never has been. All you are is the most beautiful living thing. How are you?"

"The old palaver," she said, wishing that she didn't sound so shaken and hoarse. "Obviously the Masked Marvel hasn't changed. I'm fine, thank you."

"Why are you in such a hurry? Won't you have one drink with me—five minutes? I have a lot to celebrate, if you haven't, and——"

"I can't, Noel. I'm terribly late as it is."

"It's only a quarter past five."

"I'm late, I say."

"I'll admit I'm an evil wretch, and all that, but——"

"Noel, I have an appointment at six, and I have to go home and change, it's that simple."

"Will you have a drink with me tomorrow?"

"Well, I don't know, I guess so, I can't remember at the moment what I'm doing tomorrow—anyway, tonight is just out of the question——"

"So's tomorrow."

"What?"

"I wanted to see how determined you were. Tomorrow I'll be in Hollywood. Or piled up in the Rockies, if my luck runs out."

"You're—what? Hollywood?"

"My plane leaves at nine tonight. I have to go back to the hotel and pack and clear up some business. I don't have any more time than you."

"Are you staying at the Waldorf?" He nodded. "Dear me, Noel. Holly-wood, Waldorf-Astoria . . . Riding high, aren't you?"

"On the foaming crest, kid. Healthy, relaxed, loaded with money, happy as a lark. And how are you, really? Take off those gloves. I'd like to see your pretty hands."

"You crazy fool, I'll do nothing of the kind. We're almost at the Wal-dorf, and—what are you going to do in Hollywood?"

"Take off your gloves and I'll tell you."

She stripped off her gloves in two hasty gestures. "I've never known such an imbecile and I never will. There." She made her fingers into claws. "Pretty enough?"

"Excellent."

"What?"

"No rings. I take it Dr. Shapiro isn't making good time."

"The hell he isn't," she said, and was instantly angry at herself. She covered as best she could with a mysterious subtle smile.

"Is he your date tonight?"

"Here's the Waldorf. Goodbye, Noel. Have fun in Hollywood."

"You'd kick me out of your cab and just ride off, would you?"

The cab stopped. She said, "That's exactly right, dear. 'Bye."

"How do you think I'm looking?"

"Thinner. But all right."

"I'll ride home with you."

"Oh no! Nothing doing."

"Margie, I may never see you again. You'll marry Dr. Shapiro and it'll be impossible. I'd rather look at you for five minutes than spend a life-time in Hollywood. Please. One drink. I'll put my watch on the table. When the five minutes are up I'll vanish."

"You devil, you don't care a snap whether you lay eyes on me again or not. You've been staying at the Waldorf for weeks probably, and I haven't heard a peep from you."

"I got in from Mexico day before yesterday, Margie. I knew you didn't particularly want to hear from me. However, you're right about the whole thing, as usual." His face gloomed over. He got out of the cab. "I'm being a grovelling ass. Goodbye."

She held her hand out to him through the open cab door. "I didn't mind seeing you. You're making me feel like a pig. I do have this date, Noel——"

"Margie, I honestly believe you. Goodbye and God bless you. You look wonderful. I'll write you." He shook her hand, his countenance pleasant and friendly again.

She was out of the cab before she quite realized it, saying, "You're not going to put me in the wrong like this. Five minutes is absolutely all. It's too much."

The cocktail hour was at full blast. It took more than five minutes to get a waiter, and more than five additional minutes for the drinks to come. Marjorie watched the creeping clock hands over the bar as she chatted with Noel. At a quarter to six she abandoned the idea of changing her clothes; she would take a cab straight to the hospital. She had undertaken to carve the turkey and help prepare the buffet for the doctors' Thanksgiving party. Morris was going to act as bartender. It wouldn't matter, she thought, wearing her street clothes to the party; most of the nurses would be dressed that way. The decision made her feel less harried.

Noel said he was going to Hollywood to write the score for a second-rate movie, with his old collaborator, Ferdie Platt. "Ferdie's fallen on sad days working for a quickie outfit like Panther Pictures. Too much golf, booze, and girls, I guess. I wrote him a postcard from Mexico, just for the hell of it, and his long air-mail special-delivery letter came back. Obviously he's using the temporary notoriety of *Moon Face* as a handle. I don't care. I'll have a chance to see the lay of the land. Two hundred fifty a week is a comedown for Ferdie. For me it's not a bad start."

The cocktails came. She picked up her shallow brimming glass, and a little champagne spilled coldly over her fingers. "Well, here's to the Masked Marvel, on his way to the top at last," she said. "I wish you every success, Noel. I always will."

"Well, let me drink to the one shining deed in my disorderly little life," Noel said. "To Marjorie, loveliest of the lovely, sweetest of the sweet. God bless her. And let her thank her lucky stars I was such a bastard to her."

Marjorie muttered, "Well, I don't know about all that. Let's drink."

She hadn't had champagne since the break-up with Noel. Morris habitually ordered scotch for both of them. The yeasty bubbling on her tongue reeled time backward half a year. "You vile dog, who and what are you laughing at?"

"Was I laughing?"

"I don't know what else you call baring those fangs at me. They certainly look white in that face of yours. You're black."

"Well, two weeks ago, dear, I was climbing pyramids in Yucatan. How much time left? Two minutes?"

"Don't be funny. If I gulp it I'll get hiccups. Don't remind me how late I am."

"I like the way you're wearing your hair."

"Oh, is it different? I don't remember."

"Marjorie, it's very pleasant seeing you, honestly it is."

"Well, it's nice to see you in such good spirits, Noel. Last time I saw you, you looked like the devil. I really thought you might be heading for a nervous breakdown."

"And so you decided to help a man in distress, by knocking his teeth down his throat."

He said it with good humor, but her nerves stung. She drained the glass and picked up her purse. "Well, let's let sleeping dogs lie, shall we? This has been fun, and I guess——"

"Margie, look at the time. You're hopelessly late for a six o'clock date. Make a phone call and have a cigarette and one more drink with me."

"Oh no, you fiend, none of that. You swore, five minutes and you'd vanish, remember? Don't add perjury to your crimes."

"I'll keep my promise, but I think you're making a mistake. You've been haunting me, and if I haven't been haunting you I'd be surprised. Melodramatic breakoffs are no good, Marge. They're like dominant seventh chords. If they're not resolved they hang on and on in the mind, for years, for decades——"

Marjorie said, "What on earth do you want? You're leaving in a couple of hours, and I have a date——"

"Postpone it for an hour or so and have dinner with me." He overrode her protesting gesture. "Good Lord, don't you know this is the end? Before I'm bald and you're gray? I'm never going to telephone you. I know you don't want me to. As long as we've run into each other like this we ought to talk a bit, and part friends. My teeth still hurt."

"I'm very sorry, it's a dinner date——"

The waiter brought change. Noel helped her into her coat, saying cheerfully, "Well, okay. This glimpse of you has been something, anyway."

Walking out, Marjorie saw that the bar clock stood at almost twenty-five past six. It was too late now to help with the buffet. A cab straight to the hospital wouldn't get her there much before seven. There were plenty of other girls to attend to the food; no great harm had been done. But there was no longer any real need to rush. Morris was tending bar until nine. She couldn't eat with him before then; and eating and drinking by herself in a mill of gay interns and nurses was not an inviting prospect. Morris would probably be so busy, serving out liquor to that hard-drinking crowd, that he would hardly notice her if she did come before nine. Granted that she would have to apologize for not helping with the food, did it much matter if she dined first with Noel? He could not possibly keep her longer than another hour, since his plane was leaving at nine.

She stopped at a telephone booth in the lobby and called the hospital.

The switchboard took a long time to answer. The operator was a new girl, irritable and clumsy. Marjorie very explicitly gave her this message for Dr. Shapiro: *Sorry I'm late. I'll be there about eight-thirty or nine and I'll explain then.* There were continual loud buzzes in the background, and voices breaking in on the line. The operator said nervously that she would deliver the message as soon as she could get the switchboard clear.

Noel, lounging against the wall with his coat over his arm, said, "Well? Is he in a flaming rage?"

"Just your dumb luck, if you call this lucky," Marjorie said. "If you really want to feed me, you can do it. Providing you're quick about it."

His eyes narrowed. "And you were in such an all-fired hurry——Margie, the date wouldn't have been a fiction to get away from Jack the Ripper, would it? And this phone call a dainty covering gesture?"

"Noel, you'd just as soon lie as breathe, but everyone isn't like you. I was supposed to help prepare the food for a buffet supper. You fixed that, all right. Now it doesn't matter if——" She broke off because he was laughing.

"Margie, turn off the lovely frown, or I'll fall in love again. I never knew one like you for rising to the bait."

"Oh, shut up. I think I'll go home."

"Not a chance. I'd throw myself under the wheels of your cab. Come along."

Despite herself, she was impressed at walking through the lush Waldorf lobby with a man who was actually registered there. He picked up his key and some letters at the desk, and glanced at the envelopes. "I think the best idea is for me to bang out a letter or two and pack, and check out. Then we can have our dinner in peace. Will you trust yourself in Bluebeard's chamber? I'll be ten, fifteen minutes."

"I—well, I guess I'll come up. I've never seen a Waldorf room."

It was a two-room suite. The sitting room had heavy pink drapes, curlicued gilt furniture, and pretty Watteau-like paintings. A black portable typewriter stood open on a frail gilt table, flanked by overflowing ashtrays and piles of yellow paper. "Relax," Noel said, tossing his coat on a chair. She heard him snapping luggage and sliding drawers in the bedroom. She picked up a couple of magazines printed in heavy black type, on stock almost as coarse as paper towels. "Good heavens, the *New Masses*," she called into the bedroom. "Don't tell me you're turning communist now, just when you're starting to make money."

Noel came out in his shirtsleeves, laughing. He picked up books, manila envelopes, ties, and shirts scattered around the room, and carried them into the bedroom as he talked. "Phil Yates, this sculptor I was travelling with, was a communist. Some of his junk accumulated in my bags. Boring as hell. We had some gala arguments over communism. Phil's a slow-thinking sort, so I usually tied him up. He's one of the few communists I've ever been able to stand. They're like the abolitionists. Their cause may be just, but their personalities are repulsive. I don't really know whether they're right or not, and I don't care. Economics puts me to sleep. All I care about is my own few years above the ground. I'd rather spend them with the pleasant doomed people than with the seedy squawking heroes of the future. Which makes me, in the jargon, an anarcho-cynical deviate of the lackey intelligentsia. A louse, that is." He dropped into a chair by the typewriter. "Guess I'll bang out those letters."

"Noel, whatever happened to that Hits theory of yours? Did you ever write it up?"

"If you love me, Margie, no more of that. Every man's entitled to his fantasies, especially when he's fighting off nervous collapse." He typed for a while, rapidly and smoothly, then glanced at her. "I want to tell you, though, that while it lasted, I really thought I'd stumbled on the greatest thing since the Sermon on the Mount. . . . Sit down, for heaven's sake, stop pacing. You give me the willies."

"I'm just looking at your suite. It's lovely."

"Made for sinning in, isn't it? A pity you're so virtuous and I'm so busy." He resumed his swift rattling at the machine.

When he paused again she said, "I half expect to see Imogene pop out of a closet."

An extremely startled look passed over his face. He stared at her, ripped the sheet out of the typewriter and rolled in another, frowning blackly.

"What on earth's the matter?" Marjorie said.

"You surprise me a bit, that's all." His voice was very flat.

"For heaven's sake, you're always saying the most outrageous things to me. What makes you so sensitive, suddenly? All I said——"

"It's a question of taste, I guess. Forget it, please." He typed for a few moments, then turned to her. "It just occurs to me—is it possible you don't know about Imogene?"

"What about her?"

"Why, it was smeared all over the papers. This was way back in July. Imogene is dead."

"*Dead!*"

"How is it possible you don't know? She got involved with some wretched son of a bitch of a model's agent, named Weedie, something like that—man in his fifties, with a wife and four kids in New Rochelle, if you please. She jumped out of a window."

"My God . . ."

"It's true. It was a drunk scene in a hotel room, tears and threats and gallons of booze, three o'clock in the morning, and Imogene finally went and did what the girls are always saying they'll do. Opened the window and dived. This fellow told the cops he sat in an armchair looking at her, not believing his eyes. Just sat and watched her disappear.—Imogene, the carefree cow, to whom sex meant no more than a highball." He put a hand over his eyes. "You know, I've never really thought about it—I mean as a real thing, Margie—until this second? That poor dumb girl fluttering down past one window after another, all legs and arms and flapping skirts——" He slammed the typewriter shut. "I'll pack later. For God's sake let's go down and get a drink and have some food."

Neither of them wanted more champagne. They had martinis, and Noel ordered the dinner. For a while they sat without talking, in a far dim corner of the spacious dining room, watching well-dressed couples dancing to the sedate Waldorf music. "Tell me something," Noel said. "Is the date this evening with Dr. Shapiro?" She paused so long that he turned and looked at her, nodding. "I see. He isn't a myth, then. I half thought he might be. An obscure joke, or a feminine needle, or whatever."

"Morris is no myth."

"Do you mind telling me about him? I grant you it's none of my business."

Marjorie hesitated. The Imogene story had thrown a pall over her. Noel seemed less menacing and his charm dimmer; their bygone romance was trivial rather than tragic. She gave him a matter-of-fact account of Morris Shapiro.

Noel said, staring at his martini, twisting the stem in his long brown fingers, "Sounds like quite a fellow. Makes me seem a bit lightweight, no doubt, a bit lacking in specific gravity."

"Well, you're as different as day and night, I'll say that."

"You sound as though you could fall in love with him, but haven't yet."

"You're getting slightly personal."

"What's the difference? How long will any of us live? It's amazing, Margie, how unimportant all our hot little maneuvers are. Let's you and me make a pact. Let's always speak truthfully with each other, if our paths do cross once every ten years or so. It'll be something to look forward to."

"I haven't known Morris too long. One thing's sure, he's helped me get over our—our mess faster than I ever thought I would. I'm not the least bit angry with you any more." The martini was loosening her nerves. "If it doesn't offend you, the fact is you seem like a friend of college days at this point—dashing, and good-looking, and all that, but it's perfectly okay, if you know what I mean."

"Indeed I do. Clipped claws and drawn fangs."

"If you want to put it that way."

"Well, darling, the tubby señoritas in Mexico didn't do as much for me, I'm sorry to report. But I don't mind. You and I did the only sensible thing. Sentimental regret's a pleasant enough mood. Wouldn't you like to dance?"

She said, after they had moved silently among the couples on the floor, "I'd forgotten how well you dance."

"It helps to feel you're holding a flower in your arms, not a girl."

She sensed a blush rise from her neck to her cheeks. She glanced at her watch. "Don't you think we'd better eat our dinner?"

"I'd rather finish the dance and skip a course or the whole damned dinner, if it doesn't make too much difference to you."

"Suit yourself, Noel. It's your little party."

He held her hand, walking back to the table when the music ended. "Do you know something? You're still Marjorie, for my money. I'm relieved. It does me good to know that last spring I wasn't in some queer state over an ordinary West End Avenue prig."

"You have an unfortunate way of putting things, Noel. 'An ordinary West End Avenue prig'. . ."

"But that's just what you're not. You're a dryad who's assumed that disguise for some evil reason. Probably to destroy me."

The waiter served duck and wild rice, and a red wine. She looked at her watch again. "What's happened to the time? It's after eight. You can't eat. Your plane's at nine and you still haven't packed. You have to run this minute."

"I can gobble down a few bites." He picked up his knife and fork, unhurried.

"Noel, you'll get indigestion, and you'll miss your plane."

He grinned. "Well, time to confess, no doubt. My plane leaves at midnight."

After the moment of astonishment she didn't know whether to laugh or get angry. "You hound, is there a truthful bone in your body? *Are* you taking a plane at all? Are you going to Hollywood?"

"I'm going to Hollywood, all right. And at midnight. Margie, stop beetling your lovely brows. You're getting to an age where you have to start thinking about the lines in your face. Hell's bells, you looked like such a scared rabbit when I first got into the cab with you, I thought it would reassure you to say I was leaving town at nine. It wasn't a lie. I was shading the truth by three hours. Isn't it better this way? We can take our time." He sipped the wine. "Try your burgundy. It's superb."

Marjorie said, "At exactly twenty minutes to nine I am getting up and leaving this table. Just remember that."

As they ate, he told her about restaurants in Mexico City; about palatial hotels in primitive mountain country, which served vintage wines and the choicest food. He set her giggling and shivering with stories of a maniacal multimillionaire from Oklahoma, with whom he and the sculptor had roared around the countryside in a black Cadillac limousine for a week, living like princes.

The musicians took their places again, and began to play *Old Moon Face*. Marjorie and Noel looked at each other; Marjorie pointed to her watch. "Too late. Twenty-three to nine."

Noel said, "Woman, you practically wrote this song. Your spirit guided my hand."

"I don't see myself getting any royalties."

"Dance with me, and I'll split them with you."

She laughed.

The song had been giving Marjorie chills for months. Now, dancing to it with Noel, there was only a pleasant floating languor. The light in the room was a strange dusty pink. She closed her eyes. The music modulated to *It's Raining Kisses*. "That's getting to be the standard arrangement," he said. "The Airman medley."

After a moment Marjorie murmured, "Thank God they don't know the *South Wind Waltz* too."

"Margie, it was all fun, wasn't it? Even South Wind?"

"It was fun, Noel."

"There always has to be an admission price, you know. Except you pay when you get out, the way they do on the Mexican busses. I think we got out cheap."

"I'm not complaining."

"Marge, I hope you'll be the happiest woman in New York, or the suburbs, or wherever. I won't forget you. I have no regrets, except that I'm made a bit too crooked for you. And that's an old story."

To break the welling of tears to her eyes she said, "I must leave."

It was seven minutes of nine when he kissed her cheek and put her in the cab. "Have fun in Hollywood," she managed to say as the cab drove off.

Not thinking clearly, she went home and changed her clothes. Then she had trouble getting another cab; she had to walk to Broadway. Then the cab scraped fenders with a truck, halfway to the hospital, and ten more minutes elapsed while the drivers argued and exchanged license numbers. It was five minutes to ten when she arrived at the hospital.

She met Morris Shapiro in the lobby; he was walking out in his over-coat, and the gray hat which always looked too round and too big. His shoulders were stooped. "Morris!"

He glanced at her. "Oh, hello."

"Good Lord, were you leaving here without me? Standing me up?"

"I thought something had happened and you weren't coming. It was quite all right, but——"

"Morris, I phoned two hours ago. Didn't you get my message?"

"What message? No. No message. What's the difference? I was going to a movie. Want to come? Or do something else?"

"I swear to God I telephoned, Morris. That new idiot on the switch-board—I'll strangle her—I left a message——"

He said very little in the cab. He answered her questions about the party pleasantly and he brushed aside her apologies. They went to a garish Hawaiian-decorated grill near the Waldorf. After they had danced a couple of lifeless dances and were sitting and smoking at the table, Morris said, "Marjorie, were you with Noel, by any chance?"

Stunned, she nodded.

He smiled wearily. "Talk about your extrasensory perception. I thought so, somehow. It's perfectly all right."

Then she explained: the unexpected meeting, the miscalculations of time, the taxi accident. He kept nodding. "Morris, it did me good, meeting him. I'd never have planned it, you know that. I'd have hung up if he'd telephoned. But it did me good. I realized for the first time how cured I really am."

"That's nice. You're tired though, aren't you? You seem tired."

"Well, a bit. But I'm having fun."

"Well, so am I. We'll have another drink and a dance before we go."

She tried to put more zest into her dancing. But he really was a dull dancer, and as luck would have it the orchestra played a long set of rumbas, at which he was especially clumsy.

So Dr. Shapiro took Marjorie home early that night.

She quit her hospital job a couple of weeks later, having saved nearly a hundred dollars. Dr. Shapiro had not asked her to lunch or called her since the night of the party; and while she was rather humiliated by this, she was also rather relieved. He was cordial when he happened to meet her in the corridors; and, encountering her as she was leaving the ad-mitting office for the last time, he said goodbye cordially.

Chapter 33. *PRINCESS JONES* IS PRODUCED

The engagements and marriages of her college friends, girl cousins, and temple acquaintances went on and on. The attractive ones were nearly all married, and now the less attractive ones were going. Several of the girls had babies. A few like Rosalind Boehm had two; Rosalind herself was pregnant with a third. Rosalind seemed as remote in time and in attitude now, when Marjorie accidentally met her waddling bulkily in a shop or on the street, as a grandparent. Rosalind had a little smile of secret amusement in these encounters which greatly annoyed Marjorie. Since when, she thought, was a pretty girl not much past twenty-one a pitiable freak? Rosalind, barely twenty-three, was the freak, with her big stomach, big behind, sagging bosom, and busy contented air of a woman of forty, as she juggled bundles.

The arrival of each engraved invitation touched off a fresh dirge by Mrs. Morgenstern over Morris Shapiro. Marjorie endured a bitter siege. She couldn't say that she had lost any hope of falling in love with the doctor, and that he had been wise enough to sense it and to drop her. There were no words for conveying this kind of information from a daughter to a mother. She was quite willing to concede that she was unworthy of Morris Shapiro, that he was better than a thousand Noel Airmans, that she should consider herself lucky to polish the shoes and mend the shirts of such a wonderful man. It was all true. What did it matter? Her heart had closed.

She had a multitude of dates, mostly to avoid evenings at home. She kept herself busy by taking roles with non-paying theatre groups. She even went back to her old friends, the Vagabond Players at the YMHA, and scored a real hit as Nora in *A Doll's House;* but the experience was rather depressing than otherwise, even when she was bowing to the loud applause. The auditorium, the stage, the very curtain seemed to have shrunk, like a scene of her childhood. Romances bloomed and aborted all winter, as she rehearsed with one set of young actors or another. More than once she cold-bloodedly thought about having an affair. The handsome young drifters of the theatre fringe kept assuring her that no woman who was a virgin could possibly portray true emotion on the stage. She half believed it. But none of these fellows really tempted her; they seemed hollow toy men, after Morris Shapiro. In vain they lured her to their shabby little apartments, gave her cheap rye whiskey, dimmed the lights, read poetry aloud, and played slushy music on the phonograph. Marjorie fended them off, yawning.

In more than a year of loitering around the drugstore, she had seen one girl after another become embroiled in affairs with the would-be actors. Possibly this had qualified them to portray true emotion on the stage, but there was no way of knowing. Getting rid of one's virginity was no immediate passport to a Broadway role; this was true even when the helpful man was a professional producer, as a few of the girls had found out. The visible effect on the girls was that they became tired-looking and red around the eyes, slept later, drank more, and acquired coarser speech and manners. Some became less reluctant to pose for underwear advertisements and nude pictures. Seeing all this, Marjorie concluded that if she ever did have an affair for the sake of learning to portray true emotion, she wouldn't have it with an unsuccessful young actor or a vulpine producer.

Wally Wronken occasionally took her to dinner. He was out of college, living with his parents, dejectedly making forty dollars a week in the advertising section of his father's office-furniture business. He worked on plays every evening from nine to twelve, and had already completed three farce comedies, which he had submitted without success to producers.

"Wally, you'll never get anywhere writing in your spare time," Marjorie told him. "You should devote your life to it."

"Well, I'm an adult now, theoretically. I'd rather pay for my own ties and shirts. I still think I'll get somewhere, if I can stick on this schedule. Of course it eats into my social life, but I don't give much of a damn about my social life, tell you the truth. Dinner with you is something else, of course."

The thought mischievously recurred to her at these dinners that if she were going to have an educational affair she would do well to confer the favor on Wally Wronken. He deserved it more than anybody for his fidelity and his reverence. He still made no effort even to take a good-night kiss. Bashfulness wasn't the reason any more; he had clearly learned his way around girls. But he had evidently struck, in his own mind, some philosophic equilibrium in regarding Marjorie as an untouchable divinity. He talked about the plots of his plays with her, and took her comments seriously. He always made her feel good when she saw him. It was refreshing to be treated like a goddess, especially after being treated more like a tackling dummy by some overhopeful young actor or director. But it was also rather dull. She played with the idea of having an affair with Wally mainly because she knew it was impossible.

Her mother liked Wally (having duly checked on the Wronken family), and often suggested that Marjorie could do worse than take him seriously, now that both of them were moving along in years. "He'll probably get over the writing foolishness, and there's his father's business waiting for him," she said. Marjorie shrugged this off, as she did most of her mother's broadening hints about getting married.

She did feel guilty about living unproductively at home, so she tried to keep her temper. Once, being harried to go to a temple dance, she said mildly to her mother that at twenty-one she didn't feel life had quite passed her by. "I'll be married before I'm twenty-five, Mom, I promise you."

"Who's rushing you? It's just that before you marry a man you've got to meet him, unless I'm mistaken."

So she went to the dance. She met a Dartmouth senior there, a pink-faced short boy who fell for her insanely and implored her to come as his date to the Winter Carnival in February. His father was a wealthy manufacturer of stoves. Mrs. Morgenstern gave her no peace. "What harm will it do you to go to Dartmouth for a weekend? Will you freeze to death?"

"Mom, he's a child, he's almost two years younger than I am."

"Maybe you'll meet a professor you'll like."

"I'll make a bargain with you, Mom. Stop nagging me about Morris Shapiro, never mention the name to me again, and I'll go to Dartmouth."

The mother, after a moment's hesitation, said, "It's a bargain."

February came, and Marjorie had to keep her word. She remembered the Winter Carnival forever afterward as a whirling hallucination of red-faced drunken children in crimson, green, yellow sweaters, milling, yelling, dancing, necking, riding sleds, tromping knee-deep in snow; she remembered the scratch of wool, the wet chill of snow and the burn of raw whiskey; and aching wet feet, frostbitten fingers and toes, red running nose and horribly hurting ears. Worst of all was being jammed with a dozen hideously young girls in the bedroom of a fraternity house, and feeling something between an old maid and a chaperone. Among these girls she was an object of side glances, whispers, and giggling politeness. They were mostly about seventeen. They had full breasts, they scampered around in fetching lingerie, and they talked among themselves with arrogant wisdom in schoolgirl slang Marjorie had almost forgotten. It was frightful. Even the pink-faced boy realized at last that she was suffering, and mournfully put her on an early train back to New York. Next day she went to the drugstore and bathed in the relief of being with attractive girls in their twenties, among whom she was still one of the young ones. For weeks there hung over her the nightmare scare she had had in the fraternity house at Dartmouth—the feeling of having passed overnight, unmarried, into the older generation.

She was amazed, one morning in mid-February, to read this note in the theatre gossip of the New York *Times*:

. . . An added starter in the Broadway spring calendar may be Peter Ferris's production of a musical comedy, *Princess Jones*. The author, Noel Airman, an ambitious newcomer with a couple of popular song hits to his credit, notably the recent *Old Moon Face*, has written book, lyrics, and music. Shades of a certain better-known Noel? More anent all this when producer and author return from Hollywood stints in a week or two. . . .

The shock and the thrill blew her habitual reticence apart. Housecoat and nightgown flying, she scurried from her bedroom to the kitchen. "Mom, have you seen this?"

Mrs. Morgenstern looked up from the eggs she was frying. "What now?"

Marjorie read the item aloud with an edge of triumph in her voice. The mother's eyebrows went high. She dished up the eggs and poured coffee. "Well, sit down and have some breakfast, if you're not too excited to eat."

"I'm not excited at all," Marjorie said. "But it is interesting, isn't it? I always knew he had talent. Not everybody agreed with me, but of course I'm used to that."

"Have you heard from him lately?"

"You know I've been through with Noel Airman for a year, but I certainly wish him well. Why shouldn't I?"

"Who's this Peter Ferris?"

"I don't know. Some new producer, I guess."

The mother picked up the paper and frowned over it. "*Princess Jones,* hey? Hm. You think it's going to be a hit?"

"I think it will be. It's brilliant."

"How do you know?"

"Noel read the book and played the score for me, ages ago."

"What's it all about?"

Marjorie hesitated. But there was something too exhilarating about knowing the story of an incoming Broadway show. She talked as she ate her eggs, and the mother listened attentively to the story of the American heiress marrying a bankrupt young prince, and trying to reform the cheese-making industry of a sleepy little Balkan country on the pattern of American assembly-line efficiency. After a while Mrs. Morgenstern began looking confused and wrinkling her nose. Marjorie was getting all tangled in sub-plots. She broke off. "Oh, it's impossible to tell the story of a musical show. If I told you *Of Thee I Sing* it would sound twice as crazy, and it won the Pulitzer Prize. It's a light, gay, satiric fantasy, that's all, with music and dancing."

"Well, maybe it's over my head."

Marjorie made a face, and carried her coffee with the *Times* into her bedroom. She read the few printed lines over and over. Her own name in the theatre column could hardly have made her feel more excited and happy.

She took to pouncing on the paper at the door every morning, and opening it to the amusements section without glancing at the front page. For a couple of weeks there was nothing more; then a note appeared that Noel had returned to town with the producer to assemble a cast. She walked numbly through the next few days, seeing him every time she turned a corner on the street. But there are a lot of people in New York, and the chances of any two of them meeting by accident twice within a year aren't high; she didn't encounter Noel.

Soon the papers began reporting the signing of featured players for *Princess Jones*. Several of the drugstore kids tried out for the chorus and for bit parts, with the usual lack of success. Marjorie daydreamed of going to the theatre and turning up demurely in the tryouts. But in practical fact she was too short to be a show girl, she couldn't sing, she couldn't dance, and she knew there was no speaking part in the show which she could play. Had she been Noel's girl, he might have written in a few lines for her; but it would be impossibly humiliating, she felt, to try to crawl to him now for favors. Chances were that he was entangled with some starlet or actress, and had forgotten her. And good riddance, Marjorie assured herself. She stuck to that.

Still, it gave her a secret elation to hear the drugstore crowd talking about *Princess Jones* as they did about any other incoming production. Some of the gossipers asserted that it was a sure smash hit, and that the brokers were already buying up huge blocks of tickets. Others said it was a threadbare old-hat piece which wouldn't last a week. Such contradictory rumors inevitably sprang up about all new shows. One morning, a girl who had tried out for the chorus sang several of the numbers for the drugstore crowd. Marjorie sat quiet in a corner, her spine alive with thrills, as the girl piped the familiar words and tunes, and her memories woke of Noel's Village apartment, the dying fire in the littered fireplace, the smell of beer, toasted hot dogs, and cigarettes, and Noel at the piano, singing with the remembered commanding lift of his jaw.

March 4, 1937

Dear Marjorie:

If you remember me—and if you have any use for me on the basis of your memories—would you have lunch with me one of these days? I'm engaged to be married. If I don't pour it all out soon to some feminine heart I can trust, I'll explode.

My phone number is EN 2–5784. I don't want to startle you by calling you like a voice from the dead. I'm still very much alive and I hope everything's wonderful with you.

Isn't it exciting about Noel's show?

Love,
Marsha.

Marjorie's lip curled as she read this letter. The offhand reference to Noel's show was the key, of course. Marsha wanted to pump her about *Princess Jones*. The show was in its first week of rehearsals, and Marjorie was having a hard time keeping herself from strolling past the theatre, so any distraction was welcome. She telephoned Marsha, thinking that it would be amusing to find out whether the engagement was another of her facile lies. Marsha seemed exceptionally wild and gay on the telephone. "Sugar bun, it's heaven to talk to you. One o'clock is great, just marvelous. Where? Someplace glorious. Let's have lunch at the Plaza."

"The Plaza?"

"Why not? Nothing but the best for la Morningstar, n'est-ce pas?"

"Marsha, la Morningstar is an unemployed vagrant."

"Nonsense."

"I wish it were nonsense."

"Well, darling, this is the chance of a lifetime then. I'll treat you."

"Nothing doing. If some fool man takes me to the Plaza that's different, but——"

"Margie, I'm rolling in money. Wait till I tell you. I jingle when I walk. I clank. My one problem is getting rid of it, I swear. Pick me up at my apartment at a quarter of, and we'll walk across the park. It's a gorgeous day." She told Marjorie her new address.

"I'll pick you up, Marsha, but as for the Plaza——"

"Wonderful, sugar bun. 'Bye."

Marjorie mustered up her best daytime clothes. Marsha sounded engaged, all right—engaged and triumphant—and Marjorie was in no mood to be triumphed over.

The new address turned out to be a shabby-genteel apartment house on West Sixty-second Street with a self-service elevator. Marjorie pressed the button, the red light flashed *In Use,* and the elevator whined down from a remote floor, making a noise with its cables that sounded like *No don't, no don't, no don't.* It was still whining when the street door opened and a short man with white hair came in and stood yawning beside her, holding a large brown paper bag in both arms. Marjorie smelled the spice of delicatessen, and took a second look at the tanned plump face of the man. "Hello, Mr. Zelenko! Remember me?"

The man glanced at her. His face brightened, and he extended a few fingers from the side of the paper bag. "Well! The great Morningstar! More beautiful than ever!"

Riding up in the elevator, Marjorie said, "I'm so happy to hear about Marsha."

"Yes, Lou's a wonderful fellow. You'll have to meet him sometime. Lou's quite a fellow."

A Bach fugue was resounding through the apartment, played with all of Mrs. Zelenko's old power and skill. It made Marjorie feel old to hear the Bach and smell the Turkish tobacco odor of the Zelenko home. The apartment, though larger than the one on Ninety-second Street, had much the same look. Coming into the living room, she recognized the African mask on the wall, the Chinese screen, the green Buddha and the hookah, amid some unfamiliar exotic hangings, statuettes, and lamps, and some new Grand Rapids chairs and tables. A little gray-headed man who looked like Mr. Zelenko, evidently an uncle or some relative, sat in an armchair near the window, with his face tilted toward the ceiling, his eyes closed, and the tips of his fingers pressed together. The mother broke off her playing sharply. "Margie! For heaven's sake, why didn't that fool Alex tell me you were here?" She came and hugged Marjorie. She was tan, too, and not quite as fat as Marjorie remembered; her hair was freshly waved and freshly blond. She said, "Well, you look absolutely wonderful as always, you've become just piercingly beautiful, dear, it does my heart good to see you——"

Marsha's voice, jovial and muffled, called out, "Is that the divine Morningstar? Be with you in thirty seconds."

The father came in from the kitchen, scratching his thick white hair. "Who bought all that other delicatessen in the kitchen, and why? We have enough to feed an army."

"I did," said the little gray uncle.

The father said, "Oh, hello. I didn't know you were coming too."

"It's all a mix-up, it doesn't matter," Mrs. Zelenko said, still holding Marjorie's two hands and beaming. "Darling, I know you girls are going out for lunch, but do come back and talk to us old folks afterward, won't you? I'm dying to hear all about your theatre career——"

"I can dispose of that in about two seconds, Mrs. Zelenko. It's non-existent."

"I don't believe it. All beginnings are hard, but if I ever had confidence in the future of anybody——"

Marsha came into the room, shoulders up, mincing like a model. Marjorie was truly astonished to see this slim tanned woman in a Persian lamb jacket, striking black Paris dress, and killingly stylish tiny hat and veil. Only the wide smile and eager eyes were Marsha's. "Well! My long-lost darling!" She threw her arms around Marjorie, giving off fumes of costly perfume, then stood back and surveyed Marjorie in a swift shiny-eyed glance. "You louse, why do I bother? No girl who values her ego should ever be seen with you." She had quite the largest diamond on her left hand that Marjorie had ever seen.

"Don't say that, Marsha, I think you look grand," said the uncle.

Mr. Zelenko said, "Why are you going out to lunch, anyway? We have enough food, more than enough——"

"Delicatessen, all this family knows is delicatessen," Marsha said. "If I ever nurse a baby, I'll probably give it mustard out of one breast and beer out of the other. No, thanks."

"Don't be so funny," said the mother, with a glance at the uncle. "I didn't have time to cook this morning and you know why, Miss Lazybones——"

The man in the chair laughed and said, "I bought a lot of fish and cheese, Marsha. There's a fine smoked whitefish——"

"Oh, never mind, Lou, the girls want to gab about you, naturally," Mrs. Zelenko said. "Let them go."

"How about introducing me to Marjorie, Marsh? I've heard so much about her," the man said, getting out of the chair. He wore a creased gray suit and was slightly shorter than Marsha.

Marsha glanced from one parent to another. "What? Didn't either of you two nitwits think of *introducing* Lou and Marge, for Christ's sake? Marjorie, this is my fiancé—Lou Michaelson."

The little man held out his hand. He had a friendly sweet smile that was almost boyish, despite the worn face and the curly gray hair. His small teeth were widely separated and he had two gold caps in front. "Hello, Marjorie. This is a real pleasure after everything Marsha's told me. You're just as pretty as she said. Naturally I'm prejudiced, so I can't agree you outshine her."

Marjorie was too surprised to say anything. She mechanically shook hands.

"Imagine that. You just let Lou *sit* there," Marsha said.

Mr. Zelenko said, "I was in the kitchen, trying to sort out the food. There's at least forty bagels——"

Lou Michaelson said, "Marsha told me there wasn't anything in the house to eat. I just thought I'd surprise you, and bring some lunch——"

Marsha said, "Oh, what's the difference, for crying out loud? We're off." She threw an arm around Mr. Michaelson, kissed his ear, and rubbed off the lipstick. "Meet me at five at the Plaza for a drink?"

"This is the day I play handball with Milt, dear."

"When don't you play handball with Milt? I think you're trying to cure me of the cocktail habit, my friend." Her tone was affectionate and bantering. She said to Marjorie, "These health fiends."

"Well, I can call it off today," Mr. Michaelson said slowly. (He said everything slowly.) "It's only Mondays, Thursdays, and Saturdays. Except it does me a lot of good, you know, Marsh."

"Bless you, sure it does. You just trot on up to your little old Y, and beat Milt to pieces. Meet me at the Pierre six-thirty."

"It's a date, Marsh."

When the two girls came out to the bright sunny street, Marsha no longer appeared so transformed. The heavy features of the face were the same, after all, though Marsha had quite starved away the pudginess. So Marjorie thought, as the girls blinked and smiled at each other in the first shock of sunlight.

"Game to walk, or do we take a cab?" Marsha said. "It's such a marvelous day."

"Walk, by all means."

Marsha slipped an arm through hers. They went down the narrow street, holding their hats in the gusty breeze. "It's delicious to see you," Marsha said, her voice lower than it had been in the apartment, and less brassy. Marjorie pressed her arm. They passed the gray stone walls of Central Park West and went into the park. Marsha held up her head, sniffed the air, and sighed. "What is it about this park in March? It's dead, but you can always hear the horns of spring, can't you? Look at that baby-blue sky. I could cry."

"Why should you cry, of all people?" Marjorie said. "You've got the world by the tail. I'm awfully happy for you."

Marsha said, laughing, "Just my luck, you know, that you'd practically trip over Lou in my living room. I was going to tease you. Tell you he was six feet tall and looked like Clark Gable and owned a yacht and so forth. Not but what there isn't plenty to brag about in Lou, but still—you know, now that you've seen him, it's like you'd peeked at the end of a mystery story. Quiet-looking, isn't he? He's spent a lifetime being self-effacing, but he's really clever, in his special way, and he's a thoroughly wonderful guy." She glanced at Marjorie walking silent beside her, and her grin became a bit wistful. "What did you think of Lou, really, Margie? Did you get any impression of him?"

"Fiancés are all alike to outsiders, aren't they, Marsha? I only saw him for a moment. He seems like a very swell guy, and entirely glassy-eyed over you, which is the main thing."

"You're a pretty swell guy, too," Marsha said. Their high heels went clickety-click-click on the stone walk, raising little sharp echoes. The water-stained benches were empty. Nobody was in sight but a park attendant with a burlap bag, spearing old newspapers on the muddy brown lawn. "Lou takes some knowing. He's incredibly smart about some things, and incredibly naïve about others. It's really been a revelation to me that such people exist. Not only exist, but flourish. The main thing is, as you say, he's a hell of a sweet person. And he certainly does think I'm the cat's pajamas. But imagine me hooked to a handball fiend! D'you know, when I first met him he'd just come from playing handball? This grizzled character, hairy-chested, all rivers of sweat, and grinning from ear to ear. He'd just beaten a twenty-one-year-old kid, a bruiser, six feet tall. He plays with this partner of his, this Milt Schwartz, three times a week at the Y on Ninety-second Street. What's more, he wins as often as he loses. He's fifty-two, and Milt's twenty-nine, and Milt was on the handball team at CCNY."

"Amazing," Marjorie said. "Did you meet Lou at the Y?"

"No, no, in Florida. At this hotel where my folks were staying. I've only known him a month. This has been a real abduction on a white horse, kid. I'm still slightly dizzy. I must have told you long ago that I was going to send my folks to Florida some day——"

"Yes, you did——"

"Of course. Those were my two obsessions, to get my mom a fur coat, and to send them to Florida. You don't really know them, Margie. They're like a couple of children, but they're really wonderful, and what they went through to keep me going to Hunter nobody will ever know but me. Anyway—I was going to send them to Florida or die. Well, by this year I'd saved the money, so I sent them. And that did it. Marjorie, believe it or not, my destiny actually hung on the fact that my father knows how to play fan-tan. Fan-tan, can you imagine? Lou loves the game. Don't ever call a life misspent till it's over, kid. My father has wasted years playing every kind of card game known to man, and he couldn't have done more to ensure his little daughter's future if he'd worked like a stevedore all those years. This thing is so fantastic, Marge, it depends on such a hairlike thread of coincidences, that I'm absolutely convinced it's fate. Why did I park my folks at the Vista View Hotel, if not because it's run-down and cheap? What was a rich man like Lou doing at such a joint? Only Lou would have such reasons. His mother died year before last. She started going to the Vista View thirty years ago when it was a good hotel, and she just kept going there, and taking Lou along. He lived with her all her life, you see, he's never married. So, like a sleepwalker, he went right on going to the Vista View after she died. They have a nice handball court, he says. And he and Alex got to playing fan-tan. And then he sat with my folks at meals because he was lonesome, and of course they bent his ear about their divine Marsha. And he was just impressed to death with Alex's sad old line of Voltaire and Ingersoll and Haeckel and Clarence Darrow; he thinks my father's a brilliant original iconoclast. And you can't disillusion him, because by Lou's lights that's just what he is. And he thinks Tonia, of course, is the greatest pianist he's ever heard, and that's true too, because he's never heard any pianists. So along comes Marsha, the daughter of these two brilliant personages—fortunately starved down within an inch of her life. Kid, I ran into a rush act the like of which few females have known. When Lou makes up his mind to do something, get out of his way. I never had a chance, if I'd wanted a chance. I'd known him three days when he went downtown in Miami and came back with *this*." She waved the hand with the ring. "Nothing subtle, but persuasive in its way. I held out for a week or so, because—— Well, I don't have to tell you what reservations I must have had—but that's it, and here I am, telling you about my engagement." Marsha laughed. "I'm a little more used to it now. There are some unexpected charms to it. I look forward to civilizing him, honestly. It's his mother's fault, not his. She was one of these shrewd old religious widows. Owned a lot of real estate, managed it herself until she put Lou through law school, then they both managed it, and really rolled up a fortune. She never cared about anything but business and a couple of dozen charities that she practically ran herself. Lou's still running them, by the way. So he just never learned anything. He thinks I'm practically supernatural, because of what I know about books and music and painting. And yet he's keen, damn keen, believe me, in his own way. You listen to him analyze the values in a building on Seventh Avenue, let's say, and you won't believe your ears. He knows all about it—from how good the credit of a mattress firm on the third floor is, to the diameter of the steam pipes in the basement, and all about the buildings on the rest of the block, too, on both sides of the street. I've already gone to work on him. I dragged him to the opera the first night we were back in New York. Luckily it was *La Traviata*. He loved it. He couldn't have been more amazed. He kept saying, 'Why, it's great, it's really interesting.'—Holy cow, is that *rain?*"

She put her hand to her face and looked up at the sky. "Where the hell did those clouds come from? That's March for you."

They scampered through spattering drops, holding their hats. They were hardly inside the hotel lobby when a drenching shower fell in the street. They were still laughing and panting as they settled at a window table in the dining room and ordered drinks. The gray slanting rain was driving people from the street, scurrying with newspapers over their heads. Even the hansom cabs were retreating from the plaza, the drivers huddled in ponchos, the dejected horses streaming water from their tails and drooping ears. "Am I mistaken," Marsha said, "or is it always raining when I see you? Remember your graduation? I expected to see Noah and his ark come floating past Schrafft's that afternoon."

"Seems a hundred years ago," Marjorie said.

"It's just a little over a year."

Marjorie expelled a long breath. "I know. Just a little over a year."

Their cocktails came. Marsha said, "I can still see Noel with water dripping from his hat . . . And then in Schrafft's, ordering a pear and cottage cheese salad, and saying it was a penance." She paused. Marjorie lit a cigarette and sipped her drink. Marsha drummed the fingers of her left hand on the table, and the diamond twinkled and blazed in shots of colored fire. "Dear me, and when I think how big I was still talking that day—wasn't I? Sure. A year ago I was still going to be a head buyer at Lamm's, and then a theatrical producer some day, all that. Ah, well. Here's to blasted dreams." She lifted her glass and drank.

"Marsha, you can't regret giving up department store drudgery. Why, it's horrible." She told Marsha of her brief spell as a salesclerk, making her laugh heartily with a description of Mr. Meredith.

Marsha's face became serious, and she stared out at the rain. "I can't say I regret it, sugar bun, no. Not when I've found a real sweetheart like Lou to take me out of it and look after my folks. But frankly, I was all ready for Lou when I met him. I tried for two years at Lamm's. No go. A high IQ is a drug on the market, do you know that? It only disables you for most jobs, which consist ninety per cent of doing some goddamn dull thing over and over. Of course you tell yourself at first that you're not shining in this low menial work because you're cut out to be a big shot, and as soon as you get to the top you'll show them. You tell yourself this, that is, until you hear a dozen lamebrains, misfits, and good-for-nothings all around you saying the same thing week in and week out. Then what? Then you tell yourself, as long as you can, that you're different. I don't know. I'm ambitious, sure, but I've never been able to keep up lies about myself to myself for very long. It's taken me a while to find out what I'm all about, but the long and short of it is, I ain't got it."

"Marsha, you——"

"I'm very far from pitying myself, sugar bun. But I did keep my beady little eyes open. I gradually learned that big shots mostly work twice as hard, and are twice as thorough about dull detail, as the small fry. That's the big open secret, baby. I don't know where the hell the idea got around that big shots just sit on their can and make decisions a couple of hours a day, and for the rest play golf and drink champagne and commit adultery. I tell you, for every step up the ladder, there's more work and more attention to detail, and more chances to make a big fat jackass of yourself real fast. I had my chance. I flubbed it with a loud crash. Never mind the details. I think in Technicolor, you might say, always the rosy final picture, never the dull in-between details. Oh, being the boss's son helps, we all know that. But other things being equal, I swear to God most of being a big shot is first of all being a work horse, and second of all applying arithmetic to everything in the whole bloody world, and never making a mistake in addition or subtraction. Me, I've always stunk at arithmetic, just like my dear wonderful useless father. End of Marsha Zelenko, smart career woman, envy of two continents, as she dashes back and forth between New York and Paris, the dreaded arbiter of the haute couture. The name is Mrs. Lou Michaelson, and I love it. Let's have another drink."

The two girls sat smoking, looking out at the pouring rain. When the cocktails came Marsha said, "I certainly hope Noel's show is going to be a hit."

"So do I, of course," Marjorie said.

Marsha said, "I'm not just being polite. Lou has money in it."

"He has?"

"Not much. A couple of thousand. Mrs. Lemberg is a client of Lou's. The show looks pretty good at this point, I must say. I love the songs, especially the—— Why are you looking so blank?"

"Who's Mrs. Lemberg?"

"Don't you know?"

"Marsha, I haven't been seeing Noel since—oh, I don't know, last March, April."

Marsha smiled. "I mentioned your name a couple of times at the rehearsals. He didn't pick me up on it. Just went breezily on to something else. But his face changed a bit, kid, if you're interested."

"I'm not, and I'm sure you're mistaken."

"He hangs around with a tall dumb-looking redhead from the chorus."

Marjorie hoped her face didn't show how the words stabbed. "Good for him and for the redhead. He's a connoisseur of chorus girls. That's just what he needs. More power to him."

"You're crazy, she bores him," Marsha said. "I know what he needs. But it's none of my business. Pardon the long poking nose."

"Perfectly all right. Who's Mrs. Lemberg?"

"She's backing the show. Don't you really know any of this? Oh, goody, here's the food. If you call this nasty heap of dry grass food. I'd like to set fire to it. And you, you pig—curried chicken and rice! Wait till I'm safely married, baby. Jolly Marsha, star of the freak show, four hundred pounds of quivering female pulchritude . . . But about Mrs. Lemberg . . . Lord, I'd give an eye for just one spoonful of mayonnaise on this green filth. But I can't, I just can't. With my lousy glandular system, I'd swell like a blimp before your very eyes."

Marjorie said, "Well, about Mrs. Lemberg——"

With a mischievous grin, Marsha finally told her. Mrs. Lemberg was an old friend of Lou Michaelson's mother, another rich widow. Most of her money was in Brooklyn apartment houses, formerly managed by Mrs. Michaelson, and now by Lou. Mrs. Lemberg had met the producer of *Princess Jones,* Peter Ferris, at Palm Springs. He was a handsome young actor and stage manager, who had become friendly with Noel in Hollywood; and he had talked Mrs. Lemberg into putting up the money for the production. She always consulted Lou in business decisions, so she had telephoned him in Florida about the show. "Naturally, when I heard it was by Noel Airman I jumped," Marsha said. "I raved on to Lou about how brilliant Noel was, so he telephoned back that same night, and told la Lemberg to go ahead, if she felt like gambling on Broadway. And I got him to buy a little piece of the show, just for luck. Now he's so steamed up about it and so pleased with himself he can't sit still. He keeps saying he's just begun to live. At rehearsals, he's like a child of six at a circus—— Well, that's the fact of it, baby. It's a small world, hey? If I'd ever dreamed the day would come when I'd help Noel Airman get his first musical show produced—— The craziest things happen if you live long enough, don't they?"

Marjorie shook her head, smiling, and said nothing.

"I'm going to the rehearsal from here. Come along," Marsha said.

"Sorry. I have a million things to do this afternoon." It was all a little too much, Marjorie was thinking. Marsha Zelenko—of all people in the world, Marsha Zelenko—was a personage around the *Princess Jones* production, and could come and go at rehearsals. Why was she yearning to become an actress? What was so good about being sponsored by Mrs. Lemberg, and praised by Marsha Zelenko to her little gray-headed fiancé, Lou Michaelson? The glamor seemed to be going out of the theatre. She fumbled at her purse.

In a sudden dry tone Marsha said, "I'm paying, remember? Don't fool around."

Marjorie looked at her and put down the purse. "With pleasure, moneybags. With pleasure."

"Are you really through with Noel, Margie? For good?"

"Obviously."

"Is there another guy?"

"Oh, there have been others, and there'll be others, Marsha. But no more Noels, thanks. Pixies bore me."

"How about fauns? I'd say Noel Airman is more on the faun side. Looking better than ever, by the way."

"Fauns, pixies, brownies, satyrs, you can have them all. I don't like mythical creatures. They're too airy. I don't like a man you can see through, like a double exposure. Do you know, by some chance, a nice solid man?"

"Sure, Lou Michaelson," Marsha said. She snapped open her purse, took out a twenty-dollar bill, and dropped it on the check. Lighting a cigarette in a holder with a long narrow red mouthpiece, she squinted at Marjorie through smoke. "Okay. I won't go to the rehearsal. Will you help me shop for my trousseau? I'm up to nightgowns on the check list. Help me pick out some real yummy things to please Lou."

"Well—sure, I guess so. I can do that. I'd like to."

"And you'll come to my wedding, won't you? It's a week from Sunday."

"Of course. I'd love to."

"Wonderful. Got a guy to come with you?"

"I'll provide a guy, if I want one."

"Shall I invite Noel?"

"No, don't."

Marsha's eyes glinted. "Okay, I won't."

"Where and what time?"

"Six-thirtyish." Marsha tilted her head archly. "Guess where. Just guess."

"I haven't an idea in the world. Some hotel?"

"Remember the El Dorado? Lou lives there. It'll be in his apartment."

Marjorie said, "Well, well. You're practically producing Noel's show, and you're going to live in the El Dorado. What next?"

Marsha shrugged, grinning. "The wheel of fortune, hey, sugar bun? It's all too ironic for words, but—— What are you puckering your fore-head about?"

"Michaelson . . . Did this Mrs. Michaelson limp?" Marjorie said. "A small dumpy old woman, always wore black, limped?"

"She did have a clubfoot, Lou says——"

"Why, I knew her," Marjorie said. "She and my mother were on some charity committee of the El Dorado—Red Cross, or something. She was in our apartment a dozen times. I'll be damned. You're marrying old Mrs. Michaelson's son. My mother will die."

They looked each other in the face, and at the same instant burst out laughing. They laughed very hard. Marsha touched a tiny handkerchief to her eyes. "Ah, God, it's a marvelous life, Margie, I'm telling you, if you don't get easily discouraged and cut your throat. It's a temptation now and then, I grant you. Come on, let's shop."

It was very cold in the wet sunny street after the rain. Marjorie said, "Well, this ought to be gay, shopping for a trousseau. Good practice for me, let us hope."

Marsha said abruptly, "I thought you had a million things to do this afternoon." And when Marjorie stared at her in confusion, she said, "When will you get wise to yourself? If you were through with Noel Airman you'd have gone to the rehearsal like a shot. And you wouldn't have given a hoot whether he came to the wedding or not. However, not another word from me will you hear. I'm the original genius at conducting one's love life. Taxi!"

Chapter 34. MARSHA'S FAREWELL SPEECH

Setting out for the El Dorado, Marjorie was unaccountably nervous. Her palms were wet, and she was swallowing often and hard, as though she were about to go up in an airplane, or take a stiff college final. When she emerged on West End Avenue, low black clouds covered the sky except in the west, beyond the Hudson, where the sun was going down in a dismal yellow glare. The queer light, the raw air, made her shiver. She had intended to walk to the El Dorado; instead, she caught a cab.

She had not been at the El Dorado for more than two years, but the red-faced doorman, in a purple uniform newly frogged with gold, touched his hat and said, "Evening, Miss Marjorie." It was like a dream to find herself walking through this luxurious lobby, a stranger and a visitor—a visitor, moreover, to Marsha Zelenko. She was glad that the elevator man was new. It would have been too unsettling to be taken up to Marsha's wedding by her old white-headed friend Frank. She looked at herself in the coppery mirror and saw a troubled young woman, somewhat thinner, perhaps prettier, certainly much more sober than the girl who had last looked out at her from this mirror.

Lou Michaelson lived in Apartment 15 F. The Morgensterns had lived in 17 F. Marjorie knew how the apartment would be shaped, where the hallways would turn, where the windows would look out to the park.

A Negro butler in a white coat opened the door, and the first person she saw in the apartment was Noel Airman, leaning in the archway of the living room with his arms folded, surveying the buzzing guests with a faint smile. She was not very surprised, though the sight of him made her breath come hard. His tan was gone; he looked pale and tired. His jacket was an old tweed he had often worn at South Wind.

He didn't see her as she went past him. She gave her beaver coat to the servant, and darted down the hallway to the bedrooms. Marsha's mother, in a long blue gown decked with a huge spray of green orchids, was chattering in the bend of the hall with a group of guests. She held out both hands to Marjorie. "Darling! So sweet of you to come. This is Luba Wolono, dear, you know, the great concert artist, my old, old friend. Luba's going to play for the ceremony. Luba, this is Marjorie Morningstar, the actress, Marsha's oldest and dearest friend. And this is Mr. Packovitch, and this is Mr. Maggiore——" Marjorie wasn't sure whether she had ever heard of Luba Wolono, but it sounded like the name of a concert artist, and the woman certainly looked like one: almost six feet tall, white-faced, and dressed in floor-length black, with long black hair parted as with a hatchet in the middle and pulled straight back. Luba Wolono gave Marjorie a small mournful smile. The guests stopped staring at the concert artist and turned to stare at the actress.

"Where's Marsha?" Marjorie said.

"Bedroom, first door on the right, dear. She'll adore seeing you. You look lovely——"

When Marjorie turned the knob of the closed bedroom door there were shrieks, giggles, and screams of "No, no!"

She slipped inside. "I'm not a man, relax."

Marsha stood in the center of the room with one side of her skirt pulled up, showing her thick leg, an ornate blue garter, a bare tan thigh, and most of a black girdle. Three girls were pulling and hauling at her, all talking at once. The bedroom was full of heavy carved black furniture, and a big black-framed photograph of Mrs. Michaelson brooded over it on the far wall. Marsha shouted, "Marjorie, what can you do about a goddamn lousy stuck zipper? Lend us a hand, will you? Otherwise the rabbi's going to get one hell of a thrill when I come out of here."

The girls squealed. "These are my cousins from St. Louis," Marsha said. "They're so excited they're helpless. Elaine Packovitch, Sue Packovitch, Patricia Packovitch, Margie Morgenstern." The girls stopped plucking at Marsha long enough to inspect Marjorie and chirp greetings. They varied in age from about eighteen to twenty-six, and they all looked very much like Marsha at her least attractive stage. They were dressed in terrible flounces—pink, green, yellow.

Marjorie came to Marsha's side and peered at the skirt hem jammed in the zipper. "Let's see——"

Marsha said, "Isn't it fantastic? Two years selling girdles, and I jam my own goddamn zipper on my wedding day. There's an omen for you. My hands are shaking so, I can't do anything." Marjorie wrenched and pushed deftly for a second or two, and the skirt dropped free. "Well, bless your little heart. What would I do without la Morningstar?" Marsha straightened her skirt at the mirror. "What time is it, somebody?"

One of the cousins said, "Five to six."

"Thirty-five minutes to go. God, where's my hat? It was right here—oh, there it is——" Marsha put on a small white hat with a white nose veil. "Somebody close the blinds, the wind's giving me the willies." It had grown quite dark, and rain was rattling on the window glass. A cousin snapped the Venetian blind shut. Marsha's brown eyes were brilliant with excitement; her face was flushed, and her upper lip quivered. She wore a suit of navy blue silk, unornamented and severely cut, with a white orchid on her shoulder. She said, "Okay, now. Something old, something new, something borrowed, something blue—— Wait, did I borrow anything?"

After a major squalling conference, with the Packovitch girls pressing earrings, bracelets, watches, and jewelry on her, she took a handkerchief from Marjorie, tucked it in a pocket, and dropped heavily on the bed. "Okay. The ox is ready for the knife."

Marjorie said, "How do you feel?"

"Absolutely floating, what do you think?" Marsha stared at her and smiled slyly. "Oh, listen, I'd better warn you. You-know-who is here, after all."

"I saw him as I came in."

"I'm sorry. I swear it isn't my doing. Lou got carried away at rehearsal and invited him, and then I couldn't very well——"

"Marsha, really, it's quite all right."

"Have you talked to him?"

"He didn't see me."

"Well, for crying out loud, what are you sitting here with me for? Go on out there. There are some other cute boys. Lou's partner Milton Schwartz isn't bad, if you can stand lawyers. *I* can't, but it's too late now, of course——"

The cousins giggled and the oldest, who had something like a hare lip, said indistinctly, "Marsha, you haven't changed one bit."

Marjorie said, "I'd just as lief stay here and hold your hand——"

"Sugar bun, I have a cousin on each hand, and one to hold my head if I start throwing up. Shoo. Scat. Go out and make the men feel good. Just don't start anything with the rabbi. I don't want him unfrocked before he ties the knot." Marjorie went out amid the giggling of the cousins, leaving Marsha perched laughing on the bed, her head thrown back, her knees drawn up, directly under the gloomy picture of Mrs. Michaelson.

There were rows of empty gilt folding chairs in the living room. The guests were jammed around the sides of the room and in the foyer, laughing and talking loudly. The air was heavy with tobacco smoke and women's perfume. They were a middle-aged crowd, the men running to dark suits, double chins, baldness, and cigars, and the women to fine dresses ruined by bulging figures. Obviously they were all, or almost all, Michaelson's friends and relatives. They looked, Marjorie thought, like customers in a Broadway restaurant: well-to-do, pleased with themselves, and dull, with interchangeable faces. Noel wasn't in the room. She worked her way to the window seat—the Michaelson cushion was purple, the Morgenstern cushion had been green and gold—and sat as she had sat for hundreds of evenings in her seventeenth and eighteenth years, hands folded in her lap and ankles crossed, looking through blurry panes at the black park and the flaring city. The automobiles, as always, reminded her of beetles as they ran along the twisting lamplit park roads, their headlights phosphorescent in the rain. The skyscrapers below Fifty-ninth Street loomed black, pierced with square yellow windows, and swathed in a pinkish fog. The view stirred an ache in Marjorie. This was the lost city. Here it was, unchanged, unconquered, and she was past twenty-one. She had sat like this by the window at seventeen, thinking that twenty-one was the golden time, the time when fame and money and a brilliant marriage would burst over her in an iridescent shower. It had seemed to her then that twenty-two was the start of the downward slope; that twenty-four was an autumn year; that thirty was decrepitude. She could remember these thoughts across the stretch of lost time and smile at them. But how much wiser was she now? What was the truth about herself, her life, her hopes, her dream of becoming Marjorie Morningstar?

"You're Marjorie Morgenstern." It was a pleasant voice, and a young one, cutting through the chatter behind her. The young man held two highball glasses in his hands. He wore a dark gray suit, and he had a handsome round face that might have been girlish, except for the solid square jaw. Thick black hair framed his forehead in a round line. He was about Noel's age.

"Yes, I'm Marjorie Morgenstern."

"I hope you like scotch and soda."

"At the moment I could go quite mad about one. Thank you." She took the glass and drank deeply. "This is very nice of you."

"I'm Milton Schwartz."

"Oh? Lou's law partner."

"Right."

"The man he plays handball with."

Schwartz smiled. "That's a good police-court way to identify me. I plead guilty to playing handball with Lou Michaelson." He looked at her for a moment. "You know me, Marjorie. At least I know you. We've danced. Two whole dances."

"Oh?"

"At the Ninety-second Street Y. The dance after the play. The night you played Nora in *A Doll's House*."

She regarded him more carefully. He might indeed be any one of the hundreds of boys she had danced with at one time or another since her fifteenth year; not bad-looking, with Jewish light and warmth in the eyes, and an urbane alertness about the face, the posture.

Noel Airman crossed her line of vision beyond Milton Schwartz's shoulder. Hands in the pockets of his worn gray flannel trousers, Noel was lounging through the knots of guests toward a large black reading stand in a corner of the room. She turned brightly to Schwartz. "Of course. I should have remembered. I was pretty numb that night. It was such a bad show——"

"Except for you it was pretty bad. But you were radiant."

"Thank you——"

"I'm not being polite. Actually your performance wasn't good for the show. You were so much better than the others, the whole effect became worse than it might have been. Sort of like throwing a white light on a painted set."

"Why, thank you again, that's very nicely put."

Schwartz was rolling the highball glass between his palms. "I wanted to say a lot to you that night. That's why I cut in. But then I got tongue-tied at the idea of dancing with a professional actress. I've always been a bug on dramatics, and——"

"I'm not a professional. Not by a long shot."

Noel was poking and peering at the black stand, which, Marjorie now realized, might be a piece of electric equipment, possibly a diathermy machine. What on earth was it doing in the living room?

Schwartz said, "Don't say that. I know a good bit about you. I used to work with the Vagabonds. I went backstage that night and got the low-down on you. The legal mind at work. I tried to call you for a date three or four times after that, but I got discouraged. You were never at home, and——"

She flashed a brilliant smile at Schwartz and laughed as though he had made a devilishly clever joke. Noel's eyes had moved for a fraction of a second toward her, and away again. She laid a hand on Schwartz's arm. "It was sweet of you to go to all that trouble. I wish I'd known."

He scanned her face, his mouth moving in a slow pleasant smile. "You'll think I'm a fool, but when Marsha mentioned at the office last week, quite by accident, that her friend Marjorie Morgenstern was coming to the wedding, I all but knocked her down, hugging her."

"Did you really? I must have been better as Nora than I thought. Don't forget, those were Ibsen's lines. I'm just a would-be bit player, just another West End Avenue girl. If you're cherishing any other picture of me, you'll be sorry you ever got to know me any better." She said all this with great vivacity, her eyes fixed on Schwartz's.

He said, "There's no end to how much better I'd like to know you."

"I thought lawyers were slow to commit themselves."

"You came alone tonight, didn't you?"

"Yes."

"Let me take you home, or out, or anything you say, after this is over."

She hesitated. Nothing could annoy Noel more, of course. "That's very kind of you. . . ."

"Marjorie! Marjorie, please!" Mrs. Zelenko was waving at her from the middle of the room, smiling very brightly.

"Excuse me," she said to Schwartz.

Marsha's mother slipped an arm through hers, and drew her out of the living room; Noel Airman and Milton Schwartz both looked after her. The three Packovitch girls were whispering together in a corner of the foyer. They noticed Marjorie and whispered more excitedly behind their hands. Mrs. Zelenko muttered, "Don't look concerned or anything. It's nothing at all, bridal nerves, I guess. I had a bad case of it ten minutes before my own ceremony, heaven knows. But you'd better talk to her—she's asking for you——"

"Of course."

Rounding the corner of the hallway, they encountered Lou Michaelson, with two men in black. His wavy gray hair was oiled down and sharply parted, showing freckles on his scalp. He introduced the rabbi and the best man to Marjorie. "Just a few more minutes," he said, with a flustered smile that uncovered one gold tooth. "I can't believe it. How's Marsha, Mom?"

"Wonderful, wonderful, Lou. We're just going to her."

The mother opened the door of the bedroom carefully. Marsha lay face down on the bed, under the picture of Mrs. Michaelson. She said in a strange voice, grainy and dry, "I just want to talk to Marjorie, Tonia. You can go along."

"Marsha dear, I'll do anything——"

"I'm perfectly okay. I'm wonderful. Goodbye."

Mrs. Zelenko shrugged at Marjorie and went out. When the door closed Marsha sat up, clutching Marjorie's handkerchief. Her eyes were moist and reddish. The little white hat was askew over one ear. "Have you ever been closed in on by a herd of bellowing buffalo? My dear cousins were beginning to oppress me. I had to get rid of them, or jump out of the window. And I couldn't do that. Think what the rain would do to this sweet little hat. Twenty-seven dollars shot to hell." She laughed. "Well, la Morningstar, are you nervous? I'm not. Calmest bride you ever heard of. Well? Sit down, for heaven's sake, don't stand there looking at me."

Marjorie sat by her on the bed.

Marsha said, "What time is it?"

"Twenty past six."

"Ten minutes, hey? Just time for one more cigarette." She took a crumpled pack from the bed, lit one, and inhaled with a hiss. "My last cigarette as a free girl. Next one I smoke will be smoked by Mrs. Michaelson." She gestured with the cigarette toward the picture of Lou's mother. "That was her name, too. Mrs. Michaelson. Could anything be queerer? The old girl must be turning over in her grave like a cement mixer."

"Marsha, don't say such things. You'll make a wonderful wife for Lou."

Marsha looked at her with unnaturally wide eyes. "Why is it, I wonder, that I was destined never to have anything I really wanted?"

With a catch in her voice, Marjorie said, "Look, dear, when the time comes for me to take the fatal step I'll probably have an attack of the dismals twice as bad as this——"

"It doesn't seem to me I've ever wanted so much. A friend, a good job, a fellow——" Marsha made strange sharp sounds like a cough; but she wasn't coughing. She seemed to be laughing. She put her arms around Marjorie, pressing her tight, and she cried desperately. The straw of her hat scratched Marjorie's cheek.

It was very hot and uncomfortable to be hugged by Marsha, but there was nothing to do but pat her shoulder and murmur soothing words. "I'm so alone, darling," Marsha sobbed. "So absolutely alone. You'll never know what it means. I've always been alone. So alone, so damned alone. And now I'll always be alone. Forever, till I die."

Marjorie started to cry too, yet she resented this sudden closeness with Marsha, and tried to fight down her pity. She felt that Marsha was taking advantage of her. "Don't go on like that. Good Lord, I thought you were such a tough bird. You're going to be very happy and you know it. Stop crying, Marsha, you've got me doing it. We'll both ruin our faces. There's nothing to cry about. You should be very happy."

Marsha withdrew from her and sat bowed on the edge of the bed, crying and crying. Marjorie took away the cigarette that was burning down in her fingers, and crushed it. After a minute or so Marsha blew her nose and sighed. "Ye gods, I needed that. I feel five thousand per cent better." She got up and began to work on her face at the mirror. "I've been fighting it off and fighting it off. How could I cry with those fat gloating harpies around, my sweet maids of honor? Thanks, dear, you saved my life."

Marjorie said, "Well, live and learn. I'd have bet you'd be the last girl in the world to get maidenly hysterics. I guess we're all human."

Marsha turned on her. White powder smudged around her eyes gave her a clown-like look. "What the hell! Don't you suppose I have feelings? Do you think I'm a lizard or something?"

"Darling, it's perfectly natural——"

"Oh, sure. Natural for everybody except Marsha Zelenko, hey? The girl with the rubber heart. Listen, kid, when it comes to insensitivity you're the world's champion for your weight and size." She blinked and shook her head. "Oh, look, I don't want to be mean. I'm all in a stew, you've got to forgive me——" She dabbed at her face with the powder puff. "But the hell with it, I'm going to tell you something, Marjorie, even if you never speak to me again. Lou didn't invite Noel Airman tonight. I did."

Marjorie said, "Frankly, I surmised as much. I wish you wouldn't give it another thought, that's all."

Marsha faced her, lipstick in hand. "Just like that. Don't give it another thought. Have you any idea how infuriating it is to me to think of you discarding Noel Airman? How on earth can you do it? That's what I keep asking myself. Where do you get the willpower? What runs in your veins, anyway—ammonia? It isn't blood, that's for sure. You're madly in love with the man. He loves you the way he's never loved any girl and probably never will. Do you know what I'd have given for one hour of such a love affair? With such a man? My eyes."

"Marsha, it really isn't——"

"I know, I know, I know, it really isn't any of my damned business. What do I care? I've got to say this or I'll explode. I'll probably never see you after tonight. I know all too well what you must think of my marrying Lou Michaelson——"

"I like Lou, Marsha, I swear I do, you're being hysterical——"

"I like him, too. I'm marrying him because life only lasts so long, and I'm damn tired. I could kiss his hands for being willing to take over, and be good to me, and let me relax, and give my folks what they want. I don't have a Noel Airman in love with me. If I had I'd follow him like a dog. I'd support him. I'd ask him to walk on me every morning, just to feel the weight of his shoes. Oh, Marjorie, you fool, you fool, don't you know that you'll be dead a long long time? That you'll be old and dried up and sick a long long time? You've got all of God's gold at your feet, all He ever gives anybody in this filthy world, youth and good looks and a wonderful lover, and you kick it all aside like garbage just because Noel doesn't go to synagogue twice a day or something. I tell you, you're the fool of fools, Marjorie. You'll die screaming curses at yourself. That is, if you're not too withered and stupid by then to realize what you did to yourself when you were young and alive and pretty and had your chance——"

Marjorie, her breath all but knocked out by the sudden attack, gasped, "You're just crazy, that's all. Noel doesn't care two hoots about me, and——"

"Oh, shut up, he's *insane* about you!"

"All right, and if he is, what do you want me to do—sleep with him like all his other trollops? And then let him kick me out when he's had all he wants?"

"YES, God damn you, YES! If you're not woman enough to hold him, all you deserve is to be kicked out. What do you think he is, one of your puking little temple dates? He's a MAN. If you can make him marry you, okay. And if you can't, that's your tough luck! Find out what he's like. Let him find out what you're like. *Live* your life, you poor boob. I'll tell you a great big secret, Marjorie dear—*there's no hell.* You won't burn. Nothing will happen to you, except you'll pile up a thousand memories to warm you when you're an old crock. And what's more, if you've got what it takes you'll snag yourself a husband—a bloody Prince Charming of a husband, not only witty and good-looking but rich and famous, which Noel Airman is damn well going to be. . . . Lord, look at you. You're staring at me as though I had horns and a tail. All right, *don't* listen to me. Do as you damn please. What do I care? Go to your temple dances and marry Sammy Lefkowitz, the brassiere manufacturer's son. It's probably all you deserve."

The knocking at the door had been going on for several seconds, but Marjorie, transfixed, had been unable to interrupt. Now it turned to pounding, and Mrs. Zelenko's indistinct voice called, "Marsha, Marsha dear, for heaven's sake, it's past six-thirty!"

"Oh God." Marsha whirled to the mirror. "Go out there, sugar bun.

Keep them at bay, will you? Just for two minutes while I do something about these red holes I've got for eyes."

"Sure I will." Marjorie hesitated, and said to Marsha's back, "Good luck, Marsha. God bless you."

Marsha turned, looked forlornly at her, caught her in her arms, and kissed her. "Oh baby, baby darling. Forget it, forget everything I said. Goodbye, sugar bun. I can't tell you why I've always loved you, and why I fuss so over you. I should have had a brother or a sister. I've had nobody. You'll be all right no matter what you do, I'm sure. You're God's favorite, Marjorie Morningstar. Go along with you."

Marjorie slipped out through the door, and held off the fretting mother and cousins until Marsha called, "Okay, Marge, let the firing squad in." They brushed past her, twittering angrily and anxiously.

Chapter 35. THE BREAKING OF A GLASS

A hush had fallen in the apartment; as she walked toward the foyer, Marjorie's heels ticked on the parquet floor. She was rounding the bend in the hallway when she heard a queer noise from the living room, starting low and sliding up eerily, like the wail of an epileptic. The sound rose and fell and swelled and faded, and after a few moments Marjorie realized that she was hearing some kind of music. The noises were coalescing into the wedding song *Oh Promise Me*, played on some bizarre instrument, too full-bodied to be an ocarina or a musical saw, too quavery to be an electric organ. It sounded at one moment like a cello, at the next like a flute, and at the next like nothing so much as a cat dying under the wheels of a car. She came tiptoeing into the foyer, and a long arm circled her waist: she shuddered. Noel pulled her close, whispering, "Don't go in now, wait till she finishes."

"What in God's name is that, Noel?"

"It's a theremin."

"A what?"

"Theremin. Sh." He put his finger over her lips, and moved with her to the archway of the living room. The guests were seated in silent rows, facing the windows. Luba Wolono, tall and fearsome, alone at the far end of the room, was waving white hands in the air over the black thing like a diathermy machine. It looked even odder now, because a metal pole two feet high stood in a socket at one end, and a loop of metal jutted out sidewise at the other. She was making the music simply by moving her hands in empty air. Whenever her hand approached the pole, the note became higher; when she pulled it away, it dropped, sometimes to a bass rumble. She made the sound loud or soft by moving her other hand up or down over the loop. Spectacular though the stunt was, she was either not good at this legerdemain or the machine was innately not very musical, for the sobs and slides and groans, from note to note, were hideous to hear. Noel drew her away from the arch and leaned against the wall, his arm still around her waist. "There's only one person in the world who can really make it sound like anything, Clara Rockmore. I heard her at a recital, she does wonders with it. This woman's even gotten up like her, but——"

"How on earth does it work?"

"It's an electronic gadget. You wave your hands in a magnetic field, and make a disturbance that gets translated into music, after a fashion. There was a lot of talk for a while about it being the instrument of the future, and all that nonsense——"

The theremin slid up to a weird off-pitch high note and hung there, pulsing and, as it were, gasping, *Wah wah wah*. "I just can't stand it," Marjorie said.

He patted her shoulder. "There's a hell of a moral lesson in the thing, honey, if you're interested in morality this afternoon. In theory it's the perfect instrument. You can draw out one note forever. Unlimited loud or soft effects. Infinite range of pitch, you can go higher than the human ear can hear and lower than a double bassoon. None of the reediness of wind instruments, no breathing problem. No roughness as in the strings, no bowing problem. All the virtues, no drawbacks. And the damn thing's unplayable. Think it over, dear, when you pick a husband."

She murmured, "It's a wonder you don't play it." He chuckled, and pulled her ear.

When the song ended, Noel and Marjorie slipped into seats in the back row. Luba Wolono remained immobile at the theremin. There was a rustle of talk among the guests, and the rabbi stood, placing himself between the windows, facing the aisle. Four men in black skullcaps rose, holding up a little purple canopy on four unsteady sticks. The rabbi turned to Luba Wolono and nodded. Her hands began to saw the air, and a sort of Hindu version of the Lohengrin wedding music streamed out of the theremin, in eerie keening glissandos.

Leading the bridal procession into the living room came the best man, big, bald, gold chain across his vest, chest thrown out, portly stomach pulled in. Next came the Packovitch girls with little bouquets of jonquils, staring at the theremin player, glancing at each other, and biting their lips to suppress their giggles, not with complete success. Then came Mrs. Zelenko, and Lou Michaelson. The procession piled up at the head of the aisle, and the canopy on the four sticks swayed and joggled. Marjorie in this moment changed her mind completely about her own wedding, and decided to have the hugest and most splendid ceremony she could engineer, instead of a modest home affair.

The theremin began to wail and groan *Here Comes the Bride*. Marsha came in holding the arm of little white-headed Mr. Zelenko, on whose face unregarded tears trickled. She walked past Marjorie with a dead-calm expression, eyes steady behind the little veil; paced up to the side of Lou Michaelson under the wavering canopy, and halted. At the rabbi's nod, Luba Wolono dropped her arms in mid-melody, and the theremin expired with a grunt. Marsha's father and her bridegroom, standing on either side of her, were of about the same height and build. They wore identical black suits, and their hair was almost the same color. From the back it was hard to tell which was which.

It was a traditional ceremony, and it ended in the traditional way, with Lou Michaelson crushing under his heel a wineglass wrapped in paper. At the sound of breaking glass, the guests applauded, cheered, and surged forward. "Good luck! Good luck! Good luck!" There was a rush to shake Lou's hand and kiss the bride under the wavering canopy. The theremin began whooping in a grotesque simulation of joy.

"That confounded breaking of a glass. It always shocks me," Noel said. "Doesn't it you? Leave it to the Jews to work up a spine-chilling symbol for all occasions."

Marjorie said, "My father once told me it's a reminder of the destruction of the temple."

"It's more than that. It's—I don't know, it must be something out of the mists of time, out of *The Golden Bough*. I saw an uncle of mine do that when I was four and a half years old. I had dreams about it for years. I had a feeling then, a real grisly childish fancy, that he was symbolically breaking his bride under his foot. Hell, like any real symbol, I guess it means whatever your mind brings to it. Let's go grab some champagne before the panic starts."

Soon there was a jovial crush in the dining room around a table heaped with sliced meats, smoked fish, roast fowls, salads, and cakes. Marsha moved through the crowd with Lou at her side, the center of a little travelling whirlpool of gaiety. She laughed, she hugged, she kissed people; she snapped pert answers to jokes, causing roars and giggles. In one hand she carried a glass of champagne, in the other a smoking cigarette. Marjorie, standing beside Noel in a corner, watched her, amazed. Marsha swept by them. "Bless you, my children! Grab the rabbi before he leaves, why don't you? Let's make it a double wedding." With a wave of her glass and an exuberant laugh she was gone.

"She looks really happy," Marjorie said.

"I'm sure she is," Noel said. "This fellow is quite an improvement over Carlos Ringel, and at one time she'd have settled for Carlos gladly."

"Carlos Ringel was an old horror."

Noel swirled the champagne in his glass. "Sure, but Marsha's never had too much to offer, has she? With Carlos she traded sex for attention. Now it's youth for security. When you haven't got charm or good looks, your bargaining power is limited."

"I think Marsha's charming. Very charming."

"Well, she's what you'd call the bulging sort. You know, bulging figure, bulging eyes, bulging appetites, bulging eagerness to please, bulging desire to get places. They're a type, like albinos. You run across them all the time. They attract you for a while with their energy and bounce, but they're really bores."

"I hate such pigeonholing of people. It's glib and it's false."

"Well, I don't know," Noel said. "Texans, now, are certainly Texans, aren't they? Good sports are good sports. And I'm afraid bulgers are bulgers."

"And what's my pigeonhole, I wonder?" Marjorie was feeling dizzy and loose-tongued, having drunk a couple of glasses of champagne too fast. "Oh, excuse me, I forgot. I'm the West End Avenue prig. The *ordinary* West End Avenue prig."

"Don't misquote me, please. That's exactly what I said you weren't."

"Yes, you labored under the delusion that I was different, for a while. But you found out otherwise, didn't you, Noel?" She looked him straight in the face. The crowd had jostled them close together. He looked at her rather sternly, with compressed lips curving down. It was a look she knew very well; Marsha was right, this man was still in love with her. Her body was warm and restless.

He said, "You're a prig, true enough. But then all angels are, more or less. An angel's job is being holier than thou."

"Still turning the phrases."

"Don't patronize me, you haunting little hag, or I'll hit you with a bottle of champagne."

They carried plates piled with food to the window seat in the deserted living room, where the Negro was folding and clattering the gilt chairs into a corner. For a while they ate in silence. Black rain lashed the window glass, and the wind sighed and whistled through the frames. "Nice night for a stroll in the park," Noel said. "Even the perverts and the muggers wouldn't go out in this."

Marjorie leaned her hot cheek against the window. "I love to look at it. I always did. The park road and the Broadway lights, the big hotels, they make such a wonderful show on a rainy night. I used to live in the El Dorado, you know."

"I know." He lightly kissed the side of her forehead.

She glanced up at him, surprised. "What was that for?"

"Somehow that's the most wistful remark I've ever heard. 'I used to live in the El Dorado' . . . So did we all, my darling. The golden place gives short leases."

She shrugged. "You needn't sound so plaintive. Looks to me like you're just about to move in again. How's *Princess Jones* going?"

"Very well, I think." He put aside his plate, and lit a cigarette with a new silver lighter of a foreign make.

"I was awfully glad for you when I read about it."

"Were you? You might have come by the theatre, or at least dropped me a note to wish me luck."

Marjorie saw Milton Schwartz, with a glass in his hand, come to the door of the living room and peer in. The instant her eyes met his he turned and hurried off.

She said, "Oh yes, wouldn't I have made a fine figure! Chasing after you, now that you're in the limelight——"

"I thought we parted friends last time."

"We did. I'm praying for your success, Noel. I'll probably sit up late opening night to read the notices."

"You can come to the opening night if you like. With me."

"That's very sweet of you, but no, thanks."

"Why not?"

"Well, I just don't think it's the best idea I've ever heard." She tried hard to be casual, though her throat was suddenly dry.

"I think it's a pretty damned good idea."

"Are you pleased with the production?"

"Amazingly so. Ferris isn't exactly Max Gordon. But he did have a backer all lined up, and I thought, well, an unknown producer with all this enthusiasm is better than an old-timer who isn't interested. He's mounted the show brilliantly. I think we've got a fine chance."

"It'll be a smash, Noel."

He put his hand on her shoulder. "It's strange, you know. The music's really permeated by you. I've been sitting in the dark theatre during rehearsals, thinking about you, and those long evenings in my rat hole on Bank Street——"

"It wasn't a rat hole, Noel. It had a lovely fireplace."

"Well, if it's a hit, I daresay I ought to send you a mink stole or something. You encouraged me to keep working at that show. A dozen times I'd have thrown it in the fire, if not for you. In fact you've always had a bracing effect on me. It doesn't seem fair, does it? The only girl I ever was all wrong for——"

"Noel!" The lady who called him was short, gray-headed, and plump. Marjorie had noticed earlier her thick diamond choker and diamond bracelets. She beckoned from the archway, and the diamonds sparkled. "Hurry. Some folks want to meet the famous author."

"Okay, Mollie. . . ." He said to Marjorie, jumping up, "Be back in a moment."

"Who on earth is Mollie?"

"Mollie Lemberg. She's a very good soul, really. She's backing the show, so——" He winked, and strode off.

Marjorie rolled her forehead from side to side on the cold misted windowpane. The food had not quieted her giddiness in the least. She had hardly been able to eat. She picked up her plate again, and dug her fork into a piece of tongue; then she put away the plate and the fork. Her throat swelled at the thought of eating. She was very alarmed, almost in panic, at the way things were going with her and Noel. But it was a delicious panic. It was as though she had made one misstep, nearing the top of a long mountain climb, and had tumbled and rolled all the way to the bottom, only to sit up slightly bruised, dishevelled, and laughing. She felt very much like laughing out loud.

She knew that the one sensible thing to do now was to leave the party. In a few minutes, without persuasion, without drama, without argument, without any perceptible stages, the estrangement of almost a year was gone. She was open to Noel again, and she was slightly drunk. She walked out of the living room, careful of her steadiness.

Milton Schwartz was in the foyer. "Hello, do you still remember me?"

"Of course. Handball king, Ibsen fan, legal brain."

"Right. You've been drinking champagne, haven't you? Let me get you another glass."

"One thing I don't need at this point is more champagne, thank you."

"Well, come with me while I get another highball, then. I want to talk to you, really I do. I'm dying to."

"Why, sure, but it's hardly worth dying for. I'm leaving in a minute, anyway."

They passed Noel in a circle of guests, all talking at him, the women staring and smiling hungrily. Mrs. Lemberg had her arm through his.

Milton Schwartz said to the bar attendant, "One scotch and soda, and one champagne."

"I said no."

"Well, hold it in your hand, then. Marjorie, I—listen, maybe this sounds crazy but . . . well, the best way I can put it is, I have a feeling I've known you for a long time, and am going to know you a lot longer. I want to ask you whether you've had anything like the same feeling, or whether I'm off in the clouds. This is a very crazy and stupid question, I grant you."

She wondered whether she was in some hyperamorous mood worked up by wine and a wedding. Schwartz seemed attractive to her, too. Two men could hardly have looked more different than Milton Schwartz and Noel Airman. Schwartz was dark, almost moon-faced, of middle height, and broad-shouldered. Marjorie had decided long ago that if ever she fell in love again, it would have to be with a tall lean blond man; Noel had made that figure the type of masculinity for her. On an impulse she drank half the champagne in her glass. "All right. It's a leading question, and impertinent and unfair and all that. But I'll answer it. I really don't remember dancing with you. But I think I'll remember you after this evening——"

"How well do you know that writer?" Schwartz inclined his head toward the living room.

"Very well, if it's any business of yours."

"I'm jealous," Schwartz said. "Not that he scares me, but I surmise he's had rather a head start."

"Have you had a lot to drink? It seems so."

"Quite a lot. Usually I don't drink much. But I don't think it shows. In fact, I listen to myself talk to you and I'm amazed. And pleased. I hope you are."

"Well, I'm a bit flabbergasted."

"Look, Marjorie, why don't we get out of here? A good heart-to-heart talk between the principals is usually a sound idea. I'll tell you all about myself. It suddenly seems interesting to me, my life story. Maybe we can——"

SCREEEEEEEEEE! A frightful sound blared through the apartment. Marjorie shivered from head to foot, and screamed at Schwartz over the noise, "My God! *What's that?*" Almost at once the screech changed into a mixed hideous din, as of a zoo going up in flames—growls, squeals, shrieks, barks, groans, howls. The guests in the dining room, their eyes dilated with astonishment, swarmed toward the foyer, carrying Marjorie and Schwartz with them. He seized her hand, and pulled her deftly through the crowd, using his shoulders like a football player. "Let's damn well see what it is," he yelled; Marjorie barely heard him over the cataract of horrible clamor.

Schwartz broke through to the living room, taking Marjorie with him; and they saw at once what was happening. The maniacal bursts of sound were coming from the theremin. Around the black stand the three

Packovitch girls were bounding and prancing like circus elephants, trumpeting with laughter, poking their hands at the pole and the loop; and with every motion of their hands the noise of the theremin changed. It whooped, it grunted, it screeched, it howled, it belched. Lou Michaelson was angrily fussing at the control panel of the machine, shouting in vain at the hysterical fat girls to stop. In the middle of the room, Marsha lay on her stomach on the floor, with her hat over one ear, beating the rug with her fists, kicking her heels, and laughing as though she would die. Mr. Zelenko stood on one side of her, doubled over with laughter, feebly trying to pull her up; her mother stood on the other side, obviously not at all amused, tugging at Marsha's elbow, her orchids dangling crazily. "Marsha, for God's sake, stop making such a spectacle of yourself, get *up*——"

Marjorie bawled at Mrs. Zelenko, "Where's Luba Wolono? Why doesn't she turn it off?"

"Luba *left*. That idiot Patricia turned the blasted thing on somehow, and now—— Marsha, *will* you get off the floor, you're disgracing the whole family——"

"Funniest, funniest thing I've ever seen or heard. Oh, Lord, let me perish," Marsha gasped.

HEEEEEEE, went the theremin—an unendurable scream, exactly like an ocean liner's whistle, not two feet from Marjorie. She clapped her hands to her ears and ran out of the room, fighting her way through the guests crowding in from the foyer, and stood against the wall near the doorway, panting. Noel emerged for a moment from the mill of guests and laughed, peering into the living room. "Bloody idiots!" He disappeared toward the bedrooms.

The racket stopped, all at once. The excited laughing chatter of the guests, by contrast, was like a blessed silence. Marjorie heard Lou Michaelson sing out, "What happened? Who did that? What shut it off?"

Marjorie looked into the living room and saw Milton Schwartz crawling on his hands and knees from behind a sofa. Schwartz called, "Lou, the damned thing just plugs in the wall like a vacuum cleaner. I pulled the plug, that's all." The guests broke into raucous cheers; they clustered around Schwartz, shaking his hand and slapping his back, as he got to his feet and dusted his knees.

Noel appeared at Marjorie's side, holding her coat and his own over one arm, and extending a package of cigarettes. "Here. No doubt you can use one of these."

"What——?"

"Take it. And let's get out of this crazy house before the walls fall in or the floor starts wobbling. I'm getting the horrors."

She found herself out in the hallway, lighting the cigarette. He was ringing for the elevator. She was very glad to be out of the Michaelson apartment; then she thought of Milton Schwartz. "Now just a second, Noel. Where do you think you're taking me? I didn't say I'd go out with you——"

"I didn't offer to take you out. I can't. I'm busy. I presume you want to go home, however. And not alone, in this downpour."

The elevator door slid open. She hung back, and he glanced at her, raising an eyebrow.

But she was too tired, too shaken, too giddy to take the trouble to argue with him and return to the Michaelson apartment. Milton Schwartz wasn't important to her. He would probably be telephoning her in a day or so; and what difference did it all make, anyway? She hadn't promised to let him take her home. She was very bored with the problems of being a girl. She stepped into the elevator.

Merely walking from the doorway of the El Dorado to the cab, they got wet; the wind was driving gusts of rain under the canopy. It felt very snug to settle in the back seat of a heated taxi beside Noel; snug, and familiar. The taxi smelled of rain, and their clothes smelled damp, too. The driver said, "Where to, Mac?"

Noel looked at her, then at his wristwatch. "How anxious are you to go home?"

"Extremely anxious. I've never been through anything so exhausting. Home, please."

"If you're interested, the final dress rehearsal of *Princess Jones* starts in half an hour. Why don't you come and watch it for a while?"

Chapter 36. ANOTHER GLASS BREAKS

The cab lurched around a curve, came out of the black park, and headed down Seventh Avenue toward the misty sea of light at Times Square.

Marjorie felt very much as though she were on the horse which had bolted with her in Central Park when she was seventeen. She was with Noel Airman again, despite everything; with him again, and being carried along by events in the old uncontrolled way. Yet how could she have refused to see the dress rehearsal of *Princess Jones?* She took some comfort in observing that if it was a victory for him, he seemed unaware of it. He was sunk in abstracted silence. She said, "I guess I'll never stop being amazed by you."

"What now?" he said rather wearily.

"How can you be so unconcerned about your first Broadway show? Here it was the afternoon of your dress rehearsal all the time, and I didn't know it. Nobody could have guessed. You were just ambling around that party, eating, drinking, carefree as a bird. You're really one for the books, Noel Airman."

He shrugged. "I'm not in the least unconcerned. I'd probably sing like a wire if you touched me. But what's the use? We had a knock-down conference until four o'clock. There were three dead hours to kill, I knew you'd be at the wedding, so . . ." He sank into silence again, smoking. Rain flooded the closed windows of the cab, smearing and running almost like a thrown bucket of water.

After a minute or so she said, "I'm really terrifically tired. But this is one temptation I can't resist. I'd like to watch the first act, anyway—see how you've changed it——"

"Stay as long as you like," Noel said. "We're running straight through. If it doesn't bore you, I hope you'll watch the whole thing. I'd like very much to know what you think of it."

"My opinion isn't worth anything."

"On the contrary. You're the New York audience in miniature. And you're probably as familiar as anybody with all the different versions I've done. Your comments will be very valuable, I imagine."

When the cab stopped at the stage door of the theatre, he turned to her with a slight wistful smile. "Well, here we go, darling. I guarantee you there's no theremin in it, anyway." She nervously laughed, and darted with him through the rain into the stage entrance.

Beautiful girls in frilly crimson costumes, with heavily painted faces like dolls, were bustling up and down the iron grille staircase. Noel led her to the dressing rooms and introduced her to the stars, who were fussing with their makeup at lamp-bordered mirrors. They all called Noel by his first name, chatted with him as equals, laughed at his jokes, and treated Marjorie charmingly. The leading lady, the best-known performer in the cast, was especially pleasant to her. She had a hard businesslike manner, but despite the heavy makeup she was marvelously pretty, with eyes inhumanly large and blue in rims of black paint. Marjorie was entranced. The excited chatter, the tension in the perfumed air backstage, the overpainted faces, the kindergarten colors of the costumes, gave her a feeling of walking in fairyland.

The theatre itself was dark and chilly, the rows of empty seats very bleak. A few people sat huddled in overcoats here and there in the orchestra. Musicians in sweaters or coats, most of them needing shaves, were tuning their instruments in the pit. Noel put her in a seat in the middle of the fifth row, and went off to talk to the producer in the front row. Marjorie sat working a handkerchief in her hands, contrasting this rare moment with the many times she had sat in this same theatre, one of a crowd of paying customers, looking at this same dusty gray curtain decorated with rococo knights and ladies, before the start of a play. She saw the others puffing cigarettes, so she lighted one. Smoking in the forbidden pale of a theatre orchestra heightened her dizzied sense of privilege. Mrs. Lemberg, in a bulky mink coat, came down the aisle and joined the producer.

The curtain suddenly went up on a quaint lovely setting of a European village square covered with snow and decorated for Christmas. Stagehands in dirty overalls were pushing an unsteady painted fir tree into place, hoarsely yelling at each other. For a few minutes Noel, the producer, the dance director, and the set designer took turns commenting on the placing of the tree. A decision was reached, the tree was secured in place, and the curtain came down.

"Like the set?" Noel said, returning to her.

"Why, it couldn't be more beautiful. I never pictured anything so elaborate."

"Ferris brought in a new kid from Hollywood to do the sets and costumes. They're superb, I think."

The musicians brassily struck up the overture; the curtain rose again; the setting was masked now by a gorgeous curtain, purple, red, and gold, in a cubistic pattern. Marjorie involuntarily touched Noel's arm; she had not been so keyed up in her life. "Good luck," she whispered.

Three hours went by like so many minutes.

Princess Jones, from the first moment to the last, seemed to her a rich winning fantasy; a waterfall of color, splendor, laughter, and charm. Everything about it was magical: the elegant settings, the spill of lovely costumes, the swirling crowds of dancers, the melting music, the bright lighthearted comedy scenes. She knew the story, of course, and all the jokes, and all the songs. The show had not been changed very much from the last version Noel had showed her. But it was electrifying to see Noel's brain child fleshed out and brilliantly alive—peopled, colored, danced, sung, a living thing, a Broadway show. The first dress rehearsal, according to Noel, had been very disorderly, but the troubles seemed to have been ironed out; the show unreeled as on an opening night.

When the curtain came down on the finale, a blazing whirl of color and sound—a waltz of the whole company in the grand ballroom of the palace, with the plot all unravelled and the lovers all paired off, a faintly mocking but gay end to the satiric fable—when the orchestra trumpeted a massive crescendo, and the descending curtain cut off the enchanting vision—Marjorie couldn't contain herself. She seized Noel's hand, and pressed it hard. He turned to her, his eyes glittering in the glow from the footlights. But before she could speak a word, in the first instant of silence after the final chord from the band, the producer called over in a bored voice, "Noel, did you do anything about the new duet?" Noel left her, with a nod and a smile to acknowledge her little applauding gesture with gloved hands.

He returned in a few minutes. "We're all going up to my hotel to talk. Come along."

"Oh no, thanks. It's a great show, Noel, it'll be a terrific hit. Thanks for letting me see it. I'll go home——"

"Are you so very tired? Peter asked me to bring you along."

"Well, if—who's going?"

"Well, Peter, of course, and the dance director, and the dialogue director, and the orchestra leader—there'll be about half a dozen of us. We have Chinese food sent up at these night sessions, and coffee. It's fun. We get a lot of work done, too. You can leave whenever you want, I'll put you in a cab——"

"I'd be in the way."

"Nonsense. Peter wants to hear your reactions. Come on, we've got a limousine waiting outside."

"Is Mrs. Lemberg going?"

"Of course."

"Well, I won't be the only female, anyway, then. Sure, I'd love to."

With five men and Mrs. Lemberg crowded in the limousine, Marjorie felt fairly safe going to Noel's hotel. Peter Ferris, the producer, was a remarkably handsome man, younger than Noel. His grace and his smooth manners reminded Marjorie of her actor friends; but unlike them he seemed to possess sharp intelligence, and a high charge of energy. Mrs. Lemberg frankly doted on him. He cross-examined Marjorie about the show in a good-humored brisk way, and her answers pleased him. "This girl's not only charming and pretty, she knows the theatre," he said to Noel. "You'd better marry her."

"That's what she says."

Marjorie blushed to her ears, everyone laughed, and Noel gave her a hug. The discussion of the show went on, and Marjorie was surprised at the sophistication of Mrs. Lemberg. She looked like one of her mother's temple sisterhood friends in her puffball of a mink coat, and her voice sounded like theirs, but she was bright and hard-boiled.

Marjorie made a much-appreciated contribution early in the conference at Noel's suite. A new comic song was needed, everyone had agreed, shortly before the end of the second act. The men were trying to think of a topic for the song; they were sprawled around the room—on the couch, across chairs, on the floor, in their shirtsleeves, some with shoes off. Mrs. Lemberg meantime placidly played solitaire on a coffee table, her diamonds winking in the lamplight. The silence grew long. Marjorie worked up her courage, and bashfully remarked to Noel that he might be able to use a certain duet from one of the old South Wind revues. Noel frowned, then jumped up and walked to the spinet piano. "By God, I'd completely forgotten that one. Listen to it, Peter. It might work, at that. Do you remember the words, Marge?" Marjorie remembered every word of every song of Noel's. She went to the piano and sang, acting out both parts with gestures and dance steps from Noel's original staging.

They gave her a little round of applause. "Gad, let's put her in the show, she's better than the leading lady we've got," Ferris said. "Noel, I think it's good. The words need some work, but let's try it. Marjorie, I appoint you permanent staff consultant on the contents of Noel's trunk. Let's have a drink on it."

Noel had just finished pouring very dark-looking highballs when the Chinese food came. They all drank up quickly, while the Chinese messenger dished the food. It was quite a supper. A plate of sliced pink pork was part of the buffet, along with egg rolls, chow mein, fried lobster, and rice. Marjorie had become quite free about the food she ate; but she had never yet deliberately helped herself to pork, though she had suspected more than once that she was eating it, and had gone on eating. It occurred to her now, when she saw little Mrs. Lemberg piling pork on her plate, that it was high time she shrugged off these hypocritical little distinctions of hers. She took a couple of pork slices; and by dipping them completely in mustard sauce she got them down without any trouble. Eating the pork gave her an odd sense of freedom, and at the same time, though she suppressed it, a twinge of disgust. She asked Noel for another highball.

After the Chinese food the conference grew long, and rather blurry. Marjorie wandered around the suite, washed her face in cold water in the bathroom, and glanced through heavily blue-pencilled scripts of *Princess Jones* lying scattered in the bedroom on the double bed. There was also a worn volume of W. S. Gilbert's librettos. She took the book into the living room, and scanned the pages of *The Mikado* while the talk went on, thinking of her stage debut at Hunter, and of her early friendship with Marsha Zelenko. After a while, she put aside the book and went to the window. Noel's suite was on the twenty-sixth floor. Far up the park she could see the twin towers of the El Dorado. The rain had stopped, and the low clouds were breaking up. A blue-white full moon, almost overhead, was sailing rapidly through the clouds.

Marsha's wedding at the El Dorado seemed to Marjorie to have happened not a few hours ago, but last week or last month. The whole business already was fading: the gray-headed little husband, the theremin, the Packovitch girls, Milton Schwartz, and Marsha's wild tirade before the ceremony. The present moment, here in Noel's hotel suite, meshed smoothly with the old days—before the break over Imogene, before the brief era of Morris Shapiro. It was so natural and right to be back with Noel! The period of estrangement was a queer isolated fragment of her life. She did not feel at all drunk, only a little tired, and more than a little exhilarated and tense.

The conference broke up at ten minutes of two. Ferris offered to drive Marjorie home. Noel, shoeless, in shirtsleeves and with his collar open, said, "Thanks, Peter, I'll throw on a tie and take the lady to her door myself."

"You needn't bother. I'll go with them," Marjorie said, starting to get out of a low armchair.

"Nonsense, stay where you are. I'll get a reputation as a cad," Noel said.

The others said goodbye. Mrs. Lemberg was the last to go. She hesitated a moment in the hallway, looked from Noel to Marjorie, then laughed and said in a kind but faintly metallic tone, "Don't work too hard, Noel. Goodbye, Marjorie dear." The cynical twang in a voice so much like her mother's stung Marjorie. She pushed herself out of the chair, but Mrs. Lemberg had already closed the door.

Noel went into the bedroom, and came out a few moments later sliding a maroon tie under his collar. He said nothing. He seemed embarrassed. He knotted the tie at a mirror in the hallway. Marjorie walked up and down the living room, not very aware of what she was doing. The walls were papered with a design of yellow and green flowers on gray. Her image moved back and forth in a large oblong mirror between the windows.

Noel said from the hallway, "Well, was it fun?"

"I loved it. Thanks for inviting me."

"You were very helpful."

"That old duet just crossed my mind. Lucky."

"Tired?"

"Not at all, strangely. I suppose I'll collapse once I take my clothes off."

"Like another drink before we go?" He was putting on his tweed jacket.

"I—no, thanks, I'd better not. I swear I'm becoming a drunkard."

"Sure? There's plenty of soda and ice."

"No, thanks. I'd better go home." She glanced at her watch. "Ye gods. How did it get to be this time?"

He said, "I'll probably work on that number when I come back. I've never been more wide awake. How about writing down the words for me before we go?"

"I'll be glad to, but look, Noel, I can go home by myself after that. You have too much to do——"

"Forget it. I like your company, you fool, don't you know that?" He took a pencil and a yellow pad from the piano. "Will you dictate the words? It's marvelous how you remember that junk. I've written reams of it, but the words never stick with me, just the melodies."

Marjorie sat beside him on the sofa. He poised the pencil over the pad. She stared at him, and after a second or two she said, "What on earth is the matter with me? It's gone clean out of my head."

"What!"

"Every word of it. Clean gone."

"Margie, you sang it from beginning to end an hour ago."

"I don't know what's happened. Amnesia, I guess." She shook her head violently. "Nothing like this has ever happened to me before. Is it nerves? Or what? I can't even think of the first lines, Noel."

"Well, I remember those—

She was chic, her smile was winning,
It was a very gay beginning——"

Marjorie stammered and groped for the words. "Maybe if you play the music again——"

Noel went to the piano, giving her the pencil and pad. As soon as he played a few measures, the verses came to her in a rush. She shouted them aloud in relief, and scribbled them down, laughing. "Whew! I was beginning to think I'd lost my mind."

"You'd better have that drink, after all."

"I believe I will."

She lounged at the piano, picking out the melody with one finger. He brought the drinks and sat beside her on the bench. "Not a bad little piano, is it? Rented."

"It reminds me of the one in Sam Rothmore's office."

"Dear old Sam. Let's drink to Sam." He raised his glass. "Pity it isn't twenty-year-old brandy in his honor, but here's to the fine old bastard anyway."

She said, "Do you ever see him?"

"Sam's pretty sick, Margie. He lives in Florida the year round now. He's pretty much been put out to pasture."

"One of the few real friends you've ever had."

"I know. Worse luck for him." Noel put his drink on the piano, and played the love song from the show in an idle way. "Do you really like *Princess Jones,* Marge?"

"You know I do. I always have. I can't help liking it. It's superb, Noel, truly it is."

"Maybe I'm too close to it. Tonight—and it's happened a couple of times before, during rehearsals—it all seemed a bit thin and banal. Beautiful production, not much show. I've told this to Peter. He says if I didn't have these depressions I wouldn't be a healthy author."

Marjorie laughed.

Noel said, "Well, we'll have a few weeks with audiences out of town for polishing and tightening. The *Variety* write-up will be useful." His fingers rambled into the tune Marjorie had suggested. "This melody's really not bad, do you know?" he said. "Probably a lot of the South Wind stuff will be salvageable some day."

"It's a treasure house, Noel, I'm telling you."

He began to play the old songs. She leaned on the piano, humming, sipping her drink. She closed her eyes. Scenes of their summer days together came sharp and clear in her mind—dancing in the darkened social hall at the end of an evening's canoeing in the moonlight; eating lunch at hot noonday in a dining hall full of noisy guests, with the perspiring band playing these songs in a cockloft over the kitchen; walking with Noel through fragrant woods at night; making up on Saturday night for the show, in the dressing room with the windows painted streaky blue, at the mirror cracked like a spider web . . . She opened her eyes, and laughed. "What's that one? *Moon Madness,* isn't it?"

"Right."

"First song of yours I ever heard. You were rehearsing it the night Marsha and I sneaked over from the girls' camp. Remember?"

He looked up at her, grinning as he played. "I thought you were a pleasant-looking child."

"I thought you were Apollo. Do you still have that black sweater? I hated the blonde who sang that number, because Marsha said she was your girl. Now I can't remember her name."

"Neither can I."

She reached down and struck his hands from the keyboard, as he modulated to another melody. "Don't play that."

He was wryly amused. "Really? After all this time?"

"Oh well. You're right. I can't walk around forever afraid of a song. Play the damned thing."

She turned away, arms folded, and went to the window. The clouds were gone. It was a glittering starry moonlit night. The buildings were all dark, save for a spot of yellow window here and there. The moon on the Hudson was very like the moon on the lake at South Wind. He was playing the waltz. The terrible night came back on her, as real as the room: the smell of the dewy trees, the splash of the fountain, and Samson-Aaron on the grass with his mouth open, trickling water from his Palm Beach suit. She gritted her teeth, faced Noel, and laughed. "Surprisingly, I don't mind it after all. Nothing like getting these things out of your system. I believe I'll go home."

He slid his fingers along the keyboard, came to her; he put his arm around her shoulders. They looked out at the moonlight together. He stared at the sky, craning his neck, and then pointed at the moon. "Yes, of course, I clean forgot. I think it's starting. There's an eclipse of the moon tonight, the paper said. Look at the left side of that moon, will you? Isn't it getting sort of dark red and queer?"

"I thought the moon blacked out in an eclipse," Marjorie said, peering in awe at the discolored moon. "I've never seen an eclipse of the moon."

Noel smiled. "It can't black out. The earth's air diffuses the sunlight. You just get a dull red color."

"Walking encyclopedia," Marjorie said. "Well, this is the opportunity of a lifetime, isn't it? Perfect view, perfect night. Let's watch the eclipse, by all means."

"It takes a couple of hours, dear."

Marjorie laughed. "How long before it's total, d'you suppose?"

"I don't know. Quarter, half hour, maybe."

"Well, why don't you just go and rewrite your duet? I'll watch till it's total, maybe. If I get bored I'll go home."

Noel returned to the piano. For about ten minutes he played fragments of the melody and scrawled on the pad. Marjorie sat on the arm of a chair, looking out at the eclipse. The coppery color crawled very slowly across the face of the moon. Now and then she glanced at Noel. Sometimes she found his eyes on her. She finished her drink and put down the glass. He stood. "I'll get you another."

"Positively not. Eclipse is getting there, all right. I'll have a cigarette, and then I'll go home. And you're not taking me home, either. I'll leave you to wrestle with the muse."

He brought her a cigarette, lit it, and embraced her waist with one arm. She leaned against him. They looked at the dulling moon, his cheek against her hair. After a while he said in a troubled voice, "Pretty slow kind of show, at that, an eclipse of the moon."

"It does lack something in the way of entertainment," Marjorie said, her voice shaking too.

He turned her around by the shoulders. It was a terrific release to kiss Noel. She broke away from him long enough to murmur, "It's been a very very long time, hasn't it?" They kissed again, with more passion.

Without a word he went to the hallway, and came back with her coat. "No doubt I'm being an imbecile, I'm throwing you out. Here's your coat. I love you. Good night. See you soon."

Marjorie slowly smiled, and shrugged. She started to put one arm into a sleeve. Then the coat was on the floor, and Noel was straining her to him until only her toes touched the floor. After kissing her furiously on the mouth, the eyes, the ears, the forehead, he said, "You don't exactly want me to work, do you?"

She said something, she didn't know what. He was leading her by the hand to the sofa, and she was following.

At one point, as they necked—she was quite defenseless against him, and quite without desire to defend herself—she murmured, "What about the redheaded chorus girl? Isn't she all you want?"

He said, "If you mean a kid named Carol, I took her once to dinner with Marsha and Lou. She's not quite you, unfortunately. That's always the trouble."

Soon they sat up, straightening their disarranged clothes. He took her face in his hands, kissed her on the mouth, and said huskily, "Well, now, Marjorie, my dear sweet love, this isn't what grown people do, is it? You've grown up, haven't you, at long last? I wonder. I think you have. Have you grown up?"

They stared at each other for a very long time. Marjorie's gesture at last was not even a nod; it was a slight, a very slight, ashamed dip of the head. It didn't seem to her she willed the movement; it happened. Then she tossed her head and laughed. "If you really think it's such a good idea."

He said, his face flushed and eager, "God knows I've always thought so."

"You devil. You've always known I would, too."

He stood and pulled her up by a hand. When he took a step toward the bedroom she held back; then she followed him.

Something happened at the bedroom door when he snapped on the light. It might have been the sight of the bed piled with papers; or of the open bathroom door, with the toilet beyond; it might have been that the overhead bedroom lights glared after the indirect glow in the living room, and shocked her eyes. The mood broke. She stood leaning in the doorway, while he agitatedly cleared away the books, scripts, and papers on the bed. He seemed comical to her in his excitement, as other men usually did, even though he was Noel; comical and boyish.

He tumbled the collected stuff in a heap in a chair, and turned to her. His arms dropped to his sides. "What's so funny, my love?"

She said, "You, my love."

He smiled. "The snorting pawing male, eh? Yes, indeed. Well, come on."

The smile faded from her face. She saw now something she had not noticed for a year and a half. She saw that his left arm hung crookedly. He held out his arms and came toward her. She said hurriedly, "Do you have a robe? Let me have it."

He gave her a yellow-and-red silk robe. She went into the bathroom, and as she closed the door she heard him kick off his shoes.

She looked at herself in the full-length mirror on the back of the door, in the white glare of the bathroom, and wondered in a vague way whether this girl she saw before her, Marjorie Morgenstern, this girl in the familiar blue dress with the gray trim, was really about to take off that dress in a man's apartment and lose her virginity. She wondered whether it would hurt. She felt detached, cold, and amused. Her teeth kept baring in a smile. She took off her shoes and then pulled off the dress over her head, in the same way she always took it off before going to sleep. Habit was so strong that she wanted to remove her smeared makeup—what was left of it, after the necking. But this seemed too cool and methodical a thing to do; no doubt hotel chambermaids were used to cosmetic smears on bed linen. She wondered how much of her clothing it was proper to take off. She was quite sure she couldn't go back naked to Noel. The question was, what was decently indecent for a girl of twenty-one, doing this for the first time? She took off her stockings and some of her underclothing. She kept on her slip, and hugged the robe around her as she combed her hair with his big black comb. Regretting that she hadn't brought her purse in with her, she considered dashing out and getting it, because she really needed powder and a touch of lipstick. But she was sure Noel would be offended at her appearing and disappearing again. Obviously she was to emerge, throw herself into his eager arms, and abandon all to love.

The trouble was that she hadn't the faintest desire to do it. She was, she supposed, scared; how scared, she wasn't sure. Mainly she was out of the mood for sex. She couldn't have been less in the mood had she been in the middle of baking a cake. She thought of taking a shower, pleading sudden fatigue, and going home. But in plain fact she was too embarrassed at the idea of backing out. All her reasonable objections to sleeping with Noel were gone. If she could have thought of a good argument against it, she might have come out of the bathroom and argued with him, even at this point, and argued herself inviolate back into her clothes and out of his apartment. She couldn't think of a reason. An appeal to morality was nonsense. She couldn't say she didn't love him; not after her performance on the sofa. Nor could she demand a guarantee of marriage, having started up with him again of her own accord, knowing full well how he felt, and what he was.

She knew she shouldn't have come to the dress rehearsal. She shouldn't have come to the hotel suite. She shouldn't have lingered—this was fatal —after the others had left. She shouldn't have responded so readily to the first kiss in a year. She shouldn't have used the coy excuse of staying to watch the eclipse. She shouldn't have gone to the sofa with him. But she had done these things.

She pictured herself putting her clothes back on, emerging from the bathroom, and announcing, "Sorry, I've changed my mind, dear. I'm going home. Please forgive me."

It was a temptation. It was much more of a temptation, actually, than getting into a bed with Noel Airman. She could have forgone that treat with the greatest ease. But the thought of announcing a change of mind made her feel like a damned fool. She could do it; but she feared she might actually forfeit Noel forever. He wouldn't be likely to forgive such childish inconsistency and whimsey, at this point. He had been all too patient with her, too long. It might well be the end. She didn't want an end with Noel. She wanted him for her husband. The estrangement of a year seemed never to have existed. Reality was only being with him, with Noel Airman, and life was most real and most sweet and most true when this lean blond clever man was holding her and kissing her. That was as certain as the night outside the windows. She had no other certainty to cling to. All other certainties had faded or eroded away in growing up; or she had been talked out of them; or she had read books that had disintegrated them. The certainty that there was anything praiseworthy in virginity had long since been ridiculed out of her. There was nothing to believe in, except that she loved Noel and wanted him. If her only chance of getting him was to sleep with him—and Marsha was right to that extent, things were at that stand between them, and had been for a year—so be it! She would pass through this tunnel somehow and look for daylight on the other side. Fighting it off longer was pointless.

She put her hand on the doorknob and saw herself in the mirror, barefoot, her hair combed loosely to her shoulders, in the ludicrously big man's robe through which the pink of her slip peeked. She wrapped the robe close around her and tied the cord. She stood and stared for a few seconds at the mirror.

She had a race of last thoughts. What had plunged her over the line so suddenly and so finally? Marsha's tirade? The theremin, which had given him an excuse to hold her and hug her, and then to kidnap her from the wedding? The enchantment of *Princess Jones*, the knowledge that it probably would make him rich and well known?

It wasn't one thing. She had been working toward this moment for two years. She had been moving toward her first sex act, in this bedroom, in this hotel, with this man, like an asteroid moving to collide with a comet.

What of her mother, her father? What of Seth? How would it feel after this to go home, to sleep in a bed in a room in her family's apartment?

She snapped off the light and opened the door.

At first she could see nothing but a glowing cigarette in the gloom. It made a red arc in the darkness and went out, and Noel's voice said, "Hi, darling. I was beginning to think you'd found a fire escape."

She went to the bed and sat on the edge. She could see him dimly now in the faint light from the window. It startled her to see that he wore pajamas. She untied the robe, threw it off, and got into the bed beside him. It was all very clumsy. Her movements were hurried, his were uncertain. They poked each other with elbows and knees. They kissed awkwardly and unsatisfactorily. Then somehow they settled down.

"You love me?" she said.

"Yes."

"Do you suppose we'll ever be married?"

"I don't know, Marjorie. I just don't know. If it has to happen, it will."

"You love me more than you know. You're going to marry me. You'll be a wonderful wretch of a husband, and we'll be the two happiest people in the world."

"You think so?"

"I know it."

"Okay, darling. Maybe you can read fate. I've never loved anyone the way I love you. That, I know."

She wanted to kiss him then. For a while it was tender and sweet. There was something peculiarly pleasant in the comfort and nearness of being undressed. It was not so much exciting, as cosy and intimate.

Then all changed. It became rough and strange. She was powerless to stop it. She tried to seem pleasant and loving, but she was very uncomfortable and unhappy. It became rougher and more awkward. It became horrible. There were shocks, ugly uncoverings, pain, incredible humiliation, shock, shock, and it was over.

So it was that Marjorie qualified at last to portray true emotion on the stage. Her age was twenty-one years, four months, and seven days.

Noel said, "All right, darling?"

"Just fine," she answered, trying not to sound sick.

"The cigarettes are there on the night table. Toss me one, honey."

She groped on the table. There was a clinking and a crash. Instinctively she reached for the lamp cord and pulled it. Blinking in the blaze of light, holding the blanket to her bosom, she saw that she had knocked over a drinking glass. The pieces lay glittering on the marble top of the table. "Well, that's fine," she said. "We're supposed to break a glass, aren't we? Only you should have done it with your heel, I guess. Good luck, darling."

His lipstick-smeared face, white and tired, with the hair falling over his forehead, took on a pained alarmed look. She said hurriedly, "Good Lord, sweetheart, that was a joke. Smile, for heaven's sake."

He smiled. "Let's have the cigarettes."

She passed the pack to him. With her first puff she leaned back and sighed. Her glance went to the window. The moon hung in the sky over the buildings, a solid disk of reddish bronze, without a trace of white. "Well, bless me," she said, pointing. "Look, the eclipse is total. I got to see one, after all. Makes it easy to date this night, doesn't it, darling?"

"Marjorie," Noel said, in a strained tone, "I would appreciate it just as much if you weren't quite so brave and pathetic about all this. You're a big girl. It could have been more fun, and it will be, I promise you. I love you."

She looked at him, smiling, while tears came from nowhere and ran down her face in streams. "Why, darling, I wasn't being pathetic. I'm very glad. I love you too."

She put her face in the pillow. The tears were pouring; she could not possibly stop them, and she was ashamed of herself because she was crying.

PART FIVE

My Object
all Sublime

Chapter 37. THE NIGHTMARE

One year later, almost to the day, Marjorie Morgenstern was frantically fighting her way up the third-class gangplank of the steamship
Mauretania, against a solid stream of people leaving the ship. She was
clutching the rail, panting heavily, murmuring excuses and apologies
with every step, her breath smoking in the raw fishy-smelling air. She
was not halfway up the plank when gongs sounded, and a loudspeaker
bawled, *Last call. Visitors ashore. Last call.* The ship's officer at the head
of the gangplank held out a hand to stop her as she set foot on deck.
"So sorry, miss. You're too late." The accent was like a movie Englishman's, the manner pleasant but firm.

She looked him straight in the face. He was red-faced and lean, no
taller than she. "I have to talk to my—my fiancé. Just for a minute. But
I *have* to talk to him." She stood her ground with difficulty, jostled by
dozens of visitors funnelling into the gangway.

He took in her smart clothes with a glance, and looked over his shoulder at a clock. His voice became less formal. "Very important, I guess it
is?"

"As important as anything can be."

With a bleak grin he nodded her past him, and she went running
down stairs to the lower decks.

The stateroom number was correct; she recognized Noel's luggage
piled on the berth. It was a tiny dim interior cabin on the lowest deck,
stuffy despite a roaring ventilator. She glanced up and down the passageway; he was nowhere in sight. Hurriedly she began a search of the passageways, turning here and there, not knowing which turn might luckily
lead her to come upon him. Past bashfulness or diffidence, she shouldered
into noisy cabins where farewell parties were breaking up, looked around

to make sure he wasn't in the room, and went away without a word, leaving people snickering behind her. The gongs kept sounding with startling loudness; over and over the loudspeakers called, *Visitors ashore, please. Last call. All ashore at once, please.* The passageways had been crowded when she came aboard, but they were rapidly emptying; she walked through several that were deserted. She began to run. She ran through empty writing rooms, through a lounge, through a dining room, through a bar. She made another panic-stricken tour of the passageways, finding herself in the same ones over and over, like a rat in a maze.

She had had several nightmares like this: nightmares of looking for Noel through endless twisting corridors. This might almost have been another nightmare, except that it was too coherent, too vivid, too matter-of-fact. It was really happening; she knew that. But an eerie dreamlike feeling possessed her, a feeling that she had actually looked for him—or had dreamed that she had looked for him—in just this way, through these very passageways, long, long ago. She turned corners knowing in advance that she would see a queerly shaped fire extinguisher on the wall, or a bearded steward in a white coat walking toward her; and the extinguisher, the steward, were there. She had had this weird illusion before, but never half so strongly or so persistently.

Somebody touched her arm. In the instant before she turned, she sensed it would be a rosy-faced cabin boy in a blue uniform; and it was. "You a passenger, miss?"

"No, I——"

"All visitors have to leave this minute, miss, sorry. They're taking in the gangplanks."

She looked around desperately. The passageway was empty except for herself and the boy. "Thank you." She hurried to the gangplank.

"Find your friend, miss?" said the little red-faced officer.

She gave him a harried smile, and followed a solitary fat man down the gangplank. She walked up and down the pier behind the fenced-in visitors, staring up at the colossal steel side of the *Mauretania,* scanning the waving, laughing, shouting passengers lining the rails. Great cranes reached down and plucked up the gangplanks. Sailors on the ship began hauling in the huge manila lines. A band started to play a brassy march, but the music was nearly drowned in the snorting and clanking of the cranes, and the cheers and yells that filled the immense shed.

She wasn't sure it was Noel when she first saw him, because he wore a new dark green hat of an odd flat shape; but she recognized the loose camel's hair topcoat, and the slouch of the shoulders. He was at the rail of one of the lower decks, far forward. She hurried to a point opposite him and waved from the back of the crowd. He didn't see her. He held a highball glass in his hand, and he was talking to a plump woman in a red suit, who also was drinking a highball. Marjorie worked through the jammed-together people to the fence, alternately pushing and apologizing. As she came to the front of the crowd, there were three horrifying whistle blasts. She waved her arms and shrieked, "Noel!" in the instant of near-quiet after the last blast. He heard it; he glanced along the pier, and then he saw her. He shook his head as though in wonder, smiled, and rather sheepishly waved. He said something to the woman in the red suit, pointing at Marjorie; the woman looked at her and laughed, and said something that made Noel laugh. He raised his glass to Marjorie, shouted something she didn't hear, and drank.

She yelled, "Write to me!"

He cupped his hand to his ear.

"Write to me! *Write to me,* I say!" The people on either side of her at the fence stared and smiled, but she was beyond self-consciousness. "WRITE TO ME!"

He shrugged to indicate that he couldn't hear her. He spoke to the woman in the red suit, and she shrugged too, looking intently at Marjorie. She was too far away for Marjorie to see her features clearly; she appeared to be about forty, and not unattractive.

Marjorie held up the flat side of her purse, made a gesture of writing on it and sealing an envelope, then pointed to Noel and to herself. He grinned, and shook his head vehemently. She repeated the gesture with emphasis. He shook his head equally emphatically, and pantomimed putting a pistol to his temple. Before her eyes she saw the *Mauretania's* rivets slide slowly to the left. A cheer went up from the people on the pier, and colored paper streamers rained from ship to shore. The band struck up *Rule Britannia.* Marjorie again made the writing gesture, and with a tearful smile shook her fist at Noel. He laughed, raised the glass to her again, drained it, and tossed it into the widening water between the pier and the ship. The woman in the red suit threw back her head, laughing, and patted him on the shoulder.

Marjorie took out her handkerchief and waved and waved, as long as she could distinguish Noel. She thought she saw his hand wave in answer once or twice. With the rest of the crowd she ran to the head of the pier, and watched the tugs pull the vast ship out into the muddy choppy Hudson and turn it around. It was a very clear sunny day; windows of houses along the New Jersey palisades glittered white. Far up the river the George Washington Bridge stood out sharp and gray against the blue Hudson and the green far Jersey hills. The freezing wind off the river smelled like the ocean at low tide; it cut at her legs, making her shiver inside her fur coat. She could see a dot of red at one point of the lower deck rail that might have been the plump woman, she could not make out Noel at all. But she stood and watched while the tugs pushed the bow southward to the ocean, and the water began to boil white around the towering stern. She watched the ship go down the river, getting smaller and smaller. She was almost the last of the visitors to leave the pier.

She took the letter from her purse in the taxicab and read it again on the way home. It was twenty pages long, typed in Noel's neat clear double-spaced way on his customary thin yellow paper. The *e* was awry, bent to the left and pushed up above the typing line, as it had been ever since she had started getting letters from Noel, three years ago. She had not yet read the letter carefully. Finding it at the door, in the morning mail, she had surmised at once from its bulk what it was, and had skimmed it at top speed for the immediate facts. Though he said in it that he would be several days at sea when she received it, she had at once scanned the *Times* sailing list and then rushed down to the Cunard pier, where she had pestered the pursers until she found out that Noel was a third-class passenger on the *Mauretania*.

She started to read the letter once more; but she began to feel a little ill, possibly from reading in a bumpy cab, and she folded it away in the purse.

She was glad to find nobody in the apartment when she got home. She heated the coffee that was left on the kitchen stove, and the smell made her realize that she was very hungry. This surprised her. She would have guessed she would be unable to eat for a couple of days after a blow like this. Perhaps it was that the blow, however cruel and distressing, wasn't entirely unexpected. Anyway, she was roaring hungry. She ate a roll with butter and thick chunks of cheese; then poured more coffee and ate another roll and more cheese. She ate whatever she pleased these days, and as much as she pleased. One of the rewards of having troubles like hers—a small reward, to be sure—was that she no longer had to worry about dieting. In the year of her affair with Noel she had grown very fashionably thin. Her waist was not much more than two spans around, and her hips had never been slimmer.

She went to her room, feeling remarkably good after the food; sat at her dressing table, and stared in the round mirror for a long time at her jilted friend, Marjorie Morgenstern. It was surprising how little upset she was. But this calm did not especially reassure her. Past twenty-two, she had learned something about the way she reacted to shocks. The bad time lay ahead. It might not even start for a couple of days, but she knew that when it came it was likely to be pretty frightful.

Well, she thought, contemplating her mirror image, Noel had thrown her over at last, and this time with a seeming massive finality. The twenty-page letter could hardly be more clear. And with characteristic perversity, he had discarded her when she was at her most attractive; when for the first time her career showed some promise; when she had given him all she had to give, and when he was in love with her as he had never been—though he obstinately refused to acknowledge it.

It was no vanity to believe she was looking better than ever. Though her mouth and eyes were somewhat lined with fatigue, the glass showed her a young woman who could be called nothing but beautiful. She had had a few modelling jobs recently. But for her medium stature she might have had more. She was not attractive in the stereotyped pattern of the fashion models; her cheeks weren't sunken, her eyes didn't glare or smolder, and there was nothing bony about her. But she had a well-cut face with firm flesh and good color, abundant dark brown hair, and a sweetly curved slender figure. Her best feature remained her large eyes, blue and very alive, with a touch of secrecy in them that was new, and all the old humor and sparkle. The main change in her appearance in the past year, she guessed, was that she looked like a woman, not a girl. A powerful femininity glowed from within her. She was aware of it from its effects. Men had never pursued her harder than in this year, when, possessed by Noel, she had been completely incapable of paying any attention to them. It was too bad the alteration in her had come not from a happy marriage, she reflected, but from an illicit affair, which had just exploded in her face. When marriage didn't make a girl smug and sloppy like Rosalind Boehm, or tight-nerved and falsely gay like Marsha Michaelson, it could work just such a soft charming change; she had seen it make ugly girls into pleasant women, and pretty girls into stunning women. Here she was—pretty as any, over twenty-two, and in the ash can.

But life went on, even for the brokenhearted and the numb in spirit. She glanced at her wristwatch, went wearily to the telephone, and dialled. "Hello? Is Len there? This is Margie Morningstar. . . . No, no, don't bother him, Mike. Just give him a message when there's a break in the rehearsal, will you? Tell him I'm sorry I'm late, something came up. . . . No, everything's okay, I should be there in half an hour. Are they up to my scene? . . . Well, fine. 'Bye."

She quickly changed into the warm brown wool dress she had been wearing at rehearsals because of the dank drafts backstage at the Lyceum. Marjorie had come far in the past year. She had a real part in a real Broadway play, and everyone in the company knew her as Marjorie Morningstar.

She opened her purse to put in a fresh pack of cigarettes; and there was the letter, bulky and depressing. She didn't especially want to drag the lugubrious document around with her; not to rehearsal, certainly, where she had to appear gay and fresh. She thought of the old rosewood box. It was tucked away on an inconvenient high shelf, but it did lock, and she still had the key somewhere. She found the key, climbed on a chair, and got the box down. It was covered with dust and it opened with a creak. It was so full of old junk that the papers popped up when she raised the lid. Every year or so she glanced through the contents of the box. The process was growing less and less amusing, and she had often thought she would burn it all and throw the box away. In a city apartment, however, burning papers was no easy matter. One couldn't very well do it on the kitchen range, and there was no fireplace. As a result the old rosewood box kept getting fuller, year by year. A squirrelling instinct made Marjorie think of it whenever she had a paper that she didn't want to destroy at once, or one she was afraid to throw even in fragments into a wastebasket. The security precautions she took against her mother's inquisitiveness were second nature now. Mrs. Morgenstern still poked around in the girl's room, but she hadn't found anything interesting since her nineteenth year, even in the wastebasket.

Marjorie had to double over the long letter to fit it into the box, and even then she could barely jam down the lid. The first time she tried, a few mementos slipped out and scattered on the floor: George Drobes' last letter to her, scuffed and yellowing; a frantic drunken adoring letter Wally had once written to her; a brownish clipping from the Hunter newspaper, containing Helen Johannsen's glowing write-up of her *Mikado* performance; a charming but somewhat too ribald poem Noel had scrawled on the back of a menu, in the form of an acrostic on the name *Marjorie Morningstar;* the picture of herself with Wally Wronken taken at his graduation. Stuffing all the papers back into the box, she managed at last to get it locked. She put it up on the shelf and blocked it from view with a couple of hatboxes.

Then she washed the dust of the old box full of old sad secrets—and one new sad secret—from her hands and went to the rehearsal.

Chapter 38. HOW TO DISCARD A MISTRESS GRACEFULLY

Noel's letter probably would have interested Marjorie's mother. This was it:

Marjorie, my love:
I am full of Dutch courage, having just come back from an all-night

drunk with my old boon companion, Ferdie Platt. But there is nothing alcoholic about what I'm going to say to you. In fact to make sure there isn't, I won't mail this letter until the morning. I've got so much to say that I may fall asleep before I finish it. But I doubt that. I've never felt more wide awake, nor more completely in possession of my faculties, nor more clear-seeing. There's a reason why drunks in bars always get to talking sooner or later about elemental truths—love, family, death, politics, war, and so forth. Alcohol cuts down to size the trivialities that loom so large to the sober mind. The sober mind is a man groping through a forest tree by tree. The drunk mind is that same man lifted in an airplane, seeing the forest whole. The term "high" is a wise folk symbol. I hope you get the general idea. I assert that everything I'll say in this letter is not only true, but a hell of a lot truer and more perceptive—about both of us—than anything I've ever said before, verbose as I am.

It's hard to know where to begin, but one place is as good as another. So let's begin with that moment last Saturday night when you said to me, "Why don't we get married?"

I'm not objecting to the fact that you said it. The good humor, the lightness, the way you said it and forgot about it and went on having fun, were all perfect. In fact I was a little scared, you were so clever about it. I suppose it was inevitable that you grow up in time. But I guess parents and lovers are always startled when it really happens. You picked such a perfect time to say it. You were up, and I was down. You had just gotten a job. I had just lost one. You were on the rise; I was on the fall. It was almost gracious of you at that point to ask me to marry you. What was especially gracious, you didn't press your advantage in the least. It was one of those wonderful evenings when we were both feeling in tune. You, of course, were in seventh heaven, having achieved your dream of Marjorie Morningstar, after a fashion. And I was more relieved than otherwise to have lost out on the radio script-writing job. You must have decided that the gap was at last closing between us; that the age difference was really ceasing to matter; that we were obviously and very sweetly still in love; that even our careers were falling into parallel lines. You must have thought— no, not *thought*, women don't think when they make their best thrusts —but anyway, you must have figured, somewhere deep down in your endocrine system, that NOW was the time, NOW or never. So you said it.

Your instincts didn't deceive you. The timing *was* perfect. If I just laughed and went on dancing without saying anything, it wasn't because I couldn't think of an answer. The trouble was I thought of something immediately. I had to bite my lower lip to keep from saying it. I wanted to say, "All right, set a date," and for the life of me I couldn't think of any other words. I'm not telling you this to tease you or upset you. If your encounter with that monster Noel Airman is to have any enduring value, it's as education. I want you to know how very close you came. If it was in the cards, in fact, it would have happened then and there. The fact that it didn't simply proves that the moving finger has never written this marriage and never will write it.

I just went and got another drink to keep up my energy. It's about six o'clock in the morning. There's a blue dawn outside my window and I'm so tired I can't hold up my head. But this can't wait, mustn't wait. I'll never see it all so clearly again, and I'll never have the impulse to write it again. I don't want to vanish like any decamping seducer. I believe I'm right to do what I'm doing and I want you to understand me.

Do you remember what I said to you after the first time I kissed you, back in South Wind—centuries ago, when you were such an infant I could still taste the milk on your lips? I tasted milk, all right, but I also tasted honey. The whole threat of what has happened since then presented itself to me. I said to you then, "I'll never marry you, and nothing you can do will ever make me." You must have thought I was crazy, the Grand Panjandrum of South Wind talking about marriage after kissing a kid of nineteen once, but maybe now you will grant me extraordinary perspicacity, if not clairvoyance. That same perspicacity is at work now as I bang away at this typewriter, three—or is it four?—endless years later.

As you know, I've wavered back and forth twenty times about it since then. When I went to work for Sam Rothmore, I had just about decided to marry you. When I quit and fled to Mexico I was trying to get away; I used poor Imogene as a club to beat you off with, to get you out of my system—unsuccessfully, I need hardly add. When we ran into each other and went to the Waldorf, the night you had that date with Dr. Shapiro, you'll never know what a job I had throttling off the proposals in my throat all evening. You looked to me like an angel then, that's all, a pure bright angel. Damn your respectable heart and Watteau body, you have never looked like anything else to me. When we met again at Marsha's wedding I thought I was done for. You won't believe it, maybe, but all during the rehearsals of *Princess Jones* the thought uppermost in my mind was, "Has Marjorie read about it in the papers? Will she call? Will she write?" The first thing I did unfailingly when I came to the theatre was to look in the letter box for a note from you. Well, I seem to be maundering, here. . . . Let's get down to facts.

I blame the *Princess Jones* catastrophe on you, Marjorie. That, and everything that's happened to me since. I've spent a horrible and utterly futile year at a time when I can ill afford to waste any more of my hours on earth. Now let me make myself clear. I'm not blaming you for my bad writing or for the brutal notices. I know you didn't dictate that deathless first line to Brooks Atkinson, *Noel Airman's resemblance to Noel Coward unhappily begins and ends with their Christian names.* (It's burned into my memory, you see.) I'm responsible, true enough, for the fact that *Princess Jones* was an old-fashioned piece of tripe that closed in five days. You're responsible, however, for my exposing myself and my limitations in such a wretched and crucifying way. You'll remember that while the show was still in rehearsal—that famous night of nights for us—I freely gave you credit for inspiring me to keep at *Princess Jones.* You had the credit, you must take the blame.

I'm not a librettist. It's a special, exceedingly narrow, exceedingly difficult theatrical form. Nobody's ever really mastered it except Gilbert. All current musicals are hashed up by word-carpenters. The musical show is such a charming and entertaining diversion in itself that the public forgives the stupidity of the libretto, so long as it passes muster with enough vaudeville jokes and standard love scenes. I tried to do something better. If I failed abysmally, at least I tried. The point is, I should never have tried. I wrote *Princess Jones* originally as a sort of jeu d'esprit, an imitation of Gilbert. Maybe I was dreaming of being another Gilbert some day. A young fool is entitled to dream of being anything he pleases. But by the time I met you I had pretty well reconciled myself to the fact that, if the script had any merit, it was of a slight and recondite kind, and that I'd better charge it off to youthful dreams. I didn't take the staff's drunken enthusiasm over it, that night I played it at South Wind, very seriously. But you did. You wouldn't let me forget it. Every time I read a new scene or played a new song for you, you would burst into a new blaze of excitement. Naturally, no writer alive isn't a prey to his own vanity. I wanted to believe you were right, and so I kept on reviving the damned thing and going back to work on it.

You didn't have an atom of taste about the whole thing. It was all pure femininity. That's obvious to me now, and should have been then, perhaps. But if you were in love, so was I, and I took this as proof that you weren't just another Shirley. You had the marvelous wisdom to see cleverness and charm where all the grubby professional producers were blind. That was how my mind worked.

All this is extremely unchivalrous and low of me, I'm sure. I'm a snake to state such ugly facts.

Marjorie, the long and short of the matter is, I'm tired of playing the horse to your rider, and I'm throwing you. People who didn't know the situation as well as I do would be appalled at this statement of it. You're the innocent victim, of course, and I'm the bored old seducer casting you aside. But the fact is, you seduced me as much as I seduced you. If I seduced you to go to bed with me you seduced me to go to work for you. In the long run, you came closer to making me respectable than I did to making you bohemian. You have ridden me mercilessly. Your left spur has been the American idea of success, and your right spur the Jewish idea of respectability. I have disbelieved in both ideas with all my heart since I was seventeen. But you have used the miserable fascination you had over me to make me conform to those ideas, or to break my heart trying. *Princess Jones* was at bottom *your* big bid for a house in New Rochelle, and for that reason I'm glad it flopped.

Let me make it perfectly plain that I'm not accusing you of evil intent, or deliberate plot. It all goes much beyond your conscious intent. You can't help being what you are, acting as you do, and exerting the pressures that well up in you. If you've been a most unfortunate influence on me, it isn't your "doing" in the sense that you could be arrested for it. That has made matters worse, in a way. I could always reach your mind and convince it and change it, but I could never work the slightest alteration in YOU. From the first moment I encountered you, you have never changed an iota, never deviated from your line by a hair. You were, you are, you always will be, SHIRLEY—and if I had a red strip in this typewriter ribbon, or some gold ink, I'd write that word in red or gold. There should also be a blast of trumpets, before and after pronouncing the Name.

I say you have *never* departed from your line, and I mean it. Not even when you decided to have an affair with me. That, my sweet love, was a mere gesture to my eccentric views—was it not, dear?—and to the loose ways of the day. In the old days Shirley baked cakes and showed off her sewing to get her man. Nowadays the poor girl finds she may also have to sleep with the big slob a few times beforehand; it seems to be the fashion among the smart crowd, alas. So, she holds her nose and plunges in. I'm being very brutal, I know. It's not my intention to wound or insult you by intimating that you're not a good bed partner. You know all too well what a devouring passion I've had for you. If it's any satisfaction to you, I have never known anything like it. But I have brains enough to know that a bed takes up a very small space in a house, and that you don't spend a marriage sleeping with a person but waking with her. It's the waking part with you that I will no longer endure, come hell or high water. I will not be driven on and on to that looming goal, a love nest in the suburbs. I WANT NO PART OF IT OR OF YOU, do you understand?

If I had had half a brain, the collapse of *Jones* would have taught me to flee you to Australia, or to the North Pole, if necessary. Unfortunately, you had complicated the matter by consenting to sleep with me. Nothing could have dragged me away from that enchantment, at the moment. And yet, Marjorie, what an unsatisfactory half-baked business it has been, and how like you and your ways! You wouldn't move in with me, and frankly proclaim to the world what you were doing, would you? Not you. People don't do such things. The forty thousand couples in the Village doing just that don't count, they're trash. As a result, to this day you don't know what it's like to sleep with the man you love all night, and wake up in the morning and have breakfast together. No, if it was 5 A.M., and hailing, you'd drag yourself out of bed and stagger home to sleep a formal hour or two in your parents' apartment, thus preserving the amenities. Some day I'd like to know what stories you told your vigilant mama.

When I think that one week after *Jones* fell around my ears I was working on a new musical I wonder at my sanity. But you had me completely persuaded. The pilot walks away from the crash and takes another plane into the air immediately, and all that. All the great ones started with terrible flops, et cetera, et cetera. Fortunately the beating I took had knocked some critical faculty back into me, and I soon realized that what I was writing was hopeless garbage. That was why I went to Hollywood again last summer. I couldn't face your devastating encouragement any more. It was all a lie about having an offer, dear. I had no offer. I didn't do an ounce of work out there. I just bummed around all through the summer. I did *try* to get a job, heaven knows. When I think of the crawling I did, and the scum before whom I crawled, Hollywood agents, third-rate producers, phony actors, even script girls —and all for nothing, just to prove to my precious Marjorie back home that I could still be a big wage earner—I get furious at you all over again. But enough of that. . . .

Well, by now you must have the idea. I want you to know that there is not an ounce of pique or malice in all this. Being beaten out of a contest for a radio gagwriting job—and by Wally Wronken, of all people—was not exactly pleasant, and I won't pretend it was. But again, the basic mistake was in ever trying for the job. *I am not a gagwriter.* That was you again, persuading me that with my fingertips I could write better jokes than all of Eddie Cantor's and Jack Benny's writers. The job seemed more interesting than writing advertising copy, the money of course was far better, so I was lulled into trying. But the point is, I *can* write simply peachy advertising copy. I've been proving that during these last five wretched months. If I were going to be a bourgeois provider, that's obviously the line I should stick to. And if I hate the work, and hate myself when I'm doing it—well, how many of the hordes of husbands who shuttle back and forth on the Long Island Railroad, or the New York, New Haven, and Hartford, don't really wish they were dead? This world is a vale of tears. You might as well drown yourself in martinis in Mamaroneck on a green lawn under a spreading tree, as in a cramped cell on Manhattan. The grass is better for the children.

Wally's a born gagman. If somebody else was to get the job, I'm glad he did. He's a damned clever kid. He hasn't the brains of an ant-eater so far as any thinking about abstractions or serious problems goes. But what the hell point is there to abstractions if you're not Whitehead or Einstein? My curse, the burden I carry on my back like Bunyan's pilgrim, is my abstracting tendency. And now we are coming at last to the point.

Marjorie, at the present moment in my life I'm not a composer, I'm not a lyric writer, I'm not a musical-comedy writer, I'm not an advertising writer, I'm not a gagwriter, I'm not any kind of a writer. I repeat, *at present.* Maybe I'll have a late flowering, like Hawthorne. At thirty-two, having tried my hand at everything, I'm back where I was at twenty-two. Ferdie Platt and I talked about this for six hours last night and I don't care how much we drank, it was the soberest conversation that two men ever conducted. If I am anything at all, I'm a philosopher. Now that statement looks incredibly vainglorious and ridiculous, just typed out cold, but you can go to hell if you don't like it.

I'm going back to the Sorbonne. After a while I may go to Oxford for a couple of years. There are some scholarships at both places I know I can get without half trying. Until I'm thirty-five I'm going to do nothing but study. Then I'll take a long breath and see where I am. The greatest likelihood is that I'll come back to the States and get a job teaching philosophy. Right now I can't tell you what a glorious prospect that is to me. I pant for it. But I'm willing to be patient and work like hell to be worthy of it. I'm not looking beyond the immediate moment. First thing in the morning I'm going to book out on the next boat to Paris. And to prove I'm serious I'm going back on the lean regime: third-class ticket, ten-cent cigarettes, and all the rest. The money I have from the advertising drudgery has got to *last*. And kiddo, I am the man to make it last, especially in Paris. I do that better than practically anything.

I'm not giving up the hope of doing something creative. There are precedents for men like myself, who seem to have a facility for everything and a grasp of nothing, eventually coming through with the real stuff. Samuel Butler was all over the place with cantatas, paintings, evolutionary theories, poetry, novels, philology, and Lord knows what else. All garbage. But at last he came out with *The Way of All Flesh*. Actually it was published after he died. I'm not saying I'm a suppressed novelist. I don't know what I am. Maybe I'm a defeated mediocrity salving his bruised ego, as you no doubt are about to decide in your little bourgeois wisdom. My slip is showing, hey? Well, my love, I hope we both meet, you aged forty-one and me fifty, to compare notes. I wish you the best, but I can't wish you're right about me, naturally.

Ye gods, a ray of weak sunlight just fell across my desk. How long have I been typing?

Well, I'm finished. I hope I've proved to your satisfaction that I'm a revolting heel, thoroughly incorrigible, and unreliable, and that I will never make a good citizen of New Rochelle. Actions speak louder than words. Certainly all my acts of the past three years added together should open your eyes to the cruel truth at last. But this letter should serve to document that truth, in case you begin to doubt it in weak moments. I've had my weak moments, too. Those, unquestionably, are what have given you hope. A man who makes loud anti-social noises like me, and then meekly drudges month after month at a desk in the J. Walter Thompson agency, writing extremely competent advertising copy, probably seems worth working on. So let's clear *that* up, once for all, and then we'll be through with this endless epistle, I believe. I just want to make it utterly clear that you have nothing to hope for.

Passion makes people do queer things. Now I've had a burning passion for you, and that explains all my bourgeois lapses like the Thompson job and the Rothmore job. But I want to insist, by the way, that what I told you when I took this last job was true. I am not one of these pure spirits who sees advertising as the lowest state to which the soul of man can fall. To me it's a way of selling words for money, like any other. I don't see any difference between writing girdle ads for money, screenplays for money, or stage plays for money. If you're a great artist creating enduring works, that's another matter.

Frankly, I hate all kinds of writing, it's loathsome drudgery, but I will not admit that a screenwriter or even the writer of a hit on Broadway is any better than an advertising copywriter. He's better only in so far as he makes more money. It's all horse manure. Nobody's going to convince me that the dark brown manure is spiritually nobler somehow than the pale yellow manure. I stand on that.

I took the job because my money from *Moon Face* had run out, winter was coming on, you and I were still having fun with each other (despite your moral lapses into gloom) and I wanted to finance our pleasures in style. It was the Rothmore experience all over again for me. The first week or two it seemed a simple lark, and I rather enjoyed it. And gradually it became the most ghastly and unendurable slavery. I have been at the end of my rope for some weeks now. Ferdie Platt's arrival in town was a godsend. A night of talking about the old days in Paris, and a frank cry on an old pal's shoulder, was really all I needed. Coincidentally, I daresay, losing out on the gagwriting job that same afternoon had put a sort of period to this era of my life, by reducing what I was doing to the ultimate absurdity—defeat by Wally Wronken.

Marjorie, the fever has broken at last. And for good, I believe. For the first time in three years I can truly report to you that my passion for you has waned. I wouldn't lie about this. You understand that this is the end, really the end. With the passion waned, there is no power left on earth that can ever make me into a docile commuter. Moreover, I see no chance of the passion reviving. I've been through it. I'm coming out on the other side. Nor will the like ever happen to me again. Probably it had to happen once. It's been a sort of emotional smallpox. I'm scarred, but I'm cured. And I'm immune. The reason is that I now fully understand what has happened to me. The compulsions have been dragged out into daylight, and their power is gone.

You know enough about my family background by now to realize that I'm King Oedipus himself, a walking textbook on that particular complex. It also happens that my father is a louse, a windbag, and a bore, Oedipus or no Oedipus. ANYWAY—there is a slight complication, or maybe just an extension, in the fact that I've always been extremely fond of Monica. There isn't the slightest doubt in my mind —I've never been psychoanalyzed, but I don't have to spend forty hours on a couch and two thousand dollars to figure this out—that I've been "killing my father," as the technicians would put it, by rejecting the respectable pattern of living, and being a disgraceful bum, and all that. There is also no doubt that the Shirley image I'm always talking about is my mother and my sister coalesced. Attraction-repulsion follows because of the incest theme, the association with my father, and so forth. I'm sure that my wretched behavior to a whole string of West End Avenue girls—and to some extent, the sadistic element in my treatment of you—has been a vengeance thing, the inflicting of pain substituting for normal sex relations, a childish regression. Gad, I should get a job in a clinic, I'm so brilliant at this. Well, darling, what I'm getting at is, I have possessed my nemesis. I have thereby ceased to be plagued by her. This affair of ours was probably necessary for me, or I'd always have run the risk of suddenly proposing to some dreadful Jewish dollface. You have released me.

Am I still in love with you? Love is a word. I can do without you very well. I mean to. I've gotten over love affairs before. I'm not seventeen. This isn't the end of the world. The heart is a muscle. It loosens and stretches with exercise. Mine has had a lot of exercise, and will soon snap back to normal. Yours, I'm sorry to say, will give you more pain and take a little longer. But you'll get over it too. Everybody does. Only people in nineteenth-century novels die for love—or advanced neurotics scheduled to kill themselves anyway. If there's anything you're not, it's neurotic. You're complicated, but you're made of vanadium steel. That old Jewish steel that's outlasting the pyramids. Bless your little heart, you're your mama all over again. I'm not jeering at you, my darling. You're unspeakably pretty and sweet and bright and nice, and I could eat you up. But the price is too high, and I will not pay it. I said from the start I wouldn't, and I won't. Maybe all these words have been in vain, and you think I still will, some day. Well, I won't. Don't try to stop me from sailing to Europe. I know a trick worth two of that. I'll give this letter to Ferdie to mail two days after I'm gone. I'll be on the high seas while your warm tears are staining this page. The Masked Marvel has outwitted you to the last, Marjorie Morgenstern.

And now, my valedictory to you. Once more, I will be cruel to be kind. You are not, and you never will be, Marjorie Morningstar. In time you will be Marjorie Cohen, Marjorie Levy, or Marjorie Shapiro. It is written in the stars. I knew this back at South Wind, after watching you act once or twice. I equivocated about it for two reasons. First, there seemed no point in hurting you, especially as I knew you'd never believe me. Not at nineteen. Second, you had enough sparkle and intelligence, and also my judgment was clouded enough by the fact that I was falling in love with you, to create a shred of doubt in my mind. But that doubt went, long ago. Now let me tell you the harsh truth about yourself in words of two syllables or less, so you'll never forget it.

All girls, including you, are too goddamn emancipated nowadays.

You get the idea from all the silly magazines and movies you're bathed in from infancy, and then from all the talk in high school and college, that you've got to *be* somebody and *do* something. Bloody nonsense. A woman should *be* some man's woman and *do* what women are born and built to do—sleep with some man, rear his kids, and keep him reasonably happy while he does his fragment of the world's work. They're not really happy doing anything else. I'm sorry if I sound like Harry Emerson Fosdick, but the truth is the truth, no matter how stupid it happens to sound. Anyway, nowadays even preachers don't dare talk this way, it's considered so corny. The Nazis are the only ones who've come right out with it. And THEIR saying it doesn't make it wrong, either. Two and two make four, even if Hitler says so.

Well, now, Nature gives most of you girls a burst of charm around seventeen, lasting a few years, so you can attract some man and keep this process going. It's the flower and the bee; it's that simple and obvious. But do you ever ascribe your new charm to Nature? Of course not. What's happened is that you've suddenly become a brilliant, gifted, sage individual. You've assumed a role, complete with makeup, costumes, and dialogue. And you've dressed and painted yourself with amazing cleverness, and you keep inventing fantastically witty dialogue, and there's no end to your graceful ways and arts. THAT'S how it happens that boys are starting to fall all over you. It's got nothing to do with your fresh pointy breasts and new round thighs and perky behind. It follows that you have some extraordinary talent for this kind of thing. In fact, you're an actress.

I'm not talking about you, you understand. Being an actress (or a model, same damn nonsense) has become to the average American girl what being a knight in armor was to Don Quixote. It's a process that's going on all over the country, this addling of girls' brains. That's why I call it a tropism. Nothing can stop it, until our civilization changes. Year after year troops of Marjorie Morningstars will converge on Hollywood and Broadway to be seduced, raped, perverted, prostituted, or—if they're lucky like you—to merely tangle up in fornication for a couple of years and then go home to marry the druggist's son or the doctor or the real estate man.

I say you're lucky because I've been a little more interesting and amusing, I'm sure, than the usual show-business deflowerer. It's generally some asinine chorus boy or actor, or lecherous third assistant stage manager, who does the job. Or a producer, if a girl's really worth bothering with. Or maybe a musician, or a phony Village writer needing a bath and a haircut. Some idle joker, anyway, who stays up late and has a lot of time on his hands for fooling around with the Morningstars.

Margie, this job of yours doesn't mean a thing. I am NOT being malicious. The play stinks. You know it does. You have a ridiculous walk-on part, and Guy Flamm only hired you because you're pretty and inexperienced and he probably figures he can scrounge you on salary. I don't think the show will ever get to New York, and if it does it'll close in three days. No talent scout will see you. If one does, he'll ignore you. He knows all about the Morningstars. He can spot them a mile off. Anyway, who pays any attention to a Guy Flamm production? Good Lord, you remember your first brush with him! It's a study in self-deception to see how steamed up you've become over this lousy bit part, just because you had to sign an Equity form. Well, you'll get over it. I just hope the bump isn't too hard. Actually, it's just as well you're in the clouds at this particular moment in both our lives. It'll cushion the shock of this letter. The rehearsals and all will take your mind off it. I feel a little less squeamish, consequently, about wielding the knife.

Darling, don't ever regret the theatre, once you're defeated and out. It's a quicksand, a pigsty. It's one big whorehouse extending from Forty-second Street to Columbus Circle, except for a nook here and there reserved for homosexuals. I am not abusing it because I have failed. The theatre's never had an ounce of glamor for me. The attraction always has been the money. Maybe that's an indication that I was never meant to write for it. Be that as it may, you were never meant to act in it, that's for sure. Talent is as unmistakable in the long run as red hair. You haven't got it.

I have never had such a crick in my back in all my life. I've been typing for three and a half hours. I'm faint for sleep. Go to hell, Marjorie Morgenstern. I really don't love you any more.

Noel

There was a handwritten postscript:

3:30 in the afternoon, same day. P.S.—Well, I've just read it over once. I'm sealing it up fast. It's probably the most nasty, abominable, drivelling screed anybody ever wrote. I was drunk, all right. If nothing has ever disgusted you with me before, I'm sure this will. So I'll send it as is. There is only one untruth in all these pages, all the same, and that is in the very last line. I hope with all my heart it will be true in a few days, a few weeks, a few months. Because it is the only way out for both of us. There is no hope. Goodbye, my love.

N

When Marjorie arrived at rehearsal that day she took another blow, ill prepared as she was for more evil news.

The play she was in was called *The Bad Year.* She was cast as a whore. The play was a farce about a small-town spinster of thirty-five who inherited a fortune and came to New York to live wildly for a year, before settling back into small-town life. There were complications involving city gangsters, and a doctor from the small town who was in love with the spinster. The chief comic idea of the play was that the spinster rented a room in a brownstone bordello in Manhattan, under the misapprehension that the place was a boardinghouse. It took her most of the play to be undeceived. All Marjorie had to do in the play was to sit around in her underwear with five other girls for a few minutes during each act, smoking, drinking, and in general conveying depravity as well as she could with pantomime.

In the original script each of the whores had had a few lines to speak. But Guy Flamm had pointed out to the author that as soon as an actress uttered a syllable on stage, she had to be paid the Equity minimum salary for all rehearsals and tryout performances; whereas if she said nothing, she could be signed on as an extra for a fraction of the cost. The author, a sad little bald man with limp-hanging long hands, was putting up all the money to produce the show himself. It was his Broadway debut, though he had written (so the report went among the cast) seventeen unproduced plays. He made his living as a partner in a firm manufacturing lawn sprinklers. His approach to the production was consistently frugal; and he had willingly revised the script so that there were now five silent whores, and one loquacious slut who spoke all the lines the others had had. Marjorie was a silent whore.

It wasn't much of a part, and it wasn't much of a play, as Marjorie had frankly admitted to Noel. But she had come a long way since the day after her graduation from college, when she had hesitated over taking the part of Clarice in Guy Flamm's production of *Down Two Doubled.* Her only reservation in going to the first tryout of *The Bad Year* had been that Flamm might be embarrassed at the sight of her, so that she would have no chance at all. But he had picked her out of a line of girls on the stage, along with several others, and thereafter at rehearsals had made no sign of recognition. Evidently he had forgotten his short encounter with her.

Marjorie had been haunting all the producers' offices and all the try-outs, for two years: and this was her first break. She had undergone enormous and almost unrelieved frustration. Perhaps half a dozen times she had been given the lines of some minor part to read at a tryout, but she had never gotten the part.

She was such an habitué of the drugstore, and of another haunt of the hopefuls, the bar in Sardi's restaurant, that nobody looked around any more when she came in. They could see out of the corners of their eyes that it was only Margie Morgenstern (or Morningstar—she was known by both names), the pretty girl whose boy friend had written the fearful flop *Princess Jones.* Even Renée, the hat-check girl at Sardi's, called her Margie. Renée was far from a nobody; the Broadway columnists often printed anecdotes about her. It seemed to Marjorie that all was not lost —that she did have a desperate little toehold in the theatre, after all— because this celebrated hat-check girl called her by her first name.

In such a frame of mind, Marjorie could hardly have helped regarding a chance to appear on the Broadway stage, even in a Guy Flamm production, as a turn in her luck. It was too bad that she was merely playing a silent whore; but one obviously had to start at the bottom of the ladder. She had tried very hard to get the part of the talking whore. It would have meant an Equity card, more money, a true leap into the theatrical profession. For a day or two she had actually seemed to be favored for the role by Guy Flamm; then suddenly another girl had been chosen. It was believed among the cast that the talking whore was sleeping with Flamm; certainly they were always taking their meals together, and leaving rehearsals arm in arm.

The bad news that Marjorie learned, upon coming to rehearsal the day Noel sailed, was that she was in danger of losing even the tiny part she had. The assistant stage manager, a pale thin would-be playwright, who was having an affair with a redhead playing a silent whore, had confided to his love that one of the five was going to be axed from the show to save expenses, after the dress rehearsal Saturday night—two days off. He had of course extracted a promise of secrecy from the redhead, and she had of course violated it as fast as she could get to the theatre.

With nerves already worn, Marjorie all but broke down at the news. She really feared what such a disappointment might do to her at this wretched moment of her life. In desperation she decided that her best chance for survival lay in being a little pleasanter to the leading man of the show, Dane Voen, who had been trying hard to work up a romance with her. She wasn't desperate enough to sleep with Voen, of course; but measures short of that, she thought, might serve at least to get her past the fatal Saturday axing.

Voen was a tall, fantastically vain man of forty or so, who wore a hair piece to mask a very bald forehead. He played the chief gangster, and he was an excellent actor; he made a truly fine growling villain. His one difficulty lay in understanding what his lines meant. He was virtually an imbecile. The director had to explain to him, as though he were a child of nine, what the language of each scene implied. Once he grasped the meaning, however, he read the lines with amazing clarity and force. Since the first day of rehearsals, he had been ogling Marjorie violently, all but licking his lips at the sight of her, and not in the least discouraged by her freezing indifference.

The trouble with Marjorie's little scheme for survival was that Dane already had a mistress, a vulturous dark little woman who watched all the rehearsals from a back row of the orchestra, and who looked capable of throwing sulphuric acid in the face of anyone who meddled with Dane. Dane himself feared her. He made all his passes at Marjorie in the wings, in whispers, and glancing over his shoulder. Moreover, Dane was in the process of divorcing his second wife, and was being sued by his first wife for back alimony. Marjorie had little stomach for getting involved, even for a day or two, with this bird-brained Don Juan, but panic drove her to try it.

After rehearsals were over that evening, therefore, she consented to go with Dane for a drink. The mistress had departed half an hour earlier to cook supper for him, and he was as happy, taking Marjorie to the bar across the street, as a boy with a new toy pistol. Nothing would do for the occasion but champagne cocktails; and though Marjorie choked over the raw bar champagne, which tasted like lemon soda gone bad, he kept ordering more. Voen's conversation was full of variety, in that he discussed himself from a surprising number of aspects. He described the enormous sums of money he made in radio as a baritone, whenever he wanted to. He revealed that he was a playwright and a novelist, and that he expected shortly to have a couple of his plays produced and a novel printed. He narrated the true facts about a couple of notorious occasions when he had been dropped from shows during out-of-town tryouts; what had really occurred, he explained, was that he had understood the plays better than the directors, and had showed them up so badly in analytic disputes that they couldn't endure his continued presence in the cast. He described his "methodology" in playing a part; the amusing illusion he gave of not understanding the lines was due, he said, to his methodology. He believed in reading the lines for the first week or so in every possible way but the right one, in order to dig out hidden nuances of character that had lain in the author's unconscious. The surface meaning of the lines was trivial, he said, compared to the author's unconscious meaning; Freud proved that; Marjorie ought to read Freud, Voen said, if she wanted to develop a solid methodology.

His mistress telephoned the bar in the middle of this rodomontade, asking for him; Voen told the bartender to say he had left for home ten minutes ago, and went on talking about his methodology. Marjorie began to get uneasy, but Voen talked smoothly over her attempts to break away. From methodology he switched to the subject of marriage, and in a fatherly way explained to her that his first two marriages had failed because his wives were undeveloped emotionally, owing to lack of experience with older men. No girl should venture into marriage, Voen asserted, before she had a sound backlog of experience with an older man, because an older man was tolerant and wise, and could nurture her sexual nature past all the pitfalls of shyness and repression, so that she would open like a flower into full bloom. Tenderness and wisdom, said Voen, were what a girl needed in her first sex partner, and then later on she could have a stable marriage with someone else. Halfway through his lecture, when Marjorie felt she would burst out laughing in his face in a moment or two, she told him that she had to make a phone call instantly; and Voen let her get out of the cubicle.

She actually did call home, saying she would be a little late for dinner; and it was rather lucky that she did, for when she stepped out of the phone booth, a hideous yammering was going on in the bar between Voen and his little mistress, who had arrived with her hair wild, in a moth-eaten fur coat, and had him backed into a corner, waving curved claws near his eyes. Voen was frantically putting on his Tyrolean hat and white camel's hair coat, dodging the claws as best he could, and making explanations in a rich soothing baritone voice, while the woman screeched. Frankly a coward in such a situation, Marjorie dodged back into the booth, and pretended to be talking into the telephone. She had a moment of cold horror when the mistress suddenly appeared at the window of the booth, with a face like Dracula's, making hideous clawing gestures, and shouting obscenities. Marjorie shrugged, smiled, and held the booth tightly shut with her foot, and the woman at last went away.

So ended Marjorie's feeble first effort to use sex in forwarding her theatrical career; she seemed to lack the touch, somehow. She cowered in the booth for another ten minutes, then peeked out into the bar, and went home when she saw it was safe.

Noel had certainly been right in one respect: the show did take her mind off his letter. She lay awake for hours that night, thinking sometimes of him, but mostly searching her brain for a way to stay in *The Bad Year* as a silent whore. She dropped asleep about four in the morning, having devised a plan. Her intermittent thoughts about Noel had not been very painful. Their sum was that he could go to Paris and be damned. She would pursue her career, forget him, and in the end marry a man worth ten of him.

In the morning she took her passbook to the bank and drew out fifty-seven dollars, leaving a balance of a dollar and a half. She had earned these dollars at odd times in recent months as a receptionist, a typist, a model, and a movie usher. From the bank Marjorie went to Bergdorf Goodman's and bought fifty-five dollars' worth of black French underwear heavily trimmed with lace. She put the things on in a private dressing booth, and strutted before the mirror for a while, cigarette in hand, experimenting with various degenerate leers and wiggles. It seemed to her that she made quite a fetching and vicious whore.

On the night of the dress rehearsal Marjorie's expensive underwear caused a lot of envying comment among the girls in the dressing room. She put on a robe to walk out in the wings, and shed it only at the last moment before the curtain went up. She felt ashamed and highly ridiculous all during the performance, prancing around in the glare of stage lights in underwear. She was miserably aware of Dane Voen and the other actors crowded in the wings, coolly enjoying the sight of six undressed girls, and cracking jokes among themselves. She darted for the robe each time she came off stage.

Her heart sank when the assistant stage manager came to her at the end of the rehearsal, eyes averted and face glum. "Mr. Flamm wants to see you, Margie." She braced herself and went to the cubbyhole of plywood partitions backstage which Flamm used for an office.

It was the axe, of course. His popping eyes somewhat more bloodshot than they had been two years ago, a genial fatherly smile on his face, his fingers alternately caressing his sporty green bow tie and neat gray hair, Flamm explained that the budget had been exceeded, and he couldn't afford to keep her in the show. Marjorie desperately offered to work for nothing, to forgo the rehearsal money due her, to pay her own transportation and expenses for the Philadelphia tryout. He shook his head. Her artistic spirit was admirable, he said, but the bloodsucking rules of Actors Equity, which were killing the theatre, prevented him from accepting her offer.

"Every damned actor in the show would walk out, my dear. They're a lot of money-mad hogs, these actors. There isn't a true artist in Equity. Soon there won't be any on Broadway. It's all dying, strangled by Equity and the stagehands' union. They'll be sorry, those two boa constrictors, when they find themselves constricting a rotten corpse. Then maybe they'll constrict each other to death, and the theatre will be born again. Ah, but that's far from little Margie Morningstar and her problem, isn't it? My dear, I'm terribly, terribly sorry, I truly am.—Now, no sniffles, put away the handkerchief, child. This isn't the end for you. I hope it's the beginning, and a glorious beginning. You haven't gone unnoticed, dear."

She raised her bowed head and blinked at him.

"Frankly, Margie, you never have fitted the part. If I hadn't disliked upsetting you I'd have let you out the second day you rehearsed. You just don't look like a prostitute, my dear. You're much too fresh and sweet. That underwear you had on was really exquisite, by the way. Trouble was, it made you look less a bad woman than ever. I'm afraid you looked like a nice Vassar girl fresh out of the shower, dear, in the middle of getting dressed for a big evening. Now, don't pout, don't you realize what a precious quality that is? There are a million girls on Broadway who can look like strumpets. Where did you get that slip, my dear?"

"B-Bergdorf's."

"Bergdorf's, eh? What does your father do, Margie?"

"Why . . . he's an importer, Mr. Flamm," Marjorie said, with a dim incredulous suspicion of what Flamm might be getting at.

"Marjorie dear, would it be a consolation to have a star part in a brilliant comedy, instead of a walk-on in a trivial farce? Because between you and me, dear—and we can be frank now—that's all *The Bad Year* is. Now *this* play is something else again, believe me!" And to Marjorie's mingled disgust and amusement, he brought out of a drawer an extremely worn script of *Down Two Doubled*—it might have been the same one Marjorie had been handed two years ago, the cover was a scuffed faded red—and slapped it dramatically on the desk.

He had had his eye on her from the first tryout day, he said, for a star part in this play, the most massive opportunity any young actress could ever hope for; and now, just this evening, the very charm which had disabled her for a whore's part had practically convinced him that Clarice was Marjorie's destined break into Broadway. He ordered her to absorb Clarice into her very soul, and then come to see him the day after *The Bad Year* opened. It seemed utterly beyond belief to Marjorie that he should fail to remember her, even at this point. She sat staring passively at him while he gyrated through the Clarice discovery scene, complete with whirls and eye-poppings, waiting for him to recognize her and collapse into embarrassment. She could recall every detail of that first encounter with him; he had even commented on her name, Marjorie Morningstar! How could it have passed so totally from his mind?

But the fact was, it had. The old faker had done this, or things like this, so often with so many girls that she was no more to him than a face in a parade; and she was still trying to think of a devastating way to denounce him when he shook hands and ushered her out of the office, thrusting the script into her hand as he opened the door. "This isn't an end, Marjorie, believe me it isn't. Something tells me, deep down, that it may be the start of the road, for both of us. The golden road, my dear," he exclaimed, his eyes all but starting from his head, "the glory road!"

She went to her dressing room and gathered up her few belongings, including an advance copy of the Philadelphia theatre program with her name in it. Stolidly enduring the sympathy of the girls, she turned off their questions about the red script with a shrug, and put it in her little valise. She said goodbye to the silent whores and the talking whore, all of whom shared the dressing room. The talking whore evinced a surprising sentimental streak, sobbing wildly and kissing Marjorie. Dane Voen was lying in wait for her just inside the stage door. He told her not to be discouraged; she was a great actress, and he would like nothing better than to meet with her evenings, and coach her in methodology. He offered to take her out then and there, and help her forget the setback with a little fun and drinking. She declined, pleading a headache, and she was very glad she had done so when she came out on the street. Dane's mistress was waiting in the alley of the stage entrance, with red reflections from a nearby neon sign dancing in her eyes.

It was a little after midnight. Marjorie bought a morning *Times* at the corner and noted wryly that it was April Fool's Day. She walked up Broadway in a cool foggy night. Light seemed to be dissolved in the air all around her, brilliant yellow; she was walking in a great effulgence, a universal bath, of electric light. There was no plan in her walking, she simply walked, enjoying the cool air on her hot face. After a while she passed out of the blazing square, and after another while she was standing in the misty gloom on Central Park South, the valise at her feet, staring up at the hotel where she had given her virginity to Noel Airman a year ago. She stared so, dry-eyed, for perhaps a quarter of an hour.

Then she walked up to the Fifty-ninth Street subway. At Columbus Circle she stopped beside a trash basket, opened her valise, and took out the script of *Down Two Doubled*. She glanced at the battered red script with a smile which, for complexity and secret sadness, might have rivalled the Mona Lisa's, had a painter caught it. The script fell in the basket with a dry rustle and disappeared under tumbling loose newspapers; and the girl went down into the subway.

"Papa, I'd like to work for you. Is the job still open?"

The business section of the Sunday paper fell out of Mr. Morgenstern's left hand to the floor, and he put down the coffee cup in his right hand very shakily, squinting at his daughter as though she shone too brightly. "What?"

Mrs. Morgenstern, placidly pouring coffee for herself, said, "Nazimova is in a humorous mood this morning."

Marjorie said to her father, "I'd like to go to work. Tomorrow if I can. My typing and shorthand have improved. I think I can be useful to you. I want a steady job."

Seth paused in buttering a piece of toast. "Margie, what are you talking about? You have to go down to Philadelphia this afternoon with the show."

"I'm not going to Philadelphia, Seth. I'm out of the show."

She told her family the facts lightheartedly, but she was watching their reactions. The father seemed stunned. Seth was first angered, then downcast. Mrs. Morgenstern took the news with good cheer. "I'm sorry, darling. You must be very disappointed. But from everything you've told us it was a rotten show. Something better will come along. It wasn't very nice, anyway, that part they gave you. I was almost ashamed to tell people."

"I agree with you, Mom," Marjorie said. "I shouldn't have taken it, and I'm well out of it."

"What goes on? Is Broadway composed entirely of morons?" Seth said, his jaw thrust out. "I've seen a bunch of plays this year, and I haven't seen a young actress yet who looked any better than you. Most of them don't look half as good. I've seen you act. You're better than any of them."

Marjorie leaned over and kissed him on the cheek. "That's a loyal brother."

Seth turned red, pushed his chair back from the table, and went through several grotesque gestures intended to show that he felt quite at ease. He was seventeen, he had grown another two inches, and his complexion was somewhat spotty. Often, as now, he seemed to have an indefinite number of elbows, legs, and hands. "Well, hell, I mean it. I'm not saying it because you're my sister. I don't think you're any world-beater by a long shot. But isn't it the truth?"

Marjorie said, "I'll tell you, Seth, you mustn't be fooled by my amateur work. Naturally I looked pretty good in *Pygmalion* and *A Doll's House*. Those are just about the best parts in the world. Mama could look good in them."

"No, thank you," said Mrs. Morgenstern. "I'm not ambitious like you."

"The girls you're talking about have a few dull lines in a Broadway play to create a character with," Marjorie said to Seth. "There's not much they can do, usually, with such thin stuff. If they get the jobs, they're pretty good actresses, most likely."

"Aw, if the truth were known, it probably just depends on who you sleep with," Seth said.

The mother said, "Look, smart boy, talk that way at college. Not at this table."

"I don't care," Seth said. "If you ask me, that's the one thing that's been holding Marjorie back. She's probably the only virgin on Broadway."

In the short awkward silence, a glance passed among the two parents and the daughter, while Seth lit a cigarette. Marjorie and her father both started to talk at once. The girl laughed. "Sorry, Papa——"

"Are you serious? Do you want to go to work? Because it happens I can use a girl very much right now. I just laid off my secretary, I was going to call the agency Monday."

"I'm serious. I'll start today, if you're going to the office."

Mr. Morgenstern's shoulders straightened, and a happy smile came over his tired pale face. "Well, as a matter of fact my desk is piled to the ceiling. I had no girl, so—I don't want to spoil your Sunday——"

"You won't spoil it. Let's go right now."

"Nothing doing." Mrs. Morgenstern's tone to her husband was stern. "How many doctors do you need to tell you no more Sunday work? Tomorrow's plenty of time. If you're so full of pep, we can go this afternoon and visit Aunt Dvosha. It's a nice drive to the sanatorium."

Marjorie said, "Sanatorium? What's the matter with Aunt Dvosha?"

"She got a blood condition, from eating nothing but vegetables," the mother said. "She's got to stay in bed for two months, and get injected with liver, and eat nothing but hamburgers, heart, tongue, stuff like that."

Marjorie burst out laughing, then checked herself. "Is it serious?"

"Not at all, not now," the mother said, smiling. "She's eating like a lion in a zoo."

Mr. Morgenstern said peevishly, "Since when is dictating letters work? It's less work than driving a car forty miles. For the first time in her life Margie wants to work for me, and you——"

"No working on Sundays, that's all there is to it," said the mother.

Marjorie said, "Papa, how much will you pay me?"

Mr. Morgenstern pursed his lips, trying to look businesslike, but warm delight radiated from his face. "Well, nowadays they start a girl at seventeen a week. But you can't get a girl worth a two-cent piece for less than twenty. Are you any good?"

"I think I'm not bad."

"Well, I'll start you at twenty. If you're no good I'll fire you. I don't want useless relatives hanging around the office."

"Fair enough."

Mrs. Morgenstern said, "Don't tell me we're really getting another wage earner in this house. It's too good to be true."

"Well, it's true," the girl said.

"I'll believe it after you've been doing it three weeks," Mrs. Morgenstern said. "More power to you, darling, but it's very hard work in that office and very dull."

"I know."

"Can it be that she's growing up?" the mother said to the father. Determined as Marjorie was to keep a pleasant manner—this conversation was the result of a sleepless night in which she had come to some hard decisions—this last remark of her mother's pricked her. She said, "Mom, what's our rent here? Eighty a month, isn't it?"

"Eighty-two, why?"

"I'd like to pay my share. If I keep this job, I'll pay in twenty dollars a month. All right?"

Mrs. Morgenstern stared at her daughter, and for the first time her amused look softened. "You mean that, don't you?"

"Yes, I do. That's overdue, too, I think. I'm sure you think so."

"Marjorie, as far as I'm concerned the main thing is that you want to do it. I'm very glad to hear you talking this way. We don't need your money, thank God, and——"

"We certainly don't," the father broke in. "If the time ever comes that I can't put a roof over my children's head——"

"It's all settled," Marjorie said. "I'm paying my share of the rent starting next week. Five dollars a week, twenty a month. If I keep the job."

Seth said, "She's having a soul crisis, that's what."

"It's a lot of foolishness," the father said. "What are you doing, Margie, getting ready to move out?"

"I'm twenty-two, Pa, that's all."

"As long as you're single this is where you stay."

"I want to stay."

"All right. As long as that's understood."

The mother said, "Margie, it's all very fine, and you can do it, of course, if that's what you feel like doing. But you're not being practical. You only use one room and a bath. Twelve a month is more like it."

"Fine," Marjorie said promptly, "I'll pay twelve then."

The mother smiled. "Well, good for you. Always grab a bargain."

"I think it's a bargain. But you named the price," Marjorie said. "I'm glad to have the extra eight dollars, believe me."

"Marjorie, what's all this about? Why are you coming to work?" the father said.

"She's seen the light," Seth said. "It's a conversion phenomenon. We're studying these things in psychology. The shock of losing the part in the play did it. It needs a shock to set it off, but underneath it's been coming a long time——"

Marjorie wrinkled her nose at him, and said to her father, "Isn't it high time I made myself somewhat useful in the world? Anyway, I want to save some money."

"For what?" asked the mother.

"Never mind."

"A present for Noel?"

"No. Not a present for Noel."

"A mink coat," Seth said.

"That's right. A mink coat."

"That's not it," the father said.

Mrs. Morgenstern said, "What does Noel think about all this?"

"I don't know."

Mrs. Morgenstern laughed. "She doesn't know."

"I don't."

"Where is Noel? He hasn't called all week."

"In Paris."

After a slight general pause, Seth said, "You're fooling."

"No, I'm not. He's in Paris. Or he'll be there in a day or so. He left on the *Mauretania* last week."

Mrs. Morgenstern said cautiously, "Did you see him off?"

"Yes."

"Why did he go?"

"He wanted to."

"What's he going to do there?"

"Study."

"Study? A man thirty-two years old?"

"Yes, study."

"Study what?"

"Philosophy."

Mrs. Morgenstern opened her mouth, then closed it without saying anything, rolling her eyes at the ceiling and at her husband.

The father said very gently, "Marjorie, how long is he going to be there?"

"I don't know. Quite a while. Years, maybe. He's going to go to Oxford too."

Mrs. Morgenstern said, "Marjorie, please excuse me, but I think Noel Airman is a little crazy."

"He may well be crazy," Marjorie said. "I don't know. I've only known him three years. I haven't figured him out."

The father said, "Did you have a fight?"

"No, he just went—it's quite all right, you needn't look so concerned, Papa. I'm perfectly okay. I swear I am."

"It's another conversion phenomenon," Seth said. "Delayed. That big flop he had was the shock—and then——"

"Oh, shut up," Mrs. Morgenstern said. "I'm sorry we ever sent you to college. Blah, blah, everything is a crisis or a phenomenon. You're still wet behind the ears. Go talk on the telephone for an hour to Natalie Fain."

"Who's Natalie Fain?" Marjorie said. "I'm losing track here."

Seth stood. "Thanks for reminding me, I do have to call her. Marge, Mom's jealous. Believe me, Natalie's beautiful. She's a dream. She reminds me of you."

"God help her," Marjorie said.

"It's true," Seth said. "Why, she's even going to be an actress like you. She's very serious about it. She was the star in *Pinafore* at her high school last month—showed me the write-up in her school paper. Terrific."

Marjorie groaned, putting her hands to her head. "Not *Pinafore*, Seth. *The Mikado*."

"No, *Pinafore*," Seth said. "Don't you suppose I know the difference? What's the matter with you?"

Marjorie's purpose in going to work for her father was simple enough. She intended to save money as rapidly as possible, take a boat to Paris, and get Noel back once for all to marry her.

Cruel and crushing though his huge letter was, it did not seem to her —now that she had had a few days to think it over—as final as he had intended it. Its weakness lay in its excessive finality. If he were so utterly through with her, would he have bothered to take twenty typewritten pages to say so? The man who had to cross an ocean to free himself of a girl was far from free of her when he bought his ticket—whatever he said in a letter. So Marjorie figured.

She missed terribly a friend or a counselor of some kind; she even thought of talking the problem over with her mother. Time after time Mrs. Morgenstern had been proven right in her wrangles with her daughter; even if, with her heavy hand, she had made it impossible for Marjorie to take her advice when it might have done some good. The girl believed that she was able now to ignore her mother's manner and benefit by her sense. Once or twice she made a tentative start at talking to her; but then she shrivelled and shut up. The hungry eagerness with which her mother responded, and began to pry, brought out all her old barbed defenses. It was absolutely not possible, after all, to reveal to her that she had slept with Noel, and no intelligent talk was possible except in the light of that ugly fact. Marjorie knew that both her parents suspected the truth. Her excuses for coming home late at night, toward the end of the affair, had grown pretty lame. But she decided to let them go on suspecting, lonely though it left her, rather than give her mother the victory of knowing the truth by the confession of her own mouth.

As for her father, she felt it would be easier for her to stab him with a kitchen knife than to tell him.

She considered confiding in Marsha Michaelson, and she did have lunch with her a couple of times. But somehow the meals ended quickly, the talk was inconsequential, and they spent the afternoons shopping together. It was Marsha, now, who was distant and unresponsive; she wouldn't pick up the cues for intimate talk. She chattered as fluently as ever, but there was no trace of the old gushes of warmth. It was as though Marjorie had said or done something for which Marsha couldn't forgive her. All she would talk about was plays, movies, and home decorations. After a six-month honeymoon abroad, and four months in Florida, the Michaelsons had bought a big old house in New Rochelle. She overwhelmed and hideously bored Marjorie with gabble about period furniture, modernized kitchens, the breaking and building of walls, and the depredations of rabbits and moles in flower beds. She made the suburbs sound fully as revolting as Noel had always claimed they were. Marsha had become too thin; at this point dieting made her look worse, not better. Knobby bones showed at her throat. Her face had a sunken brown look almost like a mummy's, and her lips seemed to be drawn over her teeth most of the time in a tight grin.

A letter arrived from Noel after she had been working for her father about a month. Postmarked in Florence, typed on yellow paper, it bore no return address. *I don't want to hear from you, dear,* it began. *I just thought you might want to know that I didn't throw myself off the* Mauretania *halfway across out of sheer longing for you, or anything. In fact I'm fine, brown as a peon and having a gay if somewhat confused time.* He had intended to enroll in the Sorbonne as soon as he arrived, he wrote, but Paris looked too marvelous when he got there, and he decided to put off his studies till the fall. He had already been in Switzerland, Holland, and Norway, as well as France and Italy. There was much talk in the letter of a woman named Mildred and a couple named Bob and Elaine, all of whom he had met on the boat. Mildred dominated the group and seemed to be paying some or all of everybody's expenses. *Mildred wanted to see The Hague, so she hired a limousine. . . . Nothing would do for Mildred but she must fly to Rome that very night, so back went all our clothes in the suitcases. . . .* It was a fair guess, Marjorie thought bitterly, that Mildred was the woman in the red suit. She was first angered. Then she had a spell of revulsion for a day or so when she thought she was free at last of her passion for Noel. Then that mood passed, and she was exactly where she had been before, only more anxious and exasperated.

It was impossible for her to get interested in other men. She tried. She trotted in her parents' wake to temple affairs, to weddings, even to a mountain hotel when the calendar dragged around at last to another summer. There was humiliation in being peddled here and there, a very obvious unmarried daughter; but at least she was still the prettiest girl wherever she went, so the process was bearable. Neither she nor her mother could really envy brides who looked narrowly to their husbands when Marjorie was around, and often as not slipped an anchoring arm through their elbows.

In her rounds through the marriage market—for this was what she was doing, and she didn't try to tell herself otherwise—Marjorie encountered many pleasing young men, and a couple of extraordinarily attractive ones. But with the best will in the world she couldn't warm to them, couldn't sparkle, couldn't appear alive. The ordinary responses of sex seemed to have been drained from her. There was something so forbidding about her that most of the men didn't try to kiss her. To those who did, she yielded with an unprotesting limpness that usually ended the matter.

It wasn't that Marjorie was being loyal or faithful to Noel. She couldn't help herself. She would have liked to fall in love with another man, or so she believed; that was why she gave a date to any reasonably presentable fellow who wanted one. Nor was it that all the men compared so very unfavorably with Noel. If none of them had his peculiar mercurial charm and gaunt good looks, there were several who had other attractions. Her mind and her heart were sealed shut, and that was all. She was a wife. She had long ago gotten over regarding Noel as a paragon. She knew his weaknesses all too well. Unhappily, she had committed her soul and her body to him, and now he owned her and was in her blood—marriage or no marriage.

How persuasive Marsha had been, urging her to sleep with Noel, Marjorie thought—how persuasive, and how wrong! It had all been a lot of patter from books and plays, no more. She wondered what manner of love affairs Marsha's experiments could have been, to leave her so misinformed about sex. It was all very well to prate of trying a lover, and seizing one's chance of joy, and creating sweet memories to warm one's old bones; but the brute fact was that having an affair with a man was a plunge into change, shocking irreversible change, like an amputation. It was not a dip in a pool, after which one came out and dried the same body with the same hands. And as for the much-touted memories, far from treasuring them, she found them a continuing torment, which she would willingly have burned from her brain cells. The sex had been, in the best moments, shaking, lovely; but even in those best moments it had been darkened by reservations, fear, and unconquerable shame. Yet for this sex, good or not so good, she had paid a steep price. Marjorie felt rifled of her own identity. She felt that Noel had it, that Noel was now her other larger self, that she was a walking shell. The instinct to stay alive, to preserve herself, was enlisted on Noel Airman's side; now, when her eyes were at last open to his glaring faults. That was the miserable fallacy in Marsha's arguments. Getting out of the bed, breaking off the affair, didn't end the matter at all. It was only the beginning of the heart of the experience, which was an ever-deepening ordeal of pain and depression. Marjorie found the first gray hairs on her temples—just a fugitive silvery strand or two—that autumn. They were premature; she was only twenty-three; but her father had grayed early, and evidently that was to be her pattern. The discovery was terribly depressing, and yet it gave her an indefinable twisted pleasure.

She tried not to think of what would become of her if she failed to recapture Noel. Panic swept her whenever she really faced the thought that he would never take her in his arms again, never marry her. Never! It was impossible. What could she ever bring to another man but a ransacked body and an empty heart? Her hope in life depended on getting Noel back. Determined as he was to escape her, she was yet more determined to bring him to bay.

And she believed that in the end she was going to win. All Noel's show and power were on the surface; she knew now that at heart he was rather weak. When hard-pressed he ran. A man who ran could be caught.

Noel still seemed to her to have the makings of a good husband, even if he had dwindled much from the blond god of South Wind, and the shining hero of the dress rehearsal of *Princess Jones*. She wasn't sure how much creative talent he really had, after all. She hated to concede this, even to herself, because it made her feel like the world's idiot, after the way she had praised every word he wrote, in her blind girlish worship. But the time had come for her to face facts. Advertising, publicity, promotion, probably would be his fields, as he had himself said; and he was too good at such work to be miserable at it forever. In his first weeks with Sam Rothmore, Noel had done a brilliant job. At the advertising agency his work had been superb—his superiors had told her so—until the day he walked off the job without notice. He surely had a way with words. His discourses in the long letter were vivid and bright. A sentence like *Your left spur has been the American idea of success, and your right spur the Jewish idea of respectability* was not the writing of an ordinary person. It occurred to her that Noel should really have been a lawyer. His charm, persuasiveness, and fluency, with his ability for sharp analysis, might have carried him far—perhaps to a judgeship like his father's! But it was too late for that now, of course; the question was how best to salvage his abilities, in the light of his wild temperament and spotty history.

Her hope was that this flight to Paris was the last gasp of the old Noel, the last effort to fight off "respectability." Noel cared for the good things in life too much, she was sure, to become a philosophy teacher; yet she was perfectly willing to live on an academic salary if that was what he really wished. All she wanted was her husband, the man in whose bed she belonged. She was in no hurry to follow him to Europe; he had to exhaust this fling. Instinct told her that he wanted her, at bottom, more than anything else in the world. He missed her now, and was missing her more and more. She could feel the tugs on the cord which fettered him to her across the wide ocean, in the occasional jaunty jeering letters he sent her, always without a return address, usually postmarked Paris, once Cannes, once London. In the end—this was her view in the optimistic turns of her up-and-down emotional storms—while he might never return to her of his own accord, he would be overjoyed to see her come after him; he would throw up smoke screens of cynical words to mask his surrender—to time and fate, as much as to her—but he would surrender with relief.

This was the substance of her comfort during this black, black year. It was comfort that came and went in her own mind with the shifts of her moods; comfort that was silent, never written out, never shared, never examined whole or with anybody's help; comfort spun in her brain and left in her brain; comfort that was, on the whole, pretty cold. It alternated with moods of despair and terrible pain; pain so deep that the pain in a dentist's chair, when she had to go, was a distraction and a relief. She often cursed the day she had met Noel, and her own fatuous hero worship which had enabled him to swallow three years of her life, three of her best years, the years when most girls met and married their husbands. How many chances for a happy match had gone by, while she had doted and doted and doted on Noel? Now there was no help for it; it was to be Noel, or a broken life.

She woke thinking of him, fell asleep thinking of him, and thought of him all day and all night long when she wasn't working, or reading, or uneasily sleeping (when like as not she dreamed of him). In self-protection she carried a book with her everywhere. She read at breakfast and at lunch, in the subway going to and from work, even in her father's car when she drove to the office with him. In any slack moments at the office she would flip open her novel. She exhausted the rental libraries, and resorted to the public libraries. She developed eyestrain, and got reading glasses, and went on reading and reading.

There was hardly a week during that black winter when she didn't have a cold, or a cough, or a fever. She had paralyzing headaches much of the time, and recurring mysterious rashes, sometimes on her face, so that she could not go to work. She had no appetite, month after month. She forced herself to eat, to shut off the anxious nagging of her mother and the pained glances of her father. The food tasted like straw. She faded so visibly that her parents at last drove her to see a doctor. After a long physical examination he questioned her about her emotional life, looking ironical and wise, and gave her a variety of pills, capsules, and liquid medicines. These did relieve some of the worst symptoms, but all winter long she went on feeling weak, irritable, and played out.

And all winter long her bank balance mounted. The mark she was aiming at was seven hundred dollars. For that amount, she had learned, she could go to Europe, stay three weeks, and return, travelling third class.

But she was not saving quite fast enough; this worry gnawed at her more and more. At best she could bank ten or twelve dollars a week. She had repaid her father the money spent at the Rip Van Winkle Theatre, though he had tried not to accept it. This had given her satisfaction, but it had also set back her departure for Paris by a couple of months. The last letter from Noel had come in November. As his silence stretched through January, she became exceedingly uneasy. They had been separated almost a year. Often she thought of borrowing from her parents. She had almost five hundred dollars, and another two hundred or so would send her on her way. But she couldn't do it. Noel was her problem. It was up to her, she felt, to meet the situation with her own efforts.

One evening, buying a ticket for a French movie at a downtown theatre, she recognized the cashier as one of the "kids," a clever, pretty redhead, and a good actress, though now looking somewhat worn. Marjorie chatted with her for a while. The girl was still butting her head against the Broadway wall, and meantime had been married and divorced twice, each time to a handsome unemployed actor. She was now living with a third beloved of the same variety. Movie cashier jobs were easy to get, she told Marjorie, if a girl was good-looking; there was a rapid turnover in cashiers, owing to the widespread practice of squirrelling a fake ticket roll in the booth and embezzling about one third of the admissions. It occurred to Marjorie that she could almost double her rate of saving by working evenings as a movie cashier, an honest one. With the redhead's help, she actually did get a job two days later.

Her parents protested, of course; she was too run-down for night work, they said. Mrs. Morgenstern remarked in despair that Marjorie seemed doomed to swing from one extreme of foolishness to another. The father raised her salary, hoping in this way to make the night work unnecessary. She accepted the raise, because she had been drudging faithfully in the office and thought she deserved it; but she kept on with the movie job.

It wasn't hard work, but it wasn't healthful. The heating unit in her cashier's booth was faulty; usually she was either freezing or on the verge of being cooked alive. Within three weeks, a severe grippe put her out of action. She dragged herself from bed ten days later, still coughing and weak, but panicky at the thought of all the time that was passing without any money accumulating. Her father tried to send her home from the office, but she would not go. She did a day's typing, coughing now and then in a jarring hollow way, ignoring his worried glances. At night, after dinner, both her parents objected violently when she said she was going back to the movie house; but she went, though her knees were weak under her.

She shivered and sweated through three wretched hours in the stifling booth, fearing that she was coming down with pneumonia. When the marquee went dark at last, she couldn't face a subway trip; she squandered most of what she had earned that night on taxicab fare. She came home chilled through, went straight to the kitchen, took down the brandy bottle, and drank off a stiff shot; then she threw herself on her bed with her clothes on, drawing a quilt over her shuddering frame.

"How about some hot tea?" Her father stood in the doorway in pajamas and an old gray bathrobe, his gray hair rumpled, with some strands standing up almost straight. He carried a glass of milk in one hand, a cup of tea in the other.

"Thanks, Papa. I'd love it." She sat up. The brandy had arrested her shivering.

Mr. Morgenstern sat on the edge of her bed and sipped his milk, regarding her in a disturbing way. Since she had begun the movie job she had often caught him, in the office and at home, directing this same odd look at her: inquisitive, concerned, and apparently angry. He said after a while, "Marjorie, it's enough already, isn't it? How sick do you want to make yourself? What's it all about?"

Marjorie said nothing.

"Look here," the father said, "thank God, we're not poor. Business hasn't been so bad lately. What is it you want? A fur coat? Clothes? A trip? I'm still your father."

Still she said nothing.

"Mama says you want to go to Paris. After him. To bring him back."

Marjorie laughed shortly, despite herself; and the laugh was a confession.

The father shook his head, drank off his milk, and sat staring at her. "Remember that time at South Wind? It seems so long ago. The time we talked, out on the lake, in the rowboat—remember what you said? How did you put it? You were just going to enjoy his company and have a glorious time—this was the United States, you didn't have to worry about marriage."

"I—Papa, I wasn't so very old, you know."

"It doesn't work out that way, does it, Marjorie? Not even in America."

"No, Papa. Not even in America. Not for me, anyway."

The father ran his fingers through his hair, rumpling it more. There was a long silence. He said, "Tell me, does he mean as much to you as that? Even after a year? There are so many men in the world. Does it have to be him?"

Something pathetic in his tone, and in his look, brought a catch and a dryness to her throat. "Papa," she said, "I'm a girl, you know. I can't help it."

He came and stood beside her. His hand embraced her head, and pressed it gently to his side. "Listen, he has fine qualities," Mr. Morgenstern said. "A lot of fine qualities. If that's it, that's it. He'll be our son. . . . You'll go next week. All right?"

"No, Papa, no. That isn't what I want——"

"Why not? Do you want to go, or don't you?"

"I—I almost have enough money now for a third-class ticket. Thanks, anyway."

"Third class? Your first trip to Europe? You'll go first class."

"No, I can't."

"Mama says we should send you, and right away. Enough of this foolishness—working nights, getting sick, fading to nothing . . . She's right. She's usually right, isn't she?"

"Papa, listen——"

"You'll go first class, I say. I'm still your father." His voice was taking on the harsh business tone. "It's settled. You leave next week. And since you're such an independent girl now, Marjorie, you can owe me the money. Go to bed, now, will you, for God's sake? You look terrible."

He kissed her hair brusquely, and hurried from the room.

Marjorie's parents, brother, cousins, aunts, and uncles, with a few people from her father's office, came eddying down a passageway of the *Queen Mary* all around her, and poured into her cabin, exclaiming at the luxury of the furnishings. Flowers and fruit baskets were banked around the spacious room; champagne was cooling in silver buckets on the deck; and there were trays of sandwiches set here and there on the bureaus and tables. Marjorie, in a near-trance of excitement, directed the steward where to put her bags, while her mother, glancing rapidly at the cards on the flowers, said, "Where did the champagne come from? Who ordered it? Did you, Arnold? You, Seth? What is it, a surprise party?" One after another the relatives denied having provided the wine; then a muffled voice from a corner of the crowded cabin said, "Compliments of an old friend, Mrs. Morgenstern."

The crowd of aunts and uncles parted like an opera chorus to disclose, sitting in an armchair, a young man with a large nose, in a handsome gray tweed suit, his clever eyes twinkling behind big black-rimmed glasses. There was a buzz among the relatives, inquiries as to whether this was Marjorie's boy friend, whether they were engaged, and so forth. Marjorie introduced Wally with some embarrassment to the family; but Wally, not at all embarrassed, got out of his chair and drew cheers by popping the corks of the champagne bottles. The steward passed around glasses; the wine flowed and foamed; Wally drew more cheers by proposing a toast to Marjorie. The guests fell on the food, and the party became very gay, and there was much kissing and hugging, especially among the young unmarried cousins. Neville Sapersteen, who was now a white-faced fat boy eight years old, extremely quiet and shy, drank several glasses of champagne while gobbling up a plateful of sandwiches, and was horribly sick in the bathroom about ten minutes after he arrived. Thereafter he lay on a bed moaning, with his mother stroking his head. This was the only jarring note in a highly jubilant family reunion. Neville's father amused everybody by climbing on a trunk, champagne glass in hand, and roaring several Verdi arias in succession, including a couple for coloratura soprano, despite his son's misery and wife's outraged objections.

Marjorie was surprised and touched to find among the gifts a huge bouquet of roses from Seth. Reckoning up how many weeks of allowance the bouquet must have cost, she pulled him aside and kissed him. He blushed as red as his roses, muttering something incomprehensible.

Wally came to her, bottle in hand, while she was looking at the gifts. "More champagne?"

She held out her glass. "This was nice of you, Wally. I'll never forget it."

"Got two minutes for me?"

"Three."

"Drink up, and come."

They left the party, which had spilled over into the passageway, and went to a corner of an immense and peculiarly silent salon containing acres of empty armchairs and couches. "You're looking better than ever," he said, his voice deadened and thin in the vast room.

"Well, you would think so. But thanks, Wally, anyway."

"I just wanted to tell you I've sold my play, Margie."

"Gosh! Sold a play! There's no keeping up with you, is there?" Looking at him, she thought that this must be the true air of success: no conceit or obvious triumph, but a forthright glance, a confident smile, a new erectness in the shoulders, a good-humored distant gentleness. Noel had never had this look about him, not even at the dress rehearsal of *Princess Jones*; he had always been ironical, tense, and either weary or overexuberant. "Which play is it, Wally?"

"It's a new one. I don't think I told you about it. A farce about radio."

"Have you quit your gagwriting job?"

"Hell, no. The play won't go on till the fall. How do I know it'll be a hit? I like those weekly pay checks."

"Who's the producer?"

He told her the name, one of the better-known ones. She said, "I guess you've arrived, Wally."

"One production doesn't make a career."

"Nothing will stop you. I'm proud I've known you. I'll always admire you from the sidelines."

"From the sidelines? What's happened to Marjorie Morningstar?"

Marjorie said with a smile that was brave enough, "She didn't quite make the grade. It's just as well, I guess. There's millions like me for one like you, and that's as it should be. How does the song go in *The Gondoliers*? 'When everybody is somebody, then nobody's anybody.'"

"Well, then, how about Marjorie Wronken?" He said it in such an offhand way, without smiling, that she was baffled.

"Why, sure, dear. You take my breath away. Let's get the captain to marry us, this very minute, before you change your mind."

His eyes didn't waver behind the glasses. "You think I'm fooling, of course."

"When did I see you last? Six, eight months ago? I don't blame you for rubbing it in, Wally. You always told me you were a genius, and it seems you were right. My apologies for being so slow to realize it. Okay?"

He said, "I've been hunting this deer for years to lay at your feet. Now you won't even glance at the carcass. I feel abused."

Marjorie looked in his face for a moment. "I don't know whether you enjoy tormenting me, or what. You have a cute way of putting these things, so that I'd look like an idiot if I took you seriously. If I were to turn on you right now and say, 'All right, take me, I'm yours,' you'd probably scoot out of here like a jack rabbit."

He looked offended, then he burst out laughing. "Well, what I'd do more likely is faint from astonishment."

"That's it. You just enjoy mooning over me for some obscure reason, and you know it's safe, so you indulge yourself. You've been doing this to me since you were eighteen, Marchbanks, and you're still doing it. Look, I'm beaten, I'm crushed, I'm full of repentance. All right? Obviously, I should have fallen in love with you. You're a mental giant, and you're too attractive for words. I fell in love with someone else. Shoot me."

He said, "It doesn't matter how many months I don't see you. I guess I've known a few hundred girls by now. You're not smarter than all of them. You're not even prettier than all of them. The only thing is, you're Marjorie. That seems to go on being true, somehow."

She glanced around the empty salon, took his hand and stood, then put her arms around him and kissed him. "I've left a room full of relatives and mamas and papas," she murmured. "Let's go back to them, shall we?"

"Noel hasn't been well, by the way, Margie. You're likely to find him changed."

She had started to walk toward the door. She stopped and turned, a cold thrill running through her. "Changed? Noel? How?"

"He—well, changed. He picked up some kind of fever tooting around North Africa——"

"How do you know?"

"He wrote me."

"What's his address in Paris?"

"I don't know. He didn't write from Paris."

"Is that the truth?"

"Of course it is."

"I really want his address, Wally."

"Good God, I'd tell you his address if I knew it, Marjorie," Wally said.

They walked back to her stateroom without more words.

Chapter 41. THE MAN ON THE BOAT DECK

The *Queen Mary* edged away from the pier, to the thunder of boat whistles and the crash of a brass band. The last figures Marjorie could discern in the blurring mob on the pier were Seth and Wally Wronken, shoulder to shoulder, waving their hats in the air. It all seemed to go very fast. Soon the great ship was out in the river, and she couldn't see the pier at all through the black smoke of the tugs butting the ship and squawking.

She was on her way to Noel.

The vessel began to vibrate with its own power. Marjorie strolled forward on the boat deck. Neither the raw wet wind tugging at her clothes, nor the alarming blasts of the whistle from the huge red and black funnel overhead, nor the delicious small unsteadiness of the white-scrubbed wood deck beneath her feet could give her the feeling of being on a ship, of actually being on a ship. They steamed past the Empire State Building and it seemed to Marjorie that she was in the building watching the ship go by, instead of the other way around. Never in her life had she felt so totally dislocated, so outside reality. She had expected to experience some strong emotion, passing the Statue of Liberty outward bound, but it slipped down the side, a big green statue just like the postcard pictures of it; and while everyone at the rail gawked, pointed, and chattered, Marjorie forgot it was there, as she watched a gull cruising along in the air at the exact pace of the ship, not ten feet from her face, screaming sadly.

In the widening Lower Bay the land view became flat and dull. The view out to sea was tumbling gray clouds and heaving gray water. The ship began to roll more, in a slow majestic way. The wind freshened and became much colder; the passengers drifted rapidly from the rails. Marjorie found herself standing not six feet from a medium-sized slender man with a rather young face, and grayish hair trimmed close. He was leaning on the rail, hatless, smoking a long cigar. His coat hung over his arm, neatly folded. As the rail emptied between them, he glanced at her with a slight pleasant smile. She answered with a half-smile and looked out to sea again.

She had noticed this man before at the gangway desk. He had checked in directly ahead of her. His assured manner with portfolio and travel papers, the straight way he held himself, the dressy gray topcoat and gray Homburg hat, the diagonal bluish scar across his forehead had caught her attention; she had guessed—in her generally excited frame of mind —that he might be a diplomat, or perhaps some well-known playwright or newspaper correspondent. At once she had compared him in her mind with Noel; she always did that when she saw an interesting man. In his leanness, with his tanned bony face, he was not wholly unlike Noel; but he was shorter, and if anything a bit slighter.

He wasn't nearly as handsome as Noel; but he had just the look, she thought now, with another glance toward him, that Noel strove for and for some reason missed. Possibly not being Jewish, as this man rather obviously was not, made the difference. There had always been something exotic about Noel. The wavy thick blond hair, the charged blue eyes, the height, the energetic gestures, the very handsomeness, had all given him a touch of extravagance. This man's appearance was dry, plain, adult; almost he might have gone unnoticed in a crowd. The contrast of gray hair and a young face, the scar, and a curious quiet keenness in his expression were what marked him off.

He said, glancing at her again and smiling, as he met her eye, "We seem to be almost the last brave ones. Isn't it too cold for you?"

"Well, it's all so new to me, I hate to go below and miss a moment of it."

"Your first crossing?"

"Yes."

"The weather should have been better. The city looks grand in sunlight, from the river. This is a pretty sad sailing." He strolled along the rail and leaned beside her. The scar drew her eyes at this close view: faded blue, with faint stitch marks, running from under his hair slantwise to his left eye. Somehow it was not exactly a disfigurement, but a trait, a mark, that belonged to the face.

She said, "It's just as well. I don't feel sparkling, exactly. I've never said so many goodbyes all at once. It's depressing."

He looked at the book under her arm with mild curiosity. She had taken it along upon leaving the cabin, thinking she might settle down for a while in a deck chair. "Are you an English teacher?"

"No, I'm not a teacher. Why?"

"It hardly seems you'd be reading *Tom Jones* for fun."

"Well, I've run through all the good mysteries. This is not bad. It's long, anyway. I guess I'll have plenty of time to read."

He smiled, looking down at the tourist-class deck, which was full of young people, chattering and laughing with exaggerated gaiety in the first moments of getting acquainted. "I'm afraid you will, in first class."

"Oh? Should I have gone tourist?"

"Well, no. First class looks so alluring and unattainable from below, it's better to find out how tame it really is, first time out. You'll never feel underprivileged after that."

"You make it sound unpromising."

"Do I? I guess I'm talking like this because the weather is so gray. You'll love your crossing, I'm sure."

There was a burst of laughter from a cluster of girls along the rail below, surrounded by young men. One of the men, in an American army uniform, said something with a baritone laugh, and the girls shrieked again. "I can't help feeling I'm missing something," Marjorie said.

"The joke might not have amused you. They look like college girls."

"It's fun just to laugh in company sometimes," Marjorie said, "amused or not."

"I think you're better off with Fielding."

"He's been dead such a long time," Marjorie said. "You're not a teacher, are you?"

"No, just a businessman. Chemicals is my line. . . . Am I mistaken, or did your face fall?"

"Why, not at all. Why should it?"

"Because businessmen are dull."

"Not necessarily."

"Well, yes, maybe necessarily. Making money is dull work. That's one reason why first-class passengers tend to be dull." He puffed at his cigar, and tossed it over the rail. "That's against the rules. Be sure the wind's at your back when you do it, if you smoke. Or the butt goes sailing into someone's porthole, or face, and it can be very unpleasant."

"I'll try to remember."

After a moment, resting his elbows on the rail, he said, "My name is Michael Eden."

"I'm Marjorie Morgenstern." She looked for a flicker of reaction to the Jewish name, but there wasn't any. He nodded, his eyes turned to the horizon, where the land was shrinking to a lead-colored line. She said, "I am getting cold, after all. My legs, mainly. It's a freezing wind. But it smells so wonderful, so clean and fresh——"

"You'll have five whole days of it. You may as well go below and warm up, like all the other sensible people. I like to watch the land until it's gone."

"You've travelled quite a bit, I gather," Marjorie said.

"Yes. And you haven't."

"I haven't been west of the Hudson or east of Jones Beach. I should think watching the land vanish is just for neophytes like me."

"Not at all. It's the second best moment of the trip for me. The best moment is when I see it again, the good old USA, still there, poking its big snout up over the horizon." He smiled at her. It was a peculiarly bleak, cool smile. "I'm just a Kiwanis Club boy, you see. It would be the easiest thing in the world to keep me down on the farm. I've seen Paree, and you can have it."

She said, "Kiwanis Club boys don't usually know that they're just Kiwanis Club boys."

For an instant a sharp look of appreciation flashed in his eyes. "Well, now and then I read. You can't play cards forever. Though I certainly try."

She said, pulling her coat about her, "Say goodbye to the good old USA for me, will you? I'm giving up."

She found that her steward, an amiable little white-headed man with an enchanting British accent, had put the room perfectly in order. He pressed her to have tea; she agreed, expecting a pot of tea with perhaps a few cookies, but he brought her a lavish spread of sandwiches and exquisite cakes. When she could eat no more, most of the food remained.

She was in a large double bedroom on A deck with real beds, panelled walls, and smart severe drapes and furniture, all in rich tones of brown and gray. It was the off-season, so Marjorie was travelling in fantastic lone luxury. She took off her suit, put on a new silk housecoat, and propped herself on a bed with *Tom Jones*. The bed rocked slowly, easily; far from making her uneasy, it was the pleasantest sensation in the world. She had not felt so calm, so relaxed, so good, it seemed to her, since her girlhood days, before her first fatal glimpse of Noel Airman at South Wind. There was something miraculously liberating about being on a ship.

She tried to read, but she could not; her eyes rested unmoving on the page, while her mind went over the conversation with the man on the boat deck. How old was he? Hardly forty, despite the gray hair; he might not be over thirty-five.

"Mike Eden," she said aloud, for no reason. The sound of her own voice startled her; she nestled in the pillows, and forced her attention back to *Tom Jones*.

Falling in love with love is falling for make-believe,
Falling in love with love is playing the fool . . .

It became obvious to Marjorie, on the first night of the crossing, that that song was going to remind her of Michael Eden for a long time. It was a favorite of the ship's musicians, a protean group of four who played Beethoven quartets in the afternoon in one of the smaller salons, Victor Herbert melodies at dinner, and reasonably inflamed jazz after ten at night, in the vessel's night club, a charming little oval room called the Verandah Grill on one of the highest decks, with tall windows looking out on the darkling ocean and the gently swinging moon and stars.

The musicians were playing *Falling in Love with Love* when she came into the night club with Eden for the first time, shortly before midnight. They played it twice more that evening, and several times each evening thereafter; and they sometimes obliged with it at dinner and at the teatime concerts, too. The leader had worked up a florid passage for himself in the middle of the waltz. He would step forward and soar into his solo, swaying artistically, closing his eyes with pleasure at the sounds he was making; and when it was over he would blink and smirk around at the ladies, with a roosterish pride quite engaging to behold.

The first evening they were in the night club, when Eden saw him perform this solo, he stared at the violinist with eyes so wide that Marjorie asked him what was the matter. Eden looked around at her, then out through the windows at the sea and the low yellow moon, and then at the musician again. "Doesn't he fascinate you?"

"Why? He's just another conceited musician. I've known them by the hundreds. He's not even very good."

"That's just it. There he stands, afloat on a black sea in a black night, fiddling a little song which is his pride and joy in a mediocre way, and so pleased with himself he could explode. Isn't he Everyman?"

Marjorie regarded him inquisitively while he lit another of his long thin cigars. He smoked them almost constantly; they were an odd chocolate brown, unbanded, and their odor was peculiarly rich and agreeable. She had seen him playing cards for hours after dinner in one of the salons with three elderly Englishmen, and he had seldom been without a cigar.

She said, "Do they talk much about Everyman at your Kiwanis Club?"

With a quick glance at her, he said, "We have lectures about him every Monday and Thursday. Would you like to dance?"

Eden danced rustily at first, in a stiff formal way, and seemed rather bored. But then he warmed to it, and Marjorie found herself enjoying his dancing. She enjoyed talking to him, too. While they sipped their drinks he asked sharp questions about *Tom Jones,* seeming to know the book by heart. He said the only people writing like Fielding nowadays were a few mystery writers. "Well, thank heaven somebody has a good word for the mystery writers," she said. "My—the fellow I go with—has nagged at me for years because I read mysteries."

"He's a snob," Eden said. "There isn't a mystery I won't read. I think next to doctors detective-story writers are the chief benefactors of mankind."

"He is a snob," Marjorie said. "He's the worst intellectual snob I've ever met. But at least he admits it."

"Where is he now?"

"In Paris. I'm going there to run him to earth and make him marry me. If I can."

Eden's smile was usually controlled and careful, his eyes remaining sombre, but now a wholly different look came over his face, a charming gleam of warm appreciation and pleasure. Like a sunny break in the clouds on a gray day, it came and went. "Is that really why you're going to Europe?"

"Yes."

"Well, I bet you'll succeed."

"I hope so. I've been chasing him for four years." Marjorie inclined her head toward a table on the other side of the dance floor. "That blonde over there keeps looking and looking at you. In case you're interested."

"Does she?" Eden glanced toward the blonde, who was sitting with a thickset man, also blond. At this distance she looked exceptionally pretty; Marjorie had not noticed her before on the ship. She smiled at Eden, fluttering her fingers in a small gesture of greeting. He made a small bow, then turned away, wrinkling his forehead; the scar puckered deep. When his face was in repose Marjorie hardly noticed it. She said, "You know her?"

"Slightly. I met her on the *Champlain* a few months ago, coming home."

"She's stunning."

"She's a model. German."

"Do you go into Germany much?"

"Most of my business is there."

"Then you're not Jewish."

With a cold smile he shook his head. "It wouldn't be very pleasant for me if I were, I guess."

"What's it like in Germany now?" Marjorie said after a silence.

"Not good."

"Have you ever seen—well, any of the things we read about?"

"I haven't been inside a concentration camp, if that's what you mean. I've seen storm troopers wreck a restaurant. They're like football players after a game, having a little gay horseplay. It's sort of comical to watch, really. They're laughing and joking. It's a little creepy to see a policeman go by looking the other way, that's all. Makes it seem like a dream."

"Do you think there'll be a war?"

Eden smoked for a while, looking at her. "Well, I'll tell you, Marjorie. They've built these long six-lane highways everywhere in Germany. Broad white rivers of concrete, absolutely empty, not a car on them, stretching to the horizon. The roads don't go anywhere, don't detour for any towns—they go right to the borders, straight as parallels of latitude, and stop. What are those roads for?"

Marjorie was sorry she had started the topic. She was very uncomfortable under Eden's direct gaze.

For years, now, she had been afraid even to think about Germany. Sometimes in her restless nights she had had nightmares of being pursued through Berlin by storm troopers. But it had never seemed quite real to her that somewhere on the face of the solid green earth human beings were doing to other human beings what the papers said the Nazis were doing to the Jews. She hoped that in the end the atrocities would turn out to be mostly newspaper talk, like the World War stories of the Huns eating Belgian babies. Her conscience had pricked her from time to time into giving part of her savings to refugee organizations. Beyond that, her mind was closed to the Nazis.

She said uneasily, "You know, I'm ashamed of myself. You're giving me the horrors, and all I want to do about it is change the subject."

"That's all anybody is doing about it, Marjorie."

"I'm Jewish. I should care a little more."

"Jews are just people."

She said, pausing for a moment to scrutinize his calm face, "That's the best compliment anyone can pay us. Said in that tone, anyway."

"I'm not so sure. I'm not particularly sold on people at the moment. I think, given the choice, I'd rather be a cat or a bear."

"You remind me a lot—every now and then, the way you talk—of a man I know."

"Really? A good man, or a bad one?"

"Well, some think he's a monster. He's the one I'm crossing the ocean for."

"Maybe it would be best if you didn't catch him."

"Oh, is your wife a thoroughly miserable woman?"

"I'm not married. I was." He puffed at his cigar. "My wife is dead."

"I'm sorry."

"It happened several years ago. Auto accident. That's how I got my scar. I went through the windshield. My wife was killed." He said this rapidly and dryly, as though to cut off further discussion; drank up his drink, and signalled for another. "You don't have to keep pace with me, by the way, I have an unusual tolerance for booze. . . . Isn't that Jackie May dancing?"

Marjorie looked at the dance floor. "So it is, by gosh. An honest-to-goodness celebrity after all. My trip is made." Jackie May had been the nation's favorite radio comedian when Marjorie was about fifteen, and he was still popular. He was a pudgy man, absolutely bald, with waggling eyebrows and flapping hands. He was dancing with a very pretty brunet girl about Marjorie's age, half a head taller than himself.

"That's his new wife, I believe," Eden said. "He's on his honeymoon, or so I seem to remember reading in Winchell."

"Why, he looks past sixty," Marjorie said. "Is he really married to that girl? How revolting."

"There are many theories as to why old men marry young pretty girls," Eden said. "Regressive tendencies, or a post-adolescent emotional fixation, something like that. The girl is a surrogate, a symbol, not a real person to the man, all the books say so. I have my own theory about it, though. If I had the time and the talent I'd write a book. I'm sure I'm right."

"What's your theory?"

"Well, I say old men marry young pretty girls so as to sleep with them." He said it with a straight, even dour face, looking at the dance floor.

Marjorie said, after a while, "Do you have lectures every Monday and Thursday at the Kiwanis Club on regressions and fixations?"

"I used to teach psychology," Eden said, with the same straight face.

"I see. And now you're in the chemical business."

"That's right."

"And is any of this true, or are you taking some queer pleasure in filling me full of stories?"

"It's true, all right. I gave up teaching after my accident. I wasn't much good at it afterward."

Marjorie took a less satiric tone. "You seem very strange to me. I'm not being especially stupid, am I?"

"You're not being stupid at all, Marjorie, but I believe I am. I'm sorry." He drank whiskey. "I guess I've been taking a sort of childish pleasure in mystifying you. I can't say why. The booze, maybe, though I don't think so. I've had a sort of shock today, nothing serious, but my nerves haven't been very good lately. Everything I've told you is true, all the same, or true enough, anyway. Have you ever told the exact truth in your life? It's an extremely hard thing to do. Every encyclopedia is full of lies." He looked at her, and there seemed to be a faint tinge of appeal in his eyes, curiously contrasted with the dry tone and the mocking words. "Have I scared you off, or would you like to dance some more?"

Marjorie said, "Of course I'll dance, if you like. But I think possibly it's a bore for you to keep up a conversation with me. I won't at all mind if you'd rather go back to your room and read, or go to sleep——"

"Good God, no," Eden said. "Let's dance, by all means. Let's dance till Everyman's fiddle drops from his hands. I'm having a wonderful time. I hope you are."

Chapter 42. A GAME OF PING-PONG

When she opened her eyes next morning, white sunlight was coming in a slant shaft through the porthole. It took her a second or two to remember where she was. The ship was rolling much more than yesterday; she saw through the porthole clear blue sky, then rough purple water rushing by, then blue sky again. The ray of sunlight swung up and down on the wall. She lay on her pillow, blinking at the strong light, thinking of Mike Eden. She passed a lazy few minutes remembering some of the strange things he had said; then it occurred to her to be surprised at having him on her mind, and not Noel. Thinking of Noel Airman when she woke was a chronic ailment of hers, as some people woke with raw throats. It was very agreeable to be free of it even for a day.

She rang for coffee. The steward brought it with a copy of the ship's newspaper, and told her that the clocks had been moved forward an hour; it was almost lunch time. This gave her an excuse to surrender to laziness for another hour or so. She piled the pillows, and sat up drinking coffee and reading the paper. She yawned through the news stories—Hitler was occupying Czechoslovakia unresisted—and turned to the calendar of ship's events. There was going to be a ping-pong tournament in the afternoon, a Marx Brothers movie in the evening, and a dance in the main lounge. She decided to wear her best evening dress that night, a fetching black taffeta from Bergdorf, instead of saving it for the captain's dinner.

She found herself, after a while, a bit dizzy and uneasy from the rolling of the ship. She bathed, clinging with a soapy hand to the rail over the tub, and giggling at the wild back-and-forth slosh of the steaming water. She dressed in a hurry, humming *Falling in Love with Love,* and went out on deck.

Sunglare smote her eyes, and she put on dark glasses. Marvelling again at the vastness of the ship—the deck receded into the distance, blocks long, the perspective exaggerated by the curving lines of the hull—she fell into the parade of morning marchers, gulping the sweet cool air. She rounded the far end of the port side, and came upon Eden at a ping-pong table, negligently clicking balls back and forth with an intent boy. "Hi, athlete," she said.

He waved the bat at her. "Hi. Lunch?"

"Love it."

He seemed very cheerful; he said he had been up since eight, walking the decks. They went to his table in the great ornate dining room; he depressed the steward by setting the long menu aside, and ordering a lettuce and tomato sandwich. When Marjorie asked for bacon and eggs, Eden joked, "I'm more Jewish than you are. You're the one that's having bacon." She laughed and told him how long it had taken her to get used to it. He nodded, his face serious. "It must be a powerful mechanism. It's a wonder you ever broke it down."

"Well, it's not too hard once you realize it's just an old-fashioned super-stition——"

"But you're wrong there, food disciplines are part of every great religion. Psychologically they're almost inevitable, and extremely practical. Let me ask you, didn't you feel more—I don't know—let's say at home in the world, warm, safe, good, while you were observing your laws?"

"Well, yes, but I hadn't really been thrown out in the cold cruel world yet, that's all. I was leading a pretty sheltered life."

"Religious discipline is nothing but a permanent psychic shelter. You stay inside it, and you're less vulnerable to whatever horrors happen in life."

"But if you don't believe in it, how can it shelter you?"

"How do you know what you believe? Girls don't think."

"Thank you."

"You're welcome. There come our happy newlyweds."

Jackie May and his bride were seating themselves at a table near them. The girl had a peevish look, and her makeup was too thick. The comedian, pale and smiling, seemed to be trying hard to amuse her. Eden lit a cigar and began to talk about the Freudian theory of humor. He said it might explain the deliberately childish antics of comedians: the affected high voices, the giggles, the silly faces, and so forth. References to taboo facts were forgivable and comical in children, odious in adults. "A baby's bare behind is charming and funny," Eden said. "An adult's is a shocking offense. The comedian makes himself symbolically a child, and that's how he gets the jester's freedom."

Marjorie, watching Jackie May vainly wagging his eyebrows and cracking jokes to his pouting wife, was struck by this analysis. "I never thought of that, but it's absolutely true," she said.

Eden said, "Well, I'm not so sure. The general theory of the comedian would have to be much more complex. Fred Allen, for instance, is over-adult, if anything, and he's the best of the lot. It's like the rest of Freud. Marvelous strokes of insight, but when you try to make them general truths you end up with useless dogma."

"Don't tell me you're another Freud-baiter. That's so commonplace nowadays."

"I'm not against Freud, I'm anti-Freudian. Freud himself once said that he wasn't a Freudian, and he sure as hell wasn't." The rare gleam of warmth, which Marjorie had seen only once or twice, now came into his eyes. "I spent a year and a half at the institute in Vienna. I knew him."

"You knew *Freud?*" She stared at him.

"Well, very slightly. You almost had to, fifteen years ago when I was taking my Ph.D., if you wanted to write anything in the analysis field. I saw him at a couple of seminars. I wrote my thesis on dreams in Dickens' novels. . . . What's so amazing about all this? You look as though you didn't believe a word of it."

"I don't know. It's like saying you used to hobnob with Darwin, or Copernicus."

Eden smiled. "He was a genius, all right. But he wasn't a Darwin or a Copernicus, you're wrong there. Nobody can really build on him, and that's what makes the true landmark scientist. He's got his followers, sure —the way Swedenborg and Henry George have. A sect of enthusiasts. Actually Freud was a great writer, a brilliant polemist, say like Nietzsche or Voltaire. His work will live and shed light forever, like any great philosopher's, but——"

"The blonde's looking at you again," Marjorie said with a tilt of her head. "She makes me self-conscious."

"I wish she'd fall overboard," Eden said.

"Don't be absurd."

Eden mashed his cigar out violently in an ashtray. "Did you see the paper this morning? Czechoslovakia's gone. It seems to me that if I were a German it would give me the greatest conceivable pleasure to cut my own throat. . . . I'm sorry you told me about Hilda. I can feel her eyes crawling on my neck like a spider. Let's get the hell out of here."

They went back to the promenade deck for the ping-pong tournament, in which he was enrolled. There were only half a dozen other entries for the men's cup. "It'll all be over in an hour or so," Eden said. "Stick around and cheer for me." He beat his first opponent easily, playing a steady defensive game. Then he stood by Marjorie and watched the next match, which was won by a young German named Thaler, in a green hound's-tooth jacket; Marjorie recognized him as the man who had sat in the night club with the blond girl, Hilda. At the last point the German turned to Mike, saluted with his racquet, and bowed. "Mr. Eden, at your service." He had long straight blond hair and very broad shoulders. Eden stood and took off his coat and tie, and the German grinned. "Not necessary, Mr. Eden. You are my master with ease."

Eden lost the first game, making wild slams and faulty services, holding himself very straight and raking at the ball in tense sharp strokes. The German, profiting by all his mistakes, coolly and methodically piled up points. Hilda came, halfway through the game, and leaned against the rail beside Marjorie. She applauded all Eden's good shots, and when he lost the game, she said to Marjorie, "He won the cup on the *Champlain*. He warms up soon." Marjorie didn't answer.

In the second game the German pounded away at Eden's backhand, the source of most of his wild errors; but Eden's backhand drive began to stay on the table. It was a very swift flat stroke when it worked, and Thaler had to grin foolishly a couple of times as it streaked past him. Hilda called, "That's like on the *Champlain*, Mike." It pleased Marjorie to observe that the German girl's ankles were quite stubby; the walking shoes she wore made them look worse.

Hilda said to Marjorie, "He does well, hm? Dance, talk, play ping-pong—All-American boy, no? You're old friends?"

Marjorie nodded slightly. She felt awkward and stiff, and quite unable to talk to the German girl.

"So he tells me. Nice to meet an old friend on the boat. You're lucky. He is a sympathetic person. Very cultured. Oh, we had fun on the *Champlain*——"

Marjorie felt a tiny stab of pain in her temple; a ping-pong ball bounced off her face. "Sorry, Margie," Eden called. "I wasn't trying to blind you."

Hilda laughed. "Steady down, Mike, you lose the cup."

Eden won a run of points with swift serves. The spectators—there were twenty or so, crowded around on the deck near the table—applauded. The German held up his racquet, smiling at Mike. "You make it warm for me." He took off the loud green jacket and opened his tie; the onlookers laughed, and Eden smiled coldly.

The blond girl said, "Ach, he's charming. To me he is like a typical Englishman. I lived in London three years. If I would see him in Piccadilly I would never guess he was American, let alone Jewish, you know?—*Good* shot, Mike."

The word made all the nerves in Marjorie's body contract. She calculated a slight pause, and then said, "I beg your pardon?"

"Hm?" said the blond girl.

"Did you say Mike Eden was Jewish?"

The blond girl's smile was affable. "You're an old friend of his, surely you know that? Please don't think because I'm German I care. We're not all exactly like that."

Marjorie had a strange and utterly irresistible impulse. She said, shaking her head, "Well, I'm just wondering how you got that impression. I happen to know he isn't. We lived in the same neighborhood years ago. I lived across the street from the church his family went to."

"To church? His family went to church, you say?" There was a burst of applause which the two girls ignored. They were looking each other straight in the face. The ping-pong ball clicked and clicked. The blonde's eyes wavered. "Aren't you mistaken?"

Marjorie shook her head.

The blonde glanced at Eden and then at Marjorie. "I feel very ridiculous. He never said so, I just assumed it—you see, he was so terribly sympathetic. My father had a very bad time with the Nazis, and—— Oh, I make a damn fool of myself sometimes. . . . Ach, *look* at that shot!" Eden had lured Thaler to one side of the table and slammed the ball in the other corner. Everybody clapped, and the German rapped the table with his racquet. "Gut, gut." He was smiling at Eden; his eyes were reddened and determined. He won the second game by a closer score. Eden won the third game.

The contest was best three out of five. Both men were perspiring through their shirts in dark splotches. Eden's face was dead gray, his scar purple-red. The spectators were not applauding any more, but watching in a hush. The eighth point of the next game was a fierce volley lasting a couple of minutes, and Eden won it at last with a crashing backhand shot. The German began making errors after that. Eden switched to a soft style, brought the German in far on one side, then sent a teasing spin clear to the opposite side of the table. Thaler ran for it, tripped on a table leg, and fell on his face. A burst of scattered uneasy laughter did not lighten the tension. Thaler got up laughing too, his face dark red. Eden won the game, playing with murderous vigor.

The last game was a rout. The German stopped trying, popped up the ball, and made jokes about Eden's prowess. Eden unsmilingly crashed ball after ball past him. The German said, when the score was 17–3, "I think I concede to Mister Babe Ruth." Eden shook his head and served the ball whizzing past Thaler, who made a mere comic motion with his racquet.

When it was over there was no applause. The German put on his coat, nodded and smiled at Eden, and walked out. Eden played the final round with the thirteen-year-old boy who had volleyed with him in the morning. All the sting went out of his game; the boy was an excellent player, and beat him in straight sets. Hilda left halfway through the match, as did most of the spectators.

Marjorie took Eden's arm as they walked down the deck. His shirt was soaked and he was trembling. "You'd better have a shower."

Eden nodded. She walked to his stateroom with him. He said nothing all the way. When they were inside he threw his coat across the room and sank in an armchair. "I want to puke at myself. The Nazis conquered, America triumphant, civilization saved. On the ping-pong table."

"Don't get so wrought up, for God's sake," Marjorie said. "You're warped on the subject——"

"I'm not warped on the subject at all. I'm insane on it," Eden said, jerking a cigar out of a drawer and slamming the drawer. He lit the cigar with shaking fingers.

Marjorie told him about the conversation with the blond girl. His face drawn, he stared at her, smoking, not moving. "Whatever possessed you," he said, "to tell such a ridiculous lie?"

"I really can't imagine," Marjorie said. "I just couldn't help myself. Somehow I wanted to confuse her as much as possible. She was obviously pumping me——"

"Well, that doesn't mean anything, it's a characteristic of theirs. They'll ask you about anything, including your bowel condition——"

"I'm sorry, if I did anything wrong. It certainly was a silly lie."

He got out of his chair and came toward her. She didn't know what he was going to do. He bent and kissed her mouth lightly. He smelled of sweat. "You didn't do badly at all." He went to a shelf, took down a bottle of white capsules, poured water from a jug and swallowed two capsules. "One of the privileges of being in the chemical business," he said, replacing the bottle. "Drugs are part of the game. All the happiness pills you can use. Let me know if you get nervous or depressed about anything. I am Old Doctor Happiness." He started to take off his shirt. "Don't worry about Hilda. Put her out of your mind."

"What's it all about, Mike?"

"Why, nothing at all. She's just a snoopy Teuton, and there are some eighty million of them, I regret to say. Run along. I'm going to take my shower and sleep. I didn't sleep much last night. See you at dinner."

Marjorie's first inkling that the ship was running into a storm came at dinnertime, when, with a sort of universal groaning creak, the immense restaurant slanted far sidewise, generating a din of sliding and clattering dishes, and much shrieking and laughing among the startled passengers. All the soup ran neatly out of her plate under her spoon, making a wide brown stain on the cloth, and she clutched at the arm of her chair, feeling on the verge of toppling out of it. "Heavens, what's all this?"

"It's going to get worse," Eden said. "The weather report isn't good. Let me know if it bothers you. I have pills."

Marjorie said, "I feel fine. Hungry as a bear, in fact. Natural-born sailor, I guess. I'll just order things that don't spill." And she did in fact eat a hearty dinner, while the salon swayed and tumbled and careened with slow long groans, and many passengers hurriedly left.

Afterward they went to the movie together. Marjorie found the Marx Brothers amusing for a while despite the queer heaving and dropping of the seat under her. But all at once she began wishing she had not eaten quite so much. She was very aware of her meal, heavy under her tight waist, and it was dizzying to keep her eyes on the screen. The seat seemed to be gyrating like a Coney Island ride. Reluctantly, after trying to fight the weakness off, she laid a hand on Eden's arm and whispered, "I guess maybe I'll try your pills."

They went staggering and laughing down the passageway. "Doesn't it bother you?" she said.

"I've had a pill. I'm the world's champion pill consumer. I believe in them. A man should believe in his own products."

He picked a bottle out of several which were rattling on a barred shelf in his room, and shook a red capsule into his hand. "Here. Take some water."

"How do you keep them all straight? You must be a drug fiend." She swallowed the capsule and stared at him. "How long will it take?"

"Just give the gelatin a chance to dissolve. That's the quickest stuff there is. German, I regret to say. We've got nothing to touch it."

"What do I do till it starts working, Mike? I'm an unhappy girl."

"Well, are you game to go out on deck? We'll get in the lee somewhere. There's nothing like cold air."

She hurried to her stateroom and put her camel's hair coat over the black taffeta. They went up extremely unsteady stairs, and stepped through a door into a wet icy night, full of horrid noise.

Strangely, in the spot where they stood the air was fairly calm, yet around and above them the wind whistled and shrieked, tumbling thick black smoke like a stream of waste ink down from the funnels into the gray-black sea. The waves were crashing and thundering, throwing immense phosphorescent green crests as high as the deck on which they stood; higher, when the ship rolled toward the water. Black sheets of rain waved along the deck, only a foot or two beyond their shelter, spattering and hissing, but only a few stray drops struck their faces.

"Lively, isn't it?" He held her close, one arm around her shoulders, the other hanging to a metal bracket on the doorway.

"It's terrific! Is it a hurricane?"

"Don't be silly. It's a rainstorm, that's all, and not much of one. This big tub doesn't even know we're having bad weather."

"*I* know it. My God, Mike, look how we're rolling! You'd swear we were going down."

"They won't even call off the dance for this."

"Well, I'm not going to dance, that's for sure. I can hardly stand up." They stood swaying together for a few minutes, listening to the howls and whines of the wind, and the insane crashing of the sea. "Good God, it's so eerie, Mike, isn't it? You come out of the Waldorf-Astoria, and suddenly the whole world is black and tossing and going to hell all around you. I wonder how it was when the *Titanic* went down!" She spoke in a high strained voice over the storm.

Eden said, "The Waldorf-Astoria just fools you because the sidewalk outside isn't rolling. It's in just as bad shape as the *Titanic* ever was."

"All right, shut up!" she said. "You're too morbid for me. I'm feeling better. Or maybe I'm so scared I can't feel anything else. Let's go back inside."

They stood blinking in the pinkish light of the quiet passageway.

"Back in the Waldorf," he said. "Cosy, isn't it?" His face glistened with rain.

She panted, "So, that's a storm at sea."

"I hope you'll be spared from ever finding out what a storm at sea is like. What do you want to do now? How do you feel?"

Marjorie, holding to a fire extinguisher on the bulkhead, felt the deck falling away slantwise under her feet, but the motion didn't seem to bother her. "Sort of as though I've had novocaine all over. Warm and numb. I'm not seasick."

"Good."

"But I think I'll go to my room. I'm all blown about. Come along." As they reeled down the passageway, hanging to the handrails, she said, "That pill was marvelous, Mike. The fact is, I feel a bit looped."

"That wears off."

While she combed her hair he sat in an armchair, smoking. She noticed how straight he sat. Noel would have slouched to his collarbone in such a soft chair. Again she had a strong urge to talk to him about Noel; and why not? she thought. It would pass the time, and he might say something useful. She said, "How would you like to read a twenty-page letter I once got? It's the real story behind my trip."

"Twenty pages?"

"Typewritten. Double-spaced. Easy on the eyes."

"You carry this historic document around with you?"

She pulled a small bag out of the closet and took the letter from under books and travel papers. "I'm curious to know what you'll think."

He began reading the worn dog-eared pages, laying them carefully one by one on his lap, face down. She sat in another armchair, watching his face, and thinking that this was a romantic moment indeed: a gorgeous bedroom on the *Queen Mary,* careening majestically in a night storm that rattled at the black porthole; a handsome stranger in dinner clothes, with a mysterious air and a mysterious scar, alone with her, reading an old love letter of hers; herself as pretty as she knew how to be in a black dress which disclosed all she decently could of her shoulders and bosom; two broad inviting beds. And yet, she thought, sex was as far from this room as from a hospital ward.

Mike Eden's eyebrows shot up, and he looked at her. He resumed reading, his lips curling a bit.

"Stop right there," she said. "What part are you reading?"

He took a slow puff at his cigar. "*If your encounter with that monster Noel Airman is to have any enduring value——* Is that the name of the man you're pursuing to Paris? Noel Airman?"

"Yes. It's rather a queer name—actually it's a pseudonym——"

"Tall, blond, long jaw, great talker?"

"Good Lord, *yes!*"

"I know Noel." She stared at him. "Don't be so surprised, Marjorie. Half the Americans in Europe do."

"*You* know *Noel?*"

"Noel gets around. When you meet him you don't forget him."

"I'm aware of *that,*" Marjorie said, laughing uneasily, still staring.

He dropped the letter in his lap. "Shall I go on reading?"

"As you please. . . . Well! You've really knocked my breath out."

Eden regarded her, puffing his cigar. "You and Noel Airman, eh? Interesting."

"You don't approve?"

"Battle of the century, I'd say."

"It's just about turned into that. So long as I win, that's all right too. Where on earth did you meet Noel?"

"Last year, in Florence."

"Did you get to know him well?"

"About as well as most people do. That is to say, he owes me a couple of hundred dollars."

She blushed and looked down at her lap. "That's his worst trait."

"Oh, mind you, Noel means to pay it back. Maybe he will, one of these years. It's not important. Noel's great company. We hired a car and went tooling around the Italian Alps with two other fellows, a painter and a Rhodes scholar on vacation. I paid Noel's share while he kept waiting for a check from America to catch up with him. It never quite did."

"Where is he now, do you know?"

"I can find out easily enough."

"You'll do me a great favor if you will."

"Marjorie, are you crossing the Atlantic after a fellow without knowing where he is?"

"Well, I was sure I could locate him."

He shook his head slowly, and went back to reading the letter. After a few moments he said, "I don't know. Now I somehow feel as though I'm prying."

"Oh, go ahead. Finish it. What difference does it make? Care for some whiskey and water without ice?"

"Ring for the steward. He'll bring ice."

"Not with you in here. . . . All right, grin. I'm a prude, Noel's said so for years. You'll take it without ice or not at all."

"Without ice, please, by all means."

She opened a bottle of twelve-year-old scotch from Marsha's gift basket. He accepted the whiskey and water absently, drained the glass, and went on reading. "This is quite a letter," he murmured.

"I'm glad you're enjoying it. I didn't." She refilled the glass and put it back in his hand.

"The fact is, you probably did."

"That's too deep for me." She propped pillows and lounged in the bed, sipping her drink.

He put down the last page, looking at the glass in his hand, and said, "I could swear I've already drunk this."

"Gad, you really do concentrate, don't you? I refilled it."

"Thanks."

"Well?"

"Well, what?"

"Does the letter repay all that attention?"

He laughed. "I got Noel furious one night. I analyzed his handwriting and told him he'd never amount to anything."

"What, you analyze handwritings, too? How are you on reading entrails?"

"Listen, there's a lot in handwriting analysis. We were snowed in up in the Alps, had nothing to do. I told him he had a fits-and-starts way of working, and no conscience, and a mixture of conceit and terrible self-doubt, and that he shifted between extremes of emotional dependence and independence. I'd only known him three days then."

"Amazing."

"So he said. What knocked him cold, though, was my telling him he'd been wavering for years over marrying a girl. I was cheating a bit there, putting together scraps of things he'd said. I said he shouldn't marry her because he was just going to be a charming bum all his life. Kidding, of course. He sulked all night and half the next day."

She said, "I just can't see you and Noel together. I don't know why. You seem to be out of different centuries."

"I'm a shipboard acquaintance. I'm not real. I'll vanish when the anchor goes down, like a ghost at cockcrow."

"That sounds like Noel. But then you often do. It's rather uncanny. I suppose that's what has me tagging after you."

"Well, I'll take that as a compliment. Noel's a great talker." He tapped the letter on his lap. "Also quite a letter writer. If he could write like that for pay he'd make a living. But most good letter writers can't."

"Noel can, don't you worry. He makes plenty of money whenever he puts his mind to it. All he needs is to steady down."

"And you're the one to steady him."

"I think so. That's what I'm going to Paris to find out, once for all."

"Are you sure that's the reason you're going to Paris?"

"What do you mean? Don't be enigmatic, you're not psychoanalyzing me."

He held out his glass, smiling. "More, please . . . Score one for you. It always gets me mad when my analyst friends ask me some teasing question like that. Implying they know a hell of a lot more about me than I do. Of course that's their whole game, this enigmatic wisdom. Though all it ever boils down to is that you're really a homosexual, or you'd dearly love to take an axe to your old lady. Something like that."

She handed him the drink and staggered back to the bed. The rolling seemed worse. She said, "Did you really study in Vienna?"

"Why, sure."

"I find it hard to believe. All you seem to say about Freud is old Broadway jokes."

Eden chuckled. "You sound like my analyst friends. I'll admit I make stale jokes, Marjorie. I've fallen into the habit, from arguing with them. I think I believed in it all too strongly too young. Sooner or later you're almost bound to rebel against your boyhood faith. My folks didn't have any, you see, and psychoanalysis rushed into the vacuum, once I came upon the first book when I was sixteen . . . Anyway, it's pointless to argue this subject seriously, with real Freudians. You can't win. Any position you take against Freud isn't an intellectual comment, it's a symptom of nervous disorder. Try to lick that! 'You disagree with us, therefore you're sick.' They all concur that I'm hostile to Freud because I'm in flight from some terrible subconscious secret. Unnatural urge for an affair with a kangaroo, no doubt."

Though he said it in a light tone, there was an odd quaver in his voice. Marjorie looked at him keenly. He met the look, his eyes expressionless, and said, "Like to take a chance on the dancing? You reel around and try to keep from crashing into pillars and other couples. It's fun, in a wild way."

"I'd just as soon skip it," Marjorie said. "Thanks."

Eden said, swirling the whiskey and looking into the glass as he talked, "I'm in flight all right, you know. But not from anything secret. I can date my break with psychoanalysis as exactly as you probably can your meeting with Noel. . . . In fact, I'll tell you about it. Then maybe I'll seem a little less weird to you. When I was twenty-three, Marjorie, just starting to teach, I fell for the most beautiful girl I'd ever seen, and married her in two weeks. Gradually it turned out that she was a dreadful phony. Told me she'd dropped out of college to help support her family, when actually she'd flunked out in freshman year. Told me she was taking French lessons and studying sculpture—complete wild lies. She was just repeating things she'd heard from other girls. Boned up on book-review sections in newspapers and talked about all the new books very impressively. I was so blinded at the moment that she got away with it. Feminine wiles, pardonable enough maybe, because God knows she was in love too—but a mistake. It's one thing to try to seem a little better than you are. It's another thing, and a dangerous one, to pretend you're an entirely different person.

"It was bad almost from the start. I left Emily twice, and went back each time. She would come on her hands and knees, crying, beautiful, swearing she'd do anything I wanted, *anything,* go back to college, study nights. Once we were back together it was all forgotten. She just didn't have it in her to change. She'd sit at home and look mournfully at me because I was so bored and out of love. I met a marvelous girl at school, a student in one of my courses, brilliant, sweet, good—she's married to someone else, she's a doctor now—and I begged Emily for a divorce. This went on for two hideous years. At last she actually went to

Reno. She came back after staying there three months and consuming all our savings—and she hadn't done a thing about the divorce. Not a thing, simply sat there in Reno. She had an absolutely unbelievable capacity for doing nothing and hoping dumbly for the best." His voice was becoming hoarse and shaky. "Well, this can either take two days or two minutes. In two minutes, I was driving with Emily along a highway late at night. This was shortly after she'd returned from Reno. We'd had some frightful quarrels, and then a miserable half-reconciliation. I fell asleep at the wheel. We smashed into a railroad overpass. My skull was fractured and Emily was killed instantly. Her neck was broken."

He looked at Marjorie in a peculiarly embarrassed way, with a half-apologetic smile. No words came to her dry lips and dry throat. After a while he went on, "There was quite a bit of trouble with the police, of course. It takes a lot of red tape even to die accidentally. But what with me nearly dead myself, and no insurance money, and no other woman—this other girl had married long ago—the books were soon closed. It was an accident, and that was that, for the record.

"But not for me. For me it was only the beginning. From a Freudian viewpoint there are no accidents, you see. Or rather, accidents, mistakes, oversights, slips of the tongue, are icebergs poking above the water and showing colossal masses of motivation underneath. I fell asleep at the wheel, sure I did. But falling asleep is something the unconscious mind can bring about. Drowsiness in special situations can be a hell of a clue in unravelling a neurosis. That's all too true. I had felt myself getting drowsy, had even thought of asking Emily to take the wheel. What's more, I actually remember seeing the railroad overpass far down the highway just before I dozed off. From the analytic point of view—in which I then believed, with religious intensity—there isn't the slightest doubt that I murdered my wife, getting rid of an intolerable burden in the only sure way I could, and revenging myself for years of misery and a crippled life."

The bed heaved and rolled under Marjorie. She clung to the headboard with one hand. Eden's face had gone quite ashy, though his expression was calm and even unpleasantly humorous. She said, "I don't know enough about analysis to argue—but even if it were true you wouldn't be responsible, not in any real sense——"

He walked to the whiskey and poured his glass half full. "Exactly what my analyst friends say—or almost exactly, Marjorie. I can give you the patter word for word, I've heard it so often. 'You have unconscious death wishes, but you don't commit unconscious murders. It's a silly attitude. Your wife's death isn't really what's troubling you. You're covering your unsolved neurosis by harping on the accident. Find out what's *really* bothering you, and you'll stop worrying about having murdered your wife.'

"Can you tie that, Marjorie, for obsessed mumbo-jumbo? I killed my wife, sure. But that's not what's really bothering me. Hell, no. I was taken off the breast too early in infancy, *that's* what's bothering me. And when I've gotten furious at this silly obduracy and started raving at them—I could rave now, just remembering these arguments—why, they've sat back and nodded wisely. More symptoms.

"Whenever I do manage to corner them completely with chapter and verse from Freud, they say I'm the typical psychology teacher, all book-theory, no clinical experience. All I know is what Freud *said* about these things. I don't understand the scientific facts of human nature that emerge from analytic practice to verify the theories, a little knowledge is a dangerous thing and so on, with a hey nonny no . . .

"You see, these dogma-blinded bastards have never been involved in a fatal accident. They can't imagine what it's like. They go blandly on spinning the old palaver, not realizing that the packaged comfort they dispense is sheer poison to a man in my spot.

"Ordinarily, Marjorie, you understand, the wonderful thing about psychoanalysis is that it *frees* you from responsibility and guilt. You walk into the doctor's office an adulterer, a liar, a drunk, a phony, a failure, a pervert. In due time, after lying around on a couch and babbling for a year or so, it turns out you're none of these things at all. Shucks, no, it was your Unconscious all the time. An entirely different person, a guy named Joe, so to speak. Some occurrence in your childhood sex life has festered into a sort of demon inside you. Well, you track this demon down, recognize it, name it, exorcise it. You pay your bill and go your way absolved.

"That's all perfectly fine. Unless you happen to have been in a fatal accident and killed somebody. Then this whole scheme turns upon you. It can absolutely destroy you mentally. Because don't you see—this is what my benighted friends will *never* see—it's just as horrible to believe that a demon under the surface of your brain took charge and caused you to kill, as it is to believe that you killed in cold blood. More so, possibly. Because if you think about it, the implication is that subsurface devils possess you and can cause you to commit any number of shocking crimes.

"Well, I went through agonies I won't bore you with, but the end of it all was a terrific nerve crisis, out of which I emerged unable to teach. I gave up psychology, and I've never gone back to it. It's seven years since I've glanced into a professional journal, let alone a book in the field. In fact I have a kind of horror of the subject. I got interested in making money. Making money is fun, you know, and very absorbing, I'm good at it. I started out by getting a job, and eventually went into business for myself. I play a lot of cards, and read a lot of books, and that brings you up to date."

There was a marked contrast between these casual last words and the low strained tone in which Eden said them. He was standing by the porthole, holding on to one of the metal dogs, and as the ship rolled, black water crashed against the glass, and purple lightning showed in the turbulent sky. The scar across his white forehead looked like another streak of lightning. Marjorie, greatly disturbed, said to break the silence, "It seems like a terrible waste. You must have been an excellent teacher."

"I was. Freud had been my ruling passion for about fifteen years. What an awful emptiness it left behind—and this on top of the loss of Emily! Believe me, having a sudden silent vacuum of death in my life, instead of a problem, was shock enough. Giving up teaching really did me in. For two years I was so close to suicide that—and I swear this to you—I didn't do it simply because I didn't want to give strangers the trouble of cleaning up a mess that used to be me.

"Marjorie, I've sat in hotel rooms for weeks, reading straight through Scott, Trollope, Zola, Balzac, Richardson, Reade, Lever, all the talky old novelists, just to keep from thinking. Because if I thought, the only thing I could think about was killing myself. Not for any dramatic reason, mind you. Not out of guilt or despair or anything. Simply because it was too much pointless effort to live. It was an effort to suck in air, when I thought about it. Seeing colors was a nuisance. Just to see a red and green neon sign and distinguish the letters was work, stupid work. And panic, I lived in torpor or panic, I knew nothing else, nothing, for two years. . . .

"Well, I guess I pulled out of this schizoid state, which was what it was, because I was meant to live, and not die. I don't know what else did it. And I emerged with this jeering attitude about analysis, which you call making Broadway jokes. It's second nature by now.

"Once you lose faith in all that, believe me, you really lose it. An unbelieving Catholic is nothing to an unbelieving Freudian. Where's their id and their libido, anyway? In the brain? In the kidneys? When I was a kid arguing religion we used to say nobody ever saw a soul in a test tube. Well, who ever caught an id in a test tube? It's all a lot of metaphors—and when you take metaphors for facts, what you have is a mythology. Mind you, the old man was a Homer or a Dante, in his way, quite up to writing out a mythology that would span the entire range of moral judgments. That's what his work has become. The Freudians say they make no moral judgments—I used to say so myself with great assurance—but the fact is, they do absolutely nothing else. They *can't* do anything else, because their business is evaluating and guiding behavior. That's morality. What they mean is they don't make *conventional* moral judgments. They sure don't. . . .

"All right, now I'll shut up about this, obviously it's my King Charles' head. I haven't gotten going this way in ages. In sum, Freud says I'm a murderer, and I say the hell with him, and that's my little story, Marjorie." He was pacing again. He stopped at the armchair, picked up Noel's letter, and flourished the pages at her. "Our friend Mr. Noel Airman really touched off this outburst, if you want to know. Noel's quite an iconoclast, isn't he? Probably impressed you deeply. Rightly so. He's a wonderful talker. Still, Noel is very much a creature of his time, so he takes the current myths for solid facts." He tossed the letter on the bed at Marjorie's feet in an openly contemptuous gesture. "The one thing in all those twenty pages that Noel takes seriously is the analytic explanation of his own conduct. He's right proud of it. It never occurs to him that the Oedipus complex really doesn't exist, that it's a piece of moralistic literature. He's as orthodox as your own father, Marjorie, in his fashion, but he doesn't know it. Judas priest, how well I know the type! Sweeping the dust of orthodoxy out the front door, and never seeing it drift in again at the back door, settling down in somewhat different patterns. The vilest insult you can hurl at them is to tell them they believe in something. Yet all Noel Airman really is, Margie, is a displaced clergyman. You have no idea, till you've read the literature of neurosis, how full the woods are of these displaced creatures. Brave skeptics all, making a life's work out of being dogmatic, clever, supercilious—and inwardly totally confused and wretched."

Marjorie said, startled, "Noel once talked about becoming a rabbi. He wasn't serious, really. But he worked himself up terrifically over it."

Mike Eden grinned. "It's just as well Noel didn't become a rabbi. It would have been hard on the husbands in the congregation." He walked to the whiskey bottle, picked it up, then set it down again without pouring. "I believe I have half emptied this bottle in less than an hour. Also more than half emptied my brain. I feel remarkably good. I feel like the Ancient Mariner after spinning his yarn for the Wedding Guest." He came to the bed and stood beside her. "I'm thirty-nine. How old are you?"

"Twenty-three. Twenty-four in November," Marjorie said uneasily, looking up at him. "Why?"

"When I got out of college," Eden said, "you were five years old."

"I guess that's right," Marjorie said. "I'm not thinking clearly."

"Of course you're not. I've stupefied you with words." He took her hand. "Well, maybe I've demonstrated one thing to you that may prove useful in time. Noel Airman isn't the only man in the world who can talk. As a matter of fact, Margie, it's a completely negligible accomplishment." He pulled her to her feet, and kissed her once on the mouth, a real kiss. She leaned back in his arms, astonished, unprotesting, and more than a little stirred. She said softly, "Yes? What's this?"

Mike Eden's look was tender, shrewd, and extremely melancholy.

"Plain self-indulgence, I guess. I've always liked blue eyes and brown hair, and girls about as tall as you. Good night, Margie."

He went out, leaving her rather stunned.

Chapter 43. THE PREMONITION

"Let me have a cigarette, darling." Marjorie said it without thinking, but then the endearing word rang strange in her ears. They were sitting side by side on deck chairs in morning sunlight, wrapped in blankets, reading. It was the fourth day of the crossing.

He passed the cigarettes and matches from his lap to hers without looking up. He was reading *The Private Papers of Henry Ryecroft;* Marjorie had glanced at it and thought it a very dull book, but he was absorbed in it. He had the ability to go into a virtual trance over a printed page. He read swiftly and his taste was queer; the first day he had been finishing a fat tome, *The Theory of Money and Credit,* and he had since gone through a couple of mysteries, a long paperback novel in French, and a book by Wodehouse over which he had laughed like a fool.

She liked to look at his face when he read. His brows, the lines of his mouth and cheekbones, even the scar, seemed to converge to the middle of his forehead. She admired and envied the visible concentration.

Lighting her cigarette, she studied him, wondering how "darling" had happened to slip out. Marjorie had been thinking a great deal about Mike Eden in the past few days. She was quite sure she wasn't in love with him. His occasional kisses were pleasant, and she liked to dance with him; his arm around her waist felt good; but the charming little uneasiness that she had always experienced, dancing with Noel, wasn't exactly there. Once, however, she had come to the main lounge and found him dancing with another girl, and a pang much like jealousy had gone through her. She did feel comfortable near him, and rather lost away from him. At the moment, sitting beside him in the paired intimacy of two deck chairs, she felt tranquil and in health as she seldom had in recent years. All this didn't square, she realized, with the kind of desperate love that was supposed to be driving her across the Atlantic after Noel Airman; but she had heard and read enough about shipboard romances to take what was happening with several large grains of salt. There was something dreamlike and misty about her present tranquillity—rather as though she were continually taking Eden's "happiness pills"; and she strongly suspected that the day she set foot on solid earth again the old ache for Noel would rush through all her nerves, while Eden would fade to a forgotten shadow.

Meantime, the serene peace of the crossing, however unreal, was hers to enjoy; and she was enjoying it heartily.

"There goes the Gestapo," she murmured. He glanced up at Hilda strolling by on the arm of the man in the green jacket. The two Germans ignored Eden and Marjorie, as they had been doing for the past couple of days. Marjorie said, "I suppose it was inevitable that those two team up."

"Pure blood calling to pure blood," Eden said with a grimace, turning back to his book.

"Her ankles really are pretty bad."

"Mm," Eden said.

"Mine aren't."

Eden reluctantly took his eyes from his book and inspected the bulky outline of Marjorie's blanketed form. "You're a captivating dish from head to toe. I can't tell you how much I envy Noel Airman. Especially since he's a thousand miles from here, and can read in peace if he wants to." He took a cigar out of a case in his pocket.

"You don't really envy him. You think he's a worthless worm, and that I'm throwing myself away on him." The fragrant cigar smoke drifted past her nose. "You know, I'll be sorry when this trip is over."

"Why? You'll rush panting into Noel's arms a few hours after we land, and life will blaze brightly forever after."

"Don't be so superior. I'm well aware that Noel will be as much trouble as he's always been, or more. But I feel so marvelously detached from all my problems—even from Noel—here on the boat. I haven't had such a respite in years. It's doing wonders for my nerves. I'd like to just ride back and forth on the *Queen Mary* three or four times before I tackle Noel."

"I don't think you need it." He started to read again, calmly drawing on the cigar.

Marjorie had struck one of the discursive essays in *Tom Jones*. She felt very little like reading, and very much like talking. She picked up a pad of writing paper and scrawled her name on a sheet. "How about analyzing my handwriting?"

Yawning, he put the book aside, marking his place with the flap of the jacket. "This is as bad as being married. Are you sure you want your soul to be seen into? Write a few lines. Signatures are meaningless."

She scrawled a speech from *Pygmalion*. "Pretty dull handwriting," she said, "now that I look at it."

He studied the paper, puffing out his cheeks. "It's changed quite a bit."

She blinked. "How can you know that? Did Noel show you my writing?"

"No. It's a handwriting that's undergoing change, that's all."

"Gad. Uncanny." The fact was that much of the elegance she had once cultivated had dropped out of her writing in the past year or two— the Greek *e*'s, the long heavy vertical lines, the smart initial letters.

For about ten minutes he was silent, staring at the page, now and then nodding. She became self-conscious. "Well, say something."

Crumpling the paper, he threw it across the deck; the wind whipped it out over the rail. "Sorry. I can't see a thing. Get your money back from the cashier."

"You dog, you can't get away with that."

He was looking at her with unusual warmth, a small smile in the corners of his mouth. "I'll tell you just two things I observed. Then I'm off to order some coffee. First, I'm afraid Noel's a pretty dirty son of a bitch, after all. Second, your handwriting is almost exactly like Anitra's."

"Anitra?"

"The girl I didn't marry."

At lunch he had a meager vegetable salad and ice cream. She said, "What are you, a vegetarian or something? I don't think I've seen you eat meat on this trip."

"I weigh 180 pounds. Until a year ago I never went over 160. I'm not going to balloon into middle age if I can help it."

"Curious that you, of all people, should be vain."

"You're quite right," he said amiably. "With this chopped-up phiz of mine it's ridiculous, but I never have liked fat people."

"Darling" (there it was again) "I didn't mean that. It's just that you have such an unearthly detachment about everything else, I wouldn't think you'd care."

"A man who lives alone gets fussy about himself, Marjorie. He has nothing else to fuss over."

"Do you think you'll marry again?"

"No."

"That's nice and definite."

"Might as well live out the sunset this way."

"Sunset indeed! Thirty-nine."

"I've outlived Keats, Mozart, Marlowe, Alexander the Great, and Jesus. I'm satisfied."

He had said things like this before. What distressed Marjorie most was his matter-of-fact good humor about it. He sometimes sounded like a man with an incurable disease who had become used to the idea. She stared at him as he ate his ice cream. He was a healthy, vigorous man, with clear hazel eyes and a fresh sunburned skin; only his tense movements, the rather rigid way he held himself, the habitual drumming of his fingers, were in any way abnormal; and these things merely showed excessive nervousness. The gray hair emphasized rather than detracted from the picture of vigor. She said, "Why do you talk this way? Is it a line you consider amusing or smart? I don't. It's very upsetting. It would be more upsetting if I'd known you longer. It gives me the chills, frankly."

"I'm sorry. When I talk that way I'm not thinking, it's such a matter of course to me. Possibly it's a subtle appeal for sympathy, but I hope not. I'm not aware of being in the market for sympathy."

"How can you feel in the sunset at your age? Don't you think that's very strange?"

"It's hard to describe how I feel. It's—I think it's a bit like coming to the end of a long book. The plot's at its thickest, all the characters are in a mess, but you can see that there aren't fifty pages left, and you know that the finish can't be far off. Theoretically, the thing could go on for five hundred pages more, but you know it won't. Well, of course I haven't got the book of my life in hand, or the narrow band of pages still to read. I just have the sensation. It's not at all an uncommon thing, you know, this sense of an impending end. It's a classic symptom of neurotic anxiety. I certainly follow the anxious pattern, so you can call it a symptom and stop worrying about it. People live to ninety with such symptoms."

"Well, then, you should have the sense to laugh at yourself."

"Unfortunately, Marjorie, so far as I'm concerned, expressions like 'neurotic anxiety' are just educated noise. Who really knows what the affliction is, what it comes from, what it means? It's like a wart. You can describe it and you can treat it empirically, which is a three-dollar word for 'by guess and by God.' But that's all. Some people get over it. Some people live with it, as I say, to a ripe worrisome age. Some die young, just as they knew they would. Not suicides, either. They run through the fifty pages and the book is over. Somehow they knew."

"That's pure mysticism."

"Well, I'm a mystic, more or less."

She laughed, but he didn't. She said, "Really, I've never met a mystic and I don't think you're one. Where's your sheet, your sandals, and your long hair? You're far too sensible."

"There's quite a lot in the literature," he said, "about premonitions. I'll grant that when you're engaged in a course of action that's foolish or dangerous, and hiding the folly or danger from yourself, the subconscious mind seizes on any gloomy fact like a broken mirror, or an ominous slip of the tongue, or a black cat in the way, to try to scare you into saving yourself. That accounts for a fraction of the cases. But the truth is, we don't know anything about the nature of time, and damned little about the mind. I think some premonitions are real. I can't explain why. I can't explain why an embryo grows five fingers, for that matter."

"How can you compare the two? The way the embryo grows fingers is a scientific fact. The chromosomes control that."

His gloomy face lit with amusement. "How silly of me. I forgot about the chromosomes. Well, let's say my premonition is part of a neurotic anxiety, shall we? I'm in no hurry to get into a grave, not any more. I find what I'm doing damned interesting."

"The chemical business?"

"Don't say it with such contempt. It's a romantic trade." He glanced at his watch. "Bridge-playing time. Sure you won't change your mind and come along?"

"Once was enough. I won't play with a shark like you, I feel too idiotic. Anyway, I've never liked cards much. Go ahead, have fun."

Tom Jones had never seemed duller than it did that afternoon. She read several pages over and over, alone in a deck chair that heaved disagreeably. The sky turned leaden and then disappeared as the ship was engulfed in a drifting gray fog. The sea, invisible a few feet beyond the rail, smashed at the ship with menacing deep roars. She would have liked one of Eden's seasickness pills, but she didn't want to interrupt him at cards. He was another man when he played: forbidding, curt, abstracted. She closed the book, lay back, and dozed.

"Tea?"

Eden was standing over her, wrapped in a trench coat and gray muffler; the deck steward was beside him with the tea wagon. Rain was lashing the windows and it was almost dark, though the overhead clock read only quarter to five. She rubbed her eyes and sat up. "Why sure, I'll have tea."

After the steward had gone Eden said, "Want one of these?" She took the red capsule gratefully from his palm, and swallowed it with a scalding gulp of tea. "Weather's getting wild again," she said.

He nodded. A minute or so passed. "I'm sorry, Marjorie."

"Sorry for what?"

"I should have sworn off that handwriting business years ago. I always come out with something stupid. I shouldn't have said Noel's a son of a bitch."

She smiled at him with a trace of indulgence. "Why, that's exactly what he is. The bad part is that I've always liked that about him, as well as everything else. Now if you'll concentrate your vast brain and write a book explaining why girls are drawn to sons of bitches, you'll really do humanity a service. You'll be another Freud."

He laughed, but his forehead knotted, the lines of concentration pulling in toward the center. "It's a good question. The heroes in romantic books, for instance, all tend to be sons of bitches, don't they? From Heathcliff down to Rhett Butler . . . Of course my analyst friends would say all women are masochists at heart, or it's the search for the father as pain-inflicter, and all that. But setting aside such incantations, let's see . . . One thing is obvious. The son of a bitch, considered as a type, has vitality. He's a dasher, a smasher, a leaper. There's promise in a son of a bitch. When you go to buy a puppy, you know, you're not supposed to take the sweet one that licks your hand. You're supposed to pick the most rambunctious rascal of the litter, the one that's roaring around, tearing the furniture, messing in the middle of the carpet, giving all the other pups hell. He'll make the best dog. A woman looking for a husband is in a sense getting herself a domestic animal, so it would follow that——" Marjorie burst out laughing. Eden said, "I'm quite serious. She feels something missing in a guy who's housebroken already. Instinct tells her that a son of a bitch will tame down into a guy worth having, a hubby with a little zing to him, and the vital energy to pull a heavy load a long way. She's not wrong, exactly. But she has to make sure she isn't buying a congenital and unchangeable son of a bitch. That's the big question mark. Is the pup just displaying youthful high spirits, or is he a permanent biter and messer?"

"I wonder if you were a son of a bitch in your day," Marjorie said. "I rather think so."

"In my day? I'm one of the congenital ones."

"No, you aren't."

"Don't be fooled by my company manners, Marjorie. Of course it's not my 'fault,' as we used to say in Psychology 1. I had rather bad nerves to start with, and they're much the worse for wear. However, what with happiness pills, and the general calming effect of a ship, and your balmy influence, I think I've been pretty nice so far. With luck I may keep it up till we leave the ship, and then you'll always remember me pleasantly. That's something to work for."

"Why?"

She was peering at his face, but the twilight was so dim that she could scarcely make out the features. He said, "Why, I'd enjoy believing there's someone who thinks well of me. That's all." At that moment a long string of yellow lights came on overhead and broke the gloom. They were alone on the chilly glassed-in deck, except for one white-headed lady asleep far down the line of vacant deck chairs. Eden's profile looked peculiarly familiar to Marjorie, as though she had known him in the Bronx in her childhood.

She said, after hesitating over the words for several seconds, "Mike, you're Jewish, aren't you?"

His head turned slowly, and the dark stony look of his face scared her. Then, as though at the flick of a switch, light and warmth flowed into his expression. "When did you decide that?"

"I don't know. Maybe during the ping-pong game. I've felt it, rather than decided it, for several days."

"Well, I don't mind your thinking so. Just don't go around *saying* so, please. It could prove a damned nuisance for me."

"I won't. Are you really in the chemical business?"

"Marjorie, shipboard acquaintances always shade the truth about themselves a bit, for one reason or another. I haven't shaded it to any unusual extent. And now let's get a long running start of martinis on the evening, shall we?" He threw aside his blanket and abruptly got out of the deck chair, extending his hand to her.

He played cards that evening, while Marjorie watched the movie. She then danced with a sheepish boy of twenty, travelling with his mother, who had been mooning at her all during the voyage but had never before worked up the courage to approach her. It occurred to her that at this boy's age George Drobes had been a towering adult to her. Twenty, in a man, now was clumsy adolescence.

Eden gathered her up at midnight, and they went to the Verandah Grill. He was in remarkably high spirits; they danced, and then walked the decks, talking, until three. He woke her the next morning at eight by telephoning her cabin. "It's our last day together. Don't you want to make it full and beautiful? Get your bones out of the hay."

"Dear me," she yawned, noting that the weather was lovely again and that the ship was riding very steadily, "don't tell me you're going to get all romantic and dashing now that we're practically in Europe. You should have fallen for me sooner. You bore me. I'm going back to sleep."

"Get out of that bed."

"Nothing doing. Coffee in bed on a ship is the most wonderful thing in the whole world. See you in about an hour. You're a beast not to let me sleep, just because you're an insomniac."

She hung up, rang for the steward, and went to wash and comb her hair, carolling *Falling in Love with Love*. As she opened the door of her bathroom to come out, she heard Eden's voice say, "There's a man in the room." She happened to be wearing her most fetching negligee, rust-colored silk and chiffon, passably modest. After a swift glance in the mirror and a pause to catch her breath she sailed out, brushing her hair and saying indignantly, "You're too chummy by half, do you know? Get out of here before I call the steward."

There was a coffee service for two on the bureau, with fruit, rolls, and an elaborate array of delicious-looking coffee cakes. He was in an armchair in the sunlight, calmly drinking coffee and munching on a blueberry muffin. His eyes looked tired. He wore a suit she hadn't seen before, a beautifully cut navy-blue pin-stripe, and there was a new book in his lap. He was very much the diplomat again, she thought, or else she was actually falling for him and seeing him in a golden haze. There was a quality in his scarred ugly face that drew her strongly. The word she thought of to describe it—it seemed a stupid word—was goodness.

"Do you really want to throw me out? It'll make a hell of a scandal," he said. "It'll take two stewards, and I'll go kicking and yelling. This coffee is fine, much better than what we get in the dining room. Have some."

She growled, "Well, I suppose anything goes on a ship. I've never had breakfast with a man before while I'm in my nightgown. There's always a first time." She got into her bed. "You'll have to serve me, though. Where did this stuff come from? All I ever order is coffee."

"The steward's an understanding soul. He's my steward, too. Here." He brought her coffee and a cake.

They ate in silence, and she found herself wishing that this moment would prolong itself for a week or so. After wrestling with a cautionary impulse, she told him this.

He nodded. "I needn't tell you I feel the same way. It's not merely that you're so pretty—although that helps, of course. You make me feel comfortable, somehow. You're worth several bottles of happiness pills."

"Strange that you should say comfortable," she said. "It's the word that's kept occurring to me. And yet I don't know anybody who's ever made me more uncomfortable than you have, every now and then."

The lines of concentration appeared in his face. "Well, to tell you the truth, I barged in here to have a talk with you that's overdue. But the hell with it. I couldn't be more out of the mood. Some other time. Let me read you something by Thurber I came across last night, it's side-splitting."

He read very well, and the piece was excruciatingly funny. They both laughed themselves breathless. She said, "Lord, it's a wonderful way to start the day, isn't it, laughing like that? Beats a cold shower. Let's go out on deck. I'll dress. See you in a few minutes."

"Right." He got out of his chair as she jumped off the bed; they brushed each other in passing and the contact felt pleasant. "What on earth's happening to you, kid?" she said to the mirror image that laughed and sparkled at her.

That whole day, their last day on the *Queen Mary*, was edged with gold. The sea was deep blue, the sunlight made sharp shadows on the decks, a breeze blew from the southwest smelling like flowers, and land birds cried and darted around the ship. The long broad wake of the *Queen Mary* stretched backward to the horizon, a trail of slick blue on the rough blue of the waves, like a visible ribbon of passing time. Dolphins rolled glittering by the ship all day. Everything they did was amusing and pleasant—deck tennis, talking with the captain (the weather-beaten god in gold and blue came down from the bridge and chatted with them on the sun deck for ten minutes, speaking as beautifully as George Arliss, and laughing heartily at Mike's jokes), lunching picnic-style on the boat deck in the sunshine, swimming in the ship's magnificently tiled indoor pool, listening to Mozart quartets in the salon at tea-time—the day seemed to go on and on, bright and clear and slow. In the cocktail hour, the bar being crowded, they ended at a table with Jackie May and his wife. The comedian, stimulated by Marjorie's pretty face, made an enormous number of jokes, really funny ones, and she and Mike were almost helpless with laughter for half an hour. In fact everybody appeared agreeable that day to Marjorie; she even smiled at Hilda once and received a surprised, pleasant smile in return. When the sun set at last in a holocaust of scarlet clouds, spilling red gold on the purpling sea from horizon to horizon, Marjorie, standing at the rail beside Eden, felt close to tears—not because the day was over, but because the last moments were as perfect as the rest. She looked around at the vast ship, the great red and black funnels, the line of lifeboats falling into purple shadow, and it was as though her eyes were heavily printing the scene on her brain. She said to Eden, after they had been quiet for perhaps a quarter of an hour, and the red in the sky was almost all dulled to violet, "Why isn't it always like this? For everyone?"

He put his arm around her shoulders. "It's a nice sunset, but don't get carried away. The whole world can't go riding around on the *Queen Mary*."

After a while she said, "Maybe this is just a shipboard acquaintance, but I think you'll miss me a bit when it's over. It can't be so wholly one-sided."

He said, "Marjorie, you have no idea how different, how incongruous, how unattractive shipboard friends look, once you're back on the land. It's unbelievable. Their clothes don't seem to fit. They look fatter, and their manners are phony and pretentious. You don't like the way they laugh. They're Republicans if you're a Democrat, and vice versa. Maybe you knew it on board ship, but it didn't matter. Back on land it does. They like the wrong movies. They insist on taking you to a wonderful restaurant, and the food turns out lousy, and the waiter is rude, and the wine is vinegary, and the bread is stale. You can't for the life of you think of anything to talk about, and the whole evening couldn't be longer or more awful, and that's the end."

Marjorie said, laughing ruefully, "Always, always? It seems unlikely."

"Invariably. It's a fact of nature."

"Well then," Marjorie said, "let me tell you, in case that ever happens, that you were a very nice illusion on the *Queen Mary*."

"I should be saying the pretty things to you," Eden said, "in a last all-out effort to make you."

"Don't bother," Marjorie said. "Though Lord knows you look like a wolf to me, and have from the first moment—a gray wolf, the worst kind. If you've been giving me a line, I hope you've kept notes. You can ruin girls for the next twenty years with it. Isn't it getting chilly?"

"I'll miss you all right," Eden said. "We're never going to meet again, so there's no harm in telling you that. I wouldn't see you on land for a million dollars. I don't know exactly what it is about you—you're not like Anitra, really. She's a scientist. You're a——"

"A nobody," Marjorie said.

Eden smiled, and took his hand from her shoulders. "You're right. It's damned chilly. All good things come to an end, especially sunsets. Time for dinner."

There was a festive gold-lettered menu for the captain's dinner, and the tables were full of fresh flowers. Eden ordered a vegetable salad, though the steward tried to tempt him with something more substantial. He was a short affable Cockney, and he had taken to treating Marjorie and Mike with knowing fondness, obviously assuming that they were having an affair. "Please use your hinfluence with him, Miss Morgenstern," he said. "Make him try just a bit of the roast beef, won't you? Just this once."

"I'll have the roast beef," Marjorie said. "He's hopeless." She added when the steward was gone, "I guess that's another mystery you'll carry off the ship locked in your bosom. You're probably a secret follower of Gandhi."

"Let me be," Eden said. "We vegetarians will inherit the earth. Between Hitler and Gandhi, how can we lose? We've got humanity bracketed."

She ate a sumptuous dinner while he nibbled at the salad. "You really make me feel carnal," she said. "I wish you'd break down and eat something gross—an egg or something." He only laughed.

Later in the bar she said, "Well, I guess you make up for it with liquor." He was downing a fourth double brandy, showing as usual no effect beside a slightly warmer tone when he talked. "I've never seen a guzzler like you. Noel in his best days, I mean in his worst, when he was going through some crisis or other, never equalled you. Bernard Shaw doesn't drink, does he? I read somewhere in his books that he thinks alcohol is poison. You're utterly inconsistent."

"Sure I am," Eden said. "Who says you have to be consistent? About the nicest thing God ever did was invent alcohol. He's proud of it, too. The Bible's full of kind remarks about booze."

She drank quite a bit, and she didn't remember much about the dancing except that it was heavenly. Around one o'clock in the morning they were on the boat deck, under a high blue-white moon which rocked slowly from one side of the colossal funnels to the other. The flower scent of the cold breeze had become stronger. There were a number of shadowy couples frankly necking here and there.

"Will you look at all the smoochers?" Marjorie said. "We're a pair of old fuddyduds."

"I don't know. I think there's something hugely comical about all these double shadows," Eden said. "Blob after blob after blob. Each double blob quite sure that all this squirming in the dark is a clever night's work, that they're doing something they really want to do. When they're all being shoved by body chemicals through a mindless mechanical process, like so many pairs of stuck-together frogs. Don't you agree it's funny?"

"Not at all," Marjorie said. "In fact, at the moment you sound a little like a sophomore at a dance without a date."

Eden burst into such a roar of laughter that several of the double shadows near them divided and straightened up. "If I were ten years younger and in any kind of mental shape," he said, "I would give Noel Airman a run for his money. Let's stay up till dawn and get all red-eyed and pallid and stewed, shall we?"

"Sure," Marjorie said. "Aren't the bars all closed?"

"Step this way."

Hilda, the blonde, and Thaler were coming up the stairway to the boat deck as they came down. Eden stepped aside to let the two Germans pass in silence. It was an awkward moment. At the door of his cabin Eden hesitated, reaching in his pocket for the key, and looked thoughtful. "I have a sudden positive memory that I didn't lock this door." He turned the knob and the door opened. His glance at her was sharp and worried. "I always have had a suicidal absent-mindedness. No doubt all the crown jewels are missing. Well, come in."

He looked around the room restlessly, but it was all in order: the bed turned down, a single pink reading lamp lit at his bedside. "How do you like brandy and tap water?"

"My favorite drink."

He snapped on his short-wave portable radio. After a moment of humming the loudspeaker came to life with the shouting of a harsh strong hysterical voice in German. Mike turned the sound down. The voice, barking and screaming, was interrupted by frightening crowd roars. Marjorie said, "What's that?"

"What do you think?"

"Hitler?"

"Hitler."

"Two o'clock in the morning?"

"It's a record."

Marjorie regarded the radio with wide eyes, listening to the voice. She couldn't quite believe she was hearing it. "Turn it off."

"Gladly."

He kept looking around the room as he mixed the drinks. He went to the shelf of books over the desk and stared at them; opened the desk drawers one by one, and leafed through papers and folders. The lines of his face became sharp and deep. "Marjorie, I'm pretty tired, after all. Let's call it a night, shall we?"

"Throwing me out? Can't I finish my drink?"

"Take it with you. Take the bottle."

"Catch me walking through the ship with a bottle of brandy! No, thanks——"

He slammed a drawer shut so hard that books piled on the desk tumbled to the deck, spilling little papers from among their leaves. The papers rolled on the deck, curling like shavings. A stream of bitter frigid obscenity burst from his lips as he scooped at books and papers with both hands, dropping to his knees. Marjorie put down her drink and stood, shocked and terrified, staring at him. In a few moments he sat in the chair again, the books and papers helter-skelter in his lap, and returned her stare. His face had a greenish cast, his eyes were white-rimmed, his scar looked like a fresh purple gash. She came to him hesitantly and touched his face. "Mike, what's the matter?"

He stood and, one after another, hurled the books across the room at the door. He flung himself on the bed face down, burying his face in the pillow. Marjorie realized in amazement that she was hearing stifled screams. He kicked his legs. His body writhed. She had to suppress a wild impulse to laugh; the sight was as ridiculous as it was dreadful. She thought of fleeing from the room but she couldn't. Her hair prickled, her mouth went dry, she shuddered violently, but she stood where she was. "Mike! Mike!" He did not answer; but in a minute or so he became still. He rolled over and sat up then, his eyes glassy. He staggered to the bathroom, and she saw him take a hypodermic needle from a black case before he convulsively kicked shut the door.

She threw the brandy and water into an empty pitcher, poured straight brandy, and gulped it. Sinking into an armchair, she lit a cigarette and waited, her body racked by an occasional shiver.

It seemed a long time before he came out, though the cigarette was only half smoked. He looked better, but still fearfully pale. He was in his shirtsleeves, and he had taken off the black tie and stiff collar, so that he looked half undressed. He shook his head at her and smiled wretchedly. From the shelf of medicines near the bed he took down a bottle of dark brown capsules. He peered at her face for several seconds, holding the bottle in a wavering hand. "Well, I was meaning to talk to you anyway." He took two capsules; slipped into a maroon dressing gown that lay on the bed, lit a cigar, poured brandy for himself, and settled in a chair opposite her. In that small space of time he recovered astoundingly. Color returned to his face; the hand that held the cigar was steady; and the fingers of the other hand lay relaxed on the arm of the chair, not drumming, and not trembling in the least. He said, "I've probably shocked you out of a year's growth," and his tone was pleasant and even.

"I'm a little concerned for you," Marjorie said. "I can't help that, I'm afraid——"

"I'm not a drug addict, Marjorie. I've learned to live with a pretty unstable nervous system, that's all." He looked at her, and laughed. "You're skeptical. I don't blame you. We Americans always disapprove of anything that lightens the rub of life on the nerves—anything from pain-killers for a woman in labor, to booze for the downcast. We get it from the Puritans. I can't imagine how we ever became reconciled to cigarettes. Advertising, I guess. We don't smoke tobacco, we smoke pretty girls. You know, a sensible Chinese smokes twenty pipes of opium a day and we think he's an Oriental degenerate, but believe me, he'll live longer and be happier than a two-pack-a-day man in the States." Eden yawned, smiled in apology, and began to talk about the traditional drug plants and their properties, and about the new synthetic drugs made from coal tar. His knowledge was encyclopedic, and for a while Marjorie was interested. She was waiting, of course, for an explanation of his horrifying panic seizure, thinking that this talk was a mere delay while he collected himself.

But he went on and on in this vein, calm and copious, and she began to get a little sleepy. He took from his bedside table a fat volume, *The Anatomy of Melancholy,* and read from it a long passage in wild archaic English about drug plants. What happened next she was never quite sure. When she opened her eyes the porthole showed bluish-gray, and she was lying on a bed, still in her evening dress, covered by her camel's hair coat and by a light quilt. Eden sat in an armchair beside her, reading by lamplight, freshly shaved, and dressed in the gray tweed suit he had worn on the first day of the voyage. She sat up, exclaiming, "My God!" Eden told her she had staggered to the bed midway in his reading of the *Anatomy,* muttering that she would be more comfortable lying down, and had fallen asleep in thirty seconds. "I hadn't the heart to wake you, it was only a couple of hours to dawn, anyway. We ought to be able to see land now. How about coming topside?"

She said sullenly, blinking and yawning, "I don't know which is more thoroughly ruined, my dress or my reputation. How could you let me stay here? You're a cad, that's what."

But she accepted a fresh toothbrush from him, washed her face, and put herself to rights. They went up on the boat deck, and she noted with relief that there were several weary-looking couples still in evening dress here and there on the ship. "It isn't six yet," Eden said. "Last night out anything goes. Don't look guilty, that's all. We're probably the most innocent pair on the ship."

Tired and sleepy as she was, the first glimpse of the faint greenish hump on the horizon dead ahead of the ship sent a wave of pleasure and wonder through her. She caught at Eden's arm. "That's it?"

"That's it," he said. "The Old World. You're looking at France. Over the horizon is Paris and the Eiffel Tower and, of course, Noel Airman."

Chapter 44. IN PURSUIT OF NOEL

Two days later, still dazed and unsettled by the strangeness and suddenness of her shift in plans, Marjorie was flying in an Air France plane from Paris to Zurich with Mike Eden, in a clear brilliant afternoon. She had found out with Eden's help that Noel had gone vacationing in Switzerland; and she was going to try to track him down there.

The ordered loveliness of the landscape unrolling slowly beneath her

threw her into a near-trance of sweet excitement. She could not understand why the books had not dwelled more on the physical beauty of
Europe. The continent seemed to her one green pleasure park, dotted
with picture-book cities; and smoothed and polished for centuries, by the
people who had lived and died there, to the perfection of a single master
painting. That this pretty place was the setting for all the carnage in
the history books, and the current horrors of the Nazi era, passed her
imagination. The jagged march of the Alps, purple and white against
an azure sky, shocked her with delight.

The wheels of the plane skidded on the runway; and then there was
the mess at the customs, in the crowded buzzing airport, with signs in
four languages everywhere, and people around her apparently gabbling
in seventy languages; and then she and Mike were riding in a cab in
violet twilight through a light-spangled city that looked half like a medieval tapestry and half like a futuristic movie. All this time she remained
in her state of bemused pleasure.

Then she saw the swastika.

It leaped at her eye—huge, gilded—as the cab slowed, coming to the
hotel. She touched Eden's arm. "What's that building?"

"What do you suppose? German consulate." He was irritable and glum;
he usually was, at this hour of the day, even without the fatigue of
travel.

The bellboy took their bags inside the hotel. She hung back on the
sidewalk. "Mike——"

"Yes?"

"Is it very silly of me? I want to go and look at that consulate building."

"Let's go in and register and bathe, for crying out loud. Then you
can contemplate its charm all evening. It's no treat to me. I've seen a
swastika."

"Just for a minute."

His true smile came slow and weary across the pallid face. "The bird
and the snake. Sure, come ahead, feast your eyes."

They walked down the sidewalk to the German consulate. She stood
staring up at the gilded eagle and swastika on a huge bold medallion over
the doors. After a while she said, "They're real, aren't they? They really
exist."

"Oh yes," Eden said dully. "They exist."

She went to bed that night with her spine still somewhat a-crawl,
having obtained a sleeping pill from Mike Eden. He had made no reference to the Nazis during dinner. He had talked about France, and Italy,
and about Noel Airman's charm and wit. But she knew he had been
aware of the slightly shocked state into which she had been thrown by

the mere sight of the gilded swastika. Marjorie had seen plenty of swastikas before, in newsreels and magazines; but this was the first one she had seen with her own eyes that really meant business, so to say.

For a long while the pill did not work. It loosened and warmed her limbs, and calmed her nerves, but her mind remained tight and sharp in the darkness; and at last she sat up, turned on the bed lamp, and smoked, sorting out the astonishments of the past two days. Most astonishing of all, much more so than Mike Eden's sudden casual invitation to her to fly to Zurich with him, had been her ready acceptance. But since the moment she had first seen this strange haunted man at the gangway of the *Queen Mary*—at least since the moment she had first talked to him at the rail, as the ship steamed down the Narrows—it seemed to Marjorie that she had cut her moorings from everything familiar and solid in her existence, including her own standards of propriety.

Once she had thought that Noel Airman had opened a new world to her, a world of novel manners and values; but now she was beginning to see his free ways and shocking talk as a sort of negative print of her own world; Noel's innovation had been to call the black of West End Avenue white, and the white black. Outside that limited world, outside her perpetual little tug of war with Noel, outside her girlish dream of becoming Marjorie Morningstar, there was, there had always been, a roaring larger world in which men like Mike Eden moved; by chance, blindly pursuing Noel, she had stumbled into this larger world, and it scared and excited her.

Eden had called Paris from Cherbourg as soon as a telephone line had been passed from the dock to the ship; and in no very long time—he didn't say how he had managed it—had come to her with Noel's Paris address. Noel was off skiing in the Alps, he added, and wasn't expected back for ten days. He had then offered to escort her to Paris and see her settled in a reasonably cheap hotel, before proceeding on his way to Germany; and he had been amazingly deft and quick in clearing through customs, getting French money, treating with porters, and transferring baggage from the ship to the Paris train. They had arrived in Paris toward evening, in the rain, and she had seen nothing of the city but one small quiet restaurant where she had had an elegant dinner (while Eden consumed a bowl of raw salad and a whole loaf of bread) and the dowdy Mozart Hotel, where he had put her up.

Just before saying good night to her, standing in the hotel lobby waiting for the creaky elevator, Eden had abruptly said, "You've got ten days to kill. Why slosh around Paris by yourself? This is the dreariest time of the year here. I have to spend a week or so in Zurich before I go to Germany. Come along. I'll take you driving in the Alps. Maybe we'll track down Noel. There aren't too many places he can be. It may be your only chance ever to see the Alps. They're worth seeing."

The best answer she could think of, trying to catch her breath, was, "I'm not sure that's a decent proposal."

"Of course it's decent," Eden said without a smile, "and you haven't the slightest doubt of it."

"I thought shipboard acquaintances invariably turned into horrible bores on land."

"I guess all rules have exceptions. You're holding up very well. I just think you'd enjoy the Alps. Will you come?"

In the second or two before she answered, Marjorie thought of many things: of the loneliness and strain of spending ten days alone in a great foreign city, waiting for Noel to get back; of Eden's brief but revolting collapse on the ship, and his peculiarly swift recovery; of her growing suspicion that he was engaged in undercover or illegal transactions of some kind in Germany; of what her mother would say about her travelling around Europe with a man like Eden, if she ever found out. Hesitating, she looked at his face, calm and pleasant, though unchanged in its shadowed remoteness. She was not at all in love with him. The sight of him with a hypodermic needle in his hand had withered, probably for good, any such notion that might have been floating far back in her mind; but she did feel affection, and pity, and concern for him. Despite his bizarre traits, he was, in his good moods, rare company; and if there was such a thing as a decent man, he was decent.

She said, "How shocked would you be, I wonder, if I said yes?"

"Shocked?" His smile was agreeable and mild. "I'd be very pleased. You make me feel good when you're around, that's all."

She said, "Well—I haven't any dignity left, that's one sure thing. I've chased Noel this far, I may as well go yodelling after him up and down the Alps, eh?" She laughed rather ruefully. "I guess I'll come, Mike. Thanks for asking me. It sounds like fun."

"Well, good. It will be, I promise you."

"If my mother knew what I was doing she'd kill me. But I might as well be hanged for a sheep as for a goat. I don't suppose there's a living soul who'd believe at this point that we aren't having an affair. I don't care."

"Now suppose," Eden said, a rather acid grin coming on his face, "I really ought to mention this—suppose we do meet Noel, travelling together like this? We just might."

"Oh, him. I imagine it'll enhance my glamor in his eyes. It's probably just the jolt he needs."

Perched on a bed in Zurich, finishing her cigarette, Marjorie smiled and yawned. Completely adrift though she was, her uppermost feeling was perky pleasure at her own daring, now that she was actually in Switzerland with Eden. Whatever was going to happen in the next ten days would not be dull. For all she knew, this time tomorrow night she might be dining with Noel—or with Noel and Eden together, a stimulating prospect.

The pill took hold. She slept through twelve dreamless hours.

In the morning there was a sealed note under her door in Eden's writing, with some Swiss banknotes: *"Sorry, had to go out early on business. Phoned several ski lodges. No luck on Noel yet. I'll be back for cocktails and dinner, probably phone your room about five. You can get around this town with English and your high-school French. Don't buy too many cuckoo clocks. You owe me $50, I changed that much for you. Mike.*

Conscious of handwritings now, she scanned Eden's carefully. It was vertical, clear, disappointingly plain; she had expected marked elegance from a man who had made a study of handwriting. Noel's, she recalled, was much more impressive; gracefully shaped letters, *t*'s crossed with a strong upward slant, and curious striking capitals. All one could say for Eden's was that it was very easy to read.

She went out and strolled around Zurich, feeling lost and sheepish. It was a neat, wealthy-looking city, but not exciting once she was used to the multiple-language signs, and to the slightly different look of streetcars and policemen, and to the clean clear air, which in her experience didn't go with city streets. To pass the morning, she shopped for a wristwatch for Seth and had lunch in a sidewalk restaurant, where the coffee and the little chocolate pastries were exquisite.

She returned to the hotel at three-thirty and took a nap; woke after five, and called his room. There was no answer. She bathed and dressed, taking her time; at half-past six she telephoned him again; no answer. Ready for dinner, dressed even to her hat, yearning for a cocktail, hungry, she sat reading *Tom Jones* and smoking nervously until half-past seven. She glanced at Eden's note to make sure she had not misunderstood it; telephoned his room again; and, fighting off alarm, called the desk clerk and asked whether Mr. Eden had checked out. No, came the polite reply in a moment, he was still registered; no, he had left no message for her.

At eight she went to the bar, drank a cocktail quickly, and returned to her room. At half-past nine she ordered dinner in her room, and picked without relish at the food. At midnight he still had not called. She sat up till one-thirty reading over and over a week-old New York *Times* which she had bought in the lobby. She read through the help wanted ads, the shipping news, and the financial section, becoming bitterly homesick for New York as her worry over Eden mounted. At last she turned out the light, tossed and dozed miserably till the sun came up at seven, and then slept for a couple of hours. The first thing she did on waking was to reach for the telephone. Eden's room did not answer.

She killed the morning in sightseeing, and the afternoon at a movie house showing two very old American films. Half a dozen times she went to the telephone booth in the ladies' room of the movie house and called the hotel, but there never was a message for her. Marjorie was increasingly torn between fear for Eden's safety, and common-sense embarrassment at her own melodramatic worries. One of the movies happened to be a spy story; and all the paraphernalia of mysterious blondes, papers concealed in toothpaste tubes, and sudden vanishings, so familiar in the blown-up gray images of the movie screen, made her feel exceptionally silly each time she dropped down into dry real life and went to call the hotel. That Eden had been spirited away by the Nazis—which was what she was imagining, if her vague fears had any tangibility at all—was simply too much to believe. More likely he was exactly what he said he was, a businessman dealing in drugs and chemicals; and his reticence and nervousness, if they had any meaning, probably were attributable to currency manipulations, or shading of the drug trade laws, the usual shifts and dodges of a businessman clipping corners to make more money. In a year in her father's importing office, she had learned quite a bit about this commonplace aspect of international commerce. Everybody did it, more or less.

She knew, too, that Eden was startlingly absent-minded, and quite capable of forgetting a dinner appointment and ignoring her for a couple of days. Several times on the ship he had failed to meet her at an appointed place and time, absorbed in his card games; and during one entire day he had paid no attention to her at all, sunk in a poker game that had carried over from the night before. For all she knew, Eden was off somewhere now playing cards, while her mind was dancing with lurid pictures of him being chained and tortured.

With such reasonings she staved off any action that day. Humiliating though it was, she did talk to the desk clerk at length after dinner. He was calm, amused, condescending; Mr. Eden often stopped at the hotel, he said, and went off for a couple of days while retaining his room; Miss Morgenstern had nothing at all to worry about, he would undoubtedly be back in a day or so. She went off scarlet-faced to the elevator, and spent another dismal night in her room.

The next day was a dragged-out ordeal of worry, aimless wandering, and desultory shopping. To her tremendous relief, Eden did telephone her from his room, shortly after she came back to the hotel late in the afternoon. He sounded very exhilarated, insisting on having a drink with her at once, though she protested she was grimy and tired. They met in the bar. He looked worn and rather white, but his spirits had never been higher. He had already hired a car, he said, and they would start on a week-long jaunt around the Alps in the morning. He talked in a rush, his dark-ringed eyes twinkling with gaiety. "Frankly, Marge, I may play it dirty, and do my level best to avoid meeting Noel. What the hell, he's going to have your company for the rest of his life, isn't he?"

He did not even refer to the fact that he had been away for three days; he blandly talked as though nothing unusual had occurred, nothing that had to be explained or even acknowledged. Marjorie found this disingenuous silence most awkward; she wanted to ask questions. But clearly that was not to be. There was nothing accidental in Eden's ebullient talk of the trip, and pretense that the events of the past three days were not worth mentioning. He gave her the positive feeling that if she broke into that subject she would encounter a freezing snub, and possibly an abrupt end to her acquaintance with him. Perforce she took his gay tone, as soon as she could, and kept it up through the evening.

Next day they drove up into the mountains in the midget French car he had hired; and for a week they went from one alpine resort to another, sometimes stopping a day at a hotel, sometimes two. The desk clerks tended to blink a bit when Eden asked for separate rooms, but they were always obliging. He had been joking, of course, about avoiding Noel. He made many inquiries and phone calls. Once they thought they had located him; but when they arrived at the hotel, it turned out that a man named Erdman was there.

Marjorie was disappointed; still, she went on having fun. The trip was unforgettable, from the first day to the last. The flimsy little car groaned up almost vertical mountainsides, weaving laboriously back and forth along hairpin turns, dodging past goats, dogs, peasants, and occasional huge limousines. On the afternoon of the first day Marjorie found herself looking across an empty gorge, thousands of feet deep, at a girl tending goats on the sharp green rocky slope opposite, which reflected blinding sunlight from patches of snow. She could hear the goats bleat, she could see every color in the girl's florid costume; yet she calculated it would take her less time to get back to Paris, almost, than to cross over to that girl in her roadless mountain-peak pasture. It was all like that. They drove through villages of squat timbered cottages, steeply piled along narrow cobbled snowy streets, which looked more like opera settings than human habitations. There weren't many tourists in the hotels, and almost no Americans. She became used to dining at long boards with Italians, Frenchmen, Germans. One evening a jolly drunken group of Germans in a little hotel pulled them into a songfest, with many maudlin assurances that Germany and America would always be friends, and that Hitler was not as bad as the papers said. At another hotel they fell in with a party of middle-aged French couples who pressed them into coming on a picnic, where the men did a boomps-a-daisy dance on the snowy grass, imitating Mussolini and Hitler, to the squealing delight of their wives. Wherever they went people took them for honeymooners—all but the perplexed desk clerks who knew of their sleeping arrangements.

They would drive in an afternoon from soft springtime to whistling white winter; from lilac-filled gardens to ice-blocked roads; from warm sunny cities with great department stores and clanging trolleys to black naked rock slopes in a whirl of falling snow. They ate sandwiches and drank wine by the side of tumbling white cataracts, with icy Alps all around them, receding to little purple ridges as far as the eye could see. Marjorie had never had such a sense of space, such a sense of the world as a great jagged rock covered with a layer of grassy earth, and lapped in sweet air.

Once she said to Eden, "I have to keep reminding myself that we're still on the same planet where the Bronx is. It seems to me we're on Venus or the moon."

Eden was in excellent humor all during the holiday, despite a tendency to nervous exasperation, especially with slow-moving waiters and porters. Late in the afternoon he had a way of falling into black depression, but a meal with plenty of wine usually brought him out of it.

Though their relationship was almost comically chaste, indeed the subject of much of Eden's joking, Marjorie was aware of bass notes of sex under it. They were having too much fun; the hours were too keenly edged, the lighthearted kiss at the end of the evening (seldom more than one) too sharply pleasant. She often wondered what she would do if Mike were to make a pass at her.

Had anyone told her at the start of the European trip that she would soon be traipsing around Switzerland with a forty-year-old widower she would have been insulted. Forty had always seemed to her the age at which men began to break down and retire. Yet Eden treated her as a contemporary, if a young one. A girl of twenty-four, she began to realize, was nothing more or less than a woman getting on. It was a rather startling thought. The few gray hairs she was plucking out around her temples seemed absurdly premature to her; the dances at Columbia were present to her mind as events that had happened only the other day.

They came to Lucerne, a city of green flowered gentle slopes and charming medieval houses, bordering a lake set in a ring of giant mountains. Late in the afternoon, when the town lay in shadow and the sunlight slanted pink on the snowy peaks, Mike rented a speedboat and they roared far out on the still blue lake. He seemed to be in his afternoon glum spell; he wasn't talking, or even looking at her. Marjorie was herself very tired, and the travelling had begun to wear down her nerves. The speedboat ride wasn't fun; she would rather have had a nap. She was thinking that perhaps she had had about enough of this peculiar excursion with this very peculiar man; and she could not help wondering how hard he had really been trying to find Noel.

Mike cut the motor, and the streamlined red hull drifted in silence. He lit a cigar. "Well, that's it. End of the trail. As the sun sets on mighty Pilatus we bid farewell to Mike and Marjorie, our gay tourist friends, and to picturesque Switzerland, land of lakes, mountains, and eternal snows."

Marjorie said, "I thought we had till Friday."

"Well, I made a phone call a little while ago. I have to go back to Zurich in the morning."

"And then?"

"And then? Picturesque Germany, land of Gemütlichkeit, leather aprons, beer, pretzels, song, and merry laughter."

A chill breeze ruffled the water, and wavelets slapped against the hull. It was very lonely and quiet on the lake. Strings of street lamps were already twinkling in Lucerne.

After several minutes, during which they both smoked and looked in silence at the red sunset arching across the dome of the sky, Eden said, "Noel's back in Paris."

"Oh?"

"I've been calling every day. He just showed up this afternoon. Seems he changed his mind and went to Venice, after all. Can't say I'm not grateful to him. Unpredictable fellow."

Ashamed of her suspicions, Marjorie said, "Thanks, Mike. Did you talk to him?"

"To Noel? No, he'd been in and gone out. Talked to his landlady. Woman with a thick German accent. You'll find her hard to understand on the telephone." He lapsed into silence again. He appeared sullen. Every now and then he glanced at her, a puzzling dark look. The sunset was fading fast, and it was getting colder minute by minute. At last, when Marjorie was about to suggest that they go back to shore, he said in an odd sharp tone, "I'm sorry about those three days in Zurich. Hope you weren't scared or worried."

Startled by the abrupt cracking open of the forbidden subject, Marjorie said cautiously, "Well, yes, I was worried. Pretty damned worried, that last day."

"I can imagine. I couldn't phone. I'm sorry."

"Well, you're all right, so what's the difference?"

"Marjorie, it's quite true, as I told you on the ship, that I'm going to Germany on business. But I'm also doing some illegal rescue work. I'm a fool to tell you, but I want to. I hope I can count on you not to get excited or melodramatic or anything." The words seemed to break from him in a rush. She stared at him. After a long pause he went on, more slowly, "Well, that's it. I know I can count on you not to mention it, or discuss it, or do anything at all but forget it, once we're back on shore. People's lives are involved."

"Why . . . of course. Is it very—is there a lot of danger?" She didn't know quite what to say. She was more surprised at the fact of his telling her, than at the information.

"No, very little. I mean, these things are relative. It's not as safe as studying Semitic languages at Oxford, let's say."

Thrown off balance though she was, Marjorie couldn't help smiling. Eden smiled too, and said eagerly, his eyes glittering with unusual liveliness, "I'll tell you something though, Margie, in a queer way there's a hell of a lot of fun—though that's not quite the word—in rescue work. I've been doing it for a couple of years. It's stimulating to be outside the law. It makes you look sharp, it simplifies the day's job. Above all it makes every hour you stay uncaught very pleasant. And as for depression, anxiety—all that pattern simply vanishes. The fact is, and this is the only way I can put it, when I go back to the United States I seem to be living in a black-and-white movie. As soon as I cross the German border, I'm in color again. I grant you it's a hell of a warped way to feel, and it leaves out the fact that I'm sick to the stomach with fear all the time I'm there, but still that's the truth of it." He looked in her face and laughed. "I'm shocking you."

"Nothing you say could shock me at this point. You're a man from Mars. When are you going back into Germany?"

"I'll take an evening train to Stuttgart tomorrow."

"Don't they check everybody pretty carefully on the trains?"

"That's the idea. I do everything in the most legal and obvious way, as any American businessman would."

"Are you scared?"

"I'm always scared. A bit more than usual, maybe, this time. They've checked on Hilda. I haven't been exactly an hysterical old lady about her, it seems, after all."

506

Marjorie sat up, looking at his shadowed face. "What? What about her?"

She could see his Adam's apple move. "Nothing worth changing plans for. Nobody's exactly seen her eating a Jewish baby for breakfast, you might say. But at least nobody's saying I'm seeing burglars under the bed any more. It's odd that that should give me satisfaction, but it does. They gave me such a horselaugh at first."

Marjorie shivered. The speedboat rocked in the wash of another boat going by at top speed; the boy and girl in the cockpit waved gaily and shouted something in German as they sped past. The exhaust roar echoed back over the dark water for half a minute or so, and faded to a distant murmur. Marjorie said, "Mike, who's 'They'? Or can't you talk about that?"

He hesitated. "Well, hell, I don't know why not. You've read about all this in the papers, I'm sure. It's no secret. I work with a group, an organization. . . . Remember the Underground Railway in American Civil War days? More or less the same thing. Instead of slaves, political refugees, and some Jews. There's several of these outfits, and——"

"Are you working with the communists?"

Eden wrinkled his nose. "What? Whatever makes you think I'd work with *them*? Silly bastards. Tried to peddle the Marxian brand of happiness pills to the Germans, and just got undersold out of the Hun market by Hitler with his Jew-killing superman capsule. No, this crowd is more innocuous. Just a lot of idealistic boobies who think Germany can be a small America some day. They think they're fighting Hitler. What a joke! Actually they're a lot of megalomaniacs, pure and simple, only on the right side. Their cause is hopeless. They're trying to hold back the tide with a teaspoon. But for my purposes they're not bad to work with."

A deeper twilight was coming over the lake as the last streaks of red disappeared from the snows of the mountain peaks. The nearer mountains looked almost black. Marjorie was shivering despite her new blue suede jacket; she hugged her arms, crouching on the red leather seat of the drifting boat. "You say they're trying to stop the ocean with a teaspoon. What do you think you're trying to do? Maybe you're a bigger booby."

"No, I'm not a booby at all. I have a small attainable goal, and what's more I believe I've actually achieved it, or am damn close to it. . . ."

"Mike, what did they find out about Hilda? How can you go back if——"

"Don't go building it out of all proportion in your mind. They say it's all right. This stuff on Hilda is far from definite, mind you. They've never steered me wrong yet. . . . Well, good Lord, Margie, don't look so terror-stricken. Can't you picture how helter-skelter our communications are? If we held off because of this or that vague suspicion we'd never do anything. Let's face it, the likes of me isn't wanted in Germany, and I don't suspect that, I know it. But I've been in and out now for three years. I transact a lot of legitimate business. The desk clerks in a dozen hotels know me by sight. I even know the conductors on some trains. It's very hard to describe to you what it's like, but I can only tell you it's like skiing, or serving in a submarine, or something. You have to be vigilant and there's an ever-present hazard, but also there are standard techniques and procedures, and thousands, literally thousands of people are doing it, most of them not any brighter than I am, and surviving very nicely. Moreover, I have all kinds of extra safety factors. My commercial connections, my American passport—— God Almighty, why do I have to justify myself to you, anyway?" He shot his hand forward and pressed the ignition key, but the motor didn't catch.

She leaned forward and put her hand on his, restraining him from turning the key again. "You said you had a small objective. You said you'd achieved it——"

"I think I have. I can't be sure. In any case——" He leaned back and stared at her. In the fading light from the pellucid sky, where several pale stars winked now, his scar was almost invisible, and he looked very young. She could picture him at the age of twenty-five, and it seemed to her she might have fallen in love with that ugly young man. He said, "Well, you unquestionably consider me a crackpot anyway, so I'll tell you. What difference does it make? You've got to understand, first of all, that I really have nothing in common with this group, I don't sympathize with them politically or anything, it's strictly a practical arrangement. I fell in with them by accident. When I first came to Germany in '35, travelling for a chemical firm, I was still suffering from suicidal depressions. There was an analyst living in Berlin whom I'd known in Vienna in the old days, Dr. Blum, Jewish, supposed to be one of the top men in the world, and I went to see him. He didn't help me, as it turned out, I helped him. He was trying to get out of Germany. It was easy in those days, the only question was getting your money out too. The problem now is to get out with your skin. I carried five thousand American dollars across the border for Dr. Blum in my inside coat pocket. It was a cinch, the Nazis weren't searching Americans, especially not a Nordic-looking bastard like Herr Eden, with his Heidelberg scar.

"I can't tell you, Margie, what it did for me, pulling off that little coup. To begin with, it saved my life. I didn't care at that point whether I lived or died, in fact I had a slight preference for being dead—that's why I'd gone to see Blum. And mind you, I didn't get much of a kick out of pulling Blum out—selfish frigid goat, risking his family's lives for the sake of a lousy five thousand dollars—Blum had, however, three lovely grandchildren, a blond boy of five and twin girls, real angels. When I met Blum and his family at the train in Paris, and saw those three children step safe on French soil, something came to life in me, something that had been dead since the accident. . . . Aren't you freezing? Shall we go back? We can talk about all this in a warm restaurant somewhere——"

Marjorie glanced toward the winking lights of Lucerne. "You won't talk where there are people. I'm not cold, Mike——"

"Well, Blum had friends in the same fix, and I went back a couple of more times and did it again. I realize now what a stupid procedure that was—a tourist, even a businessman, popping back and forth across the border like that. I'd have been picked up sure after a couple of more trips. But one of these birds knew someone in this group, and put me in touch with them.

"This outfit, you see, isn't primarily interested in getting Jews out of Germany, or even their own people, though they do that too occasionally. They have dizzy grandiose schemes of revolt against Hitler. They keep moiling and fussing and sneaking around, making elaborate plans, and building up arsenals, and running mimeograph machines at night, and raising money abroad and sneaking it in, and it's all a lot of pathetic nonsense, for my money. But they do have a functioning apparatus, and some powerful friends in England and America. I run certain little errands for them, errands an American businessman can bring off with the least risk, and in return, pretty much on a quid pro quo basis, they help me sneak out my few silly Jews . . . because that's all I'm interested in."

Marjorie put her hand on his. He broke off, squinting at her. "What's the matter?"

"Certain little errands, you say."

"That's right."

"If you're caught running them—what?"

"I'd undoubtedly get kicked out of Germany, for good."

"Nothing worse?"

He said irritably, pulling away his hand, "What are you getting at? That I'm not as good an insurance risk as a psychology teacher? I know that, but I might not be alive at all if I'd remained a psych teacher. The Gestapo is most unlikely to get too rough with me. They're insane butchers, to be sure, but they turn all smiles and they sweat pig grease as a rule at the sight of an American passport. Look, I'm scared enough,

Marjorie, it doesn't add anything to warn me I'm not playing tennis in Central Park. I know."

"All I'm saying is that maybe you ought to wait before going back——"

"I'd get bored waiting."

"That's not a rational answer."

"Who said I'm a rational person?" He laughed coldly. "You guessed I was Jewish. I don't even know if you're right about that. My great-grandfather was a German Jew. When he came to America he changed his name to Eden, and dropped all his connections with Jews. Our family name—on my oath, this is true—was Einstein. No relation to *the* Einstein, but don't you think that's funny? The one name that's apt to survive the next twenty centuries wasn't good enough for my family.

"But I guess my Jewish blood, or whatever it is, has stayed alive. Because I've found a reason for existing, a satisfaction I can't even describe, in pulling a few Jews out of Germany. I go after the ones that, for one reason or another, the big rescue organizations can't or won't budge. There's an amazing number of them, Marjorie, Jews by the tens of thousands, just sitting in that fiery furnace, waiting for it to cool off. It's their home, you see. They *won't* go. They can't get themselves to leave home. There are graves they can't bear to leave behind. They clutch childishly at straws of optimism. Well, I talk to them, yank at them, take jewels or money out for them—anything that'll get them moving. They're usually annoyed and not very grateful, but I get them out. Most of the ones I go after have little kids. I'm happiest when there's a kid in the picture. Who knows which of those kids is going to be a Heine, or Disraeli, or Einstein, or Freud? Or one greater than all of them?"

Eden sat up very straight, and was silent, peering at Marjorie. When he spoke again his voice had a new strained timbre. "In case you have any lingering doubts that I'm stark mad, let me ask you this, isn't the Messiah going to be a Jew? Even the Christians are waiting for a second coming of their Savior. He came to them the first time as a Jew. Why should it be different the second time? He wouldn't be self-conscious about having a Jewish name, I should imagine, like my great-grandfather. Aren't the times full of signs of a new era coming?"

Eden lit a fresh cigar, and the yellow flare of the match filled his face with leaping shadows. In the taut silence Marjorie stared at him with a feeling not far from eerie horror, as the thought came to her that he really was more than a little mad.

He startled her by saying, "No, I'm not exactly sane, and if you want further proof of it I'll tell you one more thing. For three years I've had the unshakable conviction that my remaining destiny in life was to save one child, or its forefather, I'm not sure which, from destruction by Hitler—

furthermore, that the death of Emily, and everything else that's happened to me, was part of the process necessary to forge the queer instrument to do that queer job. You don't have to tell me it's a systematic fantasy, I could write up my own case history impeccably. However, there was once an Arab stevedore who had a systematic fantasy that he was destined to start a great religion, and now a respectable part of the human race believes in Mohammed. Sometimes these systematic fantasies stamp themselves on events, and change the very nature of what's true and what's false.

"But take the thing in its worst light. Let's say I'm nutty as a fruitcake—that destiny is a primitive delusion, that nothing exists but chance. All the same, in my nutty way, don't you think I'm doing some good? Hitler's going into the wholesale skeleton-manufacturing business in a year or so, you know. Jewish skeletons. Nothing can stop it. At least I'm cutting down the number of skeletons. Especially the little skeletons. The little skeletons with small soft bones. And entirely by accident, isn't it more than possible that I actually will rescue some great benefactor of mankind? They've got the genes for it, these Jewish children, haven't they? Unless I pull them out, along with their paralyzed parents, there's nothing in sight for them but to manure the German ground."

He leaned close to her. The cigar glowed bright red. She could see the gleam of his eyes, and the wrinkling furrow of his scar. "Now I'll tell you one thing more. I have a feeling that I've already done it, already rescued him. That's the strangest part of it. I've had it more and more strongly for the past six months. It comes and goes and then comes again more strongly. I feel I've already gotten him out. I don't know who he was or when I did it, but I do have this irrefutable sense of an accomplished mission. I can't pay any attention to it because obviously, on a rational basis, it's just my horrible fear of this whole filthy business converted into a notion that would free me from having to go back into Germany any more. It's exactly like hysterical blindness in a soldier. All the same, that's what I meant when I told you back on the *Queen Mary* that I'm coming to the end of the novel.

"I've never told all this to anybody else, Margie, and I don't know why I've unloaded it on you. If I'd told this crowd I work with, they'd have stopped using me long ago. You're probably thinking right now how you can get me quietly committed. Well? What do you think? Do you feel like jumping out and swimming for the shore? Don't, I'm quite harmless."

Marjorie looked at Eden wordlessly for a long time, her breast heaving, her mind in a tumult. There was so much she wanted to say; but no sentences would form. She felt helpless, trivial, baffled and, at the same time, thrilled in her deepest soul.

She did the best she could. With a single sinuous movement, she slid across the seat to him, twined her arms around him, and kissed him. She tried to tell him with her arms, with her body, with her silent mouth, that he must not go to Stuttgart the next day, and that if she could keep him from going she would.

There was a flicker of response in Eden's kiss; then a stronger response; then it faded and he was cold. He said in a low tone, holding her gently, his cheek resting against hers, "Okay, Marjorie. Okay."

"Mike . . . Mike, you're not very well, don't you know that? You must know it. Don't go back. Not tomorrow. Wait a while, wait till you feel a little better—till you know some more. I'll stay in Zurich with you, if that makes any difference——"

He sat up, took her hand, and held it to his face for a moment. He moved away from her, resting an arm along the back of the seat. "There's something that needs doing right away. It's not at all dangerous, but I'm the one to do it, as it happens. It needs the free and easy American again. Take my word for it, my nerves are better than they've ever been. It's the truth, Margie. You've seen me as I've been for years, not at a low point or crisis, not in the least. I am what you saw on the ship, that's all. Most people can't stand me, you know, I'm a jagged, panicky, supercilious, mean-tempered son of a bitch. Yet you like me. I know it, and it's given me some new red corpuscles. But don't try to come any closer, darling Marjorie, I'm pretty used up, excellent for what I'm doing, good for nothing else——"

"Mike, listen——"

"It's exactly so. I'm doing what I'm doing not because I'm a hero, and don't go making me one in your mind, whatever you do. It takes a displaced neurotic of the worst kind, a walking ghost with no roots in the real world, to do it——"

"There are millions of neurotics not doing anything like it, Mike——"

"I know that. Therapy for me takes the form of excessively tense action, it's a known pattern, and that's what makes me useful. If I find enough wild ridiculous things like this to do, I may live to be ninety-seven, in which case I hope we'll be doddering old friends some day, but if I'm really coming to the end of the novel, Margie, nothing you or I can do will add a page to it. I'll be run over by a trolley car in Zurich tomorrow, if nothing else——"

"For God's sake don't talk that way any more, Mike, I'll start crying. It's such damned horrible nonsense, these premonitions——"

"I daresay. Don't cry, dear Marjorie, whatever you do." He took her hand, pressed it briefly to his cheek, and dropped it. "Noel is okay. I'm sure you can tame him. Really sure."

"All right."

"I'll look for you next time I'm in the States. I hope I'll be obliged to buy you a wedding present."

"Thanks, Mike." She could hardly bring the words out of her constricted throat.

He rested his hands lightly on her shoulders, and looked earnestly into her face. "Of all sad words of tongue or pen, the saddest are these: *it might have been.* . . . I've never felt the force of that overworked old jingle until now. You're a little darling, Maud Muller, a perfect darling. I've never seen prettier blue eyes or softer brown hair. Your smile, in case Noel's never mentioned it, is pure warm radiance. It just happens that I have this date in Stuttgart tomorrow, that's all. You'll have to excuse me, Marjorie. . . . You might kiss me once more, for good luck. Then we're off to deliver you to Noel."

A minute or two later the boat was foaming full speed across the dark lake to the lamplit shore.

Chapter 45. NOEL FOUND

Arriving back in Paris, Marjorie wondered whether the sun ever shone in that much-praised city. It was a cold drizzly afternoon, and Paris seemed a cold drizzly place, endlessly flat and gray, and full of dripping statues. The Arch of Triumph and the Eiffel Tower, looming out of blue mist as she drove past them in a taxicab, gave her no thrill; but the taxi did. The driver, a slumped old man, possibly eighty-seven or so, in a dirty black coat and a dirtier black cap, with a drooping big yellow-stained mustache, four or five yellow teeth, and rheumy yellow eyes, drove through the thick honking traffic with the abandon of a drunken duke. He had the unnerving habit, whenever the taxi seemed to be careening toward a collision, of dropping to the floor of the cab and twisting the wheel sharply, then bobbing up to see where he was, and how he was doing. In this fashion he mounted the sidewalk several times. Marjorie would gladly have gotten out of the cab, but in her paralysis all French left her, including the word for "stop." She arrived at the Mozart Hotel covered with perspiration, and hating Paris. The desk clerk, a fat man with hooded eyes, leered politely at her, welcoming her back, and asked in oily English whether she wanted a double bed. It was obvious that he considered her a travelling American whore, and was wondering whether he could afford the price of a night with her. The room he gave her had a yellowing cracked bath with only a trickle of rusty hot water, but the other furnishings, especially the brass bedstead, looked so medieval that the bath by contrast seemed to clang and shriek of modern times.

She bathed with some difficulty, stretching the brownish puddle of hot water a long way. It was a pleasure to be able to choose fresh attire from her steamer trunk; she was very bored with the clothes she had been wearing over and over in Switzerland. But the black wool suit, specifically bought with a hundred and ten precious dollars at Hattie Carnegie's for her first encounter with Noel, needed pressing. She doubtfully rang for the maid, and was astonished at the speed with which a smiling young woman in a gray smock appeared; was delighted at the girl's swift comprehension of the problem, indicated by her seizing the suit and pantomiming a pressing job; was enchanted by the reappearance of the girl in half an hour with the suit perfectly pressed. The girl also brought her, unasked, a pot of hot chocolate with flaky little rolls and butter. Marjorie began to like Paris better. She tried a couple of times to telephone Noel, but only became hopelessly snarled up with gibbering operators. She dressed with great care in the black suit, with a dusty-pink blouse, white gloves, black straw hat with a single pink rose, and black nose veil. Well pleased with the image in the mirror after a cold-blooded appraisal, she sailed out to run Noel down.

Eventually she found the Rue des Sts. Pères, a crooked narrow street in a shabby neighborhood, meandering uphill between overhanging houses. She was going from door to door, looking for the number Mike Eden had given her, when she saw Noel.

Hatless, in his old tan topcoat, carrying a bulky brown paper bag in each arm, he came up the steep sidewalk, his head tilted in the old way, whistling. He walked right by her; a stalk of celery and the legs of a chicken tied with cord protruded from one bag, and the neck of a wine bottle from the other. When he was a few feet past her he stopped and turned around, peering incredulously. With an impulse of mischief she brushed the veil up on her hat. "Hello, Noel."

"Jesus Christ, is it you?"

"Have I changed that much? It's me."

He bounded toward her. "Gad, and me with my arms full! Well, you'll just have to do the hugging and kissing, then, there's no help for it. Come on, hug hard."

He bent sideways, and she hugged his neck and kissed his cheek. "Well, that's all right for on the street," he said. "Ye *gods*, let me look at you. You know this is hair-raising, it's absolutely *weird*? If I wasn't thinking of you at the very second I saw you, may the devil come right up out of that sewer and drag me to hell. Christ, you're twice as beautiful as you ever were, d'you know? You're a *woman,* that's what—— Say, what in God's name are you doing in Paris, right in front of my house? I swear there's something spooky about this. Are you real? Are you just a mass of ravishing ectoplasm?"

Marjorie laughed. "Am I really in front of your house? The way they number them in Paris, I don't know how anybody ever locates anybody——"

"How the devil did you find out where I live? I've kept it from you every way I could. Bless you for breaking through, anyway—— Marjorie, my only darling, you can't, you can't begin to imagine how glad I am to see you. I never really knew how glad I'd be until this moment, but—— Well, hell's bells, let's not stand jawing on the street, let's go upstairs, slay a calf, broach a hogshead of mead——" As he talked he led her to the next house, and pushed open the door with his back. "Come on. Two flights up. No elevator, you're in Paris."

Marjorie stood at the doorway, looking at photographs in a glass display case facing the street. "Isn't that André Gide?"

"Yes, my landlady's a photographer. Her studio is on the first floor. Come along, she's shot all the intellectual glamor boys in town, you can look at the rogues' gallery she's got any time you want to." He put one of the paper bags on the floor, fished a key out of his pocket, and opened the inner door. She was glad to see that he still had his hair. It was blown about in great disorder, but it was there. She had had ugly nightmares of him bald as an egg. He said, "Follow me, it's simplest. Don't break your neck on these stairs. The dim light is strictly Parisian. You have to develop owls' eyes to get around in French hallways. Also a mountaineer's legs and lungs. Did you ever see such steep steps? If it had two rails instead of one it would be a ladder—a winding ladder——"

Marjorie paused for breath on the first landing. In letters of silver on the dingy door—the entire stairway was dingy, it smelled of dust, old carpets, and garlicky food, and the walls were grimy yellow—the name *Gerda Oberman* arched over a modernistic sketch of a camera in red. Noel yodelled down the stair well at her. "Caught in a crevasse? Shall I send out a St. Bernard?"

"Coming," Marjorie said.

The door on the next landing opened directly into a living room, very large and almost square, with cheap scatter rugs on the bare dark-varnished floor, and a glossy black grand piano by the windows, incongruously new and expensive-looking amid the drab worn furniture. The light from the windows was a dreary blue-gray. Noel flicked a switch as

Marjorie came in, and a chandelier in the middle of the ceiling lit up, a monstrosity of orange and blue stained glass. "Here we are. Sit down for a minute and let me get rid of this junk, then we'll have a drink. Okay? Can you stand scotch and water without ice? My landlady doesn't believe in Frigidaires. We have a big old lump of ice, I can chip some——"

"Scotch and water is fine. I've about lost the taste for ice."

"I won't be a second."

"Take your time."

He paused at the French doors that opened into a dining room. He made a comic gesture with the two brown bags. "I can't get over how superb you look. And how glad I am to see you. I wish to hell you'd come a week later, that's all, seeing you've waited this long."

"Why? Why a week later?"

"Well, we'll talk in a minute."

There was a framed picture of a blond woman on the piano; Noel came back in a minute or so and caught her studying it. He still had his coat on and he was carrying two brown drinks. "Here you are. What do you think of my landlady?"

"Is this Gerda Oberman?"

"Yes. Gertie, as I call her when I want to annoy her. Real Boche, isn't she?"

"I think she's quite good-looking."

"I guess so. She used to be a model before she moved over behind the camera. That's a skillful picture, it minimizes her exceedingly Neanderthal jaw. Be with you in three minutes. Drink up, there's gallons of scotch." He went into a dark hallway on the right.

"Okay," he said, returning in a few minutes in a different jacket, shirt, and tie, with his hair combed, carrying an almost empty drink. "First of all, let's clear up a few mysteries. Where did you get my address? There isn't a person in the States who knows it except Ferdie Platt, and I know you didn't get it from him."

Marjorie, in a corner of a lumpy black leather sofa, toyed with her drink. "What difference does it make? I was determined to find you and I've done it. That's all."

"Well, it's an incredible bit of sleuthing. You belong with the FBI. Freshen your drink?"

"Not just yet. Do you know a man named Mike Eden?"

He was slouching down into a chair, but he sat up at this. "Mike? Sure I know Mike. Why?"

"I met him on the *Queen Mary* coming over. He gave me your address."

516

"What? I haven't seen Mike Eden since last summer. I've moved four times since then."

"Well, he got me your address, all the same."

"I'll be damned."

They looked at each other, Marjorie smiling slightly, Noel seeming puzzled and a bit wary. She could see now what the illness had done to him. He had lost a little hair in front; perhaps that was why he was wearing it excessively long and full. On the left side, under the hair, a trace of pink scalp showed. The golden color seemed faded too, a bit ashy. Strangely, the effect was to make him appear not older but younger. He had rather the air now of a dissipated college boy. The clothes, his old brown tweed jacket and gray flannels, with a stringy maroon knitted tie, and white shirt with button-down collar, accentuated the under-graduate look. He was thinner; the flannels hung on the long bones of his thighs. He had a fresh red-brown sunburn, and the skin of his face seemed to be pulled forward tightly by his curving jaw.

What really surprised Marjorie was his apparently unchanged attraction for her. She had felt a stinging thrill at her first glimpse of him on the street; and now the old tug stirred potently in her, sharpened, if any-thing, by a touch of pity. "Noel, you don't look as well as you should."

"As well as I should? Darling, I must look like the Black Death to you. I can only say you should have seen me eight months ago. Or rather I'm glad you didn't, you'd never have recovered from the sight. I nearly died, you know."

"Wally said he'd heard you got sick in Africa——"

"Sick? I all but tore the flesh from my bones with my own nails. I caught some horrible fever in Casablanca—they say you get it from bed-bug bites, anyway it's hell on earth, you break out in a murderous itch-ing rash—I lay in the charity ward of a Catholic hospital for two weeks, up to my neck in warm starch baths, delirious half the time——"

"How awful, Noel——"

"Well, don't let me bore you with that, it's past and done with. Ac-tually I'm feeling absolutely marvelous now, especially in the past couple of weeks. I've been skiing, swimming, taking walking trips, all the corny old healthy things, for months. My strength is really all back, I'm glad to observe. What I need now is about twenty more pounds of meat just to pad out the bones. That'll come. I've even gotten back a lot of my hair. The doc says I'll get it all back. God, do I ever massage my scalp and expend lotions! I must lose two pounds every night just from massaging. But it's the only answer.—Take your hat off, why don't you? Margie, you really have bloomed. You're a picture. Did you buy that suit here in Paris?"

"I just arrived a few hours ago, Noel."

"Well, you do look New Yorkish, at that. You don't look like a Parisienne at all. New York girls have a different kind of chic. It's refreshing. I have a feeling you've just showered."

Marjorie laughed, unpinning her hat. "Bathed. In about two inches of very rusty tepid water. I'm at the Mozart Hotel."

"Oh yes, that fleabag. For the money it's one of the best. How did you know about it? Tourists usually don't."

"Mike Eden."

He nodded, and again the wary look came on his face. "So. You just got here, hey? Didn't waste much time tracking me down, I'll say that."

"That's what I'm here for, you know." She didn't want to tell him yet of the pursuit through Switzerland.

"Good old Marjorie. Ever direct. I like it. In fact I like you." He got out of his chair. "How about a kiss?"

"Sure enough."

It was a friendly kiss. His thin arms, holding her loosely, felt familiar and delightful. "Mm. Good." He kissed her again, with a little more warmth. The telephone rang, a queer shrill buzz. It was on a little table by a green armchair near them. It rang again. Noel said, "Ah well. Remind me to pick up this conversation where we left off, won't you?" He dropped into the armchair. "Allo? . . . Bon, ou es-tu maintenant? Comment? Et après, qu'est-ce que tu vas faire? Zut, et le diner?" He slouched lower in the chair, cradled the receiver with his head and lit a cigarette, rolling his eyes comically at Marjorie. A stream of rapid French was rattling in the receiver. He broke in impatiently, talking just as fast. The other voice was a woman's, high and authoritative. Noel waved a hand, shrugged, and made faces into the receiver, like a Frenchman. The argument reached a noisy, quarrelsome climax and Noel slammed the receiver down. He glanced at Marjorie, and his irritated look faded into a rueful smile. "Don't mind me. I'm getting old and querulous. How about another drink?"

"Not just yet. That was a heavy slug you gave me."

"Come off it. If you've been helling around with Mike Eden you should be used to booze. He's the original hollow-legged wonder. Come on in the kitchen. I have things to do."

The plucked chicken, yellow and a little bloody, lay on a board by the small iron sink. The kitchen was narrow and squalid. A scratched red wooden table, two red chairs, a two-burner gas stove, a wooden icebox with its varnish half worn off, and crockery cupboards painted a sickly pink left little room for moving around. The floor was greasy dark bare wood. Noel said as he ran tap water into two glasses a quarter full of scotch, "We're confronted with an executive decision." He handed her a glass and prodded the chicken with a long bony finger. "This happens to be one hell of an exquisite pullet. We can eat here and I can promise you a superb meal, but on the other hand it'll be damn dull, I should think, for you to sit around watching me cook. It's no way to entertain a guest fresh from overseas, that's for sure."

"Why, it's absurd for you to go to all that trouble, Noel. Let's eat out, by all means."

"Aye, there's the rub. I have seldom been more broke, in a career checkered with bankrupt stretches." He drank deeply. "Oh, hell, Margie, why didn't you come a week later?"

Marjorie said, "I've got plenty of money. That's no problem."

He smiled sidewise at her. "With any other woman it wouldn't be. But with you—— Or have you become more broad-minded? Maybe you have, but . . . God damn Gertie, I could strangle her. In fact, I should have strangled her months ago." He poked the chicken again. "This really is a good bird. Oh, what the hell, Margie, you've watched me cook before, you won't mind sitting here and talking to me while I put up the dinner, will you? I'm very fast." He took off his jacket, draped it carefully on a hanger on the back of the kitchen door, and took a stained gray apron off the hook under the hanger. "I hope this won't destroy my glamor, if I have any left for you. I like my own cooking better than most of the table d'hôtes in this dismal neighborhood anyway, and you're not going to go paying cab fares and treating me at one of the good places. It's no way to——"

"Just a minute, what's the exact situation here?" Marjorie said. "Is it to be just the two of us having dinner in the apartment? What about your —your landlady? Is this whole apartment yours, or what?"

"My landlady? *Damn* my landlady," Noel said, viciously whacking an onion in two with a long knife. "Just don't worry about my landlady. I can always kick her down the stairs if she makes any trouble. I've been yearning to do it for some time anyhow."

Marjorie came to him and took from his hands the knife and the piece of onion he was peeling. "Look, if there's going to be any unpleasantness, it's absolutely ridiculous for us to stay here. It's the simplest thing in the world for us to go out."

"Darling, don't worry, I'm not exposing a frail flower like you to a Parisian squabble. It's perfectly all right, she's going out for dinner. That was her on the phone." He gulped the rest of his drink, and took back the knife and the onion. "Don't get those pale hands I love all onion-smelling. What made me mad was that she was supposed to come home and bring a guest for dinner, a novelist, a little creep from Marseille who just won some prize or other. I spent two hours shopping, and then she calmly tells me she's eating out with him. Not that I give a damn, you understand. I just get a little bored with this last-minute stuff. Especially from her. She's so bloody unfeminine she can't butter a piece of toast for herself. For all she knows, I could have an elaborate dinner for three on the stove right now. If you hadn't turned up that's exactly what would have happened. It's just too boring."

He was deftly dismembering the chicken, using his crooked arm to hold it while he plied the knife with the other. Marjorie said after a silence, "She's not just your landlady, I gather."

He glanced at her and laughed, one corner of his mouth pulled down. "I've never kidded you, have I? That's why I wish to God you'd come a week later. I'm fed up to the teeth with Gerda Oberman, and if it's any comfort to you I haven't laid a hand on her in six or seven weeks. That's at the bottom of all this feeble baiting, of course, but a fat lot of good it will do her. I couldn't care less what Gertie says, thinks, or does. She could have an affair with a leprous Chinaman at high noon in the middle of the Place de la Concorde. I'd just stand by and cheer. This time next week I'll be out of here, bag and baggage. The fact is, I've been thinking of going to the Mozart myself. Wouldn't that be cosy, dear?—Christ, get that disapproving look off your face, Gerda has simply been a convenience. The fact is she actually started out as my landlady. It couldn't have been more platonic. I was to have the living room to myself and one bedroom. I was paying her, and paying a damn good rent, too. But of course all she ever had in mind when she offered the place to me was my fair white body, that soon became obvious. What do you do when you're behind on your rent and broke, and your landlady comes creeping into your room making fond little noises? Believe me, I've kept it as antiseptic as possible, Margie, I've been dry, distant, cold, you can't imagine how cold I've been. That's actually why I've been doing the cooking. From my viewpoint I'm more than contributing my share to the ménage and I can be as distant with her as I damn please. What's the difference whether the man owns the apartment and the woman cooks or the other way around? It's all convention. I happen to be a mighty good cook and I enjoy doing it, and from my viewpoint I'm completely independent here. Gertie's put on twenty pounds from my cooking. Not that that's been so good for her, she's a Big Bertha to start with, but it does show that she's been getting value for her two ratty rooms. I don't think she's eaten so well since she was born. Do have another drink."

"I don't want another drink, thank you," Marjorie said. "Is she a German?"

"Gertie? Can't you tell that from the picture?"

"Doesn't that make you feel queer, Noel?"

"What?"

"Being with a German woman."

He was dropping the legs and bony fragments of the chicken into a pan. He paused, a blood-streaked leg in his hand, looking at her. "Why should it?"

"Well, I mean, nowadays—with the Nazis and all——"

"Why, Gerda's no Nazi. She's just a smart businesswoman, as a matter of fact I think she's got French citizenship or is going to get it. She knows I'm Jewish. She doesn't object to me at all, that's very plain."

"I just thought you might object to her."

He looked at her quizzically. "That sounds a bit like Mike Eden."

"Does it?"

"Yes, indeed. Since when are you so internationally minded, baby? I'm not solving the problems of civilization in my private life, thank you. Gerda's just an individual, and I'm just an individual, so . . . Gad, look at that stony face. Mike's been at you all right. Bless you, darling, don't you know that Mike Eden's completely rabid on that subject? He's Dr. Goebbels turned inside out, nothing more or less. I can't understand him, he's not even a Jew. I told him he ought to see a psychiatrist. I've never encountered such pathological hatred. He's a three-dollar bill, that man. Well-read and sharp and all that, but there's something dead, something icy about him, isn't there? How well did you get to know him?"

"Well, a shipboard acquaintance, that's all."

"Where is he now? Where was he going?"

"I don't know. Germany, I think."

"Well, I can tell you a hell of a lot about Mike Eden. I drove all over Europe with that guy. That's when you really get to know a person, not when you're lapped in luxury on the *Queen Mary*. However——" He paused in sprinkling a splintery dry herb on the yellow poultry pieces. "See? Rosemary. Madness to put it on a chicken, some say, but not the way I surround and neutralize it. It's an Airman secret. Rosemary, you know, is an emblem of constancy. I think it very much belongs in this little reunion dinner, don't you? Not for me, but for you. I'm more moved than I can say, Margie, at your turning up. Somehow I always thought you would, too. I only wish—— Well, hell." He jerkily shook other spices on the dismembered fowl, black, red, brown. "I seem to be running on like a phonograph, when what I really want is to hear all about you. Covering my embarrassment, no doubt. Do I really look too horrible, Margie? Bald dried-out leathery bag of bones?"

"Nonsense. You look quite all right, Noel, it's just—well, it's obvious that you've been sick. What on earth were you doing in Casablanca?"

"Oh, that's another story, and a real tedious one. Hell with it. I need only tell you I was abandoned like a dying dog by some gay companions as soon as I took sick, or the illness would never have gotten so out of hand—I've about had my fill of the carefree charming romantic people that float around Europe, Marjorie, these Noel Coward and Hemingway characters. They're all selfish boors at bottom. Perpetual children, life's got to go on being all champagne and sunshine and oh so jolly madness, and as soon as any cloud comes up, any faint suggestion of responsibility or disagreeableness, they're off in a cloud of dust, and you can rot for all they care—— Where the devil is that copper pan?" He crouched at a low cupboard, banging pots and pans around. "I suppose I've been one of them myself in my time but believe me that phase is over, and thank God for that. I've changed, Margie, you'll soon realize how much I've changed. I've been thinking an awful lot about you lately. That bastardly letter I wrote—the way I decamped—pretty awful—but it had to be, sweetheart. I'd have been false to myself if I'd acted any other way. I had to have my last rebellion, I had to run off to Paris and get my bellyful. Now I've had it, all right. I really have."

"That's good."

"I couldn't be more serious, Marge. This whole year has been therapeutic for me, decisively so. I'm not even sorry, really, about my illness in Casablanca, though when I took my first look in a mirror after I got up out of bed I wanted to cut my throat. But it did me good to have such a scare. Believe me, I did plenty of thinking in those starch baths between delirious spells—mainly about you, Marjorie—and that thinking has stayed with me. It's not a case of the devil was sick, the devil a monk would be." He was browning the chicken pieces in a saucepan. He stirred them here and there, crackling and sizzling. "Smells good, eh?"

"Marvelous."

"This is nothing. Wait—the fact is, I moved into this apartment with the best of intentions. I've been doing masses of work, I really have. I bitterly resented Gerda Oberman's crawling into my life at this particular point. If I'd had a little more character I'd have left instantly, I guess, but building up moral purpose is a slow process, Marjorie. Anyway, Gerda is and has always been so meaningless to me as a woman that it hardly seemed to count. And, unfortunately, moral purpose doesn't go too well with being stone broke, so———"

"What kind of work have you been doing, Noel?"

"No, ma'am, I'm not going to say another word about myself until I hear some more about you. Christ, you must think I've become a total egomaniac, whereas the very reverse is the case—— There." He took the sizzling saucepan off the burner, and carefully poured red wine over the chicken. "Everything's set, for the time being. Let's let it simmer and go inside for a while, shall we? This is a goddamn telephone booth—— *Please* take another drink."

"All right, just don't make it half scotch and half water. You don't have to get me drunk, you know."

He threw back his head and laughed. "Alcohol's a great softener of ugly lines and sharp edges, that's all——"

"Noel, if you think I'm terribly shocked or put out you're really mistaken. I know you so well. And I'm getting to be rather an old lady——"

"Don't fish, sweetheart. You know you still look seventeen."

"Yes? Well, I've been plucking gray hairs lately, all the same."

"Shut up! What does that make me? I'll throw myself out of the window in a minute. Come on, here's your drink. What's been happening to you for a year besides sprouting premature gray hairs? What happened to Guy Flamm's play?" He took off the apron and his tie. "Whew. Hot. I'll get formal again for dinner, okay? Come in the living room."

She told him the story of the past year, describing her sufferings frankly, without dwelling on them. He was amused by the Flamm fiasco, gloomy and troubled by her account of her illnesses and long despair. He slouched lower and lower in the green armchair. He said at one point, "You're making me feel like an absolute hound. If it'll cheer you up any let me assure you I've been punished. More than punished. I've never passed a filthier year myself, it's been my Gethsemane——"

"Darling, I'm not trying to make you feel bad. You asked me to tell you all this."

"That's right. Go on. I want to know everything, it's important that I know."

When she stopped talking he sat slouched for several minutes, silent, his face drawn under the rosy tan. In his shirtsleeves he looked thinner and frailer than before. He sighed, got up and walked to the piano, and sat rippling chords. "We've really given each other hell, haven't we, Marjorie?"

"Yes, we have, Noel."

"However, there have been wonderful times, too."

"Yes, that's so."

He played a tune she hadn't heard before, a wistful tinkling ballad. "Like it?"

"Something new? I do like it."

"Ferdie Platt is nuts about it. I wrote it one night thinking about you, to tell you the truth. He thinks it can be another *Stormy Weather*. He doesn't like my lyric. He's writing a new one."

"Is he here?"

"No, he's in Hollywood. I mailed the lead sheet to him with a batch of other stuff a month or so ago, just for the hell of it——"

"Is that the work you've been doing? Songwriting?"

He caught the note of disappointment. "Not at all. I've just filled idle moments that way." He came and sat beside her on the sofa, taking her hand. "You worked for a year, saving, scrimping, just to track me down, and make me make an honest woman of you."

"Something like that, yes."

He was silent for a moment. He shook his head. "You're wonderful, really you are. You're a sweet breath of fresh air from the United States. You make me feel homesick as hell." They looked straight into each other's eyes. "However, let's not kick around such heavy issues before dinner, eh? What are your plans? How long are you going to be over here?"

"I don't know yet."

"Have you been to Venice?"

"No."

"Don't miss Venice. Maybe we'll go down together."

"Haven't you just come back from there?"

"What's the difference? I love it, I never tire of it. Would you like that?"

"How is it you went to Venice if you're so broke, Noel?"

"Oh, that." He walked to a cigarette box, lit one, and slumped in the green chair again, almost directly under the hideous blue and orange chandelier. "You may as well know all. Ferdie got so steamed up over that song, and a couple of others, that he sent me some money to come home with. We were supposed to meet in New York and work for a solid six weeks, and then I'd come back to Paris. That was the idea, and I fully intended to do it. I still do, for that matter. But—well, it's all hopelessly involved, but the gist of it is that two weeks ago I had a terrific row with Gertie, a real total blowup, over the same damn thing, money, she's a revolting miser, fights over butcher bills, et cetera—and just at that point Ferdie's money arrived, and simultaneously Bob and Elaine blew into town from Florence, the same pair that abandoned me in Casablanca, with Mildred Wills. I wrote you about Mildred. She's the divorcee from Cleveland with all the money—— Well, the long and short of it is, if I have one weakness it's that I'm a forgiving fool. They were all clamoring for a reconciliation, a lovely holiday in Venice, the four musketeers together again, and strictly because I'd had this brawl with Gerda and my nerves were so jangled I fell for it, as though I didn't know those three hysterical nitwits through and through by now. It was a lapse, but my last one, I swear. There had to be a last one. They really nailed the lid down on the coffin of my gilded youth, those three. We went to a garden party, and Bob came on Elaine out in the bushes with some slimy Argentinian, her dress half off, and he broke a plaster statue over the man's head and beat Elaine to a bloody pulp, and she did a pretty good job of marking him up in the meantime, smashing him in the face with her shoe——"

"Good God!" Involuntarily Marjorie screwed up her face.

"That's not the half of it. Oh, they're the salt of the earth, these people. Mildred Wills packed up and left in the middle of all this, and I was left to pick up the pieces. Bob and Elaine were without a cent, what's more. Mildred was supposed to be paying for them. It cost me over two hundred dollars with fines and breakage and doctor bills and all before we were through. Lovely, what? The one thing I take pride in is the fact that I never let it interfere with my plans, just went right on having my fun and in fact got a lot of work done evenings, too.—Are you thoroughly disgusted? I hope so. I am myself. It does me good to feel your disgust."

"Well, Noel, you know how I've always felt about such people—just a bourgeois——"

"Yes, well that can be overdone too, darling. I'm far from admitting even now that the only way to live is the way good citizens do on Central Park West. There's a golden mean you have to look for. But as I say, I couldn't be more through than I am with the too-too-mad set. You're dead right about them and always have been, in your sublimely simplified way——" He glanced at his watch. "Hungry? It's horribly early for dinner in Paris, but if you've been travelling——"

"I've been hungry ever since you first started browning that chicken under my nose."

He laughed and jumped up. "That was an hour ago. Why didn't you say something? I'd have hurried it. Can you be trusted to make a salad according to rigid specifications? I'll do the rest."

Marjorie had eaten dinner several times in Noel's Greenwich Village apartment. He had been a competent slap-dash cook in those days, with a couple of specialties like spaghetti and southern fried chicken, dished up any old way. But all that was changed. With this dinner there were candles, wine cooling in a bucket of chopped-up ice, a chafing dish at the table; he even found some flowers in Gerda's bedroom and made a centerpiece of roses and ferns in a shallow green bowl. He was quick and disconcertingly smooth at serving and removing the dishes. For a while the effect on Marjorie was probably the opposite of what he intended; she became stiff and self-conscious, for Noel made a distinctly odd figure, scrambling into the kitchen, serving the food, and then sitting at his place and relaxing into the suave bon vivant dining by candlelight. The first course was shrimps in an exquisite brown mustardish sauce which she had never tasted before. He claimed he had invented it. There were hot rolls, and a thick spicy soup. The chicken in wine was extraordinary —rich, almost creamy, the flesh and the tender skin coming off the bones at a touch of the fork, the taste of the fowl delicately dominant over the tart suggestion of burgundy—she had eaten nothing better in her travels. By that time Marjorie had drunk quite a lot of wine, and she was beginning to enjoy herself in a constrained way. She said, "Well, I don't know what's come over you, Noel. I can only say you'll make some lucky girl a fine husband."

He laughed, his eyes lighting with pleasure. "Not bad, really, is it, the chicken? Have a little more of the Montrachet."

"Thanks—why, it's all amazing, everything you've served. I can't imagine why you're bothering to impress me, but it's a virtuoso performance. I'd never dare try to cook for you after this."

"Well, I'm glad you're enjoying it. I'll tell you something, cooking can be a real creative art. I've just taken to it seriously in the past few months. Since Casablanca. I can't say why, exactly— Have you ever read *Jennifer Lorn*? There's a touching part in it about a young prince who is simply a cook at heart, and has an awful time getting to express his artistic yearnings. I'm not that gone on it, it'll never be more than a hobby, but I must say I get tremendous satisfaction out of it. What if the art you create gets demolished and consumed a few minutes after it's done? Does that take away from its merit? I'd give any poet a hell of an argument who claimed he'd contributed more to human happiness than a truly artistic cook."

"This isn't the work you say you've been doing, is it, Noel?"

He leaned forward, lighting his cigarette from a candle, and then slouched back, grinning. "I should hope not. This, by the way, is an American barbarism I have no intention of unlearning, smoking before the meal's over.—Despite all my peccadilloes, I've done pretty much what I told you I would in my letter, Margie. I've really dived into philosophy. What's more, I think I've come up with a pearl. You remember I've been saying for years I was going to read economics some day so I could argue with communists on their own ground—well, I've done it. And, I've come up with some astounding results. I've been through Marx and Engels, but of course that gets you nowhere, you have to backtrack through all the Britishers Marx was trying to refute, right back to old Adam Smith, and then you have to work forward to Keynes, and eventually you've got to branch off into general philosophy because economics is nothing but a splinter of the whole problem of human conduct in a material world—— You don't want to hear all this guff, do you?"

"On the contrary, there's nothing I'd rather hear."

"Well, let me get the coffee and the brandy—you'll have a bit of cheese, won't you? Sharp? Bland?"

"Whatever you have."

The cheese was a soft malodorous greenish stuff, almost liquid. Marjorie thought it was frightful. But Noel was so proud of it—evidently it was a rare and costly French treat—that she smeared a little on fragments of a hard biscuit and choked it down. The brandy, however, a strange clear yellow, slightly oily, had a wonderful taste. She drank several small glasses of it while he talked. Noel's coffee was excellent, as it always had been. He boasted that there were few places in Paris where one could get a comparable cup of American-style coffee. "That's another barbarism, the big cup, the light brew, but the Frogs can all go climb a tree with their thick thimbleful of syrup, I like American coffee and I always will—— Well, where was I? So far as arguing with communists is concerned, that turns out to be no problem at all. Marx has some damn cogent criticisms of nineteenth-century capitalism, especially the way it worked in England. But ever since oh, say the World War, he's been as dated as Ptolemy. Actually the whole labor theory of value turns out to be an abstraction, a tool, a sort of working fiction like the square root of minus one, and quite a limited tool, too. As for the modern party line, it's just a tangle of dogmatic bosh, and it has about as much to do with Marx as with Mark Twain. That's a trivial area of the whole problem, hardly worth bothering with. But the discovery I've made—and I really think it's my own, although there are hints and stumbles at it all through the literature—is something else. You know Marx claimed he had stood Hegel on his head. I think I've found the way to stand Marx on his head. If I'm not boring you insensible—I know this isn't in your line at all——"

"Well, so far I'm with you. This is unbelievable brandy, Noel." Marjorie was thinking that he was looking more and more attractive, as she became used to the slight changes in him. She was also thinking, not without a little secret amusement, that he had displayed this same kind of boyish enthusiasm over his Hits theory. His eyes were sparkling in the old way as he talked; and the nervous swift gestures, the toss of the head, the slouch with one arm over the back of the chair, the occasional run of a knuckle over his smooth-shaven upper lip, were all good to see, exciting and rich with memories, some painful, some sweet, all terribly vivid.

"Well, actually," Noel said, "like all massive ideas, this one must be demonstrated and documented in about eight fat volumes, but it can be stated in a line or two. Marx's big contribution remains the criticism of religion, morality, and philosophy as mere products of—and excuses for —economic practices. It's a truth, a brilliant comment, not a doubt of it. Its effect has been devastating. But what I've discovered is that if you dig deep enough the whole picture swivels around. It turns out in the end—this is my original insight, and I may have to devote the rest of my life to proving it, but I know I can—it turns out in the end that all economic practices *are really produced by the religious beliefs of a society* —and that all of economics, all the central questions—money, rent, labor, everything—are part of applied theology. That's what I mean by standing Marx on his head." He stopped and peered at her, both hands resting on the edge of the table. "I don't expect this to sound to you like anything but academic rubbish——"

So strongly reminded of the Hits theory that she could barely refrain from smiling, she said, "No, I follow it, but really, Noel dear, you've taken a tremendous order on yourself——"

"Tremendous? It's earth-shaking," Noel said, and the flames of the candles made glittering little yellow points in his eyes. "How about this brandy? Isn't it something? Have some more, you've hardly touched it."

"What? I'm all but fried right now, Noel—— No, not that much, please, just half a glass——"

"Oh, come on, you may never taste the like again. The Frogs, bless them, just about faint when an American buys a bottle of it—it's like selling a painting out of the Louvre. It has no fancy label, you see, no cobwebs, nothing, there's a national conspiracy to keep it from foreigners —the man who sold me this bottle was pale and trembling. He probably got ten years in the Bastille. Poor fellow, I see him now, scrabbling at the stones with his nails. . . ." He imitated a demented prisoner.

Marjorie laughed extravagantly. "Lord, you and your nonsense. It's good brandy, that's all—— Noel, have you really done all that reading? I should think it would have to take years."

"Of course it will. I've just scratched the surface. I got this idea, actually, when I was only half through *Das Kapital*. It was so electrifying that I just skimmed the rest and fairly raced through the main things of Engels. . . . A much better writer, by the bye, and a clearer thinker. It's a historic paradox, an injustice rather, that the whole thing got to be known as Marxism. I'm a great believer in the power of theatrical effect on historical events, you know. So was Napoleon, so is every other hard thinker—and I'm convinced that if Engels had had an equally long and bushy beard it would all be known today as Engelsism—but that's a side issue—as for the——"

Marjorie was choking with laughter. Noel said, "What now? What's the matter with you?"

"E-Engelsism . . . It just sounds so funny. Honestly, Noel! Engelsism . . . Ha ha ha——"

Noel grunted, his face solemn, his invariable way when one of his jokes was successful. "Gad. You've always been my best audience. But on that point I'm almost half serious. Anyway, this is leading to something important, so stop hee-hawing. The fact is, I've scanned the whole field in abridgments, encyclopedias, summaries, and so forth, enough to convince myself that in main outline this idea is absolute solid rock and absolutely original. But of course such an approach will never do, it's criminally superficial. I've got to resign myself to about four years of solid reading, and another four years of solid writing. Actually, allowing for delays, blind alleys, accidents, misfortunes, and so forth, I figure this to be a ten-year undertaking. But it'll be a labor of love. The years will speed by like days. The only question is how I live in the meantime. The songwriting's too sporadic, and anyway, to be perfectly honest, I'm losing my zest for it. There must be something thin about my talent or I'd have made it by now—I'm thirty-three, after all—what I have to solve is how I live from age thirty-three to age forty-three. Well, I've solved that, too. . . . I'm going to have more brandy, if you're not. Let's go into the living room. These chairs are too hard for long sitting."

"Don't you want to clear the table and do the dishes first?"

"Oh, don't be so damned domestic. I'm in the middle of something important here."

"It won't take but a minute—suppose she comes home? Come on, you can talk while we clean up."

"I can't do anything while I wash dishes except curse the day I was born, and as for Gertie——"

But Marjorie was already on her feet, clattering the dishes together, feeling the brandy from her head to her toes. "Shut up, Noel, and let's clear the table. I won't be able to sit still otherwise——"

Grumbling, he complied. But once the dishes were piled in the sink, he wouldn't wash them. "I'll be goddamned if I'll be pushed around any longer by you in my own household. Wait till we're married. Come along now, and quietly." He dragged her by the hand out of the kitchen. "Here. You bring my brandy inside. I'll take the candles. Sure you won't have another little glass?"

"Not a single drop, if you want me to follow your brilliant discourse."

The two candles burned low and blue as he carried the sticks into the living room. When he set them up on the piano they flared yellow again. A dim pleasant light diffused through the big room. Noel sat on the piano stool, absently rippling chords with his left hand, and Marjorie leaned on the piano beside him. Reflections of the two flames burned clearly in the black polished top of the piano. Noel glanced up at Marjorie, and his left hand picked out the notes of the *South Wind Waltz*. "Remembrance of things past, eh? You and me and a piano——"

"Yes indeed."

"Well, let's not get sentimental here. We have some serious talking to do. You didn't cross the ocean for a wallow in nostalgia. I'm not interested either. To hell with the past, I've very little use for it." He closed the lid over the keys with a dry hollow thud. "Pandora's box is shut."

"Good."

"Now then, pay close attention, because a lot is going to hang on how you feel about this." He lounged with an elbow on the piano top, looking up at her earnestly. In the candlelight he seemed very much the godlike man she had first seen at South Wind so long, long ago. "I told you I've been thinking of you a lot lately. That's a gross understatement. So help me, I've thought of hardly anything else since I got back from Biarritz. Somehow that business with Bob and Elaine really spelled finis for me —finis to Paris, to Gerda, to Europe, to bumming around, yes, even to making fun of the bourgeoisie. Darling, if I've written you one letter I've written you nine, and then torn them up, because they were too mushy and ridiculous. I think there's a half-finished one in my bedroom right now. But sweetheart, this is so much easier and better. I'm so everlastingly grateful to you for showing up. I'm ready to quit, Marjorie. That should be good news to you. All I want to be is a dull bourgeois. I've finally and irrevocably realized that nothing a man can do can make him stay twenty-two forever. But more important than that, and this is what's decisive, I've decided that twenty-two gets to be a disgustingly boring age after a while. Staying up till all hours, sleeping around, guzzling champagne, being oh so crazy, oh so gay, is a damned damned damned damned BORE." He struck the piano with the flat of his hand. "Being a shipping clerk in Macy's can't be half so boring in the long run because at least you're doing something. These perpetual twenty-twos—and I frankly admit I've been one all too long—do absolutely nothing, they're poisoned mice, that's all, running frantically in circles till they drop dead. My plans are simple. I want to go home. I want to get some dull reliable job in some dull reliable advertising agency, and I want to drudge like a Boy Scout, nine to five, five days a week, fifty weeks a year with two weeks off in August, and slowly rise to be an under-under-under vice-president. I'm more than prepared to take all the guff and endure all the tastelessness and boredom. This time there'll be no faltering, no nerve crises, because I've got real motives, see, motives that will endure, not a mere sophomoric urge to show I can play the game if I choose."

"What motives, Noel?" Marjorie said, softly and affectionately. The brandy had mounted to her brain, a pleasant amber fog.

"Two, really. First, you. Second, my writing. I must write this book, and I know I never will till I'm settled and happy and in a routine, and that means with you. You're the only one who fits in that picture, who ever has fitted. So—in short, that's the story. That's where I stand now. And I've been thinking of you so much because—well, because I love you, and because you, of all the people I've ever known, are most likely to understand and approve. To tell it to Gerda, or Bob, or even Ferdie, would be hopeless, you know."

"Of course it would," Marjorie said.

"Well, *do* you approve?"

Not knowing quite what to say, and feeling she didn't exactly have her wits about her, Marjorie said, "I've always said you could do anything you put your mind to, Noel. If you're serious, why——"

"I've never been half so serious." He took her hand, which was resting lightly on the piano top. "And you? What are your plans?"

"At this point I don't quite know."

"You want to be made an honest woman of, I gather. Correct?"

"Well, I certainly came here with that in mind."

"And now?"

"My friend, you've fed me much too much brandy this evening, do you know that?"

He laughed. "There's only one question, really. Are you still in love with me, Margie? Has it survived all the hell I've given you? Everything depends on that."

"I think there's a little more than that involved, isn't there? Noel, you know what? I wish you'd play. I think I'd enjoy a short wallow in nostalgia, right this minute."

His eyes searched her face. He opened the piano. One of the candles sputtered and snapped, and then burnt clear again. He said, "Would you mind my being sort of abrupt?"

"Well, how can I stop you?"

"I have the strongest possible feeling that you've sort of fallen for Mike Eden."

Alarm, half pleasant, ran through Marjorie's body. "Now whatever makes you think that?"

"There's been something about you all evening—never forget, dear, that you're still dealing with the Masked Marvel. A girl merely has to speak a name in a certain tone, or look a certain way when she speaks it——" Marjorie said nothing. He was staring, his hands limp on the keys. "But it's utterly incredible. A man who isn't even Jewish—you——" Still she said nothing. "Well, this is a freak change-about worthy of me, not you. Darling, I can accept anything, and I hope you'll take what I say as being utterly without malice. If you don't know yourself, I know you, and I tell you that if you've got a case on Mike Eden it's strictly a shipboard dream, and the sooner you get over it the better. If you want to throw me over, fine, it's no more than I've been asking for all these years, to be sure. But Mike—lambie pie, aside from his not being Jewish, he's such an icebox of a man, so neurotic, such a snarling sourpuss, something's really warped him very badly, and——"

Marjorie said, "This is getting a bit tiresome, isn't it? Who said I was in love with Mike Eden? I can hardly presume to argue with the Masked Marvel, so I've just let you run on. But the fact is, I'm not in love with him, and I know how impossible it is just as well as you, maybe a wee bit better. That doesn't mean, however, that he wasn't attractive to me. The fact is, I found him very attractive, and if that offends your vanity I don't much care, dear."

The puzzled concerned look on Noel's face changed to his old grin, sardonic and pleasing to her as ever. In this moment, in this flash, she felt as though nothing had changed, after all. He ran a knuckle slowly across his lip. "Gad, well said! I would like to stand up and cheer. Margie, you've come a long way. You've quite grown up, that's perfectly obvious, and I've got trouble on my hands. That's wonderful. I've needed a real challenge for a hell of a long time. Now just let me ask this, and don't hit me with a candlestick, what on earth did you see in Mike? I know he's far from a fool, but such a sneering, supercilious fish, so damn glum, so destructive—and you, of all people, sweetness and light in person—— Now I liked Mike because he's read the books and can almost argue you to a standstill on any subject if he'll warm up—not that I'm aware he ever actually won an argument from me—but——"

"Well, I found him good company, that's all. I liked his sense of humor."

"Humor? Honey, are we talking about the same man? Mike never said anything funny in the three weeks I was with him—nervous, irritable, ye gods. . . . I never saw him so much as look at a girl, what's more. I was more than half convinced he had a screw loose in that department."

"Well, you're quite wrong there."

"Obviously." He peered at her. "You know what he does, don't you?"

"Sort of a salesman, I gathered."

"No, a buyer. He buys drugs. He practically makes his living dealing with Germans, and yet he's got this foul hatred of them——"

"Noel, if it's all the same to you, can we drop the subject of Mike Eden?"

"Sure. There's a hell of a lot any girl ought to know about him who got really interested—not too pleasant things—but as long as you——"

"If you mean he uses drugs, I know that."

After a long pause Noel said, "You have changed, Margie. Quite radically."

"Well, maybe. I don't think so. I'm just getting on, Noel. Play, dear, play some of the old songs."

He began to play.

Chapter 46. THE SOUTH WIND WALTZ: REPRISE

Summertime has passed,
This night is our last,
Listen! It's the South Wind Waltz.
Once before we part,
Heart to loving heart.
Come, we'll dance the South Wind Waltz.
Time may change us, estrange us . . .

The turning on of the light came like a blow. He had been playing for fifteen minutes or more. Marjorie, softened and pleased, was singing with him. Neither of them heard the door open. One moment they were side by side on the piano stool, swaying and singing by the light of the waning candles. The next instant they both stood, surprised and blinking, in the hideous glare from the blue and orange chandelier.

Gerda Oberman stood in the doorway, one hand still on the light switch. Beside her stood a fat little fellow in an unpressed gray suit, seeming hardly more than a boy, but with a puffy debauched white face. "Mais alors, Noel, qu'est-ce que c'est, cette bêtise?" She strode to the candles, snuffed them out with two pinches of a wetted finger and thumb, then stared at the piano top and scratched angrily at a little blob of spattered wax, abusing Noel in rapid French. He winked behind her back at Marjorie. When Gerda paused for breath, he touched her shoulder, murmuring a French phrase. She looked up, and he introduced her in English to Marjorie.

"How do you do?" she said. She shook Marjorie's hand with a sudden change to brisk friendliness, a charming smile on her plump face. She had thick yellow braids piled on her head, and her jaw was powerful and square. Under her black fur-collared coat she wore an untidy bright green silk dress. "You speak French, maybe? I speak English pretty lousy." She introduced the fat young man, who said nothing but gave everyone a crinkly smile, shuffling his feet, his hands behind his back. She had another short exchange in French with Noel, this time pleasant and even a bit roguish, with a tap of a finger on his nose. She smiled and nodded at Marjorie, and took the little novelist off to the back of the apartment.

When Marjorie heard the door close, she said, "She's not such a dragon, really."

"Oh, listen, I've put up with her for months, after all. The fact is, she can be very warm and gemütlich, she's got a lot of the good German traits and as you see she's far from the jealous type——" He slouched on the piano stool again. "That was a horrible moment, all the same, when she snapped the light on. So typical too—bull in the china shop —boom, crash, I'm here, folks——"

"It's that chandelier," Marjorie said. "Why do you have such bright bulbs in it? They must be two hundred watts apiece."

"Isn't it ridiculous?" Noel said. "And she's really a superb photographer, you know, her lighting effects are very subtle—but nothing will do for her in here but a flat glare, like an operating room. And look at this dowdy furniture. She's got plenty of money, believe me she knows better. Still——" He shrugged. "You have to take people as they come." He ran his hands up and down the keyboard. "Well, where were we?" He drifted into the love song from *Princess Jones,* and grinned up at her. "Remember?"

She nodded. "I still say it's a pretty song."

"So do I. You know, I couldn't bear to play anything from that score for the longest time. Now it doesn't matter a bit. There's such a thing as mental scar tissue."

He played several of the songs. Gerda Oberman went through to the kitchen and came back a little later with two highballs, smiling at Marjorie in passing both times. Noel hammered a dissonance with both hands and slammed the piano shut. "This won't work at all, with Gerda gallivanting around—it's like trying to carry on a conversation with a dead body in the next room. Money . . . damn, if I only had a couple of hundred francs—I haven't been in the mood to do Montmartre for ages, but I sure am tonight—— Shucks, Marjorie, we're old pals, you can spare a couple of hundred francs, can't you? I can stretch a franc to ten times what it's worth to a tourist in those boites—you ought to see Montmartre once. Let's get out of this trap, shall we?"

"Anything you say, Noel."

She was putting on her hat at a mirror by the door when she heard yammering in French in the bedroom hallway. Noel appeared in his camel's hair coat, followed by Gerda, both shouting and gesticulating. The little novelist sidled in, and stood smirking against the wall. Marjorie saw him scrawl a furtive line in a dirty pocket notebook.

Noel, with a sharp final snap in French, walked to the door and opened it. "Come on, Margie, she's getting too dull for words——"

Gerda Oberman's voice became shriller as she gabbled on, shaking her finger at Noel. He was taken aback; he answered less sharply. She shrilled some more. He shrugged wearily, took Marjorie by the arm, and walked out, shutting the door on Gerda's angry talking face.

"What on earth——?" Marjorie said, as he led her down the dark stairs.

"Oh, the frantic cow wanted me to do the dishes before I left. Of all the left-footed, bullheaded, grim bores, Gerda is the queen."

"We should have done them. It wouldn't have taken two minutes——"

"Oh, shut up, Marjorie. You, too?" He hailed a cab, rapped out a direction to the driver, and sulked in a corner of the taxi, smoking.

It took the cab less than five minutes to get to the Mozart Hotel. Marjorie went up to her room, unlocked her steamer trunk, took out some French currency, and hurried back to the waiting cab. She offered Noel a fold of five hundred francs. He took it readily, with a mischievous grin. "Well, lambie, at long last you've joined the V.O.N. club. Congratulations."

"V.O.N.?"

"Victims of Noel. However, this doesn't really qualify you, as I'm going to pay you back first thing Monday. I have a check coming from Ascap."

"No hurry. It's only fifteen dollars or so, isn't it? This crazy money confuses me. Will it be enough?"

"I think so. If not I'll holler for more, never fear."

The money in his pocket affected him like a transfusion. The sulky look quite vanished, his eyes brightened, even his color seemed to improve. He chattered happily about the shops and restaurants they drove past, and he made outrageous jokes about Gerda and the young novelist. Marjorie, falling into a trough of fatigue as the brandy wore off, was hard put to it to laugh. He said, "All the same, don't sell Gerda short. She'll butter up that little slug for a week or so, and the next time the publisher wants a picture of him, it'll be an Oberman picture.—Christ, look at this fog, will you? More like London than Paris. Well, we're getting there."

The taxi was whining steeply uphill on a cobbled gloomy street barely wide enough for one car. They began to pass one dingy dim-lit night club after another. The doors of most of them were open, and Marjorie could see customers—not very many, in any one of them—singing, drinking, and dancing. "In a way this is the best kind of weather for Montmartre," Noel said. "Toulouse-Lautrec weather, you might say."

Le Chat Gris, the first boite they went to, was a tiny hot room with raw cement walls, full of long wooden tables and benches which were jammed with shabbily dressed Frenchmen needing haircuts, and badly made-up girls; all drinking beer and joining loudly in songs led by a fat man with a concertina, in shirtsleeves and a beret. The place stank of beer. The smoke in the air brought tears to Marjorie's eyes. Several of the customers yelled greetings to Noel, and he answered in French, waving and grinning. "It's the best place to start, it's cheap and always lively and you sort of get in the mood." He knew the words of all the songs, and joined in merrily. They stayed at *Le Chat Gris* almost an hour.

After that they went to a number of places—six, nine—Marjorie lost count. They never stopped longer than half an hour at any one of them, and at the most dismal ones sometimes no more than ten minutes. "The effect is cumulative, let's move on," Noel would say. "Let's try *Le Diable Boiteux,* sometimes all hell breaks loose there." But all hell did not seem to be breaking loose anywhere in Montmartre that evening. In the dim light of the boites some of the customers did look sinister enough—scar-faced toughs in ragged caps and sweaters, paint-plastered blondes who could hardly be anything but trollops, and more than a few dwarfs, hunchbacks, and cripples with evil yellow faces—but for all that, there were also invariably some harmless-looking American couples in each place: some of the seedy variety, gaunt painters and writers with untidy beards and untidier girls, and some obvious tourists, fat bald men with glasses, wives clutching big purses and staring at the toughs. In the narrow, slippery cobblestone streets the people seemed to be mostly Americans, including knots of forlornly boisterous sailors, who tended to gather at the doors of the boites instead of going inside. "Doing" Montmartre involved a lot of walking, Marjorie found, most of it uphill. She began to get very tired. She was trying hard to enjoy herself. She tried to find color and excitement in the macabre decorations of the boites, the twisted gleaming streets, the guttering candles, the queer club names, the menacing customers, the mingled smells of alcohol, burning wax, perfume, human bodies, and drizzle. She kept reminding herself that this was the fabled world of F. Scott Fitzgerald and Ernest Hemingway. But she couldn't forget that she was becoming footsore, that the smoky air in the boites was making her cough, and that the foggy wet air in the streets was making her cough even more. Her feet felt wet. Her hat was getting soggy and limp, and the curl was coming out of her hair.

. . . Candles, black cats, dancing cows, harlequins, pirates, palm trees, white nudes, Negro nudes, South Sea nudes, coconuts, red lanterns, green lanterns, blue lanterns . . . it went on and on and on, an eternity of trudging and drinking and singing and smoking and more trudging . . .

Noel was having a whale of a time. The effect really was cumulative for him. He drank more and more, became gayer and gayer, threw his arms around the proprietors as he came into the boites, sprang to the piano sometimes and played, hugged waiters who greeted him by his first name, embraced the girl singers and bawled duets with them. He knew the special liquors that each boite featured. A wink and a whisper to the waiter, and out came the special bottle with the special ambrosia— a famous old wine, an unobtainable purple Turkish brandy, an incredibly rare liqueur made of wild strawberries and flavored with mushrooms, an obscure Bulgarian drink, murky brown, with grass floating in it—he was the connoisseur of connoisseurs. The more his eyes flashed, the wider his smile and the gayer his laugh became, the farther the gulf opened between himself and Marjorie, but he was unaware of it. "I daresay you're beginning to see what I like about this miserable old town. Let's face it, it's the top of the world, in its trivial pleasure-loving way. Even if we all must say goodbye to it one sad day, eh Margie?"

It was past two in the morning when they came to the summit of Montmartre, a cobblestone square surrounded by crazy old houses, each of which seemed to have a boite in the ground floor. Cabs were crawling in a jam on the square, backing, turning, honking, and there were a lot of laughing and singing drifters on the sidewalks. The drizzle had almost stopped. A half-moon shone weakly through rolling black clouds, making irregular blue patches on the wet stones. Noel stood with his hands on his hips, looking around the square. His hair was tumbled every which way; his eyes glittered. Marjorie had merely sipped all the marvelous liquors, but he had had plenty to drink. "Well now, the question is, how much pep have you left?" he said. "This can go on all night and then some. But I recognize that you're a neophyte, so——"

"Is there a good place to eat up here?" Marjorie said. "Some food might revive me. I'm dimming out, a bit."

"At least four, my love, one better than the next." He looked closely at her, laughed, and threw his arm around her shoulder. "I see. Well, I'll have pity on you. We'll do Les Amants Rieurs, that's all, and then home to the little brown bed. Fair enough? It won't even be three o'clock. That's high noon in Montmartre."

"Les Amants Rieurs," Marjorie said. "The laughing lovers, eh? Sounds good."

"Go to the head of the French class. The laughing lovers. Just the place, what?" He took her arm in his and they cut across the square. Marjorie turned her ankle on one of the wet cobblestones and almost fell; he caught her in both arms, guffawing. "Hey! Honey, have you had that much? I didn't think so."

"Don't laugh, it hurts like hell," Marjorie said, limping. She rubbed the ankle. "That's the one I turned years ago when I fell off a horse. It's been weak ever since. Damn, it really hurts."

He put his arm under her knees and picked her up, staggering a little. "Shall I carry you, my queen?"

"Put me down, you idiot! You're in no condition for chivalry—— That's better——"

He set her on her feet, puffing. "Have you gained weight?"

"Tons. Where's Les Amants Rieurs?"

She hesitated at the door, under the cut-out wooden sign of two laughing faces, a girl and a boy in berets. "Why, it looks perfectly awful," she said, peering inside. "There isn't a soul here."

"Probably not," Noel said. "No music, no apaches, nothing to attract the dopes. Just the best wine and steaks on the face of the earth. Practically nobody knows about it. If anyone is here in a dark corner, it's apt to be Gertrude Stein, or Marlene Dietrich, or the Duke and Duchess of Windsor. The proprietor pays the guidebooks *not* to mention the place. He's a wonderful man. Come on."

It was the darkest place Marjorie had been in yet; she could hardly see where she was going. There were perhaps half a dozen flickering candles at eye level around the black walls, nothing more. A chilly draft blew through the room, so that the flames barely clung to the wicks, and the candles were all melted down sideways. A waiter in a white apron came out of the gloom, an unusually tall, almost skeletal bent man with a drooping gray mustache. "Mais c'est Monsieur Airman," he said with a sad smile. "Ve no see you long time, monsieur. Monsieur Bertie vill be glad, yes sair." He led them to a table in the middle of the rear wall and lit two candles in smoky glass chimneys on the table. "I call Monsieur Bertie, monsieur?"

"All right, Marcel, and let's have a little cognac to warm us up, meantime."

"Justement, monsieur."

Her eyes a little more used to the gloom, Marjorie looked around at the disorderly empty chairs and tables. In the far corners were shadowy customers hunched over candles, three other couples in all. Noel pointed up at the wall beside them. "Can you make it out? Brillac did it. He committed suicide at nineteen. They say he'd have been another Picasso. Got full of absinthe and killed himself over a lousy little whore of a waitress."

In the overlapping curves of yellow light from the two chimneys she could see a cubistic pair of laughing lovers, with pustular green-and-yellow eyes, and toothy purple mouths twisted up near their ears. "Not very pretty."

"Not at all. Disturbing's the word," Noel said. "Of course that's the intention. Brilliant little bastard, he must have been——"

A hand fell on his shoulder. "Mon ami. Mon cher ami."

Noel covered the hand with his, looking up. "Bertie! Marjorie, Monsieur Bertie."

The proprietor looked like any other middle-aged Frenchman, roly-poly, shrewd, sadly ironic, mustached. "Mademoiselle Marjorie, how do you do, and welcome. Alors, mon ami—et Mam'selle Elaine? Et Monsieur Bob? Et Madame Mildred?"

Noel and Monsieur Bertie talked in French until the cognac came. There was much sighing, with eloquent shrugs and shakes of the head, by both.

"Well," said Monsieur Bertie, as they drank the cognac, which was very good, "Mam'selle is a little hungry, maybe? A little bifteck, Monsieur Noel?"

"Two biftecks, what else, Bertie? A little salad, the usual, Madame's dressing," Noel said. "Champagne meantime, yes? Is there any of the Dom Perignon '11 left? I guess not——"

"There is not, monsieur," Bertie said. His eyes twinkled. "But for you maybe a bottle turns up, maybe we overlooked a bottle, hm?" He put his hand on Noel's shoulder and said to Marjorie, "He is one of the true people. There are not many of the true people left." He went away, sighing.

Noel told her all about Monsieur Bertie. He had been a flier in the World War. He was a poet. Several of the great French actresses had been his mistress at one time or another. He was an intimate of cabinet ministers, and of the leading modern painters.

Then he stopped talking and just looked at her. He looked straight at her for a long time, with a meaningful little smile. He played affectionately with her fingers. He lit two cigarettes at a chimney and handed her one without asking whether she wanted it. He kept looking at her face, as though trying to assure himself that she was really there opposite him. The little smile, the narrow-eyed purposeful look, never left his face.

Marjorie, though thrilled by the look, was also disturbed and a bit panicky. She could hardly doubt what was coming and she was unsure of herself. After five years, at the end of the long, long road, she was still in a quandary about Noel Airman! She was stimulated, quite waked up, by the tightness of the moment; yet she also felt somewhat trapped, almost as she had at the Villa Marlene with George Drobes so many many years ago, in the instant before he had pulled out the two rings.

And now Noel's hand was going to his pocket! In a half-thrilled, half-alarmed instant she thought she was going to be confronted with a ring again; instead, he brought out an envelope, and passed it to her. "I think you ought to read this letter—if you can, in this sepulchral light."

The envelope bore the address of the J. Walter Thompson company. She took out the letter, held it awkwardly sideways so the candlelight fell directly on it, and read it, squinting. It was from Noel's former superior at the advertising agency:

Dear Noel:

If you're really serious about coming back, that's good news. We all understand your urge for one more year in Paris before bending your neck permanently to the harness. If not for our wives and kids, half of us here would do exactly the same thing, and we envy you.

Let me know when you're coming back to the States. I can't speak formally for the firm, of course. But I really think you can return to your job here when you're ready. Everyone feels you did top work while you were here. And if, as you say, a stable secure future is what you are really interested in now, this is the place for you, and this is what you ought to do. You have a genuine flair for writing advertising copy, as I told you many times, and the bigwigs are fond of you, which never hurts. I hope we'll hear from you soon.

She slipped the letter back in the envelope and handed it to Noel. He said, "How do you like them apples, sister?"

"This time you're serious, Noel, aren't you?"

"This time I'm serious. Yes indeed."

The waiter brought champagne, and served it with grave ceremony. When he was gone Noel held his glass up to the candlelight, and gently swirled the wine. "Well, this is the best champagne left in our disintegrating civilization. The one fit wine, I think, for the toast I'm about to make." He raised the glass. "It's come, my darling, it's really come, hasn't it? To Mr. and Mrs. Noel Airman. Long life, and every happiness."

He put the glass to his lips. Marjorie hesitated. Still holding her glass, smiling nervously, she said, "Who's the lucky woman, Noel?"

His grin was confident and lively. He set down his glass, reached across the table, and took her hand. "Fair enough. You'll teach me yet not to take you for granted! I haven't proposed, have I? Well, Marjorie, the lady in question is the lady I'm with—the only girl I've ever really loved, the girl I want from now on—the only girl who holds any interest for me, my darling—now, henceforth, and forever. Marjorie, will you marry me?"

For five years she had waited to hear those words spoken by this man. She had dreamed of them, daydreamed of them, prayed for them, despaired of them. Now they were spoken at last, in a dark Paris bistro, by the light of two smoky candles, with all the sincerity and earnestness of which Noel Airman was capable. The picture was complete. And now, and not a moment before, Marjorie knew beyond any possible doubt what the answer was.

She was a little scared. But she withdrew her hand with gentleness, and the words came clearly and calmly. "I hope you'll believe, Noel, that I wasn't being coy. On my word of honor, I had to hear you say it to be absolutely sure. The answer is no, Noel. I won't marry you. It's impossible. I'm terribly sorry."

The cab ride to the hotel was an ordeal of silence. He slumped all the way down in the seat, his thighs sticking bonily forward, his coat open and dragging. Once, with a faint echo of his usual sardonic gaiety, he roused himself and said, "An old English proverb keeps running through my head, do you know?

He who will not when he may,
When he will, he shall have nay."

Not knowing what to answer, she said nothing.

He got out first, and helped her alight. He held her hand, peering into her face by the dim light of the bulb over the hotel entrance. "You should have come a week later, Marjorie."

"It wouldn't have mattered, Noel, honestly."

"What are you doing tomorrow?"

"Leaving Paris."

"How? Plane, train?"

"I don't know."

"Where to?"

"I don't know yet."

"I'll see you off."

"No. Thank you, but don't."

"I'm not giving up, you know, Marjorie. I'm coming home after you."

"Don't, Noel, don't. That's all I can say. Don't. Good night."

He bent to kiss her mouth. She thought of turning her cheek to him, then she accepted the kiss on the mouth. He looked hard at her, his face rather angry. She returned the look steadily. His right arm came up, and he hugged his deformed elbow. The anger faded from his face. A faint bitter grin broke through, and he nodded. "Good night, Marjorie Morgenstern." He turned and got into the cab. His voice sounded jaunty, if anything, as he told the driver, "Quarante deux, Rue des Sts. Pères."

The fat desk clerk was slumped asleep in a chair in the lobby under a red light. Marjorie went up in the squealing cage to her room, undressed and tumbled into the high ancient brass bed, and slept like a child.

Chapter 47. THE MAN SHE MARRIED

When Marjorie finally did get married, it happened fast.

Not that she was expecting it, or looking for it, when it came to pass. Quite the contrary, she was in another time of dull despair, worse in a way than what had gone before, because there was no dream of recapturing Noel to brighten the future.

Yet she never regretted refusing Noel. Once that tooth was out, the hole rapidly healed. He sent her a lot of eloquent letters after she returned from Europe. Some she read, some she tore up without reading. She answered none, and after a month or so they stopped coming.

Mike Eden filled her thoughts during the homeward voyage, and for a long time afterward. She nurtured a hope that he would somehow turn up again, and she even took a volunteer job with a Jewish refugee-aid committee; partly influenced by all that Mike had told her, but partly in the selfish hope that she might pick up news of him. Months passed. The hope began to fade, and she kept on with the work for its own sake. Most of what she did was routine typing and mimeographing. Now and then she helped a family find a place to live, or guided girls to jobs. She didn't exactly enjoy the work, but the emptiness at her heart went unnoticed while she was doing it; and at night she slept, untroubled by the sense of exasperated futility that had broken her rest during her years of haunting Broadway and battling with Noel.

Once she bought a drug trade journal and wrote to some of the companies that advertised, inquiring after Mike Eden. He had been careful to withhold from her the name of the firm he worked for. She had no luck, and she gave up the attempt; there were hundreds of such companies. After four or five months—especially after Hitler invaded Poland, and the headlines and radio bulletins filled everyone's conversations and thoughts, and the refugee work grew tumultuous—her interest in Mike lost substance. She still daydreamed and worried about him, and wondered whether he was alive or dead. But he began to seem almost like someone she had heard or read about rather than actually known.

One Friday evening early in November, Seth came home from school in the blue and gold uniform of the Naval Reserve Officers' Training Corps. It was the first the family knew of his having joined. As if this were not shock enough for his sister and parents, he announced at the dinner table that he intended to become engaged to Natalie Fain, the Barnard freshman whom he had been dating regularly for a year. Seth was a few weeks short of being nineteen. Poland had already been crushed, and the queer lull called "the phony war" had ensued in Europe; there was hope that real fighting might never break out. All the same it chilled Marjorie to see her gangling baby brother in military garb, the pink pimply razor-nicked face ridiculously stern under the white cap with gold insignia. If fighting came, this child would have to fight! As for his becoming engaged, they would all have laughed at him, and Mrs. Morgenstern would perhaps have told him to go wipe his nose—if not for the uniform. It blasted grown masculinity at them; it would not be denied.

The Friday-evening dinner at the candlelit table was different from all the hundreds of Sabbath meals that this little family had eaten through the years. The stuffed fish was as tasty as ever, the chicken soup with noodles as boring as ever, the pot roast and potato pudding as fat and satisfying as ever. But time had struck a brazen gong in the Morgenstern home. The father, whose round face had lost many worry lines when Marjorie returned from Europe cured of Noel, kept glancing at his son, and the worry lines came back, with some new ones. Mrs. Morgenstern relieved the mournful silence with brave jokes about seasickness and child marriage; and she addressed Seth all evening as Admiral, but her face was far from merry. As for Marjorie, she was simply stricken dumb. She could hardly eat. A picture haunted her: Aunt Marjorie, her wan face without makeup, her graying hair pulled straight back in a bun, serving as baby sitter while Seth and Natalie in evening clothes went off to the opera; Aunt Marjorie, the querulous fat spinster in steel-rimmed glasses, reading "The Three Pigs" to a couple of pudgy children in yellow pajamas.

Next morning she telephoned Wally Wronken. He seemed extremely pleased to talk to her, and readily made a date to meet the following day at twelve-thirty in the lobby of the St. Moritz Hotel, where Wally now lived, and to have lunch at Rumpelmayer's.

Marjorie came five minutes early for the date, dressed exactly as she had been for her meeting with Noel in Paris. She was aware of this, and slightly bothered by it; but the black and pink outfit was the best she had, and there was no point in looking anything but her best. She sat in a lobby armchair and smoked a cigarette, swinging her ankle; uneasy, almost distraught, more than a little ashamed of herself. The admiring glances of men sitting near her or walking by gave her no satisfaction. She knew by now that she was reasonably good-looking, and that it didn't take much to win stares from men; neatly crossed legs in good stockings were enough.

She was uneasy because Wally had been, if anything, too pleasant, too smooth, too glad to hear from her, too willing to take her to lunch. She greatly feared she had heard condescension in his voice. He had, of course, every right to condescend. He was the success, the young man of twenty-three with a hit on Broadway; not a smash hit, true, nothing that presaged a major literary career, but still a comedy that was in the fourth month of its run. Wally had sent her a pair of matinee tickets; she had seen the play with Seth. There had been several empty seats in the house, and she had not particularly liked the play, but the audience had laughed and applauded solidly. It was a farce about the radio broadcasting business, full of echoes, she thought, of successful farces of the past ten years. Her objections to Wally's writing remained in general what they had been at South Wind. It was commercial, mechanical; he was too eager for success, too ready with cynical imitation. But she had to acknowledge his competence; cheap and slight though Wally's play might be, it was superior to Noel's *Princess Jones*, with its precious and pallid whimsey, which she had, in her lovesick blindness, mistaken for high wit. Wally's reach was at least proportioned to his grasp. Moreover, he had set out to break into Broadway as a writer, and he had done it, while her own dream of being Marjorie Morningstar had blown away like vapor. She had not found it hard to write him a note of warm congratulation. He had answered with warm thanks, and there things had rested between them until she had taken the initiative and telephoned him.

The clock over the hotel desk crept past twelve-thirty. Her uneasiness mounted. She was regretting the impulse that had led her to call him up; she had in fact been regretting it ever since she hung up the receiver, disagreeably suspecting him of condescending to her. What was she doing, really? Was she trying to change things between them at this late date and get him to marry her, now that he was a success? It was nothing so definite or so stupid. She wasn't at all sure how she would feel when she saw him. More than anything else, she wanted to be reassured that she was still attractive, and Wally had always done that for her during the racking years with Noel.

Her conscious intention had been to tell him about Seth, and about her own fears of being an old maid. She wanted to laugh with him over the nightmare picture of herself baby-sitting for Seth's offspring, and so get herself back into good humor. But Marjorie had come a long way in self-knowledge. She couldn't be blind to the fact that she also was vaguely hoping for something more to come of this lunch, if not with Wally, then with somebody else, somebody successful and interesting, somebody whom she might meet by starting to go around with Wally again. It was this not very admirable notion that lay at the root of her uneasiness, and that made her shame and humiliation increase with each passing minute after twelve-thirty.

Those minutes lengthened. She lit another cigarette, promising herself to leave when it was smoked out. Disordered miserable thoughts possessed her. As a drowning man is said to do, she saw years of her life tumble past her mind's eye. She saw herself in other hotel lobbies, in bars, in grills, in cars, in restaurants, in night clubs, with men—George Drobes, Sandy Goldstone, Wally Wronken, Noel Airman, Mike Eden, Morris Shapiro, and dozens of others who had come and gone more casually. It was a strange set of customs, she thought, that drove a girl to conduct the crucial scenes of her life outside her own home; usually in a public place, usually over highballs, usually when she was a little tight or quite tight. As girls went nowadays, she was probably respectable, even a bit prudish. Yet this had been her story.

It occurred to her too, as the cigarette went from white tube to gray ash, shrinking fast, that whatever subconscious hope she had of winning Wally was not only nonsensical but almost depraved. She had been Noel's mistress. She knew that Wally, Broadway-wise though he was, somehow had convinced himself that this was not so. He had said things to her that left no doubt in her mind what he believed. At the time she had seen no point in undeceiving him, so she had lied by omission, by saying nothing. Evidently he had found it necessary or pleasant to idolize her; she had felt herself under no obligation to disillusion him with uncomfortable confessions.

But how could she possibly marry him, or even take to dating him again, without telling him the truth? How much of a liar was she? And yet, how could she ever tell Wally Wronken that she had been Noel Airman's bed partner, after all? How could she face the moment that would follow the shattering of his picture of her—the one good girl in a world of chippies? The fact that he made free with chippies—it was obvious that he did—had nothing to do with it. He wasn't supposed to be pure; she was. It might not make sense, but that was exactly how things stood.

The butt had been growing warm in her fingers; now the glowing end stung her skin. She crushed the cigarette out and stood, brushing ash from her black skirt. It was eighteen minutes to one. She went to the house phone and called his room. The telephone rang and rang, but there was no answer. Her face became fiery. Obviously he had been polite to her on the phone and then had completely forgotten the date. He was a Broadway playwright, and she was an aging West End Avenue girl from his dead past, trying to clutch at a shred of his glamor. He probably thought of her as little more than an autograph hunter. She put the receiver down, walked out of the hotel, and dazedly got into a cab.

The cab had hardly turned the corner when Wally Wronken, dressed as for a birthday party, with a gardenia corsage in a box under his arm, came whirling through the revolving door, scanning the lobby anxiously. He walked up and down the lobby, he walked through Rumpelmayer's, he questioned the headwaiter and the bellboys in the lobby. He went up to his suite and called Marjorie's home, but she wasn't there. He ate a cheerless lunch by himself in his living room overlooking Central Park, where the trees were bright with the colors of autumn.

He telephoned her the next day to apologize, but she wasn't in. He telephoned her several times during the ensuing week. By the time he did get to talk to her it was too late—if it had ever not been too late. She was pleasant, distant, and preoccupied. She had met another man.

It was fifteen years before Marjorie found out what had delayed him.

There was a fitting irony, perhaps, in the fact that it was Marsha Michaelson who brought her together with this man; Marsha, at times her dearest friend, at times her worst enemy; Marsha, who had greased her descent into Noel's bed. She met him at a dinner party in Marsha's New Rochelle home, the evening after her aborted lunch date with Wally. A long time later she found out that Marsha had planned the dinner with the purpose of bringing them together. He was Michaelson's young law partner, the pleasant round-faced man who had cut off the noise of the berserk theremin at the wedding by pulling the plug out of the wall. She dimly recalled that he had almost made a date with her before Noel had spirited her away on that fatal night. Placed side by side at the table, they fell into conversation easily because they had met once before; and by the time the meal ended they were talking with rapid easy intimacy, all but oblivious to the rest of the party. She hoped he would ask to see her again. He did. He wanted to see her the next day. She knew that by the usual rules she should put him off for a week or so; instead she said yes with an eagerness that made her blush a little.

After the second date, she knew she wanted to marry him. The headlong torrent of her feelings scared her, but she couldn't help herself. It wasn't at all a blind urge to get herself married off at last. Since her return from Europe she had been meeting eligible men and having as many dates as she wanted; but none of them had waked her feelings. With this man, her heart had come to almost instantaneous hot life. There was something undignified, something not quite adult, she felt, about falling for someone new so soon and so hard; after all, the days of George Drobes were over, weren't they? But her own skepticism and disapproval made no difference whatever to her emotions. Nothing seemed to matter but the fact that she was falling in love.

He was far from perfect. He was a bit short, though athletically built, not quite a head taller than herself. His speech was slow, calm, and direct, with just a touch of quiet humor, in sharp contrast to the quick nervous wit and fantastic vocabulary of Noel, and the stinging insight and mordant eloquence of Mike Eden. Marjorie had been almost sure that in the end she would meet and marry another of these wild talkers, since the type seemed to be her weakness, but Milton's measured speech and deliberate thinking seemed to suit her well enough. The fact was, some of his ideas on politics and religion were decidedly old-fashioned—she might have said banal, describing somebody else who seemed less reliable, sound, and sure. He wanted, for instance, to have a traditionally religious home, and was obviously pleased to learn of Marjorie's family background. It was amazing how little all that concerned her, anyway. The one thing she couldn't understand—that she fiercely regretted—was that she had failed to warm to him the first time she had met him at Marsha's wedding.

After her third date she was in agony, because she was sure she had looked badly, and talked stupidly, and cooled his interest. After the fourth date—all four dates were in one week, Monday, Wednesday, Thursday, Saturday—she knew he was falling in love as hard and as fast as she was, and that he was going to propose.

He never did propose. They met early Sunday morning after that crucial Saturday-night date, and were together all day long and all evening, driving in his new gray Buick far out into New Jersey, supposedly to see the fall foliage. They did drive through marvelous vistas of red and yellow flame, but they didn't take much notice. They lunched and had dinner at roadside taverns; they parked for hours in the moonlight. By the time he brought her home, about half-past four in the morning, they were discussing the wedding date, and where they would live, and how they would break the news to their parents. Only when she found herself alone in her bedroom, staring dazed at her face in the mirror—the most familiar face in the world, looking like a stranger's to her, the makeup smeared, the hair in disorder, the eyes heavily shadowed but shining joyously—only then did she begin to realize what an upheaval had taken place in her life.

It didn't seem like an upheaval. Marrying him seemed natural and inevitable, part of the ordinary sequence of things, like graduating from college at the end of her senior year. Earlier in the week she had fought against this feeling, had tried to summon objections to marrying this stranger, had tried to maintain the modesty and reserve she knew she ought to have. But her old identity had all but melted in his presence. She felt like his wife before the week was out. It was an effort to keep up the pretense that she didn't feel that way. Her relief was overwhelming when, sometime during the drive in New Jersey, he told her that he hoped she wouldn't consider him presumptuous or crazy, but he couldn't help thinking of her as his wife. It was shortly after he made this confession, and she made a similar one, that they parked in a leafy side lane and kissed with enormous gusto and began to speak of their marriage as a thing settled.

They went rapidly past the mutual delight of finding out how much they loved each other, and talked about how many children they would like to have, and what their religious feelings were, and how much money he had to live on; all the time necking as a man and a woman do who have discovered each other, but with the necking secondary, part of the exchange of confidences as it were, rather than an attempt to get pleasure for the moment out of sex. About the ridiculous speed of it all, Marjorie felt that she ought to be ashamed and worried—but she couldn't summon shame or worry from any corner of her spirit. His touch, his kiss, his hands, his voice, were all familiar, sweet, and wonderful. He actually seemed part of her, in a way that Noel Airman, despite his hypnotic fascination, never had. Nor was she too surprised to find that a man so different from Noel could stir and please her. She had learned from the encounter with Mike Eden that there really was more than one man in the world—the piece of knowledge that more than anything else divides women from girls. As long as there were two, there could be three, or ten; it was a question of good luck or God's blessing when she would encounter the one with whom she could be happy.

She fell asleep that morning dreaming confusedly and deliciously of diamond rings and bridal dresses, as the windows turned gray in the dawn.

She woke a couple of hours later to an immediate and wretched problem: when and how should she tell him about Noel?

For she had not yet done so. No consideration in the world could have brought her to tell him, before she was sure he loved her and wanted to marry her. It might have been calculating and not quite honest to let his feelings flame up without telling him. She thought that perhaps it had been dishonest. But she didn't care. Her life was at stake. She knew she would have to tell him now, and the prospect made her sick, but she was ready to do it.

The question was whether it was right for her to reveal the engagement to her parents—right away, in the next ten minutes, at breakfast—instead of waiting until he knew about Noel. Quite possibly he might want to break off with her. Clearly he had assumed she was a virgin; it had never occurred to him to question the fact. Like Wally Wronken, he had fallen into the accursed way of regarding her as a goddess, instead of realizing that she was just another girl stumbling through life as best she could. Supposing now she told her parents, and forty-eight hours later would have to tell them that it was all off? How could she endure it?

Marjorie went and did the natural, perhaps the cowardly, probably the inevitable thing. She told her parents at breakfast. This was what she had agreed with him to do. He was going to tell his parents, and they were coming with him to the Morgenstern home in the afternoon. To stop the rolling event, she would have had to telephone him and tell him to hold off because she had a serious disclosure to make to him first. Quite simply, she hadn't the guts to do it. So she plunged ahead, hoping for the best. In the whirl of her parents' joy—for they knew him, approved of him violently, and had been holding their breaths during the stampeding week when what was happening became pretty plain—at the center of the whirl, she sat in a quiet shell of black fear.

He came, radiating pride, love, and masculine attraction, the bridegroom in his hour of power. His parents were—parents: a plump short gray woman, a spare tall gray man, both well spoken, well dressed, and at first quite stiff and cold, especially the mother. The Morgensterns, for their part, were cautious, faintly defensive, and at the same time assertively proud of their daughter. Tense and scared though she was, Marjorie was able to find amusement at the way the prospective in-laws, suddenly dumped together in a room, sized up each other with hackles raised. His mother kept remarking, not always relevantly, that he was her only child, that he owned his own new Buick convertible, and that she knew of no young lawyer half as successful as he was. These statements, sometimes coming abruptly out of nowhere, tended to stop the conversation dead. The atmosphere warmed slightly when Mrs. Morgenstern served tea and a marvelous apple strudel she had baked in a hurry that morning. Then it turned out that his father was the president of his Zionist chapter; and since her father was the president of *his* chapter, that helped a lot. The first real thaw came when it developed that the mothers had emigrated from neighboring provinces in Hungary. Shortly thereafter, when it appeared that both fathers admired President Roosevelt, and that both mothers couldn't stand the lady who was president of the Manhattan chapter of Hadassah, the ice was fairly broken. It was observed, and it was considered extremely remarkable, that Marjorie resembled her mother and that the bridegroom resembled *his* mother. His father, after the second piece of strudel, swung over to extreme joviality, and uncovered a gift for making puns and a taste for chain smoking. As the two sets of parents disclosed facts about themselves little by little, for all the world like bridge players playing out their cards, it became clear that at least in background it was a fairly balanced match. True, his father was a native-born American. Mr. Morgenstern's accent sounded loud and pungent that afternoon in Marjorie's ears. On the other hand, Marjorie soon gathered that his father had not been successful in business. He spoke vaguely of stocks and bonds, became respectful when Mr. Morgenstern described the Arnold Importing Company, and made no puns for a while afterward. Mrs. Morgenstern managed to say to Marjorie, when they were together in the kitchen for a moment, that she was sure the son was supporting the parents (as usual, Marjorie was very annoyed at her, and as usual, she turned out in the end to be quite right). She also remarked that she couldn't for the life of her see what right his mother had to be standoffish, inasmuch as West End Avenue wasn't at all the same above Ninety-sixth Street, and they lived on the corner of 103rd. However, Mrs. Morgenstern quickly added—when she saw the dangerous light in Marjorie's eye—that they were lovely people, and she couldn't be happier about the whole thing.

In time Mrs. Morgenstern brought out cherry brandy, and scotch, and the occasion became reasonably lively. The parents began debating whether this meeting constituted the religious occasion in the course of a courtship known as "T'nayim." Marjorie had never heard of T'nayim before. Her parents were emphatic and unanimous in declaring that this get-together certainly amounted to T'nayim. His mother was equally sure it was far too early for T'nayim, and that all kinds of other things had to be done first, though she was most foggy as to what those things might be. His father stayed out of the argument, contenting himself with seven cigarettes in a row and a number of unsuccessful puns on the word T'nayim. In the end Mrs. Morgenstern settled the matter, in her customary way, by going into the kitchen and coming out with a large soup plate from her best china set. She called the couple to the dining-room table, and told them to take hold of the plate and break it on the table.

They did so, looking puzzled at each other. The fragments flew all over the floor, and the parents embraced each other, shouting congratulations and weeping a bit. That, evidently, was T'nayim.

The parents were happily planning the wedding, the honeymoon, and the general future of the couple when the bridegroom-to-be announced that he was taking Marjorie out for a drive. This was a tremendous joke to the two fathers, who had by then drunk a lot of scotch between them. The winks, guffaws, and elbow-nudges were still going on when they left. At the last moment, just as Marjorie was preceding him out the door, her future mother-in-law sprang at her, fell on her neck, kissed her, said she loved her, and fell into a paroxysm of wild sobbing, which she declared was due to an excess of happiness. Mrs. Morgenstern firmly peeled her off Marjorie, and the couple left her being quieted by the other three parents.

They drove out to New Jersey again. The tavern where they had dined the night before, he said, had the best food and drinks in the whole world; didn't she agree? She agreed. She said little during the drive. He did all the talking. He drew perceptive amusing sketches of both her parents, and was especially shrewd about her mother. "She's going to give me trouble," he said, "but she's all there." He told her a lot about his own parents. He pressed her to name a date for the wedding, but she turned him off in one way and another. He talked about the places they could go to for a honeymoon trip despite the war: the Canadian Rockies, South America, Hawaii, Mexico. He had an odd notion that Alaska might be fun. He wanted to go as far from home as possible; he wanted to be alone with her, he said, somewhere on the outer rim of the world. All the time he talked she sank deeper into fear and misery, though she kept up a smiling face. It seemed impossible to break into this run of pure bubbling high spirits with the revelation about Noel. Yet she knew that she had to do it tonight. They drove across the George Washington Bridge in a gorgeous sunset. He became quiet and just drove, now and then reaching over and touching her face with his hand. He was a picture of a supremely happy man.

She had her rebellious moments during that sorrowful ride, behind the smiling face. This was the twentieth century, she told herself. He was an honor graduate of Harvard; he ought to know what life was all about! Obviously at thirty-one he himself wasn't a virgin. Most likely he hadn't been at her age, twenty-four. She hadn't claimed to be one. Inwardly she raged at the injustice of his assuming that she must measure up to the standards of dead Victorian days. Virginity was a trivial physical detail, meaningless between two people truly in love; anybody knew that, all the books said it. Her guilt over having had one affair was childish. Everybody had affairs nowadays, the world had changed. . . .

In all these reasonable thoughts, however, Marjorie could find no trace of relief or hope. The fact was, she had passed herself off as a good Jewish girl. Twentieth century or not, good Jewish girls were supposed to be virgins when they married. That was the corner she was in. That was the dull brute fact she faced. For that matter, good Christian girls were supposed to be virgins too; that was why brides wore white. She couldn't even blame her Jewish origin for the harrowing trap she was in, though she would have liked to.

They came to the tavern. They had one drink, and another. He wasn't talking much, just holding her hand, worshipping her, and once in a while saying something nonsensical and sweet. She had all the opportunity she needed to talk, but she couldn't.

Then, all at once, at the very worst moment, just after the food was set before them, the story somehow broke from her in a stammering rush of words; every word like vomit in her mouth.

That ended the evening. He remained cordial, but he was quenched. She had never seen such a change in a man's face; he went in a few minutes from happiness to sunken melancholy. Neither of them could eat. About her affair with Noel, he said never a word. It was as though she hadn't told him. When the food was taken away, he asked her correctly and pleasantly whether she wanted more coffee, or some brandy, or anything else. Then he drove her home, saying nothing at all on the way. She remembered that drive for years as the worst agony she ever endured. It was like being driven to a hospital, dying of a hemorrhage.

She telephoned him early next morning after a ghastly night. His mother answered, full of concern and excitement. He wasn't at home or at his office. He had gone off, leaving a short note saying he was very tired and was taking a vacation for a week or so in the mountains. But he hadn't said what hotel, or even what town he was going to. What on earth had happened? Had something gone wrong? His mother was not successful in keeping a note of pleasure out of her voice, if she was even aware of it. Marjorie evaded her questions, and hung up.

Three days passed. His mother called every morning and evening, wanting to know if Marjorie had heard from him. This, with the mournful atmosphere in her own home, the unspoken questions and terrible worry in the faces of her parents, became unendurable. Marjorie got up very early one morning, left a similar note for her parents, and went to a hotel in Lakewood, a New Jersey resort a couple of hours from the city. It was the wrong time of the year for Lakewood. The hotel she stayed in was almost empty; the town was deserted. There was nothing to do but read, go to movies, or walk around the lake. Marjorie read magazines, newspapers, books, whatever she could lay her hands on, without the slightest idea of what she was reading. She was at the hotel six days, and the time passed as though she were in delirium. She couldn't remember afterward any details of what she had done in those six days; they were blanked from her mind as by amnesia. She came home with a severe cold and a temperature of a hundred and three. She had not eaten at all, and she had lost twelve pounds. She came home because her mother telephoned her (unlike him, she had disclosed where she was going). "He's back, and he called this morning. Better come home."

"How did he sound?"

"I don't know. Come home." Mrs. Morgenstern didn't seem very cheerful.

Sick as Marjorie was when she arrived home, she brushed off her mother's alarm at the way she looked and her insistence that she go to bed. She telephoned his office. It was four in the afternoon, a raw snowy day, already growing dark. He said abruptly, coldly, that he would like to see her as soon as possible for a little while.

In the same clothes she had worn travelling home, dishevelled and shivering, she went straight downtown and met him, at a dingy bar near his office. Naturally it would be at a bar; it had always been at a bar. He was already at a table, in a gloomy far corner.

There was a long quiet pause after they greeted each other and ordered drinks. Bad as she looked, he looked worse. He had actually aged. His face was white, lined, and wretched. He studied her face during that pause, and she felt as though she were about to be executed. When he finally spoke, what he said was, sadly and gruffly, "I love you." He opened a jeweler's box and put it before her. She stared dumfounded at what she thought must be the largest diamond in the world.

It was a good thing they were in a dark corner, because she had to turn her face down and cry bitterly. She cried a long time, in an excess of the deepest bitterness and shame, before he shyly brushed the tears from her face with his hand.

He never said anything about Noel thereafter; not for the rest of their lives. But she never again saw on his face the pure happiness that had shone there during the drive across the George Washington Bridge in the sunset. He loved her. He took her as she was, with her deformity, despite it. For that was what it amounted to in his eyes and in hers—a deformity: a deformity that could no longer be helped; a permanent crippling, like a crooked arm.

My object all sublime
I shall achieve in time . . .

The song popped into Marjorie's head as her mother was buttoning her into her wedding dress, in an anteroom of the Gold Room of the Pierre Hotel, less than an hour before the ceremony. So great was her nervous tension that, once established, the melody drummed on and on in her brain. She was holding her veil high in the air with both hands, for it interfered with the buttoning, and as she stood so, with both arms high, she had begun to hum, and then to sing, unaware of what she was singing.

My object all sublime
I shall achieve in time . . .

After a few moments she heard herself, and quietly laughed, realizing why she was singing it. She had held her arms up in just this way on the stage at Hunter College, strutting through her first acting triumph as the Mikado. The electric excitement of that forgotten moment had welded the words and the tune in her brain to the act of throwing her arms high. Six years later—the better part of a lifetime, it seemed to Marjorie —the weld was still there. But how everything else had changed!

"What are you laughing at? Am I tickling you?" her mother said.

"An old joke, Mama, nothing. . . . Hurry, for heaven's sake, the photographer should have been here long ago."

"Relax, darling. You'll be married a long, long time."

All through the photographing, all through the frenzied last-minute rehearsals of cues with the caterer's hostess in charge of the sacred formalities, all through the hot hurried last embraces with her ecstatic mother, her beaming father, both looking astonishingly young and well in fine new evening clothes—and with her white-faced grim brother, stiff and unyielding as a post in his first top hat, white tie, and tails—and with her weeping mother-in-law and desperately punning and smoking father-in-law—all that time the song ran on and on in her mind. . . . *My object all sublime, I shall achieve in time . . .* It cut off sharply when the procession began and she heard the organ, far below in the ballroom, playing the wedding march.

For there was an organ, of course. And there were two cantors, a handsome young man and a marvelously impressive gray-bearded man, both in black silk robes, and black mitres with black pompons. There was a choir of five bell-voiced boys in white silk robes, and white hats with white pompons. There was a broad canopy of white lilies, on a platform entirely carpeted and walled with greenery and white roses. There were blazing blue-white arc lights, a movie photographer, and a still photographer. There was a rose-strewn staircase for her to descend; there was a quite meaningless but quite gorgeous archway with gates at the head of the staircase, covered and festooned with pink roses, through which she was to make her entrance. There were banks of gold chairs, five hundred of them, jammed solid with guests, and with spectators who had read the announcement in the *Times* and knew the bridegroom or the bride. After the ceremony there was to be as much champagne as anyone could drink, and as many hot hors d'oeuvres as the greediest guest could stuff into himself. There was to be a ten-course dinner beginning with imported salmon, featuring rare roast beef, and ending in flaming cherries jubilee. There was to be a seven-piece orchestra, more champagne, a midnight supper, and dancing till dawn.

It was the Lowenstein Catering Company's number-one wedding, the best there was, the best money could buy—sixty-five hundred dollars, tips included. Marjorie and her bridegroom had discussed accepting the money, instead, as a wedding present from her father. Mr. Morgenstern, who had accumulated the money and set it aside for the wedding over twenty years, had diffidently made the offer. They had decided instead to have the wedding, rococo excess and all. Their decision filled all four parents with joy. It was obviously what everybody wanted.

Marjorie stood behind the closed rose-covered gate at the head of the stairs, with the perspiring hostess at her elbow, listening to the music as the wedding procession filed in below from the lobby of the ballroom. She couldn't see anything through the heavy sweet-smelling screen of roses, but she knew what was happening. In the number-one Lowenstein wedding—the only one featuring the rose gate—all the others came in first and took their places; then the bride came down the flower-strewn steps in lone splendor, white train dragging, while her father waited for her at the foot of the staircase. Then he was to take her arm, and escort her to the canopy. Marjorie had seen this pageant several times at the weddings of other girls. The day before, at the rehearsal, she had been amused by the amateurish theatricalism of it all. At the same time, she secretly rather liked the idea of making such a grand entrance. Her only worry was that she might trip on her train and sprawl headlong down the stairs. But the hostess had assured her that every bride had had exactly the same fear, and not one had ever tripped.

The music stopped. That meant they were all in place: the four parents, the rabbi, Seth, the best man, and his betrothed, Natalie Fain, the maid of honor. Marjorie could hear the gossiping chatter of the guests. She swallowed hard, clutched her little bouquet of white orchids and lilies of the valley, and glanced at the hostess. The little flushed woman inspected her from head to toe, minutely adjusted her train, pulled Marjorie's hotly clasped hands with the bouquet to the exact center of her midriff, kissed her damply, and nodded at the yawning waiter with the gate rope in his hand. He hauled on the rope. The gates swung open, and Marjorie stood in a white spotlight under the arch of pink roses, revealed to public view.

There was a general gasp and murmur below, then a total hush. The organ began to play *Here Comes the Bride*. Slowly, regally, Marjorie came down the staircase, hesitating on each step, in time to the music.

Perhaps the spotlight shining in her eyes made the tears well up; perhaps it was the emotions of the moment. She blinked them back as well as she could, glad that she was veiled. She could see dimly the guests below, stretching in orderly ranks forward to the canopy. Their faces were turned up to her. There was one look on all of them: stunned admiration.

Marjorie was an extremely beautiful bride. They always say the bride is beautiful, and the truth is that a girl seldom looks better than she does at this moment of her glory and her vanishing, veiled and in white; but even among brides Marjorie was remarkably lovely. For years afterward Lowenstein's hostess said that the prettiest bride she ever saw was Marjorie Morgenstern.

The Goldstones were there, in one row near the back; and Marsha and Lou Michaelson, and the Zelenkos, and Aunt Dvosha, and Uncle Shmulka, and Geoffrey Quill, and Neville Sapersteen in a dark blue suit, and the banker Connelly, and Morris Shapiro, and Wally Wronken—these familiar faces and dozens of others she recognized, though her eyes scarcely moved. She had taken but two or three steps downward when she also saw, in the very last row of the array of black-clad men and beautifully gowned women, the tall blond man in brown tweed jacket and gray slacks, with an old camel's hair coat slung over one arm, incongruous as he was startling. She had not even known Noel Airman was in the United States; but he had come to see her get married. She could not discern his expression, but there wasn't a doubt in the world that it was Noel.

She didn't waver or change countenance at all; she continued her grave descent. But in an instant, as though green gelatins had been slid one by one in front of every light in the ballroom, she saw the scene differently. She saw a tawdry mockery of sacred things, a bourgeois riot of expense, with a special touch of vulgar Jewish sentimentality. The gate of roses behind her was comical; the flower-massed canopy ahead was grotesque; the loud whirring of the movie camera was a joke, the scrambling still photographer in the empty aisle, twisting his camera at his eye, a low clown. The huge diamond on her right hand capped the vulgarity; she could feel it there; she slid a finger to cover it. Her husband waiting for her under the canopy wasn't a prosperous doctor, but he was a prosperous lawyer; he had the mustache Noel had predicted; with macabre luck Noel had even guessed the initials. And she—she was Shirley, going to a Shirley fate, in a Shirley blaze of silly costly glory.

All this passed through her mind in a flash, between one step downward and the next. Then her eyes shifted to her father's face, rosily happy, looking up at her from the foot of the stairs. The green gelatins slid aside, and she saw her wedding again by the lights that were there in the room. If it was all comical in Noel's eyes, she thought, he might derive from that fact what pleasure he could. She was what she was, Marjorie Morgenstern of West End Avenue, marrying the man she wanted in the way she wanted to be married. It was a beautiful wedding, and she knew she was a pretty bride.

She reached the bottom of the stairs. Her father stepped to her side. Taking his arm, she turned a bit and squarely faced into Noel Airman's expected grin; he was not ten feet from her. But to her surprise Noel wasn't grinning. He looked better than he had in Paris: not so thin, not so pale, and he appeared to have gotten back all his hair. His expression was baffled, almost vacant. His mouth hung slightly open; his eyes seemed wet.

The organ music swelled to its loudest. Marjorie marched down the aisle with solemn gladness to her destiny, and became Mrs. Milton Schwartz.

Chapter 48. WALLY WRONKEN'S DIARY

July 5, 1954.

At desk 9:40. I feel fine and I'm hoping to do a good run of work today. However, it isn't often that one solves an old mystery in one's life, so the event is worth noting before I get down to business.

Yesterday I saw Marjorie Morgenstern—Mrs. Marjorie Schwartz, that is—for the first time in about fifteen years. She lives in Mamaroneck, in a big old white house on the sound, with a lot of lawn and huge old trees, and a nice view of the water, about an hour from town.

I happened to see her by accident. I had to go to New Rochelle to visit one of the backers of the show, a real estate man named Michaelson, who'd been raising some questions about my royalty contract. He's a shrewd old character, over seventy, I'd say, extremely well off, dabbles in the theatre a lot. He understood the tax angle of my contract immediately, and made a couple of suggestions I may use. That part of it all went fine.

He turned out to be married to one Marsha Zelenko, the girl who first brought Marjorie into the social hall at South Wind, aeons ago. Marsha, whom I knew as a fat slovenly girl, more or less given to sleeping around, is now a leathery rail of a woman, bright false blond, frightfully up to date in the suburban way—expensive clothes that look out of place amid grass and trees, and dizzy bright chatter that is just a bit sour, a bit off-key, like a cruel parody of Manhattan small talk. And this drawn starved brown face, and the biggest mouthful of grinning teeth you ever saw. "Have some of this scotch, it's twenty-four years old. Do you write longhand, or on the typewriter?" And a lot of questions about the Hollywood stars I've known. That kind of thing. No children. Both her parents live there with them, and that's the ménage.

She couldn't wait to tell me that Marjorie lived in Mamaroneck, only five miles away. When I expressed mild interest, she practically dragged me to the telephone in a half nelson, dialled the number, handed me the receiver, and walked out, closing the library door with the damnedest arch look any man ever saw, all cannibal teeth and popping eyes.

A boy's voice answered. He sounded about ten. "Yeah? Hello?" I asked to speak to his mother. He dropped the phone and bawled, "Ma, some man for you."

Then she came on the telephone. "Hello?"

"Marjorie?"

"Yes. Who is this?"

Her voice sounded exactly the same: sweet, a bit husky. I'd forgotten how low the timbre was. Marjorie on the phone always gave almost a contralto effect, though you didn't notice it when you were with her. And there was the same slight hesitation in her voice—what is it, precisely? A manner of speaking half a beat late, a touch of shyness or something; anyway, it always seemed to me the essence of femininity, and it was still there.

When I told her my name, and where I was calling from, the pause lasted more than half a beat; two or three, maybe. Then, "Hello, Wally. It's wonderful to hear from you." Not bursting with joy, not even particularly surprised; very warm and sweet. Of course, I must come right over, she said; she'd be delighted to see me. Her daughter would be especially thrilled to meet a playwright, because she was so wild about the theatre.

Marsha drove me over in a yellow Cadillac a block long. We turned into the driveway of this handsome old white house, with a glass-button sign on the fence at the entrance, *Schwartz*. A gray-headed lady was sitting on a flagstone terrace out front on a deck chair—one of the grandmothers on a Sunday visit, I figured. We got out of the car and walked to the terrace, and it was something of a shock when the gray-headed lady turned out to be Marjorie. The fact is, she looks very much like Mrs. Milton Schwartz, and not much like the Marjorie Morgenstern I last saw at a much too plush wedding at the Pierre, a decade and a half ago.

Despite the gray hair (which is premature, she's not quite forty) she remains an attractive woman, slim, with a pleasant face and a sweet manner, and a sort of ghostly resemblance to the Marjorie of yesteryear. She has a fourteen-year-old daughter, Deborah, who looks more like the girl I knew than Mrs. Schwartz does. All that is to be expected, I guess. It's an unsettling thing, all the same, to see your first love a gray-headed mother of four kids. I couldn't help thinking how wise she had been to discourage me in the old days. A man of thirty-nine is *not* well suited to a woman of forty. I've been through affairs and a divorce and I still feel like a comparatively young man trying to settle down. She made a joke about her gray hair, but there was no bitterness in it; a little wryness, maybe, but a contented wryness, if that means anything.

Contented, she obviously is. There was no mistaking the look she gave her husband when he came in with their two boys from a father-and-son softball game, in old clothes, all sweaty and dirty; nor the real kiss, nor the way she rubbed her face for a second against his shoulder. He's a good-natured late-fortyish man, broad-shouldered, sort of plump, grizzled hair going at the temples. He handled the situation very well, if it was a situation, of finding me there with Marsha and Marjorie. After all, the successful old beau showing up in the suburbs is a worn gambit for comedy. But Schwartz was pleasant, even engaging; not a trace of self-conscious resentment, no snide remarks; instead, a genuine invitation to hang around for highballs, and deferential compliments about my plays. I didn't see much of him because he showered and changed and went off with the boys to their beach club to watch fireworks. The boys are standard-issue boys, eleven and nine, I'd guess. Marjorie fussed over them before they went off to the club, the way any mama should. She had to remain at home because the maid had gone off unexpectedly, and they have an infant daughter. That was how I got to talk to her a bit. I made several offers to leave (Mrs. Michaelson had gone earlier, much to my relief, because she had guests coming for cocktails), but Marjorie insisted that I stay. Later I found out why. I might have guessed. But like a fool I was flattered, so I stayed.

We had several highballs. Maybe she wouldn't have talked otherwise.

She was very awkward with me at first, though pleasant; seemed a bit awed. It turned out pretty interesting. She had a little battle with the daughter about piano practice before fireworks, and won it. The girl flung off inside and began thumping away. I was reminded forcibly of the way Marjorie's mother used to put her foot down in the old days; Marjorie has much the same dry good-humored firmness.

We sat around out on the lawn on deck chairs, drinking, watching the sunset. She asked me the usual questions about Broadway and Hollywood. But I must say she had no offensive celebrity-worshipping eagerness, the toothy bug-eyed kind of thing, like Mrs. Michaelson. I felt she wanted to know about me, and I answered frankly. Her comments were intelligent and to the point, as they always used to be. She discussed my plays well, and pleased me by praising *The Meadow Sweet*. I guess an author always has a weakness for his failures, but it's quite true, as she said, that that's the only time I stepped outside mechanical farce and really tried.

Just for the hell of it, I mentioned my encounter with Noel Airman in Hollywood. She was interested, but in an absent way; she didn't spark at all. If anything, she seemed amused when I told her he was married to a fat German photographer who's a fad with the movie crowd. She said she'd met Mrs. Airman in Paris. When I told her Noel had ended as a third-rate baldish television writer, with his wife more or less supporting them both, she nodded. "Noel was never much of a writer, you know," she said. "He should have been a teacher, I think, or a lawyer. He had a good mind, and a vivid way of putting things. But I guess he was too erratic for the academic life."

I couldn't help saying—I'll admit it was small of me—"Time was when you thought Noel was a pretty good writer, Margie."

To my amazement she denied it. She said that from the beginning, at South Wind, she'd insisted that I showed professional promise and that Noel was a mere dilettante. She claimed she'd encouraged me to become a writer, all but discovered me. She became a little annoyed when I mildly tried to disagree. There isn't the slightest doubt that she believed every word she said. She's rewritten history in her mind, and now she's the one who always knew Walter Wronken had it in him. What would have been the use of reminding her that she'd almost driven me wild once by suggesting that I study Noel's brilliant writing to improve my own? I get irritated now, twenty years afterward, thinking of that moment. But it no longer exists for her, or indeed for anybody on God's whole earth except me—and only for me because I'm cursed with a writer's memory.

I told her about my marriage and divorce. She had read, or heard, about my breakup with Julia, and was pleasantly sympathetic. What with the highballs, and the clouds all yellow and red in the setting sun, I waxed a little melancholy and philosophical about the problems of being married to an actress. At one point I said, "This much you can be sure of, you're a hell of a lot happier than Marjorie Morningstar could ever have been." She turned and stared at me, and for a flash there was contact between us. Just for an instant, the old Margie was there in the blue eyes of Mrs. Schwartz. And she said, "Good God, do you remember that? You would. You and your steel-trap mind. I don't believe I've thought of that name in a dozen years . . . *Marjorie* . . . *Morningstar* . . ." There was something extremely poignant in the way she drew out the syllables, and smiled. It was the old sweet, warm smile. That hasn't changed.

She kept pouring the drinks. Her capacity is astonishing; it seemed to make no difference whatever, except that she talked more easily. I had to beg off from a couple of refills, because I was getting a little dizzy. The only time she did anything strange was when her daughter started to play *Falling in Love with Love* in the house, not too well. She got up, highball in hand, and started to waltz. There was something slightly bizarre about that, a gray-headed woman in a swirling blue cotton dress, waltzing soundlessly by herself in the sunset, with her long evening shadow gliding behind her on the lawn. The song reminds her, she said, of a man she met on her trip to Europe, who was doing some kind of cloak-and-dagger work rescuing Jews. Something came over her when she talked about him. Her voice began to sound more like the voice I remembered (it was getting dark, too, and maybe that helped). It lost some of its flatness, some of the authoritative parent sound. Also her daughter came out about then, and got permission to go off to the fireworks, and Margie seemed to relax when she was gone. She went on for quite a while about this man. I gathered he meant a lot to her, even as a memory. Which was in itself interesting. My picture had always been that Noel was the big love of her life, and I'd been quite sure I knew everything about Marjorie Morgenstern up to the day she married (except whether she ever actually had an affair with Noel—something I simply couldn't believe then, though I suppose now she did). But here obviously, in this man she met on the ship, was a missing piece of the jigsaw, possibly even the key piece.

After that she told me about her brother Seth getting killed at Okinawa flying for the Navy, and then about a baby boy of hers, the second, that had choked to death in its crib at the age of two months, the doctors never figured out why. And about her father going broke and having a heart attack, and her husband putting him back on his feet at terrific cost, and about her mother-in-law being bedridden in her house for four years, dying slowly of some blood disease. She was quite detached, not in the least self-pitying about all this, even when she said at one point, "I've come by these gray hairs honestly, you see." It all added up to a lot of soap-opera afflictions, I guess. I can see why those programs are popular. Childless people, people without families like me, don't know about such things, but the average housewife sees herself being dramatized, I suppose. I began to be ashamed of having thought Marjorie dull and boring at first. Yet she is dull, dull as she can be, by any technical standard. You couldn't write a play about her that would run a week, or a novel that would sell a thousand copies. There's no angle.

Out of all the talk about her troubles, we somehow got on the subject of religion. She's a regular synagogue goer, active in the Jewish organizations of the town; apparently that takes up a lot of her time. Her husband is active too. They seem to be rather strictly observant; Marjorie has separate milk and meat dishes in the kitchen, and all that. I tried to pin her down on what she really believed (we'd had enough to drink by then so that such a discussion wasn't embarrassing). She was curiously evasive. She said that the professors of comparative religion were like bright kids with clocks. They could take a religion apart and show how it ticked, but they couldn't put it back together so it would work for anybody. I mildly suggested that the day was past, maybe, when religion could work for any educated person. She flared a bit; said religion still worked for a hell of a lot of people. She said her parents would never have survived the death of Seth without it, and that she didn't know whether she and Milton could have stayed in one piece after the baby died if they hadn't had their religion. At this point I was probing, perhaps cruelly, to strike bottom. I said, "Well, Margie, maybe that only proves the power of a dream." Like a flash she answered—and her voice sounded just as it did in the old days, full of life and sparkle, "Who isn't dreaming, Wally? You?"

The fireworks started around then, all green and golden and red, over the sound. We stopped talking for a while and watched. It was quite a display, what with the clear night, a crescent moon, and evidently a very large budget at the beach club for the Fourth of July celebration. Rockets, Roman candles, and burst after burst of the showering things, every color in the world, popping and banging every other second, and at the last a super-special white one that seemed to fill the sky and make it bright as day. Then it was dark, and there I was with my gray-headed old flame, both of us rather high, and her family coming home. So I went inside and telephoned for a cab.

I said, while we sat around on her flagstone terrace waiting for the cab

—figuring that it was now or never to clear this little mystery—"Well, I hope you've acquired some patience with your gray hairs. Fifteen years ago you stood me up on a date, just because I was twelve minutes late. I think you owe me an explanation and an apology. I never got either, you know."

She looked blank, as I expected. I reminded her how she'd telephoned me, and was supposed to meet me in the lobby of the St. Moritz and have lunch at Rumpelmayer's. Remembrance came over her face, with the old coquettish look, decidedly odd framed in gray hair, and yet not unattractive. "Good God, what a memory, Wally. That all happened in another century. As I recall, I thought you'd forgotten the date, that's all. I suppose I went out and had lunch at a drugstore."

I told her how excited I'd been, how I'd changed my tie four times for this date of dates, and finally rushed out to buy a new tie because I didn't like any I tried on. Her eyes became big and round, and a very strange smile hovered around her mouth. "Ye gods, is *that* why you were late? You went out to buy a new tie?"

"Just to impress my lady fair," I said. "I went out to buy a tie, Marjorie. Why did you telephone me? Why did you want to have lunch with me?"

She laughed, a low peculiar laugh, looking slowly around at the house, the trees, the lawn, the water, as though she were coming out of a trance. "Who knows, Wally? It was fifteen years ago. Probably I wanted free tickets to your show for my folks, or something." I was leaning on the parapet, smoking. She got out of her chair, walked over to me, and kissed me coolly on the mouth. "That's for going out to buy a tie, just to impress me, Wally. I'm sorry I stood you up. I can't remember why, but I'm sure it was very silly of me." The voice was the voice of Marjorie Morgenstern, and the kiss gave me a strange little thrill, remote as it was.

That's about all there was to the historic meeting. The cab was honking at the entrance to the driveway a moment later. It was only then that she came out with the real reason she'd kept me around so long, feeding me highballs. She's the president of the women's branch of the local community chest—and would I come and speak at the annual dinner? The girls had been egging her on for years to write to me, but she hadn't been able to drum up the nerve. She'd had enough to drink at this point, she said, to have the gall to ask me. Well, what could I say? I said yes, of course. As a matter of fact I don't really mind. With the show opening in a month or so, it's not a bad idea to set the girls gossiping about me in a well-to-do suburb like Mamaroneck. Those women buy a lot of matinee tickets. Though I daresay I'd have done it for Marjorie, whether it made sense or not.

And there you are. The circle is closed.

Or is it? The mystery is solved. Or will it ever be, really? Writing this entry has stirred me up in an unaccountable way. I've gone on and on, and I meant to dispose of the whole thing in a page or so. I feel dissatisfied. I haven't managed to say what I wanted, or to indicate the quality of the meeting at all.

The thing is, this was a triumph I promised myself fifteen years ago. I can remember so clearly how I daydreamed of presenting myself to Marjorie, a successful playwright, when she'd be just another suburban housewife gone to seed. Well, I did it at last, and it wasn't a triumph at all. *There's* the point I'm trying to get at. The person I wanted to triumph over is gone, that's the catch. I can't carry my achievements backward fifteen years and flaunt them in the face of Marjorie Morgenstern, the beautiful elusive girl I was so mad about. And what satisfaction is there in crowing over the sweet-natured placid gray mama she has turned into? For that matter, what satisfaction is it to the poor ambitious skinny would-be writer of twenty years ago, little Wally, the South Wind stage manager, that I met Mrs. Schwartz and got such awe and deference? It's too late. He doesn't exist either.

But why should I care about all this? That's the strange part. It's all so dead, so forgotten. Marjorie doesn't haunt me; I haven't thought about her, except casually and without a trace of emotion, in a dozen years. Seeing her now, I can only be glad she didn't yield to my frantic puppy worship. The only remarkable thing about Mrs. Schwartz is that she ever hoped to be remarkable, that she ever dreamed of being Marjorie Morningstar. She couldn't be a more run-of-the-mill wife and mother.

What troubles me, I guess, is the thought of the bright vision that has faded. To me, she really was Marjorie Morningstar. I didn't know whether she had any talent. I didn't care. She was everything sweet, radiant, pure, and beautiful in the world. I know now that she was an ordinary girl, that the image existed only in my own mind, that her radiance was the radiance of my own hungry young desires projected around her. Still, I once saw that vision and loved it. Marjorie Morgenstern . . . What music that name used to have for me! I still hear a faint echo, sweet as a far-off flute playing Mozart, when I write the name. No doubt the land is full of nineteen-year-old boys to whom names like Betty Jones, Hazel Klein, Sue Wilson have the same celestial sound. It's a sound I shall hear no more.

And if she wasn't the bright angel I thought, she was a lovely girl; and where is that girl now? She doesn't even remember herself as she was. I am the only one on the face of God's earth, I'm sure, who still holds that picture in a dim corner of memory. When I go, that will be the end of Marjorie Morningstar, to all eternity.

Yet how beautiful she was! She rises up before me as I write—in a blue dress, a black raincoat, her face wet with rain, nineteen years old, in my arms and yet maddeningly beyond my reach, my beautiful young love, kissing me once under the lilacs in the rain. I have known most of the pleasant things I can expect in this life. I'm not famous or distinguished, but I never really hoped I would be; and my limits have been clear to me for a long time. I've had the success I aimed for. I'll go on working, and I'll have more success, I'm reasonably sure. I've had the love of good-looking women. If I'm fortunate, I may some day have what Milton Schwartz has, and what's been denied me: a wife I love, and children, and a warm happy home. But one thing I know now I will never have—the triumph I once wanted above everything on earth, the triumph I promised myself when I was a heartsick boy, the triumph that slipped through my fingers yesterday, once for all. I will never have that second kiss from Marjorie under the lilacs.

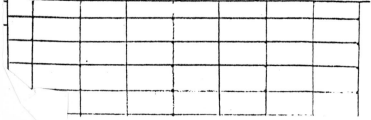